It's All
Right Now

It's All Right Now

A NOVEL

CHARLES CHADWICK

HARPER PERENNIAL

NEW YORK • LONDON • TORONTO • SYDNEY

Published in Great Britain in 2005 by Faber and Faber Limited.

A U.S. hardcover edition of this book was published in 2005 by HarperCollins Publishers.

P.S.™ is a trademark of HarperCollins Publishers.

HarperCollins books may be purchased for educational, business, or sales pro-motional use. For information please write: Special Markets Department, HarperCollins Publishers, 10 East 53rd Street, New York, NY 10022.

First Harper Perennial edition published 2006.

Library of Congress Cataloging-in-Publication Data is available upon request.

ISBN-10: 0-06-074287-9 (pbk.)
ISBN-13: 978-0-06-074287-4 (pbk.)

06 07 08 09 10 ❖/RRD 10 9 8 7 6 5 4 3 2 1

It's All
Right Now

PART ONE

PART ONE

Chapter One

For a while the houses on either side of us were empty. Then at about the same time the 'For Sale' signs were taken away and people moved into them. We live in a (just) detached house in between, which I've come to assume, perhaps my wife has too, we'll be living in for the rest of our lives . . . Well, one has to begin somewhere, on any old scrap of paper. I'm not sure what the point of it is. We shall have to see. It may take quite a time.

Webb, our neighbour on one side, suffers from too much curiosity but it lacks malice, I'm sure. On our other side live a man called Hamble and his wife who display in their demeanour a constant long-suffering which I suspect in each other's company alone they find something of a strain. Webb is married too. His wife is hunched, wan and bespectacled and seems to keep out of the way as if in her time she has been too much the object of curiosity.

I often, not all that often, wish we could afford to live without close neighbours instead of here in this unnoteworthy north London suburb where to try to keep to oneself is to draw attention to oneself. Too much neighbourliness is forced upon me in my place of work without my having to put up with it in the long periods in between. My wife would regard such theories (if at all) as anti-social. She is whatever the opposite of that is. Society is something she is decidedly pro, having theories about anyway – both the one that is and the better one we should all be trying to bring into being. She practises what she preaches – the other way round too which some might find, well, anti-social perhaps the word is. I don't. I admire what she does very much, namely good works in another neighbourhood, asking herself now and again, only in theory thank the Lord, whether she ought to be paid for them. Between us therefore you could say we are trying to bring a better world into being, a wider neighbourliness. At any rate that's the theory and I won't let it come between us.

When she sees the Webbs or the Hambles she waves briskly at them without pausing in what she is doing – mainly striding resolutely up or down our front path – and she answers Webb's enquiries with a sideways pull of one half of her mouth that only Webb might mistake for a smile. My wife does not enjoy entering into discussion about our neighbours when there are topics more far-reaching to be talked about, such as our children's progress and growing social awareness, my total lack of them (which are talked about only by implication) and the world's way of falling somewhere in between.

It wouldn't much matter to my wife where we lived, within limits of course; I think she'd prefer greater poverty and hardship to having to classify herself more evidently among the privileged. So, equally often, I am glad we live where we do, midway, roughly speaking, between the two i.e. not squalidly and not too stricken by her conscience. The neighbourhood where she works has a lot of squalor in it, about which she tells me as I go 'Ts ts', shake my head, silently count my blessings and say nothing. These are the early 1970s and things seem to be getting worse and worse which makes them better and better for her, I'm glad (sorry) to say.

Up to a point, I like to imagine that Webb married his wife purely out of curiosity, to discover what the intimacies of wedlock with someone so shy of them would be like, or because she seemed docile enough to experiment a lot with. I also imagine he is curious about my intimacies with my wife, though he might guess they wouldn't make him curious for more *ad infinitum*. One of my speculations is that when we go up to bed he is in the bathroom opposite our bedroom window with the light off in the hope that one night we'll forget to draw the curtains and turn our light out. This is not at all the kind of notion I can share with my wife. It would make her think me frivolous on top of lacking in imagination. It would also make her despise Webb for being somebody anybody could have that kind of thought about. So far I think I like Webb enough not to want him to be despised, especially (even?) by my wife. Also, without going to the lengths of hanging about in unlit bathrooms, I am not that much less curious than I imagine Webb to be to know what he and Mrs Webb get up to together. When I go to bed I sometimes slow down a lot without actually coming to a complete stop, and glance across at their bedroom to see if anything interesting is going on, on the off-chance they are more careless than we are. I mean than my wife is – it is she who draws our curtains and always with an extra two tugs to shut out the tiniest possible remaining chink of light between them. Generally speaking, my own curiosity is limited to holding myself in readiness not to turn the other way and hurry past should something going on present itself to me. When I go for walks after dark I look nonchalantly up at lit bedrooms with undrawn curtains. I've never seen anything.

I would like to satisfy Webb's curiosity without necessarily laying it on for him, by, say, appearing naked and erect in front of his bath-room window, and making a grab at my wife just as she's lowering her final undergarment or unhitching her bra, things she does in an increasingly businesslike as opposed to down-to-business manner these days. I would not mind if he saw the shadow of us on the wall doing it. Come to think of it, I wouldn't much mind other people knowing how low (or narrowly I should say) in this area my wife sets the limits of acceptable behaviour – which appears to give me and society something else in common. Perhaps Webb thinks a woman as self-possessed as my wife abandons herself utterly in the throes of being possessed by another. Perhaps he'd like to ask her to go to bed with him just to see how she would react but I doubt his curiosity is, so to speak, that all-embracing. The truth is that I some-times (very occasionally) think I'd like to ask Mrs Webb the same question, but in such a way that she wouldn't know for sure that was what I was asking (sticking my head suddenly through her kitchen window and saying 'How about it then?'), not because of her expression of shock but because she might tell Webb and excite his curiosity further, thus spurring him on to satisfy it in regard to my wife. All this is only fleetingly in my mind. Mrs Webb is skinny with a tendency towards bedragglement. I would not wish to upset her in any way. She is too timid and helpless. When you speak to her, which I've so far done only twice, her eyes describe a parabola from one shoulder to the other by way of your navel.

The difference between Webb and the Hambles, whom one always thinks of as a pair, is that if you asked Webb if you could borrow

7

something, say a screwdriver or a length of wire, he would ask you what you wanted it for. Either of the Hambles would go off in a tremendous hurry to look for it, even though they knew they didn't have it, and return later either happily bearing something else, say a pair of scissors or ball of string, or miserably empty-handed, so that you regretted not having asked them for a great deal more or something altogether different or of course nothing at all.

Webb says they emigrated to Canada when Churchill lost the election at the end of the war but soon came back on account of the prolonged absence of warmth there. Webb is probably making this up but if that is what they did do I suspect they didn't enjoy a single moment of it but didn't allow themselves even to think that, assuming that a general unenjoyability would have been their uppermost experience of life anywhere.

Sometimes I think I can hear the sound of sobbing from the Hambles' house. Perhaps they are recalling the death a long time ago of a small pet or child. They are the sort of people who have a profound sorrow in their lives they cannot overcome, who turn their grief outwards into an expression of vague loving-kindness. They are old folk, plump and grey, who came to our street to see out their retirement. I imagine they have put all their savings into their house, live on a shrinking pension and worry themselves sick about how they are going to make ends meet. They are the kind of people who go away quietly into a corner to die. I see them lying side by side, hand in hand, on the kitchen floor by a gas stove, having first made themselves comfortable with cushions. Their final talk would be of what they had lost a long time ago or of what had never happened to them, though they would believe in reunions, in spirits meeting up in lush, sunny pastures shadowed by vast oaks and cedars. They are the sort of people one cannot help because they would worry about having nothing to offer in return and because what they really need – anonymous money – would be too much for you to give in sufficient quantities, to say nothing of the anxiety caused by not knowing where it had come from. In the meantime they tend an immaculate garden in which the vegetables grow evenly and are as neatly arrayed as the flowers. I sometimes see Webb in their garden pointing and talking but I doubt if they answer his questions. They suspect he has guessed too much already. He borrows gardening tools from them and twice I have seen him come away with a packet of seeds. I am sure he borrows things from them so as to have an excuse for going back to return them. I'd like to suggest that we swap houses with the Webbs because the Hambles evidently give him more to be curious about than we do.

My wife would think I was making a joke. She never laughs at my jokes. She 'smiles' at about half of them, the obvious ones, but because I hardly find them funny at all as soon as I've made them there's no smirk or twinkle from which to tell whether I've made the other half or not. When I asked her to marry me and she agreed, I was so surprised I asked her why. I'd had the bulk of her clothing off her more than once by then (or 'we'd' and 'our' and delete the second 'her', this to remove any impression that over the years I've lost the initiative) and our gasping and grunting and doom-filled moaning had revealed no basic or physical discord leaving me in little doubt that the ultimate union would soon be reached, albeit disharmonious to all ears but our own. (Nowadays Webb would barely hear a thing unless he had an ear right up under our mattress.) So she had one reason I could be fairly confident of. But what she replied was: 'You're a very nice man. You have a dry sense of humour.'

The nicest of men, panting and flushed himself, scrabbling his way beneath straps and elastic, making soft surfaces damp with his foraging lips, having to breathe through his nose a variety of smells by no means all of which he prefers to his own, no man then should have his humour to the fore. 'Something has to stay dry,' I replied or mumbled, my ear by now in the region of her navel, then again, 'Soon I'll be in it nearly up to my waist.' There was no responding tremble of laughter in her stomach – not that she could possibly have heard me. I was glad she hadn't because, goodness knows, it was a solemn moment for me too and I didn't want her to find out yet that my sense of humour didn't rise to any old occasion, whatever the rest of me did. So if I said, 'Let's swap with the Hambles or Webbs,' she'd say, 'What a funny idea. Why?' And I'd reply, 'Houses I mean. To bring them closer together. So they don't have to try to see through us.' Or on those lines.

That is not the kind of conversation I can have with my wife. I could not even suggest we had the Webbs and the Hambles over for a meal or to watch television. Having no reason of her own to be especially thoughtful to people simply because they happen to be near by she'd wonder what reason I might have, my not having hitherto displayed much thoughtfulness of any variety. ('If it's all the same to you, dear.') She'd suspect my motives, but get them wrong. She knows I'm not one for entering into unnecessary obligations, so she'd think I was trying to put on a dutiful aspect to impress my family (what was I hiding?), whereas I'd only be watching Webb's curiosity at close quarters, in our midst, regretting that we'd so soon have to exhaust it, while the Hambles sat in an ever-widening pool of silence. I should add that we didn't go the 'whole way' that evening either when she agreed to marry me. That came later when something else had come to an end too, the death of my father to be precise. I don't feel able to say anything more about that for the moment.

I'm not being fair to my wife. I seldom am. She is an impossible woman to fault. She knows her own mind, is useful to the community, occupies her time gainfully, is an admirable parent, in short, God knows (she knows), is everything that I am not. She does not wish to nag me, let alone dominate me. It is simply that she has taken charge, has learnt to accept me as I am, an agreeable enough sort of fellow who does, alas, entirely what is expected of him. For example, we both vote Labour. In my wife's case that goes without saying. (If only it did.) In my own, it might be because I recognise in myself the acquisitiveness of the Conservative animal and am taking it out on myself for the few actual acquisitions it seems to lead to. Also my boss is a Conservative, bound to be (not free to be anything else?). Or it might be because I prefer self-righteousness to self-satisfaction for a few seconds once every four years or so, bearing in my mind my preference for the rest of the time. Or it could be simply that I vote what my wife votes. I am outwardly a better hypocrite than liar. She would never forgive me if I voted otherwise and would wish to discuss the matter, in front of the children, what's more. My cross in the wrong place would be a terrible burden for us all to have to bear. The Liberal party only makes my wife shrug. It is a word she mainly employs to go with 'helping' or 'dose' or 'share' meaning too much of a good, or bad, thing. It is a word that might worry me if I had to think about it, giving so much scope for good and bad, e.g. taking liberties. That goes for thinking too which wanders freely about all over the place and who knows where it will end? All very worrying. I should be free not to have to think about it – if it would have done me good, too bad. Let that be the end of it.

We have a small house, a small garden, a small car (which all go with the small job), two perfectly satisfactory children and every year take two weeks' holiday by the water somewhere. I have no vices. I only smoke cheroots in the garden and even then my children, undiscouraged by my wife, may watch me from the window vigorously flapping their hands. I do not drink to excess nor have yet, in fact, committed adultery. In short, I give my wife no cause for concern. (Thereby doing my bit by not taking her attention away from those it is her business to be concerned about.) When at home, I busy myself with odd jobs such as painting walls, filling cracks with Polyfilla, tidying up the small garden and cleaning the small car. The only game I play is badminton because there is a badminton club within easy walking distance. My wife does not play games, perhaps on principle. I'm not sure; I've never asked her. I would have to travel four miles in thickish traffic to the nearest golf course and anyway I don't think golf could be my game. The people who play it have a certain persistent levity that would weigh me down. Or all that paraphernalia would. Also, I have a feeling that however much I practised I would find myself quite frequently, in front of others, missing the ball altogether. Finally it's a costly game, and would trouble my conscience in as much as I would feel obliged to ask myself from time to time for what better purpose the money might be spent – not only in the sense deriving from the concerns of my wife, but also better for me, or more enjoyable – which in my limited experience (compared with my wife's) do not always (never) come to the same thing. No thank you – a case in point – I don't jog either. To be willing to be seen doing it by so many others suggests a desire for self-betterment of heroic proportions, there being no enjoyment in it, or so it would appear – unless of course that is where the enjoyment lies: in letting other people know what fun you're not having in feeling all the better for it. Even in a thick fog on a lonely moor I wouldn't, not wishing to extend needlessly my visibility to myself either; besides, it's not my body that seems to need the working out now.

Apart from the pottering and television I read books: thrillers and lives of the great explorers mainly. I fill my time quite nicely: a sort of involuntary pleasure-seeking you might say. 'You old hedonist, you,' my wife once called me. I looked the word up: 'Ethical theory that pleasure is the chief good or the proper end of action.' I was instantly heartened that my wife should have seen in me the exponent of a philosophy going back to the Greeks. But having taken the scholarly words out I was left with pleasure being the end of action, and in my case inaction is the word I would have to (become) plump for. Perhaps there is another definition for old hedonists.

I've never expected much of life, nor much of myself, which are the same thing my wife would say. I wouldn't. I am not much given to wanting to take charge of things. If I was, my life would be less satisfying, I think, because I would then be brought into conflict with my wife. It is she who brings up the children. The way she goes about it does not bother me on the whole, though she does seem to me, rightly or wrongly, to have this tendency to see right or wrong at issue when they oughtn't to be. It would not do at all if I had ideas of my own about how my children should be brought up. I wouldn't like to disagree with my wife in that sensitive area. She is a better talker than I am and I doubt if I could sustain for long an argument directed at showing she was in error. Besides, I haven't read any of the literature on the subject. She will lecture my children, too, about the distinction between wisdom and knowledge. I wish she wouldn't. All they ultimately need to know, I decide sometimes, is that wisdom is a form of exhaustion, since that makes me wiser than she is.

At this juncture it occurs to me to ask myself again why I have started writing about my life like this – except that I have time in the office to do it and it helps to make me look busy. I suppose I might be curious to know where it will take me and want to try some exploring of my own perhaps, not knowing what I'll find until I get there. In the meantime it gives clarity to, and saves the repetition of, all the talking to myself I do – no more or less than other people I don't suppose. To think of all those imagined, unwritten lives one dwells amongst . . .

I get back from work at about half past six. As I hang up my coat in the hall I shout a word or two of greeting through to the living-room where my children are watching the news. I try to vary the greeting but doubt if they notice it. 'Hi there!' 'Hallo, chaps!' 'Home again!' 'Evening, folks!' are about the extent of my range. There seldom being a response, I put my head round the door and repeat myself. My children glance up, sometimes raise a hand, sometimes smile, what is known as a ghost of one, making me feel very much in the flesh, not to say lumpish. If my wife is there too, she says, 'Hallo, dear,' and to the children, 'Say hallo to your father.' Whereupon they say 'Hi!' in chorus without looking away from the television for even a split second. They have seen me before.

I think then, as often, how satisfactory by and large my children are, how well brought up etc. – apart, just possibly, from the fact that they don't make more of my homecoming, without actually scurrying about in search of my smoking-jacket and slippers, which they would have to do since I do not possess either. It is a long time since my wife asked me if I have had a hard day. She knows I never have had. She's the one who's had that with her unmarried mothers and delinquents and the like. I never ask if she's had a hard day because I know the answer and the length of it. ('One-parent families' is the correct phrase, I realise, but I avoid it, it being too close to home.)

I cannot blame my children, therefore, for not springing to their feet when I return from work as I (my wife too) would expect them to if I'd spent my day rescuing people from fires or performing operations on the brain or otherwise making the world a better place to live in. Moreover, the news is one of the programmes in the informative category that their school and their mother encourage them to watch as a window on to the world. I can appreciate that my familiar presence, my own ghostly smile, should not be permitted to distract them from the strangeness and pain of existence at large.

Television is one of the areas of our lives where my wife is more in charge than I am. It is the only one in which I would like to be solely in charge. Just about exclusively, I have a firm preference for the escapist tough stuff like *Starsky and Hutch, Hawaii Five-O, Kojak, The Avengers* and so forth. I really do enjoy that sort of programme and look forward to it all day. I hardly ever enjoy the sort of programme that is good for my children and ought to be good for me too. My wife is right when she ticks the programmes we ought to watch and forbids the children, who have homework and other mind-developing things to do, to watch anything else. BBC 2 has a lot to answer for, in my view.

My children go to bed promptly at nine, so the conflict is only between my tastes and their enlightenment up to a point. After they've gone to bed my wife may say, 'I would rather like to watch so and so.' And it doesn't really enter my head (at the time) to reply, in a muffled manner, the lollipop roaming about in my mouth, 'Isn't that hard shit because I've a mind to watch the other thing.'

I usually don't actively dislike the informative thing she's improving herself with and sometimes have to confess afterwards to myself (out loud I merely stumble through a few worried adjectives) that it's broadened my mind for a moment or two, though I do actively dislike the sensation of shrinkage that follows it, especially when I'm reminded of how my imagination kept on interfering with my intellect, if not moral sense (the other way round?), for example with car-chases missed and fist-fights unseen.

When she hasn't ticked anything my wife often says how much she is looking forward to a good, long, quiet read. I then might say, 'Mind if I stay up and watch so and so?' To which she replies, 'Of course not, dear.' Without adding (thinking?), 'If that's the kind of rubbish you like.'

She can't sleep until I'm in bed too, which is a snag, but here again she makes no fuss when my dreadful old movie keeps me up after the time by which she would otherwise have fallen asleep. She simply turns away from me as I pull the sheet up to my chin. She does not sigh. She is not a silent nagger, having boned up thoroughly on the whole marital rigmarole. She falls asleep almost as soon as I've turned off the light. She does not brood. However, the next night she yawns a lot and goes to bed earlier than usual so I can't watch my kind of programme two nights running. My wife is an eminently reasonable woman. It is a key aspect of her eminence in general. She has had wide experience of what can happen when married couples fail to adjust to each other. She has studied the effect on their children. She does not believe in having rows. Nor do I. In so many ways we are a perfect pair. We agree entirely, without raising the subject, that it would be ill-advised to allow television or anything else, such as opinions, to come between us. I hold, generally speaking, with not arguing with people one may find oneself disagreeing with.

So when I look down at my children before pouring myself a glass of sweet, cheap sherry to take up to my bath, I may fleetingly regret the days when they were all over me when I came back from work, my son prodding me with a weapon and ordering me to fall about all over the place, my daughter hugging my legs and begging to be lifted up on to my shoulders; but my chief feeling is one of complacency. I do not scare them, they are more likely than not to be on the side of the angels. This is one of my wife's expressions – I certainly keep on the right side of her in the here and now since she doesn't believe in the hereafter; she believes this is it. She sometimes asks me to 'Be an angel . . .' or tells me my reward will be in heaven, carefully adding 'as the saying goes.' The thing is, she could conceivably be wrong, enabling me to tell her when we met up again, 'As the saying goes, I don't believe it!'. To return to my children: they will never have any cause to detest me and all I stand for since I stand for nothing – I never think 'I won't stand for it' except, possibly, when the National Anthem is played. They will grow up to be sensible, industrious etc. people over whom I will lose no sleep. I do not stay awake worrying about them now, except on occasion when worrying about whether I should be.

My son will probably marry someone like my wife because, like me, he is not of forceful temperament, but he has his mother's clarity of mind, which takes the form of argumentativeness for the time being, so perhaps he'll choose a wife who'll mainly be in charge when there's no conversation going on. There's something about him that worries me however – a certain lack of gaiety, or funlessness is it? I'd have to be a great deal more clear-minded about it than that to raise the matter with my wife.

My daughter who tends, at twelve, to a priggishness which will doubtless develop into my wife's certainty as regards good and evil, will not marry someone like me if only because she's going to be a good deal prettier than my wife and will have a wider choice, especially if she learns in the process to blur the distinction between good and evil a bit. Also, by the general inculcation of my wife's standards over the years somebody like me will have descended quite a long way below her sights by then. What my children are likely to have is purpose as well as brightness. I have aspirations for them too, because I am curious to see how far they can go. I won't mind waving until they are out of sight. As I sip my sherry, I give thanks to fate (to my wife) that I have fathered them, that they are not deformed or retarded or ugly, that they are unlikely to make demands on me. No, it does not bother me for long that they did not return my greeting.

The only time we feel like a complete family is when we are on holiday. At any rate up till now, our holidays have been happy interludes. My children have gone back to calling me Daddy, have asked my permission as well as my wife's to do things, have cavorted about with me at the water's edge and have occasionally held my hand when walking along the beach or wherever. We have forgotten ourselves on holiday. No television, masses of fresh air and exercise and long deep sleeps. Even my wife throws herself into it and thrashes about in a most untypical manner. (I speak of the water.) We are a real family for those two weeks (all we can afford, more than a lot of people can afford, thank you, dearest). I expect we are pleasant to behold, chatting away, splashing about. I see other families like us and it occurs to me we compare well with them. We have a healthy look about us. Our inner voices seem to have gone silent. Two weeks are long enough for my wife. They are of course not anything like long enough for my children. I do not mind either way. As I've tried to convey, I like the holiday mood but there is always the television to look forward to when we are home again.

Chapter Two

I sometimes think I could do with more of Webb's curiosity and the
Hambles' loving-kindness. As I've said, we live between them – two
childless couples – and wondering if they think I feel sorry for them
I sense their judgement, almost as much as my wife's, continuously
upon me.

There are times when I think of doing the disappearing trick. I
wouldn't worry about the family, oh no. But where would I go? I
see myself leaving a pithy note on the mantelpiece, stealing up the
garden path with a small black plastic suitcase, the only one that's
mine, turning left . . . then my steps falter. I see myself opening the
Webbs' front gate and going down their garden path (my wife has
taken our children somewhere beneficial like the local youth club
which they hate for the good it is failing to do them), knocking on
their front door and inviting myself in. For good. Webb would welcome me, moistening his lips with the tip of his tongue, his nose
twitching in a veritable paroxysm of curiosity. He would take me
up to a small dim attic and there I would observe through a pair of
binoculars how my family were managing without me – very well,
thanks, refining their devotion to each other by sighs and glances
betokening my lack of it. I have not worked out under what guise or
guises I would come and go without being recognised. I haven't
thought it through that far. It's the sort of thing I would have to
leave to Webb. He would keep me posted. He would enjoy that. He
has a marvellous eye for detail. I am not sure if his curiosity means
he cares. I am not that curious about other people and I do not care
enough about them.

For instance, one day I was hurrying down our front path pretending
not to have noticed his face peering through a tangle of some creeper

or other with small, undistinguished flowers that covers about four yards of our mutual fence. He had the look of some demented prowler concealing himself in the undergrowth.

'Stye any better?' he called out.

I went across and parted the creeper. He touched his right eye and I touched mine.

'Beg your pardon? We keep the little old place quite nice and tidy I always thought,' I said, baring my teeth as I tend to do when unsure how much humour there is in the air. Webb frowned.

'Young Virginia's.' With exaggerated tenderness he touched his eye again.

My son's name is Adrian. My wife chose our children's names. Virginia's other name is Clementine. Adrian's other name is Toby. I didn't argue with her. One of my suggestions for my son, having just read *Lady Chatterley*, were Thomas and John 'in no particular order,' I said. I didn't smile then, wanting there to be a lot of humour in the air, wanting it badly, my wife being little amused by now after some of the other suggestions I'd made – Randolph Dick, S. Herbert, Bob S. Leigh, Ivor Willy, C. Ellery and the like – and had already told me not to be flippant, which I thought she was being since she kept on coming up with these high-falutin' names which sounded odd on the lips of someone whose convictions rest in part on not putting on airs – though making, perhaps, too much of a song and dance of it. Aside from anything else, none of them went well with the name I'd brought into the family: Ripple. I also tried to get Edward past her, Ned for short, which she didn't reject outright at first, my having given up Spooner some while before. Vanilla and Cherie were rejected for my daughter for some reason and she was least amused at the end when I said that Virginia and Clementine together would make her sound like something unusually revolting from the new ice-cream parlour on the High Street, unless in later years she were to make her name on the cornet.

Be that as it may, I frowned too, not having noticed anything wrong with my daughter's eye, realizing too how little I actually look at her, taking into account the percentage of time when I'm around that her face is turned towards the television set or down over her homework etc. She has a sweet and innocent face albeit too often marred by expressions of sweetness and innocence and I ought to have noticed the smallest blemish on it.

'Very much better thanks,' I said.

Webb parted the foliage wider, snapping several twigs in the process, the ones I later discovered had the most promising buds on. Then he pushed his face further towards me, making me lean back.

'Some amazing ointments these days,' he said.

'Certainly are.'

'I'd watch your rear left tread if I were you.'

His little black eyes were flickering past me towards my car. He has this habit of suddenly changing the subject and often gives me advice about my car, having heard noises coming out of it which the garage had told me are perfectly normal – for a car of its age and had it received its telegram from the Queen yet? Oh very funny, I reply, and no, I don't know where the man who walks in front of it waving a flag has got to.

I winced. 'A touch of the old sciatica. Thanks all the same.' Then walked away, bent forward and with a slight limp.

I went back into the house and had a look at my daughter who was helping with the housework. Her left top eyelid was very pink and swollen over about two-thirds of it, probably as bad as it could be before it started getting better. It glistened with ointment.

'Hope you're putting something on that eye,' I shouted above the vacuum cleaner, touching my own left eyelid.

'It's only a silly stye,' she shouted back. 'I've only had hundreds of them already.'

'Just so long as . . .'

Whereupon she shoved the vacuum cleaner either side of my legs, then swivelled round to do under the dining-room table. I trotted back down the garden path, swiping hard at a Michaelmas daisy with my badminton racket and disapproving of myself for only having got so far as asking myself what a stye was to get so worked up about. Turning round at the gate I saw my daughter staring at me past the rag she'd begun cleaning the living-room window with. I thought: I bet she raises the subject at supper.

She did. Addressing her mother, she said, 'I saw Dad hitting the top off a flower with his badminton racket.'

'Sheer wanton vandalism,' I said, trying to remember what social injustice was usually the cause of that.

My son said, 'Why did you do that? He shouldn't, should he, Mum?'

'It's hardly your place to question what your father does in his own garden,' my wife said.

But she gave me one of her looks, a fleeting frown or slow blink, which is supposed to be perceptible only to me but which my children never fail to perceive.

'Practising my service,' I said, raising my fingertips to my chin and closing my eyes in a holy expression. 'Let us pray . . .'

But a solemnity had descended on the table and the chances of raising a laugh were nil. I had been guilty of undisciplined conduct. I could hear my wife thinking (she almost certainly wasn't): no wonder, he watches all that piffle on television. Beneath the calm there is violence. He is letting us all down.

Anyway, I could count on Webb keeping me informed of how my family were doing without me, the things my wife ought to be having done to the car to prevent their having a fatal accident, what success they were having with amazing ointments and so forth. I could see Mrs Webb bringing me supper in my darkened room, never saying anything, never looking at any part of me, wondering if the scribbling I was doing was all about her. Perhaps she would leave the tray outside the door. Each time I adopted one of Webb's new disguises she might pretend to herself that I had become a different person. There was the whole street to be walked up and down without being recognized by people who'd mention me to my family as having been observed behaving in a peculiar manner. The whole plan was flawed of course: Webb and I taking it in turns in unlit bathrooms, Mrs Webb not having the first idea what we were up to, whether I would have my own television set, what rent I would pay, a whole host of details like that. It is such flights of fancy, not seeing them through to a conclusion, that keep us out of trouble perhaps – instead of the down-to-earth detail of things, the sense of conclusions already having been reached, that this is it, that it's not worth the trouble.

To follow that train of thought for a bit, conclusively I hope. What I said about happy holidays by the waterside was a lie in so far as when I look back on them I imagine more intensely than usual those fatuous but exhilarating fancies that take some effort to put down. Let's see: a path of moonlight narrowing to the horizon from a beach of white sand, the rustle of palm fronds over my head as I lie back on my chaise lounge (as Mrs Hamble called it when she told the removal men, or rather asked them very apologetically, to put it by the window) and sip a mint julep (whatever that might be) while young ladies made duskier by the moonlit dark walk past me, their grass skirts swaying, then stop and stoop to top up my glass so that my eye is level with collars of flowers dangling in front of, not altogether concealing . . . the imagination should be able to manage the rest but makes a flop of it. Well, not exactly. What I mean is it's difficult to keep up or at least I have this difficulty about getting much beyond the moonlit, tropical setting to the actual action, the full exposure – beyond, that is, the nudge-nudge-pfft-there's-a-pair-for-you-whoops-get-an-eyeful-of-that stage. So that's the type of twerp one remains, is stuck with. I could not reveal to my wife that I entertained thoughts of this nature (or the other way round if you like playing with words not to mention yourself). She would only reply that that was perfectly natural/normal, dear. She would not be aghast since they did not have a 'social dimension', though 'poverty of imagination' is what is usually wrong there, she says, which is what seems to be wrong with me too, my fancies petering out like that, lacking altogether 'the creative urge' which society also needs badly, I'm told, though they may amount to the same thing as they evidently do in my case. So there again society and I seem to have something in common. Anyway, as I was about to say, I am sure my wife assumes I do not have thoughts of this nature and am contented with the few that I do have. Perhaps my fantasies would only worry her in so far as I started bringing magazines home that my children might happen upon, since she has a habit of sending them to find things that involves delving in drawers. They'd not be so fantastic then.

The magazines in question I buy in the lunch hour, hide away in the only drawer in my desk I can lock, and look at during the lunch break on the following day when I have so much on my plate that I must do without lunch. (I ought to add that I am ashamed, on reflection, not of the lust, naturally, but to be abetting the manner of life and person that satisfies it in that fashion, the degradation of women too of course. I shouldn't have needed to add that either; but 'ought to' you will have noticed. Thus one's sense of right and wrong may be muddled up in a word. That is to say, I'm not sure if I'm ashamed or not; knowing one ought to be ought to be the next best thing, but is it?)

Talking of dirty pictures, my wife has been overtly cross with me only once. It had to do with a comment I made about a reproduction of the Mona Lisa hanging above the mantelpiece in the house of a colleague – of hers, need I add – namely that I considered the expression neither wry nor mysterious nor inscrutable nor serene nor any of that, but plain horny (I swiftly added 'flirtatious' but words have a way of supplementing rather than supplanting each other). On the way home my wife asked why I had to make a 'perverse' point of reacting differently from everyone else, and in the field of the arts about which I knew little. It was nothing, I replied, thereby killing two birds with one stone. Be that as it may, I haven't accompanied her on any of her visits to houses of colleagues since then. I shouldn't have snickered, I know, thinking of finding myself at a loss in the midst of a variety of cultural goings-on in a large grassy space with a high fence around it – remembering too a silence of the most unjovial sort that fell around that lovely mischievous face and my wife receiving glances of pitying wonderment that someone like her should be married to someone like me. (I quite accept that joviality would not appear anywhere on the list of desired qualities for the kind of work my wife and her colleagues do. This is as it should be. 'How amusingly awful' doesn't sound right somehow. There are a number of phrases that will never cross my wife's lips, one of which is 'You've got to laugh.')

When the Hambles moved in we went round to ask if there was anything we could do to help. It was my wife's idea, co-sponsored by my daughter. The Hambles blushed and Mrs Hamble said to her husband, 'Isn't that kind of them, Alf?'
'It is that,' he replied.
There was nothing, they said, though even I could see there was. For example, they couldn't get their stove to work, a sink was blocked and a trunk with bedding in it had been mislaid by the removal people. As we were leaving I heard them discussing these misfortunes in that surreptitious way they have, not wanting their worries to leak out so that others would pity them, thereby allowing

them to pity themselves less. It was a shameful thought. Inaccurate too I think now.

As we returned up our front path, my wife said, 'No problems there. They'll be all right. Did you notice Webb watching from that upstairs window? Nosy little beast.'

Webb of course was waiting for us to leave. He was round there like a shot, leaving almost at once and returning with a plunger, then spent a long time with them, doubtless getting their stove to work and later bringing them blankets.

I mention this episode to show that my wife is less skilled at noticing things under her nose, while being very perceptive indeed about people further afield, or in so far as they are an example of a general social problem; which leads me to wonder, after not noticing whether I am there or not for much of the time, how long it would take her to notice that I was there for none of it – much more interesting though I might then have become as an example, while remaining the opposite of that to my children.

It was different at the outset when we were living in a garden flat a muscular stone's throw away from the North Circular Road and I made an effort to do my bit (admittedly not a lot) with the housework etc. One evening I offered to help with the supper to the extent of slicing the beans, peeling the potatoes, decanning the pea soup and putting them all on the boil. There were steaks too in a frying pan on a lower setting. Thereafter I joined my wife in the garden where I jabbed at weeds with a trowel, becoming distracted by, amongst other things, her brisk and domineering motions while raking leaves (had we so soon reached the autumn of our lives?), those other things being, in the form of a rapid series of comparisons, the somewhat idler charms of another young lady in the next garden who was only visible in snatches, though at exactly the right levels, through two missing slats in the fence. The comparison had reached the highly original notion that what is glimpsed has more allure than what is continuously beheld when my wife dropped her rake (no more than the bounder deserved, I reflected) and passed me at the trot. Indeed for an instant I believed the trots were precisely what it was because as she bounced by, the words I heard her cry were, 'Can't stop crapping.' For a second or two I stayed crouched where I was at the level of the lower missing slat until I realized she had in fact asked a question: 'God, what's happening?' So I turned and watched for a while the steam wafting prettily away through the kitchen window before following her slowly in to allow her sufficient time to make a start on sorting out the difficulty in her own way. ('We'll do it your way' became a handy phrase from approximately Day Two. No resentment to be read into that: anything to save time on a conversation whose end was clearly in view from the outset.) Eventually after a redundant pee and a meticulous hand-wash, I found myself in the doorway of the kitchen where she was flapping one arm about to clear the air and doing something with the other that caused a series of clanking sounds. 'Oh, really,' she was muttering – or was it 'Whatever next?' I do not recall. I was at a loss (witness to a funeral), could hardly charge forward into such a pea-souper without, I felt, the words and equipment suitable for a search party. The air began to clear and I opened the window a fraction wider, as far as it would go. Turning then, I saw her flushed face and the tears in her eyes.

'All mist to your grill, what?' I said.

It might have been then she said, 'Oh really,' or, 'Whatever next?'

There was no smile to detect on that pink and watery countenance, though we were newly wed and there was love between us then, a very great deal of it. Later she made light of the episode over spaghetti and scrambled eggs. I offered to clean the stove and pans with steel wool but she would have none of the rough stuff. It was so very much all right in those days long ago, any mutual occurrence at dusk or thereabouts being a likely prelude to foreplay or lifting the safety-curtain. She put a hand on my arm and smiled with forgiveness and affection, very much in that order. I grinned back and shook my head, having decided to shoulder the entire blame myself and not even hint it was all the fault of the woman next door. Virginia could have been conceived that night, along with much else. I internalized the problem, as my wife calls it in relation to her disadvantaged; the fire that might have been went to my loins. It was my passion in the end that steamed.

Perhaps Webb, Hamble and I should go off somewhere together. Webb would do the scout-work, stepping ahead, our lookout in all directions like one of those nervous, strutting birds. Hamble would waddle along behind, genial and appreciative, the beast who would bear all our burdens of body and spirit. And I, who had most to lose, would contribute nothing but a little poor wit – except that, without me, we wouldn't be there at all, going out into the world at last, myself neutral in the middle of the restless and inquisitive in front and the obliging and passive at the back. Thus I would be protected though I do not see myself lying between them in a bed. Webb couldn't be that inquisitive, nor Hamble that obliging. Also, I would have to do much of the talking. Webb only asks questions and points things out, while Hamble mainly communicates by statements of agreement and pensive movements of the head.

I suppose we'd look ridiculous, walking along abreast or in single file across a field or up a street. The trouble is I feel fairly ridiculous already, trying for example to catch a glimpse of my daughter's face, wondering how much (except on holiday) I enter my son's thoughts and feeling the eye of my wife's mind upon me, scanning me for signs of life. But without the least rancour. I give shape to whatever contentment she allows herself, thus playing my part. Compared with so many we have no troubles. I have no complaints so she cannot complain. It is ridiculous not to know why one feels ridiculous.

My wife is reading a book about immigrants and is asking herself what more she could do about them. Sometimes she tells us to listen to this. My children look worried, but they have the comfort of knowing there is nothing they can do, except try to be nicer to the darker children in their school. I am sure they are already nicer to them than most of the other children are. They try to feel guilty because their mother wants them to, as members of a society in which all responsibility for the wrongs of the world is shared. She does not say as much. She simply enunciates the sentences clearly and raises her voice at the end of them as if they were questions, looking at us in turn as if for an answer.

When she talks about what is wrong with the world I frown, which could mean either that I agree it's a shocking business and something should be done about it, or that I wish she wouldn't keep on interrupting my spy story – it's complicated enough to follow the plot as it is. Or I could be frowning because I wish that she wouldn't make it too easy for me to guess here and there what she'll look like in extreme old age, that she hadn't had her hair cropped short and done me the honour of touching up her features and complexion with some of the stuff in the tubes and jars which have needed increasingly less replenishment as the years pass, and pass they do. It is an aspect of liberation, I know, being taken for what one is, and that seems all right – though with the doubt there is about how far we should allow ourselves to be seen as we really are, there's surely something to be said for keeping up appearances in the meantime. I speak only, of course, for myself. So I end this line of thought with the observation that she has more wrinkles than she should have at her age, surely? They're from worrying too much about other people, of course; and how many more would there be if that included me? So my frown remains as I go over the various possibilities outlined above. They are a way of keeping my options open to evade her silent scanning and questioning voice. Truthfully, though, I've studied my frown in the mirror and it could mean anything. I sometimes think it's the imitation of a frown, that's all, trying to work up the feeling of how much I might care if I wanted to enough. If I smile at African and Asian people in the street and elsewhere, as I do occasionally when remembering what my wife has been reminding me of, my feeling is that they'd rather I didn't, that I was sucking up for my sake rather than theirs. Though they always smile back, that being polite. A frown of concern, while more appropriate, would make them think I wanted them to bugger off back to where they came from or similar. They might prefer that to the sucking-up – having it confirmed that there are quite a lot of shits about to have to put up with, which there are. They probably tell their children, who reply that there are children in their school who are specially nice to them because of what their mother has told them. So that becomes all right. The truth is I hardly smile or frown at them at all. I don't at anyone, not counting smiling at girls when what I'm most likely to get back is a frown, unless they're African or Asian of course.

I'd miss my family a lot if I walked out on them, less so if they walked out on me. Could that be guilt making the heart grow fonder? If I left them my wife would be sure it wouldn't be for long. 'He'll be back,' she'd tell my children, not adding 'with guilt written all over his face,' then proceed to read them an article about one-parent families, some of them doing pretty nicely actually. That would be part of the guilt: not having done enough to make them miss me more. I'm staying put therefore – the guilt imagined, the fondness to that extent too, more's the pity. Besides, it's wrong to abandon people who need you; that should be the chief part of the guilt, the pain you have caused etc. Not an aspect I've covered, the higher considerations left till last as usual, if considered at all. There's that guilt too – never taking the broader, less selfish view. 'You only think of yourself' – the commonest phrase in the English language I shouldn't wonder. Goodness me, there seems no end to it when the matter of guilt comes up. Demands a long recurrent sentence. For the rest of your natural life in fact.

It wasn't long before Webb told me that the Hambles had problems. The other day he said 'Psst!' to me through the fence, making me jump and hurry over to him lest he do it again. His thin eyebrows shot up a long way as if to rejoin his hairline and he jutted his chin towards the Hambles' house.

'They're having a job, those two,' he whispered.

'I thought they'd retired.'

'That's precisely your difficulty, isn't it? With the inflation and that, your pensions and savings . . . phut!' This with a gesture like blowing a kiss.

'Are you sure . . . ?'

He tapped his head. 'You know, I know, we all know what it's like these days. For starters, how much do you reckon they still owe on the house?'

'Haven't the foggiest. Sure they'll be all right,' I said stumblingly.

But I didn't believe it. There is something about them that smells of misfortune. They do not even have a television set. I have never seen more than one light on in their house at the same time. In winter I suspect they will try to do without heating. They never go out in the evening. I cannot imagine how they spend their time when they are not in their garden. I picture them huddled in blankets, listening to the radio, waiting for something to happen such as discovering once and for all which of them will pass on first.

'She told me.'

'Oh? What did she say exactly?'

'Well, he was out of the room and she said, (here Webb did his class-bridging voice which sounded like someone like the Duke of Edinburgh trying to imitate someone like Stanley Holloway) " 'E did so loike 'is tipple and flutter but those dies har hover and done wiv, I'm fried." She said she just didn't know the way things are going. I didn't have to ask her. She came right out with it. Almost slipped her ten quid I did. Brushed a tear from the corner of her eye, pretending it was some foreign body. I'm not blind you know. Not by a long kettle of fish. Better tell your trouble and strife to keep an eye on them. Got over her cold, has she? It's not as if I hadn't mentioned the matter.'

'It certainly isn't that,' I said with my frown. I tried to believe he was making it all up and only wanted to excite my curiosity but, as I say, the Hambles smell of anxiety and it is the smell of gas. I could hear Webb saying as the ambulance drove off, 'Didn't I tell you? I warned you, didn't I?'

Now he was only shaking his head, making sure he was the first to turn away. What bloody cold, I finally asked myself.

The windows that overlook the Hambles' house are those of my children's bedrooms so it isn't easy for me to spy on them. I never have any business in my children's bedrooms, not since I stopped reading them stories and that wasn't often. They thought my wife was better at it than I was, and they were right. I have a monotonous voice, which I cannot make distinguish between knights in armour, ogres, princesses or frogs or what have you. What would I say if either of my children came across me peeping out between their curtains? What could I say I was looking for? They would tell my wife and she would ask in front of them, 'What were you doing in Virginia's/Adrian's bedroom? I'm just curious.' Even having been given a long time to prepare my answer I would find myself cornered. Both my children have good reason to come into our bedroom, my daughter to borrow my wife's sewing things to show what a useful, practical person she's becoming, my son to borrow scissors or tweezers or pins to assist him with some creative project he's working on. They're always in and out of everywhere searching for things and, in any case, do their share of the housework here, there and everywhere, thus developing a sense of duty to family where, so my wife says, a sense of duty to society begins: what she means by charity begins at home. I do not help with the housework ('Your father more than adequately plays his part in other ways'), nor do I cook ('Your father boils a very good egg', not is one, alas) and therefore

28

share this with society too, it seems – depending as it does for its well-being on other people's sense of duty. In short, there would be an anomalousness, if that is the word, about my being found in my children's bedrooms pushing a hoover about or with a feather duster in my hand. (I have never dared ask her in what other ways I was playing my part exactly, apart from bringing in some of the money. 'Enough to be going along with,' some would say. My wife says we have more than enough. Perhaps I am also playing my part therefore by not bringing in more money than I do. The fewer lines I have the better, the less in need of prompting.)

Some time ago, on one of those royal occasions I bought a silky little Union Jack and stuck it behind the front doorbell. I should point out here that my wife has no time for shows of patriotism, a duty to society and to country being on quite different wavelengths, as she calls them. (My skill with the moral tuning-knob has made little progress; there's still too much static.) It is perhaps one of her chief virtues that she never inserts the question of national identity into the conversation, believing it might distract the children from more global concerns. I am grateful for that, in my own case being uncertain what identity I might have if I thought about it or how to set about looking for it, assuming I'd know what it was when I'd found it, while seriously doubting whether I'd want to keep it if I did know I'd got it. I have very sympathetic feelings towards my country sometimes, coming under all that scrutiny and having all those photographs taken of its derelict inner cities etc. I am not sure if I should want to feel patriotic in more rejoicing or prideful ways. Perhaps I am not sure enough of myself. No, that can't be it. My wife, as I've said, doesn't go in for patriotism and she's sure of everything, herself foremost.

Anyway, it was some time before the flag was no longer there, my wife not having wished to ask Adrian or Virginia which of them had put it there and then why, nor, by removing it herself, to have disparaged a surge of sentiment through which they must soon maturely pass. My children probably hardly noticed it. I did, a great deal, because the only other such flag on the street protruded from behind the door knocker of a house whose occupants put stickers on their car saying 'Buy British' or 'Forward with Britain' or some such and I removed ours extremely swiftly when I saw them striding down the street one day and thought they might be coming to call. So why had

I bought the flag in the first place? For two reasons: that this topic might be something worth writing about; and secondly that I wanted to know how much more beautiful the girl selling them from a stall in Trafalgar Square would be if she smiled. Very, is the answer to that. I can see her now, the shining long black hair, the tired grey eyes. She can't have been more than fourteen or so.

That evening at supper my wife wore a look of relief, believing that one of her children had now maturely passed through. After Virginia had served up the main (only) course, she (my wife, that is) brought the topic up apropos of nothing at all, 'A love of country is a perfectly healthy sentiment in its way if it means recognizing it in others and leads to wanting to make it, one's own, a better, juster place to live in. The trouble begins when people think they're superior to other people and start waving flags over it. For instance, does one's conscience allow – ?'

I dared to interrupt, to scale down my children's bewilderment (or utter boredom) and said, or muttered, 'Banners maketh man or stoppeth him rather . . .'

My smirk went unnoticed along with some chewing I was doing and I checked by a swift glance round the table, one two three, that I hadn't been heard properly, the punning anyway having let me down. My wife wore a deferred scowl, her train of thought uncoupled, my son was parting his food as if searching for a nice surprise under all that goodness, and my daughter . . . I'm honestly not sure. The twist at the corner of her mouth could have been caused by something she was doing with her tongue but she was already looking at me when my eyes reached hers and she had a knowing expression, her thoughts clearly not on any better country she ought to want to be living in – on man, for instance, and what her conscience would allow her when there was no stopping him (no banns intended). She should listen to her mother, I thought, wishing I had not ended her discourse on patriotism, having once started it. I hoped to make sure the subject didn't come up again in my lifetime. It had been a full enough year already for my wife's dissertations in that area, what with the deaths of General de Gaulle and President Nasser, the cancelling of a cricket tour to South Africa and the world not coming to an end with the election of a Conservative government under Edward Heath.

That has to do for the time being. I thought it would get easier. A typewriter might help. But I could hardly use it in the office, and at home . . . ? If you ask that you obviously haven't been paying sufficient attention. I had this vague idea that in trying to make one's thoughts visible as it were, one might begin to think less of oneself (either meaning or both). But I can already see that the opposite tendency (either or both) is also encouraged by trying to put it all down. Perhaps there is some middle way. Or is it just the clarity itself for its own sake? But to what purpose? To exhaust oneself altogether perhaps (all that memory jogging), to become wholly wise. If there's not much to exhaust, though, there can't be much wisdom at the end of it. That's when it might get even harder, getting tired of oneself with nothing to put in its place, except for having opinions ('I think what I think; you must take me as I am') or thinking more about others, becoming less heartless. Or is it best to say nothing if you can't say everything? I think not. Not yet anyway. This doesn't seem to be getting me anywhere. I suspect it never will. A topic henceforth to be avoided. Too exhausting. Bad for the heart. Unwise.

Chapter Three

Time is passing. My son has stopped asking me about my work. A long time ago he stopped asking me how strong I am. My wife was good about that, saying she had no desire to be married to a he-man, not adding what sort of man she did desire to be married to instead. Against every shred of the evidence, my son wanted to believe I was the strongest man if not in the universe, at least in the neighbourhood as far afield as he was likely to meet a boy whose father was stronger. Another blow was that I said I'd never cared for the idea of playing rugby football with all that falling down and being bumped into by others one was likely to be doing.

There is nothing remotely interesting or important I could tell him about my job without lying. I have had only one promotion since he was born and then he was too young to derive pleasure from it, being only five weeks old at the time. My chances of further promotion are slight. I hope he is learning not to mind and to transfer his need to be proud of me entirely to my wife. She is the ambitious one in the family. I sometimes wonder how she reconciles herself to the fact that, increasingly, she's doing very well out of those who aren't. The more failure she has to live with, the more success she makes of it, to say nothing of the money. That must take some living with. I'm glad I'm not useful if my conscience would prevent me from enjoying it. If one is the kind of person who sets store by being useful, it is likely one has a much stronger sense of one's uselessness than people who are of no use whatever to anyone. I am useful to my wife (play my part) in so far as I am not a drug-pusher, property speculator, fascist beast or one of those. Nor am I a male chauvinist though I do snort (when alone) if confronted on television by one of those domineering, masculine-sounding women who want to put a stop to masculine domination. So do I, as we shall see in a minute. My wife's view is that women's liberation per se distracts the attention from more central concerns, as aforementioned. I agree with that: having one's attention distracted from women per se, for example. Oops, there's your he-man talking.

I am in charge of Information Services in a large trading company with offices throughout the world. My job is to produce tables and charts showing trends in sales and the like. Marketing intelligence is another phrase for it. An agency has taken over much of the work but fortunately the company's growth has remained one step ahead of it so there's still enough figure work left to keep me and my staff – a youth called Hipkin – busy, or busy enough to appear busy. I run an efficient system of records and information retrieval. Or rather I inherited it from my predecessor and all I really have to do is not deliberately neglect or interfere with it. He had an intense fear of criticism and hence an infinite capacity for taking pains. He died shortly after collapsing on the job, on discovering a zero missing in some figures from Hong Kong which had been returned to him by the Finance Director with a question mark in the margin. The missing zero was his own, not mine luckily. Otherwise I wouldn't have got his job, but of course he wouldn't have died either.

My boss's title is Director of International Sales and I enjoy addressing him in memoranda by his initials since it is the only way I have of telling him he is hell. (Actually that was my wife's idea of a joke, at which she grinned at some length whilst I didn't, wondering what I might have said, not having consciously spoken for a long stretch of time beforehand. I'd rather have that sort of humour than my own, I think – the scholarly, informed kind, which enables you to tell a joke with a curl to your lip and a weary peer about you in search of someone as ill-suited to the crude cloth of daily life as you are. Not that my wife comes into that category in the slightest. I wouldn't want anyone to think that.)

My boss is younger than I am and one can almost hear him panting in his efforts to get to the top. He is reputed to have a good mind but all I can discern in his long reports etc. is a certain orderliness of presentation and an ability to string clichés together. Most of the vital parts (or skeleton if you prefer) come from me. Other people are a matter of complete indifference to him except in so far as he can make use of them. Perhaps something nasty happened to him at school or perhaps there is something lacking in his home life. His name is Plaskett and, to put it delicately, he is an utter or perfect shit. He is such a shit that one feels under no obligation to imagine how he might have become one. My wife believes in the 'innate goodness' of people, which only goes bad as a result of something that happens to them when they are young. Bullying offends me as much as the next man, but assuming Plaskett as a boy was anything like he is now, he might have been the one child in the history of the world who asked for it frequently, and any amount more of it couldn't have made him more frightful than he is now.

Conveniently for both of us, I'm his willing vassal. I turn in my work on time and he's never faulted it. He therefore thinks I'm a good chap and does not make enquiries of me that would lead him to conclude my job is overpaid and otherwise a complete doddle. I arm him with immaculate tables and charts and other data which he passes off as his own. I am quite happy with this state of affairs. I am glad he can depend on me because I have no choice but to depend on him. The thought of having to find another job puts me into a panic. He is my protector, for as long as I serve him well. It is a feudal relationship. God help me, I wish I didn't dislike him so much. I wish he was not younger than I am. I wish I could wholeheartedly want him to fall flat on his face. If he did, he'd take me with him and rise up again without me. I imagine myself saying to him, 'Now look here, Plaskett, I just want you to know you're an utter (or perfect) shit', or even giving him a good kick up the backside. And then I flush at the thought and tremble with terror, as if I'd actually said or done it. He has no idea what I think of him. I even think he might respect me, rather as he would respect a good clock for always telling him the right time.

Last week he gave me my annual confidential interview.

'Not much to say, Tom,' he began. 'A good solid year's work, I've said.'

'That's very kind. Thanks. I've only tried to . . .'

'I can depend on you. That's what matters.' He swivelled his chair round towards the window and I nodded vigorously, at the same time trying to compose my face in a flattered expression as he swivelled back again and frowned down at his fingernails to suggest an aura of, let's say, shrewd world-weariness.

'The heading Zeal: "A very fair day's work," I've put.'

I said, 'Missed out again on the Queen's Award for Industry, have I?'

I sometimes give him the satisfaction of being able to put me in my place, which he did on this occasion by conveying it would be best to pretend not to have heard me.

'Question is,' he went on, still studying his fingernails, his voice beginning to develop a drawl of beleaguered wisdom, 'how do we see your prospects?'

I did not have to reply immediately, thank goodness, because at that moment Mrs Hodge, the coffee lady, came in. What could I have said? 'By turning a blind eye?' Of course not. I might have said something about soldiering on, doing my best and continuing to give satisfaction. Oh yes I might. Nothing wrong with that, surely? From what little I know of religion, sucking up out of fear is a predominant part of it. And as I may already have hinted, Plaskett is godawful. It would have been truthful what's more, giving it the edge on religion. (My wife does not hold with religion, calling it hocus-pocus and a 'distraction'. I do not reply that that seems a pretty good start to me.) Anyway, Mrs Hodge is one of those people with an over-developed sense of duty. She comes to work, as she did that day, even when she has a stinking cold or worse and should be in bed. She is loyal to the company and hates to cause inconvenience. She mothers the younger staff like Hipkin, telling them to cheer up, they'll soon be dead and the like. She cleans and makes coffee etc. on our floor and the one below and cannot imagine us getting along without her. I'd say she was the mother of all of us if she weren't so servile. In my experience conscientiousness in a lot of people goes with servility. In other people, my wife for example, it goes with the need to sustain an elevated level of self-satisfaction. I didn't mean that.

'Not just now,' Plaskett said with a pout, then, 'Oh, all right, since you're here.'

That is the sort of man he is. On one occasion we had a collection for one of the typists whose daughter was badly burnt playing with an electric fire, to buy her a present with. Plaskett brushed the subscription list aside saying he was under the impression the company had a welfare fund for that sort of thing to which he'd contributed 'not inconsiderably' at Christmas. I was the only witness of the incident and didn't pass it on. There is only so much hatred in the air I can stand.

Mrs Hodge coughed, harshly, with her mouth open, both her hands being occupied with carrying the tray. Plaskett winced, twice to make sure she would see it, and indicated the cup should be given to me.

'Sorry I disturbed you, Mr Plaskett,' she said, clearing her throat lengthily before his name.

Plaskett nodded and stared her into leaving the room as fast as possible. When I had closed the door behind her, he said, 'Do I recall asking you to explore the viability of vending machines?'

He had and I'd done nothing about it, or rather I'd asked with my habitual painstakingness round the typing pool and those who didn't prefer making their own, the way they liked it and less expensive, would miss Mrs Hodge.

'I'm making enquiries.'

'I'd like some action sharpish on that. A week, seven days, shall we say? Where were we?'

'My prospects.'

'Ah yes. Well, I don't think we've anything more to say about those, do we? Keep at it.'

The interview was over. I didn't touch the coffee of course, except that as I got up I pushed it six inches towards him across the desk in a decisive manner. Right again: I did no such thing. I took it away with me and the cup gave several little rattles against the saucer in the process.

I passed Mrs Hodge on the way back to my desk and gave her a wink. It is a weakness of mine that I like to be liked. Sometimes I catch myself admiring Plaskett because he doesn't care whether he is or not. God knows what it must feel like to enjoy being feared. In short, there is much about Plaskett that is a mystery to me. Before resuming work, I wrote 'Plaskett is a huge volcanic arsehole' twenty times on my blotter in gothic letters, crumpled it up and hurled it into the waste-paper basket. Later I flushed it down the lavatory, such is my fear of him. Even then I could see him holding up the soggy ball, saying, 'Are you responsible for this, Ripple?'

I've told my wife very little about Plaskett because she'd go on asking if I was standing up to him – if not to her it wouldn't occur to her to add. I wouldn't want my children to know I had to take orders from someone like that, who didn't fire on the cylinder of ordinary humanity, one of my wife's phrases which I quite like. (I've used it when talking to my car, as one does, reminding it that its owner is only human.) I prefer my children to assume I'm my own master and take orders from no one. My wife would say that Plaskett is a product of his social environment and can't help being what he is. (She would say that I can help being what I am, though she doesn't.) I'd like Plaskett to meet my wife, say at the annual office party (which she'd never dream of attending I'm glad to say), because then he might think more, or less, of me for having married a dominant woman. I dominate him on my blotter; words do have a certain power. After all, he is not immortal, I tell myself, he is as insignificant as me in any big scheme of things, such as the size of the universe or the history of civilization. But I'm not persuaded. I sometimes wake in the small hours, wishing him harm, such as being belaboured over the head by Mrs Hodge, or getting the sack for an inaccurate set of figures I have provided him with, or being made to stand in the corner for a week behind young Hipkin's desk, or coming to me with tears in his eyes bleating, 'Oh Tom, my dear, dear friend, at last I see myself for what I am.' I dislike him most for appearing to me in the dead of night in the silliness of my imagination, against the background of my wife's calm breathing and making me grit my teeth, because that reminds me that I have nothing better to think about, like a big scheme of things, and that I sometimes have difficulty in rising above myself (especially lying on my back in the small hours.)

It occurs to me that I might put Webb on to Plaskett. 'Mr Webb,' I would say, 'there is a certain Mr Plaskett who lives somewhere in Hampstead Garden Suburb and I am curious about him.' I would add that I suspect him of vile and curious habits that are a menace to the community at large and that it would be in its interests if he no longer was. I would wear the sort of expression my wife wears when she speaks of property speculators or my daughter wears when I swipe the heads off flowers with my badminton racket. I would like to believe that Plaskett had secret vices, though admittedly if I thought he had a private life at all I might detest him less. I would like to have something on him so that I could drop hints. I think up annual interviews that take a rather different form from the above. When too much slack in the typing pool, being firmly in the saddle and not expecting praise, when the figures are good and business is looking up and one can't satisfy everyone, not in his position, when getting to the bottom of it and so forth, prompt on my part snappy words and phrases (plus a hard look into his eyes with just a tremor of a wink in one of mine) such as pinching, sniffing, the well-deserved clap, spending time in steep stairways, doing it in groups, three score and ten less one and having a smack at it . . .

I jot down the possibilities on my blotter and feel ashamed of myself, especially since young Hipkin caught sight of a couple of them and gave me a queer look, just about the only time he's looked me in the eye at all. I'd like to help Hipkin. Seriously. He is totally without ambition, drive, keenness, zeal and the rest – an extreme version of me, in fact. I have no idea what makes him tick. I do not even know if he enjoys his work or hates it. I wish he'd come up to me one day and tell me his job (entering numbers on index cards mainly) is a ghastly bore, which it is. When I ask him how it's going he says it's going all right.

Hipkin is about nineteen and not attractive to look at – a great deal less attractive even than me, for example – though we are roughly the same physical type with squat bodies and shortish legs, and lips, nose and ears which are small but protrude. Our cheeks are reddish and our complexions smooth. I do not think he has started shaving and a razor blade lasts me for ages. I caught a glimpse once of his calf. It is off-white and almost hairless like mine. Our eyebrows are sparse but scrubby offset by really quite elegant eyelashes, and our hair is of that lustreless, lightish brown colour associated with mice which goes fluffy and sticks out and up when it's washed – to judge from that, his is less often than mine, confirmed by (usually) more dandruff. Apart from the fact that my features tend to come together to make a neutral whole so that I'd be the last person you'd notice in a crowd (whereas Hipkin you'd soon notice at the edge of it, as someone who seemed to have strayed into it and was always being barged into or tripped over), the main difference between us is that Hipkin is incapable of hating people like Plaskett and would never wink at Mrs Hodge, to say nothing of the girls in the typing pool by whom he expects to be, and is, ignored.

I did not allow them to ignore me, not at first. I wish I could think of an alternative to the wink to break the ice of the official relationship between us with, or the melting words to follow it. The responding smile became decidedly frosty and I suspected they thought I suffered from a nervous tic. I therefore decided to give up winking at them. I accept it was somewhat indiscriminate and totally without purpose, other than giving me insight into Hipkin's situation of knowing it's not worth the bother, that there aren't the words. I'm back where he hasn't even started. (I've exaggerated here to make a point. My winks were hypothetical, after the one or two which each new girl got with a nod on her first morning. Well, you never know. Or do, always. We must always try to imagine how it might have been. I suspect that Hipkin can't even get as far as this either.)

How can I help him if he won't even call me by my Christian name? I could pass my magazines on to him, buy him an hour's worth of massage, invite him to accompany me to the cafeteria, enquire into his background, wink at *him*. But I fear things might then stop being all right for him because he would start to depend on me. I would like to help the Hambles too, perhaps because they would rather die than be helped, which is what may happen. Hipkin will not die without my help. He is the sort of person who'd cry out for it when the beach was deserted and the last of the lifeguards was stepping on the bus for home.

I do not wish my children to be dependent on me either, because I wouldn't enjoy their struggle against me for their independence. My wife may be in for a rude shock one day in spite of all that reading she does. I can see her not batting an eyelid, her eyes watering from the effort, when one of our children becomes less than she hopes for. If my son turns out to be a ruthless property speculator, for instance, her eyelids would go out of control and she would look like me attempting to get off with the whole typing pool simultaneously. I wouldn't mind if he became that, on the clear understanding I could reside in one of the properties he had speculated in. I wouldn't mind it one bit. As I've said, I watch too much television. Scenes from some of the worst (best) of it keep on coming back to me. I see these fat cats who have made a million or two wheeling and dealing and wonder how much and how often my conscience would trouble me if I had a villa on a cliff, a chauffeur-driven Rolls, endless girls pawing and lounging about me on a yacht and all the rest of it. And of course I couldn't stand it. I couldn't stand the thought of being found out and having it all taken away from me. I wouldn't wear my riches lightly. I wonder what sort of a conscience I must have that these thoughts should enter my head at all. I can sometimes feel my sense of right and wrong dissolving in a haze of the intensest pleasure. But then it hardens back into its usual lumpy inconsistency and I tell myself once more how lucky I am to have a wife who cannot (has no desire to?) read my thoughts. It makes little difference if my dreamt-of untold riches were obtained lawfully. To her they are equally 'ill-gotten'. I haven't told her I do the pools; in fact I've told her I wouldn't dream of it. This means we never discuss what we would do if we won on them, though once my son raised the question, beginning with a yacht as it happens, Virginia chipping in with a bigger house and a decent car. They turned to me as my wife said, 'Dreams of wealth are the refuge of the inadequate.' Ouch to that – but who is *adequate*, that's what I'd like to know? I asked my son, in the absence of foot-men, to pass the potatoes.

And in that instant I caught myself hoping he does not turn out to be a homosexual because then I'd miss the occasions I've already begun looking forward to when he'll start bringing girls home. He's going to be quite a good-looker which improves the chances of the girls being good-lookers too. I hope by then the miniskirt is back and that female emancipation has gone the full distance. I can think of nothing nicer sometimes than a world in which the man is the sex object. Nowadays, in my experience or lack of it, the wish can only father another wish and it's a bastard.

To continue that line of thought a little while longer. I've read of ugly men who have been exceptionally successful lovers – this going along with women not being much fussed about physical beauty. That's probably piffle but reinforces (exacerbates?) the pleasure of contemplating the day when the man is the sex object. I have been known to have absurd thoughts on this prospect, being glanced at, say, on the Underground as some girls are (by that sort of girl) and not glancing away, oh dear me no, slipping my visiting card into her possession by various subterfuges, or being followed up the escalator and accidentally bumped into in the street, therefrom on to a pub and thence ad libitum, to become thoroughly Latin about it. I doubt this ever happens the other way round. Men haven't got the bollocks, to coin a phrase. How much more, or less, sex would go on then, I ask myself. It is sometimes called 'casual'. The more that went on the more casual it would become surely, in the sense of impermanent rather than irregular; but 'done without care and thought' as the dictionary also has it? I should think that the more it was done the more care and thought would have to go into it if people weren't to become altogether too casual about it.

Nor does age matter nearly as much to women as it does to men, they say, when scanning the field. Why do they bother? Nevertheless I hope the roles are reversed fairly soon without changing the current discrepancies in range of preference. Perhaps then too women will be prepared to pay for it to the extent that men are now. Speaking as a nymphomaniac, I might then consider becoming a loose man (as opposed to yet another man on the loose) two and a half nights a week, say, but choosy. I would need to see their photographs first, not they mine. But I do not consider it for long. I would have nothing to do with the female equivalent of the kind of man who goes whoring now or, come to think of it, who treats women as sex objects. I would not need to be chatted up or wait to be asked. I would make it clear right away it was offered for nothing, the way I imagine it. I would in the right circumstances be an extremely easy lay.

If I ramble on a bit more like this I might get it out of my system – not that that is what it is, shambling about all over the place as it does, and as for getting it out of it, no chance of that, it being largely what the system is or would be if there was anything systematic about it. Let's see now. I am not much in favour of paying for it. One would prefer to be lusted after for oneself. Approximately half-way between the two might be an incident with a reward afterwards of a biscuit and a cup of tea as if she'd given a pint of her blood and felt good about it. Of course I am not opposed in principle to treating it as a transaction. As my wife keeps on telling my children (I think of them solely as mine when she tells them things of this sort) one appreciates most what one has to work hard and save up for. We enjoy more what we earn than what we are given etc. I am in danger here of losing the connection between sex and the other best (or next best) things in life. Except that the best sex is probably free, unless it's only with the person who can't usually refuse you it, when the freedom is without choice. I see now I've drifted away from the sense of free meaning freely available, like some kinds of medical attention and the air you breathe. My wife has enjoyed the sex she has had with me, I assume (she has done it increasingly soundlessly while breathing in more air at greater speed and fallen asleep sooner afterwards), but I doubt she has ever considered it a poetical experience exactly or even an enriching one. (There I go again. When it comes to sex I have money on the brain.) In recent times I guess the frequency with which we have done it is slightly above the mean, their being unwilling to pay for it or the preliminaries in food and drink being a factor there of course. She does not discuss these matters. As an intellectual she is not that far gone. For doing just about everything else she has to have a reason, in fact for everything that does not have to do with the natural behaviour of the body.

She would probably think it unreasonable or nugatory (one of her words which I must look up some time) to try to decide why we make love as frequently or infrequently as we do. I have a reason. If I didn't do it with her I wouldn't be doing it with anyone. I am true to her out of laziness, poverty and that absence of opportunity and initiative which some say are the hallmarks of freedom. Here we go again. Any way you look at it (freedom), there seems a price attached. If I had unlimited money, however, and could do and have whatever I liked, satisfying one appetite after another as the fancy took me, I doubt if I'd feel as free as I think I almost do simply meditating, and generally trying to be reasonable, on the subject – assuming I wouldn't be bothered with doing that too when being kept so busy satisfying the appetites. But something is wrong here: observing my fancies etc. for what they are, getting more acquainted with and in charge of myself, knowing how I'm likely to conduct myself in most, if not quite all, circumstances, the choices and possibilities begin to dwindle fast until, if I go on like this, there'd be none left at all to speak of. Knowing you're a slave or kleptomaniac (or someone obsessed with sex, not of course that there could conceivably be such a person) or whatever it is you are and having a long hard look at all you've got or are lacking, might make you a whole lot more sensible but more miserable, i.e. more freedom, if it's anything to do with knowing, could mean exactly the opposite of what could be called feeling liberated. This is going on a bit. It is what my wife calls 'intellectualizing' for which I have no aptitude on my own account (there I go again). It doesn't seem to get me very far so I might decide to give it up. It doesn't come at all easily, as you can tell. Perhaps I need only concentrate on keeping up with my wife, whom it gets a lot further; in that way I might find out how far gone she is.

Let me see, where were we? If I did have an affair, (a) I wouldn't tell her about it, and (b) she would guess immediately. What would her reaction be? One of the reasons why I'd like to have one, not the main one of course, would be to find out for sure. I doubt if she'd make any sort of fuss, sulk, weep or stamp her foot. In those circumstances she might have to seek reasons for the natural behaviour of the body (mine), a search in which she wouldn't expect me to take part. She would keep me guessing. I would never know if her search ended in her thinking me despicable, thoughtless or weak, or in her not thinking much about it or me at all. She would continue as before, even in bed. She would insist. Having gained the moral ascendancy she would wave a banner on top of it. (Silly thoughts? But knowing that does not stop one thinking them.)

If she were unfaithful to me? I wouldn't mind a bit. Wait. If she were, she'd tell me straightaway, she'd apologize for hurting me and speak perhaps of freedom, of rediscovering the basis of our mutual trust and affection and God knows what other twaddle – thereby gaining the moral ascendancy again. I would only be humiliated by the thought that in her situation words would fail me altogether. I wouldn't be put off her, or rather it, since for the foreseeable future, as I've explained, they would have to remain the same thing. I wouldn't lose respect for her (on the contrary) but I would offer constant prayers that she'd stop referring to it. Which she never would, especially when not referring to it. She'd never leave me, that's for sure. She believes in the family. In any case she's more of a sex object than I am, given that I'm not one at all. We share having no illusions on that score. As I've said, we are well suited to each other.

Which brings me back to Hipkin, who ought to have the freedom but is totally incapable of using it, who has no choices therefore and, it seems, a shortage of the necessary equipment to act on them if he had them. I wish he didn't worry me by being of such little consequence, by being too like me for comfort, without even the advantage (disadvantage?) of my self-awareness.

I might put Webb on to Hipkin too. Perhaps he is sobbing in silence all the time. Perhaps he buries his face deep into his pillow to hide his grief at what he is from a widowed mother or brutal father. Perhaps his room is stacked high with pornography and it is all he asks of life, that he be free to dream, awake or asleep, of always being somewhere or someone else.

'Everything all right is it, Bob?' I ask him.

'S'all right, Mr Ripple.'

'No problems? Done the Japanese sales, have you?'

'Fine, Mr Ripple. I think they're all right.'

'Cheer up, Bob, it might never happen.'

He goes back to his index cards. I do not see his eyes. If he ever looks at mine it is when I am not looking at his. Everything's always all right, Mr Ripple. I'll never tell him again he must call me by my Christian name. His blush was awful. Apart from anything else, it heightened his pimples.

So it goes. I do not know where Hipkin goes for lunch. Not to the cafeteria. He just goes out into the street, I think, and wanders. One day perhaps he'll get up from his desk, run towards me and hit me in the face as hard as he can. Having interfered with his life, I might think it served me right. Or perhaps one day I'll look across at him and he'll start howling, the tears streaming down his face, his eyes wide with despair, stark raving mad. Any such abnormality in his behaviour I would have to report to Plaskett, who'd say, 'He'll have to go of course.' And I would reply, 'Hold on a second, shouldn't we consider . . . ?' Of course I bloody wouldn't. I would nod and reply, 'Yes, Mr Plaskett.' Thereafter I would cover several sheets of blotting paper with my opinions of Plaskett in between sending a memorandum to Personnel Department requesting Hipkin's dismissal. When I gave him his papers I would apologize and he would say, 'It's all right, Mr Ripple.' I couldn't tell my wife about Hipkin, because she would tell me how many others there are like him who need attention and help and compassion and love that she is 'all too rarely' able to give them. And I cannot, ever.

Chapter Four

Time has passed. We are linked more closely to the Hambles and Webbs now, thanks to the children. Virginia went one way and Adrian the other. I suppose my daughter had to find an outlet for her budding social conscience somewhere. One evening at supper we were discussing . . . listening to my wife holding forth about the plight of old people who live on dwindling pensions. There was a television programme I wanted to catch and the more my wife has to say the more slowly she eats. 'E.g. the Hambles,' I said to bring the topic back to earth from those ever rising heights where the altitude is such that she stops eating altogether.

Virginia charged in then. She needed to get on the right side of her mother, who had scolded her the day before for not counting her blessings, being on that occasion three square meals a day and a roof over her head. We'd been watching a programme about the homeless and five minutes before it was due to finish, with my connivance (the tiniest nod of the head) – my wife being out of the room being outspoken about something over the telephone – she (Virginia, that is) had switched over to something else, saying (speaking my thoughts exactly), 'OK, we've got the message.' Just at that moment my wife came back, the television was turned off altogether and the lecture began. I sat there, deep in thought, while Virginia played with her shoelaces and began sniffing, which led to the reminder about her blessings. The depths I had reached were that I should never undermine my wife's authority over my children because I have nothing to put in its place, what with preferring *Kojak* etc. to having the homeless drawn to my attention. With this in mind and hoping to shift the subject, I asked, 'What was all that about?'

'One of my families on the move again.'

'You were certainly giving them what for all right.'

'That was my colleague who took them over. Wonder if he's really up to it.'

'Oh, I'm sorry.'

'That's what he said.'

Anyway, Virginia was suitably chastened (the things in her life she can do thoughtlessly for the sheer fun of them I see with sorrow dwindle away daily – no wonder she gets styes – but that goes rapidly into reverse on recollecting which of those things will be beyond the reach of the most amazing of ointments) and now had to prove to her mother that she had a warm and beating heart.

I used to search for it with her, my hand over hers, hers over mine. I can't do that now though I'd dearly like to. She's had an immaculate sex education from my wife, namely one that anticipates the questions so that they need never be asked, at the same time erasing the smutty, sniggering titillation, the wonderful, alluring mystery of finding out all about it for oneself. Only in sex education, apparently, is the 'discovery' method not yet fashionable. My wife believes in cleaning the topic up, in giving it an airing, though she doesn't apply the same principle to people's dirty laundry (some contradiction here?). She believes in making it natural and biological and wholesome, a favourite word of hers, which makes me lose my appetite for it somehow. Her other 'frames of reference' are brute lust and the end product. Oh dear, those programmes we've had to sit through showing childbirth and the copulation of livestock and monkeys etc. We sit there in tense, embarrassed silence while she tells us the naked truth should never cause tension or embarrassment. I do not care to think of myself and my children as basically animals. Personally I'm satisfied with being simply basic. Animals doing it, especially dogs in the street, disgust me. I've seen them stuck together, unable to tear themselves away. In a way my problem too of course. It shouldn't be allowed in the home.

I wonder if my children imagine my wife and me doing it. I bet they try not to. Far worse, I wonder too whether my wife would mind their imagining us doing it. I suspect she wouldn't, so that when we do do it I sometimes catch myself trying to be on my best behaviour. I'm tempted then to ask her whether they shouldn't be made to watch us doing it, on the assumption that it's perfectly wholesome etc., that all it really is is swarms of sperm chasing scurrying eggs,

46

that all the panting and physical jerks are only to set them off on their frantic treasure hunt. When they only meet up with a couple of sheets of Kleenex, how soon do they expire? What on earth is going on down there in the sewers? I am glad I did not have a sex education. Those glimpses and dirty books and playground whispers, those first feels (learning by doing, the project approach) were more rousing than the conduct of chromosomes (I'm sure they only start behaving in that exhibitionist manner when under the microscope) or films about the coupling of raw-arsed baboons and the like. I'm sorry my son won't get the same kick I got from my first sight of a live naked breast (Deirdre Perkins's), or two years later, within a week, of one female buttock and a fringe of pubic hair (Deirdre's older sister). My wife has always made a point of not concealing her nakedness about the house. She leaves the bathroom door ajar (except when on the lav; don't dwell too long on that) and expects me to do the same. Neither of my children has seen me naked. Nor will they. Oh no. If they did they might take me even less seriously than they do already.

I have not seen my daughter naked since she was about nine. I would like to again, now that it's not only her social conscience that's budding. I would like to see how hairy she has become. I would like to feel for her heart again. If I made the suggestion, she'd tell my wife who'd think it all of a piece with my impulse to knock the tops off flowers with my badminton racket. Whereas it wouldn't be pure lust, or rather it would be, compared with my desire to feel for the heart, and for places in an ever-widening circle round about it, of other girls about her age. (Is this all right if cancelled out by never dreaming of actually anywhere near doing it?) If there'd only be an element of lust in it I've no idea what the other elements could be. Perhaps my wife knows of a book which describes incest as wholesome, instancing the Egyptians; and wasn't there a Pope who shagged his sister? But even my wife would draw the line somewhere, as I do by not going anywhere near the bathroom when my daughter is having a bath in case she's left the door open and I blurt out, 'Oh, let me feel again for your warm and beating heart!'

Which she now revealed by saying, 'Can't we *do* anything for them? Oh please, Daddy?'

I was flustered. The Hambles had many of the same blessings to count as we did and I couldn't decide on a tone of voice for my reply which was neither condescending nor unconcerned.

'Just guesswork of course. They might be worried and lonely and hard up . . . er, getting on, you know . . .' I fizzled out, hearing my wife draw breath to come to my rescue.

'Your father's right, dear.' She usually backs me up like that, not realizing her support only shows how much I need it, and then went on (how she does go on . . .), 'But of course one can't know for certain. One must always hold oneself in readiness while never appearing to pry. People need empowerment not kindness, power to cope with an environment that deprives them of their rights, not kindness handed to them on a plate. One acts to lift the deprivation, to make them aware of what they can do to help themselves. Charity is a great destroyer of the spirit. Nobody likes to be felt sorry for. Self-respect and human dignity are what matter.'

I nodded in wholehearted agreement, being in a hurry to get up and turn on the television. Though I can't pretend I did agree, reflecting on how much of my self-respect and dignity I would willingly give up in the process of helping myself to what was on the plate. As I rose from my chair, wiping my mouth and still nodding, I could see my daughter working out how to hold herself in readiness, without prying. It would have to be she who found them gasping their last by the gas oven, who allowed herself to feel sorry for them only when their spirit had been destroyed along with just about everything else, by something colder than charity.

But it was to me she came a few days later, not her mother.

'I'm just going round to the Hambles,' she said.

Picking up the *TV Times*, I replied, 'That's nice. How about a drive to the park after lunch?'

'I thought I'd borrow something from them.'

'Something? You can't just breeze in and say, "Can I borrow something?"'

'I know what I want to borrow, silly.'

(I like it when she calls me that. We then feel more like a family – of three children and one parent. She never calls her mother silly. This is because she isn't.)

'What's that then?'

'A candle.'

'What on earth for? What thing are you going to switch off now?'

This referred to a current power-saving campaign. My son was in the habit of waiting outside the lavatory so that the moment he heard the chain pulled he could switch off the light. He sometimes went to the lav and had his bath in the dark. Once I turned off the light in the dining room when he was half-way to the table carrying a tray with glasses and a full water jug on it. Because I had accidentally chosen the moment when my wife was in the midst of explaining to Virginia why we should be on the side of some strikers or other, not primarily because she got the jug on her lap, the rest of the meal was spent in silence. On another occasion I nearly killed myself falling down the stairs. I had turned on the landing light on my way up to the bathroom – it can only be turned on at the bottom of the stairs – and my son turned it off just as my foot was due to touch the first step on the way down again. The other reason I fell was that I was having my pee during the commercial break in a particularly gripping television serial, one of the alternatives to which was an edifying film about famine in the Far East which my wife might have taken advantage of my absence to switch over to, and the longer I was away the longer it would take to ask me if she terrifically minded if I switched back again. It's hard to ask my wife to switch off suffering. I once suggested we might get a second-hand, cheap black and white set so we could both watch what we wanted should the day ever come when we might want to watch different things. I might have been inaudible for all the response I got. I hope I was. I wouldn't like to trouble her conscience with the prospect of our becoming a two-set family – the one blessing too many. Which reminded me that the Hambles didn't have any set at all and that I had seen a dim flickering light behind their flimsy curtains that could only have been caused by candles. If we did have a second set Virginia would see to it that that was where it ended up. It's heating that uses up the power of course. Perhaps they'll freeze to death.

'What do you suggest instead?' Virginia asked.

She spoke very shirtily so I only shrugged. There are times when I do not like my daughter as much as I do at other times, mainly when she is being shirty. But my dislike doesn't show. I do not like to bring moral pressure to bear on anyone. 'Moral' seems to have crept in there; it's a word that seems to hang about in the atmosphere, waiting to pounce. I am not of censorious temperament, especially where my family is concerned. I have no desire to change anyone, least of all the world, knowing I could not.

She went round to the Hambles while I put my head under the bonnet of my car, from where I can see what is going on round and about without drawing attention to the fact. She was in the house for about five minutes and when she came back it was with a very small bunch of carrots. I wouldn't have remarked on them had she not dangled them on a level with my eye.

'Look what I've got,' she said.

'If I hadn't known those were candles I'd have said they were carrots.'

'I found her cleaning them in the kitchen if you must know.'

'What did you say? I came for a candle but those will do instead?'

'She *offered* them, silly.'

I closed the bonnet of my car and wiped my hands on a rag, realizing before long it was a new handkerchief. I could imagine no conversation which could have led to an offer of carrots. It was well into autumn and even the Hambles could not have grown them as small and even-sized as that.

'But how did it . . . How did you . . . ?'

'I said we might be going for a drive after lunch and would they like to come too. Then she didn't say anything so I said, "What fabulous carrots!" so she just gave me half of them and tied them in a bunch. She went red in the face when I said I couldn't, I had to pay for them so I knew I had to take them.'

'I see. And what about the drive? Are they coming?'

'I already said, I don't know. I don't *think* so.'

I began thinking up excuses, a badminton court booked, the car playing up, otherwise it was a fine idea. I wished my wife was there. She's good at going straight to the heart of the matter.

'Does your mother know?'

'Mum's not coming, is she?'

'I'd rather you asked her that.'

'I said we were taking a picnic.'

'We were, were we? At this time of year? When the leaves are beginning to fall already? The forecast said snow, or was it sleet? I'd say that took breaking the ice a bit too far.'

'Couldn't *you* go and see them?'

'I'll have to, won't I?'

'You're not cross, are you, Daddy?'

She knows she's only got to say that to make me feel that all I lack is a whip in my hand.

'Of course I'm not cross. It's just that they might not want to come for a drive to the bloody park. It might be the very last thing they want to do.'

'We can't just drive off now without them, can we?' The shirtiness was back in her voice now.

'As it happens I've just remembered I'm playing badminton this afternoon. I could ring up and cancel it of course . . .' But she always knows when I am lying, or ought to by now, so I patted her on the head and said, 'Don't worry, dear. I'll go and see them, clear it all up.'

She doesn't like being patted on the head (who does?) though, for reasons already gone into, there are few other places I could have patted her and it was an occasion for some kind of physical contact, all other contact being by now the stuff that nightmares are made of.

'Oh *thanks*, Dad! I don't feel sorry for them any more or anything.'

I felt quite good then, for a split second, having let one of my children off the hook, an opportunity that comes my way but seldom. Then came the remembrance that I had to go and see the Hambles to stop them wrapping up warm and preparing an enormous hamper. Perhaps I would just thank them for the carrots, say they didn't make cars like they used to. I'd just had mine serviced, you couldn't trust anyone these days, no more than the weather, desperately looking skywards for a vast, black, gathering storm cloud. How would my wife have gone about it? Not mentioned the car for a start, that being a blessing we could count on and the Hambles couldn't. I only knew that when it was all over she would have said what I hadn't, or the other way round of course.

I hadn't been to the Hambles' house since the day they arrived. I had waved at them, called out things like 'How's it going?' and, as I've explained, glanced in their direction through windows. I knocked twice and it was Hamble who came to the door. I was still wiping my hands on what had lately become a rag and preparing myself to mumble, just happened to be passing, getting ready for the car excuse. His face seemed redder and more mottled than usual, probably from bending down to do up his winter walking boots. But in that first second while I cleared my throat, the mottles and redness darkened and I knew they were caused by me. Then a kind of timid croak came from somewhere up behind his nose, sweat began seeping out along his nose, and his mouth opened in a small round hollow as if he was blowing. Behind him a door clicked. I looked down to see that I'd tied the former handkerchief into three tight, very brown knots.

'Just called to well you know for the Virginia carrots.'

I picked at the knots and gave him that quick, closed-mouth smile with a lift of the eyebrows which I hadn't checked in the mirror lately but which is meant to convey a shy frankness, that only rarely doesn't one keep to oneself and when one doesn't, let's all flounder about together.

'Carrots? Carrots?' He took a deep breath and tugged up his trousers to create slack in his braces. Then he turned and said, 'Joanie, the gentleman's come about some carrots.'

He stepped back and Mrs Hamble appeared beside him, fiddling with the strings of her apron, and flushed also. Their similarity otherwise was uncanny too. They were about the same height and their redness was of the same hue though her blotches were pinkish as opposed to his bluish ones. The closest resemblance was between their eyes. As I looked from one to the other, their eyelids quivered and closed, then went on fluttering as though the eyeballs were darting round behind them trying to escape, but not before I had glimpsed the same grey gleam with its black centre dilating as if in a last hard gaze before the onset of blindness, as if they preferred that to what their eyes were closing upon.

'Just called to say thanks for the carrots, Mrs Hamble. Wish I could grow carrots like that.'

She smiled, her eyes opening for an instant on my neck to which my hand with the handkerchief in it went up – as I discovered later, depositing some grease there.

'Ooh, those aren't our carrots. Alf always had a way with carrots, haven't you, Alf?'

'I have that. Always could grow a good carrot.'

'Then there's his tomatoes.'

'Had one won a prize once.'

'How many pounds, was it? That year, you know, when Will had his marrow.'

'Never seen a marrow like it, before nor since.'

Their eyes were upon each other now and wide open. I might just as well not have been there. That was real tested affection all right, indissolubly joined together somewhere in memory. I half expected them to grab hold of each other suddenly. (When did my wife and I last look at each other like that? A mutual searching expression, not since we first did it, I suspect, when I at any rate was searching for an inkling of what it would be like having that other face close up, on and off, for the rest of my life. I could see the same kind of question flitting about in my wife's eyes so the search at once became for what she was thinking, no longer for any certainties of my own. Of those I had few that day for it was when my father died, and whatever I was and knew felt utterly hollowed out somehow.)

'You took other prizes. Never for carrots.'

'Never for carrots. Potatoes though.'

Mrs Hamble turned to me, her eyes closed again. The redness had gone but not the pink patches. 'Alf's got green fingers,' she said. 'Always has had.'

I wondered if they still made love and supposed they didn't. They probably didn't even kiss on the lips any more. The thought, the irrelevance, the impertinence of it, made me immensely sad.

'Virginia was delighted,' I tried next. 'Hope you didn't think she was scrounging.'

Then Mrs Hamble did open her eyes, very wide indeed, but they somehow remained small and blind. 'Oh dear me no! Fancy! Such a pretty girl. Such nice manners.'

There seemed a better than fair chance that Virginia's invitation had been taken as mere politeness so I hastened to confirm that impression.

'Always tries to say the right thing, full of good intentions, runs ahead of herself. Still a child.'

That was ghastly. The fact of the matter is that my daughter is not all that perfect. Trying in fits and starts to be the sort of person my wife would like her to be has made her something of a goody-goody, though it's usually offset by a streak of honest-to-goodness selfishness. I didn't look forward to having to tell her that the Hambles couldn't come to the park after all. Suspicious that I was lying (again) she would bring my wife into it who, by brushing the whole thing aside, would come to my rescue while making it clear to me alone that that was what she was doing.

Anyway, I had to carry out a fogging up operation so that I could honestly say I was under the clear impression they had no real desire to come to the park with us. Finally, I had to get round to working out why I didn't want them to come to the park with us, or anywhere else for that matter, other than because I'm a mean-spirited bastard.

'She's welcome at any time,' Mrs Hamble said. 'It's nice to have a child in the house, isn't it, Alf?'

Hamble didn't reply. Perhaps his thoughts were running much as mine had, but the other side of the coin as it were.

'Well, must get back to the old car,' I said. 'Was hoping to take a spin to the park this afternoon, if it doesn't rain, but can't get the blessed thing to start. Had it serviced last week, what's more.'

'They're more trouble, cars,' Hamble said.

'We had a car once, didn't we, Alf?'

'If you could call it that,' Hamble replied. He was beginning to shift about now and was rubbing his face with the inside of his forearm.

'He's a gardening not an engines man, is Alf.'

'I'm no darn good at either, couldn't sew a sock to save my life either, ha ha,' I said with that same smile I'd used before but extended now into an expression, I hoped, of wide-ranging incompetence. Thereupon I raised a hand in salute and hurried away to take the rotor arm out of my car. I found Virginia in the drawing room reading a book about Eskimos.

'Can't get the damn car to start,' I said.

'Did you tell the Hambles?'

'Did I tell the Hambles what?'

'That as soon as the car is working they can come for a drive with us.'

'We discussed vegetables in the main, seaweed to be precise.'

'But did you tell them?'

'Not in so many words.'

'But what did you *say* to them?'

'I said I couldn't get the car to start. What else did you want me to say?'

'But, Daddy . . .'

I patted her on the head and she drew away. 'Come along. They said what a nice girl you are. It's all perfectly all right. There'll be another day. Lots of other days, if the truth were known. How about some lunch then?'

'I'm not hungry. I just bet you didn't say anything about going to the park another time.'

'If I didn't know you better I'd say you were calling me a liar.'

And the infuriating thing was that she only shrugged and went back to her book. There are times when I could raise a hand to my daughter. Something I've never done, needless to say. Instead, I felt like going out into the garden and devastating the place with my badminton racket. The trouble is I have a job to find my daughter insufferable because when I might, it is myself I cannot suffer. I remembered the Hambles and their fond looks, I imagined Virginia being very nice to them, then finding them frozen or gassed to death and running back and screaming at me, 'You killed them! You killed them! Murderer! Murderer! We should have taken them to the park!'

That evening I said to my wife over my daughter's sulking head,

'Thought we might take the Hambles for a trip to the park one weekend. Virginia's idea.'

'What a lovely thought,' she replied, glancing at Virginia with pride.

Virginia smirked, avoiding my eye. She'd seen through me this time all right. Later we watched a programme about mental illness and the National Health Service. I tried to make my show of interest convincing but there's so much self-respect one can never hope to regain. That afternoon I had pulled a muscle in my shoulder playing badminton (I went to the club by bus with the rotor arm in my pocket). I was so certain my daughter was thinking 'serve you right' that I could have sworn she actually said it.

I could not dislike my daughter for long since, as so often happens, I began thinking of her being courted and getting worked up to the point of submission. A seductive fancy. In the days of our early frenzy, before we were married, my wife and I went in for a fair amount of nipping and slapping and clawing etc. (she mightn't have behaved like that if most people don't, not wanting to be one of a privileged minority) and felt sheepish about it afterwards, or rather I did. I don't like to think of my daughter being slapped or nibbled or clawed at etc. however much she is enjoying it. Indeed the more she is enjoying it the less I like it. Come to that, I hate to think of her shagging at all, however straightforwardly, of her moaning and gasping the while. I do not want my daughter to enjoy herself in any extreme fashion too far out of my presence and ken. I cannot dislike my daughter for long. Even when she is at her shirtiest I hear her saying desperately in the same voice, 'Take your filthy hands off me!'

This stuff seems to be accumulating. It's all right doing it in the office because it makes me appear I am working. Sometimes I stay on for a while and that is even more impressive, of course. I wish I could do it at home. There is a cubby hole next to our bedroom ('your father's study') and I've written a bit in there, saying I have a report to do about sales to the Pacific Rim – everyone should have one of those. But the thought of my wife or children coming across any of it is unthinkable. 'If you must know, I'm writing about my life.' What there is of it, my wife would not say. It would not even cross her mind. It does mine. There would be no getting away from it. Every little thing after that would lead to the question, 'Are you putting that in your book, Daddy?' More specifically Virginia, 'Have you put it in your book that you've agreed to take the Hambles to the park because they can't afford a car?' And then my wife asking, just the once or twice, 'When will we be allowed to see . . . ?' As I said, it is unthinkable. Let's just hope it's worth the bother and I'm all the better for it.

It was at this time my mother came to stay, but not for long. She and my wife did not hit it off at all. I'll try to deal with that another time.

Chapter Five

I do not care how much and where my son enjoys himself, provided he does. He has taken to going round to the Webbs. I cannot blame him because I am not a good father to him. I have let him down too often – when I have not read him a story, played board games with him, taken him to the cinema or to the park to fly a kite or to the Natural Science Museum or the public swimming pool or . . . If I list all the things that fathers do with their sons, to bring stimulus and happiness into their lives, I realize I have failed to do all of them with Adrian at one time or another, most of them frequently. I've done some of them occasionally of course and have enjoyed his pleasure and gratitude, largely when I am enjoying whatever it is myself. But too often, out of fatigue or a desire to watch television or sheer inertia, I've said, 'Not now. Another time.'

Hence the reason why he has begun to visit Webb so often. Webb is always glad to see him I imagine. He has a workshop in his garage and collects stamps and is never at a loss for words. I wonder what Adrian tells him about us. It is no consolation that there's so little to tell. My wife discourages nosiness except in so far as it could be described as the spirit of enquiry leading to conclusions to do with misery in the face of inequality and injustice. My children are allowed to be as curious as they like provided their consciences are strengthened thereby – an added element there presumably being their curiosity to find out where to draw the line between what is good for them and what isn't. Should they come to me for advice in this area it could only be out of curiosity.

Be that as it may, neither my wife nor I can say to our son, 'What do you and Mr Webb find to talk about?' I go on hoping he will tell us but he never does. We can't stop him from going round there. My wife can't even hint that she would prefer it if he didn't because she would have to give a reason and one, moreover, that underlined the difference between right and wrong. And there is nothing right or wrong about Webb, so far as I know. I could argue with my wife (I could do nothing of the kind) that his restless interest in other people's doings is a result of his not having anything in his own life to be restlessly interested in, his wife for example. I am not sure why my wife seems to distrust him. She does not reveal her feelings about him to Adrian. She hardly does to me either, except by the occasional grimace. I have doubts too about my son's friendship with Webb, but only for the reason that it reminds me of my failure as a father, who has no workshop in his garage and no stamp collection and who does not have an inexhaustible fund of topics suitable for conversation with boys of his age.

It was about a week before my daughter received carrots from the Hambles that my son began visiting Webb. The following afternoon Webb said to me through the tangle of creeper (though this time it was I who was clipping away at it so that I'd be able to see him from a greater distance when he was peering through it to see what we were up to, and so I'd not have to peer too to see if he was peering in such a way that I couldn't walk hastily away when I discovered he was), 'Has a good pair of hands, that lad of yours.'

I went on clipping. 'He has, has he? That's good to know. Does carpentry at school, so he tells me.'

'Not only carpentry. Metalwork too. And pottery. They're given the choice. That's what I like. Nothing like that in my day.'

I suspected he already knew more about my son than I did so I tried to keep the conversation general. 'Wonderful, the education these days,' I said, continuing to snip.

'Wednesdays and Fridays.'

'Oh yes.'

'He's working on a coffee table for his Mum. Wants it to be a surprise.'

I tugged at a cluster of branches above where I'd been snipping and revealed his face in its entirety. I could see what my wife meant. His smarminess was overwhelming. His thin, greying hair was thickly greased and combed diagonally back from a broad central parting and I had a close look too at his pencil-line moustache which was trimmed to leave a narrow gap exactly and evenly parallel to the top of his upper lip and ending exactly above the corners of his mouth, which was bracketed, as it were, by two deep semicircular wrinkles, giving him the look of someone on the point of breaking out in a convulsive snicker. The lips were made to look thicker than they were by the aforesaid gap between the top of them and the line of his moustache, and when he talked he seemed to be trying to keep them over his teeth, so to help me think him repulsive, I tried to picture just how rotten or bogus they were. But, to be honest, I was only looking at him so closely and in that way to take my mind off the fact that my son wasn't making the coffee table for me. It was I who had the birthday coming up.

'That's nice,' I said.

'It's going to be. Giving him a hand, if you see what I mean. Like the carpentry myself. Takes the mind off.'

'Nothing like a hobby.'

'What's yours then, mind my asking?'

'Not a bit.'

There was a long pause while I snipped away and made a whistling face.

'He's a good boy,' he went on. 'To tell the truth, don't usually much care for kids. Not sorry we're without. My wife said adopt but couldn't see it myself, somebody else's cast-off. You couldn't blame yourself for its faults, see what I mean? Decided to stop at just the two then, did you?'

'The population explosion and all that,' I said, blushing and swearing at myself for not saying instead, 'Mind your own bloody business.' Also, a train of thought had been set in motion about being responsible for one's children's faults, as opposed to taking credit for their virtues, and deciding the while not to obscure the issue by seeking clarification from my wife on the matter.

'Ho ho,' he said. 'Less of the old bang-bang eh?' He made a slurping sound and sniffed. 'Of course we, the spouse and I, we've given up trying. We've come to terms. So it's nice to have a boy about the place. I envy you, a good clean boy like that. Nothing explosive about the Webbs, what?' This last in his Duke of Edinburgh/Stanley Holloway voice. Then he snorted and stroked his hair.

'We wouldn't be without him.' I replied, tugging the tangle of creeper aside and starting to clip again, at a level with my knees.

'Not that she's past it,' he said.

I made the mistake of glancing up at him and he winked. Hating us both equally, I smirked. 'Some things best kept to ourselves.'

He thought about that. 'Very witty, Tom, isn't it? Not getting any younger, that's for bloody certain. Got this chum in the orifice, says getting it up is one thing, keeping it up is another.'

I clacked the shears loudly on empty air, missing what I had been aiming at, and he must have taken my snarl for another, even more lecherous, grin.

'Ouch! Though grant you, that's one way out. Heard the one about the man went to this surgeon to have 'em off, castrate him, insisted on it? After the deed was done met this mate in the hospital who said he was taking his baby boy to be circumcised – bloke snapped his fingers and said, "Bugger it, that was the word I was looking for." '

It wasn't one I'd heard before so gave a laugh, whereupon his laugh stopped and he said, 'It's not so funny when you think about it.'

'I suppose it isn't.'

There was another pause. 'Handsome-looking woman, your wife, if you don't mind my saying. The boy takes after her.'

'No, don't mind a bit. Boys look like their mothers. Girls . . . Daughter's going to be an absolute stunner, don't you think?'

He considered this proposition seriously. 'There may be a little of you in her, grant you that. What's she going to be then?'

I moved up the fence with the shears but he followed me.

'Nursing,' I muttered. 'She's keen on nursing.'

'They don't keep it hidden away, those nurses, not by all accounts. None of your shivering virgins. Not in that walk of life. My wife was going to be a nurse once, any rate so she tells me. Now she does freelance secretarial work.'

'Didn't know that. What type?'

'Never asked, did you? You've only got to ask. You get your face slapped, but you also . . .'

I looked at my watch. 'Heck, late for my badminton.' Then snapped the shears shut and turned to go.

'Keep yourself in trim, that's the way. That's my friend's trouble, he says. Any physical exercise, gets puffed. Can't keep it up. Get it? Can just see you bashing away at the old shuttlecock.'

He grinned and raised his hand half-clenched towards his navel in a spasmodic manner. I took a last look at that bracketed smirk and imagined it on his face while he questioned my son. For the rest of the day my imagination ran wild so that evening while I was doing the washing-up with my son I opened the conversation thus.

'Mr Webb tells me you're making a table for Mum.'

'It's supposed to be a surprise.'

'Decent of him to let you use his tools and things.'

'He's really good at it. He helps me. He's making a whole cupboard himself. Don't tell Mum, will you?'

'Like me to take you to the museum this weekend?'

'Another time, Dad, thanks. Actually I'm going to help Mr Webb with his stamps. Can I start a stamp collection?'

'Of course you can. That's a fine idea.'

'It's quite expensive, you know. Mr Webb's got thousands of pounds' worth. He says it excites his curiosity about the world. He's always asking questions.'

'What sort of questions?'

'Oh you know. Things. School and what I'm going to be and that.'

'I'll buy you a stamp album and a catalogue and some stamps to start with. Any time you like. How'd you like that?'

'Thanks, Dad. But if you don't mind, can I have the money instead so Mr Webb can choose with me? He knows a special shop. He says he's even got some swaps he could give me.'

'I could get stamps from the office for you. We get letters from all over the place. Japan, Brazil, places like that.'

'Where Mr Webb works they get letters from just about every single country in the whole world.'

'I see. Well, it's good for a boy to have hobbies.'

'That's what Mr Webb says. Keeps your mind off other things.'

'What other things for example?'

'Oh you know.'

My wife was out on some mercy mission that evening. I wished I knew how she would handle the situation. What situation, she might ask. Or she might hint that Webb was a father substitute and whose fault was that. She might start hinting to Adrian (my wife is incapable of dropping hints that people don't get) that he should see less of Webb and that as from tomorrow the need for a substitute would start falling away. She would look at me, as if sizing me up as the genuine article. In any case, it is impossible to make conversation with my wife when she has just returned from a mercy mission. I would not know how to bring the subject up. I bring so few subjects up, in fact none that I can think of at the moment. If I brought up the subject of Webb, it would have to be pressed to a conclusion. Which might be, 'Well, isn't that rather up to you?' So I prefer to keep things inconclusive between us. I think I'd rather live with the uncertainty of not knowing what Webb and my son talk about than have my wife expand the topic into its broader parental (moral?) aspects. I do not wish to sow in my son the seeds of suspicion. I want him to be like me to the extent of avoiding hostilities. One thing I do not find myself being ashamed of is that I wasn't old enough to be in the war; if I had been, I wonder how I could have avoided the hostility involved in keeping well out of it, thus probably ending up in the thick of it. I can just see my son's face if he knew I thought things like that. I'd like to have been a hero, fought for my country etc. so my son would be proud of me and people would look up to me. But I must remain among that multitude who will never know all that they might have been – better or worse too, of course. Everyone you meet is a hypothesis. Not 'How are you?' but 'How might you have been?' is the question that sometimes pops into my head. If I asked it, people, my son, would look at me as if I'd gone out of my mind – a hypothesis too far you might think, as if there could be such a thing.

First and foremost, I don't want my wife to tell me to wean my son away from Webb. I cannot imagine myself buying tools, lengths of timber, nails and screws etc. and turning my garage into a workshop. I would feel a fool and anyway Webb would be round all the time with good advice and soon it would be he again who was helping my son, except that now it would be in my garage. To compete with Webb's stamps, I might try collecting butterflies for example. I can just see my son's face as I pranced through a meadow waving a butterfly net. Or making model galleons, getting glue all over my fingers and breaking the spars or whatever it is that galleons have. Or bird watching when I'd keep on coming up with the same old birds. There is no activity I can think of now that my son and I could do together as pals. I wish I'd thought of stamps and carpentry first. If I had, though, Webb is the sort of man who could interest him more in butterflies, birds and model galleons.

So I have said nothing to my wife. My son still visits Webb at weekends. I cannot even tell myself that by not being more of a pal to him I am creating in him a determination to be a better father to his children than I am being to him. My father was an unsuccessful small-town shopkeeper and I thought he only tried to get to know me when I helped him in the shop and he wondered whether I wanted to inherit it; perhaps they are all like that, those who spend their lives minding their own business. I know better now, now that it's far too late. It has produced no vows to do better by my son, to whom there will be nothing to hand on, except a little money eventually. If I die first, my wife may have other plans for that, bearing in mind her views about inherited riches. Hence I have this obligation to my children to want her to die before I do, hardly a moral obligation therefore, alas – and that's before even considering what those good causes would be deprived of. It's another of those obligations to my children I can do nothing about and they are all there are.

Anyway I do not dislike Webb any longer, though I still think he is sly and a bore. Sometimes, when my wife is being too high and mighty by half (towering above me), when she turns her back on some third-rate television programme I'm thoroughly enjoying and goes up to bed, I think of Webb as an imaginary ally. I go much too far along this line of thought. I imagine telling Webb what she looks like with no clothes on, even giving him a run-down of what she's like in bed and of what she's regrettably not like. Perhaps I'm only saying that I'm not really all that much of a hater (Plaskett excepted), that I find it more relaxing to be contented with life more or less the way it is. It's just that though Webb and my wife do get up my nose sometimes the snot I prefer is my own. And of course I wouldn't dream of telling Webb anything about my wife at all. Do we not sometimes imagine the absurd, to say nothing of the obscene, so that we should find ourselves less so?

The other day my son came down from doing his homework and I said to him, 'Done your homework already? That was quick.'

'It was only geography. South America. Mr Webb told me a lot about it when we were doing his stamps. You can learn things from stamp collecting.'

'I know. You'll tell me, won't you, when you'd like an album of your own?'

'I've nearly finished Mum's table,' he said.

'That's nice. See much of Mrs Webb, do you?'

'Pardon?'

I coughed, opened the book about Dr Livingstone I was reading and repeated the question.

'She brings us tea and biscuits.'

'That's . . . Seems to keep to herself, does Mrs Webb.'

'I feel sorry for her if you must know.'

'Oh? Why's that?'

'When she brings the coffee, she doesn't stay to watch and chat or anything. She's always sniffing. She's so skinny. I catch her looking at me.'

'People can't help how they look.'

'That's what Mr Webb says. He says what matters is underneath.'

'Run along then,' I said.

'I'm not going anywhere,' he said.

I hope the outing to the park comes off one day. I see us all going out into the world together, even as far as the park. All our frailties would combine to make up a kind of fortitude. I imagine Plaskett and Hipkin happening upon us as we sit around a blanket with the good food spread out before us, munching contentedly, not having to talk. Perhaps there would be a bottle of red wine at the centre, catching the sun. They would watch us at a distance, from behind a tree. Their lives would be changed by the sight. Perhaps after all I do want to change the world a little. It is an awful place really, a vile and barbarous place, for many people. But I wouldn't want to change any of us sitting around the sandwiches and the bottle of wine. (Except myself, to a small extent, not so far that I became unrecognizable to myself of course, in fact mainly in my appearance so as to make my fantasies a trifle less fantastic.) I would not want to tamper too much with what lies beneath, thereby causing myself dismay. I do not like knowing too much. I too feel sorry for Mrs Webb, eyeing my son and wishing he was hers. I hear her tossing and turning at night, not daring to tell her husband again, so late in the day, what is still on her mind. She sniffles and tells him she's caught a cold. It does not cross his mind to wonder where she got it from. That is part of the trouble too now. I think of her imagining my son in her arms, giving him a bath, tending to his needs generally. I see her leaving to sleep in another room where she can cry in peace for all those things that life has denied her, where she can be alone to imagine Adrian in her stomach. I imagine her refusing her husband marital access, or at least I hope to God she does with my son in her belly. I never went near my wife when she was pregnant, though she told me repeatedly that it was perfectly all right, perfectly wholesome etc. I have never consciously contaminated (if that is the right word) my children, nor done anything that would make me cast an eye over them with a shudder. I would not like them to wonder what depravity I was getting up to in their vicinity before they were born.

Looking back, shouldn't that be Natural History Museum? There you have it then.

Chapter Six

More time has passed.

The other day Plaskett did for Hipkin and I found out more about myself. Plaskett had asked for some sales figures broken down into certain percentages and categories, all to do with profit margins. Hipkin had done this sort of thing before so I gave the job to him. When he handed it back it looked a pretty neat piece of work to me (there was not much of it and I was already padding out my briefcase in a hurry to get home for some television programme), so I initialled it and passed it on to Plaskett as it was, attached to some work of my own. He called me into his office the next day. It was late afternoon on a Friday when I have little on my mind except the pattern of my weekend, or rather it's a patchwork with large ragged gaps in it which can't be filled up by badminton, reading, meals and television naturally.

As usual he had his head down over his desk, as if unaware of my presence – though he'd responded to my knock with a commanding 'Come!' – this each time making me picture (want to stop picturing) him in his private capacity, or lack of it rather. He looked up, pursed his lips and pushed Hipkin's figures towards me across the desk.

'This not your handiwork, Tom?'

I leant forwards and touched my chin. 'Not exactly. I did see it though. That other job to do . . .'

'I do realize you *saw* it. One can't check everything.'

He fluttered the papers at me so I took them. Within about five seconds (it would have taken me half as long if he hadn't been staring at me, if he'd invited me to sit down) I saw that the percentages were not related to the right figures, that the figures had been tabulated in the wrong categories, that the categories were not those I had asked him for, and that the profit margins were approximately one-third of what they should have been.

'I'm sorry, Mr Plaskett,' I said. 'I'll go over these again.' And made as if to go.

'You know of course when I wanted them by?'

In front of me, at the centre of the top paper I read the words BY NOON ON FRIDAY. I turned over the sheets of paper, giving him time to continue. He looked at his watch.

'Someone's going to have to put in some overtime, isn't someone?' he said.

'Sorry about that. Would first thing Monday do? I'll see to them myself.'

If I applied myself I could reassemble the data in a couple of hours, some of it straightaway, giving me time to get back for my first television programme, and do the rest at home, thus filling at least two or three of the smaller gaps I hadn't yet decided what to do with.

'Come along, Tom. It's a wretched piece of work. Who's responsible? Not your style at all, that's for sure.'

I couldn't argue with him there. Everything I put up to him is fault-less, always that little bit better than what he asked for – an extended comparison, a fancy graph, that sort of thing. I am meticulous not only because I fear him but also because if I didn't re-check every-thing a dozen times and do the bit extra I wouldn't have nearly enough to do. My desk is in an exposed position and Plaskett walks past it on his way to the lift which bears him heavenwards to the upper floors where Top Management lives and moves and has its being. I have to make sure there are always a lot of papers on my desk and that when I am at it I have a pen in my hand and a dedi-cated look on my face. I always go home and return with a bulging briefcase with which Plaskett has seen me several times (rather than it with me), though I accept that a wodge of thick brown wrapping paper round a brick may be overdoing it a bit. Not that on his way skywards Plaskett would see me at all. I wish I could describe the look on his face as he pushed the button and twitched his cuffs. He is trying to look servile, masterful, eager, relaxed, confident, self-effacing all at the same time within a sort of aura of concerned worldliness, but the effect is that of someone who is about to wet himself. Perhaps, in his excitement, he already has. Anyway, he cer-tainly wouldn't notice then what I had on my desk, indeed if it and I were not there at all.

'I should have checked them, Mr Plaskett, but . . .'.

'But nothing. Who was it?'

'Hipkin. Mr Hipkin. Good lad. Still learning . . .'

'Well, I'd better see *Mr* Hipkin. Been with us long, has he?'

'Fairly long.'

'Thought you said . . . Long enough, you mean. Not that dreamy, spotty youth who sits staring out of the window by any chance? Well, he's clearly in the wrong job. No room for passengers here, you know.'

'I'll have a word with him. He's usually all right. Won't happen again.'

'Usually isn't all right enough. Better see him myself.'

Hipkin hadn't been in Plaskett's office before. Indeed I doubt whether they'd so much as exchanged a glance.

'Hopefully he can be given another chance, Mr Plaskett. It's the first time . . .'

'Who said anything about . . . ?' He raised an eyebrow. 'Hopeful. I should jolly well think so.'

I found Hipkin standing at his desk, making ready to go. I let him go early on Fridays but I'm sure he didn't much mind when he left, on Friday or any other day. I told him he could leave early on his second Friday and perhaps he took it as an order since he had left early on Friday ever since. I didn't know what to say to him or how to say it, but I tried, I did try.

'Bob, I'm afraid Mr Plaskett wants to see you.' I blew a raspberry. 'Those Scandinavian figures you did were a bit wide of the whatsit, mark. He's not terribly chuffed about it, to be honest. My fault. Should have checked them. Don't worry. Just say you're sorry, it won't happen again. Call him "sir" every other word. Bow from the waist, get down on your knees and give his shoes a polish. Say you'll work on them over the weekend. I'll give you a hand.' I squeezed his elbow and said again, 'Now don't worry. Apologize. Don't try to explain. Look him straight in the eye.'

It was no good, no good at all. I could feel his arm quaking through his sleeve. He had gone pale; even his pimples seemed to have drained. I was afraid he would begin to collapse in a bawling tremble and I'd have to prop him up.

'Come on,' I said in a voice an octave plus higher than I intended. 'It's not the end of the world. It'll all be the same in a hundred years.'

He smiled then, thinking, I expect, I was doing an imitation of Mrs Hodge. But I wasn't, oh no; it was me speaking all right.

Plaskett swivelled his chair abruptly to face us as we entered. I positioned myself between Hipkin and the window and slightly in front of him so as to cast some shadow on his face and so as not to have to see it myself. Plaskett clasped his hands tightly in front of him far forward on his desk.

'Mr Ripple has told you what I want to see you about?'

From behind me there was a sort of peep followed by a sniff.

'I've had a word with him,' I said, grinning inanely and giving a nod. His contempt shifted slowly from Hipkin to me and back again.

'I want to make it abundantly clear to you, Pitkin, that it isn't good enough. I'm not in the habit of presenting false information to the Board of Directors. Won't warn you again. Just get it right and if you don't know what you're doing either ask or find work to which you are more suited.'

I then said, 'If I could just say that Bob has done a pretty good job . . . the groundwork on the new . . .'

He smiled, or tried to dislodge some distasteful matter from behind his teeth. 'Thank you, Ripple, Tom. And now, Pitkin, perhaps I might hear what you have to say for yourself.' His smile vanished and he lifted his clenched hands up under his chin.

Hipkin peeped again twice, then replied in a high, weepy voice that made me shudder, 'I don't mind doing it again if I got it wrong. Sorry if I made a mistake. We all make mistakes. Didn't you ever make mistakes? Like he said, I did it all right before. You only got to ask me to do it again, say I got it wrong and do it again please. So I got it wrong so . . .'

Plaskett simply raised his eyebrows and waved us away. I placed my hand in what I hoped was a comforting fashion on the small of Hipkin's back and gave him a gentle push. I had seen the redness creeping back across his face like a stain and the quivering of his lips and was wondering how I could get him back to the washroom without anyone seeing him when Plaskett called me back. I was preparing myself to hold Hipkin firmly by the shoulders in the washroom while I told him that Plaskett was a right shit, that I thought his work was all right, I would defend him to the hilt, I'd resign myself if need be, take the matter to Top Management, plead for him at a Tribunal, organize a protest. So did I say, 'Hold on, I'll be back in a minute, Mr Plaskett.' Oh no. I went back immediately and left Hipkin standing in the corridor, looking this way and that, abandoned, a wreck.

'What a performance,' Plaskett said. 'I feel for you, having to rely on the likes of that.'

And then he smiled at me, a real smile, and I smiled back. Oh yes, I did. And not a fleeting one either, a grateful, loyal one.

'Best ease him out, don't you think? Not very stable I'd say, for starters.'

'He's not that bad actually. Can't I give him another chance? You scared the daylights out of him.'

His frown then was to counteract a grin of deep gratification. 'Does you credit, Tom, but frankly there are plenty about who'd grab at the chance to get a foot on the bottom rung here, young men who are going places. Take my own . . . Well, can't see Peterkin or whatever his name is in my chair one day, can you? Or even in yours for that matter.'

'Perhaps not, but . . .'

He stood up and began lining up some papers on his desk. 'Good, that's decided. A month's wages then. Don't want to see his face round here again.' He looked up, waiting for me to speak. I said nothing at all. 'And don't forget those figures, if you wouldn't mind. Was going to work on them over the weekend, but no matter, golf handicap needs bringing down a notch or two.' Again he smiled, ending it with a snap of his jaws as if it had been a serious mistake. 'Oh dear, can't pretend I enjoy this sort of thing, take my word for it, any more than I'm sure you do.' He showed me his palms. 'But it goes with the territory. See you Monday then. With those figures.'

He bent down to open a drawer of his desk, not expecting to find me still there when his head reappeared.

I found Hipkin at his desk buttoning up his overcoat. He looked much the same as ever and I was grateful to him for that.

'Sorry, Bob, if I'd known . . .'

'It's all right, Mr Ripple.'

'It isn't bloody all right. I tried to . . .'

'He fired me, didn't he?'

I nodded. 'A month's salary. I'll get another couple of weeks added. Nobody will know.' He showed no sign of wanting to thank me. 'I'll see you get a good reference.'

'It's all right, Mr Ripple. Honestly. It wasn't much of a job anyway.'

'That's the spirit. Miserable bugger, Plaskett. You're well out of it.'

'He's got his job to do.'

'Think you'll be all right then?'

"Course I'll be all right.'

'And Bob, I'm sorry, honestly I am. But what could I do?'

He didn't reply. He was already on his way. He wanted to go and I stepped aside to let him pass. I know what I could have done. I could have said the figures were mine. I could have taken a stand. Waiting for the lift I wondered whether I would have behaved any differently if I could have had the afternoon all over again. The answer was negative.

I tell myself that Hipkin will be happier elsewhere though I cannot imagine him happy in any work situation. I see his foot slipping off the bottom rung of many ladders. I see him picking himself up and saying to himself, everything is all right, everything is fine. I see him conveying the bad news to an invalid parent. I see him alone watching a film about tough tycoons in tall glass offices deciding the fate of millions, money, people, no matter. His gaze is without bitterness. I imagine him remembering Plaskett and me with a shrug and his shrugs becoming uncontrollable so that they continue even in sleep. I see him on a bench in a park twitching and jabbering and cursing not at the world but at himself. I see him taken away to an institution where all day long he says in an old man's voice, 'I am sorry, Mr Plaskett. Everything is all right.' I hear him crying out in his sleep that everyone makes mistakes, that he didn't mean to be stupid, that one day he'll rule the world.

He stares at us from a distance having our picnic amidst the beautiful calm landscape of the park, at our munching faces catching the red glint from the bottle of wine. My wife looks up and sees him and says she has seen some misfit lurking among the trees, there is so much misery in the world, so many folk who only have the public services to lean upon. He becomes a case. My children gape at him, hoping he's a real loony for whom it would be easier to feel compassion than any old prowler, more funky too.

Sometimes I think it is people like Hipkin who commit murders. I wouldn't quite know what to think if he murdered Plaskett, perhaps only that he ought to have murdered me instead, having seen me safe and contented sharing a picnic with my family in lovely surroundings on an early summer day. Hipkin would be more likely to commit murder on himself than on another. If he came at Plaskett with a knife, Plaskett would tell him not to be such a damn fool, and he would put the knife down as he was told. If he came at me with a knife, I would try to reason with him in the manner of my wife but he wouldn't listen to me. So I would have to punch him in the face and, it being Hipkin, I wouldn't miss. He would be slow and awkward with a knife in his hand and easy to knock down. I would leave him lying there on the grass and hurriedly phone the police. I would not leave my name or make a scene. I would not wish to confront him publicly in any court of justice.

Perhaps he will happen upon my daughter in a deserted street or other secluded place and the notion of copulation would enter his head. But she'd run away from him and he wouldn't be able to catch up with her. He wouldn't even try and the notion would quickly go away.

On the other hand he may turn out all right, get his foot on a second rung of the ladder and not slip. Perhaps the social welfare services will never know he even existed. I do not believe this, though I want to. I do not like to think of him in my wife's hands, listening to her wise advice and taking letters from her to kindly employers. My wife would know exactly how to handle him. She would have known how to comfort him if she had been in my position. She would have stood up to Plaskett. Oh my word, she would have done that all right! I can never tell my wife about Hipkin. The evening he was fired she did not ask me if I'd had a hard day at the office, nor did my children. Even though I was late home. They believed me when I said I'd had to work late, though I'd never done so before. They couldn't have cared less. They showed no pride that the importance of my job required me to behave out of character occasionally, to miss part of one of my favourite television programmes.

It was I who went to bed early that evening while they stayed up to watch something beneficial. Comfy between fresh sheets, I read more about Dr Livingstone, who carried on day after day despite great suffering of the body, inspired by the voice of God and the desire to raise up his fellow men from the cruelties of their condition and the depths of their ignorance, and by the stubbornness of his huge pride. In that way I was able to forget myself and Hipkin too of course, neither of us being much endowed with wanting to discover the source and import of things.

But despite this and that, all has been well with me and I continue to count my blessings. It might go on for ever. I can see myself growing old, all my days becoming one long weekend, without the badminton. There is a gold clock on the mantelpiece or at any rate it is gold in colour. I hear Plaskett presenting it to me with kind sentiments I had hitherto thought him incapable of, and my own inner voice, croaking now and without the basso dimension, telling myself he's not such a bad chap after all. I see the contented pottering, the endearing dither, the vagueness that follows a fatigue of all the senses. My children come to visit me, sometimes with theirs, who are charming for two minutes or so after receiving my gifts. My children smile with the strain of a duty under performance and their faces relax in the door-way on parting. They say they will come again soon. What they say when they are out of earshot doesn't bother me. I feel the twinge of surprise when I wake up to behold another fine morning on which to be alive. (The fatigue does not embrace girls etc., or rather it does in their reminding how far gone it is and in doing that becoming by the day in all respects even more lovely and wonderful.) I do not see my wife growing old and vague with me. She remains the same and her sureness is undiminished. I do not know where I would be without her. I hear the ticking of the gold clock, the birds in the garden twit-tering through my doze, the rustle of my wife turning the pages of a scholarly book, the sound of a car starting up to take our neighbours on holiday. I can even hear the sound of my own snoring.

Chapter Seven

Yet more time has passed. It was to me my children came, not to my wife.

First, my son. My wife was away attending a weekend seminar about the treatment of young offenders and round about six on the Saturday I observed him hanging about outside the kitchen door with a small saw in his hand. At the time I was mending a fuse which was preventing the television from working.

I quite enjoy life when my wife is away. It is not a parental feeling. For my children it must be like not having a parent in the house at all. They can go to bed when they like, without having a bath or cleaning their teeth if they so choose, and can eat their chips with their fingers, walking about the house in the process. They can talk sloppily, using slang and swear-words, and pinch and punch each other and not say please or thank you and generally behave like the general run of children it is impossible to have any expectations of at all. It is all very relaxed and agreeable. It had better be because I have yet to acquire the art of admonishment, first needing perhaps to perfect it on myself.

'Hi, handyman!' I called out to him. 'Time for grub and telly?'

He did not reply. Normally he didn't hang about like that and I thought he was looking forward to boiling the potatoes and turning them into mash, having told his sister at lunch that the most famous brain surgeon in the universe couldn't tell mashed potato from the inside of her head. He was looking forward too to the evening's viewing, for which I was allowing him to stay up late, in particular a film which his whoop of pleasure at the prospect of caused his sister to call him a bird-brained moron, forgetting, or not forgetting, it was a film I'd said I was very much looking forward to also. At lunch, after a morning spent working on some school project to do with rub-

74

bish disposal, he'd been in a hurry to get away to Webb's workshop where by now he had started on a chair *'with arms'*. I went on changing the fuse to the sound of what I guessed was the tapping of the saw on the window sill. Then I took another look at him. He was out of the shadow now and his face had turned a creamy colour.

'Anything up?' I asked. 'You all right?'

'Fine,' he said.

I got down from the chair I was standing on and went over to him. 'Hadn't you better start on those spuds?' I said.

Something was definitely wrong. That was obvious. I hoped it could wait until my wife came back. I hoped he was ill or sickening for something, anything that wasn't fatal or painful. For I realized by then from a second look at his face that he'd had a bad shock and it had something to do with Webb. Perhaps he'd banged his thumb with a hammer or his chair had developed a wobble, but from his third look at me, searching for something he was not finding there, I knew it was not in that category either. I should have put my arm round him and led him through to the living room and sat down with him, but I simply repeated my question in a come-on-snap-out-of-it voice.

'Something's up, isn't it?'

'It's OK, Dad. Honestly.'

He slid past me and took some potatoes from the vegetable rack to the draining board. I would have left it at that, I think, I'm not sure, if I hadn't seen that the hand which groped for the knife in the drawer under the sink was shaking. I did not fancy the thought of his peeling potatoes with an unsteady hand, getting blood all over them. No, I am not doing myself justice (how do I plead?). I was frightened.

'You'd better tell me,' I said. 'And that, Private Ripple, is an order.'

He had his back to me and all the groping, then other movement, stopped.

'Promise you won't tell Mum.'

'I can't promise that.'

'I don't want Mum to know.'

'All right. Cross my heart. The suspense is killing me.' (Why do I so often speak to my children in clichés, frequently with an American accent?)

'It's Mr Webb.'

Shit. Shit. Shit. Now I had to hear it. 'What about Mr Webb?'

His voice wavered and sank to a whisper. 'He like showed me like these pictures in a little book and tried to touch me, you know, and asked me if I ever went I mean hard . . . and he gave me this.'

He opened his hand and showed me a scrunched-up five-pound note which he then thrust deep into his trouser pocket.

'Christ!' was all I said first, then managed, 'For God's sake whatever you do don't tell your sister.'

'I wouldn't tell her *anything*, silly.'

'What else . . . ?'

'Nothing *else*,' he hissed. 'Just don't tell Mum, that's all.'

'Very well, I won't. Look, we'll have a quiet chat about it later. How about that?'

'OK. I think he's scared, Dad. I ran away. I called him a filthy pig.'

'He'd better bloody well be scared.'

The words look tough enough on the page but I hadn't sounded tough at all so I gritted my teeth, clenched my fist and struck the door of the refrigerator. Then my whole body turned cold and flabby and an ache spread across the back of my neck. And I left him standing there beginning to peel the potatoes.

I came to two conclusions in the next ten minutes or so. That my son would never go near Webb again and that Webb could remain scared out of his nasty little wits for the rest of his life for all I cared. Nothing else I thought could be described as conclusive. Except that my wife could certainly not be told. She might react in a number of ways: go straight to the police, go and give Webb what-for, no, give him an address where his sickness could be attended to, have a cosy chat with Mrs Webb. I just didn't know. But one thing I did know was that she would have sat down with Adrian for hours, questioning him as to exactly what happened and what by way of conversation and previous physical contact had led up to it. Adrian would be subjected to constant observation for signs of permanent damage and there would be no end to her discourse on the subject when alone with me, especially in bed. And Virginia could not possibly be kept in ignorance of it, indeed would be destined for inclusion in the lessons to be drawn et bloody endless cetera. The problem of Webb would proliferate like the plague.

And I would lie or sit there, looking down at my thumbs, willing them not to twiddle, thinking about how far it was my problem too.

I pictured myself as a private tutor of music or first aid, say, giving instruction to young persons not all that much older than my son (of the other sex naturally etc.) and pondering on some such similar situation, though falling well short of the risk of being called a filthy pig. My wife would gas on and on until all her pity and scorn would seem aimed at me. All of which led to a third conclusion, that whatever I said/did, did not say/do, my wife would have said/done more or less the opposite or not at all and in the end it would not be Webb I had to contend with but myself.

Meanwhile, Adrian was waiting for me in the kitchen, having by now, I hoped, peeled the potatoes, perhaps even put them on the boil.

Frightening away a pigeon, I stole over to the window to see if Webb was around. But only Mrs Webb was there, dealing with her garbage. The window was open and I could hear her singing. I'd never thought her capable of singing or evincing any joy in life. I'd never had a long look at her before, had mainly waved and continued on my way. She had the figure of a boy, slim hipped with wide knee bones and little by way of breasts. Her hair was cropped like my wife's and she had a prominent chin and large hands. More so than my wife's her legs were hairy and I imagined her with a razor in her hand, moving it up from her throat to her upper lip. I found myself making a face of revulsion. I could almost smell her. Her hollow, washed-out face was made uglier by her singing, for she sang sweetly.

She bent down to scrape away the last of the garbage to reveal Webb's face watching me watching her from the window of their downstairs lavatory. And I felt such pity for her then that she was no longer disagreeable to me; and for him, because he was spying on us both, I felt a sudden huge loathing followed by shame at that loathing for I was spying too. And then I had this impulse to wave at him, to raise my shoulders and hands in a gesture of defeat at the nature of things, to show I was sorry that the way he was feeling now, the sick fear of waiting, the self-disgust, were on our account, and that there but for the grace of God skulked I, even if only in the rankest scrubland of the imagination.

My son was standing by the stove watching the potatoes in the boiling water with a fork in his hand. I took him by the shoulder and led him away to the living-room window overlooking our garden where the pigeon had returned, accompanied by another. He stayed very close to me until I spoke.

'Beastly for you. Better not go round there again.'

He drew away from my hand. 'I hate him,' he said.

He could not see my nodding so I patted his shoulder. 'Some people are like that. Frightful yes. But unhappy people usually. Why don't you want me to tell Mum?'

'You know.'

'Because she might fuss and make it worse and go on a bit.'

'Yes.'

He drew closer then, just for a second, but more as if getting ready to pull away altogether. I had never stood with him like that before, side by side, my hand on his far shoulder. I wanted to hold him there, even against his will.

'I could tell the police.'

He shook his head. 'That's worse. I don't want to answer any *questions* about it. I think Mrs Webb would die or something. He hides the pictures and things in a secret drawer under his tool-box.'

'Poor rotten bastard,' I said, regretting there was nowhere I could risk hiding dirty magazines in my house.

'I haven't even finished the chair. It was going to be for you.'

'So you want to lower my standing in life, do you?'

No smile whatever at that. 'Can I start a workshop in your garage, Dad?'

I coughed. 'Of course you can, I think.'

'You don't know a lot about carpentry, do you?'

I shook my head. Something else had become more important now. 'Your mother would care *too* deeply, that's really it, isn't it? Frankly, I don't know what to do that wouldn't be making a fuss.'

'Oh *Mum*,' he said. 'She's just Mum, isn't she?'

There was a lot of love in that, probably as much as there could possibly be. 'Doubt if you could do any better,' I said as he drew away from me.

'Of course I couldn't, silly.' He grinned shyly up at me, then saw his sister coming up the garden path. 'Don't tell *her*, promise.'

'Who's the silly now?'

'She'd tell everybody in just about the whole world.'

I winked at him. 'Think you'll be all right now?'

'I feel a bit sick. I don't feel like supper. He had this horrid look, all sort of pop-eyed. I want him to be killed in an accident.'

78

'Look, Adrian, take it you've learnt a bit about the facts of life from school, from your mother. Lust, what we've had to watch those ghastly animals get up to, God alone knows, it gets a bit out of hand sometimes, um not very choosy, does bloody stupid, nasty things sometimes.'

'*You* wouldn't do anything like that.'

'I should sincerely hope not. At any rate . . .'

'There you are then. I can still hate him, can't I, for ever and ever?'

'Of course you can.'

Then Virginia came in. She was in one of her good moods.

'Bloody hell, he's doing supper tonight, old crap-head himself.'

'Plug your hole, shit-face.'

'That's enough of that,' I said pacifyingly, never having heard them speak such language before. Their true natures were coming out. My wife had failed. Perhaps they ought to go to a school where obscenities are completely unheard of.

'She started it, didn't she?' Adrian shouted.

I thought he was going to burst into tears but he didn't, thank God, and went back to checking the potatoes.

So, roughly, it went on until supper was over and we had settled ourselves comfily in front of the television. It was how I liked it, feet up, beer by my side, completely mindless. My son seemed to have recovered and I had given up trying to imagine what was going on in his head, in Webb's head. I found myself thinking less and less of the wrong done to my son and more and more of my daughter in relation to what folly I might be capable of (folly, you note, not wickedness) if I had less to lose, no children, a wife like Mrs Webb, and that familiar unease crept over me, greatly magnified. That is to say, I was seeing my daughter as representing many of her age and sex and undoubted charm of limb and countenance. The beauty of the flower in the bud. It didn't help (it did) that she was seated on the floor, back against the sofa, knees up, so that I caught a glimpse of her knickers. That evening I scribbled a note: They were white. What other eyes . . . ? Could she not hear my cry of warning?'

My wife returned safely to feed us up, yes, also with the much she had learnt in confabulation with other social workers in a hotel in Swindon, was it? Somewhere, she said, with nothing to take one's mind off things. She was in high spirits, 'charged with new ideas and ideas are energy.' To think of all those years I'd spent relying on the cornflakes. If she noticed a certain quietness in our son, she doubtless took it as a mark of concern for the people she was telling us about less fortunate than himself and of his growing maturity in general. From time to time he gave me a long blank look which I returned in kind, as if reassurance could be conveyed thereby.

It was a week or so before she would remark that he was no longer going round to Webb for carpentry so I was able to prepare the ground by coming back on the following Saturday morning with various tools, screws, nails, pieces of wood, sandpaper and whatnot (a basic stock suggested by the local do-it-yourself merchant) and setting up a workbench for him in our garage.

As I was setting out the tools etc. she came up behind me and said, 'Extravagant of you dear.' But I could tell she was pleased, my having taken an initiative at last.

'He's shown such an interest,' I said. 'I thought it was high time he had things of his own and stopped bothering Webb.'

'What makes you think that Webb doesn't enjoy being bothered?'

'Sheer vanity on my part. He's my son. I should provide for him.'

'Good for you!' I could imagine exactly those words, exactly that tone of voice, being used to congratulate some appalling drug-addicted petty criminal on deciding at long last to turn over a new leaf.

'Don't see Webb as the healthiest of influences,' she added, fingering the things on the bench, counting the cost no doubt. 'Pity it couldn't have waited for Christmas or a birthday. Virginia will be jealous.'

'I hadn't forgotten Virginia.'

'I agree entirely. She must learn to go beyond the child's crude conception of fairness. Giving, thoughtfulness, justice are not seasonal, not reducible, not simply a matter of equal shares for all.' She took a deep breath and put a hand on my back. 'Did you not discuss it with me because you thought I might have opposed the idea?'

'Not really. It wasn't planned actually. I was passing the shop and it suddenly occurred to me: why not? It's a nice sunny day.'

The truth of course was that I'd thought about it incessantly and hadn't wanted a wide-ranging discussion along the lines she'd touched upon above. I've found she has less to say about a *fait accompli*, when the ins and outs are examined in retrospect as opposed to in advance. (I speak of the realms of the mind, you understand.) Her hand began rubbing my back in a circular motion, making the lie seem that much more excusable.

'Sorry, dear,' I said. 'Of course we should have discussed it fully beforehand.'

'You impulsive old brute,' she murmured.

I realized then that what had happened to my son, plus having a long look at Mrs Webb dealing with her garbage, plus the thoughts that had followed, had combined to reduce the impulsiveness part, leaving the ageing brutishness to wallow about on its own. But I'd have to put up a show that night (lights out, pretend she was someone else) so I turned and kissed her on the cheek, at which she held me against her and nuzzled.

'I'll call Adrian,' she murmured.

He said, '*Thank* you, Dad' over and over again while my wife and I stood arm in arm above him. It was all very satisfactory. The brutishness went walkabout. One of the best moments ever, except for just about everything that was going on in my mind. My son gave me no long looks after that, nor did I attempt to become something of a carpenter myself. As a result of Webb's guidance and whatever went on in that school of his outside the foul language department, he seemed to know what he was doing.

My daughter sulked most of Sunday and my wife gave her a long talking-to. Poor child. After tea, she apologized to her brother for having called him a spoiled brat and for pinching his arm. Then she apologized to me, saying how selfish she'd been and I hadn't forgotten, had I, about taking the Hambles to the park?

She said, 'You haven't got to give me something too, Daddy. I'm glad for Adrian, I really am. We've got to learn the harmfulness of jealousy. Anyway, the first thing he makes is going to be for me.'

Learn the *what*? 'Nice girl,' I said, almost patting her bottom, then very decisively not doing so.

We were a happy family in those days. I sometimes glanced towards Webb's house but did not see him. There was no more calling me over for a chat through the fence, needless to say. At times I thought the price of our happiness was too high. At others I considered my raised standing vis-à-vis my wife and son and counted it a blessing for us all. But as usual there were no firm conclusions to be drawn, except that I'd lose little sleep over either Hipkin or my son, thereby gaining a sharper sense of my own shamelessness. We seem to believe sometimes there is something buried deep within us but we dig away day after day and find in the end there is nothing there at all.

Which leads me to add this before filling up my briefcase. The light was dim that night and I didn't imagine she was anyone else. The satisfactoriness was sustained. And I thought afterwards as I sometimes do (the thoughts I have tried to express are those that are harder to pin down, more rare – of which I never say to myself 'Well done!') that my debt to my wife is incalculable or does me no credit. The thing seems to be this, that women are at the mercy of the male sex, to which the only defence is that men are too. They can't help it. Women can't either of course, or as much as they'd like to, being so often on the receiving end. Helping seems to come more naturally to them than it does to us. That's so obvious it must be in the brain – not a matter of what my wife, a born helper if ever there was one, calls 'conditioning'. That was something they seem to have talked a lot about in Swindon. What I think I mean is that I wish I did not have to find myself constantly on the side of those capable of thinking as I commonly do; and I don't only mean the likes of Webb, not by a very long chalk. At the mercy of our sex, having it on the brain all right, oh yes, nothing conditional about that. Women aren't any help there, or not there even more (less?) so. If it wasn't for them we wouldn't be so bloody helpless. But if we can't help ourselves who's going to if they don't? (If you think you can just help yourself you've got a second think coming.) None of this is very helpful. Not to me. I must go home and watch television which, as I've said, I look forward to a lot. Can't help that. Saves thinking about . . . Cripes, here comes Plaskett. One of us.

'Good show, Tom, still at it,' he said.

That's about it – scribbling away and not getting anywhere.

Chapter Eight

It was Virginia who came to me next, in tears, floods of them.

After the carrots episode she took to going round to the Hambles fairly often and they evidently made a fuss of her. Sometimes she came back munching home-made biscuits with others in a paper bag for the rest of us. She'd helped Mrs Hamble make them, she said. Then it was a cake. My wife approved of this neighbourliness and a week later sent Virginia over with the ingredients with which to make another. She helped them in other ways. One day she came back with paint on her dress and forestalled her mother's scolding by saying that Hamble was painting their kitchen and she was giving him a hand. In return, Mrs Hamble gave her a handkerchief she had embroidered in one corner with an orange and shocking pink flower surrounded by lime-green leaves. Mrs Hamble was going to knit her a cardigan too, she said. She began doing other odd jobs for them. There was more painting to be done and the number of cakes grew. We had cake (chocolate-looking but not tasting of it or anything much else come to that) for supper just about every day for a month.

One Saturday morning I was looking for Virginia to ask her to do an odd job for me and saw her shaking out a rug in the Hambles' back yard.

'Isn't this becoming too much of a good thing?' I said to my wife.

'Why on earth should you say that? A limit on the good? Surely not?'

'Don't really know, just thought . . .' I didn't know of course, other than because it was me she should have been doing the odd job for, something so important I've now forgotten what it was.

'It's the most natural thing in the world. Can't you see, she's an altogether nicer person?'

'Why do you think she . . . ?'

'When dealing with spontaneous kindness it is sometimes counter-productive to examine motives.'

That was something coming from her, for whom motives in society as a whole usually loom large. Perhaps the best good is motiveless, like sheer bone idleness, both being diminished by having to work at them.

'So long as she doesn't get tired of them,' I said. 'Stop going round. Then they'd miss her, ask themselves what they'd done wrong.'

'Thank you. Good point. But I think you underrate her. She's a sensitive soul. You didn't have the same worry about Adrian and Webb. Don't see much of him these days. Wonder why.'

'Mm . . . Sure it's all right,' I said.

But it wasn't.

One Sunday afternoon Adrian was out in the garage sawing and hammering and quite ruining my sports viewing so that I wished I'd settled for stately galleons or stamps instead. My wife was out seeing about an unsuccessful adoption and Virginia was making yet another cake with the Hambles. I was in the act of switching across to cricket away from all that greenery that goes with golf when she ran in sobbing copiously, her hands to her face. Being me, my first thought was that Hamble had attempted, at best, some sort of grope.

'Oh my God!' I said. 'Not again.'

She stood by the window, heaving and gasping. I turned down the sound of the television just as a black man was striking a ball bowled by a white man very hard and very high into the air, this stopping me from turning off the picture too. I patted the sofa beside me.

'Come on, come and sit down and tell me all about it.'

But she stayed where she was, behind me, so that I had to keep on twisting my head back and forth to hear what she was saying and at the same time keep in touch with what the black man was up to, the white man's face too which was acquiring a defeated Hipkin look. It didn't occur to me to get up and stand by her and watch the game from there.

After several more gulps and snuffles she said, 'Mrs Hamble is dying, Daddy. She's soon going to be dead.'

'Come on, darling, come and sit.'

But she gabbled on, her forehead pressed against the window pane.

84

'Mr Hamble told me. He said she only just knew yesterday, he said she mustn't know I know. She's got a fatal disease. She's only got a fatal disease, that's all.'

'Perhaps it's not as bad as you think. They're discovering new drugs all the time.'

'She's got lots of pills already. She gets tired and makes these faces when she thinks I'm not looking and suddenly she goes all white and has to sit down. "A bit puffed," she says. I thought she was only tired but just now she nearly fell over when I was mixing in the butter and I went and fetched Mr Hamble who gave her two gigantic blue pills and took her to her room and then he came and told me. "You might as well know," he said. "She's not long for this world." He said only me and him knew except her and the doctors.'

I did then get up and go to her. I led her to the sofa and pulled her hands away from her face, having a thought too, oh yes, about what the schools were teaching nowadays instead of grammar.

'I'm sorry, old thing, I really am. But think, they're lucky to have you, to have each other. They think you're wonderful.'

'Oh, Daddy, she's so brave, trying to be cheerful and knitting so fast to finish my cardigan in time. He didn't mean to tell me, he said. But it was like I was one of the family now. It just came out. He said I mustn't tell a soul. She doesn't want anyone feeling sorry for her.'

'Life's a rotten bastard. It's like that,' I said.

She gave a big sniff. 'Have you got to watch the cricket?'

After yet another stupendous hit by the black man, I turned to yet more tracts of greenery, then switched off altogether.

'Soon she'll have to go back into hospital and stay there until . . . Mr Hamble said he didn't know how he was going to manage on his own but he didn't mean to say that. He pretends he can cope perfectly all right, but he's an even worse cook than you and Adrian.' With that she burst into tears again, finishing on a long, high wail. 'She's trying to teach him how to cook, not just open cans which are so expensive, and they don't even have a car to go out on outings or *anything*.'

What could I say? I've often thought about it and nothing has come to mind except what I did say. I didn't even put my arm round her. As ever, she was just that bit too far away.

'That picnic we promised. We could take them for a picnic.'

'Can he come and live in our house when she goes into hospital?'

'I'll have a word with your mother.'

'She'll only say he's got to learn to stand on his own feet.'

'Perhaps she'd be right. She usually is.' (Usually? The boldness of it shocked me but Virginia didn't seem to notice.)

'You could take him to the hospital every evening.'

'Of course I could. There is the bus, though. Door to door, just about.' (The sort of lousy thing I usually think but don't say). 'Let's talk about it calmly and sensibly when your mother comes home.'

'You mustn't tell Mum. I *promised*. Not that she's dying. I shouldn't even have told *you*.'

She'd stopped crying now, thinking hard of all the things she (we) could do for the Hambles.

'He could have his meals with us,' she said. 'He could sleep *some* nights here.'

'He might not want that.'

'He would if we asked him properly. If we *made* him. Oh Daddy, they're such *good* people. They never damaged a fly.'

Damage is one of my wife's favourite words and it's a word that so often fits. She alarms me sometimes with her vehemence, my wife does.

'We'll think of something. You must calm down. You're no good to them like that.'

'He might even kill himself or something. They could kill themselves together. They're only so quiet because they're so unhappy.'

'The poor old Hambles. I'll call round and see him. Don't worry, silly.'

'And she'll *know* I know and she'll think I'm only being nice to her and coming round all the time *because* I know.'

That was as much as she could bear and she fled to her room, wailing again. I thought she said, 'Now you can go on watching your cricket.' It probably wasn't anything like that at all. But it was what, after a decent pause, I did. The black man was still hitting the white man's ball about all over the place.

It seemed important that I should go and see Hamble immediately, before my wife came back. Walking very slowly up their path, I tried to work out what she would say but it wouldn't sound right coming from me somehow. 'Let's talk about this calmly and sensibly. I think I know what you must be suffering. If there's anything we can do, you've only got to ask. Are you a Christian or whatever, don't mind my asking?' and so forth.

He was standing in the kitchen over the kettle with his hands on his hips.

'Excuse me,' I said through the half-open door.

He didn't hear me because at that moment the kettle began to whistle and I saw him hesitate between first taking off the kettle or turning off the stove. I thought of how much space in our house he would take up. We'd keep on happening upon him on the stairs, in doorways and other confined spaces and would always be making way for each other. He would sit in the living-room and get up whenever anyone came in, not sure whether he should be there at all. He would always be apologizing, offering to help, wishing he was in his own house, opening a tin or boiling a kettle. Finally he saw me and blinked. His bluish patches had faded to grey and his hair had recently been wetted and combed. I imagined him studying himself regretfully in the mirror for a long time after putting his wife to bed. He came towards me, pulling at the skin under his chin and clearing his throat.

'Sorry,' he said.

I cleared my throat too. 'Virginia tells me your wife has to go into hospital. Nothing too serious, I hope. Anything I can do?'

He seemed to believe that Virginia had kept her promise, saying, 'That's kind, I'm sure. But nothing, thanks all the same.'

'They can do wonders these days. When's she due in?'

I followed him into the kitchen where he filled the teapot. I hoped he wouldn't invite me to stay for a cup.

'Wednesday morning as ever was.'

'I was thinking of taking the kids to the park tomorrow. Care to come along too, you and the wife?' I tried to make it sound like a passing thought, an easy offer to refuse.

'That's very kind, I'm sure, very kind.'

'Think about it.'

He looked bewildered and the hand putting the lid back on the teapot shook.

'I'll have a word with the wife, she's resting just now,' he mumbled, the redness coming back to his face. 'We are very appreciative.'

My daughter ran over to hug me when I told her and I held her arms wide to prevent any such thing. She ran round to the Hambles and came back almost at once to say they'd love to come and it was she who told my wife.

'What a nice idea,' she said. 'Haven't been to the park for ages, not since your father and I were courting.'

My son got there a fraction of a second before I did.

'We won't all fit, not in Daddy's car.'

And my daughter got there a fraction of a second before my wife would have done.

'Why not ask the Webbs to come too?'

'Good idea. Difficult to exaggerate the importance of neighbourliness in the overall social matrix. So that's decided then.' (To be fair she didn't put it quite like that. The word 'matrix' comes from another occasion. I looked it up later, thinking it might be related to matriarch, like the rest of us.)

My son and I exchanged helpless expressions and both took a large mouthful of food which we were a long time in swallowing.

'That's decided then,' my wife repeated. 'Early lunch here, picnic tea in the park. Leave the arrangements to the menfolk.'

I looked at my wife lifting her fork, from the blob of mash on top of which a long string bean was suspended, and thought, for the first time ever, 'You don't know the bloody half of it, do you?'

It was Virginia who asked the Webbs. I wished I could have seen Webb's face, or her face, come to that.

Virginia reported excitedly to me, 'He said they couldn't make it, then she said of course they could, so they're coming. I said Adrian and Mum could go with them and the Hambles could come with you and me in our car or Mum could drive our car and you and Adrian could go with them in their car or you and me could go with them of course though I want to be with the Hambles and they must go together in case she isn't well and he has to give her a pill.'

'We'll work something out,' I said, trying to put some of her enthusiasm into my voice and to think of a permutation she hadn't so far covered. I was being glad too that my son wasn't present when he said right behind me.

'Or Mrs Webb can come with Mum and Dad and me.'

'Don't you even know that Mrs Webb is shy and'll want to be with her husband?' my daughter said.

Adrian's reply was a shout. 'And don't you even know you're a pea-brain and a wooden-head.'

'We'll work something out,' I said again.

'You're a pea-brain *or* a wooden-head to think someone could be both at the same time, isn't he, Daddy?'

She gave us both that superior look which was a fair imitation of my wife's expression when winding up a matter to do with injustice and privilege, what the capitalist system has done to people, that rigmarole – except that then she spoiled the effect by sticking her tongue out.

'I don't even know if I'm going on any stupid picnic,' my son said.

'Let's have a look at what's come out of the woodwork,' I said, going past him as he made a kicking motion in the direction of my daughter, which caught me on the shin.

'Shit!' I said and my daughter giggled.

We stood side by side at the workbench and he showed me how various pieces of wood he'd cut would fit together. I was amazed at how careful and exact he was. He was close to tears and we said nothing about the picnic. There was nothing to be said. I wondered if he missed the company of the man who'd taught him so well some of the rudiments of this useful and precise skill. I was thinking too of what an ignorant bitch my daughter had inadvertently been.

'Don't worry. It'll be all right,' I said, leaving him to his woodwork and feeling thankful that my wife was coming on the picnic too to keep the conversation going. I pondered again on her ignorance, the corollary of it being that I was the only one on this occasion who knew it all. I could taste, as it were, the savour of my own moral sweat and decided I didn't care for it at all. I prayed that night for rain, for my car to break down, for any old act of a merciful God and sod His justice.

Chapter Nine

But the sun shone brightly the next day and my engine had never sounded healthier – until compared with the smug purring of Webb's next door. I lifted the bonnet and, adjusting the growl to something more like a gargle, considered snipping through the fanbelt with the garden shears. But Webb was just the sort of man to have a spare or think nothing of depriving his wife of one of her stockings. I could picture him doing so while she was actually wearing it, then bringing it to me while she stood there watching him with the flummoxed look of someone accosted by a stranger with a pronounced foreign accent. The image of Mrs Webb's stocking turning my fan and getting steadily hotter was the least erotic thought I'd had all week. I slammed down the bonnet and went to fetch the picnic bag. When I came back, Adrian was sitting in the back of the car, gazing everywhere around him, except at me. I looked in the direction of the Webbs and saw them standing on either side of their car, craning forward with their mouths open as if they were silently hurling abuse at each other. It had been agreed (decided by my wife) that she and Adrian would travel with the Webbs and the Hambles and Virginia with me.

She had said, 'A son should travel with his poor old mother to see she comes to no harm.'

I had said, 'One large Hamble and two small Ripples should fit in the back I should think.' For some extraordinary reason she let that go and that was how it was left: five in one car, three in the other – odd, come to think of it, her not pointing out the inequity in that, I mean.

Instead she now came to the car and tousled Adrian's hair before he could pull his head away. But she's not put out by that sort of thing and simply said, thank heaven, 'Never thought I'd see the day when my son would abandon me into the hands of strangers.' Start making it clear abundantly early perhaps there'd be no old people's home for her. That thought leading to being confident she'd come to see me regularly in mine, thereby to acquire ammunition for her opinions about the care of the elderly, then to wondering how often my children would ('if at all' gets added at that point), then to how much (little) they'd want to.

Virginia and the Hambles were coming down their garden path, Virginia in the middle, looking up at them in turn while they beamed down at her. I hadn't seen the Hambles walk over a long distance before and their breadth either side of my slender, green-clad daughter brought to mind a thick lettuce sandwich. Mrs Hamble was wearing a pale grey dress with blobs of a slightly darker grey distributed about it and Mr Hamble was in a baggy suit of roughly the same colour as the blobs with its blobs here and there of a paler hue due to an age of minor mishaps of food and drink or whatever, so that the sandwich that came to mind was stale as well as hunky. They looked very secure and happy together, Mrs Hamble in particular who seemed far from death at that moment, at that distance. As Hamble and Virginia got into the back with Adrian, and Mrs Hamble, very careful not to allow her dress to rise above her knee, got grunting in beside me, the Webbs passed us, he with an opening of his palm face-high, his wife with a fluttering of her fingers, and my wife with that expression of hers I can never quite identify, but somewhere between the carefree and the censorious or combining them both in a way that suggested she was determined to appear to be having fun in spite of herself – there were infinitely better things she could be doing with her time but self-indulgence was part of human experience and to deny oneself a first-hand knowledge of it smacked of, well, self-indulgence . . . Virginia gave me the thumbs-up sign and Mrs Hamble said, 'Oooh, this is fun, isn't it, luvvy? Isn't it going to be fun?'

'It is that,' her husband replied.

'We do appreciate your kindness, Mr Ripple, we really do,' she added so that only I could hear her. Then repeated it more loudly, 'Don't we, Alf?' To which he made no reply.

Virginia said, 'It's nothing,' and I saw her in the driving mirror checking to see how much Mr Hamble was really likely to enjoy himself at all. I could not see Adrian's face luckily, because that would have meant he could have seen mine which was the kind one makes while probing a sore tooth with one's tongue, and that was because Mrs Hamble's knee was up against the gear lever and I could not grasp the one without brushing against the other.

'Charming spot the park,' I said. 'Haven't been there in ages.'

At which Hamble made the first of his jokes, 'Wouldn't be so bloody charming if you had, would it, eh?'

'Oooh, Alf! Language! Really!' Mrs Hamble cried, looking over her shoulder. 'He's got a wicked tongue when the fancy takes him.'

I noticed then that the pink of her face was all rouge and that there was a thick coat of powder under her eyes hiding a darkness deeper than any bruise. Virginia gave a squeaky chuckle and, wishing my son would laugh too, I forgot to do so myself.

'Isn't this a treat?' Mrs Hamble continued.

Then there was a silence for a while until Hamble repeated quietly, 'It is that.' And I heard in his voice what to judge from Virginia's face she had heard too: and a bloody few more there'll be of those.

To take my mind off the lack of one in mine, I tried to imagine what conversation might be going on in the other car. Webb would soon have guessed that my wife knew nothing about the episode in the workshop because she'd probably have said something about how 'natural and wholesome' woodwork was and how pleased she was he'd been able to stimulate her son's interest or whatever. He might assume from that, he ought to, that therefore I knew nothing about it either but that at any time we might be told about it and then . . . what is known as a suspended sentence. Webb would be asking a lot of questions of course to which my wife, in so far as they were related to her job (and anything eventually could be made to be), would be giving very comprehensive answers indeed. I doubted whether Mrs Webb would be saying anything at all, with my wife on the one hand trying to bring her into the conversation and Webb on the other trying to keep her out of it. Finally my thoughts reverted to Mrs Webb's stocking whizzing round in my engine.

'It's like the real countryside, the park is,' my daughter was pronouncing in her most (least) adult voice. 'Perfect countryside.'

'Unbeaten record,' Hamble muttered.

I didn't want to be the one to get it first but became worried that nobody else seemed to have done. Then Mrs Hamble said,

'Honest, Alf, what will everyone think? Your little jokes.' She turned to me. 'You see. Country side. Like football or one of those. Like England. Brazil. France.'

I wondered if she knew just how hard her husband was trying to cheer her up. And if she knew, how much more miserable would it make her? Her pride in him was flowing over. Perhaps that was paramount. I found myself wishing my wife enjoyed my jokes as much, as perhaps she might if they were intended to cheer up any-one but myself. I crack them mainly to distract my children from the seriousness of life, which might cheer them up too if I wasn't also trying to endear myself (suck up) to them, and that leads back into the seriousness of life (along with reducing my chances of being taken seriously). Anyway I summoned a laugh, a little too late, and my son said, 'What's the joke?'

I said, 'Have you "been" in the park? Must remember that one. Very droll, Mr Hamble.'

Beside me Mrs Hamble shifted about and grunted again. It had been a grunt of pain, sharp, sudden and involuntary and only I had heard it. I wished that the day was over, that Mrs Hamble was in hospital being properly ministered to, that she wasn't so desperate to let her husband know he was making her happy, to let us know we were too. She wasn't going to spoil the fun for everybody else. All that. Dignity. Thoughtfulness. Decency. Courage. The lot. And there was I wishing I wasn't there to see it.

And then I heard her whisper, 'Oh God, help me!' as she turned round to her husband and quickly away again so that he shouldn't see the pain on her face.

'Tell them the one about the lady on the bus whose little boy wiped his lollipop on the other lady's fur coat,' she said. 'That's a good one.'

It was one we all knew. It had to be of course. I prayed for my children's laughter.

Hamble said, 'You tell it.'

'She said to the little boy, "Don't do that. You'll get hairs all over it." I don't tell it like he does.'

Both my children managed a kind of short laugh, though my son's was one of embarrassment, mainly. They are nice children. I laughed too, repeating the punch line, adding, 'Now that one I like.'

Not much was said after that. Mrs Hamble spoke only once, to say, 'I do like looking at other people's houses,' which must have been to explain why she kept her face averted to the window, so that I should not see it.

My wife and the Webbs were waiting for us in the car park. I may not have mentioned that my wife is a tall, well-built woman, which made me realize how small and skinny the Webbs are. I felt particularly neutral at that moment, thinking that I must be about the average of the other five adults in girth and height. Webb hid himself in front of her as we came up behind her and my son fell behind Hamble and me, leaving Virginia and Mrs Hamble to go on ahead. I hung back so as to be with my son and muttered to him, 'Cheer up, kiddo.'

'It's all right for you,' he said.

The grouping remained much the same when we were well inside the park except that Webb and my wife walked further ahead. It was difficult to tell who was keeping up with whom. Mrs Webb dropped back with Mrs Hamble and my daughter, and I took up the rear beside Hamble, with my son keeping more or less level with us on the grass verge kicking a tennis ball.

The three carrier bags containing the picnic things were being carried one each by the men. My wife had a blanket over her arm. In front of me Mrs Hamble briefly took Virginia's hand, swung it and let it drop. I wanted to get Webb on his own for a moment to tell him he wasn't to think I didn't know even if my wife didn't, and to watch it (what?). Then, having thought it through like that, I had no wish to do anything of the sort.

Adrian's tennis ball rolled in front of my foot. I gave it a hard kick through Hamble's legs and it finally came to rest a yard or two in front of my wife who glanced at it and strode on. For a few seconds she was talking to herself because Webb put his carrier bag down, picked the ball up and took two long paces towards us, his arms outstretched in front of him, hands joined in a fist inside which was the ball. Then his right arm looped over his head to toss it at us, making Mrs Webb, Mrs Hamble and Virginia hasten aside on to the grass verge. Hamble and I leant forward, hands out ready to catch it, but it came at us in a swift underhand lob from Webb's left hand and our arms flailed in the air as it bobbed up between my legs and hit me in the balls.

'You devil, Webb!' Hamble called out, grinning and red in the face.

Mrs Hamble chanted 'Butter-fingers! Butter-fingers!' and Mrs Webb clapped her hands but was not smiling, giving her appreciation a qualified look.

I grinned, I think, and went red in the face too when I saw Webb open his mouth wide and stick his finger in the air, while my wife eyed us all warily like an over-dutiful playground supervisor. My son picked up the ball and said, as much to Hamble as to me, 'He's just stupid. I've only seen that thousands of times.'

But Hamble went on smiling, now at his wife who had her arm round Virginia and was whispering something to her.

Trying to make sure my grin looked like a grin, I said to my daughter, 'Why don't you and Mrs Hamble scout ahead to find us a nice picnic spot?'

Mrs Hamble did not hear me. She was looking vacantly across the parkland and up at the sky as if puzzled that anything could be wrong if she was having such a good time on such a nice day. Then with Mrs Webb at her side and giving Virginia a gentle shove ahead of her, she returned to the centre of the path and took a few paces after Webb and my wife before turning and coming back towards us, leaving Mrs Webb and Virginia to carry on on their own.

As she came up to me, my son threw the ball from behind his back and Hamble lunged for it, missed and fell sideways. He sat there chuckling for a while, then put out his hand for my son to pull him to his feet, grabbed him by the leg and dragged him, chuckling too, down on to the grass beside him. Mrs Hamble gasped and I turned to see her holding her stomach. Her eyes were moist and screwed up as if the tears were having to be squeezed from them.

'My God,' I thought, 'she's having an attack!' and nearly called out to my wife.

But oh no. She touched me on the wrist and whispered, 'I can't remember when I . . . I'm so *happy*. It's all so lovely suddenly, seeing him . . . we're having such a . . . God is smiling on us today . . . He would have made a wonderful father.'

Well, yes. I have no religion (or so I believe) but as I watched Hamble on the grass with my son, she brought to mind a fleeting image of God, jolly, red-faced, a romper on lawns with children who had to watch His paunch and twinges . . . But not for long. God the Father who suffered little children because only they were not yet old enough to know what an appalling amount of suffering He could put up with. A fat, crotchety old fool, laying the law down, who'd done sod all for mankind over the centuries except smile sorrowfully down and watch it behave badly, or surprisingly well on occasion, all things considered. Christ alone knows why on earth we should wonder whether He would have made a wonderful father . . . Meanwhile Mrs Hamble, ignorant of the staring passers-by, watched my son pull her husband to his feet and her tears began to flow. So I led her away to catch up with the others.

'Here,' I said, giving her my handkerchief. 'Who'd understand why you are crying? I mean, you're all right now, aren't you?'

I've tried since then to think up two questions more stupid than those but haven't got anywhere near it.

She quickly recovered so that I guessed there had been pain too in that moment of joy. 'I can't tell you what a good man he is,' she said. 'Sometimes I see him left on his own and I feel like going and having a good cry in the lav.'

She hurried off to rejoin Virginia and, looking at my wife striding ahead with the Webbs, I thought that if I did the disappearing trick before she did, I'd have a good cry in the lav too, knowing how well she was coping and what she was saying about me. Good-natured, unassuming, decent and the like I'd become. And I'd grip the handle, not needing then I suppose to use it, and my crying would turn into a ghostly growl that she hadn't known me better because from her angle there wasn't anything to know. I'd leave mysterious bits of dust about all over the place and the odd, luminous turd in the lavatory bowl. I'd stop her somehow telling my children what a good-natured etc. chap I'd been.

We'd passed through an area where groups of people were sitting round tables and seemed from their hunched and downcast demeanour not yet to have registered they had ventured out of doors.

Mrs Hamble said with a small gasp, 'Wouldn't have sat at a table, would we? It's not the same, is it, Alf?' That being followed by a silence she went on, 'I like to be right down close to it. Mother Nature they call it.'

'Should have sat a damn sight harder on *her* mother's nature, I can tell you that,' Hamble muttered to Virginia and me, but Mrs Hamble heard him, was meant to of course.

'Alf, you shouldn't, not about the dead, should he, Mr Ripple?' she said with a sniffle or giggle perhaps.

I didn't answer but tried to look amicably at them both. I quickly saw that it was no use so far as he was concerned, his having been reminded among all that thickness of green under the bare blue heavens that there was death in the air and foliage wasn't the only growth that was having a good flourish that day.

We finally fetched up beneath a cluster of trees of the pine or fir type where my wife spread out the blanket she'd been carrying. We sat down round it in a circle as follows: Mrs Webb, Webb, my wife, Mrs Hamble, my daughter, Hamble, myself and my son who was half behind me so as to avoid being in Webb's line of sight. There were six plastic boxes of various foods, three of them brought by the Hambles, with us supplying two packets of biscuits, four bananas and some paste sandwiches, and the Webbs some other sandwiches. Mrs Hamble opened her boxes to reveal the selection of a classy miniature cake shop: coconut buns with cherries on top, date squares, those cornflake things stuck together with chocolate, oatmeal biscuits, flapjacks and macaroons. Those are the ones I immediately recall some two months later and all of them made by herself of course. We had each brought our own flask of liquid.

My daughter and Mrs Webb began passing the boxes about in a polite manner while Mrs Hamble pointed and listed what the contents of hers were, interspersed with comment mainly to Virginia about their recipes. The confusion was such with the boxes changing hands and conflicting with my attempts and Webb's to pour orangeade and coffee respectively from our flasks that, after thirty seconds or so of exasperated gazing, my wife finally felt the need to take charge, prompted in the end by my attempt to hold a cucumber sandwich on top of a date square with one hand and with the other pour orangeade, so that a splosh of it dropped on the sandwich, making it sag even more soggily than it was otherwise doing and soon fall in half on to the grass.

'Why don't we just put everything in the middle and dig in?' she said.

'Keep an eye out for Jerry. Your turn for sentry duty, Private Ripple,' Hamble said to Adrian.

Nobody got that reference and in the silence that her brisk tone of voice had otherwise caused, my wife grouped the boxes in a rough circle at the centre of the blanket. I saw that Hamble was smiling to himself and it cheered me up a lot that he didn't seem to mind, unlike me, if his jokes were missed. I was hoping to smile at him, perhaps wink, but he was not looking my way, only at his wife, checking up on her. He wanted to go on amusing her somehow. The signs of her tears were still there smeared across the top of her right cheek though it might have been a streak of light that had found its way through the trees. She seemed happy enough, holding up an oatmeal biscuit and telling Virginia something about rice paper.

'This is the life,' Webb said.

Mrs Webb was munching one of her own sandwiches, as I was, though they required virtually no jaw movement, having the texture of mashed potato without the odd lump. Mrs Webb was looking hard at hers between glancing up a lot too, each time at a different person, as if to check how much she was under observation. Eventually it was my turn and she discovered she was, whereupon she flushed and I was not nearly quick enough to turn my stare into a smile or whatever.

Webb was saying to her, 'Change is as good as a rest they say', then to me, 'Often do this, do you? Kids make the difference. There's your incentive.'

I nodded, turning it to neck trouble on remembering I was meant to be ignoring him, then watched my wife offering Mrs Hamble one of her own plastic boxes which she took and passed on to Virginia.

'We've got a nice day for it, no question about that,' I said.

'Isn't it lovely?' Mrs Webb said wistfully, as if about to break into song. 'I can't remember such a lovely summer.'

At which Webb slapped her on the knee and said, 'The old girl's forgotten the season of our wedlock. The sun shone every day for a month. Hand in hand we walked across the broad sunlit uplands, like the saying goes.'

Mrs Webb tutted and dropped her head as if nodding off, or overcome with shame, but did not move her knee away from under her husband's hand.

'That was Winston,' Mrs Hamble said accusingly, her face taking on an almost delirious expression and she turned it to her husband, recalling perhaps their own wedlock and walks hand in hand in the sunlight.

My wife, I fear, was looking at Webb with disgust or rather with that kind of hard smile people have when there is silence in company and someone has made a smell or when, standing in a bus queue eagerly looking for the next bus as it comes round the corner, it turns out to be some other sort of heavy vehicle altogether. I remembered then our own marriage during a drizzle and that second when our own joined hands felt like a single, knotty, paralysed fist. The only country walk I could recall was one along a narrow path beside a ploughed field. We had tried to walk side by side but the grassy tufts and clumps kept on making us lurch. We did not visit broad, sunlit places like the park.

'Good old Winston,' Hamble said.

Under my raised elbow I saw my son twiddling the furry top of a blade of grass against his knee and wished he would say something. I reached for one of the boxes and offered it to him. He picked out one of the cornflake things and took a big chomping bite out of it.

'No pleases and thank-yous today then?' I whispered good-humouredly.

'Gee thanks!' he muttered.

I put a hand above his head as if to protect him from the rebuke he'd be getting before too long from his mother who dislikes sulking as a sign that people might have stopped counting their blessings.

Webb said, 'We could do with another one like that, don't you think so, Mr Ripple, Tom?'

He was holding up a macaroon, about to take a bite out of it, and I thought for a moment it was that to which he was referring. But my wife had raised her chin and seemed about to let loose one of her fully-fledged opinions which would not do at all in present company, so I managed to get in swiftly, 'Quite a guy, Churchill.'

'He only saved us, led us to victory,' Mrs Hamble said, but it was more like a cautious final shout. She took a handkerchief out of her sleeve, arranged it in a neat pad and blew her nose. I thought she was going to cry again.

It was Virginia who spoke next. (Until then, I'd never been able to blame her for periodically trying to keep up with, on the right side of, her mother who now looked proudly down upon her.)

'Mummy says he made a lot of mistakes, didn't you, Mummy? And he wasn't elected after the war. He was too bossy or something and a member of the ruling classes.'

I could see Hamble going red in the face and was sorry my wife couldn't see it too, though I doubt if it would have made the slightest difference.

And sure enough, off she went, 'He might have been right for his time. But he wasn't a believer in fair shares for all exactly and I'm not sure in any case that hero worship is good for any society if it is to undergo radical reform from the bottom up.'

Hamble spoke very quietly and very audibly as his wife moved her handkerchief down from her nose to her mouth, 'I reckon I'm working class and I'm not any damn Tory but he did have style, he was big, bigger than all the rest of them put together.' Then he muttered so that only I could hear him, 'Bottom up bollocks.'

I looked at him, raising my eyebrows as far as they'd go, followed by a frown indicating that anatomically that might require some thinking about. He got all that and after a glance at my wife gave me the briefest, happiest of smiles.

My wife slowly unscrewed a flask and began pouring from it into a paper cup, her face wearing a completely expressionless look, or clearly expressing that orangeade was more deserving of her attention than Winston Churchill, now or at any other time for that matter. She offered the cup to Hamble.

'I may not have put enough water in,' she said.

Hamble took it, steadying his hand with the other at the wrist. 'I'm sure it'll do very nicely.' His hand began shaking and he put the cup down on the grass.

'He likes it strong,' Mrs Hamble explained.

My wife was smiling now, having put Churchill in his place. Or so she thought.

'You can't say Churchill wasn't big,' Mrs Hamble mumbled.

'He had a lovely way of putting things,' Mrs Webb said.

'Fight on the beaches, all that,' Webb said.

This had to be put a stop to so I said too loudly, 'For a square yard of sand and a deck-chair more like it nowadays.'

The redness was fading out of Hamble's face but he did not smile. My wife did not catch the resentful look he gave her. I could imagine her saying once again at the supper table that evening, 'It's sad the way the British had this Churchill worship, the bulldog mania lingering on in the minds of ordinary working people.'

Mrs Webb said then, 'He went a bit funny in the head, didn't he, gaga like, in the end? It was in the *Sunday People*.'

'So'd you be gaga at his age,' Webb said gently though his face was set in a snarl.

Mrs Webb addressed her reply to me, 'I hope I'm dead and gone long before that, all dribbling and mumbly. Life's long enough as it is. Too long sometimes if you ask me.'

'We didn't,' Webb said.

Then there was a long silence in which nobody looked at anyone else except me, to observe the fact. Under my elbow my son had stopped twiddling the blade of grass. My wife was crunching antagonistically on a coconut thing and looking about her to fit the other folk who were enjoying their afternoon out into one category or another. We munched and sipped and gazed around us, or up at the sky. There was discomfort in the air. Except for Mrs Hamble. That was the extraordinary thing. She was radiantly happy as if she knew you only have to be that once in your life to be ready to die. I wished a small dog would come along to which I could throw Adrian's ball. I wished there was a game we could all play. I looked around for a piece of wood of appropriate size, then said, 'Let history decide. How about . . . ? Run along, Adrian, see if you can find a bit of wood to play cricket with.'

'It already has,' Hamble reminded me as Adrian hesitated long enough to make it clear he thought it was a rotten idea and see if he cared before slouching off with his hands in his pockets.

My wife said, 'Not so sure about that,' her eyes and Webb's following Adrian while I watched Webb until he realized it and we exchanged looks of wariness on his side, contempt (I hoped) on mine. It was I who lowered my eyes first.

Meanwhile Mrs Hamble and Virginia had struck up a conversation about the cardigan Virginia was wearing and Hamble leant forward to listen to them. I was glad neither had seen the look that up till then he had been giving my wife. There was one member of the working classes who henceforth might be looking out for another spokesperson, or deciding to manage without one altogether thanks. (I could hear Hamble asking me, 'Often shoving her spoke in like that, is she?')

Then Webb said to his wife, 'On your sixty-fifth birthday then I'll give you a bottle of sleeping pills and a length of rubber hose, how about that then?'

Mrs Webb thought about that as if they were being offered to her there and then. 'I'm not frightened of death, don't you ever think I am. I'll know when I'm good and ready.'

Both Virginia and Mrs Hamble heard that, I think, for they raised their voices and their conversation switched abruptly from the cardigan to the penultimate oatmeal biscuit which Mrs Hamble snapped in half in order to make a point about its consistency in the middle.

I thought by now the orangeade had done the trick but the cup had tilted over and much of it had spilled on to the grass. Hamble looked hard at my wife and I thought he might apologize for that, ask if there was any more.

Not a bit of it. 'I'll tell you something about Winston Churchill,' he said. 'If it wasn't for him, we might none of us be sitting here now, you won't find that in any of your history books. Hitler wouldn't have stopped at the Channel or anywhere like that. You won't find that in the history books, the *Graf Spee* moored in Southampton harbour. Where will you find that in any of your so-called history books?'

With nothing whatever worth adding, I nodded. 'Hitler couldn't have lasted much longer. He was a complete nut.'

Guessing that my wife was about to apply her mind to all that at some length and/or knowing her husband had a lot more to say where that had come from, Mrs Hamble gave him a long, imploring look.

He nodded at her. 'So, you could say, was my old Aunt Hazel.'

Mrs Hamble beamed at him. 'Really, Alf! You never had an aunt called Hazel.'

'I did that. She was a proper witch.'

And Mrs Hamble began chuckling, holding her sides, until a few more tears flowed. 'Ooooh, ooooh!' she moaned.

Then she hoisted herself to her feet, gave Virginia a hand up and led her off by the shoulder in the rough direction Adrian had gone in. Virginia looked back at me, raised her eyebrows and shook her head. I deflected the look on to Hamble, who shrugged. Then I did laugh at his joke and he shrugged again as if someone else had been responsible for it. And I laughed a second time, because my wife had missed it altogether and was making it known by the length of her silence that the entire occasion was one she'd not have minded missing either.

So she wanted to get back into things. 'It's easy to say that too much fuss is made about dying, now that much of the pain of it can be avoided. So, frequently in my experience anyway, people cannot accept that their days are numbered and the calm and resignation are perhaps less common than they were, once having deleted the religious factor of course. People do not go gentle . . .'

She was saying all this to me fortunately, thus again missing the way Hamble was looking at her. There was no mistaking the spasm of hatred. To myself I muttered, 'Pompous, insensitive cow.' I never want to see an expression like that again on any man's face, especially one as kindly and helpless as Hamble's normally is. I never want to think that about my wife again either.

My son appeared, bouncing his ball up and down on a piece of wood, and waited for us some distance away.

'Cricket?' I said to Hamble, getting to my feet.

'What about you?' Hamble said to Webb.

Webb had his mouth over his hand, which was catching crumbs from a too large piece of flapjack he had bitten off, and shook his head. My wife lay back on the grass, tugging her skirt down over her knees, putting her hands behind her head and closing her eyes. Seen upside down she had the look of a bearded tyrant caught in an off moment. I hoped I would not thereafter always see her like that. The last glimpse I had of the Webbs before we started playing cricket was of them sitting forward with their arms round their knees, contemplating the debris of our picnic as if it might have been their own lives spread out before them. Virginia and Mrs Hamble were nowhere to be seen.

My son was very keen on hitting the ball hard and soon had Hamble and me running about all over the place. Mrs Webb came and watched us with an absent look and once fetched the ball and tossed it to me, overarm in that awkward way women have, using all their bodies. After a particularly strenuous spell, Hamble put his hands on his hips, took a deep breath and said, 'Used to prefer French cricket myself.'

'Come on!' my son called.

I was pretty puffed myself and said, 'Can't imagine the French playing any sort of cricket somehow.'

Hamble tossed the ball to me over my son's head. 'Rugby and long-distance cycling is what they're best at,' he said.

'Come *on!*' my son repeated and I caught him with a real stinger half-way up his thigh.

'Got him!' Mrs Webb cried.

At which my son threw the bat on to the ground and sauntered off with his hands in his pockets.

'It's only a game, lad,' Hamble called after him.

Virginia and Mrs Hamble then emerged beyond Adrian between two exotic red-leafed trees, spoke to him for a moment and, Adrian in the middle, they came on towards us.

'We don't stand a ruddy chance with that brother of yours,' Hamble said to Virginia. 'He's a proper demon with the bat, call him Dracula we ought to.'

All of us smiled, even Adrian, Mrs Hamble directing hers at Mrs Webb who was coming to join us. As we ambled slowly back towards my wife and Webb, I looked around us at the day and realized it was one of exceptional warmth and brightness with enough wind and clouds about to keep on changing the light and heat, making our silences less noticeable. Mrs Webb and Mrs Hamble began humming different tunes, hymn tunes they sounded like and entirely appropriate, then stopped after a line or two as Virginia skipped away a few paces ahead of us. Hamble put an arm round his wife's shoulders and gave them a quick squeeze. My son chucked the ball which hit the centre of the trunk of a small tree at about the height a very tall batsman's balls would have been. I drew a square in the air around Adrian's face, feeding Hamble his line.

'A perfect pitcher,' he said and we both laughed while Adrian beat his chest.

Mrs Hamble waddled on and caught up with Virginia, smiling more widely than ever. Mrs Webb had fallen behind and had begun humming a different hymn. In no hurry, we moved towards Webb and my wife. Webb was leaning back on his elbow, facing away from us. My wife was still lying on her back with her eyes closed.

'Here they are!' Webb said, jumping to his feet.

My wife did not move until we all started clearing up the picnic things when she sat upright and said, 'This is the life! I could lie here for ever.'

'I'm bloody sure you could and every bloody where else,' Hamble's expression conveyed until Webb said, 'And catch your death in no time, Mrs Ripple.' Only Mrs Hamble managed a smile at that.

A great weariness suddenly seemed to come over us as Virginia put the last of the plastic boxes in Mrs Hamble's carrier bag and my wife folded the blanket and led the way home.

So the day ended. We drove back in the same cars we had come in. The Webbs had deposited my wife by the time we got back and waved to us from their front door as I drove up to our garage. The Hambles were profuse with their thanks and seemed in a hurry to get home again. Virginia and I watched them walk up their front path and Virginia held her arm up ready to wave but they did not turn round. Adrian went off into the garage to do some more woodwork and I was glad my daughter did not try to say anything. There was nothing I could have said to her in reply.

My wife was in the kitchen thinking about supper. There was already a packet of fish fingers on the draining board. I hoped she wouldn't say anything either – for my children's sake and not only because Adrian was due for a scolding for having sulked but also because Virginia was showing signs (twiddling her hair and chewing her nails) that the day had been too much for her. For my sake too, because I had thought ill enough of my wife for one day. Nor was there much on television to keep the conversation neutral: just two old cowboy films I'd seen before, a famous orchestra in rehearsal (yet another repeat) and punishing stretches of enlightenment with light entertainment in between. A dismal prospect.

My wife spoke little over supper and the children went to bed early. There was a moment when she said something about what a close couple the Hambles seemed to be and I switched the conversation to, of all things, Plaskett, describing him merely as a man I had heard about and making the point that it was a fair bet a man so nasty was unhappy, for your ordinary, decent, sensible person couldn't possibly enjoy ordering other people about.

'Was Hitler unhappy?' my son asked sagely. My wife didn't attempt to answer that.

Indeed it was my children who did most of the talking, mentioning characters in their schools who were less than nice and having doubts about the consequences of being especially or unnecessarily nice to them.

My only contribution was, 'Nice people are nicer than nasty people.' I'd read this somewhere as having been said by a famous writer, I forget who now.

'That's silly, of course they are,' Virginia said. My wife looked at her and nodded, just the once so it might not definitely have been taken as that.

Even last thing in the bedroom she had little to say.

'That was a bit of an effort,' she said finally. 'But the weather was nice.'

'The Hambles certainly seemed to be enjoying themselves.'

'Did you think so? Perhaps. Must say I found myself rather beginning to like Webb. Restless type. Needs a challenge. Rather a drab wife, poor soul.'

'She can't help that.'

'Of course she can't. That's precisely the point I might have gone on to make.'

I kept the bedside light on late that night in order to finish the life of Dr Livingstone, knowing it might stop her from sleeping, me too come to that, and serve us both right.

The following evening I saw Mrs Hamble slicing string beans in her garden so I went over to the fence and said, 'String beans for supper I see.'

She waved the knife at me. 'French beans we used to call them.'

Then Hamble's head appeared a few yards down the fence where he'd been doing some weeding.

'Or runners,' he said. 'Only their legs. Frogs' legs.'

Mrs Hamble lowered her knife, sucked in her lips and began shaking her head. I smiled at them both, waiting for him to continue.

'Human beans,' he said, running his tongue over his lips and blinking so that his whole face seemed to twitch.

'Honestly, Alf,' Mrs Hamble said, 'what next?'

'I'll tell you what next. When we Brits get into that Common Market, we'll eat them up.'

That is what I remember now of that day. In years to come, who knows? The dying of Mrs Hamble or Winston Churchill or my son twiddling a blade of grass, or a silly image of God or a paper cup spilling orangeade on to the grass?

I ought to add this. What I said earlier about my wife's reason for visiting me in an old people's home was both unkind and untrue. She would believe, as I would, that she was visiting me largely out of love, albeit with some pity in it. The confusion of these two might trouble me, rather than the opinions I was helping her to form about what I and my surroundings were an example of, to be held forth about. I wouldn't give a bugger about all that, not in my condition, make that clear to her, becoming then even more pitiable and to that extent more (less) loveable; but by then too something far larger will have loomed across it all – to do with the sad inevitability of things. The most we can do about that, I suppose, is try to set an example – that of course also going for those in charge of the surroundings – but stay quiet and not hold forth about it and perhaps thereby to eradicate the pity. Which brings me back to the Hambles, though none of this really explains why, suddenly, I do not feel pity towards them at all.

Nothing happened worth writing about between the outing to the park and our holiday by the seaside. I saw much more of the Hambles. The hospital only kept her for a week. Every time I was in the garden, trimming and weeding and turning the soil, they were in theirs and we exchanged views on this and that: greenfly on the honeysuckle, fertilizing the roses, dandelions in the grass, things of that sort. Mrs Hamble sat in a deckchair beneath their living-room window, knitting mostly (something for Virginia, probably, so I couldn't ask, that leading to how much longer it would take) and glancing up very often at the bent body of her husband.

Sometimes they sat side by side drinking tea, talking a little and gazing about them. They reminded me of a couple in an advertisement for life insurance, looking their last on all things lovely I think the expression is. I began to wonder if Virginia might have been mistaken but, naturally, could not ask her. She still went round there often and entered without knocking. They treated her as one of the family, even sending her on errands, but in the nicest possible way I'm sure, asking, not taking advantage.

My son kept himself busy in the garage and my wife seemed to have a particularly heavy load of casework at the time, carting it back and forth in *two* briefcases. She read and wrote a great deal, using the dining-room table, her spectacles perched on the end of her nose over which she peered questioningly at me when I entered as if in the hope that I was merely passing through. The television had to be turned down so far that the rest of us were forced to take a much closer look at it, making it more obscure: which is true of people too, come to think of it. ('Speak up, I can't hear you.') Thus my wife obliged us to have a closer look at 'the medium itself' too and the harm it might be doing to 'the independence of our minds' along with most of the rest of humanity – everybody, that is, who had television sets. This went along with talk in the air at the time about the medium being the message – the message for me becoming that independence is being able to watch it at a distance in a state of complete mindlessness while doing no harm to anyone, whatever harm might be being done to oneself.

Webb spent less time in his garden than I did and usually now had his back to me. Mrs Webb came out from time to time to put pieces of bread and other fragments on a small bird house built like a straw hut. I never saw her doing any gardening. I imagined her watching the birds from behind a curtain all day long. I never heard the sound of a typewriter coming from her house.

At work some people had had their holidays and walked about listlessly, their tans fading, and with a tendency to be short with those who still had their holidays to come. There was less work to do than usual, even though there were fewer people to do it. I therefore built up even higher the pile of files and papers on and around my desk to give the impression of carrying at least double my usual load so that when I grabbed the holiday I could ill afford to take (somehow managing to fit it in, that is) I was trying not to leave an intolerable burden on those who remained, who would not have nearly enough to do either, solely because Ripple (good old Tom) had got through such an incredible heap of the stuff before his departure. But it was equally important not to leave behind a clear desk which would remain clear or near it throughout my absence, raising the question of what on earth I would do on my return. Working all this out took up a lot of my time and I left for home a little later than usual with additional ballast in my briefcase.

Plaskett returned from his holiday with a more pronounced spring in his step and a sun-tan that lent his complexion an almost human swarthiness. His first morning back, he actually gave me a wave as he emerged from the lift (I had been staring at it, waiting for him) and called out, 'Morning, Tom.' He really was glad to be back, the rat. I for one most need a holiday when I have just returned from one. The same probably goes for everyone else, except Plaskett. He called me in.

'How's tricks?' he asked, rubbing his hands, I swear it.

'Oh, pretty steady. Had a job with the Brazilian figures. All that inflation.'

'Can't think why we bother with Latin America, can you?'

This seemed promising, since the less he was bothered by the less he expected me to bother him. I said, 'Nor can I, frankly. Never been better than marginal.'

Being precisely the words he'd once used to me, they caused him to nod and mumble, 'As I've always said.' He glanced at a couple of summaries I'd done for him to await his return. They had no intrinsic value whatsoever but were presented in a novel manner I'd picked up by chance from an obscure American business management journal which I hoped would impress him. A twitch of his eyebrows. No more than that.

'A change of scene makes all the difference,' he said.

'Have a good holiday then?'

'Perfect. Feel a new man. Took this little place on Ibiza. Been there?' I shook my head. He knew bloody well I hadn't, of course. 'Hotel with chalets near by. You know the kind of thing. Marvellous swimming pool, plenty of golf, amazingly good food and far too much of the cheap local plonk. And goodness, how one slept! Kids loved it. You should try it some time.' There was a long pause while he stayed looking away from me out of the window. 'Not that pricey, either . . . Well, anyway, not considering what you get for it.'

I tried in that brief moment to imagine him as a father, the behaviour leading up to it and with whom. I had never found him so revolting. Perhaps it was the image of him taking a dive from the top board of the marvellous swimming pool after a round of golf playing well below his handicap, not that he could regard himself as having such a thing. I wondered if he had hairs on his chest and, if so, in what quantity. I wondered what sort of bathing costume he wore and how he looked with wet hair plastered sideways down over his ears and temples. I saw him singing loudly in a shower. What became repulsive then was that, after all that, he couldn't wait to get back to his job. He was eyeing the pile of files in his in-tray with the kind of eager leer most of us would keep for the amazingly good grub and a fair scatter of the other folk who were using the marvellous swimming pool. Naked envy beginning to sully the purity of my hatred, I took a harder look at him.

'. . . Back to the old grindstone,' he was saying with a sigh, forgetting fortunately to ask where I would be going on holiday and when. I minded little the prospect of his invisible sneer about the English seaside, this overshadowed by the prospect that on the afternoon before my departure he'd send me a long list of tasks 'for completion as soon as possible after your return.' I closed his door muttering, 'You're such an utter prick, Plaskett,' which I wrote twenty times on my blotter before having another look at the Brazilian figures and turning them into a graph which made me feel slightly seasick. I almost left that evening without removing the sheet of blotting paper. Every time I thought about this during the holiday that followed I broke out in a sweat, this making up for his not after all asking me to do anything at all as soon as possible after my return, though this became ominous in its own way, going together with the thought of the impression made by my ball-point pen on the sheet of blotting paper underneath.

We had an excellent holiday, similar to the others. Carefree, apart from the above. Even my wife giggled occasionally and my children got on well together. We went to the cinema, to the funfair, for walks on the pier and along the beach, for car trips in among the scenery and to a couple of stately homes from which my wife drew no historical/social/political etc. conclusions at all, beauty winning out over truth perhaps – though that's not the kind of conjecture I am able to take very far without my wife's assistance which I do not often ask for, having no way of knowing whether there might not be some quite different direction someone more, or less, acquainted with the subject might be taking me in. My son spent much of his time on an air mattress thing with paddles and collecting pebbles and shells with which to adorn his next piece of furniture – a sewing box for his mother's dressing table. He also acquired a num-ber of friends, rather nice friends, with whom he played clock golf, shuffleboard and cricket. My daughter had now reached the sun-bathing age and lay about on the beach, mainly face down. One or two of the boys who seemed to spend their entire time sauntering back and forth along the beach and never getting wet, scrutinized her at some length. It wasn't hard to see why. She was still a child, though, when it came to eating ice-cream or riding on the roller coaster. We breakfasted independently when the spirit moved us which usually meant in this order: my wife, my son, my daughter, myself. We had lunch and supper together, however. Only once did Virginia spoil our enjoyment by saying how much she wished the Hambles were there enjoying it all too.

My wife also sunbathed and sported about in the sea. She spent much of her time gainfully too, reading. She read three books on that holiday of an uplifting (depressing) nature, but did not try to interest us in them. She was in a contemplative mood on the whole and showed me unusual affection, in frequency rather than novelty or depth. We made love four times, the first three times with her on top because she had got too much sun on her back. Astraddle me, upright, her eyes closed, it was as if she fancied herself galloping blindly up hill and down dale in flight or pursuit, blissfully (if one can judge anything by appearances) unaware that her steed also had a sore back from too much sun. But it was she who did the snorting and I who once called out, 'Yoicks tally-ho!' The fourth time she told me to be slow and gentle and I was. The weary horse munched and nuzzled, the shudder in its sweaty loins coming just in time, a second or two before, in our different ways, we dropped off, she then keeping me awake a long time, deep in sleep practising the horse's part. The third time, at the start, I watched her breasts swinging before my eyes, giving one of them a light slap to make it swing more and said, 'Ding dong bell, pussy's in the . . . well?' She did not smile at that either, simply closed her eyes tighter in what conceivably might have been ecstasy. A thought at this point. Why am I writing this down if there's not the slightest chance anyone else will read it and if there were I wouldn't be writing it? For myself, then? But why shouldn't it be enough simply to think things? It is for most people. Thoughts. Words. All vanishing alike into thin air.

I see that holiday now in snatches: my children splashing each other; my son drawing a piece of wet seaweed over the back of my wife's legs; my wife transfixed by the sight of our daughter at the top of the big wheel; my son digging his spoon under a cherry at the top of a spiral of ice-cream; the twitch of my daughter's buttocks as a bandy-legged, greasy-haired lout walks past her, moistening his lips; one of my son's big hits knocking over an old man's thermos flask; my wife taking off and handing me her glasses, closing her book and handing that to me too and skipping off like a child down to the sea; my daughter rubbing cream into her thighs and her face turning from pink to gold; my son taking his first dive off the side of a pool, arms rigid, clamped close to his ears, bending forward and simply dropping in; the dishevelment of dripping hair; sand in the fair down on arms and legs; and everywhere beyond, the broad expanse of the glittering water.

I have no memory of the surrounding crowds. I do not see us as a family among others. The bandy-legged lout, the old man with the thermos flask, our dim dawdling waitress with the notebook and pencil dangling from her apron and her ravishing, innocent smile, the almost tearful frown of one of my son's new friends on the day we left – these I can recall with an effort but between the foreground of my family and the tumbling waves all the bustling and noise are but interruptions in my mind. Indeed I cannot recall the sounds at all, neither of the water, nor of the crowds, nor of our speaking. Apart from the above and other such snatches I cannot remember anything any of us said until it was all over. I assume our happiness from the deeper silence when we packed and loaded our suitcases into the boot of the car: as it had been, I mean, the speechless sadness a measure of it.

As I was putting the car into gear and turning round before pulling away from the pavement, my wife put her hand on mine and said, 'That was a lovely holiday, dear. Thank you.'

'Don't thank me,' I replied. 'I should be thanking you, all three of you.'

And I suppose I really meant it. I did, I did. For turning round the other way to look through the back window, I saw my children's faces, dark, healthy, weary and content and they grinned at me and did not need to thank me. But had to when my wife said, of course, 'Say thank you to your father.'

'Thanks, Dad,' my son said.

'Yes, Dad, thank you *very* much,' my daughter added.

They both meant it and I replied, 'It was my pleasure.'

And it was, that day, it was.

I remember too my last look at the sea as we drove away and it started to drizzle. The water was grey and choppy and there was no one on the beach save a tall man with a spaniel, striding straight into the rain without a raincoat, prodding his walking stick deep into the pebbles. A local inhabitant, perhaps, who was coming into his winter's possession, who was glad of the rain. And it is at this moment that I think I know why I am writing this down. It is not just preservation – the photographs can do that, evoking much else besides – it is the feeling of mastery it gives over the passing of time, though it's only temporary.

My mood did not remain on that elevated plane. During the drive home, in between the intermittent chatter and silent contentment of it, I decided the time had come to decide what my values might be – beginning in love and gratitude and humility and thoughtfulness or thereabouts. I had spent two marvellous weeks at the seaside with my family, like hundreds of thousands of others, simple, homely, suburban, liberal, decent people, all of us. What better time could there be for starting to ponder on higher things of the mind and spirit? But my thoughts turned almost at once to Plaskett, and then to the image of leaving a dead rat on his desk. I realized then that it might be difficult to lay my hands on a dead rat, particularly one long dead, which I could take to the office by public transport without drawing attention to myself. Might I settle for a mouse therefore? We had sometimes caught mice in traps around the house. (My wife and son are the ones who set the traps and extract the victims. My daughter and I refuse to have anything to do with it, my daughter out of compassion.) If a small thing, I thought, is a symbol of a big thing, a mouse could be the symbol of a rat. But Plaskett might altogether miss the significance of finding a dead mouse on his desk, thinking it had come there by chance and died of awe. Whereas the presence on his desk of a dead rat (a live one in a cage would be better still but more difficult to smuggle in of course) would be difficult to miss the import of. I couldn't see myself enquiring of anyone how I might obtain a rat, nor taking possession of one, so I settled for hanging a placard on his wall which said, 'Plaskett is a rat.' In my mind. Only in my mind. All this and more besides on the way back with my family from the seaside at the end of a wonderful, sunlit holiday. After such a fine beginning, that was what became of my decision to search for my values. Most of the way back, amongst the chatter and silence and remembered happiness, my thoughts turned to dead rats. It was hatred that took over, not love etc. So much for the mastery. What is that power it has, hatred I mean? No wonder some people believe in the devil. I don't. It doesn't seem necessary. There appears to be something black and foul in the soul or wherever, which was there first, before any light shone on it. There's that line at the beginning of the Bible about what it was like before the creation: when darkness was on the face of the deep. (I remember this because that's what my mother used to say to my taciturn father when he needed a shave. More about them anon.) You need hardly any historical knowledge at all to realize how much hatred there has always been about. You don't have to look far for it. The devil is something to blame, I suppose, instead of us . . .

So the journey ended. I tried to recover how it had begun but to no avail. Plaskett lingered. The silence prevailed. That night before my wife turned the light off she said again what a good holiday it had been, spoiling it by adding, 'And now back to the serious business of living.' It didn't seem the right moment to recall country houses and seek clarification about beauty and truth, for instance.

Chapter Eleven

All that seems a long time ago now. I've had other things on my mind and there's some catching up to do.

Not long thereafter, Plaskett offered me promotion preceded by a management training course. I was to head a new Sales Operation Section, following the take-over of another company. He was going up in the world, he said, and wanted to take me with him. More responsibility, more money, more power. I cannot now remember whether he actually spoke these words out loud as he gazed out of the window, his mouth twitching in and out of a smile, his eyes then closing, dazzled by his prospects perhaps. There would be some travelling for me, he went on. To faraway places. I thanked him, or the noises coming out of my mouth ought to have been that, as my mind pranced about among queen-sized beds and meals wheeled in on trolleys, of expense accounts, of opportunities for waywardness – that thought not entering my head in quite those words. I would buy a new suit, two, three new suits, and little white cards to put in my wallet to hand to clients. Finally he stood up, came round his desk and put a hand on my shoulder. The little squeeze was intended to be such that I might have imagined it – or was that only in my imagination?

His voice took on a tone I'd not heard before, having a shot at something he'd read about leadership, perhaps: firm and decisive, just you watch it whatever your name is, but not lacking the common touch. 'You've soldiered on. You're a cool customer, Tom. You're loyal. You're conscientious. You've got a good, clear mind.'

Was I blushing or had I turned pale? Both, it felt, my complexion perhaps therefore staying unaltered. Cool, that was it exactly. Somewhere in between – genuinely aware what a fraud I was. I decided very quickly I hardly disliked myself at all for finding Plaskett much less dislikeable, no longer a rat; or only one of the small, harmless, white, pink-eyed variety that lives in a cage, which like the rest of us to a greater degree than we may care to believe cannot help what it is. I thought of my family's surprise that I was more than they took me for . . . No, that isn't the truth. I liked Plaskett then. A lot. Myself too. I gave him the slightest of winks. He gave me the slightest of smiles, then the thumbs-up sign. This I returned. His smile remained. Oh yes, by jingo, what a jolly nice chap he was after all.

And so it was. My daughter gave me a hug and my son slapped me on the back and my wife said, 'Well, well! I knew your day would come.'

I responded with a smug smile as if all along I'd known something they hadn't. I took them to see *The Mousetrap* to celebrate, enjoying that little joke, making it clear it was to be my show this time, my wife not having pressed the case for Shakespeare for more than most of a Sunday lunch. I thought of the gifts I would bring back for them from those faraway places: leather handbags, scent, jewellery, stamps for my son etc. (The only snag was that, with the travelling and coming home late I would be doing there was all that television I would miss. This would do wonders for my active independence of mind etc. as previously discussed – what other influences, if any, would fill its empty spaces I'd just have to accept as they came.) I imagined myself smoking cigars and growing portly. I was immensely pleased with myself, even more so for not being too pleased about that. I even imagined taking up golf and eschewing all thoughts of waywardness, of becoming the perfect family man, boasting in foreign restaurants of my children's achievements, of my wife's work for the poor and needy, then showing photographs of them to complete strangers. I imagined appearing before the board and heard Plaskett saying, 'Tom Ripple has just returned from Brazil and I thought should speak to us about his findings in person. You have his report before you . . .' And the chairman would add, 'And a jolly thorough, well-written job of work it is too.' I would look them all in the eye and speak slowly in a clear, quiet voice and make firm recommendations, Plaskett nodding sagely beside me the while. Behind my back they would say, 'Man to watch, Ripple. Coming along nicely.' And so forth.

And so, roughly, it turned out and with all this success going to my head there's not been the time or need to do much thinking, or any at all, come to think of it. In making something of myself it has mattered less, if at all, what I've bothered to make of others. A question of priorities, Plaskett would say. So back to where I left off.

Virginia had been right about Mrs Hamble. A couple of weeks or so before my promotion and the start of my new life, she was taken away in an ambulance. It was during the early hours and nobody saw her go. That evening Hamble came to the door when we were settling down to a television programme. I turned the sound down enough to hear him say to my wife.

'Just to tell you Mrs H has gone into hospital and she was sorry not to say goodbye.'

My daughter joined my wife at the door and said, 'When's she coming home again?'

His reply sounded matter-of-fact enough. 'She'll not be coming home again. She's dying, that's what she is. She's a goner.'

My wife said, 'Oh I *am* sorry. Do come in, just for a moment. Please do.' She sounded wholly sincere about it, which must be much harder (easier?) for her, when to sound (feel?) it is an aspect of her profession, in a manner of speaking.

'I won't do that, thanks all the same. She said specially, remember me to Virginia.'

There was further mumbling before I heard the door shut and turned the television up again. Virginia went straight up to her room. She did not cry, then or later, until the end came. She had been expecting it for a long time.

My wife came back into the living room and turned the television down.

'Poor old dear,' she said. 'Isn't that rotten?'

I had nothing to say. I looked at my son who asked, turning the television up again, 'What's the matter with her?'

'Cancer, by the sound of it,' I said. 'The poor bastard.'

'It's too . . . We shouldn't try to say anything,' my wife said, wise woman that she is.

My son frowned at the sound of his sister's footsteps overhead.

'I suppose you're right,' I said.

I imagined the Hambles together in the hospital, holding hands, also speechless. I hoped Virginia would somehow be spared . . . but what? Visiting or not visiting Mrs Hamble in hospital, the reality of dying or picturing it, beyond her competence?

'Is she going to die?' my son asked, turning the sound of the television up further to offset the noise his sister was making (pacing up and down, so young, so free of care).

'We don't know,' I said. 'These days . . .'

'Sooner or later, dear,' my wife said to him. 'Oh do turn that sound down. There's no use pretending, hiding behind euphemisms. As one grows old . . .'

Since I could tell by the way she drew herself up that she was intending to go on a bit about geriatric matters, I think they're called, and since, too, a new murder film was beginning, the first crucial details of whose plot I did not want to miss, I pointed a finger at her and said, 'I thought you said we shouldn't try to say anything.'

I had never spoken to her like that before, never dreamt of it. I do not know how she took it. Except that she looked sorrowfully down at my son who was following closely a scuffle and fatal stabbing and guttural screams of agony in a back alley somewhere in the United States of America, as if resigning herself to the fact that with a taste for all that and me for a father his life chances had dipped into the sub-zero category.

It was round about then, as I've said, that the days of my prosperity began. There's not a lot to say about those. I have acquired a paunch, a fattening under the chin, my bald patch spreads. I began looking out for a house with more space round it in a tree-lined avenue, something with a porch or fancy diamond window panes or a heavy studded door with a big brass knocker and a long sloping lawn where the sprinkler would play on long summer evenings. I thought about acquiring a cocktail shaker with which to make myself a Manhattan to go with my cheroot. I even entered a shop in St James's Street and tried on a maroon velvet smoking jacket with a satin belt and tassel. I once had a manicure at the same time as a haircut. I even began to detect in my wife's superiority a touch of reticence, as if she had begun to wonder whether capitalism might not have something to be said for it after all, if not out loud of course. I even fancied that my children lowered their voices when I hung my furled umbrella with the ivory-looking ('Yes, I'm quite sure, Virginia') handle on the coat-stand.

I hadn't intended to write about that other life at all. I know far too much about it already. It is too easy to imagine, too hard to forget. I even joined a golf club and took lessons. I acquired a handicap, just, and can hit a ball not very far but down the middle. My strength is on the greens. I have acquired the lingo suitable for the clubhouse bar and am slightly more generous about paying for rounds than I need to be. People put their hands on my back and I no longer mind.

I have heard my voice among others mocking the unions, sneering at the politicos, quoting the unemployment figures, repeating productivity horror stories (the more people produce, the more my company sells, the more money I make), bemoaning the rise in the cost of living, at the less and less I can afford (while spending more and more), discussing property prices and telling smutty stories.

People at the golf club like me. I judge that by the number of times a hand is put on my back and I am called over and asked what I will have. I am careful not to be too generous about paying for rounds; otherwise I might become worried that the frequency with which I feel a hand on my back and am summoned to the bar has less to do with how much people like me than with what they like me for. There is always company at the golf club. I am not sure if it is friends I have made there. At the office (more than once I've heard myself say 'Back at the ranch') I tell Plaskett that I've met so and so, the MD from Curious Chemicals or the Chief Sales Manager from Fattening Foodstuffs who told me this or that about the market here or a merger there, and he nods and adds to my intelligence an item of his own, or it is the other way round. I have even begun, in the most agreeable way, to disagree with him, and twice have caused him to change his mind though the first time he changed it back again. ('Had second thoughts about that, Tom, old chap. Should have trusted my instincts.' 'No you shouldn't, you revolting little egomaniac,' I replied. I did nothing of the kind.)

There's the other thing to be got out of the way too, in the sense of spoken about, because it can never be got away from, as opposed to with, though that too – or not invariably rather. On my trips I have sometimes been untrue to my wife (true to myself), though not of course in line with my former fancies. The reality invaded the dream. I hadn't much minded, in this area, not being a handsome cove with gaunt features, tall with a stoop and a limp and greying at the temples etc. because in the fancying department I could have whom I chose and for such as me there is little choice otherwise or none at all.

Travelling about, I began to realize in full measure what a truly colossal number of pretty girls there are in the world. What I had known was the tiny tip of a boundless iceberg. That's not right. If there was an iceberg, it was me, smouldering under the surface, adrift in hot water . . . or, try again, going down arse over tit, all hands at the ready, women and children first . . . Oh no, that's just what they're not. No comparison there.

Let's just say then that the smouldering stops the moment I put my hand on the hotel bedroom doorknob and open the door. It's never as fancied, as young, as lovely, as unobtainable – it's the old, old story, all make-believe and anticlimax. (Come now, what do you take me for?) Then the preliminaries, the bargain struck, the money counted, the undressing – the harder for me, the easier for her, getting it up then over and done with. It's been all right on the whole. No point going into it further thereafter, not without taking precautions. Then what? The businesslike march to the bathroom, the hasty dressing, the goatish smile turned sheepish, the final courteous goodbye between, once again, total strangers. Most of the fun, as we've known all along, is in the expectation, 'most' in the sense of duration, that is, not of intensity. I've been called 'dulling' once and have caused the odd gasp but nothing to write home about, simulation and dissimulation there becoming one in thoughtfulness, I nearly said bedfellows. I did write home on my trips – on postcards showing shopping centres, cathedrals, children's playgrounds, ancient monuments, anything that came to hand. I have bought gifts too. I was mindful too of not giving my wife a dose of the clap (better safe than having to say you're sorry), though she might figure she caught a crab from the lavatory seat in a slum she'd been doing good in lately.

I don't know why I go on like this. I began, then, to feel sorry for my wife. It would serve me right, I thought, if she was unfaithful to me. Little did I (do I) know. I have felt no excitement handing money over to a woman who is likely to call me 'dulling'. It must be that sort of occupation, not unlike most, doing it joylessly only for the money, saving up for what is increasingly not worth saving. In regard to my children, would I mind them reading all this when I'm dead and buried? By then they'll be glad, despite my wife, of the money I've passed on to them, it crossing their minds perhaps that, had it not been for the carryings-on there would have been that much more of it. They'd not want to picture it – people don't, certainly never between their parents. Though where would they be without it? There's an awful lot we don't like to think about: the infinite accident of things, multiplying out indefinitely, the wonder of it. It doesn't get us anywhere, there's no end to it, except in the coupling of our parents; that must be why we soon give up pondering all the rest, not wanting to think about how it will end, in a desperate cry of surrender to God Almighty as often as not and no wonder. Picturing me in a hotel bedroom handing money to a stranger – they'd probably then lose interest, the picture too coming to mind of a bank statement, that too overdrawn . . .

In short, I've had it off from time to time and there is still a truly tremendous lot of it about still to have it off with, though this is not what I'm reminded of when I've just had it off, only that what I've just expended represents that much less to pass on to my children and that the day is fast approaching when there won't be much expending left for me to do. Another reflection then inserts itself: that I shall continue to rise in Plaskett's esteem as I become less capable of rising in other respects. When I can't get it up at all, perhaps I'll be chairman with more power to my elbow and hardly any of it everywhere else.

It seemed important yesterday – a silent, lonely, utterly sexless Sunday afternoon – to get all that out of the way, to bring out the tawdriness, the commonness of it. To get back to where I was. I returned one evening to be told that Mrs Hamble was dead. The funeral would be on a day in the following week when I would be in Montreal. She had died the previous morning, quietly in her sleep. Virginia had been weeping and sat as if stunned at the end of the sofa, pale and pink-eyed. As if I had committed some dreadful crime she turned away from me when I entered. My son, who also did not get up, was sitting on the carpet running a small motor cycle round his knees.

'Poor old Mrs Hamble's gone,' my wife said.

'Oh dear God, I'm sorry,' I said.

At which, for the first time ever, Virginia burst into tears without running from the room. There is a first time for everything, I reflected, including death. I sat next to her on the sofa, intending to put my arm round her, but my wife shook her head, wrinkling the skin between her eyes where her deepest lines were forming. In old age, I reflected too with my usual sensitive sense of occasion, she will appear to be permanently in a bad temper. I did not know what to say to my daughter, except that she'd brought a great deal of pleasure to Mrs Hamble's last days. I could not speak of the life to come, of encounters in paradise because my wife was still present and had purged all 'mythical rubbish' of that nature from my children's minds.

'She went peacefully,' my wife went on. 'Mr Hamble said that when he last saw her she seemed so happy, "not all there" was how he put it. She kept on talking about our picnic in the park where she'd had a glimpse of heaven, she said.'

I stood up. 'What will become of him? He's such a decent old chap.'

'There's a brother somewhere,' my wife replied. 'I've been in to pack up her things. Her clothes and other oddments. He sort of asked me to. I might get a bob or two for them.'

She had clearly been a tower of strength, her work bringing her into contact with many similar situations.

When she left the room, I told Virginia she'd be of no use to Mr Hamble if she went on like that. Her grieving, I said or something like it, would only add to his.

She nodded. 'I don't know what to say to him.'

'He doesn't want you to say anything. He doesn't know what to say either.' I sipped my sherry and lit my cheroot. And felt guilty. 'I'm sure he'd rather be alone,' I added.

'*Please* go and see him,' she said finally. 'Mum did. I bet she knew what to say.'

'Yup,' I replied, standing up and leaving her there staring up at me with eyes again about to brim over.

I found him in the kitchen and he invited me into the living-room. The dust already seemed to have gathered thickly on the threadbare furniture and faded, pale-brown carpet. A number of ornaments had been collected together and dumped on a mat in front of the electric fire. He pointed at them and said, 'I'm going to bury all those in the garden. I'm going to dig a ruddy big hole.'

'Is there anything we can do?' I said. 'You've only got to say.'

'For starters,' he whispered, 'you can bring her back to me, you can bring her back to life.'

'I'm so sorry,' I said.

'Christ!' he mumbled. 'As if I thought you were Jesus Christ or something.'

He knelt beside the ornaments and began lifting them up one by one and fingering them. His broad back began shaking but his whispering voice held steady. 'I remember when and where we got every single bloody one of these.'

He held up a plain wooden clock and studied its face as if the numbers were a complete mystery to him. 'This stopped the minute she died,' he said.

Whereupon he raised it above his head and smashed it down on the fender. Then he lifted it to his ear. 'It's started again but it won't tell the time any more.'

The glass had shattered and he slowly removed the hands, bending them back until they snapped.

'She bought me that when I reached my half-century. It kept perfect time. A lovely clock it was. Only had to wind it once a week. Wound it Sunday mornings before taking up her tea. I'll go on winding it but it won't tell the time any more. Just the numbers standing in a circle, midnight to midnight.'

'Come round and have a bite with us,' I said.

He shook his head and got to his feet, a yellow china vase the size of an egg cup in one hand and a small brass gong in the other.

'You've been too kind already. I don't want to be a burden.'

'You be just how you like.'

'That girl of yours would stare at me. Never could abide being stared at.'

'She's heartbroken, Virginia is.'

'She's a good lass, I'm not saying that.' He went over to the window. 'She was a fine woman. Having all those years of her, I can't complain.'

'Anyone could tell that.'

'Anyone couldn't. She was an ordinary woman. No use pretending. She was familiar. I never loved her, not in that deep way. I ought to have loved her like she did me. We went on doing it a long time, I'm not saying that. She thought the sun shone out of my backside. Can't think why. Sod all I did for her except cheer her up sometimes. We had our good times, plenty of them, like that in the park. She never stopped talking about that. She said she was a lucky woman. She'd not want me to go into mourning or anything like that. She'd want me to lead a normal life. She was always calling us that, normal. She'd want me to keep the garden going and that. She'd not want me to bury anything in the garden or smash anything up. I shouldn't have smashed that clock. That's the silliest bloody thing I've ever done in my whole life.'

He still had his back to me and I couldn't tell whether he expected me to reply.

'Like I said, Mr Hamble, any time, anything. You're to believe that, really. It's a message from the whole family.'

He wasn't listening. 'I'll try to keep the place tidy as she would have liked it. I won't let anything run to seed in the garden.'

'Just say the word.'

He turned then. The tears had been streaming down his face and it shone all over. He sniffed and licked some of the moisture away from around his mouth. I looked quickly away.

'Quite a sight I must be. I won't go near the mirror till I've had a good rest and wash.' He mopped at his eyes and cheeks with his shirtsleeve. 'You'd better be off. You won't want to be listening to any more of this. Everyone's turn comes in time. Yours too. You've got more to lose than I have. You could have. Your kids could be killed in a car accident. It's a bloody sight worse for many. It would have been a bloody sight worse for her if I'd gone before she did. She loved me more than I did her. Would have killed herself more than likely. I talk too much, she used to say but she liked it. It was to her, you see. There wasn't anyone else I might be talking to. She'd have liked it too if I'd never have spoken a bloody word . . .'

He turned his back on me again, the words petering out and then he began to sob. I raised a hand to place it on his back but decided he'd rather be left alone.

At supper I said I thought that Hamble needed company but not too much, that he should be visited once in a while but not fussed over. My wife said nothing but she didn't nod either. Virgina was pale and thoughtful, working out what she could do for him. I was proud of her then, as someone who'd follow in her mother's footsteps and serve her fellow man. I could see my wife looking at her with pride too. I saw my daughter dressed as a nun being seized by cannibals. My wife saw her as a young woman with a dawning conscience.

Later, my wife began talking about the various reactions to bereavement. Some people, she said, went to pieces. Others 'discovered themselves', became resourceful, found new interests. Others faded away before your eyes. That sort of stuff. I wondered how it would be when either of us died. My wife would hold forth to herself just as she was doing now. She would certainly not be in the category of those who fade away or go to pieces. And I? God help me, I wasn't sure but I was pretty certain I wouldn't go around smashing up clocks. I might learn to cook and would keep my garden going. I doubted if I would weep much. I certainly wouldn't bother the Webbs for groceries and other small favours. That's what I thought then but, having returned to the past from my present life and now coming back again and having another look at all that about golf clubs and women in hotel rooms, I have different concerns besides imaginary bereavement. I ask myself how it would be if Mr Hamble became a widower today, whether I would put my hand on his back now that I'm on my own myself. Probably not. But I might have lingered longer on the threshold.

Chapter Twelve

Now, as winter ends, I see Hamble pottering about in his garden, looking from a distance like a contented man. I sometimes go and chat with him especially since I do not have a family around any longer. There is no one else to talk to. The 'For Sale' sign is up again outside the Webbs' house. It will be up outside mine shortly. I give prospective buyers of the Webbs' house a sly leer if they happen to look in my direction, wondering about the neighbours. I do not want them to assume they will be as congenial as I am. Best to prepare them for life. I turn up the television with the window open or give a series of thick, bronchitic coughs which is not altogether put on, being the daylight version of the cough that sometimes keeps me awake at night, the result of smoking too many cheroots. Or I stare at them wide-eyed and scratch myself around the groin, which goes well with the cough, and turn away with a snort of contempt, cackling to myself.

Hamble has become redder of complexion as well as fatter. There is a glow about him. He grunts while he works in his garden, bending and straightening and jabbing his fork into the dark, rich soil. He is a one-man monastery of the order that speaks as little as possible and goes in for small-scale agriculture. Talking to him over the fence, I admire the neatness of his garden and express interest in his plans for it. We do not mention mine which is becoming neglected and for which there can be no plans now. I wonder how so large a man can be so unobtrusive, how someone so lonely does not make one feel sorry for him. He does a piece of work, the snipping of turf down the edge of a flower bed, the raking of soil round a newly planted shrub etc. and gazes at it with deep satisfaction, mopping the sweat from his brow as if content at last to lay down his tools and die. I can see what he means. All neatness is a conclusion. One minds less going away when all behind one's back is orderly. That is my experience. One cannot sleep in peace on a muddle. That is why I sometimes go to bed in the early hours of the morning, my report perfected. Otherwise I might lie awake all night, thinking I was about to be found out and the whole of my waking life was a lie There is no need now to pack my briefcase with bricks.

The Webbs' garden is a shocking mess. I can see the prospective buyers tidying it up and laying out turf and shrubs and rock gardens in their minds. I wonder if the agent has told them about Webb and how he no longer came to be living there. I wouldn't go so far as to tell them after contracts have been exchanged and the removal van has drawn up at their front gate. I never discuss the matter with Hamble because I know he has no desire to discuss it with me. He is creating for himself a modest paradise surrounded by a fence. I sometimes imagine when I've just returned from a trip to some hideous, noisy, modern city that the seasons have stopped changing around him. It is as if he is seeing something perfect that is taking shape inside his head. We do not mention my family either. I wonder what they said to him. I wonder how Virginia said goodbye to him. I would feel like an interfering intruder if I brought up such subjects as Webb or the whereabouts of my family or sought his opinion on some event that had been in the news lately. I would remind myself of the golf club nosy parker if I enquired into, say, how he was coping on his own, implying some similarity between my state and his own. As for entering into discussion about the nature of existence, its nasty surprises, the tricks it plays or what meaning it might have, inserting some potential spiritual dimension, I would be taken back to my last visit to the golf club when a man recently made redundant was told by the aforementioned nosy parker, 'Be philosophical. Don't think about it.' That sums it up. It was redundant I felt in Hamble's presence. The only safe topic of conversation is often (almost always) the weather, everything else seeming too far-reaching or chancy. Oh all right, but it's certainly a useful topic when talking to gardeners.

There was a photograph of Webb's house in one of the daily papers. They did not give the actual address, only the name of our suburb and, as I said at the outset, the house, like ours, resembles hundreds of others. I could imagine people strolling about in their thousands, pointing and saying, 'Is that the one?' I'd been away for a week and my wife showed me the paper one evening after the children had gone to bed.

'You'd better read this.'

'Well, well, well, you never know,' I said eventually.

For years, it transpired later, he had been visiting playgrounds and such places in the hour or so before dusk and persuading children of both sexes by offers of cash to accept his fondling or scrutiny in quiet corners where there was a tree or other obstruction to shield him from the general view. A wise (or clever) boy who had been frequently warned by his mother of such persons was told by his sister there was easy money to be obtained, had accepted his payment too (could he, I have asked myself, have got away with less, how generous was he?), then gone off untouched, made a note of his car number (being a child too who had recently won a competition with an essay on 'Your Police Force and You') and reported him via his mother to the authorities.

The episode was connected with similar reports from elsewhere. The dozen or so parents concerned were those who had discovered unusually large sums of money about their children's persons. At his trial Webb put himself at the court's mercy and asked for twenty-three other offences to be taken into account, thus prompting comment by the judge about the Gross Materialist Age We Live In, with parents being so unacquainted with the sources of income and spending habits of their children and what, inappropriately I should have thought, he called their cupidity. He did not specifically say, he did not need to, that there seemed therefore to be approximately two dozen children who had taken the money and run, and what – bearing in mind the vastly wider variety of temptations that were to come – did that tell us about the proportion of the population that was on the fiddle or had their price? Which brings me back to Webb, whose plea that he had inflicted no pain, nor caused any fear, had only indulged in a little touching, a little seeing, carried no weight with the law or, one may assume, the public at large.

What added interest to the newspaper story was that when the police were taking Webb out to their car, Mrs Webb had followed them with a frying-pan and struck him hard on the head with it, crying out, 'He doesn't owe me a penny, the horrible little sod.'

It was silly of me to have grinned. 'Is that all you have to say?' my wife enquired. Then, 'Adrian has told me, you realize?'

I clucked. 'Yes, I know. I should have . . .'

'Didn't it occur to you that in the public interest . . . ?'

'I couldn't have done that to Adrian, to them, no, I mean . . . The police asking questions. I simply couldn't face it. I mean, Adrian . . .'

But I had no hope of persuading her of the purity of my motives – which may be a contradiction in terms, for me certainly, perhaps for everyone. And I would have been out of my depth in no time if she had pursued the public interest angle.

'So long as *you* were spared,' she said.

At which she left the room, closing the door too emphatically to hear me say, 'I can see I might have saved the poor little sod a lot of money.'

Virginia told me the whole story over again, or rather mainly the bit where Mrs Webb rushed down the path and brought the frying pan down on her husband's head with a 'huge big clang'. She said it served Webb right for what he'd done, he was a dirty, horrid beast. I wondered if she knew he'd tried to do it with her brother too. And then I wondered whether he'd spent his fiver and what on, on what part, for example, of my wife's sewing box studded with shells and other ornamentation. If he'd asked my opinion, I think I would have advised him to add it to his savings. I would have said it seemed immoral (moral?) to donate to charity a sum of money obtained as a result of an immoral act. All I said in response to my daughter was that it was best forgotten about (be philosophical, don't think about it), it takes all sorts to make a world (or bag of sweets, I added, that bringing a smile to her lips or possibly that before it became a grimace of disgust), a man was innocent until proved guilty. In law, I didn't add; the opposite being true in real life.

I started off by telling my son that his mother had shown me the story in the newspaper and his sister had gone over it a second time. There was no need to say any more.

'It's all over and done with now,' I added. 'If you must know, and I can't help it, there's a part of me, a very small part, that can't help feeling sorry for him – what'll happen to him in prison to start with.'

It was quite a large, if far from predominant, part actually, but I desperately wanted him to agree with me, if only reluctantly, even with a shrug or that sharp, single nod of the head and curl of the lip he gives when he can't have his way.

But he said, 'I hate him. I'm glad he'll go to gaol in the public interest. I don't care what they do to him there. She should have hit him on the head with an axe or something.'

'So you told your mother in the end?'

'I thought *you* would, that's all.'

I told him then that he ought to know I never broke promises and I was going to ask him what he had done with the fiver but the tears were coming into his eyes and he said, 'Oh, Daddy, it was so disgusting. Why do you have to go away so much these days? Mrs Webb looked so sad when she went back into her house with the frying-pan dangling from her hand.'

'I expect her heart was finally broken,' I said.

He nodded. 'It didn't matter any more if I told Mum then.'

'No. You're quite right. That's when it became in the public interest. His making a habit of it . . .'

'Nobody knows where she's gone. Nobody saw her go. She was ugly, wasn't she?'

'Well, yes. I suppose she was, a bit.'

'I don't feel the slightest bit sorry for him at all,' he said finally.

'No, Adrian, you're right. It isn't necessary for you to feel sorry for him.'

My wife made a point of being extraordinarily pleasant to me that evening (she has always been ordinarily pleasant.) She insisted I watched the crappy television of my choice and sewed up a tiny hole in the sweater I wore to the golf club. In my absence she had bought me a new face flannel and a bar of expensive soap, mauve in colour, which she told Adrian to fetch. She brought me a cup of hot chocolate in bed, put her hand on my forehead and asked me if I was sure I wasn't sickening for something . . . Before supper, Adrian had been making a racket drumming with a wire brush and wooden spoon on the draining board and she had told him to show his father some consideration after one of his long and tiring trips overseas. At supper she asked me several questions about my work, enabling me to bandy some sales figures about. She told my children I was an exporter of British goods and thus had my part to play. She explained how the balance of payments affected employment and the strength of the economy and hence the scope for extending the social welfare services. Something was up. It was as if the downtrodden had ceased to be her overriding concern all of a sudden. It wasn't long before I

131

found out. What was being trodden down on was the accelerator pedal, a new destination already in sight.

My children hid their boredom (a rare ability which makes me prouder of them than just about everything else) and I found my attention wandering too, to the idea that it wouldn't be long before my daughter got a good deal more than the equivalent of a fiver for a good deal more than a look and a feel, and that it wouldn't be long after that that my son would be exploring ways of getting the lot for nothing. Thus my thoughts returned to the balance of payments, giving it fresh meaning. And tottered on to reflect on the equivalent in Dutch currency of fifty-four pounds I'd added three nights before to the trade deficit in the course of taking a foreigner off the streets and making myself that much more likely to be in early need of the social services.

Well, that was a bit worked up. The flippancy doesn't flow so well when I'm not saying the lines to myself in my wife's presence, imagining how she'd react if I said them out loud. In that sense I miss her. I no longer have to keep my silent wits about me. Once I pottered about muttering, What do I do, where do I go next? And answered to myself, Nothing, nowhere. Overheard, I would be humming. And felt contented. Living in a family it was easy to feel without consequence.

My dozing life is altered too. Not so much now the tropical darkie stuff but young ladies who approach me in crowded places and lead me into dim alleys. Sometimes they grow rapidly older the darker it becomes but usually they grow younger and at the other end of the alley in the bright sunlight they become children, sometimes uniformed and sometimes my daughter and sometimes both. They only rarely remain what they first were and only then might a good time have been had by all.

There are times between sleeping and waking when I wonder how my life might be different. From the little reading I've done and watching rural scenes on television I sometimes imagine myself in other surroundings. I see those broad, sunlit uplands or a vast, flat park with small clumps of trees in the far distance and the grass thick and rich and freshly mown, where I stroll about and happen on weddings which end in the bride coming out of the church and singing, most gloriously, an operatic aria. I wander in amongst small flocks of sheep and cross muddy streams. I lead a young donkey across gravelled paths and tether it to an abandoned village pump. I am not going anywhere in particular. I am a stranger there. Simply by my presence I am occupying an estate. I am not preparing it for anyone. My family will not visit me there. I am hoping it will be safe one day for me to leave it and visit them. The sheep are few and their wool is pure white but scanty. I have only the one donkey. The only bird there is a large owl with one of its eyes shut, the other having a decidedly blind look about it.

I have these dreams only when I am at home. On my trips I take sleeping pills and dream leadenly of pages of figures and of cranes unloading cargoes in foreign harbours. I count export tonnages not leaping sheep. I attend meetings at which men with similar gold cufflinks and recently shampooed length of hair suddenly all stop talking at the same time and turn to me, the only one who is listening, for they have noticed I am still in my pyjamas. There are no young ladies taking shorthand in that dream. The air is musty with cigar smoke and I wake up with a headache, dreading the day until the evening when I shall eat good food and drink good wine at the company's expense and after that to bed with a good (wait for it) book . . . But no, there is all that scribbling I have done, all that figure work, to be rendered orderly, there is my report to begin drafting, there is what I think about to take my mind momentarily off all that – which is what all that has not taken my mind off more than momentarily throughout the day, what with the need there has been for someone there to take shorthand, hand round coffee and the like. Where was I? A good book. I always take one with me. A page or two before I drop off. I am into Captain Cook now. The high seas and faraway countries. Waking or dreaming, the mind is seldom taken off by those. It is not apparelled for the big wide world, as it were. It is still in its pyjamas. The light is turned off and there, unexplored, so near yet so far, are the legs of young ladies taking shorthand etc., leading to what damp, dark forests, what jungle noises.

So venturing into those undiscovered regions I gave no thought to what was going on back at the homestead. Her parting letter was a well-written piece. There is nothing between the lines, no acrimony, no condemnation. The only thing wrong with it is that there is nothing wrong with it. Otherwise I might have been able to respond to it.

Anything I said could only lower the tone. She only feels kindly towards me so how can I feel other than kindly, and gratefully, towards her? The difference lies, I suppose, in the one-sidedness of the gratitude. My word, it is such a good letter! It seems extraordinary I could have been married, still am married, to a woman like that, who has a clear, informed mind and does good in the world. Here it is.

My dear Tommy (remember I used to call you that in the early days?)

I hope you will be able to forgive me for not being here on your return. You will find enough food in the refrigerator and larder to keep you going for at least a week. But I most need your forgiveness for having taken the hackneyed course of leaving a letter on the mantelpiece and for not giving you more warning. Yet I find it hard to believe this will come as a great surprise to you.

It would be easier if I could pretend I had been unhappy with you and do not say that because I have had other things, my work and the children of course, to keep me occupied. Nor, I think I would be right in believing, have you been wholly unhappy with me. Our 'sex life' has continued with no negligible pleasure on both sides and no less regularly than should be expected, according to the literature, of couples of our age and familiarity. I regret nothing and am grateful for much. You have many qualities that a woman may cherish: the equability of your temperament (I do not think I can ever remember you raising your voice), your complete lack of pomposity and pretence. And I for my part believe I have made an acceptable home for you – at any rate far better than many that come my way in the course of my work. And yet . . .

Have I not once or twice detected a flicker, a wince (if I am right, it is a measure of your considerateness that it was never more than this) to suggest you were becoming discontented and ill at ease with my Weltanschauung, for what it is worth. It would be dishonest of me not to admit that your own interests and manner of life were diverging from my own. (There is of course no question of right and wrong here, or at any rate in the private sphere.) In short, on the surface of our lives there has developed a neutrality and tolerance which had begun to invade their depths to the point where I think we both felt equally it would be a mistake, an imprisoning of the potential of our natures, to continue our cohabitation any longer. Perhaps we will one day want to come together again. But I doubt that somehow.

134

As regards the children, they too, I think, had begun to detect an incompatibility between us which, wouldn't you agree, might have become more damaging than a separation. I have told them we have decided to live apart for a while. They are wholly convinced there is no ill feeling. I am determined, as I know you will be too, to ensure our separation is a 'civilized' one – a word I wish I could avoid, having as it does such class associations. There is no other man in my life in the usual sense, though I have a colleague who has become an especially close friend. It was at his house, if you remember, you made an unusual observation about the Mona Lisa. And I would hope that, at least for a little while, there will be no other woman in yours for them (the children, that is) to have to come to terms with. But this is only a hope, not a moral statement. I only wish for your happiness (and your continued success) and should another woman become important for that then you must not hesitate on my account, and only slightly longer on theirs, for they only want your happiness too. They'll soon become accustomed to the idea. To be candid, I do not expect the male sex, knowing of my availability, to be queuing up at my door exactly. (Neither of us, it would be fair to say, I think, enjoys any overwhelming immediate appeal to the opposite sex though I did have my hand squeezed in a car the other day!)

Dear Tom, I know you will not be bitter because it would be out of character. I do not think I even have to ask you to forgive me if in any way I have said or done anything that has hurt you, and that takes a great weight off me. We will of course keep in touch and remain good friends. The colleague mentioned above has an unoccupied floor available in a large house he owns in the 'unfashionable' end of Islington. It is fully furnished with two large bedrooms for the children and a pleasant garden with a hut in it I can use as an office. It is perhaps rather more 'modest' than we are used to but closer, in both senses, to my work. It goes without saying that the children long to see you as soon as possible after you get back, when you can spare the time because I know how busy you are now flying about the place striking deals or whatever it is you do.

With fondest affection, your mate and companion for seventeen far from wasted years, your loving wife.

I look in the mirror and try the flicker and wince but they only make it appear I have a mote in my eye or something sticking in my gullet.

I wonder if there was anything I said. Perhaps I talked in my sleep. If so, of course, there's only the one thing I could have talked about. I was not hurt or bitter. I did not sulk, weep or stamp my foot. I am glad too that I'm not weighing down on her and vice versa glad too, very. On the whole I think she's got it right. I couldn't have said it better myself, which she might just as well have said too. I have this forestalled feeling. It is not as though I wanted the last word, because there would have been so few, if any, left to choose from. I try the wince and flicker again and see some sniffy, evil-minded monster making for the undergrowth. 'Not immediately, overwhelmingly attractive to the opposite sex.' Too bloody true, but ouch nonetheless. I must look up *Weltanschauung* some time. I did enjoy 'especially close friend'. And not a word about coming across a packet of French letters in my sponge bag, so to this day I do not know if she did and if so whether it would have made the slightest difference. And oh yes, heigh ho, what a wonderful thing it is for the potential of my nature to be no longer imprisoned.

Chapter Thirteen

More time has passed.

Plaskett asked my opinion the other day about a young trainee sales executive. I sighed, gave my head the briefest of shakes, said nothing.

'Yes, I entirely agree. He must go,' Plaskett said. 'But, dear God, how I do hate sacking people. Too soft-hearted, that's my trouble.'

'Well,' I replied, extending the vowel sound.

'I think of the day when my youngsters will have to start making their way in the world. Pity their poor parents. Can't hang about, though. Got to face reality.'

'Most definitely,' I said.

'Admire you, Tom. Remember that pathetic young man, Higgins, Hope, Pitkin . . .'

'Hipkin.'

'If you say so. Good memory for names too. Anyway you gave Hipkin pretty short shrift, if I remember rightly. None of the bleeding heart about you.'

'This other chap,' I immediately suggested. 'Give him a pep talk, another chance?'

'No, Tom, you're quite right. Can't carry passengers. Tell Personnel, will you? And thanks.'

I lost no sleep over that, promising myself to find out what had happened to Hipkin; that I knew perfectly well I wouldn't should have kept me awake even longer but one can't look oneself in the eye in the dark and the shaving mirror gives back defeats and failings of a less particular nature. The next day, seeing Plaskett ahead of me walk past the doorman without saying good morning, I gave him an especially friendly greeting (the doorman that is; Plaskett always gets that) – indeed winking and putting my hand on his shoulder. For the first time ever he did not respond, turning his back on me. I know him to be a thoroughly nice man, contributing most when there is a whip-round for a colleague in need, a wedding present or whatever. What had become of me, I asked myself? A sucker-up and willy wet-leg, an arsehole by association, a condescending one to boot – all that becoming increasingly hard to visualize as I reached my office to find Plaskett standing outside it, a file at the ready. He did not actually look at his watch, merely revealing it with a stretch of his arm. He did not say good morning to me either. He never does. It's straight down to business. When I went out at lunch the doorman gave me his usual wide smile, making me feel good about myself again; you're not such an arsehole after all, Ripple, I muttered, at once telling myself not to be so bloody condescending about it.

It's been all right, spending the day with my son. There is always somewhere he agrees to be taken – a museum, an exhibition, a funfair, a film. As often as not there is something out there to engage us in conversation. I do not look forward to the day when his voice finally breaks since I'm sure it will be much deeper than mine (I nearly wrote 'than my wife's') and it will not be clear who is in danger of talking down to whom. He is gaining in confidence and can talk about his successes in school without bragging and embarrassment. He is still good with his hands. He has produced several small wooden objects for me – last Saturday it was a painted carving of an old man in, I think, an Austrian costume. I do not know if he is considered bright at school, form orders having been abolished so as to discourage children from thinking that some of them may be more or less industrious/intelligent than others, thus raising self-esteem in some by reducing it in others, thus too failing to teach them to accept reality – and quite right too, unacceptable as it usually is, which should make us wonder if that's how it must be and thence imagine it otherwise. Perhaps that's where education comes in: showing as many alternatives as possible in the past or elsewhere, in books and art etc.; alternatives perhaps too to day-dreaming – of prowess/looks and girls/boys mainly (almost entirely?) – which takes up almost all the time left over by reality at that (any?) age and over which, like reality, we have no control and so can't be its opposite, not like the imagined alternatives. So, if I've got it right, schools should be teaching children to see reality for what it is, to imagine more and stop dreaming about being the best and coming on top, so to speak; to hold others in the same esteem as they would like to be held in themselves, thus making it possible to bring back form orders, to be thoroughly unrealistic about it. I used to come about half-way down the class in all subjects so who am I to talk? My son gives the impression of being clever. He will not let examinations worry him. He says he enjoys school. When I ask him about it I think he suspects me of looking for problems that do not exist. Perhaps he is among those for whom education is simply passing the examinations and having the choices that brings, between making money in one way or another and the more the better. Virtually everything else is seen to follow from that, prowess, girls, whatever. What other reality there might be is hard to imagine sometimes.

He is relaxed with me but there is still that perfect timing between us that keeps us from looking each other in the eye for more than a second or two. In museums he asks me few questions, not, heaven forfend, because I wouldn't know the answers but because he can rely on the printed explanations that are normally found on stands in the display cases or stuck to the glass. He reads, stares and passes on. Perhaps he will develop into a shrewd person with a cold eye and with little passion in him. I cannot guess how much he likes being with me. I would like being with him very much more (less) if I could. I fear he is only being dutiful, that my wife will have had a word with him. We barely touch at all, even when saying goodbye. I then use original expressions like 'Keep up the good work!' and 'Keep smiling!' and 'See you again soon.' Perhaps with a wink, that one. I always remember to stuff a pound note or two into his top pocket and to tell him to give my love to his sister and mother. I'm sure he never does. We never talk about home, past or present.

The first time I took him out I muttered it was a shame it had happened, it was one of those things, then something about disagreement. I did not say what 'it' was so there was no immediate reaction. Then he nodded routinely as if I might have been referring to the photographs of the Second World War we had recently been looking at, or I had shifted into some unconvincing philosophical mode. Also, I had tried not to sound melancholy but, as can happen, had to clear my throat half-way through. The other reason why he did not react promptly was that he was munching a Mars bar in a museum cafeteria at the time and I had chosen a moment just after he'd taken a large bite out of it. As he swallowed, I said, clapping my hands, 'Well then, me old chum, where to next?'

He looked up at me from the Mars bar as I looked down at it.

'It's all right, Dad, honestly. Sometimes we don't only choose between right and wrong.'

So he'd known all along. It was his mother speaking of course. I do not know what she can have meant by that. I'm sure Adrian didn't. Perhaps she meant that it is harder to be certain about right and wrong in the private sphere than in the public. True, no doubt. I just hoped that she wasn't unsettling him with big questions like that when the simple ones were already making him unhappy enough. I could imagine her briefing him as she did up his raincoat buttons and stroked his hair sideways. Perhaps he is not being dutiful. I can't have him feeling sorry for me, oh no, so adopt a brisk manner and make jokes about the objects in the display cases – the historical costumes and skeletons and ancient household goods. I hope I do not sound like Hamble cheering up his wife in the park. He does grin at my jokes, after a fashion (such as when I said that in the course of asking if he'd like an ice-cream after viewing a costume exhibition), but I have only once succeeded in making him laugh out loud. He never calls me 'silly' now.

He asks me about Hamble and all I can say is that he seems to be getting by, which is true enough. I tell him I am selling the house and taking a flat in Kensington. He says, 'Mr Hamble will be sorry, won't he?' I say I don't know, that he seems to live in a world of his own. I don't say that he will hardly notice my going now that the rest of the family is no longer there, particularly Virginia, of whom they were so very fond. I do not want my son to hear me underestimating myself. I want to go up in his estimation, if anything, only because that is what he wants for both our sakes. As a rule, though, the higher people are in their own estimation the lower they are (should be?) in that of others, the opposite not seeming to be the case, however. I don't want my son's estimation of me, therefore, to have anything to do with my estimation of myself, or what he believes that to be. I'd like us both to have a simple humility without knowing we had it, without having thoughts along these lines at all, which go round and round, darkening the page. He never speaks of the Webbs, wishing no doubt to spare me tension and embarrassment.

In that respect too he does not tell me how often his mother is in the company of some hand-squeezer or other; nor would I tell him of any other woman I'd taken up with. Once or twice he may have seen my glance stray – no, purposefully prowl – around the crowd in search of the usual . . . to take my mind off those wearisome display cases being a subsidiary reason. It would be surprising if he had not. Perhaps that makes him feel sorry for me, that I am lonely. I would very much rather he felt sorry for me than that he should catch me in the company of the sort of woman I tend to be in the company of on one of my trips. I've got nothing against them of course but that sort of woman does have a way of looking as if she's been specially put together and got up for the benefit of just my sort of person – how did my wife put it, where is that letter? – who does not enjoy any immediate, overwhelming appeal to the opposite sex? He'd note the protrusive and partly exposed bosom and the quantity of camouflage especially about the eyes and might then feel sorrier for me, that I'd had to travel so far in flight from solitude. So I'd rather he pitied me without any evidence and let me go on cracking jokes, even though that may remind him of Hamble in the park cheering up his wife. Of course I can have nothing against such women (I would not have to explain to him) since they do everything for me in short, and very short indeed it is too.

I would not want to have to introduce my son to another woman though, as I've said, he's a cool customer and would reveal neither shock nor disgust. He would appear to take note of her rather as he takes note of the objects in the display cases, having read the explanatory card. He would not change colour. Whether she did so or not would depend of course on the extent of the camouflage. How far I did would depend on that too, on how much I thought she (I?) was having to hide. Perhaps then he might feel less obligation to let me take up so many of his Saturday or Sunday afternoons.

I wish I could find a plainish, jolly, straightforward, friendly, flexible, virtuous-looking etc. girl who'd like the same sort of television programmes I like and share other simple pleasures – the sort of woman who would patently change colour, whom my son could mention without a qualm to his mother, not having not to say, 'Dad's taken up with some dreadful tart.' Then he might not feel sorry for me any longer (if he does) and I would be cleared from his conscience, from my wife's too (which may still largely be the same

141

thing, if not for long). If he worries about me, it may be because she does, or seems to in asking how I am. Of course, all this is in my imagination. I don't know what he thinks. I doubt if I ever will. He'll never chance to see me with another woman. I shall see to that. I am unlikely to meet up with the sort of woman who'd insist on accompanying me to museums. I imagine surprising him only because that makes it easier for me to guess how he feels towards me.

The truth is, I believe (I know), that first and foremost he loves me and misses me and looks forward to our meetings, because I am his father. He cannot express that love, no more than I can. He is not relaxed, he is not a cool customer, I see that now. We are matter-of-fact, uneasy, jokey with each other because of that love. I hope. I don't know. I sometimes think I'd like to hold him for a long time in my arms in silence, his head against my chest, as used to happen when he was very young and had come to some minor harm in body or spirit. He too surely must remember those times of closeness, the warmth of my hold on him, my deep steady breathing? And shudder at the thought? There are many years to go. We will know each other as men. I am sure we will get on all right when we meet for a drink and speak of matters of moment, the state of the economy and so forth. In the meantime we wander side by side among crowds and keep our eye on the time and for much of that do not have our minds on each other at all.

I told Plaskett I had been separated from my family.

'Sorry to hear that, Tom. Families can be a bedrock. M'a family man myself.'

I said it was one of those things.

'Of course,' he went on, 'it takes the mind off the job too if the old marital boat has started to leak. Better a clean break than . . .'

He did not finish that sentence, reaching for the file I'd brought in to him. He knows, if anyone does, that my mind is still on the job – if anything, to keep it that way, I'm more loyal and single minded than ever. He doesn't give a toss about my private life. I respect him for that. Why should he? I don't give a toss about his, while being quite curious about it. How can anyone, particularly a wife and children, stand the sight of him? But as I've said, I can, now. Very much so. It is clearly possible to like people, love them even, or even more so, despite their faults. If that were not so how much more virtuous everyone would be. Affection, love, have a lot to answer for; without them how much less hateful and nasty people would be.

Why do I deceive myself about my son? One day we will sit opposite each other as men and irritate each other for this reason or that, but from within an overriding affection, I hope. Now, when I take him to the Underground or drop him off at the corner of the street where he now lives (I do not drop him at the door because I might be invited in by the especially close hand-squeezer, assuming they are the same person.) I watch him going away from me and when he is out of earshot I say something, anything, out loud to clear the clogged feeling at the back of my throat. I close my eyes because they have started to sting a little. The sensation soon passes. It is then in particular that I imagine us sitting together discussing the state of the nation and being irritated, if only a little, by one another's views or ways of expressing them. Seeing him walk away, I tell myself he will have no difficulty finding gainful employment and a nice wife and will create a pleasant home and family, all of which will occupy his time of which there is no reason he should have much, if any, to spare for me. If I were not my son's father, I would not find him remarkable. I do not see myself in him, nor his mother. I wonder if he is becoming a better loser. I am sure he will should he start to turn into one of life's winners. When he walks away from me I am sure that I love him, even though all afternoon at a museum or wherever we have been keeping an eye on the time and have had difficulty in conversing other than about what is there on the stands or in the display cases. And even though, however hard I've tried, I've only once succeeded in making him laugh.

It is different in the case of my daughter. I sometimes have serious doubts about how much I love my daughter. The first time I took them out together they bickered incessantly. Never again. We went to a boat show and my daughter is even less interested in boats than I am. Her feet began killing her at the first sloop or whatever it was. My son was fascinated by all that craftsmanship and ran his hand over the wood-work and other smooth surfaces which are a feature of boats. Apart from the murder that was being done to her feet of which she contin-ued to remind us, my daughter told her brother, then me, that after all a boat was only a boat, wasn't it? I might have agreed with her if it

143

hadn't been for my son's interest in the things and if there hadn't been a number of under-clad (over-clad) girls hanging around them, showing them off as it were, or drawing attention to them, making associations in men's minds to do with cruising about on calm waters and bunking down in small cabins. They had nice, saucy, come-aboard smiles, some of those girls (all of them come to think of it), and bodies which in clambering about between booms and tillers, bollards and hatches would cause constant inattention to what the charts said about reefs and sandbanks, leading as luck would have it to shipwreck and desert islands. Equally important, they contrasted with my daughter's body, clad in patched and fraying jeans, more grey than blue, and an upper garment of once-purple stuff that bobbed and gleamed obscenely (to me) over her bra-less breasts. (Surely they shouldn't hang so low, so young?) She was a bit pimply that day too. I accepted that her tattered running shoes may really have been causing her feet discomfort but not that much. I couldn't get out of my mind how much they must stink. Perhaps in her new womanhood she was being harassed by her biology. (It was not only her feet I visualized when she complained about them.) We had to leave her on a seat because she said she felt faint and my son said, 'Ts! Bloody spoilsport.' Later she said that the boats were only for the rich, couldn't even he see that, and the show was an offence to the poor and underprivileged. As I was supposed to, I overheard and nearly added something about what the girls were only for too, but instead said that a bicycle show or shoe show on the other hand would be even worse for our soles. My daughter pouted, and my son laughed. I'd made him laugh, hooray, and it was at my daughter's expense.

I do not take my daughter out often. I cannot think of outings that would appeal to her. She is not much interested in clothes except in garments she can buy off racks in boutiques in back streets, which have previously been worn, or worn out, or look as though they have been, by someone else, of either sex. I give her money which she can spend as she pleases. I give her more than I give my son and tell her not to tell him. I want to make up for that laugh perhaps. She says she spends some of it on pop records which are similar to the kind of things I sometimes hear by accident on my car radio. She is a reflective, soulful girl, or wishes to be thought that, and I am surprised she has a taste for the hysterical din and just about wordless vocabulary characteristic of those songs. Perhaps their shrillness offsets her own lack of confidence. I don't begin to know. I myself have never liked being shouted at or other people being shouted at and I don't like to think of my daughter being bombarded by noise, especially with all that pre-language swilling about in it.

I wish I knew what to talk to her about. We usually go to the cinema and have coffee or something in a café before or afterwards. I prefer having it before because then we don't have to talk so much about the film, its greatness or grottiness about which I am always careful to agree with her. I do not wish to discover how little we have in common now she is nearly a woman. When she is one she will become a mother too and I hope then she also has a husband or at least a man who is continuing to take an interest in her, for whatever reason, even if it has nothing to do with his fatherhood. I love her that much. What I'm getting at is that I do not want her to be laid and left. I particularly do not want her to be laid and left after she's been careless. If one is very careful indeed, as careful, that is, as one always should be, there is more likely to be that chance of coming and going. On the other hand I do not want her to get 'involved' or to tell herself at the crucial moment that she isn't when she is or is when she shortly won't be after he's come and gone. In point of fact, I don't want her to get laid at all, ever. Not even by her husband. Though I'd like her to have a child or two. To that extent too I love her. I like the idea of her as a mother and me as a grandfather, but more to my son's children than to my daughter's. Do I mind thinking of my son in the act of intercourse? I only ponder the matter when considering the prospect of becoming a grandfather. And now, after a fairly long pause while I try to think of something else altogether – cranes lowering cargo in foreign harbours, anything – I find that the thought of my son undressing the sort of girl I would shortly be on the lookout for at his age, being exactly the sort of girl I am on the lookout for at my age, is a satisfying one, though I limit its duration to the stage up to the girl's complete nakedness when my son has not even removed his jacket and tie yet, the stage when I intend to take over the proceedings.

I simply cannot imagine either of my children growing up to that extent. I sit opposite my daughter in a café, wishing she wouldn't eat cream cakes because of her spots and praying that no harm will ever come to her. The thought of her in tears is intolerable. I want her to be fulfilled without being touched. I do not want those primitive young men to be shouting into her ear and banging their drums against the rhythms of her heart. In no circumstances should she ever be made to gasp. I see her in a country cottage, unkempt, glowing, with brats toddling and gurgling about her. Her husband is a country doctor. He is a very gentle man, devoted to his family and hard-working. He is also a perplexed doctor because all her conceptions have been immaculate and he assumes her to be a virgin, having had no way of finding out. In his spare time, of which he has little, he is composing a learned article on the subject for *The Lancet* but which in the end is only accepted by *The National Enquirer*.

I think like this about my daughter afterwards. At the time we chat quite pleasantly and I find myself not caring for her nearly as much as I should. Perhaps she misses any show of affection on my part which would be brought about, I suppose, by talking about 'us'. I pity her for only having her mother to rebel against. Being so understanding in general and knowledgeable about youth in particular, she'd analyse and explain the rebellion long before you'd trundled the first heap of rubble up to the barricade. And if you rebelled against the analysis and explanation she'd analyse and explain that too and so on *ad infinitum*. My daughter is discontented about something and I feel I may be letting her down by not being an aspect of what she's discontented about.

We talk about her school mostly. I feed her with questions like 'How's Mr Phipps lately?' That sets her going. Mr Phipps is her chemistry teacher and I think she has taken a fancy to him. She relates anecdotes about what he said when an experiment didn't work out as he expected it to. I do not only see my daughter immaculately conceiving in a country cottage. I also see her blown to bits in a chemistry laboratory. I do not pursue enquiries about exactly which of Mr Phipps's experiments have not worked out as he expected them to.

There are two girls, Angie and Sprog by name, she mentions quite frequently too. One of them has access to pot and the other is aiming to become matron in a large London hospital. One is good at the high jump, the other at playing the cornet. One is amazingly pretty, the other is a duckling but more fun to be with. One has a father in the kitchen implements business. The father of the other one is dead. I mix them up in my mind and wonder what they think of my daughter. They do not wear uniforms in her school any longer which I regret in the process of trying to envisage them. Those pleated skirts and white blouses with ties are things I miss in a more general sense, nowadays, the idea of them. Gymslips etc.

I cannot bring myself to talk about what she wants to talk about. I would have nothing to add to what her mother will have told her about why we broke up and I wouldn't say it nearly so well – and not only because I am not as sure about it (anything) as my wife is. She will have put my point of view with complete fairness, which is remarkable since I'm not at all sure I've got one, not to speak of. When we are together, my daughter and I, I see now that I care for her largely to the extent that I recognize she wants it to be known that she cares for me. She sometimes mentions the old days, saying, 'Do you remember when . . . ?' She recalls that afternoon in the park with the Webbs and the Hambles. It is in that context alone that she remembers them. She sighs for the past and assumes a world-weariness and wants me to have a wallow with her. I don't know why. Perhaps she can't feel sorry for herself and others on her own and needs my support in deciding that the world is a cruel place. Just to make her happy I am sometimes tempted to say how sad it is we are not all together again and that things couldn't have gone on as before, pretending I didn't quite know why.

She would like it best if I put my hand on hers when she remembered some touching episode from the past, some fun here, some sorrow there, and my eyes blurred with a faraway look and I said something like, 'Let bygones be bygones. All I want is your happiness. We had some good times. All in all, life has been kind to us and the future is full of hope. I love you no less and like to feel your love for me too is undimmed though our ways have parted and the sun has gone behind a cloud and we are learning to tread alone up to the foothills of wisdom towards evening before the night falls and a new day dawns.' If she didn't at once call for an ambulance, her eyes would fill with tears and she would say, with the deepest sigh (revealing the full droop and magnitude of her bra-less bosom), 'Oh, Daddy!'

It is when I think she would like the conversation to take this sort of turn that I find myself caring for her less than I ought to. Or is it myself I do not care for then? Because the truth is I would like, I would like very much indeed, to be close enough to my children to

147

get away with having that sort of conversation with them. I fear my daughter's sentimentality and world-weariness because she enjoys them and they aren't enjoyable to me at all. I am not self-indulgent so far as my emotions, as opposed to my appetites, are concerned. (Distinguishing between those in each instance might help one to decide how far one should indulge oneself, though doing that would be pretty self-indulgent of course.) She is ready to wallow up to her neck and I don't even want to get my feet wet. I imagine her saying to Angie and Sprog that her parents are separated and her eyes filling up. And either Angie or Sprog replies, 'But *my* father is dead.'

I cannot be fair to my daughter when we are together. I doubt her capacity for sorrow. (I don't doubt my son's but have more reason to.) When we are apart, I think of things happening to her in a science laboratory or a haystack. I hear her gasp and cry out for help. When we are together, I look at her pimples and the poverty of her attire, I hear the whispering forlornness of her voice, and my manner towards her is hard and matter-of-fact. My hand keeps well away from hers. It is difficult to keep her at a distance without giving the impression that I am only doing my duty by taking her out to the cinema, that she is a bit of a drag and that whatever mood she is in the sooner she snaps out of it the better. But as soon as the outing draws to an end, I begin not to feel like that towards her at all.

And by the time she is going away from me (flat-footed, broad-bottomed, not my type at all, particularly when associated with the bra-less bobbing and dangling that is going on at the front) I am feeling that all I want on earth is her company back again. I suspect there are tears in her eyes. I can hear her talking to Angie and Sprog about me, making me out to be a sad creature which quite clearly I'm not, ho ho. I am ashamed of myself for doubting whether her emotions are genuine. I remember how fond she was of Mrs Hamble and know, but do not feel, that she has a kind heart and is generous in spirit. My doubt is utterly disgraceful. I have no cause to question her genuineness. My wife's often saying, 'I genuinely (or honestly) believe (or think or feel) . . .' casts a long shadow, however – that so often, in general I mean, it must be assumed that believing etc. are a complete fake. I only wish my daughter didn't look so damned miserable all the time we are together. I wish I could make her laugh, or even smile, other than wistfully. She would only think I was trying to cheer myself up. (She would be right.) 'My father is always trying to crack jokes,' she would say to Angie and Sprog of whom one would say in reply, 'My father does not crack jokes at all, because he is dead.'

We had one very happy afternoon together, my daughter and I, playing 'Guess the Prices' at Harrods, the object of which is to get within twenty-five per cent in three guesses. The game ended when I sat down, legs outstretched, and tested the weight of a black leather brief-case with gold trimmings and a salesman of stern but subservient mien with a grey waistcoat and suede shoes to match approached me with a glance at my blushing, filthily-clad offspring which rapidly lost its subservient aspect. I gave him no time to offer his help by patting my wallet and saying, 'Any reduction for the pair, run one up for me, could you? Never mind. I'm not in a hurry. Legacy not quite through yet. Don't have any in real leather, do you by any chance?'

'Actually, sir, they happen to be Finnish. Reindeer hide,' he replied while my giggling daughter scuttled away and studied an oblong lampshade she told me later was made from a camel's bladder. (Light at the end of the tunnel, I suggested.)

'Oh, what a shame, so none left then,' I said, getting briskly to my feet and tugging down my jacket. 'In that case, in brief, you should-n't tempt people. I'm not surprised the poor creatures do in the least with all those Santa Clauses after them to lug their sleighs about.' Then made for the lift, gathering my daughter up on the way.

She was very red in the face by now. With my hand on her fore-head, I yanked her round to face the salesman so that he could see how feverish she was and therefore in need of my attention. How he reacted when she stuck her tongue out at him I cannot say. I was proud of her then. If only she hadn't burst into another fit of the gig-gles. It was her own little private demo but I was glad too that that was likely to be all the rebellion. Otherwise the humour might not survive the discovery that out there in the world there is really nothing to laugh at at all. This is what my wife knows so much more about than I do – from first-hand experience, that is. Unpreparedness for reality sometimes seems to become more important by the day.

I thought my son might enjoy the same outing the following week-end. But he didn't get the point at all, trailing behind me and feeling sorry for me that there were so many classy things in the world I couldn't afford. For why was I there at all if not in search of something to buy?

'Can't we try somewhere cheaper, Dad?' he asked. 'I don't even *like* any of these things.'

'Yeah, boy,' I replied, 'there are cheaper places but always start at the top and work your way down. That way it's easier to come to terms with what you can't have or can't afford, becoming less envious perhaps. It's a matter of self-respect really.'

He glanced up at me with a frown but didn't, I'm glad to say, ask me what I meant by that. I'm not sure I know. I did not say 'disgust at ostentatious wealth, conspicuous consumption or the unacceptable face of capitalism' – he'd be getting that indignant perspective on things sufficiently from his mother. I suspect though he won't be much more of a rebel than I am. I wish I could begin to guess what will become of him. Perhaps I simply hoped he wouldn't get all worked up by contemplating what he'd never have, that in his dreams whether of night or day, he would live by himself alone, however extravagant his fancies. That would not be to rule out the scope for indignation of course. For our self-respect, none of us can afford not to say (or think) sometimes: Oi, stop it, we can't have that.

Try as I might I couldn't get a smile out of him that day. It wasn't so funny for the reindeer or camel he reminded me. He was bored and weary. I was too. We both wanted to get home, however boring and wearisome that would soon become too, making us look forward to our next time together. Uppermost, though, I suspect, was that we felt responsible for each other's happiness; and could not live up to that. (The same, as I've tried to show, goes for my daughter but her own happiness gives her enough to be unhappy about.) That would always be the reality which nothing could have prepared us for on each such occasion to do with other people, when getting a smile out of anyone is the closest you're likely to get to announcing what you know you cannot live up to. I got laughter out of my daughter and not a smile out of my son. This has nothing to do, I suspect, with which has the better sense of humour.

150

Chapter Fourteen

Yet more time has passed.

Plaskett has invited me to spend a few days at this little place he's bought on a lake. Needless to say, I accepted. I have met his wife briefly. She and their two children, both boys, came to meet him at the airport when we were returning from one of our trips together. She is a trim, lively woman with long black hair and large eyes that gave me a friendly look of the sort that seems to have been there already for someone (everyone?) else. She might have been French a long time ago and was trying too hard either to or not to still sound it. The children seemed very nice or at any rate they had nice manners. I could see why Plaskett might not want them to come into contact with people like himself later in life. There seemed to be no tension or embarrassment of any kind in the Plaskett family. They chatted in the car very freely and brought me into the conversation from time to time. Mrs Plaskett looked round at me more often and longer than she needed to, I fondly conjectured. What had Plaskett told her about me? It crossed my mind that it would be possible to fall in love with her. I imagined becoming her burden of frantic and silent shame. I imagined blurting out the moment we were alone together, 'Let me be your albatross,' then, 'Care for a shag, lady?' I wished my eyes, instead of thoughtfully drifting off, would search hers in return. Of course I wouldn't take the smallest step towards discovering whether Mrs Plaskett would like to be flirted with, by me or anyone else for that matter. I would have no compunction about chasing after her in principle – that's what matters in the long run, my wife used to say, sticking to one's principles.

But I'm not secure enough in my job, not yet. (Not ever?) In the meantime it is pleasant to picture us entwined together in a bedroom in their little place by the lake, while Plaskett and his nice children splash about in the water just within earshot. The idea of it is sufficient, will have to be. I stretch back in a deckchair on the veranda, having accepted a Pimms from him with a nod and a smirk, still smelling of his wife, giving her a wink behind his back and making her blush. Later when the children are tucked up in bed, we sit watching the reflection of the full moon making a silver path along the water, Plaskett totally unaware that his wife's mind and my own are barely at all on whatever his seems to be on to judge from what we all seem to be chatting about. This is all the revenge I need. It is better than leaving a dead mouse on his desk. It is more than enough to betray him in spirit while he continues to carry me ever upwards to wealth and success. I remind myself that he only likes me because I am useful to him. He needs a right-hand man, a 'yes' man. I imagine looking him in the eye one day and saying, 'What's more, you twerp, I've said "yes" to your lady wife too, and it's been all right, that's been.' Well, I'm not serious about any of this of course. I am only concerned to make sure I don't hide from myself all the thoughts that fleetingly cross my mind and linger there for a while. Plaskett values me as an honest man. I would not wish to betray that trust by not admitting that I fancy his wife. I wish to remain true to his opinion of me. (The invitation, by the way, was not repeated, nor to be taken seriously. What gives me away is that that was how I took it at the time.)

I drove up our old street the other day. It was only a short detour. I wouldn't have done it otherwise. I saw Hamble in his garden still pottering. He looked even redder and plumper than before. As I passed, he straightened, stared at me, then down with that small, uncertain smile of his at what he was doing. Then he scratched his head and frowned with puzzlement but the smile remained. Wasn't I someone he had seen somewhere before? Hardly important. It was as if he couldn't quite believe his luck to be so happy on that bright summer afternoon in a place where once to have experienced happiness with another was to go on sharing it. I did not wave at him. If I had, he would only have waved back, neither wondering nor caring who I was.

In our garden two small children were playing on a swing and a tricycle respectively. My thoughts did not dwell on them. Unlike my daughter I derive little pleasure from reliving years gone by and reflecting on the passage of time. Looking out of our living-room window and seeing my own children at that age playing in that garden, I doubt whether, continuing to be honest, there was much more in my mind than the thought, if that was what it was and not just a wordless picture, 'There are my children playing in the garden.' Whereupon I probably looked at my watch, hoping it would tell me it was close to their bedtime and that it wasn't my turn to read them a story so I could watch television instead.

The truth is I don't think about my wife much, except when I accidentally remember a scene from the past in which she took part. When we last met, my daughter told me they'd moved in with another man.

'That's all right by me,' I said and meant it. I asked what he was like so as not to have to make guesses about him.

She told me he had bushy eyebrows, a Scottish accent and a beard, that he wore half-eye glasses and shared my wife's interests, being in the same occupation. Also he smoked a curved pipe and had a weakness for liqueur chocolates. They chose their books together at the public library and when they had finished them they would carry on a discussion about them. Sometimes they read aloud to each other. They were writing a paper together about aspects of stress among teenage children which was to be delivered at a conference in Manchester. The man was also writing a book and was assistant editor of a journal. My daughter told me he was more careful than my wife was to make sure that she and Adrian were not left out of the long conversations they had together. ('So not interminable then?' I forbore to interject. 'They've got to go to bed some time.') Often he asked them what they thought about this and that and my daughter agreed with me it was likely he was checking up on something he intended to say about teenage children in his book, since he had none of his own. Lucky for them, I thought, not having to explain all the time how they felt about everything until the only feelings they had left were about having to explain them. He was always cheerful, my daughter said. He took them on outings and sometimes put his arm round them. At that I raised my eyebrows.

'Oh, not like *that*, Daddy,' she said. 'He's perfectly harmless.'

I was glad she wanted to reassure me. I didn't say that I was sure he wouldn't do them any lasting harm, but no one was perfect and so far as she was concerned, it was always to a greater or lesser degree 'like *that.*' Always.

It has remained all right with me that my wife has taken up with another man whom my children seem to like, or not to dislike. My son did not mention him so I told him Virginia had told me about him and he seemed nice enough. My son nodded and I looked for an aspect of stress, wishing I could have sight of that paper so as to know what to look for.

My son said, 'He's looking forward to meeting you, he said.'
'That would be nice,' I replied.
'I think Mum wants to marry him.'
'That's all right by me. Provided it's all right with you too.'
He shrugged. 'If you don't mind I don't mind.'
'So that's all right then.'
'I suppose so. I just wish he didn't ask so much about what we feel about things.'
'Because you're not sure?'
'Because I am, silly.'
Thus my son and I discovered what a virtuous circle is.

My children are growing away from me. They are at the threshold of their futures. I think of them in clichés like that or dream of them. I see them stepping up into the dark hallway of a small house and going through it to a french window, beyond which is a large flat green park like the one in that other dream. It is too dim to see whether they have turned round to wave. I can see them faintly in silhouette and getting smaller. They are joined by people of their own age and the silhouettes grow broader and become agitated. I turn away from them and go through a back yard with a dustbin, a pram and an old bicycle in it, beyond which are conference rooms thick with smoke and airport lounges and swinging doors leading from deafening, stifling city streets, and hotel bedrooms into which trolleys are wheeled with food and drink aplenty.

I think little of my wife and her new man. They are trying to bring a better world into being. It is a world I would like to live in provided it left me alone to be what I am. I'm quite happy to contribute to that world my share of taxes. I can see that the world's well-being costs money. I'm not one given to thinking, 'Screw you, pal, I'm all right.' If I had no choice in the matter, I'd not begrudge making my contribution with my time as well as my money. I am a good functionary. I would not resist the revolution even in my mind, except in detesting the people who'd brought it about. I wouldn't mind selling my services to the state, as my wife and her man do. I would like to feel I had done something, anything, for human suffering. But I have had the choice and have not used it. (I am not generous enough when giving to charity, though to be very charitable indeed at least to myself, I am not ungenerous either. People say they give what they can afford or choose one charity and refuse the rest. They seem to need the excuse, hovering between feeling good and not feeling bad about it. They do not take the risk of giving too much and feeling so good that they then catch themselves later feeling bad about it. They can't afford, really, to think about it at all.)

Anyway, I suppose that better world would have to coerce me, leave me with no choices. But then, of course, I wouldn't derive satisfaction from the little I'd done to relieve human suffering. Satisfaction comes from having had alternatives, from having been left to choose for ourselves – and that's almost always who we do choose for. I suspect that, if I got round to working it out properly, had another go at the subject, I want to have my cake and eat it. I had the choice of putting my finger in Plaskett's eye, of taking an interest in carpentry for my son's sake, of doing voluntary community service for my wife's (of what for my daughter's?) and did not take them. The list is endless. I think I wish to be left alone not to have to make any choices at all, envying no one for what they do for others or what they do entirely for themselves, unblurring that distinction for a moment. I cannot pretend I am jealous of my freedom.

My children are travelling away from me. My wife arrived there a long time ago. Their bodies and minds have detached themselves from mine altogether. In so far as I think further along those lines my sentiments are those resembling disgust. Now that my daughter is nearly a woman, her blood and body hair and smells and natural functions are what I find myself thinking of, not her freshness after a bath before her womanhood began. I refuse to imagine my son erect or my wife copulating with another man, or with me come to that, now that I'm no longer the man I was. When I cannot help it, as now when trying to decide what there can possibly be left for me to ponder upon, I catch myself on the point of chuckling out loud. By God, if Webb had had his way he would have found us ridiculous! Gasping and grunting and heaving. They're first-class comedians, he would have thought of us, they can't get any funnier than that. In the natural, wholesome etc. course of events we'd leave our wildest antics to the end and they'd be a scream.

In trying to forget about my wife I'd prefer not to find her funny. (I do not mind finding myself funny provided there is nobody else to share the joke.) I do not like to think of my wife thinking of me laughing behind her back. I do not like to think of my wife thinking of me thinking of her body in the throes, with somebody else. Not that I suppose for a moment she would. Though I hope she does so that I can go on convincing myself I don't like to think of it.

I want us only to have in common as the years pass the knowledge that we had children (how would become a distant, unconsidered mystery) who'd turned out pretty much all right in the end. I want us only to remember at the very end of our lives the days she brought them home from the hospital, the fussing we did of them (even my wife fussed the first few days after she brought our babies home), how I shook too much at first to take Virginia in my arms and woke her up in the middle of the night, as all fathers must, to make sure she was alive, she looked so frail and insubstantial and was sleeping so peacefully. I thought then, 'The world is too rough a place for this one. She will never be ready for it. I have not passed on to her sufficient sturdiness and strength. There is not enough of her mother in her.' Indeed, I thought her mother was altogether too rough and ready with her except when she brought out her breasts and Virginia guzzled at them. She was very serene and tender then and I hoped she would pass that on too. I never watched her feed Adrian because by then her breasts hung too flat and loose and insisted on comparing themselves with those in the glossies that were coming more and more on the market at the time. And now it's my daughter's parts and their comparability I try not to think of when I catch sight of those explicit photographs in the windows of newsagents, particularly in some of the larger foreign cities – Scandinavia springs to mind for some reason I can't for the moment put my finger on. I am no longer a respectable married man but all this, I know, demeans me. It's just that that is the sort of thing I have caught myself thinking in respect of breasts. Is it any less demeaning to prevent thoughts from entering one's mind at all? Of course it is.

The first days after my wife brought our children home, I remember those. I have had many good times. I have had a laugh or two, but those days were the best. I was beside myself then, saying to myself in the mirror, 'Can this really be happening to you?' I loved my wife then. I was grateful to her for making me aware that I was capable of such love. Perhaps in later life I'll remember in the same way the days when my children got married, the days they made me a grand-parent. I cannot visualize their mates. I doubt if I will approve of them entirely (at all?). Perhaps I'll say to my daughter's husband as he leads her down the aisle or out of the registry office, 'All right so far, old chum, but just you keep your hands off her.' But she'll only have eyes for him. She'll let him do what he likes to her. I will try not to think of her too much (too much of her) after that, after I've given them whatever I can afford otherwise to get them off to a flying start – a deposit on a house for instance.

And this train of thought leads me to think too about Hipkin. Once I thought I saw him selling hot dogs from a stall outside Victoria Station. I crossed the street so as not to have to be sure. It was too easy to imagine the conversation we would have.
    'How's it going?' I would ask.
    'All right,' he would reply. 'How's it with you then?'
    'All right, all things considered.'
    'That's all right then.'
    I wouldn't give him news of the office, for example that Mrs Hodge died suddenly. He might not even remember who Mrs Hodge was. There is not much I can remember about her either, except her sniffling and her smell. I do not even know what she died of – heart trouble perhaps. She was taken off to the hospital one weekend and we had a collection to buy her flowers, the doorman making it possible for a second bunch to be sent, of twelve red roses. I do not remember if Plaskett contributed. Or rather, I remember not finding out because that was about the time I had persuaded myself he might not be such an utter shit after all.

Chapter Fifteen

Again, time has passed.

The divorce is going through. My wife's man phoned me as I was getting out of the bath. He sounded a decent enough sort of chap. There had been a car accident, he said. Nothing too serious. My wife had a few cuts and bruises, nothing to detain her in hospital for more than a day or two while they carried out tests. Adrian was unharmed. Some bones in my daughter's leg were broken. She was out of pain now.

'Who was driving?' I asked.

'I'm afraid I was.'

'Well you're a fucking idiot.'

'Don't be like that. I'm sorry, truly, but it really wasn't my fault.'

'They never had an accident with me, all those years.'

He sighed so deeply I thought he must have put the telephone right up against his mouth to do it.

'Don't you sigh at me,' I said, much more quietly now.

'I wish there was something I could say,' he replied. 'But honestly, it wasn't my fault. This maniac came straight out of a side turning.'

'It wouldn't have happened if I'd been driving. I mean I wouldn't have been driving them there then, would I?'

'I suppose it wouldn't.'

'Well, anyway, thanks for telling me.'

There was a pause. 'I want to marry your wife,' he said. The Scottish accent made him sound assertive and plaintive at the same time.

'Go ahead,' I replied. 'And give them my love. And drive more carefully in future.'

'For Christ's sake, I *was* driving . . .'

I hung up. I hoped he wouldn't tell my wife and children how I'd spoken to him over the telephone, setting a bad example. I wouldn't want there to be any bitterness in their lives on my account. I wondered if when it happened my wife was having her hand squeezed.

I went to see them in hospital. My wife had a cut down one cheek and a large bruise over her left eye.

'What a sight I must be,' she said. 'I haven't dared look at myself yet. I've got some beauties on my body too.'

Decidedly not saying it was all right for some. I pointed at the gash on her cheek. 'Will that be a permanent you know . . . ?'

'I'm too old to be worrying about that sort of thing now.'

'One's never too . . . It could have been a lot worse,' I said. 'Count your blessings. You could be dead.'

She smiled and winced. 'Oh yes, it could have been a hell of a lot worse.'

She didn't ask after me, assuming no doubt that my life was as it always had been. I told her I would do what I could to get the divorce through as soon as possible. She touched my hand.

'You're a sweet person,' she said.

'He sounded a nice man on the telephone.'

'He is.'

There was a bit more talk about settlements for the children and keeping in touch with them. I told her to get well soon, her problem families would be missing her.

That only made her frown. 'Oh don't remind me! But it's society that's got the problems, not the families.'

I told her I was sure she must be right and said goodbye, avoiding the little lecture that might have followed since I still had my daughter to see in another ward and a plane to catch. Perhaps for the last time I thought, 'She does talk the most awful drivel sometimes.'

My daughter was very pale and the nurse said I wasn't to spend too long with her because the shock hadn't worn off yet and she had to be seen to. There was no damage to her face but under the frame over which her bedding was spread I glimpsed a long expanse of plaster up to her waist.

'Lazing about as usual, I see,' I said as I kissed her.

'This is the life,' she said. Her voice was faint and high and she smiled sheepishly at me as if she'd done something wrong. I could tell how glad she was to see me. I kissed her again.

'It doesn't hurt any more,' she said.

'Only when you play games,' I said.

I gave her the books and magazines and box of chocolates and silver locket I had bought for her, then remembered the chocolates had been meant for her mother.

'The chocolates are for you and Mum to share,' I said.

She liked the locket very much. It was an elaborate construction of onyxes and crescents of silver and the chain was silver too. It was clear it wasn't something I'd popped into Woolworth's for.

'It's lovely, Dad. Honestly, it's really beautiful.'

'Yes, but God knows why I'm bringing presents to a girl who's been daft enough to get herself involved in a traffic accident. Still, you see I was doing this plumbing job in this duchess's flat near Hyde Park and happened to see it lying there on this dressing table and I thought to myself . . .'

'Don't, Dad,' she whispered.

She was looking down at the thing and fingering it and I could tell from the flickering of her eyelids that she was becoming tearful. But I went on. I don't know why. I'm not always that selfish.

'Actually she was a marchioness. You know, one of those little women from another planet with one eye and aerials instead of ears and I said to her, if you don't fratefully mind, I'll be 'aving this 'ere what-d'you-call-it for some bird-brain I 'appen to be hacquainted of who can think of nuffink better to do on a fine spring morning but loaf about in bed heating chocolates, pretending like she's sprained 'er hankle or some damn thing. And the marchioness, know what she said? She said, "Lock my don't touch it and you'll never strip my dropping paps again." Whereupon, not taking no for an answer . . .'

By now she was crying properly and the nurse came and gently asked me to leave.

'She's had a nasty shock,' she repeated, then went away again. I bent over and kissed my daughter's forehead a third time, ran my thumb round under her eyes and told her not to be a silly billy, I'd be in to see her again soon, and even then I couldn't leave off, adding that I was going to Cologne and Paris (which I was) and would bring her back an odour and something to get plastered with even if she didn't have the manners to jump to her feet and see me to the door. And I went on, 'People have funny beliefs in Germany, some of them. I was at this party and heard this bloke next to me

160

going on about little round red Jesus, smelly blue Jesus, smooth holy Jesus, Jesus for mice and Jesus that keeps you awake at night and cauliflower Jesus . . .'

She got it then and began to giggle which made her cry again.

'And then I realized what he'd been talking about all the time was . . .' and we spoke the word together, smiling broadly for the photographer who wasn't there, who's never there when he's wanted, '. . . cheeses.'

Then I winked and left.

Perhaps it was having imagined her battered and bloody and dead by the roadside that made me want to make my daughter weep. Because the expressions of love are rare and hard to come by before it's all over and done with. That's my only excuse for the greed of my love and makes me no less ashamed of it. That's what I think about, that and her body bloody and twisted and sprawled across a road, in the shorter and shorter gaps between the times when I find I'm no longer having to think about anything much.

That should be enough for the time being. All good things come to an end. Everything is all right now really. I have met a nice woman who laughs at some of my jokes and has a personality which is known as lively. My guess is she doesn't have much of a figure but I'll be finding out more about that shortly and of course it won't matter a damn, not then. She says she has no desire to have children which is one of the reasons why she's left her husband. She is in her mid to late thirties or so. She is a prattler and gets pleasure from little things (not like me in the slightest in that regard, ho ho). If I said I was going down the road for a newspaper she'd say what a fabulous idea that was and ask if she could come too. When we walk down the street, she puts her arm through mine and clasps her hands together and leans against me. My wife was built in a manner that made it impossible for her to do that without causing me discomfort. I hope she gets pleasure from what will happen when I find out most of what there is left to know about her; her getting pleasure from just about anything ought to modify mine but won't, at any rate not at the time. She is a wriggler. She is much younger than her years. She has the capacity to tire me out, I fear, but in the process I'll be finding out more about my own capacities, which can be no bad thing in theory; though in practice knowing what little one is capable of can be, if this is the word, incapacitating. (She does not have what could be described as a public conscience. She does not read newspapers much, as opposed to magazines, or keep herself seriously informed about what is going on in the world. But then who does? At any rate anywhere seriously enough to match up to the seriousness of it. It is the feeling that there's absolutely nothing one can do about it – incapacity, in a word.)

Another thing she has a capacity for is spending my money. That means there'll be that much less of it to hand on to my children. It is a dilemma I must learn to live with. I miss her very much on my trips. If we get married I'll take her with me though I dread to think of the additional expense (having taken the savings into account). I must work more noticeably harder so that someone other than myself begins to wonder why I do not make more money at it. I must keep in with Plaskett who has just been made a director and he won't stop there. Despite my lively companion I still catch myself lusting after Mrs P, especially on my occasional business trips with her husband when it is abundantly clear he is too much occupied with the profit at hand to be thinking about the loss of anything further away. I do not miss my former family, not with any constancy, no more than I miss my father who is long since dead and buried now. My mother lives on and I do not think nearly enough about her either. (Does the rest of the world think as much about themselves, and therefore as little about others, as I do? My guess is most certainly yes, to judge from what they talk about.) Mostly when I'm away, as I've said, I miss . . . it doesn't matter what her name is. I watch less television nowadays, though we enjoy perforce the same programmes, watching them together, that is, not primarily because of the programmes themselves.

The large green landscape in my dreams has shrunk, is now no more than a dingy park surrounded by small detached houses of the kind that are commonly found in the less seedy north London suburbs. The dream has turned from green to grey, from sunlight to dusk. The park is very quiet and there are no animals in it, not even squirrels, not counting the occasional homeless-looking dog lifting its leg against a leafless tree. Sometimes I am in it with my children but never with a woman. My children have become younger and walk silently ahead of me. Sometimes I have to run to keep up with them though they are still walking. I want to catch up with them to make sure they are my children. But I never do. Eventually I give up calling their names and sit down on a bench and watch them disappear through a gate towards one of the rows of houses. I am usually alone but sometimes Mrs Webb is there too for some reason – hovering reproachfully on the edge of my vision. At the gate my children turn and wave but by then they are too far away to recognize. There is no reason to suppose my children are not happy, assuming they are my children. I am a little worried that they are not warmly enough dressed, that is all. They are wearing clothes that are suitable for warm weather by the seaside, sometimes only bathing costumes. I am clad in a thick overcoat, a muffler and gloves and become too cold to stay seated there. I open my eyes and move closer to the woman who may become my wife, who is always warm, but not so close as to wake her. I usually only imagine these things when we have made love and I do not want her to get ideas, given she is likely to be wanting to do it again in the morning i.e. on Saturday or Sunday when another, relatively trivial, imperative does not force itself on us instead – utterly trivial by comparison I should have written: work, I mean, and the serious business of living. She sleeps very soundly, apparently without a care in the world.

In the day-dream my children seem to walk slightly above the ground. They glide in front of my plodding run. When I am fully awake, cold and shivering, I remember my daughter has a limp since one of her legs is slightly shorter than the other now. Or I see my son running away from a garage. It seems strange to me, therefore, but not wrong, to be moving closer for warmth towards a woman who is not their mother. As a matter of fact, they have met her and seem to like her, quite. She is just the same with them as she is with me, lively, hardly ever stops talking. It may become easier to take them out when she is there too.

(Added later. That didn't come to anything, alas. Perhaps having met mine, she wants her own children before it's too late and has now gone back to her husband. No hard feelings, though I cannot of course speak for him. Sounds bloody tolerant to me, and would be all the more so, I suppose I should add, if he'd met me, not (in every single respect anyway) the sort of rich, dashing, handsome bounder who'd sweep any God-fearing woman off her feet. I've met a blonde woman to take her place. She is in banking. Between them they've rather taken my mind off this writing I've been doing, but if it's a substitute, I shouldn't mind that too much, should I? Or is the word 'sublimation'? Like a number of my former wife's words I've no idea what it means but, by the sound of it, suspect it couldn't be that or one wouldn't be much bothered with women at all when bashing away at it, in sublime ignorance most of the time.)

Everything is satisfactory on the whole. I have no complaints. Except for my daughter's limp of course. But it's only slight, she's getting prettier by the day and I have this idiotic notion she'll meet a kinder, less grope-fingered, goatish man because of it. She doesn't seem to mind it. It could all have been so much worse. Just as my former wife said. She was right about so many things, perhaps about everything. I'm not sorry I married her or anything like that. There was a lot she taught me, reminding me of reality. Except for getting older (all the spasms of despair in the small cold hours) I have no regrets really, given that I am what I am, though it is a very good thing indeed there are enough people not like me about who believe to the death in the liberty of man, who build bridges, clear minefields, teach children, mend bones and the like; those too especially, the quite unknown, who care for the afflicted in faraway places, day in, day out, whose compassion is just what they do, not something that brings them acknowledgement other than from those whom they care for and not always then.

That's as far as I've got. I still don't know the point of it, though it's taken quite a time.

PART TWO

PART TWO

Chapter One

Thank you for your interest.

Fiftyish or thereabouts I was coming up to when I wrote earlier that it was all right then. Much more time has passed. We have Channel 4 now, for instance, and Mrs Thatcher has been our prime minister for what already seems a very long time indeed but is only a couple of years. For those I met in my recent employment it could never be anything like long enough and I don't only mean those who had had or wished they'd had nannies and could imagine her smacking their bottoms. 'Recent' is the word that will have caught your eye. The handshake was respectable enough, though hardly what you'd call handsome. My former boss, Plaskett, went with the new American company which bought us out. I'll never know how hard he tried to take me with him with whatever energy he had left after doing all right by himself. I took my leave just before Christmas, the season of good cheerio you could call it, the office party being combined with a farewell party for me and two or three others, all of them older and less senior than I. This is what I wrote about it at the time.

I withdrew my hand from Plaskett's final grip sooner than he was pretending he wanted me to, his spare hand on top of our joined fist giving the second of what might have developed into a series of squeezes. He was moving his mouth less to talk and there was a new twang in his voice. 'Gush, Tum, I'll sure miss you. We all will. A darn fine innings, a real dandy . . .' There may have been a wink at this point, or a blink hinting at feelings resolutely under control: '. . . cruising along and well into your second half-century . . . no great shakes at this sort of thing but I'll tell you one thing, straight up, on the level, you were a real brick . . .' There was another blink then as I got my hand completely away and his went to my elbow. 'What'll

167

you do then, stashed away the odd buckaroo if I know my Ripple? These take-overs, shucks, I mean . . .'

No need to dwell further on what was passing through my mind, that it was my chance to tell him what a perfect shit I'd always thought him before it became all right and hardly less then except that I allowed myself to think it less; that a real brick was what I had in my briefcase to give the impression of having to take a lot of work home; that into one's second half-century almost straight up it might be but not so often and how was his lovely wife doing on the level these days? What I said was, 'It's been a privilege. Oh yes, enough to get by on I hope. We discussed, remember, what to do with it, quite often in fact, the best way to hoard the stuff I mean, units one could really trust, ho ho, and what with the family off one's hands and moving into the country and, well, it's not having to last for ever . . .'

He gave my elbow a last tap and began moving away to one of the several people he'd been looking over my shoulder at. 'Good on you, Tom. And remember to keep in touch or why not come . . .' He didn't risk a second time reminding me about his cottage by a lake to which he might have forgotten he'd once invited me without getting round to the details, like a date. I mumbled to his jaw, then his shoulder blade, 'Good luck then and keep the old flag flying, and since you ask I'd hate to come and stay in your stinking hovel. How about the weekend after next, you appalling little nerd . . . ?'

He winked twice, gave me a backhand tap, then a punch on my upper arm and sped through the crowd, arm outstretched, calling out, 'Oh, hi there!'

Nobody else catching my attention, I slunk off, a few quick hand-shakes, palms on backs, mine on two where bras are fastened. I glanced back from the doorway but no one was looking my way. Plaskett was impressing the new American MD, trying out more of the new lingo no doubt or going over aspects of the new corporate plan, three of whose five appendices (the brilliant, conclusive ones) were my parting handiwork. Not that my recommendations were adopted in their entirety, the one tucked away in a footnote for instance which found a place for me (new job title with almost double the salary) in the new set-up. Clearly they weren't read with sufficient attention to the fine print. From the look on his face, the American seemed to be learn-ing to hum a complicated tune while making it known what astonish-ing strides the dental profession in his country was making.

At the lift I found I still had most of a gin and tonic in my hand so went back to put it on a table just inside the door. The last I saw of them all, of the bulk of my life so far, was of open mouths and eyes gaping into them, amazed at how all those words were managing to tumble out against the constant flow of food and drink. It was a relief for a change, intermittently, to be getting out not off nor on to a good thing nor into anything I'd regret later (fat chance) and the rest of it. One pair of eyes held mine for an instant, those of the typing pool superintendent whose bra fastening I'd recently fingered. She raised a hand and twiddled it at me. There was no wedding ring on it now as there had been the Christmas before. She was not seeing me off this time – or was rather. I verified this by raising an eyebrow and beckoning but she turned away and gave the man she was with a peck on the cheek, or did she whisper in his ear? Oh no, not that toad-faced lecher from Accounts, it couldn't be . . .

There is more besides but that's the remnant of the old life and leads nowhere. I leave it in more or less unaltered because, so far as I can judge now, it gives an idea of my mood at the time. I doubt if I gave the occasion much thought, what with counting my assets (discount-ing my liabilities seems to be taking longer), deciding which way to drive to find my property in the country, making phone calls to my children and former wife to tell them I'd chucked it all up and taken early retirement. The active ought to have been the passive voice, I know, but there were certain habits I wanted to get into before tear-ing the last strip off myself so to speak. Anyway, none of them was in. I thought what self-sufficient lives they led but might still want to phone me, my children just for a chat (poor Dad, all alone – a loan being increasingly all I was good for), their mother to dish out a lump of that exhausting old wisdom. So I decided instead to drop them a note, but didn't for several weeks. And had the phone disconnected. Not fair otherwise on the head hunters who'd keep on ringing back, or on Plaskett who'd had a change of heart and couldn't hack it without me.

There were several things I liked at first about this village twenty-odd miles from the Suffolk coast more than I disliked about it. I had only the vaguest idea why I was taking this step beyond knowing what I could afford and wanting to find out if a spell of solitude would make it easier for me to write again about what is less than all right – beyond, that is, the impurely personal, the inconstant here and now. If it didn't work out, I could probably get a job of a kind. Plaskett would give me a reference: loyal, tidy-minded, a way with organizing facts and figures – enough to obscure my lack of qualifications if you didn't count the equivalent of four O levels, two reasonably good CSEs and an A level in Ancient History. However, here I still am, becoming less re-employable by the day and London's not the only capital which isn't what it was.

I chose a cottage on the edge of a village green. That's how I'd always dreamt it, waking from my doze by a lattice window and through the roses seeing someone coming up to bowl. The grass had spread through the gate and most of the way to the front door towards which the estate agent preceded me, slashing away with his walking stick and just missing me with it since I was right behind him when he turned to say, 'Garden needs a bit of seeing to but good rich soil if and when you ever get through to it.'

So did the front-door lock, not that it mattered he had brought the wrong key because the kitchen door only needed a shove and we could have entered by any of the windows. As we stumbled our way through the 'living' quarters (spacious drg rm, dg rm, box rm/study) and then up to the two 14' x 11' bedrooms, he handed me a card with the name of a building contractor on it and said, 'Take it from me, may not look it but sound as a bell. Fit for a queen, I'd say, but for a couple of raging poofters who got so far as having a survey done, then one of them went and snuffed it so no future in that. Needs a coat of paint or two, a few screws here and there, don't we all, a bit of carpentry, reroofing. That plus a c.h. job won't set you back more than the odd thou.'

I said I'd think about it, which wasn't easy with all that dusty dankness in the air and mingled stench of a century's various small droppings or whatever.

'If I had a quid for every time . . .' he began, hunching his shoulders and pinching his nose. 'Oh never mind, offers considered . . . it's not such a frightful little village. Dumps like this being done up all over the place. East Anglia on the up and up. Can't lose on the investment. That's the kind of thing us lot say, isn't it?'

His exertions had made him breathless and something reddish and scaly seemed to be taking him over, the raw flakes on his bald head beginning to infect his forehead and breaking out around the ginger tufts on his cheeks and the sides of his neck. Suddenly he turned his back on me and, slashing away again and half sideways, made irregular progress back to his car, or rather my hired job which he had both legs into before he realized it wasn't sufficiently familiar. It wasn't even roughly the same colour. I went most of the way after him, waving, and he shouted back at me, 'Give us a call, or don't on the other hand. Wish I had this one off my books, I can tell you.' And he drove off, wincing and revving a lot.

I'd asked him who'd lived there before. 'Before what?' he'd replied with his half-grin or sneer. 'Estate under dispute since the Korean War or thereabouts. Used to get calls from a snooty little twerp from Cromer way with a cleft palate. Couldn't understand a word he said. Family bought it for a superannuated nanny or someone. Like I said, make me an offer.' So I made one so low I'm surprised it was audible and the place was mine.

The contractor did a good job on it: no complaints there, once I'd got the hang of the currency in use in Suffolk (learnt to convert thousands into the odd thou) and mastered the thirteen-day East Anglian week – a calendar I also adopted in my dealings with the perfectly obliging folk who were buying my flat in London.

While the men were 'at work', I used to drive up for a day or two, hack away at the grass, replace bricks in the front path, lay out a flowerbed, plant the odd shrub: a bedraggled clump with off-green leaves it was which the label said turned a shimmering gold in autumn but instead came out a week later in little pink flowers which along with most of the leaves almost immediately fell off. The truth was I had nothing else to do and hoped to unsettle the contractor by peering round doors or leaning on implements and generally assuming a homeless demeanour. But they all thought I wanted a chat and usually I did, though I drew the line at pulling up a chair, putting my feet up, buttering scones to go with the tea all day and giving the playing cards an especially thorough shuffle. 'Lonely, bored old bugger,' you could see them thinking and they were dead right much of the time. The rest of it I spent wondering what I was going to do about it.

Now, having just moved in, I look out over the garden and imagine I see my children there playing about in it, wait for my wife to ask if

171

I've nothing better to do with my life, not that she ever said anything remotely like that, quite. But I don't want to return to that way of thinking. Then, nothing was about to happen most of the time, but for life carrying on indefinitely, up to a certain point. Now it's as if I could start making things happen if only I knew what and how, given that what I know already is fast becoming all I can ever know. What about village life and the other folk here?

Apart from Sidney, the estate agent, and the people in the village shop I've met a retired colonel and his slender American wife at the health centre two miles away. I've also bumped into a man called Jenners who informed me at once he had lately retired from the Department of Trade and Industry and gave me his card which told me what his address was and that he had an OBE. We were in the shop at the time and after telling me I must call round he embarked further on how well he'd done in life so that I began to wonder why he hadn't done a great deal better.

In a pause he wanted me to fill with some accomplishment of my own, I muttered with a quick look at the card, 'It's nice to meet you, Mr Obe.' For Jenners could only be a name in use among his familiars. All this in a blindingly idiotic flash, but it flummoxed him enough that he reached hurriedly for his tin of ham, dropped it into his carrier bag and bid me good day with a courteous but uncomradely smile which won't have lasted long beyond discovering his ham had turned into my Dark Red Kidney Beans. (I accept that I may make an indifferent first impression on people. Twenty-seven years in export/import seem to have given me no definite opinions to speak of and I'm not what you'd describe as a striking figure of a man. I look somewhat ordinary in fact and no doubt sound it with my way of flattening my Midlands lilt and talking with as small a gap as possible between my unceremonial teeth. Enough of that; I've made it clear at some length previously that common enough is what I am.)

'Common' was a word my mother sometimes used in the shop about customers while my father did the accounts at the back. Or 'vulgar'. That was what she began calling my father's habits too as he grew older and sicker, drinking and wheezing and belching and puffing away as if old age was a phase to be got through as fast as possible and only then need he bother with a change of garments. Once I saw her hold her nose when he came near her. She noticed I was looking and pretended she was only rubbing it but she knew it was too late. Yet when she watched him snoring by the fire in the evenings it was with a stern pity and longing, not disgust. And it was with a glimmer of pride she told me he was 'poring over his books again'. So that, I thought, was why he had to fill his glass so often from the bottle of golden liquid and soda siphon on the sideboard. And when there was more talk than usual about burning candles at both ends and making them meet, I imagined his drenched books blazing up around a great snake of flame and sizzling wax while my parents looked on with a mad desperation in their eyes. They sometimes called me their 'one and only', my father once adding, 'Damn near killed your mother, you did, coming into the world.' On another occasion he told me the doctor had warned him he might have to choose between us. So that I felt constantly under scrutiny for lack of uniqueness and gratitude and spent a lot of my time hiding my dismay that I was nothing much at all but flesh and bones and thoughts floating about in my head that could have been anyone's. It wasn't until I was well into my teens that I came to terms with how un-unique I could ever hope to be, especially in the flesh – out and out randiness, I mean, as you will have guessed, because it would never be out and out nearly enough etc. So I became furtive with strangers, like a suspect for a crime I had yet to commit, and got into the well-worn, protective habit of keeping myself to myself. Though in the latter years of my success I learnt to lay a hand on a back or arm in the club or boardroom with the best of them and ingratiation, I think that's the word, became a way of life. Common wasn't in it. My mother wouldn't have been proud of me. Or would she? I wish I knew. I wish that now more than anything. But it is that sort of an evening. When the wind batters at the door in midwinter and a tall bush sways across my uncurtained window, fitfully lit by the moon. I shall put this near the beginning, I think, because the least merciful memories are of what was always absent and can never be brought to completion even in death. They lie among the shadows to one side or rear up beyond the reach of words: like love, for instance, unless that is merely something not dishonest and not uncaring. If I am to write anything at all, therefore, I must aim well short of what can never be lived again.

On to events recorded at the time, or shortly thereafter. About three weeks after I took up residence, the vicar came to call. He made it easy for me, I'll give him that. He didn't try to nudge in alongside me as it were though I rather wished he had because perched opposite each other on the packing cases in my 'study' and having to lean forwards, it was difficult not to look him straight in the eye. If soul searching was his business, he seemed to think he'd best start by giving me access to the whereabouts of his own, for the windows on to it were wide open unless that was only to furrow his forehead, thus counteracting the untroubled plumpness of his countenance further down. There was a contrast too between the bagginess of his tweed jacket and his gleaming toecaps, the frayed dog collar and his sharply creased cavalry twill trousers. Only about thirty, I guessed, but in a hurry to add on a decade or two. And the way he compressed his lips and clenched his jaw when he smiled suggested a grim and gristly sort of faith he hated to inflict on anyone else on a damp February afternoon. First thoughts those, while I wondered how soon to tell him this lost sheep was grazing much too far away on a barren plateau on the other side of the hill.

'Look', he began, 'make a point, you see, of calling on the new-comers, leave a number, the absolute least one can do . . . Your charming little church up the road, can only get to it fortnightly, doubling up as we do nowadays. Matins. Check on the wear and tear. Well, who knows there may be a great revival of faith one of these fine days and it might be needed? You aren't by any chance . . . ?'

I shook my head. 'Sorry. Not really. It's not one of the things I . . . Seem somehow to have managed without it, mucked . . . Special church, is it, antique . . . ?'

'Oh dear,' he interrupted, 'not like that in the slightest. In fact, it's remarkable really how so many people do seem to muck, rub along without it, or anything much at all out there beyond. But then I've got this big caboodle that holds it all together and lets in the light. Couldn't shake that off in a hurry . . .' He stared at me and bit his lip, preventing a smile that might have turned righteous. 'Sometimes, you're absolutely right, I do see it from a distance in a fearful flash as just a huge miscellaneous chunk of sustained imagining down the ages pretty tightly held together by language. Though that isn't quite the point, is it? Yes, it *is* a rather pretty little church but then in their way they all are, special you said. Each has its history. Not unlike people in fact.'

'Would you like a cup of tea or something?'

174

He straightened his back and hesitated. 'Thanks awfully, but no. Must get on. There are those who wait for me. The dying, for instance. Always a few of those around. Anyway, keep an eye on the place, slipping tiles, let me know. If there's ever anything I can do. And, this should have come first, I hope you'll be happy here.'

On the way in I'd told him the basic facts, or some of them: a business career, grown-up family, early retirement, place in the country, so the conversation was rounded off nicely and we could get to our feet. At the front door he gazed out over the flat, smeared landscape and said, 'I'm not from these parts. Cotswolds, hilly bits, slopes and copses. Too much sky, don't you find? The eye doesn't rove, less to distract from the end of things, clouds blown about. Time's rolling smithy smoke, know the phrase? Larkin.'

He was looking at his least playful then so this was lost on me at the time. No point explaining one had to fetch up somewhere, that price came into it and having to be not too far from the sea, where not too many people who resembled me had to be too, and not so remote there might be doubts about the television reception (to say nothing of nobody being within miles when there was a creaking on the stairs, a whisper, and the telephone line was cut). But why the sea? Something to do with those holidays with my family all those years ago when it was more all right than at other times, some enactment of happiness that might approximate to the real thing when we and those around us seemed to come into our own, to be living up to ourselves more, despite a lot of silly behaviour. So all I managed was, 'Yes, certainly but one can't go on searching for ever. Having lived in cities I don't mind the sky. And don't worry, I'll keep an eye on the church.'

He turned and shook my hand. The furrows and grim smile were back – how he wanted me to remember him, which brought on another spasm of conscience. 'The faith thing, the churchgoing. I didn't come for that, to sound you out, badger, once I could tell you weren't whatsit. But you could have been, you see, and if you had . . .' He looked again at the sky, getting blacker now more broadly and lower down. '. . . I do a nice line in weddings, baptisms, funerals, we all do. None of the unspeakable new Bible for me. I'm a sounding brass and tinkling cymbals and charity man myself. Oh yes. Last unction. On my mind. It's all our fault people don't ask for that any longer, though they like a chat, because nobody's sure about the extinction, are they, phut, curtains. Why don't they ask us? Because there's been too much damned unction all along the line. Thanks awfully for the tea . . .'

He began moving down the path towards his car, nearly tripping over the rake I'd abandoned there the day before when the rain began. Would he remember that I hadn't given him tea, feel foolish about that later? So I said, 'Sorry I only had the china.'

He appreciated that and nodded. 'The gallons of the stuff I get through in this job, you wouldn't believe it.' He raised his palms and studied the raindrops on them for a moment or two. 'Oh Lord,' he said finally, baffled shepherd counting his flock. 'Let's say it all together: it's the thought that matters . . . Read the newspapers, do you? Every day the quite unthinkable suffering, beyond . . .'

He trotted towards his car as the downpour began. Once inside he wound the window up, then down a few inches for a twiddle of his fingers along the top of it, then up again. After much grinding and roaring the car sloshed away with a lurch and I was left alone to pick up the rake and go back for some more unpacking and three hours or so of television. In my notebook, I jotted down: 'Vicar called. Don't expect to see much of him. Tried to put him at his ease but he has far too much on his mind.'

It must have been round about then I wrote to my children and their mother to tell them what had become of me: short, descriptive letters – the measurements of my rooms and garden, the distances between here and there and a sketch map of the village. To my children I said, 'You see, I've got it all sized up, the measure of my life.' To my former wife, I added, 'I'll let you know when I've become a case; it'll be a revelation.'

I didn't write to the blonde woman with whom I was getting on famously when I wrote that it was all right then. She worked in banking, a teller, and how. I suppose we'd known all along it couldn't last. Nothing dramatic happened to bring it to an end except that I discovered I wasn't the only man in her life. God alone knows, nothing wrong with that except that sharing means less for oneself. It's a long time ago now and but for its finality hardly worth bothering about. Belongs near the beginning perhaps.

In her flat that evening I'd found a condom wrapping under her bed and a week before that a few curly black hairs caught on the grid inside the plughole of her bath. (I was trying to persuade her to let me move in with her and sharing the chores was meant to clinch it.) There were also the phone calls when she listened for a bit, then said, 'I'll ring you back'. And told me it was only so-and-so, the name of a woman who from far off had a very deep voice. Shacking up together, let alone marriage, had increasingly become an item on the agenda which made her less and less impatient to get on to other business. Left till last, that remained absorbing enough even if it seemed to be the proceedings themselves, rather than my part in them, which aroused her interest, so that I exhausted the topic too early, my final motions were unseconded and the adjournment was agreed before deciding on the date of the next meeting.

I started the conversation like this, 'There's other chaps too, not so? Still, I mean. Not my affair or not only, but does it, is it likely to carry on like this, your carrying on . . . ?'

We were side by side on her sofa at the time, not touching anywhere except, just, at mid-thigh and upper arm. She was about to get up to open the bottle of wine I'd brought along with the pizza, I think it was. (Yes, anchovy and tomato. I can see it now, shreds of mushroom too. It looked disgusting lying there on the table in front of us, like drying vomit. I wish I'd never brought it up, I thought.) At once there was a gap between us everywhere so I hastened to add, 'I wish it weren't so hard to take, so objectionable. Not that in my shoes I'm in any position to object, with the thoughts men have . . . I'd rather you didn't that's all. Much . . .'

That was followed by a longer pause than in retrospect seems plausible. Then she got up, tugged down her skirt and plonked the wine on the table in such a manner that a black plastic ashtray with one of my cheroot stubs in it leapt off on to the floor. Where I'd just hoovered, I coolly observed.

'So now I'm hard to take, am I? Objectionable, am I?' she said, swinging round to face me and swinging back in a way that produced a breathtaking effect on her skirt, bottom and hips.

'I didn't say *you* were . . .'

But it was an eternity too late. I just wanted her to say with a touch of graciousness or at least not too hurtfully what she'd been waiting for a chance to say for longer than I dared to imagine. Meanwhile, cheering myself up, I started to do a calculation of all she'd cost me, deducting from that what she wouldn't any longer. It was beginning to add up and I suppose there was a grin in my voice when I said, 'I hate to think what this is costing me.'

'Comical is it? Well, take it from me, it's pathetic what you've got in the bank. Sod all interest it gives me and only weakly what's more. Couldn't live off that and shrinking dividends . . .'

I tried to guess from her voice how less lovable than usual she was looking, the eagerness in her eye turning into contempt, but could only see her struggling to get the lines right, quoted from one of her banking chums no doubt. They were quite promising. Pity she muffed them so. Please don't feel on my account, I was about to say but instead stood up, put my hand on the small of her back or lower and mumbled, 'Better be off then. Can't deny it, inflation getting less as the years pass, dwindling assets. We couldn't have got by . . . There had to be more than just the screw. You . . .'

'Screw you too!' she shouted. Was there a sob in her voice which I might have seized on with a sob or something like it of my own, moving my hand downwards instead of into my pocket to find my car keys? We had had such good, enlivening times together and I'd often congratulated myself on how, well, bankable they'd be, memorable, however faintly, on long, late, terminal winter evenings. I took out my car keys and moved two paces towards the door.

'Dearest,' I said, 'I didn't say . . .' Now at the door, turning the handle, I had a last try. 'Look at me,' I said. 'Let me see you for the last time, as it was in the beginning.'

But she didn't turn. She was holding her breath, I think. I wished she'd say outright, 'It wouldn't have worked, Tom. There's somebody else. There'll always be somebody else.'

No, I didn't wish that at all. I was glad of any reason at all not to like her when loving more than ever what I was about to lose. I turned the doorknob and she gave a sort of half-swirl of her hips, then pressed her hands slowly downwards from her waist as if wiping off the last traces of my repetitive fingering.

'You're all right,' she said gently. 'I'm sorry but you alone, me alone, it would have been boring, so boring. For you too.'

I went back and reached beyond her for the wine bottle. 'Speak for yourself. Don't mind if I take this, do you?'

And that was that. I brushed her bottom with the bottle and left. Neither of us phoned. Memories remained, and how. That incomparable swirl, the bumping of the bottle on her tautened flesh, and all that early eagerness which so much flattered me and brought tunes of a kind to my lips and gave me backache and a new lease on life and made me nod at myself in the mirror in the mornings and tell myself to take that conceited smile off my face.

As I stepped out into the street I realized just how mean I had been to take away that bottle. To have been made happy for a while by someone, and pleased with oneself, deserves at least a parting gift from one of the priciest vineyards in France.

Early March and spring in the air: a counsel of despair if ever there was one but let it pass. Both my son and my daughter have phoned and are coming to see me some time. That is the best of news but all is not well with Adrian, I could tell from how cheerful he sounded . . . What do I do all day? Sometimes I drive nowhere in particular, often to the coast where I watch the fishing boats being hauled up the beach and buy some fish. Lunch in a pub perhaps. An hour in the garden, tea, a thriller, television. Just these lines will have to do today. Yesterday there were two attractive women in the pub, with men. Both smiled at me. I had been staring at them. I sang on the way home. Just that little bit of encouragement, well well. Can invent a scene or two on the strength of that to send me off to sleep tonight. Or nibble a little blue pill if that doesn't work. Mustn't masturbate. Try to prolong the invention into my dreams. When my children come, keep my notebook out of sight. I did truly love her. I shouldn't have minded who screwed her so long as . . . This could go on for ever. No future in that, so wind back the reel a bit. Nothing is ever complete. Few memories are that merciful.

A couple of weeks after the vicar called I went to have a look at the church. There was a booklet which told me its history and a lot about the village at the same time. Rather like looking back over one's own life, there was the original core you had to take on trust – a stretch of wall here, a beam there – then a series of additions and amendments down the years but making up a whole which at a glance you could believe had been fashioned by one person or a small team over a fairly short space of time. The oldest thing there was the font, most of the writing on it worn away with the stonework. I ran my hand round it as thousands had done before, with love and hope in their minds, and continuity and new life, so that a string of compendious words like that began multiplying in a way that left me, well, standing there. The lectern was another notable feature. It had figures crawling up it in spirals, mainly animals, towards a gathering of saints and the like who were holding up the Bible. That was a beautiful thing too and I was surprised it had been left out and open. Hence the little brown blotches, insect droppings perhaps, which had accumulated over the centuries. Or rusted spots of damp. All the pages were much the same.

There was a small circular stained-glass window above the altar through which the sun was shining. It portrayed Jesus in the lap of his mother and beside them a shepherd holding a lamb. All wore haloes of the appropriate size. The sunlight made the blue so vivid as to be unbelievable, though that must have been the idea: to remind you when you next saw a deep blue sky which made you catch your breath there might be a lot more to it even than that. Likewise, the red of Mary's robe was redder than any blood. However, the booklet said it was a late Victorian addition and rather dismissed it, using the word 'garish'. This was to draw attention to what was lost when the Puritans had a bash at the place. Before that, the stained glass had been exceptional by all accounts. One of the walls had been chipped away at to reveal about a square yard of a very pale painting in pink of the bottom two-thirds of St Christopher's face and his shoulder with a crook over it. His eye was just in and looked thoroughly fed up but resolute with it. The whole figure had been plastered over to hide it from the Puritans and there was no hope now, the booklet said, of getting at the rest of it.

There was one other stained-glass window, divided into three panels with the words 'Suffer The Little Children' underneath. There were five adults and seven children in it with Jesus at the centre. They were dressed very gaudily in purple, royal blue, olive green and a rich brown like the soil I was beginning to get through to in my garden. There were also two trees, one bearing orange cherries, the other red avocado pears, and above them was a great elaboration of silver leaves and yellow stars and gold and red curlicues. A prosperous scene in short in which everyone looked very pious and pretty insufferable, especially the children.

In the rows of pews there were a few prayer and hymn books and only half of the hooks had hassocks hanging from them. On a board above the pulpit three hymns were listed. I looked up the first: 'The day thou gavest, Lord, is ended.' I went back to the lectern and turned back to the Old Testament where there was a long white silken marker in the page and read the words: 'Lord, who shall dwell in thy tabernacle, or who shall rest upon thy holy hill?' I then spoke the whole psalm out loud in my ordinary speaking voice. ('Speak up a little, would you mind, Tom,' Plaskett used to say to me at board meetings when it was his case I was making for him as it always was.) It seemed very audible in that emptiness, however, and from time to time I looked up and behind me to make sure nobody else was there.

From the few occasions when I'd been to church with my father it wasn't hard to imagine faces gazing up at me with a kind of shameful but honourable intent so that, all in it together, their individual sinfulness became nothing worse than an average falling short or a bit of bad luck. On finishing my reading, I looked all around the roof then took a stroll outside but found nothing I ought to phone the vicar about. I went back and put a fiver in the box for the restoration fund. It seemed ready enough for a revival of faith and I thought I'd be quite happy to be around then (especially if it didn't happen in my lifetime) and watch the people sitting or kneeling or raising their voices so that I appeared to belong there even if whatever it was could never belong to me.

Then I wandered through the graveyard. The headstones were all a bit skew-whiff and mottled with moss and fungus. They told little to nobody now. No recent burials but as in other graveyards I'd driven past, there was plenty of room left. Someone was keeping it tidy and though winter was not yet over there was a smell of mown grass in the air. There were several yew trees here and there which needed clipping in places but not all that much. Sparrows were hopping about and a few more colourful birds of about the same size. Closing my eyes, I realized how much chirping was going on. Then a real song started up which I now know was that of a blackbird. Another bird took it up, but differently, more showily – a thrush? Above, rooks wheeled about, frightened by something. Not long and we'd be into another April. I looked out across the flat fields. In one direction a tractor inched along. In another some cows were clustered and a horse stood apart, looking over a fence. I sniffed for the smell of the pig farm on the far side of the copse next to the field where the tractor was. But what little wind there was came from the opposite direction. For a moment or two I couldn't help imagining the turf had been stripped away and the earth piled up beside the graves in a sudden reverse upheaval of time, the bones laid bare with worms and insect life swarming through and around them. Then I had another look at the horse, still there though the cows seemed more closely crowded together.

Nothing new altering the landscape, I looked up at the sky where the main mass of clouds, flimsy and only tinged with black, was slowly approaching the sun. Not much wind up there either. A tattered forerunner had already reached it and a faint shadow slid across the graveyard, trailing sunlight behind it like a robe. I thought of the old font then and wished I could have my life all over again, as one does, wanting to be that tiny distance further away from the dead. Pure greed of course and who says I would have led a more uncorrupt life the second time round, if with a different range of better intentions. In fact if a second chance meant any of the hindsight becoming foresight it would probably have been that much more so, corrupt I mean. I felt as un-unique then as I had as a child. But that's probably only what graveyards do to you, especially when spring is in the air. My own skull would soon be indistinguishable from all the others, gaping skywards with that yell of terror or is it a quite uproarious laugh? I hurried home then, thinking that visiting churches, if you're not accustomed to it and don't know what to look out for, can be a dreadful mistake. Perhaps this is what I should end with – so different from where I last ended, in light-filled but shadowless pastures where there was no death at all, only an eternal meeting-up and reconciliation.

Chapter Two

Spring affected me in other ways: drawing attention to my lack of companionship for instance. I'd made several attempts at drafting something about myself for the 'Eye Love' column in *Private Eye* but found it extraordinarily difficult. The combination of choosiness and self-satisfaction does make for a certain unlikeability, and wouldn't you always be asking yourself how truthful the prospectus had been? When the witty non-smoker chewed gum non-stop between cracking stale jokes, the devilishly handsome stockbroker misinvested all your money, the ambitious, attractive female (22) looking for passion, friendship and romance could never make up her mind in what order, the shy Sidcup motorcyclist seeking a soulmate tinkered and revved all day and never said a word, or the uninhibited, versatile, virile, discreet, sensual, adventurous, dependable, generous, easy-going, reserved, intelligent, single community worker seeking fun-loving, solvent, slim, humorous, compatible, attentive, tolerant, successful, cuddly, quiet but dynamic dog-walking graduate with a passion for opera turned out to keep snakes or to fart a lot. There really is a terrific follow-up job to be done by some nosy psychologist doing research into ways of getting let down. All those outdoor activities, all that squash playing and mountain climbing, film- and theatre-going, wining and dining, my word what good times people are after out there and not getting, and what a job that universally required sense of humour must be having to keep on stream the caring, affectionate, sensitive aspect.

The best I could manage after more hours I shouldn't wonder than I've spent on this account so far was: 'Middle-aged man, single, house in the country, Rennie shareholder, top-heavy, flat-footed smoker, keen on at least some of the same things as you or you wouldn't be reading this, prefers indoors, never had a single drink in his life, churchgoer, tone deaf, snappy dresser, humour optional when the money runs out, immensely distinguished looking, perfect eyesight, likes poached eggs, antique furniture and watching other people gardening.' Not a word of untruth there except that I'm not all that flat-footed, have no views about furnishings and wouldn't know a Chippendale chair if I clambered up on to it to change a light bulb.

It was so awful, artful I believe the word is, that it could only prompt a reply from someone as desperate as I was in danger of becoming if I spent any more time on such self-regard and showing off. What else am I doing scribbling away like this if not to rid myself of all that? I didn't send it in of course, settling instead for: 'Once certified accountant. Early retirement. On his own. Cultivated. Small garden. Hobbies: Cooking. Books. Running. Rackets. Anti-smoking smoker. No particular tastes. Religion immaterial. Photograph optional. Any Takers?'

The first reply I got a week later was this:

Dear Box 1611

You do sound doubtful about yourself, don't you? Here's a photograph but I was younger and slimmer then. I'm writing this letter because this has not been a good day for me and I wouldn't dream of replying to any of the others. In fact, if you must know, I've never done this before. Anyway, my attributes don't seem to be what people expect.

I have a good job but I've always worked hard so I think I deserve it. I don't believe in people feeling sorry for themselves and the world owes them a living. I was very fond of a man once but he died. He was very clever at doing screeching tyres when he was driving and things like that. I was also married but not for long. I try not to be a misery. You don't crack jokes all the time, do you? There's a tenor in the choir does that but nobody thinks they're funny. It is very embarrassing. The man I went with said being a misery is worse, truthful maybe but not very becoming in a person if all your bits and pieces are in place and you're the right size and shape and not about to die. As he was then. He never looked for sympathy. I don't know any jokes really. He told me quite a few but I've forgotten them, that's the trouble, though I pride myself on my sense of humour. My doctor says there is nothing wrong with me and I never take pills. My main interest is classical music, especially vocal, and I sing soprano but only in a chorus. I vote for the Conservatives.

Yours sincerely,
Box 927
P.S. I'm the one with the bicycle.

She was at the centre of the photograph, leaning against a fence and holding a man's bicycle at arms' length. To one side was another woman standing in profile with her hand flat above her eyes, gazing high into the distance, perhaps at an aeroplane. Her face was thus invisible but her shape was well shown off. It was a summer's day, because they both wore flimsy-looking dresses and their shoulders were bare. The woman with the bicycle had her mouth open, not with laughter but displaying a gaiety she did not feel. I put the photograph to my nose and it smelt of lavender. Closer up, the face became care-free, the happiness genuine, but held at a distance again it now seemed the laugh was to attract attention to herself, a jolly good sport used to being left out of things. Perhaps the joke had to do with the sea, for I now realized that the shed in the background was a bathing hut and the fence was a breakwater. I looked at the face again, the dark hair blown across it, but could not tell how pretty it was. Breasts obviously biggish – she'd wanted me to notice that – and one knee bent across the other so as to narrow herself down there and not show too much of her legs. But why did she hold the bicycle away from herself like that? Because she knew the other woman's body, posing and flaunting itself, the dress wrapped round it by the wind, was what the picture was all about, and she was only there to set it off, imperfect and clumsy and learning not to care any longer.

I received other replies. They were all quite factual and were accompanied by passport-type photographs, leaving little to guesswork. They all looked helpless and eager but full of kindness. I thought of them sending these photos out all over the place for inspection by complete strangers to be judged against standards as high and irregular as a mountain range, to say nothing of their desires, only to be left grinning in the wings like dud competitors in a charm contest. They all had neat handwriting and their letters had obviously gone through several drafts, all the pains taken to please and impress. One said she would simply love to do the gardening but perhaps we could hire someone to do the heavy work. Another so preferred plain cooking. A third went on at length about hypnosis for giving up smoking and liked a good joke on a rainy day. The least attractive of them told me that looks weren't everything but that didn't mean one shouldn't dress smartly. And the prettiest and youngest told me she hated those 'muscleman types' and 'some of that music you're always hearing nowadays nearly drives me potty, I'm not kidding you.' Then there was the teetotal Christian who would remember me in her prayers and run with me laughing up the pathway to the sun. Finally there was the woman with thick glasses who told me how much she loved the feel of old things but up to now she hadn't been able to afford them. They all pleaded for my attention. I felt a shit after thinking for a while it was compassion.

I waited for a while before replying to Box 927, wondering if there might be more replies to come – people away on holiday in the south of France, that sort of person – so it was some six weeks before we finally met. In that time various other events occurred which I shall now try to relate so that the love-story element in this account is not as continuous as it ought to be. One wouldn't want to raise expectations, though, and no one would seize from the shelves a romance entitled *Tom and Maureen* (for that was her name).

In the meantime I attended the church and met a few more people but first another short interlude. The last time I had been to church was the Sunday before I finally left home to become a trainee clerk in the firm in which the bulk of my working (?) life has so far been spent. On one side of me, my mother had her arm through mine through most of the standing-up parts, but she did not cling for it was she who had urged me to get out while the going was good and make my fortune or God alone knew what it would make of me. On my left, my father cleared his throat much of the time, especially when he attempted to sing.

It was my mother who insisted we should mark my departure by a visit to the church where I had been christened and which she hadn't attended since. 'It's where you got your name when all's said and done,' she said. 'We couldn't agree on it. Had our doubts, you could say, so Thomas it was.'

'A right old fuss you made too,' my father added.

'No he didn't,' she replied. 'It was only after your breathing all over him or that ho-ho-hoo-ha vicar, creeping Jesus with hairy nostrils.'

My father used to sneak off to church sometimes, leaving his account books spread across the kitchen table as if to find something that added up for a change. So he knew the tunes even if he couldn't sing them, or only in throaty snatches. My mother stared ahead of her, grimly silent, as if she knew them only too well. The last hymn was about fighting the good fight. I remember that because my father sang loudly then as if suddenly reminded that courage was something he'd forgotten to tell me about.

We left for the station immediately after the service. After I'd kissed my mother, holding her for a couple of seconds before she pushed me away, my father put his arm round my shoulders, which he'd never done before, holding on through a spasm of asthma and finally managing, 'That's it then, lad. The shop'll be waiting for you if you ever want it, when you've got a bit of experience.'

'He'll need more than a bit of that,' my mother added with one of her rare smiles.

There were tears in his eyes, more than the asthma would have brought on, I told myself. My mother looked at me sternly, as if she expected me to disappoint her, just prove her wrong. 'Onward Christian soldiers then' were my father's parting words, apropos of nothing. 'Onward Christian fiddlesticks,' my mother added as I climbed on the train. When I'd found a seat I looked out of the window for them but they were already half-way to the exit. How happy it would have made me then to see them arm in arm but she was walking ahead of him and he was reaching in his pocket for something. It was as if nothing had ever happened to them, as if nothing ever could.

The last time I saw him he was in the hospital. The cancer had reached his bones and he lay very still, his hands hidden. It was as if he dangled there, letting go of his flesh so that it would never trouble him again, would stop reminding him of what couldn't hold it together much longer. I wished there was a hand I could lay mine on, just the once, now that the awkwardness would hardly notice alongside the rest of it. His face, always hollow and drawn, had thinned further, the skin slackening down from his eyes and mouth, enlarging them out of the last of their fragile certainties. I wondered if he knew how much he was staring at me as if making sure who I was. I thought how much his complexion resembled one of his favourite smooth, off-white cheeses with a Stilton effect in the hollows of his unshaven cheeks. Such thoughts one has at the end of things.

'I'm a goner,' he said, opening his mouth wide and biting it shut.

'Nonsense,' I said. 'They're going on with the treatment, aren't they?'

He flinched, parting his lips as if waiting to hear what the reply ought to be. 'Don't know what's worse. None of it's a laugh. Two ways of feeling bloody washed up, that's all. The shop. You don't want it, do you?' His voice was drowsy, each sentence broken up into words on the point of losing connection with each other.

'I'm not sure, Dad. Do you care that much?'

'All I mind is having to lay around here. Sodding whatsit, crawling about inside me.' He paused for a long time, searching around my eyes as if some fresh reason for living might be obtained there. 'Hanging about for the whole rotten shooting match to whizz off. In a million pieces.' He smiled fleetingly. 'That's a thought. Meanwhile little shops all over the world. Carrying on their business. Make more of it than what I did. Then you mightn't. Before you get carried off on a whizz of your own.'

'Mother could keep it on. Get someone in.'

He began pulling his hands from under the sheets but changed his mind and was still again. His face began to flicker but he slackened his jaw and the flickering stopped. His eyes moved to the window where it was beginning to snow. I thought how little I had seen them, how little he had ever looked at me and then only to check whether I was paying him any attention. And now I had no way of telling from them what I could ever hope to say that would make the slightest difference: there was anger within them suddenly and a disciplined pity for himself and a terrible envy of which he was ashamed. But it was so unsingular to him, to us, all of it. I looked down at the bed cover where his legs were shifting a little.

'She'll suit herself,' he said loudly. 'Doesn't help knowing this happens to everyone. One time or another. Don't you believe it. Snowing again, I see. Your mother never brings flowers. Not like the others. Only make me want to be outside. Watching them grow.' He gave a short laugh or cough and winced again, his eyes moving down to his body. 'Believe in the after-life, do you?'

'Oh yes, I should think so, Dad,' I lied.

'Buggered if I do. Your mother doesn't. Changed her mind when I took sick, though, didn't she? Sent the vicar to see me. New bloke. Didn't mention Jesus once, or the flesh. I should bloody well think not. Told me to take it easy.'

'Well, you shouldn't do anything daft, like rush off to church.'

It was my last little joke for him. He used to enjoy them, even the lavatory schoolboy kind I brought back from school, probably the same ones they'd told in his day. Perhaps it was because my mother told me she could do without my guttersnipe smut, thank you. This one was a flop. Will I ever learn the limits of humour?

'I'd fancy seeing the inside of a church again. That's one thing I'd really like. Some of the Bible and hymns and that. I used to like a good sing . . .'

He drowsed off then, his head slowly dropping away from me. It was then I laid my hand on his and felt it stir beneath the bedcover. And realized in that instant that my being there meant little to him, that I and my mother and the shop had never meant anything to him much. Or perhaps we had meant everything but it was nowhere near enough. I went down the corridor passing small groups of people coming the other way, some with tightly bunched flowers held close to their bodies as if it would be extravagant to part with them. There were also nurses in pairs, chatting cheerfully. How could it be that I didn't have a clue what mattered to my father, what he could not bear to lose?

The church was on the way to the station. I had time to spare but I didn't go into it. My mother was at her sister's in Leicester. There was singing coming out of it, a choir practice perhaps because they kept stopping and starting. It sounded out of tune to me and there seemed to be too many men for the women or boys. I imagined my father clearing his throat amongst them and hurried past. I had a long wait at the station because my train had been cancelled. I was impatient to get back to London, away from him, from the nothingness in his life, as though death was simply its continuance. I couldn't stop muttering the word to myself: Nothing, utter nothing. How much less could we have been to each other? I was also impatient to get back to the woman I later married, the chance, the certainty of going the whole way with her that night.

It turned out not to be. She said that with my father dying, the frame of reference, or was it in a sense the context, was somehow not apposite. I remember that because I misheard her, insisting that it was precisely because it was the opposite . . . so we stayed as variously close to each other as clothing permits while she tried to comfort me. I dreamt that night of being with my father in a vast church, a cathedral, filled with singing and sparkling with candlelight. We shared a hymn-book and with his spare hand he proudly gripped his lapel while he bellowed out the tunes, though I couldn't hear him, only the whole huge sound.

About two weeks later I heard he was dead. I did not tell my wife-to-be and that night we made love for the first time. Very apposite it was too, I don't mind telling you.

'How's your father?' she asked when it was over.

'Died about eleven hours ago as it happens.'

'Didn't you . . .' she began. 'Weren't you . . . ?'

'Not really,' I said. 'In fact I forgot all about him.'

'I should hope you had,' she said, hopping out of bed to make coffee but not getting far with that and soon returning for more.

'It won't be any good now,' I said. 'Now I've remembered.' But it was, it was longer and better and I begged him out loud to forgive me.

'For what?' she whispered, biting my ear. 'You were wonderful. We were both wonderful, weren't we?'

From then on it was plain sailing, into marriage and beyond, as I've recounted elsewhere – the seas never worse than choppy, she doing all the steering while I idled about in the cabin, drifting in the end onto the sandbanks and clambering out on opposite sides, she first while I stayed below poring over the charts. (My very own Tiller Girl was one of my secret names for her.) From that nothingness into very much something, not just anything, it was at first: love and a family, a house and a car etc.

I sometimes went up to see my mother where she lived with her sister in Leicester but she only came to stay with us once. She and my wife didn't get on at all. My wife tried to draw her out with a questionnaire about working-class life in the Midlands and I could see mother thinking she should mind her own business, once saying, 'I'm not a clever woman, you know.' She would never have commented on how we should bring up our children. She just watched them listening to the relentless enlightenment as if waiting for the end of a long-winded television programme. Several times, when the questioning became too persistent, she looked down at her knitting and muttered, 'It's not really for me to say, is it?'

My wife told me how much she admired her self-containment,

her sturdy sense of privacy and the like. My mother said how nice everything was but I don't honestly think she gave a damn one way or the other. Not once did she play or chat with the children, though on her last morning she bought them both two large bags of assorted sweets, a smug, overfed-looking doll for Virginia and a wind-up armoured car for Adrian.

'Don't know if you like this sort of thing,' she told them, not quite adding, 'And whose fault is it if you don't?'

For my wife she bought an expensive potted plant, an azalea I think it was. My wife said it was perfectly lovely, she shouldn't have and tried to embrace her. 'Should or shouldn't but there you are,' my mother replied, buttoning her cardigan up to her neck as if my wife's move towards her was a sudden puff of cold air.

The day before her departure was a Sunday and she offered to take the children to church.

'Oh no we *never* go to church, do we, Mummy?' Virginia said, her manners losing out to her righteousness, not for the first time.

'Never did anybody any harm so far as I know,' my mother said, unoffended.

'Well, there is a danger, a real sense in which . . .' my wife began.

I got in there pretty quick, as you might imagine. 'Good heavens, mother, you never used to be what I'd call a paid-up member of the Lord's Day Observance Society.'

'No more than I am now,' she said, almost smiling her thanks at me, a tiny instant of conspiracy. 'But there's plenty as are, they tell me.'

'Hocus-pocus house, isn't it, Mummy?' Virginia twittered on. 'Anyway, Dad never goes to church, do you, Dad?'

'I've tried, scores of times,' I said. 'But they wouldn't let me in. Enough sinners clogging up the system already.'

'What's a sinner, Mummy . . . ?'

'Nothing for you to worry about, dear,' my wife replied with stunning inaccuracy.

And so that conversation came to an end. My mother had already turned away, saying she would go for a nice little walk alone if we didn't mind. My wife and I watched her walk up the path. We said nothing at first. She looked sharply about her as if carrying out an inspection or seeing things for the last time, cataloguing them. It wouldn't have surprised me if she never came back.

Then as she turned the corner, my wife said, 'Sad.'

I did not reply. I saw no sadness there, not even loneliness. She even seemed rather pleased with herself. Having made up her mind about things, that to most of them she was indifferent, she was entitled to her little share of freedom. I wished I'd offered to go to church with her but she would probably have told me there was no need for that and not to be soppy and be my age.

And so it was that when I went to the village church that day I wished I was not alone. I arrived early and hung around by the font, running my hand over it again, then helped myself to a small fat red book and a thinner blue one, both with pages falling out and, as I discovered later, some missing. Give them another century or so and they'd be about the same colour, brownish-purple with paler patches where the cardboard had worn through. I then sidled along to the end of a pew at the back where there was a hassock. Impossible to tell what colours and patterns it might have had when new, freckled varieties of grey now and the stuffing knotty and flattened. All those shifting knees over the years, all those insects abandoning their nesting places. I leafed through the books as the others came in and took their places in pews nearer the front, putting their heads in their hands for a moment then sitting upright and gazing around at the windows as if to remind themselves they wouldn't have to stay there for long. I missed my father then, looking forward to having a good sing, missed him greatly, so that I heard myself say, 'Oh, Dad, what am I doing here and what were you thinking of, buggering off like that?'

About twenty people had gathered by the time the service started: the Colonel and his wife with two other, younger people (children down for the weekend?), Jenners and his wife and another woman, the couple from the village shop, Sidney on his own. In the first row were four elderly people, neat and well wrapped-up in greys and browns whom I haven't seen since. On the other side was a trio of grey heads similarly cropped and wearing loose spotty garments as if they'd been standing under a tree in a storm and bits of bark, twig and leaf etc. had settled on them. I remembered seeing two of them come out of the clinic when I was going in and hearing the Colonel's wife say, 'The local crafties, aren't they just too sweet?' Then there were five others who, at the time of writing, I've only seen once or twice since but not to speak to, including a couple in their Sunday best who had a stupefied look as though they rarely spoke to each other and had fetched up at last in a place where that no longer mattered. And finally there were two women and a man who were dressed for the golf course. They sat two rows in front of me and the man's hands in prayer had one thumb over the other which he twitched from side to side as if practising his short chip shots. The women whispered a lot and I thought I caught the words 'foursome', 'seventh' and 'open' though that may have had to do with finding their place in one of the books.

On top of everything else, the vicar played the organ and got a desperate noise out of it which largely concealed the little singing that was going on. I started off line one of the first hymn ('There is a book who runs may read' – an Optional Guide to Jogging?) on the high notes but dropped down among the others and beyond when two heads turned. I was alone too in not going up to the front for communion. On their way back they all glanced guiltily at me as if I'd caught them out doing something sham or sleazy, except for Sidney who gave me a semicircular wave in front of his plum-coloured waistcoat. I was in my board meeting charcoal grey pinstripe suit and my hand went to my neck to hide my floral yellow and mauve tie, the last gift of the lady who'd taken up with a banker or two. What had she said? Liven you up a bit? Give you a bit of colour? The sham and sleaze became my own.

These thoughts led nicely into the sermon whose text was 'Blessed are the poor in spirit'. In projecting his voice to the back, the vicar seemed to be addressing his remarks mainly at me. So far as I could tell, the drift of it was that we shouldn't think ourselves up to much because then we might find ourselves not really up to it while other people (God too) might start worrying about what we thought we were up to. Humility meant needing the Lord and losing the sense of self, moderation in all things, not trying to be sufficient unto oneself and generally avoiding show. These are the words I jotted down in the notebook I now kept on me, ending with 'our mediocrity in the world, our commonness' to which I added, 'Bad choice of tie, bet she got it off one of her Flash Harry moneybags, who do they think they are . . . ?'

While the collection was taken the last hymn was 'There is a green hill far away without a city wall.' It wasn't until the end that I stopped wondering what might be so distinctive about that. The collection was taken by the Colonel who hesitated before coming all the way along my pew just for me. Being the last, I could see what everyone else had given. Mine was the sole tenner. It was the only note I had in my wallet other than a one-pound note which I'd torn in half by mistake that morning in pulling it out past my expired credit card and which I'd stuck together with Sellotape. It was otherwise a filthy, crinkled thing and I'm pretty sure he shook his head when that was the one I seemed to be selecting. He left me in no doubt about the pleasure the tenner gave him, giving a quick nod and smile as though we'd come through a lot together. It occurred to me that as an acting lance-corporal in the Pay Corps I might once have calculated his pay. But now we were pretty much other ranks together in the eyes of the great Commanding Officer in the skies, to say nothing of having had similar signals at the clinic from the Grim Reaper.

For a while he stood beside me waiting for the right moment, his fist pressed against his mouth trying to control a cough. Then with a final bark, he pulled my donation from the edge of the plate to the top of the pile and marched back down the aisle with it, the plate held out far in front of him as if to show what a splendid example I'd set.

I was the first into the porch where the vicar was waiting for me. He questioned me briefly ('Settling in all right, are we? How *nice* to see you.'), enough to cause a bottleneck and two unnecessary introductions: the Colonel and Jenners. I escaped down the path and was struggling with the gate which only needed a shove (it turned out) when the Colonel caught up with me and invited me along for a drink, introducing me by their Christian names to his son and daughter-in-law who fell behind with him, leaving me to lead the way along the grass verge with his wife. Behind me I heard father and son talking in code about types of weaponry, that or the roads around the camp where the son was stationed. Then they got on to Northern Ireland. 'No end in sight there,' the Colonel said. 'In our line of work, never is,' the son replied.

I listened for the daughter-in-law to speak, for the voice to go with the face, of which more anon. Meanwhile the Colonel's wife was saying with that nasal, plaintive American voice, 'Do I miss it? We met in Washington and now, look, as far as the eye can see . . .'

I said I knew what she meant but one had to end up somewhere – something like that as she charged on ahead and had to turn round several times to see if I was still within earshot. 'I was a hostess, public relations, if you can believe it, all social whirl, my gush, the propositions I had, you wouldn't believe. Men in uniform are the worst, or the best, depending . . . then that gorgeous British accent and twinkle in the eye. So here we are. I absolutely adore it, part of the time anyway, spent talent or whatever, roots put down but withering . . .'

She went on like this, tossing her blonde- or grey-streaked brass-coloured hair and showing me several aspects of her tanned or coated face which moved so much I couldn't decide how attractive she still was, had been rather: but little doubt about that, given her tall and striding shapelessness, large daring eyes though surrounded by too much adornment at any rate for the open air, and well-fleshed lips which, barely added to, the web of wrinkles converged on to little avail.

We arrived at the house up a side road ahead of the others who lingered in the front garden, as well they might on that early spring day, so various and ordered it was, with shrubs etc. arrayed in multi-shaped beds, two dazzling white wooden seats, a gleaming lawn and trimmed trees. All this glimpsed from the french window where she soon brought me a gin and tonic. Or that is what I asked for and it tasted much like it, though it had a yellow tint to it and the two slices coming apart round the circular ice cubes looked more like tangerine. A shortage of fizz too.

The others then started to arrive. Jenners engaged me in conversation, or rather I overheard him talking at the garden about trade and industry but, two years into retirement, he told me several times, the old brainbox was beginning to rattle a bit. He seemed to be holding me personally responsible for something that I ought to have realized long ago. Keeping my end up, I mentioned the take-over and he nodded sagely as if he knew the American company well, though twice mispronouncing it.

His wife came and stood beside him, a small woman whose short steely hair had a much-patted look. Her mouth twitched as if still getting used to not answering back. 'Perhaps, dear, Mr Ripple doesn't want to hark back, do you, Mr Ripple?' she said in a voice several tones lower than her husband's and twice as fast. She squinted at my chin or tie, fearing the worst there too.

Then our hostess came over, followed by the estate agent. 'Being anti-American again, is he?' she said.

Jenners made a gasping face. 'Ooh no, need you far too much for that. Necessity the mother of affection.'

He gave a long, booming laugh, tilting his drink so that some of it splashed on to the carpet, then stooped and dabbed at it with his handkerchief, spilling more in the process. I knew from what little furnishing I'd bought over the years that it was the most expensive carpeting you can buy, an inch thick and as close to pure white as something walked on can get. Mrs Jenners hurriedly left the scene making a chirping noise and Sidney said, 'Didn't know bureaucrats could stoop so low. Your obedient servant . . .'

Jenners grunted and our hostess waved her hand in the air and crooned, 'Oh do leave it please. These new carpets so washable, don't you find . . . ?'

The Colonel joined us with his son and daughter-in-law, frowning down at Jenners and saying to me, 'Piddling come and meet some people.' And led me away by the elbow to meet the trio who'd been in the front pew of the church.

They ran the crafts centre he explained, but no need to tell me that since they had about them a fair range of the crafts they might be involved in: frilly leather purse, chunks of jewellery, wicker bracelet and woven tie which might have been a strip of unfinished rug. There were clay stains on their sleeves which were unusually long and frilly or frayed, almost hiding hands held tranquilly between breast and navel though in the case of the women it was difficult to be sure. It was one of them who wore the tie and the man the bracelet. They were telling me I was welcome to visit the centre at any time and why didn't I sign up for a course? The Colonel passed by us several times and looked at their shoes and the powdery sheddings round them, thinking no doubt this mightn't be a good day for the new carpet. The shoes, if not home-made originally, had had things done to them over the years and might be aiming in a few more to become sandals. In the meantime the holes could be filled with bits of clay or tufts of wool sprouting through them from the socks beneath.

They were telling me how sensible I was to be getting away from it all and what an opportunity it was to do something creative when the Colonel's son joined us and said, 'Back to nature. I'm all for it, doing your own thing, working with your hands . . .' He petered out then, looking uncomfortably spruce with his probably regimental tie, dark grey suit, suede shoes and general neatness around the head.

Then he smartly pulled himself together, looked one of the women straight in the eye and said, 'Did your husband, I mean, did he always, or was it something you came to late, after, I mean, having a bash, sort of, were into something else?'

Both women looked at him, or rather most of the way up at him, and gaped in slightly different ways. The man, who was the one with the beard, watched them patiently, expecting them to get it right. Then the one with the widest sample of attachments said, 'Oh he's not anyone's partner nowadays, are you, Geoffrey? Or are you?'

'Having a bash,' the other woman said. 'We keep ourselves *far* too busy for anything of that sort.' At which she gave a squeak and moved all parts of her face as if to rearrange the inside of it.

The young soldier blushed and the man said, 'What he meant was, did I ever work in a bank and chuck it all up? Not quite. Used to design conveniences and the like for the London Borough of Camden.'

While they explained in turn, mainly to each other, how things had come about, I noticed the young soldier's wife appearing beyond his shoulder. We grinned at each other. Nothing nicer had happened to me all week, or longer: the hint of mischief in the eyes (grey? green?) and the strands of honey-pale hair straggling down across her lashes and the tongue that touched the gap between her two front top teeth – enough of trying to pin all that down, though vivid as anything could be, even now; to say nothing of the guesswork that was going on too about what was infinitely alluring further down. Yet there was a weariness about her and I wondered if it was of anything more specifically nasty than life.

I turned to her husband who was recovering with talk of Salisbury Plain and said indistinctly, 'Keep your filthy hands off her or you'll see what you will see' – this not interrupting a set of opinions about hippies and Stonehenge. I looked for her again but she had gone out into the garden where she joined the vicar and one of the golfers who was looking at his watch. Just beyond the french windows the Colonel was drawing the estate agent's attention to something in the garden and saying, 'Better get a move on . . . What was that you said? . . . Pig-shit, get used to anything.'

His wife meanwhile was a few yards away with Jenners and they seemed to be talking mostly at the same time about Vietnam or tourism, very politely disliking each other intensely while Mrs Jenners blinked from one to the other as if they were discussing revolution in a language she was beginning to learn from a phrase-book.

The vicar came to join us, starting a long way off, 'And how are the cottage industries doing these days? What an assorted little congregation we are to be sure. Grimshaw over there, scratch golfer, yachtsman, video rental I think he said, not forgetting those who allow us to sleep soundly in our beds at night.' He turned towards me and finding nothing to add there, went on, 'Four senior citizens from the next parish at church too today, isn't that nice? Saw Buckley's photograph in *The Times* on Saturday, record profits, no he goes to St Mary's. Sometimes. And then the omnipresent God-botherer . . .'

One of the craftswomen was explaining about government grants and youth schemes which prompted the Colonel's son to say something loosely in praise of, or hopeful about, Mrs Thatcher. The rest, who now included the Colonel's wife and a female golfer on her way out made conflicting sounds and faces, so the vicar took over, rapidly at first, then slowing down, 'On the whole, it's been the party that binds us to custom, not much time for ideas. What do I mean by that? The other lot, well, holier than thou sometimes, even than Him.' He pointed at the ceiling. 'Knowing what's best for one and all, you see . . .' He wagged his finger at me. 'You see, takes away from responsibility for oneself a bit, doesn't it, thinking we'd do better, be better, if the common good were *required*, a lot of equalizing up or down depending where you're looking from that's, well, flattening, dispiriting, can be? Whereas this lot, they think they know what makes most people tick, and the awful thing, the Christian thing is, that they're right, sheer greed for starters. Take the seven deadly sins now . . . no, that's going a bit far, some public morality has to be imposed of course, otherwise . . . So privatizing everything, including morality, I'm not at all sure . . . Interesting thought that. Not for a moment, don't get me wrong, do I believe that compassion, justice, that sort of stuff, co-operation, shouldn't be at the centre of things. There's no *competing* for places in the Kingdom of Heaven, now is there? Helpful, perhaps not . . . ? Difficult subject, one reads the thinkers, Mill, Rousseau, Paine, Burke . . .'

These last two names (looked up since) were spoken to me, then the young soldier, making us fiddle with our ties while the others wore that concentrated look of inattention associated with sleep-walking. Seeing he'd lost us and fearing it might be for good, the vicar gabbled to his conclusion, 'God preserve me no. Politics and original sin, you won't tempt me into those treacherous waters. Pelagianism, you're thinking. No, no, the Church must keep its distance, don't you think so, Mr Ripple?'

I took over his desperation. 'I can't imagine for an instant any of my sins have been original in the slightest but if you'd like to run a check . . .'

The young soldier obeyed his own command to smile and the craftspeople exchanged glances, deciding if any humour might be allowed in just yet or if it counted as that. Then one of the women said, 'Can't abide the bloody woman myself,' and the vicar swiftly went back to talking about the Church.

I escaped at this point, hoping to find the young soldier's wife alone but there was no sign of her and I said a few goodbyes. In the hallway I found Sidney rummaging through the pockets of the overcoats. 'Sodding fags,' he said.

'Don't use them myself,' I replied, taking my raincoat from the rack with his hand still in it. If he wasn't drunk he was taking pains not to show it. In tugging his hand out of my raincoat and delving into another, he said, 'They got this place for a song. I could go for Mrs Yank, couldn't you? Bit of a nympho, wouldn't surprise me. How you can stand that willy wet-leg ponce of a sky pilot Christ alone knows . . . Oh well . . . How's the cottage? Bumped into Nanny Phipps on the staircase, have you, or aren't you into ghosts as the wanker said to the lecher. Does things to me that woman. Jig-a-jig with the Brig, doesn't bear thinking about. Slope arms! About turn! Roger! Out! As for the daughter . . .'

I became aware of the Colonel hovering by the entrance to the drawing room so I raised a hand to him and left Sidney to talk to himself, still rummaging. 'Sodding fags,' he continued to mutter. More than a few feet away his words were inaudible and he seemed to be clearing his throat by numbers. I closed the front door and there, half-way down the front path, looking down at a flowerbed where there was nothing to see but soil, was the young soldier's wife. She delayed moving aside just long enough to encourage me to say, 'When might we see you in these parts again?'

'It'll be a while, I'm afraid. We're posted to Germany next week.'

The world-weariness I thought I'd detected was in her voice too, close up like that pepping me up no end.

'That's not far. The odd long weekend, with the folks, churchgoing, this lovely garden. Nice to know it's always there . . .'

She shrugged and sighed, a brief impatience with me, and why not? 'It's not that simple, is it?' she said.

Which could have been worse, unlike what occurred next as she parted her hair with two fingers, first one side then the other, and tossed it back, her face wholly unhidden then, the eyes clearly light blue, the mole on her chin, the moustache, where the lips puckered and eyebrows faintly joined, becoming the past almost at once, the remembered blemishes of a forgotten perfection.

'*Auf wiedersehen*. And have a good journey. I won't attempt to translate that.'

She made a face but there wasn't what you'd call much of a smile in it. 'I'm sure I will. And I hope you like your life here.'

'It's been with me so long I'm beginning to get used to it,' I said with the old wail having its say as I glanced back to see her husband and father-in-law looking up at the top of a cedar tree where a branch had torn away. We looked up at it too.

'Goodbye, then, and try to be happy,' I said, moving on slowly, my hands deep in my pockets and very clenched.

'Goodbye,' she replied and turned to her menfolk with a quite different smile from the one she'd given me, not having to pretend goodwill at all.

That was written up not long afterwards. It gives some idea of the village life I was avoiding and why I decided not to go back to the church on any regular basis. From other jottings at the time, I seem to have dwelt a great deal on the past and crossed most of it out. The trees were coming into leaf and my garden was beginning to show what little it was capable of. I made several trips to the garden centre and bought the smallest variety of rotary mower. I enjoyed each new day because in early spring there is always something fresh to observe and listen to out there. The thing is not to take your eyes and ears off it for too long because then you start remembering it's all happened before, it won't have anything new to say, as it were. But generally it was all right then. I read some exciting thrillers and there was some pretty good television at the time – that sort of thing.

About a week later I answered the doorbell one afternoon to find the Colonel standing there.

'Ah, there you are. Good. Thought I'd drop by to see if there's anything, you know, hope you wouldn't hesitate . . .'

'Won't you come in? Cup of tea, drink, please do.'

'No, thanks frightfully. Agnes gone ahead to the shop. Sure there's nothing, only have to ask . . . ?'

He turned to study my garden, about one-fifteenth the size of his, then looked up at the sky which held his attention for far longer but there was nothing noteworthy going on up there either: more cloud than blue but not by much, though covering the area where the sun might have been. He sniffed and I noticed how the untrimmed top of his moustache had joined up with the bristles inside his nostrils. For a moment his pose was commanding, then he closed his eyes suddenly and opened them, looking lost. Perhaps something high and wide out there had reminded him of other times, the smack of rifles on a parade ground, manoeuvres on a rain-swept moorland. He recovered, like somebody adjusting his lapels after being shoved to one side. He turned back towards me, his pale eyes still puzzled but there wasn't going to be any damn nonsense about working out why.

'Garden not up to much yet, I'm afraid,' I said. 'Sure you won't come in?'

'Nice little place. Queer old cove in black used to live here. Saw you coming and turned her back on you. Thing is, when one's been around and about, can get a bit lonely. Hustle and bustle one day, sky and silence and bugger all the next if you get my drift. Anyway, just drop by, we'd like that.'

I went up the path with him. He walked straight-backed, chin up as he had in the church, his gaze not taking in anything below the horizon.

'That's very kind of you. The same goes for me. But you'd only come for the PG Tips, not the gardening kind.'

We had reached the gate and he looked down the road towards the pub which was hardly that any longer, though it still served drink to go with the shrunk billiards, noise machine and usual pub smells, these barely perceptible now, the door to the gents having been taken away for repair in the early days of the Attlee government perhaps and never replaced.

'There's the wife, I think,' he said but still lingered.

'Son and daughter-in-law safely arrived in Deutschland, I trust?' I asked.

'My word,' he said, putting a hand on my arm and letting it rest there, 'you didn't think . . . He's the in-law. Poor old Susie, no escaping it, was there, the army life? Attractive little so-and-so, isn't she? Her mother would have much rather . . . Still he's not a bad egg, not such a bad egg at all. There she comes now. Doesn't she move . . . ? Quite a gal, years younger than me of course. Noticed, have you, how fit some Americans are? Can't imagine why she tumbled for a thicko like me. We're going to walk back the long way round, might catch a lark or two in Hodgson's pasture, they don't notice the pig-shit, birds. Work up an appetite, thirst hard to quench without a good few goes at it.'

'Very kind of you to call,' I said finally, then had to add, 'Hope things work out all right on the Rhine. Could be further, more dangerous. Get leave often, do they?'

'Dear Susie. Always was a charmer . . . oh well,' was all his reply as he marched off to meet his wife, raising his hand high above his head about twenty yards away as if to stop a sudden surge of heavy traffic.

Perhaps I could jump ahead a little here. The next time I saw his daughter was at his funeral service, which can wait until later. I mention it now because recounting the above now that he is dead, I see him in other surroundings and now blind to mine. In the notes I made that evening there is nothing about him looking skywards for the sun and I'm not at all sure how much he said about his daughter. I met him several times afterwards, not knowing how little time was left to him. On three or four occasions it was in their garden where Agnes, as I shall now call her, touched me and brushed up against me a fair amount, but in full view of him. He didn't mind. The last occasion she wasn't there, having returned to see her folks in the States. On another occasion he told me what a shame it was I'd just missed his daughter by a couple of hours. Something about her had saddened them because they changed the subject (to the song of larks, as it happens) when I asked how she was. Saddened wasn't the word for me as I stood by the mantelpiece where there was a photo of her

202

as a teenager steering a boat, on the Norfolk Broads perhaps. They say that photography is faithful. If that is so, it is likely she has known no greater happiness before nor since, unless somebody had just told her a tremendously good joke. Anyway, the point I want to make is that much of this, though finishing off what will probably turn out to be the second chapter, was written near the end, to distract me from an unhappy lunch I'd just had with my son, so it may be tainted with untruth, a kind of apology to the less and less memorable, to what I tried to make of it at the time. Of course I could go on imagining about Susie and her father to my heart's content, but that's hardly the point.

Chapter Three

Now, I think, Nanny Phipps, my daughter and Maureen in that order.

To judge from the state of the cottage, Nanny Phipps had left a long time before and all that remained of her was an old leather suitcase in the cupboard under the stairs. Needing the space, I reminded Sidney of it more than once. He gave me a phone number but nobody answered. 'Just chuck it out if I were you,' he said finally. 'Where she's gone, among the angels or creepy-crawlies, she won't be needing her bits and pieces there.' But it was in excellent condition so I decided to keep it after getting rid of its contents.

These consisted of a plain black dress, two aprons, several china ornaments of domestic animals, a broken travelling clock wrapped in tissue paper, three gilt or gold-coloured photograph frames with no photographs in them, a maroon shawl, a prayer-book, a Bible, a necklace made of seashells, a pair of thick-heeled ankle boots with one heel higher than the other and the laces missing, a willow-pattern saucer wrapped in a yellow silk scarf, some children's storybooks, a small hip flask, a mauve cellular blanket and a photograph album.

I took the album into my 'study' and slowly went through it. The photographs were mainly of three children growing up over a period of six years against a background of a garden, a three-storey house and the seaside. Their names were Sarah, Lily and Harry in that order. Sometimes there were adults in the picture, clustered self-consciously for a christening or some other get-together, but usually it was just the children, doing the usual things and appearing happy: on a swing, holding a new toy, fondling a dog or cat or rabbit, coming from a swim, dancing in a sprinkler, standing on their heads, dressed up, on a bicycle or tricycle etc. All the pictures were slightly blurred and tilted as if taken by a bad camera on the spur of the moment. The most indistinct were of Sarah on her own. She always had her head on one side and squinted or frowned as if facing the sun.

(Looking through the album reminded me I had no photographs of my own children growing up and I wondered why – I mean, photographs were taken but I had no idea what had become of them, no memory of the camera with which they were taken either. So I looked with envy at these clumsy black-and-white snapshots, each neatly labelled in white ink with names and a date. And yet not, because the more past I had to dwell on, the less time I would spend doing other things, surrendering even more of my decrepit grip on life to the passing of time, to an incontinence of the imagination, the dribbling on and on of it and there's no prostate operation you can get done on that.)

There was only one picture of Nanny Phipps herself. She was wearing a black dress, perhaps the one in the suitcase. Underneath it was written: 'Sarah, Lily and Harry. 7th May. With Yours Truly. Flower-gathering!!!' She was standing with her back against a big, knobbly tree in a meadow and was holding a large bunch of what looked like weeds. The two girls were sitting cross-legged at her feet with wide mock-smiles, each holding up a long stalk with which they seemed to be tickling their nostrils. Harry was standing to one side making a fierce face at the camera and throwing something at it which created a small cloud around Nanny Phipps's midriff. It was her face that held my attention: offended and stern, as though the person behind the camera had no business there, interrupting a nature ramble. I put the album back in the suitcase with the other stuff but kept out the Bible and prayer-book. They were bound in black leather which overhung the gold-edged pages. Inside them she had written 'Beatrice Phipps' in a large bold hand but there was no date. They were beautiful, weighty things and I put them on my bookshelf where they looked reproachful next to the paperback thrillers etc. They are still there. It is not that I stole them. When I finally returned the suitcase, I forgot to replace them, that is all. I look through them from time to time, particularly the prayer-book, trying to find there the consolation etc. which Nanny Phipps had found. There's some astonishing language there, plain but with a grandeur to it. They don't write like that nowadays so far as I know, but if they did people would think they were coming it on a bit strong. Perhaps there just isn't the same confidence about.

Mid-April now and my daughter has just been to see me, dropped off for the night by a fiancé who had business in Ipswich. She was more her mother's child than mine, which I say without resentment, my son likewise. This meant, again in brief, that they were actually brought up, they didn't just amble unescorted through adolescence into adulthood as they would have done if I'd had any non-say in the matter. Even now I have no opinions really about the rearing of children (other than keeping up with them at a sensible distance: a long reign but slack, if you get me) and I certainly wouldn't want anyone to bear my imprint for life. (My wife had very definite views, but then she had read a large number of books on the subject and knowledge confers the right to know better than those without it, I suppose. Otherwise, what's it for? Just to remind: my speciality was commercial statistics and overseas markets etc. and that is fat all use to children unless in persuading them to start saving up now for their escape in later years to foreign parts from one long rainy day.) Any imprint, I should add, beyond having been loved go though that did with a lot of getting let down. Hardly an opinion that, merely evidence of love in having sometimes reflected on it, not in itself but what it has a right to expect of others. Anyway, I don't want to go over all that again, other than to sketch out why my daughter was neither that much for me nor against me. In this area, flesh and blood aren't all that vital, not in my experience. Coming to see me was the decent thing to do if it could be conveniently fitted in. For the rest I must refer you to what I've written elsewhere.

I hadn't seen her for about eighteen months. She did her speech therapy training at the City of Birmingham Polytechnic, followed by an MA in Speech Sciences at Leeds. When she came to London she only had time to visit her mother or I was on one of my trips and, whatever I may have written earlier to boost my morale, she had no time for the woman I took up with when my wife left me. (The one, remember, who will now be active round and about the City of London getting her share of the Big Bang.) However, she did phone me from time to time, reversing the charges, whenever she needed money off me . . . a rotten thing to say. I wish I hadn't said that but I've just remembered the research I once did into the close connection between unusually large entries in my telephone bill and the letters OD in my bank account. Don't get me wrong. I didn't mind that. The bigger the bill the more chatting we'd done and there's no limit to what one owes one's children if all one has to give them in the end is money. Having her feel grateful to me was a lot better than having her feel nothing at all. I always gave her more than she asked for, therefore, so she probably thought me a soft touch too. And that's all right, in this general realm anyway.

The other notion I let run on a bit as their car sped up the motorway (other than worrying about safety belts and the like) was that they think less of you (speaking temporally) than you think of them. And why not, their becoming more and more of your past the less and less future you have and your becoming less and less of their future as that turns into their past with others increasingly in it crowding you out? And while I was about it I could remove those two words in brackets in my case, for my life (doing my bit to keep Britain tidy) was not littered with achievement exactly. Not that love is affected by opinion, though opinion can be rendered senseless by love.

The house was looking quite nice, or at least orderly – the fifty or so paperbacks lined up on the shelf between Bible and prayer-book, an extra effort in the garden, a good dust, hoover and wipe everywhere, even a roaring fire or as close to that as one of those imitation gas jobs can look. I met them at the gate, kissed my daughter and shook her fiancé's hand. The only impression I formed of him was that he was forming an impression of me in comparison with what he'd been led to expect: respect, say, for his future father-in-law getting overtaken almost at once by wondering what there might be to be respectful about. His car indicated he and/or his firm were doing all right thank you. There were a lot of tapes and other paraphernalia around and among the equipment that enabled him to drive the thing safely which I took a closer look at. Nothing else being said, I tried a joke.

'Got it all taped, I see. Music to your gears.' No good that, so far as I could tell, so I went further, 'Give us a brake.'

That was even worse but it helped Virginia to snicker and punch me lightly on the arm and say, 'Oh, Dad, you don't change.' Then she kissed me hard on the cheek and all other thoughts slunk away into the shadows as the good times flooded back, sadly under-recorded, when I said it was all right then. The only thought left, in short, was: this is my beloved daughter and he is clearly a sane, honourable, decent sort of bloke, kind and conscientious and a sense of humour isn't everything – if he can't joke his way out of difficulties he is less likely to get himself, or her, into them in the first place, and he will care for her, attentive to a fault, so long as that doesn't mean his hands coming anywhere near her. One of which filthy objects I grasped limply before the revolting lecher got back into his machine and sped off on his way to Ipswich.

Going up the path, Virginia looked around the garden and said, 'Nice, Dad. Don't see much though to have a swipe at with your badminton racket.'

And so she remembered that from all those years ago and we kept along those lines: the Webbs and Hambles, our neighbours in north London, the day in the park, visiting her in hospital after her accident, and her mother of course and how was she rubbing along these days, by the way?

She told me about speech therapy and the job she'd applied for at a hospital convenient for the Bakerloo Line. She'd been the best student in her final year, she said without boasting, and her MA thesis might become a book one day. To give the gift of speech was a privilege, she said, but she wondered if she had the patience, the detachment from unshareable pain. We looked each other in the eye (which we hardly ever used to do because of a new stye or worry or unreal hopes of me I might discover there), so I gained a good idea of the sort of person she had become, outrageously beyond the range of the chap with all that stuff in his car or anyone else for that matter. (Bloody reclining seats the thing had too.) During a commercial break while I poured more drink, she said she was sorry she hadn't been better about keeping in touch. I said I'd drink to that if she'd do the same on my account. Which helped to start things going wrong, there being some obvious joke there I didn't make.

'And your mother,' I asked. 'Still putting the world to rights?'

'She's getting quite a reputation. Do you read the *Guardian*?'

'Certainly not. Well, not all that often. It makes me feel I shouldn't be let loose on the world without it.'

'She's written twice in that. Has a book coming out.'

'You must be proud of her. And she of you.'

'She sends her love. Her bloke sits there puffing his pipe and nodding. I can't make him out. As if he knows everything already but isn't letting on.'

'I know, wisdom is like that. Anyway, give her my love back. It was hers in the first place.'

She laughed, turned the sound down a bit further, then came right out with it. 'Dad, you wouldn't have the odd bob or two to spare, would you? A thou or two or whatever? The down payment's murder. We'd pay you back . . .'

That Suffolk currency again. I did a series of things. First, I waved my arms high and wide as if to say: this is all I have, the accommodation I stand up in. Then I took out my handkerchief and pretended to sob into it. Then I flipped a fifty-pence piece on to the table. Then I looked at my wrist without the watch on it and muttered something about the pawnbroker. Then I took a stub of cheroot from the ashtray and relit it. And meanwhile did some quick calculations and cursed myself for all that maudlin introspection while they sped down the motorway, instead of preparing my magnanimity the moment we were alone, thus: OK Virginia, you're getting married, I know how killing these down payments are. Can't spare a lot but would you settle for X, one doesn't get married every day of the week . . . And then all the chat and old jokes etc. wouldn't have been leading somewhere, have later seemed to have been. What I said was, 'Of course, whatever I can but . . .'

'Every little counts,' she replied and came and kissed me before going off to bed, this time on top of my head or rather just above my hairline, not so as you'd know the difference.

'We haven't talked about Adrian,' I said. 'What line is your mother taking? He'll be needing the odd thou too in time . . .'

'Eventually, perhaps,' she said, not quite adding, 'When it's his turn.' The old shirtiness was in her voice, or what higher education had turned it into: perfunctoriness? (Thank you again, Monsieur Roget).

So I stayed up with a glass in my hand, hearing her run a bath, walk about overhead, then settle down after several spasms of creaking and indecision which echoed my own. By the time I tiptoed up to bed, sliding myself up the stairs with my back to the wall, I had persuaded myself that all that mattered was that she was there again under my roof and if you can't ask your old Dad for a bob or two and she really was somebody and I couldn't take it with me and I wish she hadn't had to ask and who did she think I was, Arishtotle Onashish?

(I tried these last lines on Maureen the day she came to visit. She didn't find them funny. She asked me about my children and told me

I was luckier than I knew. She didn't ask how much I gave Virginia in the end. I explained I wasn't really drunk but in writing up her visit soon afterwards, I could see the lighter side. I didn't want her so soon to expect too much of me.)

So what is the truth? Now, some time later, I can say calmly that the next morning I wrote her out a cheque and haven't seen her since. She has phoned me a few times, the last time to tell me she was pregnant. The previous time she told me about the semi they'd bought and they'd love me to come and see it. Perhaps this is how I should end this second account of my life so far, with a bit of unfinished business, a threshold of the future? However, to continue with what I wrote at the time about the following morning.

Her fiancé was due at about ten and she came down to breakfast shortly before nine. I had it all ready: a choice of grapefruit and orange juice, several cereals, fried eggs, bacon, tomatoes, toast, coffee, a table laid with a table-cloth, napkins in rings, cups with matching saucers. A cup of herbal tea and half a slice of brown bread would do fine, she said.

'Is that your whole meal then?' I quipped.

But her smile was wan until underneath her cereal bowl she spotted my cheque at which she stared for rather a long time before coming round the table to give me a squeeze, but no kiss this time. I had no idea what she was thinking. Was it much more or much less than she'd bargained for? From counting the noughts perhaps, she wore what must be meant by a nonplussed expression.

'Good old Dad,' she said eventually. 'What can I say, thanks a lot.'

Had the squeeze been perfunctory too, or not? She went to the kitchen to make the tea and called through to me about a house they had their eye on in Colindale, mentioning the astonishing price more than once. When she was back opposite me, I changed the subject by remarking to myself that first thing in the morning was not her time of day: eyes narrowed by the swellings under them, hair which showed which side she'd mostly slept on, and that brief squeeze had told me that brushing her teeth still came after breakfast, something else I hadn't taught her. Coming down the stairs, her limp wasn't improved by not wearing shoes, and the stretched greyness of her face in the morning light, with pink patches here and there like signs of skin trouble, gave the impression of drugs no longer counteracting

210

pain. Again, glad to have a proper breakfast to keep my hands and eyes occupied, I was not looking at her much as she began talking about her Richard, his prospects and the like, but mainly about his widowed mother who didn't have two pennies to rub together because, roughly speaking, her two other children were always having them off her.

'... so poor Richard is always having to shell out. It gets him down and means he drives himself too hard. Still, we'll manage.'

'You'll go on working, will you?'

She nodded and made a face or was it just tongue clearing crumbs from gums? Then she scratched between armpit and waist. 'We'd like to start a family some time, when we can afford it.'

Two questions were swilling loosely about in my mind now. What had her mother given her – two healthy salaries there – but how to ask that without the risk of hearing a sum I hadn't matched? And secondly, there was the envisaging of Richard – his uprightness, his coming into his own and having to work too hard – so that by the time I'd finished my second fried egg I was seeing not the house she was telling me more about, nor the farm implements he sold, but his entering her room and beginning to unzip his trousers . . . No, I mustn't exaggerate. They were already off along with everything else and he was driving himself too hard, her beloved Dick . . .

'... by the sound of it,' I heard myself saying, 'he's doing all right, really getting stuck in . . .'

'... it takes a lot out of him,' she was adding.

'... you must both get pretty shagged.'

I was getting up then to take my plate to the kitchen when we heard his car draw up. We went out together to meet him, the day swarming and fluttering with sunlight. While he and Virginia were being affectionate, I took another look at his car, surely having had an expensive wash and a polish since the previous evening? I took out my hanky, gave it a shake and flicked it over the gleaming cedar-green boot.

'Just thought I detected a speck of dust,' I said with a chummy grin, taking him by the elbow to steer him to the front gate and offering him coffee and leftover grapefruit, etc. Anyway, he didn't seem pleased, because he shook his shoulders free of his neck and a flush appeared under his ears and jaw, though it might have been there already of course.

'It's a company car,' he said plaintively.

Virginia put her arm through his, briefly laying her head on his upper arm and saying, 'But it might just as well be yours, darling.'

That soothed him at once. 'I like to look after it, the more so because it isn't.'

'Did you have a successful trip?' she asked.

'So so,' he replied. 'Mustn't complain.'

I went ahead to plug in the kettle which too soon (not soon enough) drowned out what I strained to hear them whispering about in the drawing room. She was telling him, naturally – too bloody naturally if you ask me – about my cheque. I joined them with the coffee. Virginia still had her arm through his and was smiling happily, the fresh air having done wonders to her complexion or, on reflection, thrilled to bits by the cheque. None of that, of course, just profoundly content to be with her man again. His expression was very similar. They were both staring at me so I was glad of the tray of coffee cups to put down somewhere after pushing the *TV Times* and a couple of paperbacks out of the way and removing a dirty glass with a third of a whisky and soda still in it. Time now to put all matters right, be pally, fatherly and the rest. Hard this, because while back in the kitchen to fetch the sugar I heard more whispers and a treble ts sound which might have been kisses, oh well, or a verdict on my stinginess. Giving them their coffee, offering them milk, then sugar, were rigmarole enough to keep my voice steady.

'It's marvellous to see you both. Hope you can make a habit of this. East Anglia on the up and up. So so today, reap reap tomorrow . . .'

He responded eagerly. 'Oh yes, Mr Ripple, I'm sure you're right. The agricultural support industries have a great future. I think I may say that your daughter and I are confident we can build a good life together.'

'First a tractor, then fertilizer eh?' I ventured. Virginia spotted that at once and gave a quick giggle. I wonder if by now she's managed to explain it to him.

'And I just wanted to say, Mr Ripple, that Virginia's told me you've given us something for the house and we're really and truly grateful.' And at last he gave a hesitant half-smile which showed me again, with the other half added on, what a nice man he probably was.

'It was nothing,' I said. 'I mean it was the most, the least . . .'

I took a hasty sip at my cup of coffee to end its rattling in the saucer.

I was thinking: what, about £175 less income per annum down the tubes or thereabouts away? What had that British Airways package to Rome cost?

'We're really going to make it on our own, Mr Ripple. It's only a loan, really. We insist, don't we, Virginia?'

'Of course,' she said. 'Of course. Of course it is.'

'Stop there,' I said, pouring myself more coffee though my cup was three-quarters full. 'I'm already beginning to lose interest.' A pause as they leant forward attentively. Not worth repeating, that one. 'Seriously though, that wasn't a loan. I want you to have it because soon enough I'll have had it. It's there to be spent, enjoyed. When you finally close my account, wind up my assets, don't want you thinking: what did the old fart need all this for when we could have done with it and don't any longer. Might as well shell out on the cherrywood coffin with gold trimmings. He always did have money to burn . . .'

Virginia put down her cup and went over to the window while Richard began saying something about starting his own business one day. The sunlight framed her as she stared out at the level landscape, the shadows of clouds crossing it as if we were adrift on a shallow sea. He looked across at her wistfully as if she was about to be snatched away from him.

Then he went up beside her as she said, 'I wish you wouldn't talk like that, Dad, bringing it nearer and just when we have to go, so that's what I'll remember.'

He put his arm across her shoulder and said, 'It's certainly a nice spot you've chosen, Mr Ripple. Windy in winter, I expect, though.' He turned. 'We really must be going if we're to reach Norwich by . . .'

It was a timeless moment as they stood side by side, wanting to be alone together as soon as possible. Virginia came and kissed me and I held her, too briefly.

'Run along then,' I said briskly.

Richard stepped forward like a volunteer, saying, 'Again, thanks, Mr Ripple, we really do appreciate it.' He went out into the hall, took Virginia's bag and walked alone down the path. We watched him from the doorway.

'An excellent bloke altogether, I'd say . . .' I began.

But she wasn't, then, thinking along those lines. The exasperating piety of her early teens had become a melancholy I'd never noticed before: a lifetime ahead of her of helping people to speak for themselves, while those of us who can have a gift we constantly misuse – something like that.

'I wish you and Mum hadn't broken up,' she said quietly.

'We can hardly start on that now, can we? At least there wasn't any bitterness.'

'I mean you all on your own out here.'

'Oh that.'

I looked around the sky, clear blue now, the milkiness falling away from it and seeming to settle on to the trees to bring on the blossom. She had a point.

'Well, if I don't like it, I can always move back to London. Down payments there, though, quite killing. Lend me a couple of thou, could you?'

She giggled and it was all right then for a moment or two as we walked down the path, her arm through mine. Richard was behind his wheel and had turned on the engine. I took out my handkerchief, licked a corner of it and rubbed away vigorously at an imaginary spot just above his windscreen wiper. Virginia got in and fastened her safety belt. I put my face against the windscreen and my hand through the window he was rolling down, palm twisted round and face up for a tip. He put a five pence coin into it and I tugged a lock of my hair. Then the car slowly pulled away and their hands fluttered at either side on top of it like tattered pennants. I went on waving until they were out of sight, my hand high above my head. Oh well, I thought, if you can't have everything, this will have to do instead. Or so I say now. But then, as I walked back down the path, it wasn't only the loneliness, it was feeling £1500 the poorer and why hadn't I made it much more, love and love of self getting thoroughly mixed up the while. And then it suddenly wasn't all right at all: my daughter travelling away from me, the things I hadn't said and didn't know how to say and never would.

Perhaps that should come at the end. Other things have happened since but one remembers things simultaneously and brings them to a close each time in a different way, as if asking: if this moment were to be my last, how would I choose to sum up? Waving goodbye to my daughter, a breath of warmth in the air at the end of winter, a patch of sunlight on a dark, unpainted wall, some bird singing alone long before daybreak – these things or things like them instead of the guilt,

214

the failed joke, the thoughtlessness, the self-pity, the fear in the early hours of being dead, when the sun will rise one morning without you and other hands will smooth your rumpled sheets. So moments like that, the raised fluttering hands, are snatched out of the blue and vanish. And so it was I drank another cup of coffee before taking a rake and going out into the garden, with no notion of what needed doing there. And the air was blank and ordinary again. No, these won't do either as last words: a bloke going out into a fine Suffolk morning with a gardening implement in his hand, not having the first idea what to do with it. I'll tuck it away in the middle somewhere where it won't notice much. There is far too much unravelling still to be undergone.

The following day I went to the village shop to buy tinned anything and learnt a little more about Nanny Phipps. At the counter Mrs Jenners was being tiresome about a price. After greeting me with a sigh, she remained near the entrance, overhearing us while bruising oranges one by one in a tray by the window.

'Some people, I can tell you,' the shopkeeper began loudly. 'Settling in, are you?'

'So far as I know, yes.' I replied, plonking down my tins of corned beef and asparagus tips.

'We got used to Miss Phipps in here most days more often than not. Not what you'd call a gasbag, wasn't old Phipps. Had nothing against her myself . . .'

I wanted to know if she'd died in my cottage. 'Live here long did she?'

'When I came here she was there already, wasn't she? I wouldn't call her shifty, not exactly.'

'What would you call her?'

'The postman said she was a nanny. It's the sort of thing what postmen know, isn't it?'

'You mean a bit bossy?' I tried, handing over my money, thinking Mrs Jenners had a point, in fact a very good point. Behind me I heard a tinkle, then a bang and click.

'Not like that Mrs Thatcher. More put upon, and skinny with it.'

'She didn't die here, anything like that?'

She folded her arms and leant forward on the counter. 'There's nothing quite like that, is there, dear?' She put out a finger to touch me on the wrist, then thought better of it, making a thlsh noise, hiding her upper teeth with her lower lip and showing her gums. 'I'm just telling you this. All skin and bones she was, a real skeleton, not well covered at all, wasn't Miss Phipps, not like some I could name.' Her bosom sank on to the counter as she reached for something beneath it. 'It's the winter when you need the flesh on you, fat . . .' Whereupon, arms across her breasts, she pinched her bare upper arms. 'In winter her eyes watered, like she was having a good cry, like she had troubles, but the water had nowhere else to go, did it? They say we're nearly all water. She sniffed a lot so you never knew, did you?'

'So what happened to her?'

'Well, she got old, didn't she? Will that be all? I had some frozen cutlets in. One day a car came for her, one of those big shiny ones, black, and it was up for sale.'

I thanked her. 'So she just went away?'

'In the middle of winter. Just before Christmas. No, just after. Round about then. Then it was like she was never here, except she made you feel warmer. I don't know why she bothered.'

'Bothered what?'

'Well, I don't like to say it. Bothered with hanging on. But she wasn't bossy, not bossy, more like keeping to herself but not a lot to keep, I'll say that for her. Will that be all? I had some nice, juicy cutlets in.'

I thanked her again and left. I have met Nanny Phipps since then. Maureen was with me. It wasn't an occasion to lift the spirits, but I must leave that till later. I had a curiosity to satisfy, that was all, or more or less all. It was something the shopkeeper said and then there were the photographs. There is no photography of my life. If there had been, might I have thought, the more's the pity? Must press on now. Maureen. This is going to be difficult. I've rather been dreading this.

Chapter Four

I replied to her letter just to say let's meet, let's give it a go, if you're asking me, I definitely prefer the one with the bicycle. I suggested the steps of the National Gallery, a date and a time, no need to confirm, I was going to be in those parts anyway, which wasn't true. I told her she'd have no difficulty recognizing me, just look out for someone immensely distinguished who'd shaved off his beard and with a red carnation in his buttonhole. If it turned out to be dislike at first sight, I thought, we could look at the pictures, safely mutter, 'Now there's a painting,' from time to time and go our separate ways.

I've had a look at the notes I made at the time and can already see there's going to be a problem. There's a good TV programme coming up in five minutes, just time to put on more comfortable shoes and pour a drink. So I return now to the notes one grisly morning when it's pissing with rain and the clouds are so low the further trees seem to be shrivelling under a grey sea. The problem roughly is how not to alter what happened in the light, or shadow, of what happened later, how not to impose a pattern on it so as to feel wise after the event, get increasing satisfaction the more one writes from the composition itself, make a fiction of it in fact so that if a change occurred from the first to the third person singular you'd hardly notice the difference. By then anything goes and you don't have to worry about the real and the true, a yarn is being spun and all for the sake of the finished cloth to be fashioned at will, which isn't anything like the snagged and tattered and altogether scruffy garment you were wearing and picking nervously at at the time. Later. The rain has got worse if anything. No drive to the sea today. The roof is leaking and I've just put a bucket on the landing to catch the drips. I've run out of whisky and cigarillos. It wasn't a comfortable night: the storm noises, bladder, anus, heartburn, nothing serious – unlike the central heating system, still under guarantee? Check that. Tell it how it is. Tell it how it was?

I had some lines ready to break the ice with: 'Fancy bumping into you.' 'Shall we go inside or would you rather go to the pictures?' 'If you can't stand the sight of me, let's make it a blind date.' Or waving a hand across Trafalgar Square: 'Sorry about the unholy mess but, as you can see, St Martin's in the fields.'

In the event I said none of these things. I arrived early to find a vantage point from which I could look out for somebody who was on the lookout for me, my red carnation not in its buttonhole mainly because I was wearing a jacket that turned out not to have one. There was a striking, forlorn, fair-haired woman at the foot of the gallery steps, her face raised to the sun but her eyes were closed tight, expecting nothing. Wherever I stopped was too near or too far, too exposed or too out of sight, so as the minutes ticked by, I prowled about with a purposeful air, walking up and down the street, looking at my watch, joining the bus queue, perusing one of the fifty-five blank pages of my diary, lurking behind a lion to do up a shoelace, studying notices outside the church, waiting for a gap in the traffic to cross the road to the square, waiting to cross back again, all the time glancing across at the gallery and fiddling with the flower in and out of the side pocket of my jacket and then standing at the bus stop again, or rather against the wall at a point where I could take in the gallery entrance on the way to or from looking skywards to reconfirm once again I hadn't made a mistake in leaving my umbrella behind. Finally I walked up the steps in a businesslike manner and into the gallery to attend a meeting for which I was late and came out a few moments later no less briskly, having attended the meeting which had proved a waste of my time. I was pausing to adjust my tie at the base of the steps when a voice behind me said, 'Excuse me, but are you Mr Ripple by any chance?'

I leapt several feet into the air and landed facing the other way to see before me a lady holding out a carnation that might have been fresh plucked the previous summer if a flower was what it was.

She didn't look a bit as she had in the photograph but I had seen her somewhere before. Which of course I had. She had been the other person at the bus stop who hadn't been peering towards

Canada House to catch an early glimpse of the next bus, indeed had had her back to them; and also the woman who came up behind me to study the programme of the lunchtime oboe recital so that when I turned for another look at the gallery, we bumped into each other and our first words to each other were 'Sorry' and my first thought about her was, 'You silly cow, can't you look where you're going?' She told me later she'd spotted me early on, revolving in front of the recital programme, moving my lips as if learning it by heart, someone wrong in the head or a jealous oboist, but it was the flash of red at my hip while I looked everywhere but at the open pages of my diary that had clinched it. And then when the flower fell at her feet as I came out of the gallery, it wasn't only that she plucked up, I later suggested.

'Oh!' I said. 'Oh dear, haven't we . . . ?' And offered my hand into which she put the carnation.

She nodded and looked down at her handbag which she unfastened and fastened again. Then for a very long time indeed, almost three seconds, we looked each other straight in the eye except that she was four inches taller than I, not counting hair. Then I was touching my face here and there and she was testing the clasp of her handbag again.

'Would you like . . . ?' I began, looking past her to where people were gathering outside the church. 'Or St James's Park. Or take in the gallery, go for bust?'

She turned towards the church. 'I quite like oboe music, don't you? Then we could . . .'

'Most definitely. I'm certainly not hanging around here any longer. You never know with these postbags.'

And so we spent our first hour together at a lunchtime recital. Twice I glanced sideways at her and she smiled back at me. I was thinking: is she enjoying this music as much as I am not, does she do this often, what do we do afterwards, say afterwards about the music, about anything at all, is she hungry, does she think I like her, does she think she likes me, what am I thinking about her, about anything, what the hell am I doing here listening to an oboe with a complete stranger, etc. . . ? A range of questions too shifting to dwell upon and moving from those to recalling her letter, the photograph, and imagining how she or I would put it if what we meant was, Thanks but no thanks, I was after someone, well, more . . . less . . . not so . . . absolutely nothing like you at all . . .

I tried to spare myself too much of this by paying attention to the oboist who seemed to get by without breathing other than via his instrument. Which brought me back to the condition I was in and looking down at my thighs, I registered that I could see hardly more than a third of them and from there I observed past her parted coat that she had quite a mound there too, covered by a tight-fitting skirt, the bottom part of a suit which was probably her best, sleek but tweedish, composed of two slightly different shades of humdrum green like fine woven grasses going brown and needing rain. Higher up, remembering the photograph, I couldn't see without looking, but recall a heap of white frilliness done up to the neck, fluffing out and encouraging guesswork like all that rear-end gathering of cloth in the last century or whenever. Then I began to focus again on what I'd say when the oboist stopped doing his breathing exercises through his instrument. So that when we stood up and she buttoned up her coat and I buttoned and then unbuttoned my jacket, I said, 'That was pretty good but then I expect he's had lessons. Especially the Albonino. Old favourite of mine. Keeping the fingers and tongue together at that speed. Quite a lick as the ac . . .' We moved into the aisle. 'How about a bite to eat? Pasta a nice little Italian place . . .'

'Albinoni,' she said quietly, touching me on the sleeve and giving a nod which left her eyebrows behind.

'Haven't been to Al's in a long time,' I replied.

I studied the forthcoming concert programmes muttering mispronunciations of some of the other composers' names – Cuddly, DePussy, Faure Reicha for poorer – and made her smile this time, but only with that kindness that likes to spare feelings.

We said nothing that I can recall until we reached the steps of the gallery again, apart from comments on the weather, basing those on past experience. I looked skywards at where the sun emerged from behind a cloud and said, 'The sun's trying to get through again. Second coming long overdue, as the bish . . .' Whoops, I thought, inaudible, pray to God . . .

We sat opposite one another in a wine bar, eating smoked mackerel and getting through a carafe. She told me she was a Senior Executive Officer who supervised a registry in a government department. She had taken a day's leave. She lived in Clapham, alone. She had a married sister and divorced brother and four nephews and nieces. She liked her job. She sang in a choir. She took package holidays, last year to the Canaries. 'That figures,' I said. Not quite a smile but one of the commonest quips in choral circles I shouldn't wonder.

She didn't see much of her brother and sister. Not much in common, not really. Her parents were still alive. I exchanged some information of my own, wishing I'd brought my Rennie tablets. And slowly there began what Plaskett used to call 'a thorough appraisal' meaning I should dig about for what was in it for him. She looked at me more continuously than I at her, her eyes wide on the edge of alarm, her plump lips drawn in or hidden by a napkin as if those couldn't speak for what there might be to be alarmed about: not much mauvish lipstick, high forehead hardly lined other than between the eyes, ample cheeks beginning to hang, hair three-quarters black, the rest grey, swept back, unremarkable ear-lobes, complexion well planned but too pink in the sunlight, a sudden but short-lived smile, and once I made her chuckle which revealed broad, long teeth and almost as much width of gum. What a crude, heartless inspection, I was thinking, but also that this was how two people might meet for the rest of their lives, neighbours they could depend on to cheer each other up and depress each other no end, one of whom, with little grief, would attend the other's funeral. But I was finding her attractive too, so wanting her to find me attractive in a way that ruled out the sort of inventory outlined above. Not, thank goodness, that women judge by appearances like that, other than their own or other women's perhaps. Towards the end of the meal, I loosened my belt and concealed a belch, fumbling in my pocket again for my antacids. Apt that.

'Heartburn,' I said, a bit squiffy by now. 'Since you ask, a five-centimetre hiatus hernia.'

'How unpleasant.' I had no time to correct her. 'With me it's my back.'

'We all have our little complaints.'

'Oh I'm not complaining. It's not serious. Do you play games?'

'How very generous of you. Badminton, but a long time ago.'

'Were you good at it?'

'Oh my yes. Gave it up. Didn't have the heart. Not fair on the others. What about you?'

'As I said, it's my back. For years now, ever since . . .'

'One of those long-playing discs,' I ventured.

'That's what my doctor's always saying.'

'Ah,' I replied. She gave me that kind smile again. 'Golf too,' I added.

'That's nice,' she said.

And so we first became acquainted with each other. We made no plans to meet again. The encounter tailed off. A tiredness crept over her, reflecting my own. She aged. As I paid, she put a handkerchief to her face but did not blow her nose into it, just held it there. When she took it away, there was an instant of despair in her eyes but then she sniffed and it was gone.

'That was very nice,' she said. 'I enjoyed meeting you.'

'The pleasure was mine,' I replied.

We parted outside the tube station. Shaking hands, we held on a little as if to fasten on to some dim understanding we had of each other. Just being there together, I thought, the way we had met, gave us more in common than could ever divide us. If you had seen us you would have thought: sad-looking, commonplace couple, not much written in *their* stars. Which would have been bloody condescending of you. I watched her buy her ticket and walk to the escalator, lonely and dignified. Was she thinking: well, that was a let-down, I'll never do that again? I was, but not for long, not after wandering in and out of some of the bookshops in that part of town. It doesn't take long to rediscover that bodies aren't everything, quite something most of them, but not everything. I began to miss her.

The gas fire is flickering tonight and the wind is blowing fiercely, nothing in its way across the Russian wastes and the North Sea. Are there small ships out there still, I wonder, drenched and lurching, the waves mounting hugely above them, and will some go down tonight? At this hour I sometimes listen to the storm warnings on the radio and then remember what my father once said when my mother reminded him the shop was barely afloat: 'Think about they who go down to the sea in ships and occupy their business in great waters.' 'The Bible won't help you to pay the bills,' she replied. 'It's the Book of Common Prayer,' he mumbled, lighting up and shuffling towards the bottle. She shrugged. 'Too common by half, all that kneeling and no action. They're your undoing, that's what prayers are.'

But I must not be distracted. I put on a record that Maureen brought for me when she came to stay. I barely glanced at it at the time. It has on it several violin sonatas by Mozart. They seem too simple for great music, like a small voice trying to say something clear and final. But my antique record player produces a lilt of its own and the wind is too loud, rattling the windows and making the door bang. So I take the record off. We never listened to it together. I think again of the fishermen and of their wives and children too who are sleepless as I am, but with fear, whose depth of happiness I can never know either when the ships come back in the morning, the sunlit water bubbling behind them.

I look back on my first description of her and it is not what I remember now it is all over and she is what she has become. That first shyness, shutting her eyes when she turned her face to me, fluttering them, then bold for an instant before turning away again. The smile quick and cautious as though she doubted whether that was what she ought to be doing rather than frowning. Then her face softening to unseam the wrinkles. Her lips too large for her thin voice, the fragment of mackerel to one side of them, which she missed each time she dabbed them with her napkin. The sweep and intricate fastening of her hair and the few, frail, symmetrical curls, which must have taken her hours. Her long hands clasped tight, showing the bone.

Tired now, too tired to go to bed. I think of the fishermen again, holding on for grim death as the wind howls louder. I think of the fish slithering in the holds and a small fragment of one of them ending up at a corner of Maureen's mouth. We shall never listen to Mozart together, or Albonini come to that. I wish she were here, very much, but if she were, I would wish she were not. The wives and children are at the quayside. The dawn comes and it is calm but there is no sun. The boats approach in the distance, black like silhouettes. The gulls have gone. At my sunrise the ships break through the night air without glint or shadow and all around them the waters do not stir. The ships are counted and the women and children have drifted home. When I wake up I shall still be wondering what the builder would charge to fix the windows and doors to stop them rattling, install double glazing and do all the other things that need doing for the price of Virginia's odd thou. To bed now in this safe house.

Another interlude.

Time has passed and we're into early summer now. The trees are large with leaves, silvered and whitened by the wind. The cows in the pastures stand further apart and the horse is where it used to be. The clouds are few and flimsy and widely scattered to little apparent purpose, like my thoughts but too high and not grey or drifting enough either. I've done a little work on the garden, planting out the second lot of cuttings Agnes gave me, tactfully not asking about the first, though looking hard for them. She recommended a potting soil or was it peat, not too much sun or was it not too little? However, it's not all bad. There are some exceptionally fine rosebuds dotted about and things that Nanny Phipps might have planted are doing well: honeysuckle I recognize, a small apple tree which later shed its apples when they had reached the size of a pea, two infant rhododendrons with bare stalks whose three flowers reached and passed full bloom during the night and a mass of morning glory mixed with clematis along the fence. This last is not all it should be because, in trying to thin it out, I snapped or cut through several, if not all, of the branches which when followed through turned out to have the most promising endings. I've planted two or three other so far unsuccessful shrubs, bought at random from the garden centre. In between there is a lawn with more grass in it (if you include the hay-coloured patches) than other growths, excluding clover, daisies and dandelions. Agnes gave me advice about that too, lending me some very fine blue powder which I cast about on an almost windless day so that it wafted away via my shoes to fertilize the front gate, the tarmac beyond and places round about, or lay in patches like puddles of diluted ink. In mowing the lawn, I was sorry to decapitate the daisies, its best feature by far. (When I told Agnes this, she squeezed my bare lower arm quite hard and said, 'Getting old is like that, I guess – in smoothing things over and cutting them down you lose the brightness in life.') I've also distributed some dollops of peat across some of the flower-beds together with some white pellets. It made the soil look very healthy when dug in, but before that like a crowd of sweating Africans coming out in spots.

I should mention that when Agnes left that day she said to me at the gate, 'What do you all do for sex by the way?'

'There are still quite a number of us, I'm told, who go to bed with women,' I replied, catching sight of the Colonel in the distance striding towards us, brandishing his walking stick and shouting at a white or very pale orange dog which danced about him in a frenzy.

'Doesn't tail off, does it?' she said, as if to herself, posing sideways to me. I counted four layers of cream on various parts of her face, including the rouge. 'Well?' she said. 'Do I pass?' She gritted and showed her excellent teeth.

'Most definitely. With distinction. You must carry on and get your Master's.'

She liked that, touching me just below the far side of my waist and giving a loud laugh. Then she nudged me and said, pointing at her husband who swung his stick in the air, 'Well, darn it, if that isn't a fine figure of a man coming this way. Do you think if I ask him . . . ?'

She ran her hand up my back and skipped towards him, putting an arm through his as they wheeled round to cross the green. With a loud halloo the Colonel gave another high circular wave with his stick before throwing it an astonishingly long way for the dog. Agnes's slacks, I noticed, were loose fitting but pulled up fairly high and there was a lot of movement the other side of them which resulted in a fury of labour – pinching off a few dandelion heads, snapping with shears at the ex-clematis, wiping the lawnmower blades, digging away at what might one day become a vegetable bed. All this leading to an ache in my back which needed supporting with two small cushions when I watched television that evening and then to my trying to watch it from the floor from which I developed a crick in the neck. All very much to the good this, a coming to my senses as I saw the stick descend and the dog leap at my groin. What had the doctor said, no sudden movements, no exerting yourself? What a fortunate fellow I was. I drank repeatedly to my own health.

All that was just before my first meeting with Maureen and round about then Sidney called by. 'Just for a check-up, as the doctor said in the brothel,' he said with a toss of his scalded head. I ignored that as he peered about the place, making humming noises, or perhaps actually humming

'You could sell this for a tidy profit already,' he said finally.

'Like Jeremiah with a new suit and haircut?' I quipped unwisely.

For he chortled, then guffawed, then doubled up, seizing me as if to take me with him in a dying bronchitic spasm. Then there was no stopping him. Had I heard this one, then that one, stop him if . . . Three in the Irish category, one about a cross-eyed bull and another about Jayne Mansfield's breasts, burning with self-delight and helping himself to a whisky the while. So it was some time before I could steer him back down the path and then he came all the way back, his hands cupped in front of him saying, 'Got one yellow ball in one hand, one yellow ball in the other. What have I got? Heard it have you?' I shook my head. 'The undivided attention of a Chinaman.'

I smiled, as one does, but then rapidly reminded him of Nanny Phipps's suitcase. I was testing my limits of tolerance, where disgust began. No (this added later), nothing profound or moral like that. Just getting steamed up for a whistle and hoot in the empty air, stuck in a siding with nowhere to go. Half way back up the path, still gasping, he pointed towards the Colonel's house, its roof just visible through the leaf-laden trees.

'If it's satisfaction you're wanting . . . As the saying goes: age shall not weary them nor the years condemn . . .' He held a bicep and raised his fist. 'What think you, Ripple?'

I stared into space and said nothing. I know little poetry but those lines I did know and had always found them very beautiful but not true, for how many of us remember so often those who have laid down their lives for us?

'You horrible little pisser,' I said, but it wasn't out loud. Perhaps I am more tolerant than I like to believe.

After our first meeting Maureen and I let time pass. Then we both wrote on the same day so our letters crossed. They were much alike.

Mine said: *'Dear Maureen, I very much enjoyed meeting you. Thanks for introducing me to Albert Bonino. In case you didn't notice, music is not my bag. Perhaps, as the American sailor said, I could come and hear you sing one fine day? Weren't we lucky with the weather? That's more than I can say about today: horizontal rain. I don't want to go into that. Please say if you'd like to meet again. Regards, Tom Ripple.'*

Hers said: *'Dear Tom, I was glad to meet you and I hope you didn't mind the concert too much which I realize is not your 'thing'. Music always cheers me up, especially singing. It is not a very pleasant day today, weather-wise.*

Perhaps it is even worse in Suffolk? If you are ever up in London again and have some time to spare, perhaps we might meet again. Best wishes, Maureen Hurton.'

A week or so later, I telephoned her and we arranged a second meeting. We went to Greenwich by riverboat after a stroll round Westminster Abbey. All that cleaned-up fame and history, one felt one was being lied to, but too much patriotism is like that. The boat was waiting at the landing stage ready to move off, as if we'd planned it all along. But it wasn't like that. It was she who suggested we meet at the Abbey, an obvious place for a rendezvous. Then we wandered and there was the boat. Such is life, haphazard, not like a book, least of all a detective story. But whatever the events turn out to be, it's still us experiencing them, making something or nothing of them in our own way. However, we're just coincidences too of course, a great multitude of freaks, even if that's not how we feel. We feel special, choosers if not chosen exactly, though it must also be true that we've all been killed in car accidents or whatever that haven't yet happened.

There was a cold breeze coming off the water and we were not dressed for it, so much of what we saw was through unclean glass. Being below decks made her uneasy, for she did not stop fidgeting and once she fumbled with her coffee cup and knocked it off the table. She also kept on looking about her as if fearing to be recognized. We soon ran out of things to say to each other and I sat with my hands in my pockets, indicating or asking about the odd landmark with that eagerness which covers up boredom. Out on the deck, her hair was blown loose and she kept on trying to pat it into place. Once she put on sunglasses and immediately took them off again. She seemed discontented with herself and when she turned to me it was as if to an old friend who was letting her down.

'Perhaps this isn't such a marvellous idea after all?' I said.

'Oh no! Aren't you enjoying it? I'm having a lovely time. It's just all these tourists everywhere, gawking and staring . . .'

I wondered too how much she had been wooed by other men, had wanted to be, or not wanted to, up to or beyond the point where she or they were found wanting, too much, too little or too soon. I mustn't seem eager lest she should believe I thought I had little chance of ever now doing better than her. The jests and nonchalance then became a disguise, equally too of my own doubts about anyone who had little chance of ever doing better than me. Then too there was what at most and best I had begun to imagine doing with her compared with what at least and worst she might not want to imagine having to do with me, my additions becoming her subtractions: in short, it was a calculating business altogether.

We had a look round Sir Francis Chichester's boat and the *Cutty Sark*, followed by a late lunch and then a walk past boutiques and antique shops. She admired a brooch of a green-winged dragonfly which I went back to buy for her and pinned on her lapel, having told her to close her eyes thus to imagine her sleeping beside me.

'Oh you shouldn't, Tom,' she said and kissed me briefly on the cheek.

That seemed to cheer her up. Until then our conversation had been chary and intermittent, a little information, no views, no likes and dislikes: getting along not off, in a word. The exception was Mrs Thatcher and the Falkland Islands. Safe territory this, you'd think, in a manner of speaking. She told me the Argies had been taught a damn good lesson. I had a problem there, another lesson being the damage to the principle by the rejoicing, to the bravery by the boasting, so that it couldn't be all that good if it was so bad for us. I had wondered what my parents would have said and knew that in this, if in nothing else, their discomfort and silence would have united them and now united them with me. But I said nothing and changed the subject by drawing attention to a headline in the evening newspaper about squandered riches.

'What would you do with a windfall on the pools?' I asked.

'I've never really thought about it.'

'Nor me. At my age, does rather suggest autumn leaves on stagnant water.'

She'd like more space, a garden, she said thoughtfully. Once she'd lived in a basement flat and her sitting room had been flooded by a burst pipe from next door, ankle-deep in places it had been. She had sued for damages, one of those foreign landlords from Asia or somewhere like that.

'Kept you wading, did he?' I asked.

'He paid every penny,' she said earnestly. 'He was very sorry. Quite nice really. But there were such hordes of them and the food they eat. The smell. Yuck. I tried to get on with them.'

'Curry flavour, you mean?' I said.

She'd rather have gone on talking about immigration or Mrs Thatcher, I could tell. She knew I had changed the subject.

'That brooch looks so pretty on you, catching the sun, it's almost real,' I said after a long silence while we sat waiting for the riverboat.

She did not reply but laid her hand on mine, the getting off suddenly leaping ahead of the getting on, the meeting of minds postponed to another day. Hand in hand we wandered about *Gypsy Moth* and the *Cutty Sark* again. It had become one of those days when the sun shines brightly and then there is a burst of rain, a day for rainbows. And the blue and grey reminded me again of my childhood: one moment my father letting me count the cash or slice the cheese, his hand steady and warm on my back, the next my mother chiding me about my homework – Sunday afternoon ruined by dread of Monday morning. This interrupted my thoughts of ships on the high seas, the standing before the mast and holding on for grim death, of lives lived valiantly and hardened by the elements. Then, to end another silence, I ran a hand over a gunwale and said, 'You have to take your hat off to them, the daring, the sheer – what's the word – tenacity?'

'Fortitude,' she added. 'That's the word. That's what I admire about him most.'

'Absolutely, what with one's sixtitude looming . . . ?'

She laid a hand on my arm but this time clearly telling me not to try so hard. She had a point.

We spent the journey back below decks, the rain now falling steadily. Maureen sat upright, her hands in her lap, her cup of coffee untouched. Then she leaned sideways against the wall and closed her eyes. Small drops of rain glinted in her hair and the tip of her tongue showed between her teeth. Towards the end she looked away from the blurred riverscape of warehouses and tenement blocks and offices and palaces and caught my eye, for I was looking everywhere but at her. Then she touched her dragonfly and nodded. I gave her the thumbs-up sign. The calculations collapsed and there was a sudden warm ache between stomach and throat which did not make me reach for my Rennies. The roll of the boat contributed and I went up on deck to breathe the fresh air. When I returned her eyes were closed again, a fingertip resting on the dragonfly as if to stop it doing a flit.

We parted at a bus stop in Parliament Square. She had a choir practice to get back to. They were doing Haydn's *Creation* with a wonderful new conductor, the Rattle of the future, she called him, which I'll admit perplexed me at the time.

As the bus came round the corner she said, 'I'm sorry, I've been a bit of a misery today. One of my headaches.'

'Oh you haven't at all. Not a bit of it. So long as it wasn't me.'

'Let's keep in touch,' she said.

There was no attempt at a farewell kiss. She got on the bus and turned to wave from the platform. A large bald man coming from upstairs to get off in a hurry cursed at her as her raised arm caught him on the chin. My wave ended in a snook cocked at the retreating back of the man in a hurry. Then I blew her a kiss but she did not see it because she was having words with the conductor. The last I saw of her were her behind, then legs, then ankles as she mounted the stairs. And that I play back now, over and over again, as if it is all fresh and recent and I do not know yet how it will end, like a snapped branch of my clematis bush, nor how much I will change it as I change, or hope to, over the passing years.

Chapter Five

The following day I went to church again, though my memory of it is dim. I sneaked in when the service had already started and left when the queuing for communion began. I felt lost and woolly headed, sheepish in a word, but sang lustily enough, dreaming of Maureen: 'Let me to thy bosom fly While the nearer waters roll . . . Freely let me take of Thee; Spring Thou up within my heart, Rise to all eternity.' And thought too of my father and of my former wife who wouldn't be seen dead in such a place though it might be another matter when I was.

The sunlight came and went through the stained-glass windows as if in that brief time we worshipped through many dawns and many dusks. The vicar read a lesson about being compassed about with so great a cloud of witnesses and we should lay aside the sin which doth so easily beset us and run with patience the race that is set before us. Well one would, wouldn't one, be on one's best behaviour jogging along in front of all those people?

That from my notebook: more jests and nonchalance to hide what more in another sphere of hope and love. And as I put a fiver in the box for the church restoration fund, I remembered my wife again, her scorn for 'established' religion: 'The rich man in his castle, the poor man at his gate, God made them high or lowly and ordered their estate.' Recited God knows how many times to our children, the other world, she said, usually a pretext for doing nothing in this. Oh yes, she preached too and I did not disagree with her and said nothing and made jokes at her to myself. Then too, the words were spoken with such sureness there must be truth in them, some clue to the heart of things turned upside down by jests and nonchalance.

Once my father said to me, 'Whatever you say, it's a refuge, a consolation, isn't it?' Mother overheard him. 'Refugees is it, we are now? What are you running away from? And consolation, I thought that was something cheap they give to losers.' My father blinked and shrugged and could not look me in the eye, humbled again. That was why I started wanting there to be humour in the air, I suppose, that and wanting to be a believer in just about anything. Thus I sang out, as if to give voice to my truest feelings while my thoughts meandered off in other directions to find words equally as sure, for example, as saying I have observed a horse standing alone with its head over a fence or there is a smell of mown grass in the air.

That's that out of the way, hardly worth mentioning, having no faith in myself as I looked out over my garden and didn't see Maureen in it, bending over a shrub or feeding the sparrows. No more church-going, I reckoned. There wasn't any humour in it any longer. Futile vacant little garden . . . Thoughts to that effect when there was a knock on the door. It was the Colonel.

'Ah, Ripple. Care to come to the pub? Saw you in church. Heard you too. Don't know why I bother sometimes. Hope some of it might rub off. A bit spare today. Agnes in London. Then Jenners of all people invited me back for a drink.'

'I'd like that very much,' I replied.

'Didn't invite you then?' he said as we got into his car.

'Not that I can recall exactly.'

He engaged gears with a fierce shove. 'Not that lonely. Jenners doesn't agree with me. What in God's name do you think he got his OBE for do you think?'

'Can't imagine.'

'Exactly.'

We drove in silence for a while, then he said suddenly, 'Don't know how you stand it, all on your own out here. Never married, anything like that?'

'Yes, actually, once upon a time.'

'Sorry, old chap, didn't mean to pry.'

'That's perfectly all right.'

'Not snuffed it or anything, don't mind my asking?'

'No, nothing like that at all. Just the usual, there one moment, gone the next.'

'Like leaves leaving a tree, blown off some of them, others fluttering down. And there it is, naked against a winter sky. Stark. Read that somewhere. Rather well put, don't you think?'

'Very.'

We arrived at the pub, where I hadn't been before, and I bought him a double gin and tonic, a single for myself.

'No,' he said when I joined him by the fireplace as far away as possible from the din going on at the bar. 'Jenners, if you must know, doesn't agree with me at all. He was quite senior, you know. Did a Defence White Paper, he told me. Good with words, those chaps. Knows it all. When we first met he said to me, "Aha, a member of the conventional forces, I see. Keeping our powder dry under the umbrella, are we?" Something like that. I ask you. "Keeping you occupied, that's the thing. What would we do without Northern Ireland? The way things are going, we'll need you on the streets yet." You know the sort. Can't help feeling sorry for his lady wife.'

'I thought he was Trade and Industry.'

'They chop and change. Made out all right, did you, in your line of work?'

He leant forward, then far back and glared at me. I felt on parade.

'So so,' I replied as we both drank deep. 'Not that you'd notice. Export/import, in that general area. Then a take-over, a handshake, you know how it is.'

'Pfff. I didn't make full colonel either. Care for another?'

He took his empty glass and my half-empty one to the bar where he had to wait a long time before he could lean through two muscular shoulders and give his order. Behind his back, one man circled an eye with thumb and forefinger and the other twiddled an imaginary moustache, neither moving an inch.

'No,' he continued on his return. 'On the Defence Staff in Washington. Couldn't blame the old girl for thinking I'd make brigadier plus. Trouble with Americans, don't you find? Posh voice, tight swanky uniform with stuff on it, think we come out of some bogus damn flick or other. All want to be shagged by a Lord. God alone knows, I didn't put it on, but that's part of it. Understatement, know what I'm driving at?'

His voice was getting louder and I glanced across at the bar to see the two louts staring at him, nudging each other, their cheeks puffed up in ridicule, flicking their fingers under their noses.

'Better keep my voice down, you're thinking. Nothing I can do about it. Short back and sides. Regimental tie. Only wear the damn thing to church. One good reason for going there.

Be myself for a change. Sentimental, but it was my life.'

'Wish you'd done something else?'

'Good God no! Not what you'd call work. Wish my daughter hadn't married into it. Lovely girl.'

'So I'd noticed.'

'Got any children, have you?'

'A daughter and a son.'

'That's nice. Or is it? Not into things, are they, nothing like that?'

'No, they're fine: speech therapy, accountancy.'

'Very sensible too . . .' He looked at the bar where the louts were staring at him and making upper-class noises and faces. 'We'll soon see to them.'

I put out a hand to restrain him. 'We could go somewhere else . . .'

He winked at me and went over to them, staggering a little, and talked to them for a long time. They shook their heads several times, shifted about on their stools, then began nodding. Finally he gripped them each by the arm and came back and they turned back to the bar where the barman pulled them each another pint.

'What was all that about?' I asked.

'Invited them over, asked if they knew a good builder, handyman, ironmonger. Did they know where I could get a second-hand chicken run, bought them a drink. Where was I? Not ambitious enough maybe. Not like Jenners and his bloody OBE. Trouble with buggers like that, if you ask me, is it's not their *career* that matters, but *their* career, if I make myself clear, probably not. Sour grapes, you're thinking. What I was getting round to was I nabbed the old girl under false pretences and she had money all right, tons of it, and now we're nobodies . . . Don't mind that one bit but you see, there's less and less of the what-d'you-call-it, life, to make up for it . . .'

My turn to get the drinks now, in a hurry too. When I returned he was gazing into the empty fireplace.

'God, not another,' he said. 'I shouldn't.' He slapped me hard on the knee. 'Not very soldierly, is it, you're thinking? Swapped one mess for another, what? How about you?'

'I manage, just about.'

'Fit, are you?'

'So far as I know.'

'Well, I'm not.'

'Oh. I'm sorry.'

'I don't mind, so why should you? Early seventies. Lucky to be alive. Simple as that. She takes my arm when we walk round the garden, beautiful garden, out of this world. Everybody's idea. I feel happy then, a day by itself, forgetting there are others to come, then none.'

There was a long silence as we sipped our gins. Then he began telling me about his daughter, how she'd always wanted to be an actress, got the looks for it. 'And then the silly old ninny fell in love with a soldier, in bloody tanks, what's more.'

'He seemed a decent sort of chap,' I said.

'Lovely girl,' he said, returning the wave of the louts as they left the bar. Then, abruptly, he stood up and braced his shoulders. 'Better go. Afternoon nap. Good of you to come along. Doesn't do to think about Jenners, does it?'

I led the way to his car, wondering if I should offer to drive. He concentrated hard on the way home and I didn't want to interrupt that. When he dropped me off, I thought for a moment he had fallen asleep, or worse, for he did not turn to say goodbye and was leaning forward over the steering wheel. I bent down to wave before closing the door and he looked up at me and said, 'What a load of bollocks that was. That's why I go to church: wear my tie, stop myself thinking bollocks for a while, or a different, more elevated sort of bollocks anyway.'

I too slept that afternoon and dreamt he gave his daughter away to me in Westminster Abbey. Though by the end of the service she became Maureen who got into a limousine on her own and vanished. The Colonel and Agnes walked away in the opposite direction, the two louts in tow, leaving me alone in my morning suit and top hat until my former wife came up to me and took me by the hand saying, 'Don't be so serious, you're so serious sometimes.'

It might be of some interest, though it's of no conceivable interest to me, to recount how my days are normally spent. First thing in the morning I have breakfast: an orange, a bowl of nuts, dried fruit, oats and other roughage which I buy in bulk and mix myself. I have read somewhere that this is wholesome and can quite believe it. The crunching and chewing helps to get the day off to a determined start. Also, my bowels have never functioned better. I then browse through *The Times*, hastening towards the crossword which I can't resist. I've been known to study it for hours without getting a single clue. Once I got it out altogether but that took me the best part of three days of doing little else. Usually, I do up to a third of it and give up around ten-thirty.

After that, I sometimes do what I'm doing now or potter in the garden, or drive to the shops and the library, or do things about the house, a bit of painting, crack-filling, banging and screwing. The standard housework I do on Sunday mornings before settling down to the newspapers which take up most of the day. On some afternoons I go for a drive, to the coast or to one of the larger towns where I visit antique shops from which I buy small, inexpensive, insignificant objects like egg cups, ill-assorted pieces of flawed china which I distribute about the place on ledges, shelves and window sills. I also buy old photographs and postcards, the faded brown ones, sometimes in chipped silver frames, which I hang on walls. Many of them are of people so that I am surrounded by others' loved ones who stare out at me as if I ought to be someone else. They look proud and confident but cheated somehow, especially the stern young men in uniform wanting to be remembered at their most handsome and manly like that. There are other photographs too: of formal gardens (two), fishing vessels (three of those), a pier, a sundial with a pet rabbit on it, King George V and Queen Mary in a carriage waving but not smiling as the royal family, I can't think why, seems to have more reason to do these days, a bad-tempered Alsatian with a Siamese cat lying across its paws, an African chief in layers of regalia, and four of naked women posing in veils on or against furniture, plump bottomed and small breasted, with a saucy immodesty unlike the blatancy of such portrayals these days which I can do without, what though? There is a place where I can buy cheap frames to put these pictures in and sometimes I change them round. Thus when I wander about my house, my windows on to the past give it an impermanence, while the dim brown shadowlessness adds a fading constancy to things.

The books I borrow from the library are still mainly thrillers or deal with the lives of the explorers. I read very few novels mainly because it is too easy to see through the cunning and the characters aren't true to life, being mainly their authors' playthings. The young men in the photographs have set me reading about the First World War. I do not comprehend the full senselessness and horror of it, but it is within my

236

reach unlike so much else that has happened and is happening all the time. It is every day in the papers and on television, a cruelty and terror beyond imagining. There is one photograph of men lining up to enlist in 1914. There are a few women and children about, grinning too or not worried about much as if gathering for a parade or watching their menfolk queue up for a football match. Everyone is having a good time. I can look at that. There is so much else I can't. My mind just casts it out.

But in between it doesn't bother me at all. It forces itself on my attention and then I forget all about it. I wonder if other people are the same. Some have it well under control, Jenners for instance. I once met him in the library. He told me how busy he was keeping, serving on a committee for the protection of the countryside, an enterprise something-or-other, the regional United Nations Association I think he said, and 'of course our dear little church', absolutely crucial as that was to some research he was doing into local history.

'Well, one did acquire a few serviceable skills, organized the odd Royal Commission, put one's thoughts for what they were worth into some sort of order, didn't one? Learnt what made the system tick, set the old wheels in motion . . .'

I was thumbing through a colour supplement at the time, which had an article on Cambodia and another on mentally ill people released into the community. He had definite views on both these matters which he expressed with little movements of hands and eyebrows to indicate the bounds of common sense . . . on the one hand, on the other hand, such a pity but mind you . . . Finally he said, 'Do drop by whenever you feel like it, but best give me a call first.' As I say, there was nothing exclusive about him, his misgivings were all-embracing.

As for the rest of the day, it's usually soup with leftovers in it for lunch, something ready-made with potatoes for supper, reading or dozing off in the late afternoon, TV in the evenings, perhaps a little more of this writing before going to bed with a milk drink and a bite out of a sleeping pill. I have very neat handwriting so cannot see the advantage of getting a typewriter which would interrupt the sound of music on the radio in the background, the classical kind so that at least I'm coming to know the names of the composers. Some will take more getting used to than others, Mussorgsky and Khachaturian, for example. I suppose that's the trouble really, Maureen. In this small house music and television couldn't satisfactorily have taken place at the same time.

After our trip to Greenwich I waited ten days for her to phone me, wondering if she was waiting for me to phone her. Guesswork is such a labour of love or lovelessness. She answered at once.

'I came down with such a cold the next day. I was a misery, wasn't I?'

'Absolutely not.'

'I had to give choir practice a miss that night.'

'Wouldn't a married woman have done instead?'

She laughed and I saw her front teeth fully showing. 'We're short enough of altos as it is. We need more tenors too.'

'I thought you did it for nothing.'

A shorter laugh this time, understandably. I thought I heard a voice in the background. Let her be listening to a man on the wireless, I beseeched. But he could not be the only other person there unless he was telling her constantly to put the phone down. We nattered comfortably for a while, neither saying, 'When shall I see you again?' (The only advice my father gave me about girls was, 'Never seem too keen.' To which my mother replied, 'That's the idea, is it? Show your hand and they'll tell you your fortune.' She had a way with words sometimes. My father enjoyed that too, repeating it often for several weeks but never in her hearing.)

Finally I said, 'Let you know when I'm next in town and if you were free for lunch or something or dinner or . . .'

'That'd be nice,' she replied, her voice untrembling with excitement.

Well, fair enough, the flag wasn't flapping away at the top of my mast either.

In the end it was she who took the initiative, sending me a notice about the performance of Haydn's *Creation* with a note scribbled across it, 'Any chance you could come? Yours Maureen.' Underneath that was what under the magnifying glass turned out to be not a very small x, but a bit of sloppiness on the part of the printer. The event was two weeks away so I phoned at once to say I had to be in town that day and I'd love to. Whereupon she invited me to her flat for a bite to eat beforehand, the church where they were performing being only walking distance away. Well, well, things were happening at a rattling pace, weren't they?

I tried to find out from the library how long *The Creation* lasted. That is, if it started at seven-thirty, when would it be over by: too late for a postponed pudding, given some rule against singing on too full a stomach? I tried this out that evening after a supper of fish fingers and two baked potatoes, sliced bananas and yoghurt and the usual imperfections of my voice were decidedly more so, not to mention the muffled and timeless accompaniment down there in the wind department. Meanwhile my mind's eye behaved erratically, needing a variety of lenses in quick succession, mainly in the short-sighted range. The girl in the public library had a magnificent sense of humour, replying, 'Six days, if you can believe it.' A call to the local choral society perhaps: 'Excuse me, you don't know me from Adam but, as he might have put it, how long did *The Creation* take before the real cock-up began?'

All this written the day after my call. It reads squalidly, and so it should, ending as it did in reviling myself twice over followed by purging my guts on the lav, bare feet on the lino floor, a sore throat and an ache in my back which launched lightning attacks on my shoulder blade. Like the world before it all began, I was in no form at all and void, Godless and wordless.

Over this period I had a call from my son Adrian. For reasons I've given elsewhere he's always been the one I was most worried about. He is studying accountancy and business management at a polytechnic in the Midlands, not far from my home town, in fact. He'd always sounded lonely and abandoned, this time especially so. His studies were going well, he said. 'How are you, well, off for money?' I asked. 'Bearing in mind that I'm not.' It wasn't that, he said. He only wanted to say hello and how was I getting on? 'I'm not telling you that,' I replied. 'So you'll have to come and see for yourself. Enjoying the life, are you?' 'Everything's fine,' he said in a way that told me it wasn't one bit. Soon he'd be looking for a job, there were several possibilities. 'Like me to pull a few strings?' I said. 'Or wouldn't that be fair on the others?' His small laugh at that could only have meant one of two things, alas. I said goodbye to him, wishing I'd said more, had had more to say.

A week or so before, I'd spoken to his mother about him. She phoned me.

'How *are* you, Tom, in your country retreat?'

'Still limping along, my back to the enemy.'

'The same old Tom.'

I left a pause. 'Enjoyed having Virginia here with her bloke. She seemed pretty got together, adding her bit to the sum total of human happiness, following in her mother's footsteps. You did a good job on her. Gave her a conscience . . .'

'To a large degree, though, they have to give themselves that,' she interrupted. 'But I do so agree with you that it's right-wing claptrap to maintain that people must be held responsible for their own actions. We've been doing research into a group of non-achievers and . . .' A male voice sounded in the background. '. . . under-achievers and what we're beginning to find is an intriguing correlation between a random class sample on the one hand and on the other a sex . . .'

Her voice gathered speed, the pitch rose and we were getting into a fully-fledged keynote address.

It was my turn to interrupt. 'I'm with you. Another throw of the dice and it would all have been different, but the older you get the more you are only all you might have been.' I looked out of the window. 'The more so on days like this, sunlight and things, a mown lawn . . .'

'No, Tom,' she said patiently. 'Everything in one sense can be *helped*. Necessity, chance, these are not the determinants of choice, but its enforced contextualization . . .'

Again the voice sounded in the background. I tried to change the topic, if that was what it was.

'Our son called, by the way. He seems all right, but difficult to tell with him. Is there any particular line you think I ought to be taking?'

'Well, he's a case, isn't he . . . ? Let's put it this way, I'm not sure I would have chosen commerce for him. Might it take him out of himself as it were too *far*? To what extent, as we keep telling him, does he *trust* himself?'

'I see the snag there, for a chap on the track of whoever's fiddling the books.'

'That's not what I meant, quite. We try to tell him, Bradley and I, that, relatively speaking, he has all the up-front advantages, and to the extent that that is true, self doubt is, how shall we say, too readily trivialized. We really do try to draw him out of himself. We point out how the Webb episode, that general frame of reference rather, has an obsessive minimality in the *scale* of things. Terminal individualism is the extreme case of that.'

'Oh, if that's all.'

'You realize of course that he may be homosexual?' There was a pause here while a conversation went on at the other end. 'To put it simply, it's the mattering of that that matters, you do see that, don't you?'

'Well yes, but it could matter to him a lot if he'd rather not be bug . . . bothered with the whole thing.'

'But isn't that just the point? You do see the point, don't you?'

The waters gathered above my head as I imagined Adrian there, adrift on the deeps of their calm, incomprehensible reason. And what did I have to offer in its place? If you're going to be gay, at least try to be gay about it. Outside/inside plumbing, whatever turns you on/off. Worked-up stuff of no use to anyone. Time to bring this conversation to an end.

'Anyway, I'm sure between the two of you, you've got it all worked out. Just so long as you leave him with a leg to stand on.'

She took this as a reference to why Virginia has one leg shorter than the other. The other voice came closer, saying something that sounded like 'parental imbalance'.

'You mustn't be bitter, Tom, it isn't like you.' A pause, waiting for my response. 'Are you there?'

'Sure. I wondered if . . . I only meant his own two feet . . . You're the pros. You're not averse to . . . Oh scrub round it.'

'That's exactly it, Tom, the balance between directness and caution. Brad and I give encouragement in every way we can. You see, when a person is undelineated by what we've decided to call an unresolved self model and the parental model, or models rather, are discrete (ee tee ee), less than complementary (with an ee), when, for example, shared assumptions are unexplored, the borderline between family responsibility and state res . . . Are you there?' The mumble resumed in the background. I left a longer pause this time. 'Are you there, Tom?'

'Ooops, sorry,' I said. 'Milk coming to the boil. Now where were we? Oh yes, well, that. Sounded spot on to me. I'm sure he'll be all right so long as, in theory anyway, he's spared the theory.' I heard in the background what was about to lead to another interruption. 'Anyway, so long, keep up the good work. Regards to Brad.'

'Bye, Tom. I think we're more or less agreed the overriding factor . . .'

I hung up, then sat there for a long time, head in hands, wishing it hadn't been me when Adrian had his first experience of lust in Webb's garage all those years ago. My wife had made it her business to make life happier for people and must often have succeeded in doing so, very often indeed. And that went with believing and understanding a lot, whereas those of us who lack belief and understand little tend on the whole to achieve nothing. Fine. I didn't want my son to be a case of anything, that's all. I haven't been fair to my wife, I know, getting the jargon wrong and muddling it up, though unmuddled it was no less muddling to me. Bloody Brad in the background hadn't helped exactly. The thought of him holding forth about my son, and to his face, was what kept my head in my hands, my eyes tight shut, for as long as they were.

Now there's AIDS too. I see my son's pale, melancholy, fated face on those with the disease who are interviewed on television. I find myself then loathing homosexuality for the risk it puts him in of becoming like them. I think that if that is how he dies, I would not want long to outlive him. And if it came to that, how hugely much better use to him his mother would be for she would have many things to say to him, while I would have nothing, nothing at all.

Chapter Six

I reached Maureen's flat about half an hour early, having booked into a hotel in the region of King's Cross: no questions asked. A couple were signing in when I arrived and the woman was giggling because the man had written Mr and Mrs Roger. He didn't look that imaginative, too like me in other ways as well, thickening everywhere except on top, looking forward to a little bit of future before he was even more past it, his impatience already touched with remorse. On the way to the lift she turned to me and twitched at her silken black dress where the base of her knickers was so I wasn't sure which got there first, my glimpse or her forefinger. She winked, an occupational habit which made me wish she didn't have to carry on with the likes of me until those eyelids, dry with disgust, all the rest, finally stuck fast . . . Oh God, the sooner I saw Maureen again the better. If only to discover there was still another side to myself.

I walked the streets around the house where her flat was, imagining her life there: some unfulfilled trees, dustbins with their lids off, people hurrying back from work, children on the roads like bored gladiators wanting the traffic to try harder to knock them flat. There was a stench in the air of cement dust and rehashed stew left too long in ovens. The houses had a splintered look, the splashes of paint here and there like last attempts to stop them falling apart. This was Maureen's world into which she stepped handsomely every morning, not giving it a second glance.

She lived on the top floor but one and as I pressed the entryphone button, a curtain parted a few feet away and a child stuck out his tongue at me. The door buzzed and up I went, not hurrying but still puffed when she opened her door and pulled me towards her for a peck on the cheek. She was in a glossy long blue dress with a lavender sash at the waist and was sufficiently bare from the neck down to show how and how far her breasts dangled. Her hair was tightly

243

drawn back and piled up and pinned together in a knot of astonishing complexity.

'We have just over an hour,' she said. 'I always treat myself to a cab on these occasions.'

'You look grand,' I said. 'In good voice tonight?'

She answered this by holding her hands to her stomach and letting forth a series of descending notes which let me see quite far into where they came from. Then she poured me a sherry and strode off into the kitchen, her dress swishing and hinting broadly . . .

There was some choral music quietly playing from concealed loudspeakers. It was a comfy room: two rows of records and three racks of tapes, matching sofa and armchair profuse with meadow growth, a desk with its lid closed, two other chairs newly upholstered in dark red velvet, a bound set of unopened-looking books of the sort advertised in the colour supplements, striped off-purple and tarnished-gold curtains, and three paintings on the walls. The first, above the boarded-up fireplace, was of a village in a valley, slightly blurred so perhaps an over-enlarged photograph. The second was of a youngster with long blond hair in green breeches with a large-eyed, big-eared dog at his feet and some thick, vague woodland in the background. The third portrayed a long-haired white goat stuck in the mud by a lake about to give up the ghost and add its bones to the others lying about – this might have been a photograph too, in which case perhaps there was still hope for it.

She called through from the kitchen, 'We're having lamb. You're not vegetarian, are you?'

'Goodness me, no. It's gambling with one's health, I know, but I love a good stake.'

'Help yourself to another drink.'

I did so and had a closer look at all those records.

'Quite a record collection,' I called out though she was now right behind me, about to lay the table.

No candles. No wine glasses either. But a vase containing six roses had appeared, which ought to have been brought by me, and the table-cloth was made of lace or at any rate had that intricate see-through quality.

'They keep me sane,' she said.

'I'm a terrible ignoramus in this area, as you've discovered,' I replied, pulling one out at random. The sleeve was taken up with the face of Kathleen Ferrier.

'I've heard of her,' I said. 'My father had a ghastly old gramophone and hardly any records but two of them were of her. He played them often in a sort of trance. "There's your father's bit of crackling again," my mother used to say. I don't think he was listening to the music itself – mother was right – I think it just reminded him of things.' But by now I was talking to myself because she was back in the kitchen again.

The meal was very nicely done, proper dishes for the vegetables with gravy jug to match, mint sauce and roast potatoes. She told me about her choir, that she had been one of its founding members, then she dabbed at her lips and said, 'We'll have to leave the dessert till afterwards. Do you like mousse? Mousse is my forte.'

'Not chocolate mousse, by any remote chance?' I asked. 'I'd eat that even at my age.'

She was looking down at what her fork was doing with the last three or four of her peas, pensive perhaps about what might or might not be allowed to occur after the afters. But no. Without looking at me, she said softly, 'It helped me to get over my marriage.'

'Whipping up the odd mousse, you mean . . . get a move on, you horny beast.'

'Joining the choir. He didn't care for culture. He thought I was getting above myself.'

'I see. Putting on all those airs . . .'

Still not a trace of a smile, and no wonder. 'He thought I looked down at him. He wasn't a tall man. I hate to say so but he wasn't very educated, beer with the lads, West Ham United, rubbish on the telly all night. And when there was an opera or concert I wanted to watch he called me culture vulture and artsy fartsy.'

'Not a whole lot in common, in fact . . . ?'

'He began hitting out sometimes. I lost a child and couldn't have any more. At the same time he lost his job and his big joke was that he was looking for another one putting wheels on miscarriages. I was very young. I hated him and I've never used my married name since, never.'

Her voice was very quiet now and I could see a pinkness gathering at her neck. After all those years married to a well-informed woman, could I do no better than say, 'When people feel inferior, threatened, they either get nasty or try to be funny. The two can get mixed up . . .'

But she wasn't listening and the tears were beginning to form. 'Then there was this man I met in the choir, a base . . .'

'. . . fellow,' I interjected.

She glanced at me patiently, dabbed at her eyes and plumped her napkin down on her lap. 'We must think about going,' she said.

'Will he be there tonight, the man . . . ?'

She shook her head. 'When he passed on, sixteen years ago it was, do you know what my husband said? "Just picture him belting it out in the chorus of bloody angels. His idea of heaven, I should think." Then he put his face right up against me and laughed. By then he hated me but I was never unfaithful or anything like that.' She stood up, patting her face with her napkin in various places. 'I shouldn't burden you with all this.'

She went to the window to see if the minicab had arrived. I saw a street lamp come on and across it a drift of light rain. In the brightly lit room of a house opposite a woman was leaning out of the window, elbows on the sill, and looking up at the sky, one of the multitude with nothing to do and nowhere to go that evening.

'I'm sorry, Maureen,' I said, 'I have no story to tell like that. My marriage came to an end too. With regret perhaps but no hatred. Unless you include the telly, culture didn't come into it. Things are upsetting enough already without that. What I mean is . . .' But I didn't know what I meant.

She drew the curtain as the woman opposite seemed to shout something with extreme loathing but it was only a yawn.

'There's the cab now,' she said.

I helped her into her coat and she stayed between my hands for an instant before leading the way through the door and down the steep stairs. Fleeting thoughts the while about the mousse, my artlessness, the long stretches of misery in her life, the dead man with a deep voice, my rotten jokes, the word pathfinding for the flesh. And so, in the cab, I kept my hands firmly to myself, thrust between my thighs, keeping a good distance between us.

'Nervous?' I asked.

'A little,' she replied.

I reached across to give her hand a squeeze but, like her mind, it was elsewhere and my spasm of affection was wasted on a handbag.

I sat fairly far back in the church but could keep an eye on her because she was the tallest in her row by a long way and her mouth opened wider, as if trying to hold the conductor's attention, warn him of trouble ahead if he didn't calm down and concentrate on one thing at a time. The only other singers with larger mouths were both basses who seemed to be in competition with each other regardless of what else was going on. I counted eight singers who only seemed to be singing part of the time, apprentices perhaps or there to keep an eye on their loved ones. The orchestra had no choice in the matter and that's how they looked; assuming they were being paid they were only there for the notes, as it were. By contrast the soloists sang for all they were worth.

I then studied the rows of women more carefully, imagining some of them equally passionate in other situations. A higher proportion of the men had beards than in the population as a whole and I tried to guess their occupations; mainly in the public sector, I guessed, adding a bit of energy to it here and there. But then, my eyes closed or closing, I listened to the music for quite long stretches instead of dreaming beyond it of other things. And it made me happy – that and the thought of people coming together for some such purpose from time to time and being so wholly revived by it.

We walked back to her flat and I told her how much I'd liked it, I could see how much she was enjoying herself. She talked about technical things, where the tenors got lost and the second violins didn't come in and the altos were out of tune in the third chorus. While I thought about chocolate mousse and what was for afters.

We sat at opposite ends of the sofa, listening to the same music sung by one of the best choirs in the world, culture once more disturbing the natural order of things. I ate a great deal of mousse and before turning the record over she told me more about herself: her father an insurance agent, now retired in Bournemouth, her mother once a nurse, a brother in Australia who had to give up cricket because he had a drink problem. The other end of the sofa might as well have been the other end of the earth too except that here there wasn't a drink in sight. The mousse was finished, the coffee pot empty for the second time. She stood up and put the record in its sleeve. Not risking that she wouldn't put on another, I stood up too.

'I ought to be going. You must be tired. Can I help with the washing-up?'

She shook her head. Then, as I was about to open the door, or was hovering thereabouts, finding nothing to say, she came over to me and put her palms on my chest. It was all so sudden that I toppled against the door.

'I'm falling for you, you see,' I said.

Her hands went back there but slightly lower. 'Thank you for coming, Tom. You have been very sweet.'

'Eaten a lot of it too . . . It's been . . .'

The word became flesh and I took her face between my hands and we kissed, not hard, in fact barely touching and mouths closed.

Pushing me gently away, her eyes were shut and her head was bowed as if in prayer, leading me deeper into temptation.

'It's a terrific cheek, God knows,' I mumbled, placing my hands round and just below her waist. 'But what would you say if I made a pass at you . . . ?'

She thought for a very long time, putting her arms around me until we were up against each other, or in my case prevented from being. My hands descended further where her body hardened, then softened, and I pressed her into me. We kissed again, my mouth open, hers not much but enough for my first taste of her, the last of the mousse. Then she pushed me away and began to pray again. My hands stayed where they were.

'I'm being rather hard on you, I'm afraid,' I said.

She liked that and gave her sudden, chuckling laugh. 'I've got to get up early tomorrow to catch a train to Bournemouth. I'm going down to see my parents.'

'Oh Lord! Then I'll have to watch myself. Though it's not quite the same thing.'

'It's a very early train . . . And I . . .'

' . . . I understand. Carried away on the transport of delight I missed my connection.'

She was drawing away from me, less now to be drawing away from. 'No, Tom, it's not that. It's . . . We don't know each other. We might regret it. Think, that was that. You do understand, don't you? He loved me too in the beginning.'

I nodded vigorously. 'But you don't mind the pass having been made?'

'No, of course not.'

'I find you attractive in all the ways . . . so long as you know that.'

I went over to the window, holding her hand, then letting it drop as if she would sense from it I had started to lie.

'It's not raining. I think I'll walk for a while,' I said.

'You're not cross, are you?' she whispered, putting a hand on my back.

'Absolutely not. I've been very happy this evening. Still am. It's just that . . . Do put another record on. My father's bit of crackling, why not?'

She bent forward to put on Kathleen Ferrier. Her dress clung and cleaved. She turned, still bent, and caught my leer, then ran her hand across her buttocks.

'You'll keep in touch, won't you?' she said, fetching my coat.

'Won't hold it against you, not this time,' I said, kissing her on the cheek. 'No hard feelings,' I added, rolling my eyes and making a rapid, rather stooped, escape to the sound of her chuckle and the voice of Kathleen Ferrier singing about the lamb that taketh away the sins of the world.

Back at the hotel the woman was waiting in the lobby, in conversation with the night watchman. They fell silent when I asked for my key and waited for the lift. As the door closed, I saw her watching me with one eyebrow raised, her tongue between her lips. I shook my head but grinned. If there had been a knock on the door I do not know what I would have done. Thoughts of Maureen soon sent me to sleep, of her ardent singing and silken haunches. It was clear I would see more of her, but when and how much? I awoke the next morning with the same expectancy but left it well alone. It was pouring with rain and I discovered I had not packed my razor and both taps ran with lukewarm water.

In the following weeks I went up to London on two occasions, returning home the same evening. We went to an afternoon concert and to a matinee at the National Theatre. Sometimes we held hands in various mobile ways. Having tried to go too far too fast before, I wanted her to know, I suppose, I wasn't after only one thing, or that only by the wayside on a longer journey. But as I am writing this after all the rest, when the journey is over and I have only a few notes to guide me, I cannot tell whether I deceive myself that she was not then being deceived. I did little to make myself known to her, giving her the freedom to make herself known to me, for example sharing views with me to which I responded with none of my own, or hardly.

On the first afternoon we passed some youngsters on the street, presumably out of work at that time of day but with a smartness and swank about them nonetheless.

'Yergh! They could find work if they wanted to. They ought to bring back National Service,' she said vehemently.

'I did National Service,' I said. 'And I've never looked for work since.'

'They think the world owes them a living. All take and no give. All please and no thank you. As if they owned the place, no respect, no self-discipline. Or am I being unfair, showing my age?'

I said nothing. One of the youths hooted at us behind our backs. It was a cruel sound and I did not know what I might have said. We were passing through a street strewn with garbage, which she stepped round in exaggerated fashion, sensibly though, considering the dog-shit in amongst it.

'These ghastly, loony Labour-run councils, what do you expect?'

That needed verifying and again I said nothing, studying the rude words scrawled on the walls and then drawing her attention to a gleaming silver car with the following words scratched into the paintwork of its bonnet: 'Wats the difference between a BMW and a hedghog? The prickes are on the outside of a hedgog.'

'You see,' she said. 'The politics of envy. If they could spell they wouldn't think like that, would they?'

I told myself she was only fastidious and good luck to her as she spoke further of Maggie and we made our way past grand and grimy old buildings which looked pleased with themselves, reminding of times when we had the confidence or enterprise or whatever it was to tell the rest of the world how to conduct itself. And what was I to say, a man wishing to fall in love, when she spoke of the money some of the London Boroughs were spending on blacks and gays and lesbians and not on stamping out drugs and hooliganism and all the real evils of the world? 'Surely you agree . . . ?' she would begin or end with. But most of the time we talked about other things and I got away with an 'Oh dear' here and a 'ts ts' there, hearing the sound of my wife's voice taking to task the ignorant and uncompassionate, trapped between this righteousness and that. My poor Maureen, don't listen to her, I cried or want to cry now. As I cried silently once between the Webbs and Hambles, Plaskett and Hipkin, my children and their mother.

I feared she would ask me how I would vote, for the truth was I wouldn't know for sure until my hand was poised above the ballot paper and I tried to recollect what I had read in the newspaper or seen on the telly that day or the day before that had impressed me so much. I'm one of those the party political broadcasts are aimed at, for each convinces me of something at the time always including, in part, the condescending frightfulness of the broadcast itself. And then I reflect that all of us have something in us that corresponds to everything all the politicians tell us, so that on Friday evening or Monday morning we might vote quite differently, taking a rest from it all on Sunday when one would rather not be bothered with any of it at all. Personalities influence me too. There is a part of me that goes along some of the way with whoever is doing the talking, though it soon becomes baloney according to someone else so that if you listened to everyone they'd all be talking baloney all the time. It can be very disturbing, all that variety of moods and opinions and attitudes. So that one ends up not knowing who one is or what to think except when one stops having thoughts along these lines and settles for not having any new experiences at all. If you recall, I once tried to clear my mind of all this by thinking about liberty. However, that also means a few people being free to muck many more other people about while equality, it stands to reason, leads to preventing almost as many people from being as free as they'd like to be to prevent other people being as free as they are. But then there's that third French notion of fraternity which, as I've indicated, I've sometimes got the feel of, though it's only a dream, what might be, and never you forget it. I don't mean the warm, fuzzy American version that Plaskett would now be well into – a man who never had the liberty of mind to think equality worth minding about. No, I mean the seaside in the old days with my family, the clumsiness and confusion of it, the very old and the very young and everyone in between gathered together in the open air, a vast silence and stillness beginning just above and beyond their noise and movement, the pockets of people, their private caring made public. Or Maureen's choir united in singing forth about a new created world and heavens telling the glory of God, or the market day I found myself wandering among two weeks ago. Well, none of that helps me to decide how to vote though I get closest then to understanding what I might believe if I had the imagination and tenacity or whatever to believe anything. Political conviction doesn't seem to come near that. Perhaps politics has little to do with the uncertainties of life. There is even greater doubt about the politicians themselves of course.

When I went to see my father in hospital there was awkward gathering and coming and going of a different kind. Each time I saw him, I was reminded of the seaside, the sea air, the sparkling water, a ship or two in the distance, the dozing and prancing about and making buildings in sand, the wind constantly altering the clouds and the water so that every day was different and for some was always the last. The people were the same as those in the hospital coming and going with flowers and paper bags of fruit, hushed and overcome with anxiety at bedsides. It was he who reminded me, just by lying there, because that was when he had been most happy, despite what my mother said about the idiot we'd left in charge of the shop and all the other idiots who had come all that way and were spending all that money to make sure we wouldn't enjoy ourselves as much as we otherwise might have done.

My father lay with his blind eyes gazing at the sun, trousers rolled up to his knees, his hands caressing each other at his waist. While my mother sat and knitted, looking about her for something else to find ridiculous and no better place than the seaside for that, so she had quite a good time too. Neither swam though my father paddled, treading the shallows with a kind of stealth. Almost his last words to me were, 'Let's go to the seaside again, Tom lad, when I get out of here. Just the bloody blue sky and water going on for bloody ever and a nice breeze blowing. Wouldn't mind so much if it caught up with me then not like here, a bit of rooftop and pissing down more likely than not.'

That is how I most often remember my parents, at the seaside. I don't know how they voted. My mother may not have done so at all and hardly a day passed when she didn't say that was the sort of daft thing the government would do or some politician or other ought to take that self-satisfied expression off his face. My father used to say, 'Politics, take it or leave it, I can. Somebody's got to do it.' (If they did cast a vote, his would have been the opposite of hers, his one chance every four years or so to cancel her out.)

You probably skipped most of that. I sympathize because so did I when Maureen finally did ask me about Mrs Thatcher, adding that her parents had always worked for the Conservatives which in Bournemouth must be rather like offering the groundsman at Wimbledon the use of your nail scissors. We were settling into our seats at the Festival Hall and some Elgar was on the way for starters, Pomp and Circumstance March Four, and the best I could manage in place of the above was, in my ventriloquist's voice.

'She gets my goat . . .' (Which she doesn't actually, or not always by any means.)

And that was sufficient as the orchestra tuned up and she laid her hand on mine and I remembered my father humming the better known march as he prodded away at his own bit of hopeless, inglorious land at the back and whispered the words 'mother of the free' when she brought him out a cup of tea and told me to run along and buy him a flag.

'My vote too, she's so *right* for us,' Maureen hissed as the conductor took his bow and she gave my hand a squeeze.

I nodded, we turned to each other and smiled, our secrets unshared. Her hand squeezed tighter as the march progressed and I was glad it wasn't the other one because then I might have let out a yell unparalleled in the annals of public concerts. But it was rousing nonetheless as it led me through undergrowth with the prospect of open country beyond.

That happened next. It was a piano concerto by Beethoven, the slow movement of which is much loved even by those who don't much love music. A long, dreamy stroll it made for out in the open country, nothing imaginably more perfect. But it wasn't just the music of course, it was hearing it with her as she leant forward, head a little on one side, eyes closed, lips damp, a curl of hair encircling her earlobe etc. so that it was hard to tell which was doing most for which. Or, put another way, if this was love could it only be sustained at that pitch by going about in her company with one of those Walkman machines dangling from my shoulder? Would it go on keeping out the dread of what was looming up on the horizon, the black clump of trees, clouds massing above them and with no other path than the one you are on going right to the heart of it?

It was only a short stroll out in the open country through meadows in the sun, with cattle grazing in the middle ground and beyond them fields of wheat flowing up to the sky. Or some such until the mind became the old darkening battlefield again, the factions changing sides with no prospect of truce, and memories picked their way among the casualties like nurses, failing to console or heal. The spirit, like the flesh, could not be kept up indefinitely. Beethoven in the end only set up a new series of skirmishes, the old hanker and wail set to music so that when it came to an end, the ridiculous was even more so, having passed through the sublime. Nothing left then of clumps of trees or sunlit wheat fields.

However. We were brought closer. Let that be enough. Desire crept up on the companionable, or rather the clearing slowly extended into the undergrowth to reveal it amiably crouching there. I chatted easily with her, our hands interlocking as often as not when walking or waiting somewhere so that when the conversation eventually led up to her visiting me in Suffolk it was no rash leap in the dark.

We were sitting at supper after having seen *The Three Sisters* by Chekhov. Her view roughly was that it was difficult to feel sorry for people who moped about so much, no wonder they killed each other for no good reason and Communism served them right, the way that woman treated the servants, they had it coming to them. I didn't disagree with her, obviously, but also because the characters had pissed me off too while at the same time taking part in a play that managed to be both tragic and comic, wholly depressing and wholly satisfying, at the same time. And then it was she who paid for the tickets. I'd taken the trouble to read a few of the reviews which had been mainly about the acting and the production rather than the play itself which chimed with what I'd seen of theatre people on television, wanting only to talk about themselves, how they were doing, not what they were doing and who wrote it. In fact they talked about their careers much as Chekhov's characters did about life, never getting outside themselves. Anyway, the reviews hadn't helped me to say anything about what the play was about, giving me scope though to say, as I dug decisively into my last chunk of forest cake, 'That youngest sister, I feel like her sometimes, wondering what I'm missing in the big city, like seeing a great deal more of you.'

She mopped her lips and covered my hand with hers. 'And I long for the country. I was born in the country, or nearly, Rickmansworth actually.'

'Why not come out for the day? We could drive to the sea, look at the fishing boats, there's a nice . . .'

'And stay overnight . . .' she said, feeling for where her handbag wasn't beneath her feet.

I spluttered into my napkin, depositing there the sickly evidence of consumption.

'Certainly. There are a couple of nice little hotels. Or . . .'

She looked at me steadfastly, absolutely not winking or letting anything happen to her features at all. 'Provided the bedroom door can be locked or bolted,' she said.

'Or better still both,' I replied, my own face up to goodness knows what unsteadfastness. 'You'd sure have to knock first.'

Well, she laughed at that as I did too, its humour quickly escaping me. We fixed on a date there and then, three weeks hence. It was a fond parting, a kiss on the mouth, lips given time for a little promising mobility. And both hands held long thereafter.

The next three weeks were expensive. I'd had a peep at her bedroom whose pale blue and green frills and glossiness, unclipped white woolly rugs, tall triple mirrors, flowery curtains and sculptured lampshades set a certain standard. I settled on golds mainly, including the towels and sheets, but the counterpane was a patchwork of most colours, deep brown predominating, from Morocco or thereabouts. This distracted attention from the coat of magnolia paint I gave the walls, which needed at least one more, still does. I also bought flowers, chocolates, bath salts, scented soap, a red furry lavatory-seat top, lilac air freshener, lavatory-brush holder, soap dish, two china shepherdesses, an antique set of glass and silver dressing table things for which I then had to buy an old-looking dressing table to put them on. Bringing the place up to scratch increased the itch and, after much experimenting with the wattage of light bulbs, the scene was set. Not hard sometimes to understand the appeal of the theatre, why the people in it are so taken with themselves. Plenty of food for thought otherwise, which reminds me I also bought a colourful recipe book.

In the course of all this, I decided to let it be known she was my sister. I enjoy tittle-tattle at least as much as others might enjoy it about me so I didn't want anyone whispering behind our backs as I showed her round, giving her an idea of a way of life we were already within distance of wanting to share so that if we did, its predictability held no surprises, forgetting the even spicier tittle-tattle that would give rise to.

Sidney was the first to be told. He stopped by one evening while I was at work in the garden. I was in a mucky state since I had been trying to pull loose a thick, superfluous root.

'Nice,' he said. 'Very nice, I'm sure. Seems a shame to keep it to yourself. In a manner of speaking.'

'My sister's coming to stay so I thought I'd . . .'

'Oh yes?'

'Tart it up a bit.'

It was the wrong word. He looked me up and down, running his tongue along his fillings, his eye resting on where the button level with my navel was missing.

'Stopping long, is she, this er sister of yours?'

'The weekend.'

I can't be sure he winked then because his eyes went quickly down to my muddy hands, then on to my knees.

'Dirty,' he said distinctly, grinning with a growling sound. 'So that's your story,' he seemed to be saying as he looked me in the face for the first time, still moist and flushed from my exertions, 'but your secret is safe with me.'

'Piss off, you horrid little turd,' I said. Out loud I said, 'It's a messy business,' and flicked a shred of mud off one of my knees. 'Must get cleaned up.' And turned to leave him as he said, 'Hope your sister enjoys it then.'

No telling what expression was on his face, but I thought I heard the growl again. It was all in my mind of course. Paranoia, my ex-wife would call it. Common or garden self-regard I would.

One of the women at the crafts centre had scolded me in the shop for not having visited them so I went there one changeable late afternoon. They occupied a farmstead about a mile away with four small barns or outhouses around a farmyard that had a pig, a goat and a mixture of chickens in it. The same woman came to the door to meet me wearing a calf-length grey night-shirt so that I realized what they'd worn to church hadn't been their working clothes at all. Unless it was the thing she slept in, had just got lopsidedly out of bed in, so that one breast was more clothed by it than the other. A great deal more. It was less rudely therefore that I peered past her into the room as if wondering what might be lurking in wait for me there.

'Come along in,' she said. 'Pretty filthy but that's how it is.'

We settled down to meadow-cuttings tea and a home-made biscuit or muffin while she told me about the centre. I looked around me. Not Maureen's scene at all. The room was a kitchen mostly but also a dump or a transit depot for every practical household object I could think of, skipping over a good few of the others. The place was also a pet shop. As the woman talked, her arms under her breasts shifting the burden off on to me, two of the cats joined us on the table while one dog sniffed my ankles and another licked her outstretched bare foot. A third cat joined us and travelled between us, deciding after a long sniff against the tea but finding other things to lick at on the way. The first two cats had a disagreement, then explored each other and thought better of it. Looking away from the breasts yet again, I glanced downwards. It was as I suspected. There were two dogs smelling my ankles and the sock I could see had threads of moisture across it. I also glimpsed the head of a puppy moving about a lot, one of my shoelaces stuck between its teeth perhaps . . .

'So you really must enrol, you see. Everybody can do *something* . . .' she was saying.

She led me across the courtyard, still barefoot, while I stepped cautiously to avoid the leavings of animals, birds and bad weather. In the first workshop her brother or husband or neither of these was supervising a young man who was making a music stand. He raised a hand to me as if he'd seen me around the place before. There were seven or eight other people working at various stages on classy-looking furniture. The only thing they had in common was that they were all very busy. Side by side working on identical bedside tables were a girl of somewhere about fourteen in black and silver with upright hair whose colours she was still making up her mind about, and a recently barbered elderly man wearing a white shirt with cufflinks, a dark blue tie with golden oak leaves on it and sharply creased twill trousers with turn-ups. At the far end of the workshop were several finished objects: a grandfather-clock case, a small roll-top desk, two matching chairs with high backs and a nest of tables. The woman was telling me about government grants and retail outlets and I asked how much the things would fetch. 'Whatever people are prepared to pay,' she replied defiantly.

In the next workshop, people were working on cloth, weaving it or making it colourful. The other woman was there and showed me round or rather went round giving advice to which I listened in. The people here were the same cross-section, though more female than male or perhaps not because there were two of them it was hard to be sure about. There was some standard fabric to be seen but I had never been into shops or houses where one was likely to find the accidental-looking colours and designs of most of the other stuff. Nobody took the slightest notice of me.

Then on to workshop three, jewellery and leatherwork; and workshop four, pottery. This had the most people in it and their products were all over the place and of every conceivable shape, size, purpose and state of completion. In the far corner I recognized Mrs Jenners, her hands cupped on a turntable round a lump of clay which rose up between them like a thick brown wonky flower coming into bloom. Then, as we were about to leave, a man with his back to us bent forward to do something in an oven turned and straightened his shoulders with a deep breath. It was the Colonel. He came over to us, carrying a broom and wiping his other hand on an apron.

'Won't shake hands,' he said. 'Come to sign up, have you?' He turned to the woman. 'You'll fix him up, won't you, Ruth? Made such a mess of the woodwork put me on jankers in here. Still, get a lot of free wobbly ashtrays and leaking mugs out of it.'

Ruth gave him a punch in the chest, which brought on a fit of coughing. His face turned deep red with some purple in it but he stopped before it became purple all over. 'It's the clay dust,' he finally managed. 'But better than shovelling out the pigs, disgusting brutes. Whatever Ruth here tells you, don't take a blind bit of notice. They're not what they seem. Cheap labour, that's what it is, exploitation.' At which he turned abruptly and busied himself again with his furnace.

We went back into the sunlight. Some chickens gathered round, followed by the pig, then a second. The woman shook her finger at them.

'No you don't,' she said. 'I'm Gwen by the way. He can't tell the difference. Comes here twice a week or so, drops by to tidy up, puts up shelves and generally gets in the way. It's not true about the carpentry. He was incredibly painstaking. Worked for weeks on a table lectern thing, panels on hinges on which he'd begun sketching and carving four figures, the saintly sort you see in stained glass windows but there were limbs and hands and heads all over the place. Suddenly dumped the thing in a corner and forgot all about it.'

I pointed at a building on the other side of the yard. 'More things going on in there too?'

'It's where we can put people up. Some just drift in for a couple of weeks, bored, curious. You don't like to turn them away. But we want the long-termers, proper apprentices. The Colonel hasn't really got the hang of it, thinks we're one of those communes you're always reading about.'

We had now reached the gate and either the bright sunlight or brisk wind had brought tears to her eyes. I thought of my son and what happened to him when he went to learn carpentry from a neighbour. I wanted to see him again soon, though it was only his enduring misery I would see. I tried too to think about Maureen and all we would do together but it didn't last.

'I'm afraid I'd not have the aptitude for any of that. But it's . . .'

'Stuff and nonsense,' she said.

We stood on the damp verge by the track leading to the road where I had left my car. The high trees above us were rustling noisily in the wind, the laden branches threshing about as if to make more room for themselves. The sunlight came intermittently through them and danced at our feet. Seeing her in her night-shirt made me shiver and I pulled my jacket collar up and closed the lapels under my chin.

'Aren't you a bit chilly?' I asked though her face and arms were pink as if she'd lain in the sun too long.

She glanced at me impatiently. 'Everyone can do something, if not well, well enough for them not to be unhappy while they're doing it.'

'I always thought happiness had to do with expectation. Or perhaps that's another kind?'

'Aha!' she replied. 'Fulfilment's desolate attic. The more deceived.'

'Oh yes?' I gave her a mystified smile. 'Have to think about that, won't I?'

She offered me her hand and it was a relief to see goose pimples forming along her upper arm. 'Come back any time. You'll always be welcome. In fact, very welcome. It was kind of you to take the trouble.'

Clearly she meant every word of it and I thanked her. 'That's better,' I said as she buttoned her night-shirt up to her neck. 'Which reminds me, my sister is coming to stay shortly. Perhaps I could bring her along?'

'Of course,' she said with a final plump smile and waddled back towards the house.

On the way back, I thought of taking Maureen there, all done up in some smart outfit, picking her way among the debris. It was out of the question. I made myself a cup of tea and had another look at the spare room, now almost ready for her: the dance of sunlight enfeebled on the confectionery colours, the stench of fresh paint and damp timber and scented spray too thick for the fresh breeze through the open window. The room gleamed smooth and pure, enticing and deceitful. I stood there and watched the wafting of the flimsy lace curtains and thought of the sails of galleons billowing out on the high seas.

Chapter Seven

The day before Maureen's arrival I called on the Colonel to replace a bag of fertilizer his wife had given me. She was away for a few days and he greeted me at the door waving a large cigar about and with the other hand clearing the air. He brought me a cup of coffee with a shaking hand and I told him my sister was coming to stay.

'That's good. Bring her round. Really ought to be in bed but things to do before the old girl comes back. She likes to come back to a house full of flowers. Don't have the odd bunch lying about do you?'

'I could easily pop down to the garden centre . . .'

'Wouldn't hear of it. Can't imagine what she gets up to on these jaunts of hers. Well, that's all right if . . . if what? Mrs Jenners is the one I feel sorry for. Had dinner there the other night. Kind of them of course.' He went out into the garden and threw his cigar away with a slow, bowling motion. He came back, peered into my coffee cup and said, 'More? No. Where was I?'

'Your wife on one of her jaunts.'

'Lots of life in her yet, I can tell you. Damn sight more than me. Where was I? No, that wasn't it. Jenners. From his book on the village, his little monograph he calls it, straight into disarmament without a break. As if it was all my fault. Well, listen, this is it, he caught his old woman yawning and he said, wasn't that just the trouble, the great British public bored out of their insular little minds? She just sat there, poor old dear. If Agnes had been there, I can tell you. She says what she feels like, what she does is her affair.'

He began coughing again and struck himself on the chest. 'Another coffee?' he managed finally. 'Something stronger?'

'I'm sorry,' I said. 'I'm keeping you up. Is there anything I can get you?'

'Decent of you, Tom, isn't it? You're right, a spot of kip. See yourself out can you?'

'Only in the mirror,' I replied, looking downwards at my paunch as he waved and went towards the stairs.

Three steps up, he paused reflectively and gave a series of short wheezes before turning to face me with a gasp, his shoulders beginning to heave.

'Gracious me, Ripple! You can't mean . . .'

I left him standing there making noises I didn't like the sound of at all.

I drove straight to the garden centre and bought two substantial bunches of flowers and a potted plant which I left on his doorstep with a note: 'Herewith some combinations of bloomers. Worth the odd knicker.'

He never offered to pay for them. One of the last things he said to me was, 'You who brought the flowers. Full marks she gave me. Damn good of you.' It was a gratitude more than enough.

Before I write about Maureen's visit, further mention of Nanny Phipps's suitcase. I'd once more asked Sidney about it when I met him in the village shop, immediately then in a frantic rush as a sly look slid up his face and he looked either side of him, leant forward and said, 'Heard . . . ?'

That evening a man phoned. He didn't have a cleft palate, though admittedly with that class of person it's not always easy to tell. His voice was high and drowsy as if the process between thought and word was a tedious squeeze.

'Poor old Nanny,' he began. 'You've bought the cottage. In a home for the elderly near Ipswich. Hate to say it, but not quite all there. Sorry about her belongings. Do drop them off though, if it's not inconvenient. Not a bad place, nor it should be if the bills are anything to go by.'

'You must be the Hal in the photographs,' I said.

'Henry, actually.'

'Devoted to you, I expect?'

'Sad, really, but what does one do? One grows up, gets packed off to school. Life marches on. Tries in one's modest way to do right by people. Sad, really.'

He gave me the phone number of the home and I thanked him for his trouble. Later that evening I spoke to the matron who haughtily told me Miss Phipps had little room left in her life for 'things'. They might upset her but then they might not. 'The more they have, the more they know what will soon be taken away from them. Who can tell what goes on in their heads? Well, memories of course. But those are just as likely to make them bad-tempered, what is missing from them, what they can't remember any longer . . .'

'So an old photograph album might help?'

'Please, Mr Ripple. It is kind of you. But reminders may be worse, showing up what never could have been otherwise.'

'So you'd rather . . . ?'

'I look forward to seeing you. You can decide for yourself.' It was only then I realized she was not haughty but very tired.

And so I decided how we would spend part of Saturday when Maureen came to stay. The rest was becoming unimaginable. What we'd do getting churned about by how and whether we'd do it and forty-eight hours became not the beginning of a lifetime but the life-time itself. The village suddenly became very empty and uneventful, my garden shabby and shrunken, the landscape flatter and more endless, the concert halls a long way away. I moved here and there, touching things with mounting distress – a shortness of breath as the summit loomed.

I wanted to set a tone, casual, self-sufficient, courteous, tolerant of my surroundings, urbane I believe the word is; though in grey cor-duroy trousers, tartan shirt with the top two buttons undone (letting show what might be guessed to be the outer fringe of a splendid thicket but in fact was just about all there was of the thicket itself), a leather-elbowed tweed jacket, and with hair astray and grains of earth under my fingernails, perhaps I should try Roget for another. When she rang to confirm the time of the train, I said, 'Remember to get out at Diss station, not De other one.' Worked out beforehand of course and worth one of her endearing chuckles I'd hoped.

That was the first time in my life when my watch stopped because I had forgotten to wind it. No theories about that, thanks: the way I drove to the station must have disproved them all. So I arrived to find her standing there, raincoat over arm, too large a suitcase surely, and looking pissed off, disconsolate even. So that by the time I'd hurried towards her, bent to lift the suitcase, straightened to kiss her cheek, bent down again, tied an undone shoelace, breathed in deep and said how sorry I was, bloody traffic, my pricking flesh and its damp patches and crevices made me feel I was wearing some loofa material which had not yet dried out. It was a muggy evening, or was it? As we reached my car, I noticed she had reddened too and wasn't saying much. Naturally we only had one thing on our minds or rather several things closely connected or not yet.

I drove home with care but dashed through erratic traffic and only cursed once when a brand-new mauve Japanese job with two dents in it already came to an abrupt halt in front of me. 'You f . . . !' I expostulated, putting an arm out across her body, then back against it protectively, too high though. The driver was a woman with a high head of hair.

'Women drivers,' I said. 'They drive you to drink, then they don't like the pub and want to drive you back again.' Silly, because in my experience men are nastier drivers than women, though usually niftier which is much the same thing.

Eventually we passed the car and the driver turned out to be a Sikh. 'They've got as far as East Anglia, I see,' Maureen said. 'Don't they look fanatical? It's a wonder they ever pass the driving test.'

And they scowled at each other. Did she realize he'd stopped suddenly like that so as not to hit a dog?

'Their driving does tend to be a bit hair-raising,' I said. 'The older they get, you see, the taller the turban.'

'Yergghh,' she replied.

I explained to her that she was my sister. 'You know these villages, everybody minding everybody else's business.' It was only then I asked myself what if we do stay together? They'll point out my cottage and say: that's where Tom Ripple lives, bloke who late in life shacked up with his sister.

But her intentions were no more advanced than mine for she smiled contentedly, the flush now fading. 'Take no thought for the morrow . . . The sermon on the mount.'

'You mean like, Thou shalt not look a gift horse in the mouth?'

Which I thought funny but she laid her hand on my knee and said, 'You shouldn't underestimate yourself.'

We spun down the country roads, the traffic thinning. I told her I'd heard on the radio the concert she said she was going to the week before and had listened for the sound of her clapping. She asked me what I thought of it and I said I'd thought mainly of her, which was true as I waited for the infrequent tunes, so much thick and impenetrable stuff around them, like streams suddenly emerging down the side of high, wooded mountains. She then said something about structure and harmony and the rotten week she'd had in the office what with absentees and temps and other riff-raff. I could see why she went to concerts. We began to relax and I prepared her for what we were having for supper.

Our ease with each other expanded into the evening. We took a walk along the village green and across to the edge of a meadow where the landscape spread out before us. A horse ambled towards us with a series of snorts. Maureen backed away and told it to shoo, flapping her handkerchief at it. It stopped and looked round as if expecting reinforcements, then cantered off in the other direction. It was old and might have been a racehorse once and was showing off once more to the cheering crowds. I had caught a look in its eye, disappointed we weren't somebody else. There was little wind. The sky seemed flattened, the blue whitish as though it had sucked up the clouds. And suddenly the sun burst through below a bank of black clouds lying above the horizon, splashing the browns and greens with silver and gold. She took a deep breath, opened her arms wide and closed her eyes.

'This is so beautiful, so fresh,' she said. 'I could stay here for ever.'

And she was right. It was one of those moments when there was nowhere else one could possibly wish to be. Come off it, Ripple, I told myself, it's only a rare moment of flawless weather and the sun will soon be gone. I put my arm round her and she nestled against me. Well, not really since there was no closer she could get but that's the sort of talk which goes with women and sunsets. She tilted her head towards me and made a long mmm sound.

'I'll run and get the tent,' I said.

Then her arm was round me and for those few minutes the sun stood still. A good variety of birds sang excitedly everywhere and one of them high up at the centre might have been a lark. The world was laid out beautifully like a banquet of all the calm colours and shades of light as the sun was again covered by clouds. And we said nothing, as if anything spoken then could only be less than truthful.

On the way home we passed Sidney's house. He was in his garden with another man and a woman and raised a hand to us. Then, as Maureen dawdled to finger a rose, he lurched over to get a closer look at her. I introduced them and he searched between us for the likeness.

'Come to check up on big brother, have we? Join us for a drink, why don't you?' He was not yet blind drunk but from the way he narrowed and widened his eyes clearly had a terminal focusing problem. Not enough of one though, for he added, 'Can't see the shlightesht reshemblansh myself.'

'Thanks, but no . . .' I replied, beginning to lead the way home.

Maureen stayed put, pulling the lapels of her jacket together as he sized her up. Indeed he might just as well have got out his tape and taken her measurements for a tight-fitting trouser suit. She was transfixed.

'Coming to the Jenners for a church after drinksh tomorrow?' he asked, giving the tape a last little tug at her left nipple. Maureen turned to me and I took three paces further on.

'Come along . . .' I began. 'Or we'll . . .'

Sidney waved his whisky towards his house. 'This the life, eh? Come along along, jusht a quickie-do-do.' He pushed out his stomach and took a step backwards, spilling more of his whisky, then came to attention, clamped his elbows into his waist and let out a belch. 'That's better,' he said.

Maureen, at last, began to come towards me with a contempt on her face I could learn to dread.

'Thanks, Sidney . . .' I began.

He followed us along the fence. 'Your brother boyfriend who gives a shit thank me for his bijou residence, told you that, did he? Bijou froggie for jewel. No English word for bidet is there though? Ever ask yourself *pourquoi*? Extra-ordinaire, promenade on a summer soirée, *le whisky and soda*, hors d'oeuvres for work-horses . . .'

The ensuing doubled-up chortle threw him off balance and he came to attention, trying to click his heels but his feet were too far apart and his knees buckled. His scaly complexion was oozing all over like a layer of ointment. I looked across at his guests who were whispering to each other. The woman looked at her watch and they both got to their feet. Sidney turned round and did a little dance towards them, waving his drink in a circle.

'Come and meet . . . Don't skedaddle for Chriss . . . Not even a petty capot de nuit?' he bleated at us over his shoulder.

I raised my hand and said, 'Another time.'

He took another long look at Maureen and attempted a leer but the effect was of a startled lizard preventing itself from being sick. Then he staggered towards his guests, calling, 'Don't *go!*' before stumbling forwards and falling. As we hurried away, Maureen muttered, 'Serve the revolting little beast right.'

I caught a last glimpse of him being helped to his feet by the man while the woman flicked her hand down the front of her skirt where the last of his whisky had ended up. Maureen went on a little way ahead and I heard him groan loudly, '*Mon dieu, quelle catastrophe. Oh chers amis*, how would I manage *à trois* without you? Umpty pissed. Sister *mon derrière* . . .'

He looked back at me and waved. I waved back. We were like old chums saying goodbye for the last time after a wild binge, sharing a shame that over the years would turn to revulsion.

'Yerrgh!' Maureen said for the second time that day when I caught up with her.

A lot of work will have to go into the next bit but I'd much rather skip it, for I have become less and less sure of how truthful it can be. Anyway, here goes.

As we reached my cottage, the sun finally left the sky. Maureen went up to have a bath and change while I set the scene, moving the candlesticks an inch closer together on the dining table, turning on and off and on the two lamps, adjusting their shades, putting on a record: a Schubert Impromptu if you can believe it. When she came down she was in a full white dress and had a red cardigan round her shoulders. She had let her hair down and drawn it back so that it curled round her ears and framed her chin. I could imagine her appearing like that at the foot of the stairs for the rest of my life – not much made-up except round the eyes, which glinted in the candlelight as though filling with tears. She looked lovely. I held out a glass of white wine, which she took, sipped, and put down on the table. We stood facing each other.

'Glad you came?' I asked.

She nodded. 'Mm. Are you?'

'Mm. Very. Can I ask you a question?'

She took her wine glass but her hand was shaking and she put it back again.

'All right,' she said. 'I don't promise to answer it.'

'Can I kiss you?' I put out my hand and she took it.

'I don't know about that,' she mumbled, looking down at our locked and restless fingers.

'It's very simple really. Our mouths touch for quite a long time, for as long as they feel like it in fact.'

I pulled her towards me, her eyes still lowered, until we were holding each other cheek to cheek, giving me time to say, 'Just so as you know how beautiful you are to me.' I said that, not having to ask myself then whether I lied or not or how much.

She shook the cardigan off her shoulders and the age-old procedures began. 'Hold me, hold me,' she murmured when her mouth was free and my wandering hands obliged, pressing her against me, back then waist, my fingers finally splayed across her buttocks, as compliant as they were ample. Such words come long afterwards. At the time, there was only the dizzying smell of her, the softening stubbornness of her flesh, our hands moving round and about between us. There were then no truths to be spoken. Someone listening in would have heard the noises of a small, unselective but contented zoo shortly after feeding time.

Dinner ensued eventually and I doubt whether either of us paid much attention to what we were eating and a good thing too. Steak and baked potatoes I vaguely recall. Our appetites were otherwise engaged. Maureen gave up on hers about half-way through, pushing her plate away.

'Can't do this justice,' she said.

'It's criminal, I agree. Putting it inside hardly seems fair on the system.'

She smiled at me in a way that had nothing to do with the joke. The soup had been all right – lukewarm water with a faint flavour of salt and parsley – but the rice pudding was not, its dollops when finally shaken from the serving spoon with black, brown and yellow shreds stuck to them resembling early organisms giving up on evolution. The wine was all right, the coffee and brandy and mint chocs too. We talked about things: Sidney, the village, filing systems, the cold winds from Russia, potted plants, *The Messiah*, the prime minister, rising damp, while my mind skulked about on other business, ending up in a din of speechlessness. There was only one way this eloquence could end.

Don't think we slept together. The three-footer I'd bought to go with the sheets I already had permitted other things but not without protest, squeaking and creaking until we finally cried out and moaned and laughed and silenced it. I was asleep when she left.

Then, shortly after daybreak, we were together again. She brought me a cup of tea and sat on my bed, watching me wake up. Her unfettered hair hung loose about her face and she bent to kiss me as I held her breasts through her night-dress and lowered them down towards me again.

'Your tea will get cold,' she said, standing up and letting her nightdress slither down round her body with a shake of her hips. I reached out for her, keeping my fingers moving there until she sat again beside me and her fingers found and fondled me with exquisite precision.

'Oh dear Almighty God,' I sighed, almost without the consonants.

'Shall I go and get you another?' she said, raising my fingertips to her lips.

'I'll come with you,' I said, half sitting up, but holding her hand there. 'Or not, because that would mean not going anywhere just yet.'

And so we caressed and fumbled our way into Saturday morning, laughing a lot and beginning sentences we did not finish, my dissolute sister and I: Tom and Maureen, grinning and groping and holding hands, persuading ourselves of life eternal, like a couple in an insurance advertisement, easy to swindle with bargains, seizing each instant on the never–never. Going up after breakfast to get dressed for a walk to the village store, we made love again.

'I'm utterly zonked,' I said. 'Perhaps we should go to bed.'

And so it was that night and morning. We had not even drawn the curtains to see what the weather was like. It was a clear day at the height of summer. The light blazed through the windows and we were suddenly silent. We could not even look at each other. I gazed down at my garden and she stood close behind me and did not put a hand on my shoulder. We were as distant as if I were showing a stranger round the house, a prospective buyer. The landscape opened up to us independently, our worlds distinct. And yet she was then less singular to me, just another woman, making us separately pitiful. It was this, not all that had gone before, that made me love her more then, not less as it surely ought to have done.

'You have had your way with me, Tom,' she said quietly.

'It was a wonderful journey. The destination every bit as good as it's cracked up to be and lots to do and see along the route.'

She still did not put her hand on my shoulder.

'Looks like a fine day,' she said.

'It goes on and on,' I said. 'Backwards and forwards. So vague really. You can see the rain coming from a long way off.'

'It makes a nice change from London,' she said. 'All those foreigners.'

At the village store we met Mrs Jenners who confirmed the drinks invitation. I enquired after the crafts centre. Disarmed, like a small girl, she said she had never done anything like that before, was a terrible rabbit. I introduced Maureen, my sister up from London.

'For a nice restful weekend? Away from the rough and tumble,' Mrs Jenners said.

Maureen caught my eye and I put on a very solemn expression, nodding safely. 'Oh yes,' I said, 'there's nothing like it. Such a release. Getting it away umph away from it all.'

Before going into the shop, I'd remarked about Mrs Jenners that she suffered from too much breeding so the rabbit remark with the help of a nudge from me was all too much for Maureen who went over to the window to gasp and snort over the fruit and vegetables, watched in astonishment by the shopkeeper as if she could see the droplets sprinkling on them like dew. It was too good to let pass. I said to Mrs Jenners, 'Your husband did well in life. Now it's your turn to make pots, ha ha.'

'Woodwork I'd prefer,' she replied.

'Oh absolutely, so would I but there just aren't the jobs these days.'

She smiled in a way she'd learnt from her husband, imitating the face she might have made if she'd found it funny. She patted her handbag after putting her change in it and said goodbye to me, her eyes downcast, as if what she'd bought, what she was, would soon enough be found again to be miserably inadequate.

The shopkeeper was now joined by her husband, seen briefly in church. They looked past me at Maureen who had followed Mrs Jenners into the fresh air. I went over to the window to choose some carrots, a bunch of onions, a couple of grapefruit. Outside Maureen gesticulated and pointed, indicating what I should buy else. So I opened the door and flapped my hands at her in a shooing manner, then returned to pay. The woman took my money cheerfully and her husband gave me my change, both saying, 'Lovely day.' Then the woman said, 'Your friend took bad, was she?'

'Up from London, is she?' the man added.

'My sister actually,' I said. 'It's the fumes. All that carbon monoxide, you know.'

'Smog,' the man said, putting his hand to his mouth, then to his chest.

'Fumes,' the woman said in a doom-laden voice. 'Don't know how they stomach it.'

She looked back at Maureen who now had her nose in the air.

'Does wonders to clear the lungs sometimes,' the man said, clearing his throat for five or six seconds. 'I worked in Manchester once. Gawd, I can tell you.'

'Until I rescued him, didn't I, Frank?'

'Yer, in a manner of speaking.'

'I was the price he had to pay, what with me having the shop come to me and that.'

Which he didn't deny, even when she gave him a nudge. But no need to because he had his hand on her somewhere behind and a serenity came over them. I thanked them very much and she gave him another nudge.

'Can't deny it,' he said with a smirk. 'A terrible price it was.'

'Now when he don't count his blessings I send him down to tidy the graveyard.'

'Puts me in my place she does.'

She leant further forwards with a wriggle and I left them to it.

I joined Maureen up the street outside the old village school, now being converted into three flats by the builder who'd done up my cottage. Through one of the windows I saw the head of the tall plumber at waist level. He waved at me, then his head disappeared, deciding on his next card perhaps. It was approaching the lunch hour. I told Maureen I'd been explaining she'd been let out for the day as a result of the new mental health policy. She had recovered now and stared at Mrs Jenners who was getting into her car about fifty yards ahead of us.

'Can't stand those hoity-toity people,' she said. 'I nearly died when you made fun of her like that.' While I was reflecting that those who are easily made fun of have lived in an unfunny world since the laughter was part of some forgotten hurt and there I'd gone on and on as if to bring it all back to her. Well, laughter does us a power of good and heigh ho for anyone in the way. 'And those shopkeepers,' she went on. 'The way they *stared*. I felt like a freak.'

'Just natural curiosity, surely?' I began but she shrugged and I let it pass.

We had a late lunch, after which Maureen studied a 'score' for half an hour or so. We had agreed to go for a drive that afternoon and return the suitcase. I wanted her support (and admiration?); less selfishly, it would be a way of becoming more deeply acquainted too perhaps. She had gone through the suitcase the evening before, several times saying, 'Pathetic.' While I waited for her I sorted through it again, tidying it up, and imagined Nanny Phipps sneaking behind a bush with her hip flask, taking her eyes off the children, feeling doubly guilty.

At breakfast I had asked her, 'That photo you sent me, by the seaside, with your bike. Were you happy then?'

'I hate the past,' she said. 'I don't want to talk about it.'

'You seemed to be putting a brave face on something or other. Do you mind me asking, were you a virgin then?'

'Oh dear, must you?' she replied. 'Then I was. The following morning I wasn't. And he married the other one, the conceited little tart.'

'You were well out of it perhaps?'

'How do I know? Haven't I told you enough?' she said sharply.

And she was right. I wouldn't have wanted her to question me, even if we both had more of the past than of the future and had to live with it, so to speak. But in trying now to keep hidden the snarls and snares in this unravelling of ourselves, what infidelities might we not be guilty of, to ourselves I mean, in not telling the truth? It was all much too comfy to risk any of that.

We stopped off at the crafts centre but I saw at once it didn't interest her. Gwen offered to show us round but she said, 'Another time. I'm not really dressed for it. But thanks very much, I'm sure, all the same.'

'Looked a bit chaotic,' she said as we got in the car. 'Odd little creature. But they do a good job, making people self-reliant, keeping them out of trouble.'

The journey through country lanes gave us little else to talk about. Maureen looked about her, imagining perhaps those being her surroundings for ever, this being the kind of thought the Suffolk landscape lends itself to. It was as if she was looking for something exceptional to comment on and not finding it: fields, animals in some of them, trees, hedges, some houses more attractive and/or larger than others, a greater variety in the clouds than usual but difficult to draw attention to those without getting on to the weather. I hummed, wanting this to be enough, this to be the life. But thought, if this isn't enough, it would become less and less so, bearing in mind the eight or so years' gap between us. If only we could suddenly turn a corner and happen on a choir singing in a field.

Then we reached the sea with a bird sanctuary near by, an expanse of high reeds or grasses renowned throughout the world. There were some bathers and walkers in the distance and one or two people lying on their backs nearer by. The sea was crinkled and unglittering and we stumbled down towards it into the wind which wrapped her dark green dress around her and made her hold on to her hair. There was no sunlight now; in fact the bathers were beginning to pack up and the walkers were moving fast inland. The people on their backs stayed put. There wasn't a bird or ship in sight and no smell of the sea at all. Suddenly nothing was happening.

'All pretty uneventful, I'm afraid,' I said as I took her hand and we plodded down over the pebbles towards the water. 'In the afternoons the fishing boats come in further up.'

She held my hand tightly then let it go. 'The sea scares me when it's like that, when it's not sunny or anything and there aren't people in it. It makes me not know what to think about anything.'

I took her hand again and said, 'You mean all the wrecks under it, the drowning. Worse than stars for making one feel very insignificant indeed. We haven't the faintest idea what's going on down there. If there's a God, that's His element. A smooth enough face much of the time but savage and pitiless underneath.'

'I didn't mean that,' she said. 'I don't know what it's got to do with God.'

We stood in silence as the sea receded with a gentle, slooshing sound. Then she led the way back to the car, hugging herself, clambering up the slope, beautifully ungainly, the reminding it did.

We reached Nanny Phipps's home at about four-thirty, having stopped at a tea-room on the way. I thought at first the waitress was making eyes at me, but it was only to tell me she knew what I was up to, pulling back Maureen's chair, taking her cardigan, asking if she minded the draught. When Maureen went out to the toilet she stood above me, letting me smell the scent on her, telling me about her cakes. Such a pretty, blue-eyed lass, egging me on with her pity: this is a body you can never have, you tired old fart, you'd give anything, wouldn't you . . .

'Chatting up the waitresses, were we?' Maureen said when she came back.

'Absolutely not. I spotted her game right away, buttering me up for a tip. Queer, if you ask me, some of these youngsters these days, what they're into, the absolute bottom.' I glanced at the waitress who was leaning forward to place our order at the counter. 'The cheek of it.'

This was vulgar, in the worst sort of taste, like the stale cakes the girl eventually brought us. Maureen and I did not look each other in the eye then. She knew. I knew. We all knew. Neither of us found it in the slightest funny, though I grinned. Suddenly I loved her, in that instant of her primness and disapproval, remembering the night before and what she had so freely shared with me, when I could have said anything at all and made her laugh.

(Must one go on, several months later now, dwelling among these idiotic doubts like a house of rickety rooms whose doors and windows creak and constantly swing open as if they were inhabited by ghosts? I listen to the wind outside and would rather now be standing at the sea's edge under a full moon, watching the waves wrinkle and break across the path of light, never anywhere the same, a constant rearrangement of eternity, ever onwards and outwards, beyond all reach of words such as those; instead of sinking inwards and downwards, dredging up the old muddle and fancy. I'm truly sorry, Maureen: at this moment I miss you more than I can ever say.)

The home was a country house set back from the road. It looked Elizabethan or had a lot of dark timber showing. There were ornamental trees in the garden in among benches, rectangular and circular flower-beds and gravelled paths. The man from Cromer went up in my estimation. The sun was out again and the freshly mown grass shone in swathes like a vast velvet curtain laid out to dry. It made Maureen's dress of roughly the same shade seem cheap. A gardener was taking the last pile of grass and tipping it on to a vegetable garden.

The woman who opened the door to us immediately afterwards looked at her watch. I said we'd brought Miss Phipps's suitcase, which caused her to look at her watch again. The hall where she left us was panelled and very grand with a wide staircase and dark gleaming banisters, the effect of this spoiled by half a dozen sand-coloured imitation leather chairs covered in cracks and bumps as if some luxuriant fungus was about to break out all over them. We sat down some distance from each other and did not speak.

Faint noises reached us from the two corridors leading off the hall: a long reluctant whimper, an abrupt chuckle, a clatter of something falling followed by a whooping sound, a high snatch of song tailing off into a groan. Maureen hugged herself and looked out over the lawn.

'Oh please let's leave it and go,' she said.

But then the matron came with the other woman making apologetic noises behind her. She smiled a brief welcome, her hands clasped stiffly at her waist. 'It *is* a bit on the late side, Mr Ripple, but so kind of you. I told Miss Phipps you were coming but I fear the old dear . . .'

'She's asleep, matron,' the other woman said abruptly.

'Well, we'll just have to wake her up, won't we? They doze all day and then at night when it's hardest to cope they can't sleep. She hasn't had visitors for I don't know how long. You'd like to see her, I expect?'

This was more to Maureen who was still at the window, looking out over the lawn. She half turned to say, 'We can't really stop . . .' as I said, 'Well, if you're sure . . .'

Maureen shook her head vigorously at me. The matron saw it and went on smiling. Then she suddenly frowned as though dismissing some triviality she'd overlooked. 'Off we go then,' she said briskly. 'She'd love to hear about the cottage, I'm sure.'

'Honestly,' Maureen said very distinctly.

The matron glanced at her. 'Come along then. Go and warn her, Margaret, look sharp now . . . She always thinks strangers have come to take her measurements.'

I lifted the suitcase and followed them down the corridor, not looking back to see if Maureen was following.

'Everyone comes here to die, that's all you need to know,' she said quietly. 'They hear the ambulances drive up and drive away, the murmuring and shuffling in the corridor. The next day you can see them in the television room, trying to puzzle out who's not there any longer.'

We stopped while the other woman went ahead of us into a room at the far end of the corridor.

'Give it a few minutes,' the matron went on. 'I've been doing this job for years and I still can't begin to guess what goes through their minds.'

'When my father was dying,' I whispered, 'he told me it was like always being somewhere else. Like wandering around empty rooms at dusk, he said, looking for someone to have a good chinwag with but everyone's gone off to the seaside or somewhere. He said he came across himself once, with his back to him, looking out over a park where people were strolling about a long way off. It was a lovely morning, he said, but he knew if the bugger turned, forgive me, matron, he'd be a goner. He told me happy memories were sod all use to anyone, not in the end.'

The matron nodded and smiled at me as Maureen came up behind us. 'I really admire you working in a place like this,' she said too loudly.

'There are far worse places,' she replied, touching her on the arm. 'The young especially. Such damage, such cruelty, you and I couldn't imagine enduring it for a moment. Oh well, life of some sort has to go on.'

The other woman appeared and beckoned to us and we went into the room. The matron leant forward across a deep armchair that faced away from us and did some tucking and rearranging.

'Come along, Miss Phipps, we've got visitors.'

I moved past the chair to the window. I was blocking out the mid-summer evening light so all I could see at first was the shawl and blanket like a heap of dumped bedding. Then suddenly I became aware of her eyes glistening at me, wide with panic, until the matron moved between us and spoke soothingly to her, explaining. I glanced at Maureen in the doorway examining the room, avoiding my eye.

There was little to see: a tidy bed with a patchwork quilt, basin and tooth mug, wardrobe and chest of drawers with a red check cloth and empty candlestick on it. On the mantelpiece above the boarded-up fireplace were a vase of small artificial daffodils hardly more yellow than grey now and a china shepherdess missing an arm being looked up at by a sheepdog and a ginger cat. There were no photographs anywhere. The only picture was of a castle on a hilltop with a crimson sun bursting above a cloud and illuminating a muscular white stallion which seemed to be waiting for the drawbridge to be let down, its nostrils, tail and mane smouldering away as if about to burst into flames.

The matron had stood aside and Nanny Phipps was still staring at me, or past me to find where the light had gone. The matron nodded to me.

'I'm living in your cottage now, Miss Phipps,' I said. 'And I've brought your suitcase.'

She said nothing, still searching for the light but her hands moved to her chest and began twitching at her shawl.

'He's brought your suitcase,' the matron repeated loudly. 'Isn't that kind of him?'

I knelt down and opened it, worried she would notice at once the Bible and prayer-book were missing.

'Here are all your old photographs,' I said, putting the album in her lap.

Still she said nothing and did not touch it. Then she twisted her head round suddenly and said distinctly to Maureen, 'Lily and Harry. Sarah's dead, you know.'

She began to slide sideways and the matron gently eased her upright, saying, 'No, dear, this is Mr and Mrs Ripple who are living in your old house. They've brought your suitcase.'

'All your old photographs . . .' I said, standing up and reaching forward to open the album.

Her withered hands emerged from under the blanket and began to tremble as she held them out to me. 'Come and tell your old Nanny, Harry,' she murmured. 'Where have you taken Sarah?'

Her hands reached out further, steady now, until her arms were outstretched. I held out my hands and she gripped them tightly. Her blurred eyes, blue or grey once, gaped at me as if she wanted me to see some fear or longing in them she could no longer express.

'You'll have to speak up,' she said, her voice cracking. 'I'm deaf you know.'

She tapped a pink contraption in her ear, which made her jump. Her eyelids drooped and her mouth hung open and I thought she was about to fall asleep.

'I'm afraid I can't tell you about Sarah,' I said.

She sat up with a start. 'I'm not a fool whatever you think. I knew she was dead when she stopped coming. You've changed, Harry, getting on in the world, are you?' She began shaking my hands up and down and I felt the cold skin sliding over the bones. 'You must get on, that's what I told you. And you need a haircut. I'm not blind. They like you to look right.'

'Sarah. When did you last see her?'

'Killed in a car accident, that life she led, rushing about. Those film stars . . . Don't say I didn't warn her.'

'Would you like to look at the photographs?' I said, pulling my hands away. Slowly I turned a few pages but she didn't seem to see anything.

'Little Sarah,' she murmured. 'Poor pretty little Sarah. You were jealous of her, weren't you, Lily?'

I looked across at Maureen who had her hand to her mouth. Then she beckoned to me and pointed to the door. The matron had her back to us, arranging something in the wardrobe.

'Well I can tell you,' Miss Phipps went on, clutching my hands again, her voice thin in the stale air, 'I'm not dead yet. They charge too much, Harry, living in a cupboard and smelly toilets. Matron, there's one who fancies herself. Bossy boots. That's what you called me. Bossy boots. They hurt my teeth with their fancy this and that . . .' Her voice became slurred and her grip relaxed. Then she clapped her hands together, making no sound. 'The food gives me a runny tummy. How can I put on weight for the winter? You shouldn't pay for the food, Harry.'

'You mustn't worry about that,' I said.

She plumped her hands down on the album. 'You can take this horrid stuff away. We're not allowed things. Old rubbish, they call it. Tomorrow, Harry, you can take me to see Sarah in her beautiful home. I'm too poorly today. I'm glad you didn't bring Lily.' She began beating time. 'Silly Lily, Silly Lily.'

The album began to slip off her lap and I caught it and put it on the chest of drawers. Matron came over and pulled the shawl round her shoulders, letting her hands rest there.

'It's old bossy boots again,' she said, twisting her half-open mouth and hunching her shoulders, all that was left now of laughter. 'I know perfectly well who it is and there's no need to shout, thank you. Come to measure me again. I'm getting smaller all the time, the food they give you.'

278

'Is there anything I can get you?' I asked.

But she was drifting off and I doubt if she heard me.

'She's gone again,' the matron said. 'Into her dreams.'

But her eyes opened again and she looked up at us, then round at Maureen, as though seeing us all for the first time. She smiled happily. 'Everyone is so kind, making a fuss of me. They spoil me. Now I must go and see what they're up to in the garden . . .' Her head fell to one side and she stared past me at the window. 'Look at the sunlight on the trees. The leaves are falling. Perhaps I am getting old. Come along, Sarah, you and I . . .'

And she fell asleep.

'Thank you both for coming,' the matron said as she bid us goodbye. 'You gave her a little more hold on life but there'll be questions. She likes to tease us.'

'Do please let us know if there's anything,' I said.

'Thank you. But that won't be necessary. Her only physical needs now are those we can easily satisfy.'

'Was there . . . Did something happen to Sarah? And is Lily . . . ?'

'Lily, I believe, is in Canada. Not even a Christmas card. Sarah was her favourite, as you could tell. Her brother told me she was retarded in some way. She didn't live long. The others went to boarding school. They kept her on for a while, then . . . the scrap heap.'

'So the photographs, she might not really have wanted them?'

'Probably not but then, who knows . . . ?'

She looked at us in turn as she must have looked at her patients countless times, with a painstaking cheerfulness, then closed the door behind us before our backs were turned.

Chapter Eight

On the drive back Maureen was silent for a while. She'd offered to cook the supper and there was much else to look forward to, a short stretch of intense living that dying shouldn't be allowed to interfere with. I wonder sometimes how people have acquired the knack of thinking about anything else, that and sex, both separately and together. She was upset about something and whatever it was had to be got out of the way.

'Sorry to inflict that on you,' I said eventually.

'I hope when I get like that I'll have the sense to give up the ghost.'

'What a haunting thought.'

That she ignored. 'I couldn't stand seeing my parents in a place like that.'

'Oh I'm sure they'd find you somewhere to sit . . . Sorry, that was a joke.'

'And not a very funny one in the circumstances.'

'You're absolutely right. It was all rather depressing, that's all.'

'Then you shouldn't joke about it. You're always cracking jokes, aren't you?'

'Yes, I know. I'm sorry.'

Instead of changing gear, I put a hand on her knee and the car shuddered.

'You're driving me crazy,' she said, putting my hand on the gear lever.

I gave a laugh that didn't sound much like a laugh at all. Too late to do it over again.

'Very good,' I said. 'But don't you get into the habit. One fryer in the family's enough. I'll crack the yolks, you lay the table.'

'There you go again,' she said.

Back in the cottage she began busying herself in the kitchen. I hung about, still wanting to talk about Nanny Phipps: such were the sorrowful things we would have to talk about if we were to grow old together, those and what else we would have to talk about as we grew old together. But I was only in the way and could think of nothing new to say, so decided to phone the Henry chap in Cromer.

'Ah, how very good of you. Much appreciated. As well as can be expected, as the saying goes?'

'Yes, except she seemed to think I was either you or the undertaker.'

He laughed at that, a yolluch yolluch sound followed by some inconclusive nose clearing. 'Afraid I stopped going quite a long time ago. Didn't know me from Adam. Anyway she left us when I was about ten. The years trundle on, what?'

'I didn't say anything.'

'I see. Place seem all right to you? Look after her all right?'

'Oh yes, in good hands there.'

'Oh good. No complaints, then?'

'She seemed most interested in Sarah, your sister.' There was a pause. 'Just thought I'd mention . . .'

'That's perfectly all right, old chap. Poor Sal. She was the oldest, a bit mental, in fact, quite a lot mental if the truth were known. As she grew older she began realizing it in her funny way, us learning to read, going off to school, that sort of thing. She and Nanny were together a lot. The old girl used to tell her stories. We kept out of the way. We were jolly embarrassed actually. You know how kids are. Then father did a bunk and mother was always out and about, putting on a brave face. And then Sal began to realize she wasn't a dancer or a princess or any of the things in the stories and Nanny had to keep her away from mirrors. She wasn't very pretty, if you know what I mean . . . Sorry, am I boring you?'

'No, please.'

'She began crying a lot, throwing tantrums, you know the kind of thing, until mother decided she couldn't cope and she ought to be put into a . . . anyway, it never came to that.'

'She died?'

'That's it, yes. There were other things wrong with her, always sniffly, getting colds. One night mother was out and she had one of her fits, screaming and gasping, and Nanny went in to calm her down. Lily and I were in our beds blocking our ears, it was pretty ghastly and then suddenly everything went quiet . . . Nanny came and said goodnight to us. I remember how calm she was, tucking us up, read us a story. The next morning, Sal had gone. There wasn't any fuss. A quiet funeral. Father came for it and decided to stay put. Lily and I sort of vaguely knew . . . People came and went.'

'I wish you'd told me. I wouldn't have . . . I'm sorry.'

'It's all over now. What can one do? She stayed on for a bit but after the court case there was nothing for her to do so father bought her the cottage . . . That's it really.'

'Poor old thing.'

'Thank you for phoning. It was good of you. Must go and see the old girl again but you see . . .'

'I do see.'

We said goodbye and hung up. I turned and saw Maureen in the kitchen doorway.

'That was a long call,' she said.

'Just thought I'd let him know about Miss Phipps,' I said.

'Her again.'

'It's a sad story.'

I put out my hand to hold her round the waist but she wiped her hands on her apron and moved away.

'Keep an eye on the potatoes. I'm going to have a bath.'

'He was telling me about Sarah.'

'I'm not sure I want to hear about it. As if there wasn't enough trouble already in the world. You don't have to make it your business.'

'He just began telling me, that's all, and I . . .'

But she was already half-way up the stairs, the belt of her apron pulling her skirt above her knees. Her haunches swayed and wobbled and I went to look at the potatoes under the bubbling water, a turbulent longing stirring under my heart.

We ate, drank wine and watched opera on television. Into the third bottle, she told me I drank too much. When I lit up another cheroot, she got up and opened the window wider. I had run out of Rennie tablets and while she exclaimed about the music, that mighty passion in extremis, I endured a heartburn of my own. Unrelentingly they sang for me, the hellishness of it in Maureen's heaven.

For a while we lay together in our night garments. With one hand behind me to stop me falling off the bed, I kissed and caressed her as efficiently as I could but she remained unaroused, watching me examine her unresponding nipples etc. My hand moved further down where nothing much was happening on my side either, or happened briefly too soon. She took my hand off her as it returned once more to her breasts and sat up on the side of the bed.

'Not feeling like it?' I asked considerately.

'We're both too tired. It's been an emotional day, and those ravishing voices still ringing in my ears.'

I slid my hand up her back under her night-dress. 'I'll wait for a bit, then give you a yell,' I said.

She turned and smiled suspiciously. 'Is that another one of your jokes?'

'Good heavens no. It's just that I know nothing at all about opera. I'll have a good bone-up the next time.'

She stood up, not letting my hand linger, and went to the door from where she blew me a kiss. I spent the next minute or two rummaging in my clothes for Rennie tablets and found three in the pocket of an old cardigan. Munching them it was not long before my heart stopped burning and along came a waitress wearing only an apron under which, staring me in the eye, she fumbled away my tip. Sorry, Maureen, I muttered as sleep took hold of me, but there are no heights without depths, Covent Gardens without scrubby allotments. I awoke the next morning to hear her downstairs making the breakfast, singing an aria with great fervour but in a language I couldn't understand.

That final morning we went to church together, then afterwards to the Jenners. It was a fine day but not bright, the clouds whitening the blue like unwashed stretches of muslin and a chilly breeze that came and went just as you thought a heat haze was building up. The village converged on the church, hands raised here and there, one or two groups chatting around the graveyard. A sensible distance away, I unlocked my arm from Maureen's and she sighed and said she was getting her period. 'No jokes please,' she added.

Agnes was back and greeted me with especial warmth, her hair freshly streaked, her complexion a new depth of sun-tan, most of the cracks smoothed over like partly restored antique furniture. As I introduced Maureen, Sidney came up looking sheepish and then suddenly not when he seemed to think that, in avoiding his eye, Maureen was admiring his hairy celery and cress suit.

'A touch of the sun, I see,' I said to Agnes.

'Two weeks in Florida,' she replied. 'Absolutely gorgeous.'

'Isn't she?' Sidney said, leering at them in turn.

The Colonel glanced up at the weather vane at the top of the church spire with a harrumph noise followed by what sounded like 'Silly bugger.'

'I don't tan easily,' I said. 'I just go pink. Florider, in a word.'

The Colonel nodded down at me over his specs and Agnes showed us her teeth, darkening her tan by at least two shades. Sidney was close alongside Maureen, not actually sniffing her, of which she pretended to take no notice while faking an interest in the church's architecture.

We moved towards the porch where the vicar was waiting. Another introduction. 'Coming to check up on big brother, are we?' he said. 'Well, you've got a nice day for it. God's in His heaven, all's right with the world. Not the slightest truth in that of course.'

Maureen told him what a pleasant little church it was, she liked its proportions.

'Small but perfectly formed, you mean? Ha ha.'

Maureen raised her eyebrows at me, looking suddenly pale in the shadow of the porch. We went on in. There were more people than before. I recognized the shopkeepers, the trio from the crafts centre and the golfers who were already on their knees, wanting perhaps to hurry things along so as to bring closer the green field far away. There were about twenty or so strangers, mostly elderly or approaching it, sitting very upright as if waiting for their names to be called for some disagreeable appointment which in a way I suppose they were. Maureen seemed overdressed in her yellow blouse and charcoal-grey suit, her hair furled neatly and nobly beside and above her head like one of the enraptured matrons of the night before. The church glistened as if recently given a good scrubbing, filled haphazardly by the sunlight. We moved into a pew about half-way up and Maureen at once knelt and, head high, closed her eyes. I leant forward in an attitude of prayer and began counting backwards from one hundred. Reaching seventy-six, I murmured: whatever this might be, let it last.

The service began and the first hymn was 'New every morning is the love.' As I feared, Maureen sang out. Indeed, it was more like a solo with the rest of us mumbling our several ways into some sort of accompaniment. At least once everyone had a jolly good look at her while the vicar leant towards her at the organ nodding his head in a circle to keep her going. Once when I looked at Agnes she gave me the thumbs-up sign. Beyond her the Colonel was on parade, staring straight ahead of him, after the second verse becoming hardly less audible than Maureen. Gradually they gave the rest of us confidence as the vicar swayed back and forth, occasionally waving his right arm about, aimed chiefly at the crafties in the front row who, heads down, seemed not to be singing at all. Even I bellowed a bit, trying to stay up in the right octave but settling in the end for somewhere in or around one of the middle parts. It all ended on quite a crescendo with Maureen holding out longest and just as we were about to close our hymn-books, the vicar said, 'Why don't we sing the first verse again. Begin afresh. Let it rip!'

And so we did: 'New every morning is the love, our wakening and uprising prove.' I nudged Maureen but she took no notice. I wished I hadn't. Schoolboy humour, I thought. As the years pass I don't seem to find it any easier to rise above myself, not as hard either, leaving this sentence in for instance.

The vicar took the text for his sermon from the lesson the Colonel had read: 'Take no thought for the morrow for the morrow taketh thought for the things of itself. Sufficient unto the day is the evil thereof.' The point he seemed to be making was that if you're always worrying about the future you're likely to miss what you ought to be worrying about now. He also quoted a poet: 'The world is too much with us. Late and soon, getting and spending, we lay waste our powers.' I am still thinking about these ideas, trying to reconcile them. Easier to understand when younger perhaps. I was now spending what I'd once got and wasn't getting any more of anything much and the morrows therefore had little evil left in them, just about none at all, in fact; worth taking thought for that surely? Gripping the pulpit, the vicar leant forward, which pushed his shoulders up because the pulpit stayed where it was. After a long pause he began talking about the Great Beyond up and/or out there which comprehended the long littleness of life.

It was then the Colonel had one of his coughing fits. At first he tried to stifle it, hunched up and with a handkerchief to his mouth while Agnes patted him on the back. Then he straightened up, thumped his chest and had several clears of his throat, his handkerchief a few inches from his face, which darkened from deep red into the colour of a bruised and speckled plum. 'Bloody, God-forsaken tubes,' he said loudly before a final heave and splutter, much of the outcome of which must have missed the handkerchief and added, though not noticeably, to the triangle of speckled, beigish stuff hanging down the back of one of the craftswomen in front of him. Meanwhile the vicar fumbled with his notes as though about to rectify a major theological blunder and had just started up again when the Colonel raised a hand to him and said, 'Sorry about that, vicar. Carry on.'

Nearing his conclusion, the vicar's gaze wandered to the upper church windows through which the sun blazed for a moment, then vanished. Maureen's eyes followed his and she wore her radiant look, lips parted, teeth too. Throughout the whole proceedings she had avoided looking at me once, even now on the way down from one of the stained-glass windows. She believes in all this, I thought, wish I did. I wished too my father was there instead, and that my mother was waiting for me at home with one of her 'good square meals or as good as you'll get this side of last Christmas'. The vicar came to an end. 'We can but live in the here and now with all its commonplace trials and pleasures though in the eye of eternity there may be nothing new under the sun . . .' The Colonel loudly cleared his throat, hastening the end . . . 'In the name of the Father, the Son and the Holy Ghost, Amen.'

Then it was time for Holy Communion. Maureen looked at me and I shook my head. She brushed past me and was third in line after the shopkeepers. She knelt very upright, the word being made flesh, and how. When she returned she smiled at me as if I didn't know what I was missing. I smiled back at her and she licked her lips, a final taste of what she'd just sipped and nibbled in memory that Christ died for her or, would you believe it, his actual body and blood. The last hymn I sang fervently: 'O wisest love! that flesh and blood/which did in Adam fail/Should strive afresh against their foe/Should strive and should prevail.' Should but didn't. Leastwise in my mind's eye her taut grey flanks at the altar rail loomed below the tall church windows and all my aspirations sank into a groan.

At the end she knelt again to pray so we were last out and she took my arm briefly as if to rehearse our wedding, then thought better of it. Behind us, the vicar came to the end of something bouncy from what sounded (but only just) like *The Sound of Music*. Outside, the people were already dispersing and cars were pulling out, three times causing other cars to hoot, whose weekend drivers so enjoyed those nice, quiet winding country lanes they couldn't get out of them fast enough. Mrs Jenners scurried back to confirm we'd be coming for a drink.

'Must trot along to do the goodies,' she twittered. 'Edward's poorly . . .' And off she went again, tumbling into Sidney's out-stretched arms.

Sidney then went off with the Colonel and Agnes, the Colonel ahead after biffing his chest, waving to us and raising an imaginary glass. Sidney's hand hovered in the region of the small of Agnes's back, or lower, and she signalled to us too with a high beckoning motion.

For a while Maureen and I dawdled among the gravestones. She had her back to me.

'All pretty rustic I expect you find it?' No reply to that. 'You were in smashing voice today. Had a look at the windows on the way out. No new cracks so far as I could see.' She moved a little further away from me. I thumped a gravestone. 'This Christianity's really got something going for it. Beginning to get the hang of things but like the what's-it-called Eucharist, difficult to swallow at first and as for the Holy Ghost can't make head nor tail of it. Still, I do want to learn. I'm not saying . . .'

Too late again. 'I'd rather you didn't joke about things you don't understand, Tom,' she said.

And I followed her to the gate thinking what a lot of humour that put paid to.

We walked to the Jenners' house in and out of the sunlight, the trees swishing and fluttering overhead giving teasing glimpses of the Great Beyond. I wished that we had just met and could start all over again, that she'd say what a perfect day it was and weren't we lucky, that for some of us the Lord could settle for saving us from ourselves. From time to time she stumbled up off the road on to the damp grass verge to let the cars pass and there was no getting close to her.

'I don't like these clergymen these days being all chummy and breezy,' she said. 'Sucking up to people and making it all singsong and fun. It's so undignified, don't you think?'

'I've never been that sure about dignity,' I said.

'I have,' she replied. 'Anyway, it's wonderful to be in the country. Makes me feel a new woman.' That was better. Reaching a broad level stretch of verge, I put my arm through hers. '*Please* don't say it,' she continued.

'I wasn't going to.'

'I bet you would have done.'

'You wouldn't consider becoming my old woman would you?'

'There you go. You always spoil it.'

And so I proposed to her and she turned me down. An itch started up in my anus which wasn't helped, or rather was, by the occasional furtive dig and scratch, and a callus under the right edge of my right foot was making me limp now that the verge was narrow and lumpy. Spellbinding stuff this but life's little irritants often help to keep the mind off life itself.

We were last at the Jenners' and, wiping our feet on the gold and dark-green semicircular door-mat, if that was what it was, we heard the hubbub beyond and caught a glimpse of a garden into which people had begun to drift. Mrs Jenners greeted us with a tray of sausage rolls, which she removed from under my outstretched hand saying, 'You must come and meet everyone. Now, who don't you know?'

We followed her into the drawing room, which was tastefully and amply furnished like an antique shop of the sort where the proprietor asks if there is anything in particular while running a slow check on what your clothes were likely to have cost you.

'What a quite delightful room,' Maureen said, damaging her vowels by trying to raise them a class or two.

'Oh, isn't it? We so love stumbling on things,' Mrs Jenners replied as she wove her way through it all saying, 'Now come and meet . . .'

Then it happened. We were making our way to where Mr Jenners was standing at the centre of most of his guests on the patio beyond the french windows when he boomed out, 'Ah, Ripple, and goodness gracious if it isn't Miss Hurton from my old department. How *are* you, Mabel isn't it? What a nice surprise! What brings you to these parts?' Then he turned to the others, the boom unlowered though we were now alongside. 'Let me introduce Mabel Hurton. Joined us from the Patent Office, if I recall correctly. Soon put some order into the place. Best Registrar we ever had by miles, or should I say files ha ha.'

People mumbled their names, some offering their hands and in the silence that followed, Mrs Jenners said very distinctly, 'Miss Hurton is Mr Ripple's sister and she's staying with him for the weekend. Isn't that nice?'

Jenners had stopped listening to her years ago and rambled on. I had a quick glance round the others, who included the Colonel and

Agnes, Sidney close beside her and the vicar still with his mouth open, struck dumb in full flood. There were also one or two people from round and about I knew to nod to and they all began searching reflectively around feet, sky, flower-beds, foliage, Jenners, as if taking part in some guessing game. Except for Sidney who raised an eyebrow at me and smirked at Maureen, back and forth like a comedian failing to get a laugh. I could sense her beside me steaming.

Jenners was introducing me to somebody who was somebody with Somebody and Somebody in the City and then to a man who had recently decided to add a market garden to his pig farm. 'Solves the problem of waste what? Yeorgh yeorgh,' he said, tapping his stomach. 'Wish I could. Yeorgh yeorgh. And his good spouse, got to master the jargon, does sterling work for the National Trust and Jonathan here, lose track of what Jonathan's up to . . .'

They were looking at me now as if I'd just managed to squeak into company at this level but there might be more to me than met the eye, one never knew these days. I mentioned the name of my old company at which they nodded, the blood slowly finding its way through their sun-tans, fading in the neck region to the colour of their pink gins. The Colonel raised his glass to me with a shaking hand and Agnes yawned. Then the conversation turned, or turned back, to the prime minister and several sentences began which didn't augur much broadening out of the topic somehow.

'Whatever you may say . . .'

'There's no arguing that . . .'

'No doubt now who's running the show . . .'

I was asked what I thought as a businessman and I spoke about export curves. ('Like the Miss World contest?' Jenners suggested, spoiling it with a long guffaw that seemed to get lodged mid-nostril.) The Colonel and Agnes had drifted off and Sidney was now alongside Maureen. I could not bring myself to look at either of them, so smiled instead at the vicar whose mouth was now closed, in fact had been clamped tight since Jenners started enjoying his own joke so much. Mrs Jenners then returned with a quadruple gin and tonic for me and for Maureen what looked like a ginger ale plus fruit I didn't remember her asking for. She was trying now to escape back into the drawing room but Jenners stayed with her, saying over his shoulder, 'Oh now, Frank, don't you underestimate the bureaucracy. Thanks to the likes of our Miss Hurton here, can be damned efficient when it wants to be. How is the old gang keeping these days? Still keeping them on a tight rein, are we?'

We were now grouped either side of the french window and a tall man with half-eye glasses joined us, stooping and ruddy-faced like a scholarly butcher. Agnes was within earshot, the Colonel too who was doing something in his ear with a matchstick. There was a pause while everyone except me looked at Maureen and she said, 'Since you left us, Mr Jenners, things have really improved . . .' She checked herself and then, to change the subject, took a deep breath and added, 'When you're far away in the country it makes such a lovely change.'

Now I did look at her as somebody snickered and the woman from the National Trust said, 'How too delicious for words,' and Jenners made a noise I hadn't heard before, somewhere between a dog yawning and a small motor mower puttering to a halt. She was blushing deeply but it wasn't this that held my attention, for her hand with the tumbler in it was beginning to shake and shook more when she put her other hand round it. With a show of bumping against the arm of a chair, I lurched against her and knocked her tumbler to the floor, muttering, 'Oh God, I'm sorry. What on earth did you put in this gin, Mrs Jenners? Never could hold my liquor, runs in the family, eh Sis?'

Together we stooped to retrieve the mess while Jenners called out above us, 'Never mind that. Darling! Where on earth has the woman got to . . . ? Ah there you are. Bit of an accident. Run along and get a cloth, there's a . . . No lasting damage I hope . . .'

'Let's get out of here,' Maureen whispered to me as I gathered in three ice cubes, two cherries and two half-slices of lemon and plopped them back into the tumbler which she held out to me, unbroken except for a small triangular chip which I ran my hand over the carpet to find.

'I'll do that,' Jenners said sharply, waving a tea towel above us, then kneeling down as I lifted Maureen upright by the elbow and told her not to worry, more loudly apologizing again and then again. Everyone else had now moved away back into the garden and we turned to follow them with a last look down at Jenners on his knees mopping up and crying out 'Ouch!' as his forefinger caught the fragment of glass and he knelt upright and picked it out from under his nail.

Sidney was blocking the way into the garden and turned to us.

'Pissed again, Ripple, I see.' He twitched his mouth at Maureen. 'Needs a good woman to take him in hand, wouldn't you say?'

We moved round him into the garden where the vicar was indicating something in the distance to the man from the City and Mrs Jenners was in deep discussion with the crafts centre people. The others were fairly close by having something pointed out to them in a flower-bed by Agnes. The Colonel came towards us and gave Maureen a pronounced wink. He looked tired out as if at the end of a long campaign that had gone wrong from the outset.

'Got him on his hands and knees, I see,' he began, pointing at Jenners. But then he started coughing and with a wave walked briskly to the far end of the garden to have it out. I saw Agnes watch him for a moment with an expression of despair, then anger.

We joined Mrs Jenners who said, 'Had a little accident, did we? Aren't we lucky it wasn't coffee? That carpet is our pride and joy. We got it to celebrate his OBE.'

At this point the vicar joined us and she said, 'Vicar, I don't believe you've met Miss Hurton, Mr Ripple's sister, who's spending the night with him and used to work for Fred . . . ?'

One of the craftswomen then said, 'How come your name is . . . ? My name is Stutchbury and so's his but he's married to her, good as, and I'm not his sister or cousin or hers, far from it. She was a Stutchbury once of course. Perhaps . . .'

Which set the vicar off, talking very fast, 'You do really have a remarkable voice, Miss Ah . . . It's what we sorely need . . . to praise the Lord with a bit of oomph. The music's there, isn't it? So might as well make the most of it. Sound as if we meant it, or wanted to mean it. It's the joining together, isn't it, deriving succour one from another, adding our voices to the voices of the past, a community of the living and the dead? Even if you don't believe every word of it. Mind you, there are dangers, the strength in numbers aspect, not much of a problem here though . . . Sing in a choir in London, do you, Miss Ah . . . ?'

'Yes,' said Maureen. 'We're doing *Elijah* next.'

'Oh how perfectly lovely,' the vicar said.

'When I sing out,' the man from the crafts centre mumbled, 'one of them always nudges me.'

'But you can't sing a note in tune,' the two women said almost simultaneously.

'Which do you think God would prefer?' he went on. 'That every-one has a more or less tuneless bash or one should keep one's wrong notes to oneself?'

The vicar paused. 'Well now, I think we must assume that God has the highest aesthetic standards, it could hardly be otherwise, could it? However He also, how shall I put it, makes allowances. Otherwise where would we all be? He surely likes *triers*, people to have a bash as you call it . . .'

The man from the City had now joined us and said, 'Look at it this way. If God were an investment trust manager, He'd look at His port-folio as a whole, expecting some stocks to perform better than others, wouldn't He, vicar? A drop here, a slide there, wouldn't bother Him, provided He had overall capital growth . . .'

I got in here because Sidney was approaching with his eye fixed on Maureen from the neck downwards to about her knees, then slowly up again. I brought myself to look at her now and she was more flushed than ever. She turned away from me, glancing at her watch as I said, 'The old man in the sky with long white hair and a beard . . .'

The vicar got that, God bless him, for he gave me a quick nod then turned to the man from the City with what would have been loathing if his face wasn't so trained in charity. 'I listen to money singing. It is intensely sad,' he said.

Nobody had the faintest idea what he was talking about but that didn't matter because one of the craftswomen repeated, 'Overall capital growth geddit? And the vicar likes us all to have a bash,' and all three of them chuckled. The man from the City began, 'I don't care what you say . . .' then cleared his throat and was silent.

Sidney put his hand on Maureen's shoulder and said, 'Tom's a lucky chap, having a erm sister with a voice like that. Pretty hot stuff, eh Tom?'

Maureen looked at her watch again and said, 'We really must leave.'

Mrs Jenners then bustled up and said, 'More drinks everyone? Aren't gardens such a joy? So far away from everything. Isn't it pure heaven? Oh sorry, vicar . . .'

We nodded our goodbyes, thanked Mrs Jenners and escaped round the side of the house. Turning for a final wave, I saw Sidney gazing after us and the Colonel and Agnes together at the far end of the garden, heads almost together, her hands on his. I guessed she was trying to persuade him to go home but he wouldn't hear of it.

That was roughly how it happened. I wrote it up as soon as I returned from taking Maureen to the station, to take my mind off things. She caught an earlier train than she had planned. As it pulled out, the rain began. I hadn't brought a raincoat or umbrella and had parked my car several streets away. Much later now, I remember her face indistinctly, as it was in the photograph, much put upon, brave and reconciled. I remember her too walking ahead of me back to my cottage saying over and over again, 'That was awful . . . I can never show my face here again.'

Over lunch she spoke about 'that vulgar little estate agent', 'those snooty business people', 'the smug artsy-fartsy crowd', the 'so-called vicar with his clever-clever talk and vulgar joke about God's hair' and Jenners who was 'probably the most pompous man in the world'. As for the Colonel he was 'like a ridiculous caricature. All he needed was a monocle.'

I said I was sorry and little else until we were on the way to the station. 'I hope you enjoyed some of it?' I took her hand but immediately had to change gear again.

'Well, a visit to an old people's home and a village pottery are hardly . . . I know I must sound ungrateful, Tom, but . . .'

'Not at all. For my part, I loved having you. Thank you for coming.'

There was a long silence after that. It wouldn't have been funny at all. The countryside looked particularly beautiful that morning with the storm clouds building up and the last of the sunlight clinging to the leaves as the wind tossed them about and bared their branches. Nothing at all would have been funny then, not even I myself trying to find something funny to say.

As I kissed her goodbye at the station, I said, 'Please come and stay another time, despite everything. I care for you deeply. I always will.'

When did that become a lie? The moment I said it, I think.

'I'll give you a call,' she said.

And as soon as the train had pulled out and I'd finished waving I missed her greatly, couldn't put out of my mind the memory of her kneeling at the altar and the vicar murmuring, 'This is the body . . .' And of much else before that, all of her, without the intervening cloth and without the words which always somehow went wrong, became untruthful and stained the air with their peculiar incomplete ugliness.

I drove back through the wet early autumn evening, taking corners too fast, cursing the narrowness of the roads, the bloody garage for not fixing the windscreen wipers properly. Not that there was much wrong with those that a good blow of the nose and a good night's sleep and good long hard summing-up couldn't fix. And did. And even now, late into the night, into yet another drink, listening to our old chum Albonino played on ancient instruments, I think harshly of us both, what we were at our worst, to save myself an unmanageable remorse.

When I awoke the next morning it was pouring down. Peering down across my garden I could just see my car, just enough, that is, to see I hadn't wound up the front windows which I'd opened between showers the evening before to let out the remaining smell of her cheap, exquisite perfume.

The rain hardly let up over the next few days and when the sun finally shone for an hour I sent her a short letter which consisted mainly of the most neutral bits of the several long letters I wrote her. I wanted to be truthful and say beautiful things at the same time but the two are hard to reconcile in my experience. The result was this.

> *My dear Maureen,*
>
> *The house has seemed empty without you, and I don't only mean one of the main items of furniture upstairs. I should imagine you've been having much the same weather as I've been having so nothing to remark on there. I realize you didn't enjoy yourself as much as I wanted you to, though the sun did shine. I still hear your voice in the church and at other times too. We had our moments, didn't we, but there were so many things we never got round to talking about. Perhaps in my own setting you got to know me more as I am? Thank you for coming to see me.*
>
> *Love,*
> *Tom*

I phoned her before posting the letter.

'Just wanted to check you arrived back safely,' I said.

'Must rush off to choir practice. I'll phone you early next week.'

'In this weather wrap up well, won't you?'

'It's all right, I'm being picked up.'

'All the bloody time, I shouldn't wonder.'

'There he is now. Thanks for phoning, Tom. Bye-bye.'

'Wouldn't do to keep him waiting, unless he's in the restaurant business . . .'

But she had hung up. She replied to my letter as follows.

Dear Tom,

Many thanks for your letter. Please don't think I have any regrets but it wasn't really my scene as they say. I have such a full life here and our next performance is of Elijah (by Felix Mendelssohn). Frankly, I wonder sometimes whether we have quite enough in common to consider a permanent relationship though I'm not saying it wasn't fun if you know what I mean. It was. No hard feelings on my behalf. When you are next in London do call me and perhaps we can go to a concert or something. The Elijah's on 4 October, at seven o'clock this time.

Yours affectionately,
Maureen

This was a sad letter to get but then it was pouring with rain at the time and I had backache. Later that day the sun came out and I felt hugely relieved. Indeed I was singing a hymn in my garden when Agnes came by.

'Well, haven't you got it looking nice at last?' she said.

'Coming from you that's real flattery,' I said, putting a hand on the small of my back which had stopped aching. 'Like to come in for a coffee or anything? Well, not just anything exactly.'

She laughed. 'Well, isn't that just too kind of you, Tom. But thanks no. Another time.'

'Who says there'll be another time? I'm thinking of giving it up, coffee I mean of course.'

She laughed again. 'My word, we are in high spirits today aren't we?'

We raised our hands and I watched her walk away. She turned back once, did a little dance and I imitated a swoon. All right all this except that it brought on my backache again.

Chapter Nine

I must now write about my son who phoned me one evening as I was getting into my bath. He usually called about once a month, when there was some news: a change of flat, an examination passed, a part-time job, he'd been sick but was better now. After establishing we had nothing more to say to each other, I always asked if he had enough money and he always said he did. All the same, I usually sent him £25 or so the next day just in case.

This time it was different. Could he see me before term began while he was down in London staying with his mother for a day or two? So I arranged to meet him at a restaurant near the park where we'd taken the Webbs and Hambles for an outing that day, if you recall.

'It'll be on me,' I said. 'But let there be no misunderstanding. It's only a loan with all that money you'll be earning one day. The only meals on wheels I'll settle for then, I can tell you right now, will be on a trolley at the Café Royal.'

'Dad,' he replied after a pause, 'I really want to see you again. Have you changed?'

'Not yet. Actually I'm standing here stark naked while my bath's going cold. Mod cons are not expected to reach these parts until the late 1990s. Still, I can always boil another kettle.' I raised my voice. 'It's not the deafness I mind so much as the incontinence. Share this outdoor privy with a neighbour you see, family of five, eleven including the children, nothing you can teach me about control of outgoings I can tell you.'

'That's revolting, Dad. You don't seem to have changed at all.'

I clicked my teeth together. 'Like I said, stark bollock naked. Can't you hear the dentures chattering? Off you go then and see you soon.'

'OK Dad. Look after yourself.'

We sat opposite each other at this restaurant, changed since the day I used to take the family there for a treat, perhaps after one of those uplifting films they were sometimes allowed to see. Or to give my wife a break from what she called home-wage-slavery. In those days you received a bit of personal attention like a clean table-cloth, indeed a table-cloth at all, and only got the ketchup, sugar, mustard, Worcester sauce and pepper when you asked for them and couldn't tell from the cutlery that today's menu was the same as yesterday's. Now it was all booths with Formica surfaces which at least you could tell had been wiped the once. An absolutely smashing place, in short, at which to make a fuss of one's only son after not having seen him for a year or more. He was all neat and combed and generally spruced up and looked perfectly ghastly.

The waitress stood above us, pencil poised over a pad, looking uneagerly from one of us to the other like a ticket seller at a mainline London railway station. She yawned and I said, 'I can see we're going to have a job deciding. Place beginning to fill up, is it? The lunch-time rush.'

And I raised myself up sufficiently over the partition to confirm we were still the only people there if you excluded the disconsolate chap with a tartan cap lolling at the counter and gazing at the coffee machine, who perhaps fetched up there after Scotland lost its last football match at Wembley. Which is what I said to Adrian as the waitress muttered, 'Please yourselves,' and left us. Doubtless she was underpaid or tired or had much unhappiness in her life, some of it caused by customers like me who were a lot better off than she was and were rude to her or took the micky as I had. Aren't people a scream, the lengths to which they'll go to cheer themselves up?

I began by asking him how his mother was.

'Really busy,' he replied. 'And she seems to be getting quite famous, a borough councillor and all that.'

'Labour of course.'

'Oh gosh yes, they both are. Sort of into Militant.'

'Pretty talkative that must be I shouldn't wonder.'

'Yeah. They do want to change the world rather.'

'Your going into commerce, the City possibly, makes for some getting at you, does it? Though the left must need people who understand money. No point knowing what's best for people if you can't balance their books too. I mean . . . What do I mean?'

'I don't care about any of that, Dad. I just want to do a good job. The thing is I'm quite good at it, taking extra exams and things and one or two of the big firms are already after me.'

'That's wonderful, Adrian. I expect it was the name that did it though.'

But I could tell things weren't wonderful at all. It was worse than the taciturnity of his childhood, which made it hard for me to be a good father to him, though doubtless it worked the other way round. No, he was simply and utterly unhappy. His face was sickly and lumpy, as if cold dishwater with little blobs of muck in it had seeped in under his skin. And his eyes: well, easy to describe those – on the verge of tears and he'd avoided looking me in the eye once. Then he said, 'I'm sorry you and Mum broke up, Dad.'

'Well, so am I in a way. At least there weren't any hard feelings. It was a bit of a mismatch, that's all. I admire her. Always have. She was a good woman, a good mother.'

He fiddled with the menu, curling up its corners. 'I remember when you took us out and the harder you tried to cheer us up, the worse it got. Do you remember the day at Harrods?'

'Indeed I do. Guessing the prices. So you felt sorry for me, did you? Look, I didn't, don't, feel sorry for myself. Might have been sorry in a more general sort of way. Then found this happy-go-lucky woman who turned out . . . Never mind about that. Remember her, do you?'

He made a face now, beginning to part the menu in two. 'Oh her. Ts . . . I just minded your not being there all the time any more. Virginia not so much. She was into things then.'

'And I was worried silly about what things might be into her. Still, she seems to have got herself a nice bloke so that's all right . . . You're not in love too, are you, nothing daft like that?'

It was at this point that something more than mere unhappiness spread across his face like a shadow and he nodded vigorously. The waitress came and stood above us again and I shook my head. When she'd gone, I said, 'I suppose we'd better order. A choice between the unspeakable and the uneatable. Who said that? Wasn't it that old qu . . . ?'

Sharply, he interrupted me. 'Dad, you ought to know, I'm gay.'

'Yes,' I replied with a shrug, 'your mother hinted at that. So you won't be having the breast of bird or either of the tarts then?'

My voice held pretty steady, I thought, but now it wasn't him who wasn't doing the looking in the eye. So we held each other's gaze for an instant and I moistened my lips and tried to grin.

'You don't mind or anything, do you?' he said.

'Of course I bloody mind. I mean, just look at you, how miserable something's making you. Instead of having a high old time or whatnot with girls. Or before long expecting to. While now, or for ever, well, I know everyone's very liberated about it these days and lots of famous people, not all of them actors by any means, are like that, whether you flaunt it or not, lisp or wear a ring in your ear, it'll be at the centre of your thingummy moral and mental stage – you won't be able to keep it apart so easily. I mean not like us demented heteros who have it on the brain too to be sure but not always on about itself in addition to what it's always on about . . . hold on a minute. What am I saying? What I mean is it won't be a laugh a minute exactly, will it? Nothing wrong with that of course but well furtive or something . . .'

He was beginning to smile but such as when weeping is soon to follow. I had my hand on his and when the waitress returned, squeezed it and kept it there.

'Darling boy,' I said, 'we must order or the lady will be ever so cross with us.'

'I see, it's like that, is it?' she said. 'Take your time, dear, it's all the same to me.' And again she left us to it.

'Seriously though, Dad, you don't *mind*, do you? Mum says things like the ultimate irrelevance of sexuality. The truth, she says, is its superfluous individualism, something like that.'

I took my hand away and tapped him on the chin with my fist. 'Does she indeed? Well, don't know about that. Possibly. The truth just isn't very beautiful to me in this instance. Why pretend? I don't like thinking of you "with" another bloke. Not in the slightest. Whereas thinking of you with a girl. Don't like thinking of that either, except more generally, like move over you lucky sod. Oops, sorry!'

He smiled again. It was becoming all right and he blinked away all but one tear that stuck to his eyelash.

'So it disgusts you?'

'That's it, yes.'

'A lot?'

'Yes, a lot. But you don't disgust me at all. It could make you tougher, more tolerant. Provided you don't make a thing of it, let people get to you, become bitchy or bitter or sly or anything that takes you away from yourself and others, me for starters. Like, look at you now, Adrian . . .' I took his hand again, seeing the waitress return. 'Honestly, what a wreck. Not disgust, no, just fear . . . A coffee for me, thanks.' Adrian nodded. 'Two coffees.' She waited. 'A fried egg and chips.' Adrian nodded again. 'Two fried eggs and chips. That's one egg each.'

She pocketed her notebook and looked at our clasped hands, narrowing her lips.

'Sorry to disturb, dear. But you won't be able to handle the egg, will you, not with one hand? The chips yes, but not the egg.'

'My son and I aren't very hungry. Used to come here in the old days.'

'Your son, is that what he is?' She winked at Adrian, nodded sideways at me. 'Whoever he is, tell him from me, what he needs is a good square meal. Bringing him here, that's not treating him proper, is it?'

'I'll have a glass of milk too please,' Adrian said.

'Sure he can afford it?' she said to him and left us.

'You were saying, Dad. Disgust.'

'Look, Adrian, I don't want to have this conversation any more. I mean, if one were to draw up a tremendously long list of the nastiest things in the world, what blokes do with each other wouldn't be on it. When I think about you, which isn't often, but a whole lot more than you think about me, what with your studies to worry about and, well, other blokes, where was I, I want to think of you more often now, which means your phoning me more often, like at least once a month or send a postcard . . .'

'There's something else, Dad.'

'Oh no, not something *else*, for Christ's sake.'

'It's what happened with me and Webb that day in his garage.'

'Don't remind me. I was bloody feeble, wasn't I?'

'Yes, you were. But you see, there was part of me that enjoyed it. He didn't touch me or anything.'

I raised my hands to my head and dropped my elbows to the table with a thud and groaned, 'Now he tells me! Is that what started you . . . ?'

'No, I mean the pictures he showed me. They weren't so frightful. Not like some of those I came across in the magazines you thought you'd hidden away where we couldn't find them. I thought they were awf . . .'

300

I groaned some more, shuddered, struck my forehead with my fist, sobbed, shook my clenched hands, dabbed my eyes with my paper napkin so that by the time the waitress returned we were both convulsed with giggles, spluttering all over the place. I don't know who started it, Adrian I think, and then it got worse when we looked down at our eggs with the chips around the top of them and we simultaneously tousled our hair and covered one eye and stared back at our plates with expressions of horror.

'Glad someone can see the funny side,' the waitress said with a loud sigh. 'There's a nice bit of cheesecake to follow.'

'Where?' I managed, peering round the edge of the partition. 'Where did she go?'

This was too much for Adrian who was weeping all right then. Gasping into his handkerchief he hurried out to the toilet.

'I'm sorry,' I said to the waitress. 'That was bad-mannered of us.'

'It's not easy for your sort,' she said. 'You have a nice time while you can.'

When she left I rearranged both the eggs and all the chips on Adrian's plate and gave them ketchup ears and lips, a mustard nose, a Worcester sauce moustache and sprinkled salt on the chips to give the beard and hair a hoary look. When he came back and sat down it wasn't for long and with a great wail he had to go back to the toilet again.

We left shortly after that, having eaten nothing. I left a ten-quid note for the waitress. I hope she didn't think I was a rich man. Some people it is impossible to thank enough. It was a late autumn day and we wandered through the park, kicking leaves. Not much more was said that I could recall later. I told him to give my love to his mother. He told me more about his studies. He was doing astonishingly well, no doubt about that. I told him about my house in the country, my ten-acre garden not including the banks of rhododendrons and the two orchards. He told me he was ambitious, but not for power or wealth. He didn't want to make things happen so much as stop them from happening, like insider trading, the very rich getting greedy and the very greedy getting rich, he didn't despise money, only what it did to people – that kind of thing.

A cold wind got up so we didn't dawdle in the park as much as we wanted to, remembering the day with the Webbs and Hambles when we played french cricket and he got into a sulk. The leaves blew across our legs and clung to our trousers and what was left of them on the trees didn't hide what was fast becoming a black sky. Towards the end we sat huddled close together on a bench, our hands in our pockets and watched the last of the blue diminish and then vanish as a strong gust of wind shook free about half of the last leaves on the tree above us. For a while we jumped about trying to catch them (Adrian caught two, I none, or not a whole one) and then we made our way to the Underground station.

'What's the meaning of it all, Dad?' he said.

And I told him a story the Colonel had told me a few months before. A taxi driver is speaking: 'I had that philosopher Bertrand Russell in my cab once. Turned to him and said, "You're Bertrand Russell, aren't you?" "Yes," he said. "So what's it all about then?" I asked him. "He didn't say a bloody word."'

He pinched his lips, touched my wrist and turned away. No sign of a smile. I had tried too hard again. As it was all those years ago I watched him walk away with fear for him that blocked my throat and a spreading shame that I was no longer there beside him. I had seen him as he must have been often on his own, weeping his heart out.

As I look back over all this now, a long time later, AIDS is getting worse and the Big Bang has happened. Adrian seems to be doing well out of it. I've seen him a couple of times, looking dapper with horn-rimmed glasses and dark-blue suit. No spots at all. He didn't refer to our meeting that day. In fact he was in a bit of a rush, was making time for me. But that was all right. He showed me a photograph of his flat in Canonbury, which I shall go and see when I am next in London. He actually offered me the odd hundred quid if I needed it. I said I'd let him know.

I asked him what his mother thought of it all. He made a face. 'She disapproves but isn't very good at hiding she's a little proud of me too. She once said, "We socialists don't condemn personal riches, not as such." Wouldn't dare tell her what I'm doing for privatization. She's all right really, Mum. Doesn't lecture me any more. Her man stays quiet, always looks down at heel, just for my benefit, I suspect.'

On the second occasion I had to ask him. He looked me straight in the eye.

'Fingers crossed, Dad. I know two blokes who've died of it. One of them I was in love with – that day in the restaurant, you remember. But I never actually . . . I got scared just in time. So there was no . . .'

'Buggery.'

He nodded. 'I was going to say danger. And now there's this girl and I've had the test. Twice actually. Christ, Dad, I'm so fucking lucky.'

'Subtly put. This girl, so the magazines didn't . . .'

He looked at his watch and I wondered how much it must have cost.

'Let's say, I'm looking forward to trying. She's very sweet, very understanding. She's guessed, I think. Not a great looker but stylish if you know what I mean. We both think we're on to a very good thing indeed.'

'I see.'

He looked at his watch again. 'Sorry, Dad. Must rush. Another Japanese invasion on the way. Have to try to stop them taking over the world.'

'One last thing, Adrian. When I'm next in town, take me shopping in Harrods would you?'

He caught my second glance at his watch and smiled. Now it was his turn to put his hand on mine. Then he readjusted his tie and specs and left. Four days later a watch just like it, in fact better if anything, arrived in the post.

So that's Adrian out of the way. I like books to have a happy ending. I like the idea of reunions and the giving of gifts. Because life isn't like that. It's all separation and loss and everything gets taken away in the end. When the watch arrived, telling me the right time, so the leaflet said, to the nearest hundredth of a second, I held it tight and blessed my son and his good fortune. But I never wear it. There's nothing wrong with the watch I've got, when I remember to wind it.

Into winter again now and the evenings are long. I have finished raking the leaves, thereby tugging up clumps of grass which leave patches of bare earth I can do nothing about until the spring. Agnes gave me some winter lawn dressing and told me what to do with my roses. When most of the leaves had fallen I phoned the home about Nanny Phipps and stopped by there late one afternoon. The matron received me in her office.

'No point seeing her now. Strangers alarm her more than ever. She doesn't think they're undertakers any longer but detectives or priests in plain clothes. She spends most of the time talking to those photographs you brought, or rather to Sarah with whom she goes on adventures. She smiles and chatters away and seems not to notice the incontinence, all that. I would call it happiness if there were any reality, any truth in it. Perhaps that is what happiness is . . .' She chuckled. 'Impossible to imagine being happy at the centre of such aching and stench. Oh well, we'll find out soon enough, when such questions no longer occur to us.'

I asked again if there was anything I could do since I too had time on my hands. 'Even if it's money.'

'That's all taken care of,' she said and stood up. 'Please don't think me rude. But there's so much to do and we can't keep staff these days. Don't worry about her. She's quite in command of herself most of the days saying, "Off we go Sarah, my beloved. We'll never get there if we dawdle." '

'I've come across her old Bible and prayer-book. Do you think she'd like them back?'

'I shouldn't bother if I were you. Then she'd really think they'd come for her.'

As I write now she is still alive. I phoned yesterday and the matron said, 'She has so much to live for now, waking up at all hours to be with her Sarah, all that travelling they do together . . .'

If only there was some way I could have told Maureen all this. I still don't quite know what went wrong, not right at the heart of it. The jokes could have been better or shouldn't have been necessary and the truth may be in there somewhere. Any fault I find is usually with myself. As my father once said, 'You shouldn't want what you can't have.' To which my mother replied, 'You shouldn't have what you don't want either.' Increasingly, therefore, I avoid looking too carefully at girls because I don't like feeling sorry for myself.

It was the Colonel who died. For two weeks or so I did not see them and thought they might have gone away for the winter. It was the woman in the shop who told me he'd been taken to the hospital but was now home again. I phoned at once and Agnes told me he was getting better.

'Bollocks,' he said loudly on the extension.

'Just rang to ask how you were. I'd no idea . . .'

'I'm feeling shit awful.'

'Don't suppose the weather helps.'

'The weather doesn't make a damn bit of difference. Notice the way the birds scarper off when the going gets rough.'

'Some of them hang on.'

'Can't imagine why. I'll tell you one thing. Here's one old soldier who won't be gathering bloody lilacs in the spring again.'

'Leave them where they belong, on the bush. Quite right too.'

'You know what I mean. Anyway, how's the love life? Handsome woman, I thought.'

'My sister, you mean. You surely don't imagine for a moment . . . I may be vegetating but I'm no Swede.'

His laughter became an uncontrollable cough and Agnes said, 'Thank you for calling, Tom. You must call round when he's a little better.'

'What's that?' he spluttered. 'No shagging where I'm going. How many angels can you have on the prick of a . . . ? And we shall rise again . . . To hell with Jenners, that's what I say.'

There was a pause then while she went up to join him and I heard her say faintly, 'Drink this, darling. Steady now.' Then she let out a little shriek. 'Don't *do* that!'

I put the phone down and she rang back about ten minutes later. Her voice was still laughing at the edges but was choked and hoarse for other reasons as well. 'Sorry, Tom. I've given him something and he's asleep now. That was rude of us.'

'Very. I can't think why I ever bothered. When can I call round?'

'I'm not sure if he'll have to go into hospital again. I guess not. He's very sick you know.'

'Is it . . . ?'

'It is plural. Rather a number of things, apart from the cancer I mean.'

'Can I . . . ?'

'I'll be in touch, Tom dear.'

'Give him fond wishes.'

'I'll do that.'

He died a week later. It was Jenners who told me. 'Ah, Ripple, thought you ought to know. The old soldier's handed in his kitbag and joined the big regiment in the skies.'

305

You could see he'd thought about it, subtle bit of drafting that. Still, people would be telling other people about him one day and other people about them and so on *ad infinitum*. A bit of phrase-making always helps, but that wasn't all.

'Hung up his boots, taken his last salute you might say . . .'

'Thanks for telling me.'

'After the last post the reveille, and there's always . . .'

I said goodbye, thanking him again. Later that day I phoned Agnes and she told me he was to be cremated the following morning. She and their daughter wanted to be there alone but there would be a memorial service in the church on the following Saturday. I can't remember now how she sounded except when she told me he hadn't wanted flowers and any contributions should go to the church restoration fund. For a moment she seemed almost cheerful.

'He was a strange old thing in some ways. Only once said he loved me, when he proposed: "I shall love you until the day I die and that's all there is to it." He absolutely always charmed the pants off me. He was true to his word. It breaks my heart no longer suddenly to love and be loved like that . . .'

Her voice trailed away. I had nothing to say and that is how it is, as it is tonight when one's done with the scribbling, a sense of having said and done just about nothing.

About thirty people turned up for the service, old comrades in arms, the usual crowd from the village and round about. The shopkeepers had decorated the far end of the church with many varieties of flowers, which looked especially bright and out of place on the filthy winter's day it was.

We began with the hymn 'O God our help in ages past.' The old comrades sang out but I could not sing at all, watching his widow in the front row, her head bowed under black hat and veil. Her daughter was beside her, staring in front of her, not singing either. They were arm in arm and I wondered if they wished they were alone.

One of the old soldiers read a lesson with the lines: 'What shall I cry? All flesh is grass, and all the goodliness thereof is as the flower of the field; the grass withereth, the flower fadeth.' But he read it abruptly as if the opposite were true or had nothing to do with why they were there.

Then we sang, 'The Lord's my shepherd, I'll not want . . .' and towards the end the widow and daughter joined in, holding each other closer. After that the vicar read a couple of short prayers, his head down as if rehearsing them to himself, testing their truth. Then we chanted a psalm, trying to follow the vicar as he clutched at handfuls of notes to change the chords but there were only two lines of tune so we soon got the hang of it: 'God is our hope and strength, a very present help in trouble . . . He maketh wars to cease in all the world: He breaketh the bow and snappeth the spear in sunder.'

He did not go up to the pulpit for his sermon but walked a few yards up and down the aisle, looking mainly up at the windows awash with shadows: 'Whatsoever thy hand findeth to do, do it with thy might; for there is no work, nor device, nor knowledge nor wisdom, in the grave whither thou goest.' He told us where the words came from so I could check them in Nanny Phipps's Bible. He thanked us for coming, some of us a long way and some who had doubts about the words we had heard and sung.

'In this place we do what this place is for and what has been done in it for hundreds of years and with a bit of luck for hundreds of years to come. As for the man to whom we have come to pay our last respects, I only know that he was fond of it and gave it much of his time and money. I do not know what he believed. He said to me once, "Like to put in an appearance from time to time to make sure it's still there. Got to keep things going." I cannot speak of his character which is customary on these occasions but I had the impression he was a deeply kind and truthful man. It could be assumed he was a brave man, though until today I did not know of his decorations. On another occasion he said to me, "By profession, padre, I'm a trained killer and I always wanted to be where the scrapping was. It was where my thinking led me, for what it was worth, on to some battlefield or another. My conscience will never let me explain that away, for all the killing we wanted to prevent." I had no answer to that. And at times like this I must confess I sometimes feel that for all the magnificence of the words I have no answer to anything. We can only come together with the certainty that we must try to share the sorrow of others and in that sharing join ourselves to the past. Blessed are they that mourn for how can they ever be comforted? For as much as he was a peacemaker, he was a child of God and until He does get round to making wars cease in all the world and I fear He never will, we shall have need of soldiers of honour and conscience who ready themselves for battle but do not seek it. We cannot leave everything to God. Dear Jesus Christ, how I wish we could. I see so little evidence of His justice and His mercy. And so we must constantly look to those who consider others and are truthful according to their best lights . . . He that doeth the thing that is right, and speaketh the truth from his heart . . . he that leadeth an uncorrupt life . . . he that setteth not by himself but is lowly in his own eyes . . . How does it end? . . . Whoso doeth these things shall never fall. And now his favourite hymn: "Abide with me, Fast falls the eventide, The darkness deepens, Lord with me abide." '

And the darkness did deepen as we sang. At the end of the verse, the vicar paused at the organ and we heard the rain beating down on the roof and against the windows and he left the organ to turn on the lights. Then we started singing again and for a second or two I missed Maureen, who would have drowned out the sound of the battering rain, the onset of winter. I missed my father too and then my son, their anguish I could never share and that, then, was all my own. Agnes and her daughter were singing loudly now and I remembered the Colonel saying to me in the pub that day, 'She's a lovely girl.' Across the aisle, on the far side of her mother, I saw her only in part, but then as she came out of her pew she smiled sweetly at me out of her overruling sorrow, and it was the turn of my thinking, my unthinking, to be led on to the battlefield where no peace is declared and no mercy shown.

This added later, you understand, trying to tell the truth but lowering the tone. Agnes caught my look, read it, smiled too as if to say, Life must go on. The dead man's daughter: blue eyes, lips parted, cheeks flushed, a face perfectly clear and at peace, despite the shadows cast by her hair, the little scars across her forehead and beside her mouth. She seemed, in that glimpse, not to belong there, a nervous child standing by a piano getting ready to sing, of whom too much is expected. And then a second glimpse as she moved up beside her mother to take her arm again, and stooped to straighten her skirt so that, close enough to touch, I saw her breast hang and her blouse tighten round it . . .

Around the entrance, people were putting on raincoats and wrestling with umbrellas. They were going back to the house for tea and I heard the vicar tell Agnes that he had to rush off. She thanked him and turned to me, 'Do come, Tom.'

But I refused too. She should be alone with old friends. Her daughter had gone ahead to fetch the car and I let them all go, muttering and fussing. The vicar went back to turn off the lights and we reached the door together. The rain was teeming down and the bare trees were threshing about, their glistening trunks caught in the car lights. He gave me a lift to my cottage but only said what fearful, godless weather it was. I invited him in but he shook his head.

'I'd love to but I'm late as it is.' Then he smiled broadly as if by mistake. 'I've buried three people so far this week and there'll be a couple more by the end of next. He was the oldest by a long chalk. Nothing much to be said about the others. Nothing commonplace, though, about the varieties of grief. What a godforsaken job this can be at times.'

The weather cleared the next morning and it was fine enough to walk to the shop. I met her on the way back and we stopped at my front gate for a while. She wore a scarf round her head and in the uncertain grey daylight she looked distracted as if someone had tried to swindle her. Perhaps she had wept the night before or not slept or had a cold coming or not bothered with make-up or all of these things. Her face unadorned and unshadowed by her hair was flushed and faintly dappled as if she was coming out in a rash which had infected her eyes. She wasn't beautiful at all any longer, she was flawed, off balance, ordinary, hurt, unspeakably lovable.

'I'll stick around for a few days to be with Mum,' she was saying in reply to some question I had already forgotten.

'Will she stay on in the village?' I asked.

She shook her head, distracted again, looking around the sky as if seeing there nothing but waste and despair.

'Not exactly thrilling, is it?' I added.

'No, she'll go back to the States. She always wanted to after Dad retired but he couldn't have borne it.'

'They seemed happy, I always thought. Very, in fact. Close, I think it's called.'

She sighed. 'Oh yes. Well, that's all over now. She couldn't stay here without him. It wasn't easy for her.'

I opened the gate but she showed no sign of wanting to move on, was still looking about the sky or where it met the clumps of trees along the horizon like heaps of thorns.

'I hardly knew him but, if I may say so, he seemed an exceptionally nice man.'

She nodded impatiently and I thought, she doesn't want to talk about any of that.

'I just wonder if I'll always miss him as I do now. They waited for me so long, you know.'

She looked at me accusingly as though that might stop the grief getting the better of her again. I looked at the sky and saw the desolation now whitening, promising a short spell of fine weather.

'I didn't miss my father much at first,' I said. 'Getting married, having children, that kind of thing. Now I seem to, more and more. My mother too, come to that, though she's still alive. I'm more often reminded. My children too, though I can't help wondering if I ever loved them as much as he did you. And you must greatly have admired him. That would help. Unless love simply grows of itself and isn't a condition of anything else.'

'His bravery, you mean?'

'Yes or rather more generally. He was decorated, the vicar said.'

'The Military Cross and a DSO. Even Mum never knew quite what for. When I was little his sergeant once told me he was the bravest man he had ever known. When the subject came up, he quickly changed it as if he'd done something he was ashamed of. But it had nothing to do with his being my father . . .' She put a hand on my arm. 'We shouldn't try to explain these things. And me with a baby on the way. I'm sorry he never saw his grandchild, that as much as anything.'

'I am glad. Congratulations.'

But I wasn't of course, not as I should have been. (That added later. The child will now have been born and is suckling at her breast. Compared with this moment, midnight, into another autumn, the leaves unswept, a fresh bottle broken, the stub of a cheroot relit, what I felt then was the merest blemish of innocence. Oh Maureen, forgive me, why did I ever pretend . . . ?)

She put her hand on her stomach. 'It doesn't notice yet, well hardly.'

I looked higher and wider at where there was nothing to be looked at at all but the same old messy passage of clouds. She seemed to have drawn closer to me and to be shivering.

'Would you like to come in for a cup of something?' I asked.

'I really must go. Mum is at sixes and sevens, putting the house on the market, deciding what to sell and what to keep. All the legal things . . .'

She moved away a few paces and stood looking over the fence at my dingy garden.

'Mum says you must come and help yourself to whatever you like.'

'What, after the dreadful things I've done to the stuff she's already given me?'

Suddenly she flung off her scarf and shook out her hair and held her face up to me, the strands of gold tumbling across it, catching all the dull light there was in the air to make a great blaze, as if to say: you see how beautiful I can be, how I can dazzle if I want to, this is how you will remember me. She moved away and I raised a hand, the fingers splayed as if to ward off a great onrush of wild beasts on the rampage.

'Good luck,' I said.

'Same to you,' and she turned and strode off.

I watched her for a dozen paces and she turned to confirm that that was what I was doing, raising a hand with a final valiant smile.

I went inside and made myself a nice cup of tea and remembered what my mother used to say when my father asked for that: 'You wouldn't expect me to make a nasty one would you?' Well, that was what I was drinking, a very nasty cup of tea indeed. Which helped me to come to my senses and I lay on my bed with a Ruth Rendell and dozed until dusk.

A few days later the 'For Sale' sign went up outside their house and over the next weeks I saw a variety of cars parked outside it and, once or twice, Sidney's. It was he who told me that they'd left, after telling me what the asking price was. It was a bitterly cold day and he wasn't wearing gloves but that wasn't why he was rubbing his hands so much. Funny, I thought, Agnes didn't phone to say goodbye but, as it happens, I was less on her mind than she was on mine. Then Sidney said, 'She told me you could have whatever you liked from the garden. But don't overdo it, old fruit, it's a selling point. I'm having a gardener in.'

'Did she leave an address?'

'It's like that, is it? Better ask her solicitor.'

I wrote her a note which simply said: '*I'm sorry I never conveyed my condolences in any sort of proper manner but I've given something to the*

311

church, a poor token of my regard. I miss you both. The village is not the same without you. I took only one shrub from your garden while the going was good. It'll probably die like all the others. It was after dark while Sidney was changing sentries. I hope you are finding happiness in your new life. Affectionately, Tom Ripple.'

Not one of the great letters, you're thinking, but I wrote it on a large greetings card with a painting on it called *Frosty Morning* by Turner. I preferred that to a lavish, sunlit bowl of flowers by a French painter, choosing the true over the beautiful. Though I should imagine both are regarded as having almost as much of one as of the other at the point where they become indistinguishable, or perhaps it was just that I couldn't say it with flowers.

She wrote back from the States on an ever larger card on which a girl with long hair was gazing up a hill at a tall, plain wooden house. It was a beautiful idea but not truthful somehow, sentimental in other words. Inside she had scrawled: *'Thank you for your darling card. I'm so sorry I never said goodbye but I was too confused and shook up even to think. I hope you are keeping well. You all seem a long way away already and it's good to be back in the good old U.S. of A. I hope Sidney shoots himself in the foot. He was a crook and a lecher. No proof, but he seems to have helped himself to things. As for the rest, you always were a gentleman.'*

So that was that. As I write now, I remember them with affection, still miss them. When I drove past their house today I saw several small children running in and out of the front door so I assume the new people have moved in. I am in a quandary. Do I go there to satisfy my curiosity, saying, 'Welcome, I live down the road, do let me know if there's anything I can do.' Or if I did, would they think: some nosy old twerp come to satisfy his curiosity. Give them an inch and you'll end up running a mile . . . I have no idea what impression I make on people . . . I think that on meeting myself for the first time, I would not trust myself very much. Too little to go on somehow . . . Why am I going on like this? To fill the time of course. I've run out of things to say concerning the other people I've tried to write about.

Out and out it travels through memory and arrives nowhere. This must be why I stay here where there is so much sky, messed over and often concluding in nights of filthy, noisy weather. I am making myself useful at the crafts centre, sorting out the accounts, travelling about putting stuff into shops, deciding on prices. I spend two afternoons a week at that, sometimes visiting a bank to ask for a loan or applying for a government grant. There's a whole world out there, I'm beginning to discover, of what's called economic renewal through community development, training schemes, helping people to help themselves. Next week I shall put the finishing touches to a modest expansion plan. I've visited other such centres and see no reason why ours shouldn't be as good as any of them. When I go there I wear a suit and tie and I suspect they smile at me behind my back. I'm beginning to get to know what will sell and what won't. I'm invariably right. I drink their home-made wine and pretty dreadful stuff it is too. I make my own beer now, with brown sugar: Ripple's Forest Brown I call it. My paunch grows larger. Tomorrow I'll wear a waistcoat with my suit and polish my shoes. That'll cheer them up.

Loose ends to tie up. A call to Maureen. I promise to go to London to hear her sing again but I know I never will. Now I listen to quite a lot of music at home. I have that to thank her for. Good old Albinoni. I think she was quite impressed when I told her what records I'd borrowed from the library.

I've also spoken to my former wife. I told her about the crafts centre. She was enthusiastic, very. Until I said that Mrs Thatcher would approve: self-reliance, self-help, making it pay and they were coming on their bikes from all over. She thought I was taking the micky. Well, I wasn't, or not much. She rang back a few days later, having checked with Brad perhaps, to say that Mrs Thatcher was stealing clothes and something about conceptual hybridization (?) and the Prince of Wales. She always had a problem with royalty, wanting to take strong exception to them against the inclinations or indifference of most of the rest of us.

'The Princess of Wales is something else altogether,' I said.

'But such a distraction from reality,' she replied.

'Precisely,' I said.

She sighed. Somehow we'd avoided mentioning our children at all.

My daughter. Everything is all right there. She has told me about her new job and sent me things to read about it. Some of the deaf children she's teaching to speak are blind too. In our own way we all need someone like that. It would be marvellous to get clear through to others, as Mozart can. He almost seems to be saying something but if we knew what it was there'd be nothing more to say.

Sidney's left the area. I hardly ever see Jenners. His wife persists at the crafts centre but has yet to produce anything saleable. She tells me her husband is still at work on his little monograph. She's always the last to leave in the evening, I'm told. When I last bumped into him he gave me his views about various things with which I found myself agreeing. I was very pleasant to him and with a tap on the shoulder told him to keep up the good work. He seemed to have no answer to that.

I have nothing more to say about my son. Pretty busy, he sounds, when I phone him. Marriage isn't mentioned. Doubtless he'll spring it on me one day. You can tell he's all right. He also talks down to me, just a little. I don't mind that in the slightest. I bet he still doesn't dare to talk down to his mother.

I have to end somewhere. With spring in the air again I have done some strolling. The man who bought the Colonel's house is in High Tech. They have three small children who think me an extremely old man. When walking near their house I try not to look like one, swinging my walking stick with a jaunty air, putting no pressure on it. I've bought an ingenious German contraption with which to shave down my callus. The village is part of their estate. They will soon grow up and stop coming round to scrounge biscuits and the like and some little time beyond that there won't be me any longer to come and scrounge off.

I even came back the other afternoon to find them sitting on the floor in front of my television. It was an old cowboy film – absolute trash which I thoroughly enjoyed watching with them for a while. When I asked them about the plot, they just said, 'Ssh!' They didn't even look up at me when I came in.

Nor did they say anything when I went out and fetched them Coca-Cola and Jaffa Cakes. 'Sod you lot,' I thought. But they thanked me later, when the film was over. They usually remember to do that, not always, but usually. They're nice kids even though they do watch far too much television, almost as much as me I should think.

314

Once the girl brought me a small, uncoordinated bunch of flowers or rather wild greenery with some colourful bits in it which came, I suspect, from my garden. It's the thought that counts – though as a rule it doesn't begin to add up. (A joke I've made before, I think; high time I brought this to a close). All this is practice for being a grandparent. Virginia is sure to have a baby soon and one day Adrian, who knows?

I visit the church quite often. People are beginning to think I have some sort of official status at the place. Jenners has become a bit offhand with me. Or rather, he barely acknowledged me when I passed him taking notes from a gravestone and asked him what in the devil's name he thought he was up to. Never mind that. In those surroundings I can do without his sort of certainty. I wish I took religion seriously. I still don't believe a word of it, though it is astonishingly beautiful and right-sounding, the words and the music. But is it true? That's the only thing. Of course it's not the belief itself that people really think about but the survival. At least that's as far as I've got, that and being able to keep up a sort of daydream of fine feelings untroubled by what's going on in the real world outside.

I have a number of wishes: that I could have said to Maureen, 'I find that I still need and want you. It was a miraculous event that early autumn evening, all right through and through but what happened when we came out on the other side?' I'd like her to be there in the church with me, singing the way she does. I have read her first letter again, the sadness behind it, and am ashamed. For I have used her, in all this too, over and over again.

The vicar remarked on her absence last Sunday. I shrugged and looked embarrassed.

'Can't have everything, can we?' he said.

'Good God,' I replied. 'Since when? I always thought it was there to be had for the asking.'

I've even been known to go to the garden centre to buy large bunches of flowers with which to adorn the altar and thereabouts. They don't add enough extra beauty to help bring out the truth or anything like that. So if they're not just the boost I need for my leap of faith, they're wondrous to behold while standing or sitting there and wiggling my toes.

Mrs Thatcher has just got in for her third term. I know how eager you will be to learn whether or not I voted for her.

My mother is still alive and perfectly well considering, though hard of hearing which makes it pointless to phone her. She never phones me. When I have been to see her she has taken little interest in what I am up to as if I would have to disguise it was no good. She has nothing to tell me. She always hated gossip and never talked about the past. She has never mentioned my father that I can recall. As for current affairs, she distrusts everyone and everything. With so little in my own life to tell her about I do not stay long. When I told her I was taking early retirement she said, 'And so soon after you got started. Still, work isn't everything, though I don't know what else there is.'

PART THREE

PART THREE

Chapter One

So what happened to bring my rustic sojourn to an end? On this damp winter's evening in Highbury, I look at my notes and at this moment wish myself back there. The Colonel stands with his daughter at the bottom of their garden and it blazes up around them. She takes his arm as he starts coughing. Tears come to his eyes and she smiles up at him, then at me as he hunches forward and splutters into his handkerchief, his heaving and shaking gripped in her love. Her smile is helpless and unexpected and I turn away from them. They do not want to be seen like that. I hear him cough again with deep grating sounds and when I look back at them, he is standing rigidly to attention, head back, and says, 'Bloody bronchials, never did trust the buggers.' She is stroking his hand. I am no longer there so I do not know if there was such a moment.

Then I am alone in the deserted church and shiver as I breathe in the chilly air of old stone. I stand in the porch and wait for the rain to pass. I smell the pig farm and see in the mid-distance two horses, side by side and head to tail beyond a padlocked gate. A tail flicks and then they are quite still again as the sky darkens and descends. I do not know why they seem to have significance for me, just two horses standing together at nightfall. The bedroom window of the flat on the top floor of the house where I now live looks out on the backs of similar houses. It is where I have my desk (and binoculars) and I wish I was now looking out instead over flat brown fields, sniffing at pig dung. But not for long as I sort through my notes and recall why I am here not there.

Among the notes are some jottings I made towards drawing up a business plan for the crafts centre but these are largely indecipherable now and can be destroyed. I spent three or four afternoons a week there and dabbled with a craft or two of my own, soon acquiring several wonky mugs, ashtrays and small vases or pots, things which as often as not began as one thing and ended as another. Odd jobs indeed. That not seeming to be leading to better things, I then spent a couple of days in leatherwork before moving on to tie-dying one memorable morning. The former was all knives and needles and stretches of skin and it soon became apparent it would be difficult to achieve much at that while keeping one's hands well clear of it. As for the latter, it was not only my tasteful pale blue knitted tie that became deep mauve in small patches but also the trousers of my best pale grey suit and my new cream St Michael shirt I had ironed that morning in order to be fittingly attired for sustained figure work in drawing up the second draft of the afore-mentioned business plan. I look now at my fingernails and am sure they are still not the colour they were. The trousers and shirt I still wear at times such as this, late at night under a dim lamp, when I'm not expecting company.

And so I transferred finally to carpentry and began work on a three-legged milkmaid's chair with a back the shape of a heart. I worked in a corner with my back to the room and Geoffrey and his womenfolk used to pass behind me from time to time, touch my bent back and say, 'Fine, Tom. Keep up the good work.' Or words to that thoroughly condescending effect. They had not dwelt at tiresome length on the quality of my pottery either. 'Come to watch your favourite sitcom?' I used to riposte or 'You take the chair, I'll take the minutes.' This while they hastened on to other parts of the shop where the serious work was going on, on things to which a price or the word 'promise' might be attached. And as I worked, I sometimes remembered Adrian and Webb and what had come crawling out of the woodwork then. I wondered if that was what he did in prison to keep his mind off things or to remind him of them.

One day, regarding the chair as nearly finished apart from having secured its parts together, I was standing back to admire it as Gwen was passing. With a whoop of congratulation she plumped herself down on it, the whoop soaring an octave as the chair collapsed beneath her and ending abruptly as she hit her head on the corner of an unfinished bedside cabinet belonging to someone who had left the centre under a cloud and to which I had decided to turn my attention next. Slumped against the wall, she was unconscious for several seconds, her grey/brown irises looping back and forth like trapped marbles behind her eyelids as I tried to raise her to her feet without taking too decisive a grip of her. Eventually she came round, seizing me round the thigh with one hand and holding her head with the other which then grasped at my collar as I attempted to loosen her hold on my leg, ending as that did with her fingers scrabbling about in the flaccid region between anus and scrotum. Geoffrey had now arrived on the scene as had several others who watched him while, elbowing me aside, he lifted her upright. My apologies were lost in a murmur of what might have included anything from consternation to unconfined delight.

'Are you all right?' he asked with a swift and visible grit of his teeth.

'Oh, crikey!' Gwen moaned, but starting to giggle as she looked down at my chair and said, 'And look what I've done to his master-piece, poor old Tom.'

It had in fact come entirely apart but for the snapped-off top half of one leg, which was still in its socket. 'I can easily make another,' I said.

'Too bloody easily, if you ask me,' Geoffrey mumbled. No sorrow or morale boosting there that I could detect.

Then Ruth, his sister or sister-in-law or cousin or wife or whatever, arrived and began dabbing at her head with a pad of cotton wool which looked as if it had been used for some equivalent purpose on two or three previous occasions.

'Let me,' Geoffrey said. His voice was shaky and he seemed to sway as he bent over her. 'Nothing to worry about. Heads are known to bleed heavily.' He turned to smile at me or it might have become that if it hadn't got stuck while he said, 'Can't imagine why, can you, Tom? Where it comes from, I mean. Hair, skin, then skull, not much room for a lot of blood in between, shouldn't have thought.'

He had spoken loudly as if to a wider audience and I looked behind me to see that the onlookers had begun to disperse. Gwen touched my arm and looked at me almost with tenderness while Geoffrey pressed the pad to the wound.

'I am sorry, Tom, it was coming along *so* nicely,' she piped.

Geoffrey showed me the bloody pad. 'See, only a small wound. Stopped already. No harm done.' By then he was staring down at what was left of the chair and not adding anything at all.

At that moment, Ruth saw my neck and collar. 'Cripes, Tom, you're covered in it!'

It was all gasps now as I pulled out my shirt collar and saw a partial set of Gwen's fingerprints in blood, the clammy sensation on my neck accounting for the rest of it.

'A sticky end to my career in woodwork, how absolutely bloody,' I essayed.

Some tittering then, Geoffrey's a good octave shriller than his womenfolk's, prompted I would soon confirm with hindsight by a good deal of tripartite winking and nudging. I caught a whiff of whisky on Geoffrey's breath. It was not yet quite teatime. I thought then how jolly it all seemed, how much I liked them, how lucky I was. I did not give a toss about my chair.

We then adjourned to their unconverted farm cottage where Geoffrey briskly applied a fresh pad and plaster to Gwen's wound while Ruth made tea which remained in the pot since as she was about to pour, Geoffrey brought out the whisky bottle, not intended as an alternative. Gwen insisted I should take off my shirt and began scrubbing at the collar with a nailbrush in the kitchen sink. Meanwhile there were noises going on like nose clearing plus sucking through an empty straw. Sitting there at the table in my low-slung vest, I was grateful to them for not taking more than fleeting glances at it, as undarned but not nearly as unlaundered as it might appear to be, or around it at the excess of ill-nourished and under-exercised flesh, the moles far too closely resembling old spots, there being a fair sprinkling of those too among the current half-dozen or so. The four or five dogs wishing to make themselves even better known to me and the cats on the table sniffing at my hands round my whisky glass prevented me from remaining as motionless as I would have preferred to be until I had my shirt safely back on. I began to wish the agitation would stop, the sight of blood and the whisky not sufficiently explaining it.

I should add here that these people were still a puzzle to me, in particular the relationship between them. Geoffrey's grizzled, blond-grey hairiness could have put him at any age a fair distance either side of forty-five, say. He had a lumbering, clumsy manner except when he was at one of his benches when he concentrated on his work with a remarkable slow precision. His eyes were deep-set and his beard made it impossible to tell what his mouth was doing, or saying for much of the time for that matter. He treated me with a sort of blurred courtesy, which seemed rather overdone, if not shifty. There was nothing I could guess about his relationship with his women-folk, such as which of them he slept with, if either. Or both for that matter. His manner towards them was offhand but that could have been businesslike or the consequence of too much familiarity. They were alike in plumpness and stature and could have been about the same age, though Gwen's hair was grey and cropped short while Ruth's was the colour of oak-stain and done up in plaits round the back and top of her head, this difference however cancelled out by Ruth having the more wrinkles and lower breasts. Both had pink complexions – Gwen's as if she had just come in from a long walk along a cliff in a high wind and caught a chill, Ruth's the sort associated with onset of extreme embarrassment, patchy and rising from the neck. This went with her almost permanent smile as if she could not be sure otherwise when it would be needed. Gwen's smile was frequent but brief, alert but easily disappointed. Their voices were much alike, hushed and hasty and pitched for persuasion. I had seen little of them off duty but they had made it known early on they were ex-Labour Greens or the other way round and I was quick to agree with them about the rape of the planet and the greed of men, not only because I feared their going on even longer about it in that saintly tone of voice, but because mainly I did. Towards Geoffrey, Gwen was slightly the more deferential, patting him on the arm from time to time. Towards each other they were brisk, supplementing each other so that when one spoke, the other wanted to have the last word. If they were rivals, they had not yet come to terms with it. I cannot remember now whether they ever looked each other in the eye. They always seemed to be side by side, never face to face. With Geoffrey it was always difficult to tell. When they held forth and said, 'Don't you agree, Geoff?' he stared at them non-committally as if he couldn't be bothered to distinguish between them. Most of the time their talk was technical and in that they were all they professed to be. They were good teachers and their students greatly respected them. They were perfectionists. They had written handbooks and articles that could be found prominently displayed in the centre's reading room. They were a team. I should have mentioned all this before but as you will soon see why, my memory of them now has a veil drawn across it. I have tried to be fair and accurate. At the time, it was simply that the noises off had seemed out of character. What had been building up of course was a fit of the giggles.

To resume. As the second round of whisky was poured and Gwen scrubbed away at the collar of my shirt, I asked if I could have a wash. Geoffrey was holding an empty bottle of whisky up to the light and Ruth broke into another titter, I forget about what, to say, 'The loopy-loo. Through that door, along to the end of the corridor and facing you on the right. Don't try shutting the door, it's off its hinges. Pick up a damp clean towel from the so-called airing cupboard opposite.'

'If there are any,' Gwen added. 'Sort of yellow or were. Among the sheets which are whiter, or some of them.' She made a noise into her hand like an imitation of a steam train starting up.

'The chain, a sharp jerk, then a long slow pull,' Ruth said, demonstrating the action. 'Well, more or less.' She looked at Geoffrey for approval, but he was staring down at Gwen's head where the Elastoplast stuck to her hair was lifting the pad away from her wound. The pink tingeing of her hair around it suddenly made her seem much younger. He pressed the plaster hard down with the tips of his fingers.

'Ouch,' she said.

'Hardly bleeding at all.' He sounded disappointed.

'Oughtn't you to have put disinfectant on it?' Ruth asked in the solemn manner of a drunkard aiming to sound sober. 'Dettol or something?'

'What's Dettol?' he said, and they all turned their backs on me for further rehearsal of their sound effects.

I left them to it but as soon as I was into the corridor, I realized I had left my comb in my jacket pocket and was about to return for it when I heard them conversing as follows, indeed could see them since the door was not quite shut, as they settled down round the table, heads forward like conspirators.

It was Gwen who began. 'Poor old Tom Tiddler! We do get some duds but the way one keeps on bumping into him and that perplexed, sort of willing look he always wears!'

'And those dreadful wisecracks,' Ruth added.

'I hope to God that's put him off carpentry,' Geoffrey said. 'Over to you next for a bit of weaving, Ruthie, I think.'

Ruth let out a throttled shriek. 'But I had him for pottery! There was this absolutely amazing object, did you see it, which I took for a spoutless teapot but which he told me was to become an ornamental cockerel. "Give it a chance before you fire it," he said. Joke, see?'

324

They groaned, as well they might have. Gwen continued, 'You might have stopped him making that damn silly chair, Geoff. Three legs, honestly!'

Geoffrey opened another bottle of whisky. 'No raging creative talent there, grant you. Odd he didn't give up out of sheer pain, his face set in a sort of permanent wince. All fingers and thumbs, I've never quite known before what that meant.'

'Poor, poor old Tom,' Gwen repeated. 'But he does have his uses. Done wonders for our accounts, but talk about fuss. I mean measuring all those lengths of timber and claiming a rebate of what was it – £2.97?'

Geoffrey poured generously. 'Come on, you two, he's not so bad. Aren't we supposed to be bringing a love of the arts and crafts to the common man? If we can civilize dear old Tom, we can civilize anyone . . . Remember the Colonel and be thankful.'

'Or Mrs Jenners,' said Gwen, causing Ruth to let out another shriek.

There was some clinking of glasses as I turned my head to one side to listen more closely. Ruth's face had been verging on the purple. She had tried to speak but had only managed what a death rattle might sound like. I oughtn't to have remained there, I know, but seeing ourselves as we are seen by others, we can't have enough of that. The whisky was now having a sobering effect as they got down to business.

'The way he looks at us. Have you noticed? Nonplussed isn't in it.' This was Gwen.

'Perhaps he fancies one of us,' Ruth said eagerly.

'Or both of us, why not?' Gwen added. 'He looks at our bodies as if comparing.'

'Or thinks we're gay,' Geoffrey said. 'He looks so dreadfully shockable.'

'I think he's taken a shine to you, Geoff,' one of them said.

The other said, 'He can't make us out at all, can he? He's trying to please without having the first idea how to go about it.'

I glanced back at them and saw Gwen say, 'Without his shirt, all that flab on him. Why is it so hard to feel sorry for him . . . ?'

I decided then that it didn't hugely matter whether I returned with my hair uncombed and went to wash the blood off my neck. My uppermost thought was that it had clearly been a teapot. I had only said it happened to look like an ornamental cockerel *at that stage* in its evolution. Such people you can't trust. But never mind. It cracked fatally in the firing.

When I returned whistling down the passage, I found them still round the table looking guilty as if that was the verdict they had reached all too easily. Gwen gave me my shirt and Geoffrey poured me a glass of whisky. Then he went over to the sink while the women began doing aimless things in other parts of the room. They all had their backs to me again.

'You're a real friend, Tom,' Geoffrey began, then after a long pause, 'We've been talking. Wondering if we shouldn't be going our separate ways. Things aren't . . .'

'You must have noticed,' Ruth interrupted, turning round very briefly, not smiling for a change but then doing so or giving her gums an airing. Well, not quite all the joke was now going to be on me.

'What a pity,' I said. 'You seemed, it seemed a happy sort of team thing, and all you're doing to bring a touch of enlightenment, civilization to ordinary chaps . . . even including me.'

Gwen busied herself at the sink and did not turn round. Her voice seemed to quiver between glee and remorse. 'One cannot keep up appearances for ever. You're too good a friend, Tom . . .'

All three of them turned round as I began trying to tuck my shirt under my belt without unbuckling it. They turned back quickly and the triple snicker I heard might not have been united empathy, if that is the word.

'I'd just like you to know', I said, 'that it's given me a lot of pleasure. You know that. A stroke of luck, really, fetching up here, being able to make myself useful. Not much of a carpenter, grant you, not yet, thick as two planks in that direction so far, not cut out for it perhaps . . .' I pulled my hand out from under my belt. My fingers were moist with sweat and the touch of my groin was cold.

Writing this up now from my notes I can see it all from a distance and say my opinion of myself had taken a bit of a knock, but I could console myself by deciding they were pretty frightful (deluded, condescending?) people one way or another. Or could I?

At the time I simply felt sorry for myself, as if something had served me right but you will be a better judge of that. I wonder sometimes if we can know ourselves any more than we know other people, which is precious little, though we may surprise ourselves less. The trouble is that how others see us matters to us the more we guess they have got us wrong, so that those who give us the benefit of the doubt are likely to seem indifferent, with little opinion of us at all, and reciprocating that makes for a certain boredom of spirit. All this worked on a bit on a chilly black evening as a few snowflakes begin to fall. I wrap my dressing gown round me and catch a glimpse of the flab and pallor down there above my pyjama cord. Well of course at the time that was what I minded most, the reminder of my unappealingness if you will, and as I wandered home I made vows to take more exercise, do press-ups, give up smoking and drinking, expose myself to the sun, bathe more often, eat less and more wisely. So when I got home, I poured myself a large whisky, lit a cheroot and prepared a large dish of fish fingers and chips which I kept on putting into my mouth for most of the rest of the evening. There was the other sadness too, that I couldn't go back there now, that I really had been enjoying myself, working out where I would put my milkmaid's chair, varnished and polished: a place for the telephone books beside the telephone, under the mirror in the hallway. So my creative instincts were not entirely to be mocked: dreadfully inept perhaps but wanting to make something lasting and useful. Anyway, it was one of the most introspective evenings of my life so far and it didn't get me anywhere except drunk.

I didn't turn up at the centre for the next couple of days and the following evening Geoffrey and Gwen breezed in without knocking like old chums, Geoffrey saying, 'Where's the bottle then, you old reprobate?'

Gwen fell backwards into my settee and looked up at me fetchingly, running her hands up her thighs and pulling her dress up with them. 'We missed you today, Tom,' she said. 'Had to crate for Diss. You hadn't forgotten, had you? Not like you at all.' Then she glanced at Geoffrey's back and winked at me.

'Sorry,' I said. 'Feeling a bit out of sorts.'

Geoffrey found the bottle and poured for them both. Then they chatted on, I forget about what, as if nothing had happened at all. No, not quite that. They were being especially nice to me and I'd have said they were trying to make it up to me if they had not seemed to be trying equally hard not to laugh. I wished they'd say, 'Sorry about the other day, Tom. Silly of us.' But they weren't even thinking it. So why were they there? Curiosity and pity? Or some vague qualm perhaps. Above all, I wished that Geoffrey had poured me a whisky too in my own house and that they would address one or two of their remarks to me, not to make me feel it was I who had dropped in unannounced on them. Geoffrey was pouring himself a second drink when I heard myself say, 'Actually, I'm thinking of moving on myself.'

After a silence in which they stared at each other more than at me, Gwen said, 'Oh no!' to which Geoffrey added, 'Oh dear!' I gave them ample opportunity to expand on all that before, moving in slow motion, I took the whisky bottle from Geoffrey's hand, screwed the top on very tightly and put it back in the cupboard.

'I know this must come as a shock to you,' I said quietly. 'Need to be nearer the family. Old mother and all that.' Though she had been dead for six months, about which I will try to write presently. 'However, there we are. You'll just have to try to manage without me.'

After several sideways movements and a breathy heave, this brought Gwen to her feet, leaving an indentation in my settee, I calmly noted, which could only mean a serious displacement of its springs. A distinct raucous ping verified that as she came across to kiss me on the cheek. It felt wet as though what she had given me was a quick lick.

'We'll miss you, Tom,' she said.

'Certainly will,' Geoffrey added.

'I'll miss you too,' I said and in that instant believed it, though it was myself I would miss in that setting before the shadow fell across it. So I added, 'My aim was true enough, just fell a bit short, that's all. You were very patient with me.'

'Not at all. You know you'll be welcome at any time,' Geoffrey mumbled through beard and knuckle or something like it. Bloody relieved he was, no doubt about that.

Then they took each other by the hand, locked fingers and left, leaving the front door open. Watching them going down my garden path, arms interlocked too now, I wondered what they were saying to each other. I wished they didn't seem in such high spirits. Totally out of keeping with the occasion. Surely I had made myself useful to them on the business side at least? 'Pricks,' I muttered. Then, 'Why do they wear those shaggy, bedraggled clothes as if they wanted to identify with fucking nature after a thunderstorm?' They did not turn back to wave. Gwen pointed in the direction of the church and I listened to their peals of laughter until they were out of sight.

There was another factor in my decision to leave Suffolk which had occurred a week earlier. There was to be a third two weeks later. Let me have a look at my notes.

I hadn't seen much of my dear old friend Jenners, indeed nothing more than to wave to, avoiding more than that on a couple of occasions by a brisk change of direction. Disgracefully antisocial, I know, but I had not quite got round to responding to several circular letters he had sent me about the Church Restoration Fund, the Liberal Democratic Party as it had then become, the founding of a Village Arts Society and an Environment Action Group, to name but a few. I was coming out of the village store with a melon and tin of tongue as he was coming in.

'Ah er Ripple, Tom,' he said. 'The very chap I was looking for. You wouldn't have a moment, would you?'

He joined me in the street outside and peered at me over his half-eye reading glasses like a tatty file on some trivial matter he had every intention of delegating as soon as he got round to it. No sign of a book anywhere which rather undermined the shrewd and master-ful effect.

'Wonder if you got my note about the bypass?' he began. I made a series of noises that had no complete words in them. 'Good. You see, we've absolutely got to get a decent campaign together. Every signa-ture we can muster. Circulars to be taken round. Meetings to be arranged. Secure a full hearing, that's the thing. You do twig, I trust?'

I stood my ground nobly. 'Tell me more,' I said.

He peered a good six inches closer, smiled and raised one eyebrow, the judicious effect being offset by the sudden gritting of his discon-tinuous, splintered-looking teeth.

'Sorry, Tom, how did you mean exactly?' he said.

'I mean, why is the bypass such a bad thing? On balance, I mean, would it . . . ?'

I had said this quite neutrally or so I hoped. All I knew was that it would take traffic away from a small town and two villages and would cut through the pig farm, the reduced stink from which when the wind was in the wrong direction being considered an environmental plus. There was also the small matter of a container lorry having ended up on top of a cash register and the girl who operated it in a new supermarket in the small town and one child mown down in the narrow streets in each of the two villages.

'For heaven's sake, surely . . . ?' he began on a high note, then closed his eyes and calmed himself down. 'Now look, Ripple, take it from me. I'm not without some tiny experience in these matters. Been on the other side of the great divide most of my life. Conducted not a few enquiries myself if the truth were known. You may remember . . . well, perhaps not. No use, you must see that, in having a moan above a handful of illegible signatures. Start off by having a damn good look at the relevant legislation. They're no fools, you know. Some of the best brains in the business. What do you say?'

I readjusted my melon and took a pace back. 'Oh, I'm sure you're absolutely right, Mr O . . . Jenners. It's only that I'd like to have a thorough look at the facts before I start licking envelopes.' He stared at me in astonishment, then did a brisk, semi-contemptuous thing with the ends of his mouth. 'Could very well be', I went on, 'I'd be the very first to lay myself down in the path of the bulldozer but then on the other hand . . . I'm sorry, I don't know but . . .'

'Fine, Ripple, fine,' he said, his voice now squeezed through a tightened throat. 'But if you want my opinion, and I could be wrong of course, all we hold dear in this fair land of ours doesn't conserve itself, you know. Down the years, it's taken the likes of me and y . . . us who care, really and truly care, for our heritage to stand shoulder to shoulder and speak out for the generations to come.'

'Community spirit.' I hazarded.

'Exactly. Mustn't let progress roll over us and I've done some rolling over in my time, I don't mind telling you.'

I imagined him tumbling about in a meadow with Mrs Jenners. 'I couldn't agree with you more,' I said. 'I'd be the first, the last . . . If I could just study the pros and cons I might . . .'

He gave the longest sigh I had ever heard. 'They've been all over the local newspapers for months. Surely . . . ?'

'Then there might be other petitions too?'

'That's hardly the point, now is it? That's their business. It's a matter of principle, don't you see? Do you want a bypass running through your back garden or don't you?'

I patted my melon. 'Don't particularly want a bypass anywhere though when the time comes I might not have the heart . . .'

He made it clear with a grunt that this was wasted on him. 'Please yourself,' he said. 'But I must say I think you're . . .' And at that he turned abruptly and went into the shop.

I stood there, clutching a melon to my chest. I was not pleased with myself. He was only being an active citizen. He wasn't just sitting around polishing his OBE. He'd invited me to be treasurer of the Church Restoration Fund and as I was composing my first appeal he told me over the phone ('no disrespect intended, old chap') that he'd drafted in one of his City chums who knew 'a thing or two about the old fund-raising palaver'. Well, they changed the plan for the bypass, moving it to bring misery to the people of another village fifteen miles away. Is he raising a petition against that too? I suspect not. A heritage too far.

Remembering these events now from a safe distance, I wonder some-times whether I should have stuck it out there. I look out over the houses opposite with the expensive binoculars I bought in Suffolk to watch birds with, as is expected of country dwellers. I only used them once, to watch the delivery of a worm, and never had them with me when I might have a lark or buzzard (?) in view. Anyway, I rarely use them now either and in all my years of looking through windows I still haven't seen anything. I put the binoculars away and think of all those people living on top of each other, mile after mile, as if imprisoned in huge dormitories and released daily to hurry along predestined routes to other places of confinement, their minds on some release other than death or on times gone by before they started doing whatever landed them there. And worrying a lot. Hope is not something one sees much on people's faces in streets and on buses etc. It is at times like these as night draws in and the television is turned on all over the land, flicker-ing away through their frantic, unchosen dreams, a shared oblivion, that I remember the church and my last visit there. I had already told the vicar I was leaving and that morning Sidney had told me my house was sold. My notes tell me that that was where the conversation began as he squeezed in beside me in the front pew.

'The "For Sale" sign taken down I see. Changed your mind, I trust?' I shook my head and made more room for him. 'Well then,' he went on, 'a whacking great profit, I hope.'

I nodded. 'An absolute killing.'

'So it's final then,' he said, glancing at me for an acknowledgement. I said, 'Ouch!' Which caused him to lean forward with a frown and close his eyes, to say a prayer for me, I assumed.

After a long pause, he sat back with his eyes still closed as if something disagreeable had entered his prayer which would come to life if he opened them. 'Will you miss it a little, do you imagine?' he asked finally. He had spoken too loudly and a bird flitted across the roof with a cheep. We both looked up at it and he did not wait for my reply. 'Often ask myself what becomes of them. You never see the corpses, do you? There must be millions of dead birds lying about all over the place, at this very minute.' He leant forward again but his eyes were now wide open in wonderment as though whatever it was had turned out not to be disagreeable at all.

'Yes, I think I will,' I replied. 'This at any rate. I haven't the faintest idea why. Except of course that it does go back a bit. Sad therefore one doesn't see people flocking here exactly.'

'Have to make do with all those souls departed instead, you mean. Try not to think too much of those, myself. Too depressing by half if you ask me, eternity that is. Or infinity. The great belittler. Like learning our galaxy is six million light years in diameter. Milky Way a mere hundred thousand light years across, a light year being six million million miles. And at the last count there were a hundred thousand million galaxies.'

'Phew,' I said, 'you're not making that up, are you?'

'A few noughts either way, perhaps. I must say I do wonder sometimes what God thought he was up to. Got a bit carried away, if you ask me.'

'He certainly thought big,' I contributed.

'But quite why so big, I ask myself, unless to indicate He might know what He's up to in other, littler matters. Or it all got out of hand.' He stood up and pointed sharply sideways. 'Just look at that light, what's left of it, through that stained glass. Gaudy Victorian piety and cheering up. The figures treading in some perpetual morning.'

'They look cheerful enough to me. Aren't they in paradise or on their way there or something?'

He ignored that and walked towards the altar. The bird did another flit across the roof. Then he sat down abruptly on the altar steps, his hands clasped around his knees. For a while he looked all around him with an overwhelmed expression before focusing back on me, the best there was of the here and now but a relief nonetheless.

'It's always sad when someone does the disappearing trick. Don't suppose you'll ever come back, lend your voice. Bring that sister of yours. Now there was a real voice for you. I remember that Sunday. We really did seem to be having a good worship that day, didn't we?'

His gaze wandered again and I began thumbing through a hymn-book. 'A thousand ages in Thy sight are but an evening gone,' I read out loud and he waited for me to continue. 'Back to the galaxies and all that. It's way beyond me, I'm afraid.'

He swivelled round and had a good look at the cross on the altar. 'How right you are. Perhaps it's all simply in the participation and putting yourself at the mercy of the thing. Blind faith. Like being in hospital, dreading the operation, the needle. Utterly helpless in the wise and routinely compassionate hands of others. Surrender. But you're not alone in it. Others in the same boat or a damn sight worse. No longer responsible for one's own life. Ruddy heresy, that's what that is. But it's true. Not being able to *do* much about anything. Or not so heretical. The difference is in the how much.'

He stood there picking off the dead heads of flowers in the vase on the altar. Several petals fluttered to the ground. Suddenly I missed the Colonel again. I had not heard from his widow though I had responded to her card, mainly on the subject of Sidney and the plants I'd seen him digging up as soon as she left. I also told her I'd seen him carrying away what looked like a bundle of curtains. Finally I asked about their daughter. I remembered her too then very vividly, my last sight of her, pale and small and desperate beyond her grief. And the sadness then was in not knowing what happens to people: Hamble, Webb, Hipkin, even Plaskett. Or Nanny Phipps, probably dead by now. They all slide away so easily into the dusk. I had to speak then because the vicar was staring up at me from the dead flowers in his fist, as if trying to make a connection.

'Ways of feeling insignificant, you mean? In fact, not feeling anything else most of the time.'

He crossed the aisle, looking for somewhere to put the dead flowers. His voice was loud and his fist was raised, as if trying to work himself up into defiance.

'Oh Lord no! I can't have meant that, can I? Saw bodies lined up, one diseased soul after another, on the great conveyor belt of time. Come and have a look at this one, nurse. That's four vanities in one morning already. No lunch for gluttony over there. As for sloth, pack him off home tomorrow. We need the beds.'

I laughed out loud at that and he lowered his fist with a grin. He'd clearly had several of these worked out and nobody else to try them on.

'What treatment for lust, do you reckon?'

He struck a cluster of notes with his fist at the bottom end of the organ.

'If only one knew *that*! There's always aversion therapy, I think it's called.'

'Laying on a series of fearful bonking sessions with matron, you mean?'

He ignored that, slowly opening his hand to let the petals fall, now reduced to a sprinkling of dust. Then he struck a resonant chord and said peevishly, 'I'm sure He doesn't do it deliberately. When I'm here alone and one's head isn't filled with the words and the music, the most dreadful irreverence seems to go on.'

He tapped his head vigorously. 'They say that's the devil. I seem to have forgotten the correct view about that. What do you think?'

'Evidence is that Satan or whoever he is has a pretty free run of the place most of the time. Not interrupted by words or music or anything else, come to that.'

'Or little crucifixes stuck up here and there, you mean?'

He struck another chord and suddenly seemed very angry.

'I'm afraid I don't know anything about that,' I said

'No reason why you should. The thing is that looking at my congregations and gassing on about the varieties of difficult goodness, I find myself wishing I was a left-footer and had confession to look forward to. Penance. Especially girls'. Why am I telling you all this?'

I pointed up at the roof. 'Perhaps because you know I haven't got a line to anyone.'

He turned towards me, pressing his hands down on his knees.

'Lordie me, no! We're not allowed to make distinctions like that. Everyone's on the telephone in His book. Nobody gets cut off. Can you imagine the size of the switchboard? Probably what they do with the lesser clergy for the first thousand years or so of eternal life. Telephone duty.'

334

'You are being held in a queue. Your call is important to us.'

'Better than just hanging about feeling righteous. On a bad day like this, I just feel I'm drawing my pay, glad it's not a penny more. Doing my duty hardly more than sucking up to Him, counting on His mercy. And then in trying to convey some sort of consolation to others, sucking up to them too. Like what I'm doing to you now.'

'Surely not. Not me.'

He looked at me thoughtfully. 'I'm pretty jolly keen for you to like me. If you couldn't give a toss about my faith, wouldn't want you to think less of me on that account.'

'Well, that solves my insignificance problem for a moment or two.'

He sighed. 'Here I am in this wonderful place. I should be trying to win you over. Like one of the new evangelicals.'

'What are they when they're at home?'

'Well, that's precisely where you're not very likely to find them. Drums and guitars. Dancing in the aisles. Rapt faces. If Bath and Wells gets the top job people like me had better watch out. Lots of pure faith. Lots of Bible. A user-friendly Holy Ghost . . .'

'That's rather out of my . . .'

'Hold on a minute. You see if he was fully Man, as He was, you can't just stop there, can you? The questions that can't be avoided. The theologians get themselves into a terrible tizzy. Erection and Resurrection. Did He only rise from the dead?'

'Actually,' I muttered, 'you hear that mentioned quite a lot, especially in parts of London. Jesus effing Christ.'

'It wasn't me who said that,' he replied grimly. 'You've got to stop asking questions somewhere.'

He was now very upset, so I tried a topic I'd been reading about that morning.

'Women priests. Are you for or against?'

He gave a sigh of relief. 'That's a problem. There's a danger of confusing the imagination. We're supposed to represent Jesus, you see. However, there's a view that he was gay or rather, being fully Man, a bit of both. Queen as well as King of the Jews.'

'You've lost me there. I can see it might be distracting. Confession. Come unto me all ye who are heavy laden and I will refresh you . . .'

He groaned, but it didn't seem to be at me and began pacing up and down in front of the altar, his head bowed. Then he stopped, opened out his hands and gazed at the roof.

'I so love it here, you know, places like this. It is filled with such trust we call Hope, such ignorance we call Faith, such coming together we call Charity. The words. The music. Not a word of truth in them of the usual factual sort. Oh how wonderfully humanity has dreamt and invented in His name! The galaxies of the imagination! Where's the sense of awe nowadays? The reverence and wonder?'

'We've lost our marvels, you might say.'

Ignoring that, or not hearing it, he came down the steps and put a hand on my shoulder.

'But it's not enough much of the time. Must go. Come and see us. Forget what I've said. Totally off the rails. Prattle.' He squeezed my shoulder. 'And God bless you. I mean that.'

I was half-way to my feet to shake his hand but he pressed me down and shook his head.

'In places like this one never says goodbye. We must become as little children, that's the secret. God is love. Try to get back to the beginning.'

I thought he was only saying his lines. He was being dutiful. It gave him a pious air, which did not suit him.

'No parting messages then?'

'Only be true to yourself, keep your chin up, that sort of thing. Who was it wrote, one of the great Romans: speak the truth, laughing? I mean how could we bear it otherwise?'

He tapped me on the shoulder and was half-way up the aisle when he turned and said too loudly, as if trying to create an echo, 'Or is all the humour and ha-ha and sneering only the devil's way of making us forget the appalling cruel mess he has made of God's world. It's a thought, isn't it?'

Then he left me. The bird fluttered several times across the roof, in the darkening light no more than a trick of the shadows. For ten seconds or so it cheeped continuously and then fell silent. The hymn-book was still open on my lap and I flipped through it. All those bold, worshipful lines. Inside the back cover, someone had drawn one of those bald creatures with a single hair sticking up with crosses for eyes and its nose over a brick wall. 'Wot no miracles?' the caption said. I was surprised no one had torn it out. Perhaps too recent. Some bored schoolboy forced into church during the holidays. The door clanged shut. The church was utterly empty. However long I stayed

336

there the ghosts would not murmur. The crucifix on the altar sank back into the shadows and all I could believe was that the story had ended there, a brave shot at something bigger and better but fallen terribly wide: a moment of history, or not even that, and all the rest a credulous hunger of the imagination. I wished the vicar and I hadn't talked as we had, that somehow we could have summoned the communion of the dead, there was so much unspoken grief in that cold air. As I went out, I took a final look at the last shimmer of blue in the stained glass, the worn font and its indecipherable inscription, the surplus drawing pins on the notice-board in the porch, the faded appeal for starving children in Africa. And I thought I should never come here again, nor to any other church. Too much to aspire to, too far to go, too many voices, the unfinished yearning of the dead.

Nor did I dawdle in the graveyard, beginning to shiver and thinking, 'This will be the death of me.' It seemed for a moment as if snow was falling in the distance but it was only the last of the sunlight falling across the trees in a sudden gust of wind. A storm was on the way and the sky opposite the sunset was pitch black. There was a flicker of lightning along the horizon and I thought that if the bypass went through there would be flickering along the horizon all night long for ever.

As I walked home against the mounting wind, building up to its persistent Suffolk norm, I looked back at the church, its silhouette like a vast cluster of boulders against the dying colours of the sunset. Jutting above the bank of clouds, the rusted weathervane stood still against the wind. A last bird chattered. And so my mind drifted to other things: where would I live until I found my new home, where would I store my worldly goods in the meantime, how many of them should I sell or leave behind, how would the money last out which had to do with the lasting of life itself? And then slipping away from all that into what I was going to do about supper, what was on the telly, how soon would I be in bed with my new Ruth Rendell, oh yes and had I run out of Hamlet Miniatures, surely there was a half-finished packet in my corduroy jacket – no, wasn't that at the dry cleaner's? Did I have a cold coming on? Serve me right sitting in that draughty church for too long 'doing a bit of communing' as my mother called it when I was in one of my rare reflective moods. Or 'he's probably in one of his communes' she used to say to my father when I dawdled over some errand. I could not stop shivering. Had I remembered to turn the hot water on? Throat lozenges. Aspirin. Night Nurse. Rennies. Shit. Forgot to get another bottle of whisky. And thus my commune dribbled away into little worries following on from one another at random which in my experience are the substance of life, except that that is the very last word for them, with nothing to bind them together, just fluttering and wittering on and on. As I opened my front gate I thought too of the crafties and what a pity that was, the splitting apart of lives that had come together by accident for some useful purpose, the bitterness that forms and is always in some measure, but never sufficiently, deserved. That was how Satan worked, surely, not through talk of fucking in church. If his main job was creating enmity between tribes and nations, his hobby was stirring it up with envy and grievance and thoughtlessness between ordinary people. That was where the fun must be, as opposed to the sense of achievement.

Such were the thoughts I jotted down that evening as my cold took hold and I filled myself with brandy and aspirins before going to bed. There is a good side to everything: not a cheroot to be found anywhere but as I searched, my sore throat worsened and by the time I gave up looking, smoking was something else I decided to give up that night. But there is another note too: no sign of the yuppie children, alas. I miss that, the remnants of them when I return to my empty house or finding them there cross-legged in front of my television set, the Coke and Jaffa Cakes to hand or, more often, consumed up to the quantity I had left out for them on top of the telly to prevent them from rummaging about in my kitchen cupboards or anywhere else for that matter where certain sorts of reading or pictorial matter might still be chanced upon. My last note says: the vicar said we should become as little children. What on earth can he have meant by that? The insatiable wanting what we can't have? The curiosity? Or something called innocence? None of that, surely?

But by now they had stopped visiting me, it should be obvious enough why. And I suppose it was this, or rather all that went with it, that decided me that Suffolk could probably get along without me.

One evening in late summer when they had been to my house on a dozen or more occasions, their mother came for the first time to collect them. I used to ask them when they had to be home by and they were always pretty scrupulous, at least about that, reminded by their immense and elaborate digital watches and the various signals they emitted, some of them in the form of martial-sounding tunes like *The Star-Spangled Banner*. There were still about twenty minutes to go and I was shirt-sleeved in my garden at the time for what purpose I cannot imagine, other than not enjoying what they were watching at the time, which usually I did and not wholly on their account. I had not seen much of their parents other than to wave to across the road and once or twice at the village store. They had seemed perfectly agreeable, his breeziness trying to make up for her reticence or boredom or the impression she gave that he, along with everything else in life, was slightly beneath her. Our first encounter at the store went something like this.

'Settling in all right, are we?' I began. 'Do let me know if there's anything . . .'

He grinned as if I'd asked something shocking.

'Oh definitely! Away from your actual rat race and that.' He glanced at his wife as if to check he'd got the voice right, then added, 'Quite splindid.'

I was then treasurer of the Church Restoration Fund and was able to thank him for the cheque for £15 which the children had brought round in a used airmail envelope with a Belgian stamp on it. From the way she glanced at me then I guessed she'd beaten him down from a lot more than that.

'We're not great on churchgoing, if you want the honest truth,' he said. 'But we can't have these heritage places cracking up, can we, sweetheart?'

She was pinching avocado pears, neither I nor heritage anywhere in her thoughts.

'It was fratefully decent of you to chip in like that. Jolly good show . . .' That was how it came out, I regret to say, so I added, 'Vicar most appreciative . . . Called to see you yet, has he?'

She passed between us to the counter. I noticed how scrupulously planned her face was, the lip-coloured lipstick and hairlessly symmetrical eyebrows. These now shot up.

'We didn't know what on earth he was on about, did we darling?' she said, the drawl keeping her voice a class above his.

'I wouldn't quite say that, poppet. Gave us something to think about.'

'Speak for yourself. He was very charming, I'm sure.' She wrinkled her nose. 'Don't they want us to *confide* in them?'

Her husband glanced down at her exact-fitting blue slacks and I guessed what more there might be to it, some Saturday morning tiff he was well on the way to deciding was more his fault than hers, or entirely if he knew what was good for him.

'We're not really into religion, that's the thing,' he said.

'We've all got our jobs to do,' she said, a sigh reinforcing the drawl. 'Shopkeepers. Sky pilots.'

There was then a long pause as she searched for money in her handbag and I chose some tinned goods and a loaf of bread. He came up behind me, going through some loose change in the palm of his hand. Suddenly they seemed united. I had become some cheeky or sleazy foreigner.

And so I floundered into it. 'Has to go easy on the throttle, joystick . . . Soaring up then taking an awful nosedive, loop the loop . . . Only a quiet spin above the treetops, then zooming heavenwards through the clouds, out of contact with air traffic control, running out of fuel . . .'

As all the gauges showed zero, he rescued me, handing his wife the change, her fingernails, I observed, matching the lipstick.

'Good bloke, grant you that,' he said.

'Come along, Jerry,' she said. 'The children . . .'

'Oh how are the children?' I asked eagerly, stepping aside to let them pass. 'Such delightful . . .'

'We must see more of you,' he said.

Again her nose wrinkled. 'Bring the vicar to tea. Tell him we're atheists or Buddhists or one of those.' She spoke as if she couldn't stand the sight of him, or me.

'Cheerio then, Mr Ripley,' he said. 'Must scarper. You know how it is. Kids.'

'Allah be seeing you,' I quipped as they reached the door.

She turned and stared at me for an instant as if she had noticed something very unpleasant about me but couldn't quite put her finger on it. I handed my money to the shopkeeper. My hand was shaking. I did not know if I was flushed or pale or a bit of both.

'Are you sure you're all right, dear?' she asked

'Perfectly all right,' I replied.

'I'd say you got carried away there a bit,' she said.

Now, confronting me half-way up my garden path, she wished to appear in a businesslike hurry while scanning my unweeded flower-beds as if they had something to tell her about me, the dearth of colour at once giving the show away, her own floral get-up and immaculateness in general setting the standard. Insult to bloody nature, I told myself.

She bit her lip. 'The children . . .' she began.

I nodded in the direction of the house. 'In there, or were when I checked a moment ago. Programme's got about ten minutes to go, refreshments likewise.' I looked at my watch. 'Seven and a half minutes. Like me to call them?'

'*Would* you please?'

They were squatting as usual right up against the TV, glasses of Coca-Cola tilted. Both were picking their noses.

'Come on, you horrors,' I said from the doorway. 'Your mother's here.'

'Oh *no!*' they groaned without budging an inch.

I had not realized she'd followed me into the house and she now barged past me, switched off the telly and yanked them to their feet which caused about an inch each of Coca-Cola to end up on the small, cut-price imitation washable Persian rug I had recently bought. (Later I discovered the crumblings of at least half a packet of Jaffa Cakes scattered over the greater part of it. That was the day my second-hand hoover broke down, refusing no doubt to go over that gritty and sodden ground yet again.) They grumbled briefly but stopped when she took their glasses, put them on the television set and gripped the girl's wrist, forcing her hand open to reveal the remains of a Jaffa Cake or rather a thick, crumb-flecked chocolate stain that covered most of her palm.

'You know you shouldn't spoil your supper. How many times do I have to tell you?' she muttered as she grabbed them both by the upper arm and hurried them out.

I stepped aside and caught a glimpse of the girl's face, which looked terrified out of all proportion to the gravity of the event.

'I'm sorry, Mummy,' the boy said in a high whisper.

'You're hurting me,' the girl whimpered.

When they reached the front door, I called out, 'Bye, kids. See you.'

But it was the mother who turned. The trace of apology in her smile could as well have been a sneer of warning. The bloom had gone from her face and I thought better in that instant of my garden.

'Say thank you to Mr Ripple,' she said, shaking them, and that is what they might have mumbled as she let them loose and they ran down the path ahead of her.

I stood in the doorway and held my hand in the air ready to wave but it was never needed. I remembered my own children at that age and thought how a damn sight better brought up they were, though such a situation in our house could never have arisen: letting them watch crappy television, I mean, instead of actively learning something or otherwise doing themselves good. Then I remembered Webb and suddenly that expression on her face made sense, going along with what was much in the news at that time: the trace was of revulsion, not apology. But my uppermost thought was what colossal cheek it had been to turn off the television in someone else's house for what may well have been the first time in the history of mankind.

They did not return after that and I only saw them at a distance. Once they were playing with a rubber quoit on the green and I waved but they pretended not to notice. I ambled towards them but they backed away so I stopped and called out, 'Hey, it's only me, Uncle Tom, the Jaffa Cake man.'

They froze, the quoit falling to the ground between them. The girl half raised her hand and I knew that if I moved any closer they would run away. So I veered sideways with another wave and then, very stupidly, blew them a kiss. I could have been seen from their house, but perhaps that was why I did it. I did not look back until I reached the store and by then they had vanished.

They had been warned of course. Nothing personal, I'm sure, but stories of unbelievable nastiness were then being told, still are for that matter, about child abuse, and the moral of them all is that you can't be sure of anyone, not even your Mum and Dad, especially your Dad. That had been the expression on the mother's face, ugly against ugliness, nowhere near giving me the benefit of the doubt and quite right too. Oh, Mr Webb, you and your kind, what have you done to the rest of us who can hold ourselves in check? Or so I scribbled frantically in my notes that evening.

A week or so later, I returned to find a jam jar on my doorstep with some flowery weeds in it, plus two spent rambler roses. They did not seem this time to have come from my garden. A scrawled note read: 'Dear Sir, Thank you for the tellyvishun and things and Coke.' Not a word about the Jaffa Cakes. Oh yes, they were such very pretty children too.

After that, so far as I can now recall, there was some more waving from a distance when they were all together. To an onlooker it would all have looked very neighbourly. I consoled myself, it appears, thus: 'There are no hard feelings. I wonder what goes through their minds. How can the good things in life be brought so inexplicably to an end? "Never trust strangers." "Why, Mummy, why?" "Because you never know." "Never know what?" "Sometimes they do naughty things to you." "What things? Spoiling our supper?" "No, other things." "What other things?" "Sometimes they steal children or make them do things they don't want to do." "What things, what things?" Then there is silence. I seek an image of danger, of the thing they should fear. Tonight I looked at myself long and hard in the bathroom mirror and saw beyond all the sagging neutrality and fatigue what that thing might be, which no wink or grin could dispel. Webb leered back at me. I was nothing like Hamble. I did not look benign and utterly harmless though I am becoming more so by the day, I hope. But the truth is that though I never touched them, I wanted to – a bare arm, a cheek, a bare leg, to lift them on to my knee . . . There is no more I can admit to myself. Their mother was right. It was Webb's face I saw, somewhere between guilt and lust. I must stop feeling sorry for myself . . . The pleasure was mine in their presence, not in the pleasure I gave them. A touch the beginning and end of affection . . . We are not free to please ourselves in our ways of giving pleasure to others, particularly children, for unless there is perfect love, we cannot know where the understanding ends and the damage begins. That is where our ignorance lies, along the border between shame and selfishness. It is better we should remain as strangers to each other . . . Become as little children? The hell with that . . .'

Thus my Suffolk notebooks dribble to an end. While finding this flat I spent a night or two with my son. His wife Jane is the nicest person I know and not only because of her love for him. She is a plain girl, or so people would say, with a fringe and glasses, too heavy and short to have much of a figure, who wears colourless clothes and smiles only at some delight at life, not often but unexpectedly, unconditionally. For instance, and I'm being truthful here, she really does seem to enjoy my dreadful puns. His groans are real.

Jane is a financial analyst who, like my son, works in the City. He is more the practitioner and is now well established in a leading firm of accountants. She is cleverer than he is, not that this ever notices. I doubt if she is even aware of it. You can tell from the way she enjoys the play of ideas for their own sake and questions fundamentals. She does not hold opinions like weapons in an armoury. She starts off by believing she may be wrong. She sees the necessity of the way things are, a world ruled by money and those who move it about while trying to keep as much of it as possible for themselves: all that, all the evils my wife used to go on about in the twilight of socialism or which in certain circles you were then expected to go on about while people like me went dizzily round in circles with people like Plaskett hovering at the heart of them. Jane understands the system, indeed helps it along, but she shakes her head from time to time as if she wished people weren't so willing to put up with it. She trots out the names: Trafalgar House, Burmah Oil, IDC, Bradman, Shamji, Lyons, Guinness, a couple of Sultans, Ronson, Fayed, Polly Peck. Much of what she says is above my head but she knows how to make it easier for me to understand something, even beyond the point when she knows I never will. It is sleaze and greed on such a brazen scale that her calm amazes me. It makes Plaskett seem like a small boy trading in gobstoppers. Perhaps it is just that she has the measure of human nature and expects no better of it. Her superiority of mind and spirit is without vanity as if, like her dress, she had come across it by chance. She makes no effort at all. Adrian watches her carefully as if he still cannot quite believe his luck. For it is his love that she wants, not his good opinion or respect. It is in his direction that her shrug or smile end up, the way of the world having been pushed to a distance. With anyone else, I might embarrass him, increasingly seedy as my appearance has a way of becoming as the evening wears on, the clink of ice in my glass, the whiff of cheroots filling the air, the slur and inconsequence of my speech revealing the cogency of my mind at its soberest. Though she has work to do, she means it when she urges me to stay another night. I wonder how much gratitude too there is in her love for Adrian. What else there is in it, I dare not guess. I cannot help listening out for the sounds they make when we have gone to bed. I hear the murmur of quiet conversation and then there is only silence. I wonder if they intend to have children. I hope so. She would make a marvellous mother. Jane and I share his secret. I think this confuses him, when she puts her arm around him for instance, or touches him or takes his hand. He avoids my eye then, as well he might, but he avoids hers too. It is as if he still has too much to learn from her and they still have a long way to go. They are devoted to each other. He is a lucky lad. I try not to let my own happiness show, remembering that day in the café, the fried eggs and the last leaves falling. That's all I feel like saying about Adrian for the time being.

What I have omitted to write about is my mother who is dead now. After all those years with her sister in Leicester, she had moved back into a room above the shop, which she had rented to Asians called Ranasinghe. I visited her twice during my sojourn in Suffolk and used to phone from time to time. She had no telephone of her own and took my calls in the office at the back of the shop. 'She is coming very soon, Mr Ripple,' one of the Ranasinghes used to say but she was clearly not in any hurry. She never phoned me. I asked her how she was, but that was a waste of time for she would never complain on her own account. I gave her news of Adrian and Virginia and she always asked after my former wife about whom I had nothing to tell her. Though they had little in common, perhaps she wanted to remind me that our separation had been all my fault, some silly frivolity or lack of stamina, and she had 'seen it coming a mile off' as she used to say about any mishap which others would put down to chance. But none of this was said and each time she simply remarked, 'You must do whatever you think best, as per usual,' the last three words preceded by a pause.

I learnt most about her from Mr Ranasinghe or one of his womenfolk. 'Don't be worrying, Mr Ripple, we are looking after her,' they would say or 'She is actually one of the family.' I fear she did not respond much to their kindness and when I went to see her she was reluctant to mention them at all.

On my last visit, I said to her, 'They do seem awfully nice, mother, really quite fond of you.'

'I don't know about that,' she replied with a sniff. 'You shouldn't call them Ranasinge as if they used to be fancy barbers. It's Sing.'

I had never called them anything else and I thought at the time she still took pleasure in correcting me, that it was the only pleasure left to her. But I see now she wanted to cheer me up by telling a joke. How many of the grim, dismissive things she had said over the years were for her own amusement or laid up in store for me, to be remembered when she was long since gone?

'The shop seems to be flourishing,' I said.

'If it wasn't, they wouldn't keep on with it, would they? The things they sell nowadays. I don't know about flourishing.'

It was now a newsagent's and stationer's which also sold sweets and tobacco and ran a newspaper round. The range of magazines included the usual erotica and I had assumed that on her way in and out of the shop she pretended not to notice the half-concealed breasts and bottoms above head height along the top row.

'Cater for all tastes,' I said, unnecessarily tweaking my trousers.

She sat upright, her hands clasped on her lap, and stared at me as I began pouring the tea. Was she about to remind me for the umpteenth time it should be milk in first? But I believe now she knew we would never see each other again and an occasion should be made of it.

'In your father's day,' she said in her most matter-of-fact voice, 'it was those nudist camp magazines. That was all there was in those days, that and *Lilliput*. Liked a good nipple, did your father.'

I had never heard her talk like this before and hastened to ask how much sugar she wanted. I glanced up at her and there wasn't a glimmer of humour in her eyes, the old black sharpness in them blurred as if by some sorrow it would be absurd to express.

'You know I don't take sugar. Caught you at it once. Can't think why he bothered to hide them away.'

I handed her her cup of tea and stirred mine vigorously though it had no sugar in it either. 'I don't remember that,' I said. 'Did you . . . ?'

'I didn't anything. It made you popular at school, showing it round, shouldn't wonder. Saw you stuffing it into your satchel. Your father thought I had thrown it away. Sheepish he was for a few days, I can tell you. I couldn't tell him what he'd done for his son's reputation when he was so worried you weren't what he called "making your mark". He had ambitions for you, did your father, more's the pity, but I suppose you've done all right, him not there to see it.'

'Well, mother, it's . . .'

'There's a new word these days. Bonking, they call it. Your father didn't, you can rest assured about that. A rude word never crossed

346

his lips. He was very respectful was your father. Not so businesslike was he with the shop.'

Our eyes met and we stared at each other for what was to be the last time. Was she asking me if I understood what she was driving at, or was she telling me that she too could see the funny side of it all and that was where love might be found, in the way I remembered her?

At this point, Mr Ranasinghe's wife or other relative came in, bearing an immense square chocolate cake with many apologies that she should be disturbing us. I thanked her and looked at my mother, waiting for her to do the same. She made room for it by the tea tray and said, 'We were talking about sex.'

'Very welcome, Mrs Ripple. I am not interrupting your family business again.'

She smiled cautiously at me and I followed her to the head of the stairs with more profuse thanks. She took my arm and whispered, 'Mrs Ripple is a very good lady to us, a very fine lady.' Then she smiled again and this time there was no caution in it at all as if to tell me that that was a very intriguing and proper thing for a mother and son to be talking about. 'She is a very rightful lady too,' she added.

When I returned, all my mother said was, 'You'd better take that with you. I don't care for chocolate cake. Never did.' She was becoming tired, her head tilted slightly and she closed her eyes for a moment.

'How kind of them,' I said.

'Oh yes,' she said, 'they are kind, all right. I grant you that. Can't imagine . . .' She paused and sat stiffly upright again as if she had suddenly made up her mind about something, the invincible futility of it all perhaps. 'Now you'd better be off if you're not to miss your train and leave the cake if it's too much trouble. I shall eat it if I have to.'

I went over to kiss her but, as always, she turned her head away and drew back. When I looked back from the doorway, her eyes were already closed. I left the cake though not on purpose but decided not to go back for it. Mr Ranasinghe told me again on the way out what a lovely lady she was. He clearly meant it. Another woman was with him and three small children who looked up at me with awe, that I should be the son of such a fine lady. That was the last time I saw her, as she had known it would be. Nothing of any importance had been said, no questions asked, no summing up, as though there were enough illusions in life already without any of that. We had not mentioned Adrian or Virginia, for this would only have deceived us into finding refuge in the continuity of things. I only wished she had met Jane, who would have known what healing there was to be done.

I realize this is not a satisfactory way to report on the death of one's mother. There seems to have been little love between us, the way I have told it. Can I have counted so little to her? I shall never know: you are on your own and it has nothing to do with me any longer – could it have been as simple as that? I have not mourned her, though she is constantly in my thoughts. The Ranasinghes helped generously with the funeral arrangements and paid me handsomely for the freehold of the shop. I did not believe for a moment that that was why they were so good to her. I am sure she did not believe it either, for she would have hinted at it otherwise. She took their decency for granted as if that was the way things ought to be. Somewhere there, perhaps, lies her judgement of me. And sometimes I am sure that at the end she was doing me the kindness of trying to meet me on my own ground or what she thought it might be – plain smut – and there must have been a certain affection in that.

Last Christmas I exchanged cards with the Ranasinghes and we will continue to do so. Theirs read, 'We miss your lovely lady mother and so do the children also. She was never cross with them and too kind always though they were always being so noisy and interfering with her.' This is an aspect of her life I cannot imagine. She died suddenly and had been ill, so I learnt at the funeral, for a long time. It was a weak heart. She had given up going to church, which never really suited her. That is how it must all stay in the mind. She made no will. Whenever I think of her, I find myself talking to her, trying to justify myself. I never talk to my father as if from the beginning we had always understood each other perfectly well without it.

When I went up to finalize the sale, I opened a small building society account for each of the Ranasinghe children for with the sale of my Suffolk house I was now as well off as I would ever need to be. They were all assembled in the shop for a little celebration: four women this time and at least two more children than I had seen before. The champagne they had bought was the very best, though they wouldn't

348

touch the stuff themselves. When I handed over the building society pass books, Mr Ranasinghe put his hands together as if in prayer and said, 'Oh no, Mr Ripple, kindly please. Mrs Ripple was already such a wonderful gentlewoman.' The women and children gazed at me with unqualified wonderment.

When I left, they had difficulty expressing their thanks or anything much at all. They wanted to share my grief but at the same time were overcome with happiness, having come into their dreams. The woman who had brought the chocolate cake that day gave me a large square box in Christmas wrapping paper which was about the right size for it. I did not open it until I had returned home. It turned out to be a magnificent golden bowl inlaid with patterns of many colours which is beside me now on the window-sill next to the binoculars, blazing away and glittering as if caught in the sunlight though it is one of the darkest days. It has its own light within it and does not need the sun.

There was one other gift I brought with me from Suffolk. The Post Office van delivered a slim parcel from the vicar containing a volume of poetry by Philip Larkin. He enclosed a note which said, 'These will help to keep your pecker up in your new life, or spirits should you prefer (if it can't be both). Just the opposite, I fear, but extremely beautiful nonetheless.'

Chapter Two

I moved into this flat on the day Mrs Thatcher ceased to be prime minister. I had no strong feelings about that except in vaguely wondering whether people might now find themselves less able to focus on the distinction between right and wrong, politically speaking of course. If it meant that a Labour government was less likely next time round, one would have to go on wondering that much longer what difference the change might make to the conduct, say, of certain people in the City Jane has told me about, though she thinks with sadness it would make no difference whatever since they would go on doing and being what they did and were whoever ran the country and if they didn't and weren't, whatever pickle the country was in would be that much worse. Perhaps my former wife's views will come into vogue again and people will demand very much higher taxation on the rich without the risk of their taking their money elsewhere or doing whatever they do with it to make sure nobody else gets their hands on it, or of people not working so hard since there would be less to gain from it and therefore less to tax. Or the change might mean a general raising of the tone of the place, but no hope whatever of that, Jane thinks. A pity that equality got itself a bad name as opposed to liberty, a preference, someone said, for flattening rather than fattening, but put like that, no wonder. What worries Jane most are private health and private education where liberty conflicts with public solidarity and produces what she calls 'the causes of estrangement'; and 'mind your own business' has more than one meaning. Anyway, it was an era over, people said, and the difference between right and wrong in public affairs can become blurred again, though in that respect it didn't help that Mrs Thatcher put herself on the wrong side of the argument the more right she believed herself to be or even was.

Now to my new abode. I have the whole of the top floor of this house to myself: two spacious rooms, a kitchen big enough for a very small table or two chairs, a bathroom and a separate lav (an increasing advantage this). It is freshly converted and without character and I haven't so far succeeded in giving it any of my own: just my mainly grey and brown Suffolk stuff, the framed photographs of the lives of others picked up in antique shops and nothing you might call art-work, except for the Ranasinghes' bowl of course, an imitation bronze bust from Nigeria or wherever and two unframed reproduc-tions: two lovers by Picasso and another called *The Awakening Conscience* by William Holman Hunt, but better known, I suspect, as *The Domestic Goose*. I read more than I used to so there are more books around. In contrast to the bowl the imitation Persian carpet has lost its glow and is too associated with Jaffa Cakes and all the rest of that. I have a choice between looking out over the houses opposite and their gardens or at the fronts of houses facing the street. It surprises me sometimes how little there is to see in either direction so that I might as well be in Suffolk. No Webbs or Hambles. I am in no hurry to acquire a sense of neighbourhood, not again yet.

The other occupants of the house are as follows: on the next floor down live two seriously undernourished girls whose names, the entryphone tells me, are Michelle and Annelise. They are ballerinas and I watch them step out down the street as if already rehearsing, heads high, toes out and not quite touching the ground. I fear for them in a high wind. I have not met them properly yet. When they come in I hear the key turn twice in the lock and the sound of a bolt being rammed home. I hope they already did this before I moved in and not after catching sight of me on the landing above on my second evening, laden with three bags containing sufficient provisions with which to stock my six-foot fridge-freezer until the danger of earth-quake passed or spring came round again. They did not respond to my 'Hi there!' though the sight of me peering out between a French loaf and a couple of cos lettuces cannot have been wholly reassuring. Certainly it was not enough so for them to have rallied round when, as they fumbled for their door keys and I began fumbling for mine, the middle bag clutched to my waist released a series of apples and tangerines which, hunched forward as if struck between the legs, I managed to arrest the flow by letting the bottom bag (the one with the eggs in) drop to the ground. 'Shit!' I said, but by then their door

351

was being decisively shut and they may not have heard that or even seen much of my initial clutch and stoop. The giggle was in my imagination, I told myself, as I began the process of reassembly. Most evenings they are out dancing. I have never been to the ballet but have seen snatches of it on television, entirely by accident. I must go and see them perform one day, unbeknown to them of course. I wonder if I will be able to distinguish them from all the others. With what they show, it would seem rude to try.

On the ground floor lives a man called Foster. When I called on him he told me that, apart from my flat, the whole house was his and he was thinking of selling off the others too. This must make him quite a rich man. I could see he had been about a bit because of the exotic objects that surrounded him, his coarse complexion also suggesting long exposure to harsh climates. The objects looked valuable and were mainly delicate like egg cups and miniature china statuettes and small items of brass and silver and inlaid receptacles, none of which encouraged me to light up the cheroot I took out to go with the dry sherry he gave me without being asked for it. While I was there he received a phone call during which, with his back to me, he said such things as, 'Well you can tell Monty from me the deal's off' and 'Fifty K, piddling peanuts' and 'His bloody lordship can take a running jump so far as I'm concerned.' When he put the receiver down he turned and stared at me as if to make up his mind whether I could be trusted. His voice rasped as if his mouth had dried out and the blank scorn in his eyes seemed to disown the rich surfeit and delicacy with which he had surrounded himself.

Towards the end, however, he told me the room had been furnished by his wife. 'She had an eye for beauty,' he said and from the abrupt way he spoke I assumed she was dead and he kept the room as it was, with its dark red brocaded chairs and gilt mirrors and gold tasselled velvet curtains, as her fading memorial.

'We travelled the world together,' he said finally. 'What used to be called the Empire, more's the pity. Good times those were on and off, I can tell you. Been about yourself much, have you?'

'Not a lot. Business trips to the Continent, that kind of thing.'

'Ah well, doesn't do to hanker, I always say.'

Beyond that, he showed no interest in me. Perhaps we both understood we would be living together under the same roof for a long time and it might be wise to get to know each other gradually

352

or hardly at all. That was certainly the case on my side and more, I feared, could only mean worse: the gleaming brown brogue shoes, the sharply creased twill trousers with turn-ups, the olive green cardigan, the pink striped shirt and mother-of-pearl cufflinks, the dark blue tie with gold oak leaves on it, seemed designed to aggravate. There was an air of hostility too in his neat grey moustache and hard-set mouth but above all in his unwavering pale blue gaze. I was under scrutiny, fair enough, but there was more to it than that, as if my own downright shiftiness by contrast hid some nasty secret he would soon get out of me. Afterwards I realized that what had most disturbed me was his stillness and the fact that he never smiled; somehow I could not imagine him even attempting it as though it might turn at once into something else, savage and out of control.

As I was leaving, he said, 'Met our pretty little dancers, have you?' I nodded. 'Well, I've told them no bloody thumps in the night and to turn down the Harry Tchaikovskys or whatever the stuff is.'

'Ah,' I said as he gripped my hand to remind me what a real handshake was.

'They were nice as pie but then so was I,' he said. 'Knocked on the door, then straight out with it. I'm out a lot so let me know if they give you any trouble. You won't be bothered by the folk in the basement. Superannuated Polacks. Separate entrance. Good thing too with all that coming and going. Regular doss house it is. Youngsters working illegally, the lot of them. Got nothing against Poles, who could have? Funny lingo they speak like talking in sneezes. The old boy does odd jobs. Likes to be asked if you're ever in need. Won't talk about himself. People don't who have something to tell. Her, you hardly ever see. Anyway, make yourself at home. Wife used to keep her junk up there in the old days. Tarted up quite nicely, wouldn't you say? Nearly took it myself but you know how it is . . .'

Then he turned abruptly and went back into his room, closing the door with a bang. That was about three weeks ago. Perhaps he expects me to invite him back but I doubt it somehow. I see him get into his Volvo at odd times of the day and night. He is dressed just the same but with a tweed jacket instead of the cardigan and a variety of silk-looking cravats. Once he looked up at my window and caught me staring down at him. He did not wave. Yes, it is impolite of me not to have invited him back. I wish I knew what it was about him. His pale eyes might as well have been blind. He was going through the motions. He couldn't have cared less.

Yesterday evening when he was out, there was a lot of thumping down below and the music was anything but Harry Tchaikovsky. I was glad when he returned at about eleven because almost as soon as I heard his car door slam shut the noise stopped. Next time, I must bring myself to knock on their door too and be as nice as pie about it. I shall start rehearsing my lines now.

That was two weeks ago. This morning, the strip bulb in the light above the bathroom mirror didn't work so I replaced it with another and that didn't work either. I had not realized how much I needed to see myself clearly every morning when shaving and running a comb through my hair. It is a Sunday and I had been looking forward to a riveting day: the newspaper, a walk, a drive to the park, lunch, television, tea, more television and somewhere along the way picking up a magazine or two of some sort or even two of the same sort. After cutting myself twice I remembered what Foster had told me about the Pole in the basement.

The dancers had come in late with a particularly loud slam of the bolt and moved around a lot, bumping into things and talking fast and high, possibly in argument. But no thumping mercifully. So I went down the stairs on tiptoe so as not to wake them. As I reached their door, taking exceptional care to avoid the creaks, it opened and one of them was right there up against me, but not for long. She was wearing a short white dressing gown clutched not very high up her chest and her black hair clung lopsidedly to her head like a damp wig. But above all I was astonished at how tiny she was, how extremely little there was of her anywhere, especially where her hand held her gown together, but also her face in relation to her eyes, bare of all adornment in the morning light, hollowed out, white as her gown and awash with miniature pimples like beads of sweat. Once beautiful at a distance, she now did not have long to live. She looked with a gasp or hiss at whatever sight I was with the two unshaven patches surrounding bloody tufts of cotton wool or simply the general blear and puffiness looming over her, then turned with a trim swirl, pulling her gown round her so that I saw too in dazzlingly precise outline the stiffening of her haunches and below the hem of her gown her muscle-shaped calves hard as fists. I'm not sure if that gets any-

354

where near it. I never am. At the time, I was mainly aware of her gasp, then mine, and the glint in her large black eyes of what might have been disgust or fury. As much as anything then (well, almost) I wanted to make it up to her, whatever it might be. For she had seemed a cruelly treated little thing, above the waist at any rate. She had looked up at me as if now at last she had reached the limits of her endurance.

I made my way outside to the basement flat. There were steep, narrow steps leading down to it which were slippery with unswept leaves and the handrail wobbled. Under the window were two new dustbins with their lids propped up against them. Both were empty. On the window-sill was a pot of what might once have been a gera-nium, now only a forked twig with three shrivelled leaves clinging to it. I rang the bell and after about ten seconds or so rang again. I could see nothing through the net curtains except, in the gap between them, a small statue of a man sitting very upright on a horse. I was about to go away when the door opened. My first impression of the Pole was one of haughtiness and he reminded me in that instant of my mother, his tired eyes watchful but unexpectant. He was well into his seventies and was dressed in a new-looking dark suit as if on his way to a busi-ness appointment. His large, powerful face seemed not made for any show of feeling, except perhaps indignation. His short grey hair was brushed back and in the shadow of the doorway, his face was the same colour, sleek and metallic. For a while he stared at me, long enough to discover everything he would ever need to know about me.

'Yes? What can I do for you?' he said finally in a voice that sur-prised me with its meekness.

'I am sorry to disturb you,' I said. 'But I recently moved into the top flat and I can't get one of the lights to work. Mr Foster said . . .'

'It will be a pleasure,' he said with a slight bow and a smile full of frankness and welcome. 'Marek Bradecki. It is no trouble at all. I shall come in a minute.'

'I'm Tom Ripple,' I said. 'It is really most kind of you.'

The smile vanished and he shrugged as if to say it was no more than his duty, everyone was the same. Then he shut the door as if I were no longer there.

On the way back to my flat, I took my Sunday newspaper from the front step and saw that the dancers' *Observer* was there too. This was my chance, so I took it too and knocked on their door. The same girl opened it but now her hair was drawn back and tied in a dark green ribbon and her face was smoothed over with cream with a tinge of colour in her cheeks or where they ought to have been. She had changed into a white T-shirt: as I had surmised, no breasts at all. But nipples, most definitely. I hoped I had taken her away from an enormous breakfast.

'Your newspaper,' I said. 'Sorry about earlier. I didn't want to wake you after the late night you had.'

'Oh, it's you,' she said, taking the newspaper with an aimless frown, which gave me the nerve to say, 'I do hope I don't disturb you, the floor or ceiling depending on how you look at it being so thin.' Subtle, I thought, two birds with one stone. But it fell at my feet.

'Not at all,' she said deliberately. 'Don't take any notice of us.'

Her friend hovered up behind her, even smaller and whiter-faced with deep black shadows under her eyes. She seemed to have spent the night weeping. 'Who is it?' she said, then 'Oh!'

And the door was shut. 'It's no trouble,' I said to it. 'I had nothing better to do.' I was, I realized, smiling well into the range of complete idiocy. I felt as if I had exposed myself.

About an hour later, Mr Bradecki knocked on my door. He was still in his dark grey striped suit and was carrying a bag of tools. I took him straight to the bathroom and pulled the cord to show that the light didn't work. He replaced the shade, pulled the cord and the light came on, then took off the shade to show me the metal plates that made the connection. I shook my head and he gave my elbow a quick squeeze. Not a word had passed between us and I asked him if he'd like a cup of coffee. He nodded and went over to the window looking out over the street where he stood very erect, his hands clasped behind him, pulling his shoulders back. He had moved briskly as if to show how youthful he still was.

'Have you lived in London long?' I began.

He continued to gaze down at the street as if waiting for someone. 'Since the war,' he said. 'Always here in London. This now is my home.' From someone less assured his voice would have sounded ingratiating.

I wanted to ask whether he had ever gone back to his homeland but thought better of it. There had been a lot in the media about Poland, more than enough to tell me there was far too much there to lend itself to polite conversation, a variety of hopelessness and misery that could not be conveyed and certainly not shared. Best not to pry and yet when he sat down on my sofa and began noisily sipping his coffee, gripping the mug hard as if I was about to snatch it away from him, there seemed nothing else to say for it was all he could possibly care about, the history of it which they must all carry about with them like piles of unwanted baggage.

'That's a long time. Plenty about Poland in the news lately. It must make you happy that . . .'

He gazed into his coffee as if trying to read the future in it and I went over to the window, wishing I had said something altogether less or more trivial.

'Yes,' he said finally. 'But not happy. Never happy. Bad in another way because once there was hope in it. Hope is the mother of fools, we say. The young people think always of making money in the west. Money instead of slavery. You can never have enough money. The new politics, they don't trust that either. Democracy is other people wanting power, money, superiority.'

I turned round and his face was taut as if with the strain of holding his hands still. He was hunched up and his lips were drawn back as if now he wanted me to see him as an old man whose time was finished.

'Politics the same everywhere, I suppose,' I said. 'There are other things to worry about like . . . well everything really.'

He glanced up at me wearily. 'Forgive me, Mr Ripple, it is not the same. You have democracy like the scenery, like nature, like a big playground . . .'

'I've never really thought about it, to be honest.'

'Just so, just so.' He sounded angry now, but with himself. 'We have no experience of democracy. It was like a vision of religion in suffering, something to pray for, pray to, like heaven on earth, how do you say, a slogan. And like a religion, they say there is only one truth, one point of view. Ours. Christian or Communist, the same. We believe everyone should be equal as in the eyes of God. Do you see? They only want to be told what to do, like by the priest, or the Party boss. Democracy is salvation, not being responsible for our own lives. So we look for Messiahs who bring promises as if they were hope which we never had. On this earth, the enemy are people in authority. We do not ask, what is best for everyone? You could have in Poland the people choosing a fool who offered them paradise and said all the powerful of the earth were cheats and liars.'

'Well, there is an element here . . .'

'Oh no, no . . .' He paused and suddenly relaxed, smiling down at his coffee and then sipping it as though he had discovered it was something else much nicer. 'What does it matter now? Those of us who are old must try to die in peace. Everyone tired. Everyone frightened. That is all. Fight for peace and liberty we said and now what is this liberty? It is my wife now . . .'

Then he suddenly put down his mug, looked at his watch and left abruptly with a slight, correct bow. An old soldier. I guessed. What had he done since? His hands were large and rough. There had been swank and swagger there once but now reduced to the remnants of manner, a semblance of honour. He had looked at me with infinite patience as if I could not possibly understand, comfy in my own assumptions. And lucky. Very lucky. He was right. We had confronted each other in pity and there was no going far beyond that.

A few moments later the music started up down below. I tried to read the newspaper and a piece about the Polish presidential election but could not concentrate on it. The music thumped slightly faster than the beat of my heart, which began catching up as I convinced myself that a bit of the rough stuff was what they needed between long evenings of *Swan Lake* to which Maureen introduced me that memorable evening, its lush sweetness playing on in the distance, conducively enough until we had laboured through to the arid pastures on the other side. That sort of music. I checked the street. No Volvo. I'd bloody well tell Foster. Come right out with it. The music stopped for a while and I went on reading about Lech Walesa, a man on horseback, the piece said, who sat on his horse as if, like the man in Leacock, he was about to ride off in all directions. Then the music started up again, even louder, and I decided to get out despite the wintry weather. I couldn't blame the dear things, I told myself while wondering what the procedure was for obtaining a firearms licence. The Volvo would be back by the time I returned, a car I was learning to love. It would be a long Sunday. However, now I could have a decent shave and see myself clearly in the mirror. How terrific.

I drove to Hampstead Heath which I had not visited since the old days when I went there with my family. Now in the heart of winter it had not changed, the same people fiddling with their tackle by the ponds and dreaming of big fish lurking under the ducks, the same scruffy, intellectual-looking folk striding along and putting the world to rights, then the long curving slope up from the ponds between the trees past patches of old snow reminding of sunlight. I sat for a while watching paunchy men playing football, deadly serious, yelling out, becoming what they were not. They might have been the same men I had seen playing there all those years ago when Adrian and Virginia had squabbled and their mother had tried so hard to get them to see reason and I had only sighed. They were fond memories, increasingly so, but it was as if we knew something was going wrong already and we had drifted off the right track of our lives, and it was the same for everyone, the footballers too, booting themselves back into their boyhood.

Now, the bare trees dripped and stood tangled and frayed like huge dead thorns against the foggy damp of the sky. Had the days I had come here with my family been more frequent, in both summer and winter, for now I could only remember high clouds and gusts of wind whitening the trees dense under the sun? And then, suddenly, the laughter. Have I sufficiently recorded that here too at this very place when the wind blew off the ridiculous black cardboard bowler hat which Virginia, then aged about seven, was wearing and it landed at a footballer's feet, he brought it back and put it on her head with a deep bow. Which reminded me that Christmas was coming round again and I had not decided whether to accept Jane's invitation to spend the day with her parents who lived somewhere in Hertfordshire. I thought too about Virginia who was well into pregnancy now after one false start and wondered whether her mother would be going up to stay for that event. Or should I offer to, or shortly afterwards, intending to relieve the administrative burden but only not quite managing to offset what I was adding to it? My former wife would take over without interfering at all. How tactful and caring she had been towards me when our two were born.

Or so I mused this afternoon as I walked among the low clouds on Hampstead Heath and decided to spend Christmas on my own, pleading what excuse – that I had been invited by friends I had made in Suffolk? Christmas with the Jenners. I could just imagine that: the seasonal review of the state of the nation, the envelope licking for good causes, the dredging up of a life of service. No funny hats. No crackers. I could assume Jane's parents would be very nice indeed, he a family solicitor, she a teacher of mathematics. Adrian calls them 'mother' and 'father' and that is how it should be, all things considered. So why do I not spend Christmas with them? Perhaps to save Adrian the embarrassment of having to cover up my dreadful Christmas jokes, of worrying whether I felt out of place, was about to make a complete ass of myself. Poor Adrian, who had gone on laughing that day, long after the footballer had pretended to take a hefty kick at Virginia's hat and it was back on her head and we had begun to make for home. It was I who told him the joke had gone on long enough while my wife laughed too, intermittently, not taking sides, her arm round Virginia in the back of the car, soothing her anger. I do not remember Adrian laughing at any other time. It was not, I think now, at his sister's discomfiture. It was simply the sight of a flushed, fat, middle-aged footballer bowing and putting back on a young girl's head a miniature cardboard bowler hat. And so it was that I shared Virginia's annoyance while my wife delighted in Adrian's unusual display of gaiety (that once rare, good word then in its rightful place) knowing it might not come again. Why did I make her out all those years ago to be so humourless, such a prig? Why do I not go back and cancel all that out, rewrite it with hindsight and kindness, begin all over again? Is the truth so much less important than truthfulness?

About two weeks have passed. The launderette on the corner has asked me to put its books in order on one afternoon a week, but not yet. They have shown me the office at the back from where I shall be able to watch the people watching their undies etc. going round and round as if it was another sort of television – the intimate repetitions of the lives, the numbing, non-stop documentary into which they dream their dreams. When I go there, I watch the swishing lurch of my own sad invisibles and their haunting confusion, wishing they weren't tumbling about there on their own, that in amongst them were the thingummies of others. That's an idea. When asking the ballerinas to make a bloody sight less noise please, I could offer to take a bundle of their washing to the launderette. All our bodily trappings in there together. Easy enough to sort out afterwards. Life is not like that.

As I write the world is overwhelmed by the danger of war in the Gulf. There are only a few days to go. I read and hear all the arguments and predictions. There is no way through them to any certainty of right or wrong. I wish I knew what my wife was thinking. I wish I could have a chat with the Colonel or the vicar. I wonder what Hamble would say, or Hipkin. But not Plaskett. When I phoned Jane to wish her a happy New Year and to thank her for the bronze fish they had given me for Christmas, she called me 'Dad' for the first time. I noted down what she said then with such melancholy in her voice, adding in now what she has said since: that there would never be a world where competition for honour and riches and power did not drive everything along. But how far did we not behave like that in our own lives, according to peaceful visions, free and orderly among ourselves? There could be no new world order while individual wills collided, no common civility could come from such a host of personal greeds and jealousies. If we cannot perfect ourselves, what hope is there for collective humanity? Meanwhile, I read that people are postponing suicide because the bloodshed is something to look forward to. It is for others too, whose lives are more precious to them.

A week ago I invited Foster up for a drink. He accepted without enthusiasm. I gave him a gin and orange, his fourth choice, while he looked scornfully around my room as if carrying out an inventory until something less tedious turned up he could be angry about. I began by mumbling something about the Gulf.

'I don't know what they're waiting for,' he said. 'Why do you ask? Bang in there and get it over with.'

He couldn't care less what I thought, so I told him I had met the Pole and had liked him though he seemed to have more on his mind than he could cope with.

'Huh,' he replied, 'it's the way they are, in my humble experience. You should meet his wife. Poland. I don't know. Sad really. Always has been. Curse on the place. Better now, I suppose, but doubt it somehow, frankly. Met a few around the world. They've got style, grant you that, but clearly a bit mad. Their business now, if that's the word.'

Again, no hint of wanting a discussion so after a long pause I broached the noise question. He went on gazing about the room, still not finding anything which interested him. I thought he hadn't heard me.

'I'll mention it, if you like. More than bloody just mention it.'

'Oh no,' I said hastily, imagining them face to face. 'If it makes them happy. I can always go out for a walk or something.'

'Suit yourself. Me, I wouldn't stand for it. Turn it off or piss off.'

'It doesn't seem a very healthy occupation. I was never one for ballet myself,' I said.

'Glorified leg-show to music, is that it?'

'Not exactly. It's just that . . .'

He settled back into the sofa and gazed at the ceiling. 'Used to take the wife. She loved it. When we were on leave, it was what she most enjoyed, going to the ballet. After darkest bloody Africa, made a change from the native stuff, drums and stamping, all night some-times, some damn funeral or wedding ceremony or what have you. Once lived on the banks of the Zambezi, couldn't sleep a wink. I was away all day, tsetse control, game management, that line of work. Wouldn't interest you in the slightest. Sometimes spent the night up a tree watching the elephants. That wasn't for her and who could blame her? Used to shoot them for the Afs. You could smell the stench of the meat drying in the sun for miles. That was elephants for her. Stink. I don't think she ever saw one in her life. Hippos too, come to that. So ballet was quite a contrast, collecting nice things, etcetera. Only got leave once every three years in those days so there was a hell of a lot of *Sleeping Beauty* and *Giselle* and concerts and that sort of stuff to be got through. Didn't mind it myself if it made her happy, that's why I went. Too bloody much to make up for, not just looking forward to it, I mean, but playing it on the gramophone, batteries of course, so out of tune more often than not. Wobbly. She didn't seem to mind that. Anything to fill the black African night instead of crick-ets and drums and tree frogs and noises of animals. Had an Alsatian puppy once, name of Bertie, got taken by a lion. We wondered what it was. Awful shrieking sound buggering up one of the soppier bits in *Madam Butterfly* or one of those. She loved that pup . . .'

He fell silent and shook his head. 'Sounds perfectly dreadful . . .' I said.

'Christ no. Those were the days. It wasn't only Tchaikovsky and getting through gallons of this stuff.' He held up his glass, which was empty, so I took it and poured him another. 'Sweated it out almost at once. Bloody hard to get pissed for starters. The ladies don't sweat as much, do they? It was that and the Tchaikovsky took her out of her-self. Other things too. Schubert she liked or was it the other one? Both probably. Poor old thing . . .'

Another pause. 'The people. Did they listen, gather round?' I asked.

'The Afs. Good God no. My wife used to say, "I wonder what the

Chocolates are thinking." Our peculiar habits. Medical supervisor, name of Dickenson, used to say, "Black magic probably." His idea of a joke. Knew how to make her laugh all right. Only mistake was to bore them. Loved the Andrews sisters. Came for miles when the information van went round. Couldn't give a stuff about malaria and dysentery but *Chatanooga Shoeshine*, that was a bloody marvel. Those were the days, I'm telling you . . .'

He was now gazing out of the window above the roof-tops. Why did he suddenly frighten me, for he had only been seeing the past? Or was it only his own fear I saw: the Volvo coming and going at all hours, the mysterious phone calls? Why had he told me so much about himself so soon? To impress me? Surely not. He was getting up to go, draining his glass.

'Let me know,' he said. 'I'll tan their little bottoms for them, or close as dammit.'

'No, no please,' I said. 'It was nothing.'

'Oh no, my friend, music isn't nothing when you can't do without it. To answer your question, they should smash our friend Adolf Hussein into invisible little bits, the sooner the better. I'll say this though. We never made enemies of the Afs. Ballet music and chopping up elephants, you can't do better than that, now can you? God knows what we need elephants for. We manage all right without dinosaurs. Ever considered that, have you?'

And then he left. He did not thank me for the drink. He was already miles away. I do not think he had looked at me once. When we had met in his room he had hardly taken his eyes off me.

I have forgotten to mention that Virginia's daughter was born on New Year's Day, at five o'clock in the morning. It was her mother who phoned me, a little too soon after that. We had not spoken since she called me in Suffolk as I have recorded. From her tone of voice, we might have continued in daily contact all our lives.

'Hallo, Tom, it's me. Your ex. We have a granddaughter.'

'Oh good. Both all right are they?'

'Very.'

'What are they going to call it?'

'Just Ann, I think.'

'Sounds enough to me. Totally all right in all departments, you're sure of that?'

'That and extra. I promised Ginny I wouldn't tell you this, but she looks just like you, she's got your . . .'

That absolutely couldn't be allowed to continue. 'Thin on top, you mean. I wouldn't worry about that if I were you, not yet.'

She laughed. 'It's good news, Tom. Takes me back . . .'

It did me too, God alone knows. 'Can I speak to her?' I said.

'Virginia?'

'If Ann's tied up . . . Tell her to give me a call. Give her my love.' I was beginning to gabble, hoping she wouldn't go on as she did.

'Doesn't seem so very long ago, does it, that you and I were alone together and then suddenly Ginny was there too?'

'That isn't my recollection at all. In those days one had nine months' notice, or seven and a half months or whatever it was. Something called pregnancy.' I had tried to sound jolly but it came out differently, as argumentative.

'Oh, Tom . . . I wasn't *too* much of an opinionated old prig, was I? Not all the time. I was only trying . . .'

'No, of course you weren't. I was on the Heath the other day. Do you remember Virginia's black bowler hat and Adrian couldn't stop laughing?'

'No, I don't remember that. I remember watching the kites and Adrian wanting one so badly.'

'And I wasn't having any of that, I suppose?'

'Oh no, you promised him one but somehow then he seemed to forget and we never got round to it.'

'No. I never got round to it and he had to forget. I remember it now.'

'The bowler hat. Yes, I do remember. He cried a lot that night and I couldn't understand why, not at the time . . .'

And so our conversation petered out. I thought how there could never be bitterness between us again. Ann had put a stop to that. It was kinder to forget, though the past is all we are and we cannot choose what to remember, we cannot redeem it by picking out a bowler hat, fooling about at the seaside, the first sight of one's child, laughter, falling in love, a kite against a single black cloud. We do not think at the time: this is to be remembered, this will last and this will be lost. Perhaps that is why I am trying to write about my insignificant life, to restore the past and make it whole. It doesn't add up to much but if I had a gift for it, I would make it more satisfying or beautiful or whatever, but not true. Thoughts like these were going through my mind when to bring the conversation to a close I said, 'And what about you? Are you all right?'

'Brad isn't at all well. In fact . . . I try to keep busy but there's a new generation. I've had my share. And you?'

Well, there was a time when I would have had only one answer to that. My share of what, for Christ's sake? Nobody thinks they've had enough of that, do they?

'Fine,' I said and then simply, 'Goodbye and thanks for calling and give her my love.'

Together, I suppose, we might have had a message for Ann, that from the very beginning she should cherish life, every minute of it, lay up treasures. But she won't of course. The treasures will have to be found later, by chance. At the time tainted, ignored, overshadowed, unmemorable.

Two days later, Virginia phoned. Before she told me her husband had been laid off and there was no other job in sight, I told her a cheque would be in the post the next morning. It was for quite a lot but certainly not more than I could well afford. Nice to have something for Ann when she might need it, but by then of course she and Adrian would have inherited the whole bang shooting match. Anyway, there wasn't to be any familiar thou talk on this occasion. I said how sorry I was about her man, though he was still a filthy goat so far as I was concerned. About the money, she said, 'You shouldn't, Dad, honestly.'

'How would you like it laundered then? If you don't want it, give it to this Ann person who's come to live with you and can't even pay the bloody rent. The scroungers these days, it beggars description. Oh forget it . . . You OK?'

'Oh yes! She's a beautiful baby, Dad.'

'Looks like me, your mother tells me.'

'Not that beautiful, not by miles.'

'No, well of course . . . Listen, Virginia, I'm thrilled, that's all. The bad news is that I'm coming up to decide whether you're a fit person to look after it. When would be convenient?'

'Any time, Dad, you know that.'

We said goodbye and immediately afterwards I phoned Jane. I called her auntie and wished I hadn't. But any sort of envy in that, or any other, direction was not her style. That day the US Congress had given President Bush permission to go to war. I mentioned this but she didn't want to talk about it. I wished she'd tell me what to think. Everybody else was. I said that what I most dreaded was the ghastly bellicosity of the tabloid press. All the gung-ho and gotcha. But she did not respond to that either. 'Adrian and I are so happy for Virginia,' was all she said.

A few days later I met the Pole in the street. He was in conversation with two young men and they fell silent when I approached. It was a fine day with an entirely blue sky and I spread my hands and looked up at it.

'Can't complain,' I said, as one does.

His smile was brief and the two young men drew away from him and began whispering, making the Polish language sound even more than what it does already.

'The worst things start happening in good weather,' he said to them rather than to me. 'Have you heard about Lithuania too? But I must not detain you please.'

'Yes,' I said, 'that's pretty awful too.'

'The more patriotic the Russians, the more dangerous.'

The young men were grinning at us. One of them nodded, the other shook his head as if they were disagreeing about how best to appear shy but clever. I thought he wanted me out of the way so I left them to it but about an hour later when I was unlocking the front door he called up to me from the bottom of his steps.

'Now it is your turn to come and mend my fuse box, Mr Ripple.'

Night had already fallen and he came slowly to the top of the steps so that I saw his face in the light from Foster's flat, chalk white with three black holes like a skull. 'Come,' he said and then disappeared.

The door of his flat was open and in the darkness all I could see for a moment was a news broadcast on the television. The air was dense with the smell of cigarette smoke. Then I noticed two heads outlined above the back of a sofa and heard Mr Bradecki say, 'Shut the door, please.' He was standing in the doorway leading to a corridor beyond and switched on a dim bulb behind his head. Tall and erect, he seemed to be naked and the light was like a Christmas paper hat dangling above him. 'Come through here,' he said loudly. 'The boys watch television, nothing else. The wonders of the capitalist West. When they are not washing their dishes.'

I followed him past a closed door to a small room whose walls were covered with framed photographs and various badges and insignia. There was a desk under the window facing me on which he sat, then pointed to the only armchair in the room, of some dark-brown material worn grey with age.

'If you sit there then you are soon ready for vodka,' he said cheerily. 'If I do not give you vodka then you will be thinking I am not Polish at all.'

He reached behind him on the desk for a bottle and two small glasses which he filled to the brim, handing me one and almost immediately tossing back his own.

'Isn't it Russian as well?' I mumbled, which was fairly silly but I had to say something.

'One day I will explain the difference. The more they drink and tell you how much they love you and all mankind, the less you should trust them.'

'I don't think I've ever actually met a real Russian,' I said.

He let out a single long 'Aaah' and drained his glass. 'You have the Americans instead. Do you like that?'

'Well yes.' But I didn't understand what the question meant and he seemed to lose interest in the subject. While we spoke I glanced round the photographs on the walls. Most were of people in pairs or family groups but there were two or three larger groups above his desk of what appeared to be airmen, all smiling. There were also several of castles, large houses and churches. At my shoulder was a galloping horseman and above it an aeroplane, easily recognizable as a Spitfire. To the side of that was a large gravestone covered in flowers and candles. The largest of the badges and crests was an eagle against a red background wearing a gold crown. I leant forward to get a closer look at two cameos of heads with long hair in profile. My main thought was how to get off the unpromising subject of the Americans.

'At this moment you are gazing on Chopin and Paderewski,' he said.

'Ah yes of course.'

He waved his hand across the walls. 'How silly, you think, the great Polish traditions we keep alive in foreign lands, except it is all dead.' He spoke bitterly, without pride. And then he jabbed his finger at various photographs and reeled off a string of names that meant nothing to me at all. He came over to fill my glass, which was still almost full, tilting the bottle so that I had to cover the glass with my hand. 'The rest, my family, my ancestors, places they lived, landmarks. You can see how it was. Memories of nationhood. Pictures stuck up to hide a blank wall. Never once have I painted it. If I took them down there would only be shadows and cobwebs.'

He drained the bottle of vodka into his glass and went to find another. I turned to look at the wall behind me. Under the ceiling was a row of books and beneath it the photographs were all of devastated cities and flat landscapes littered with smashed machinery, guns, a tank and gutted trucks against a background of torn and twisted trees like scratches made with a broken pen-nib. And in some of them were people, huddled and vague and staring at the camera in exhaustion.

'Those . . .' I muttered vaguely as he returned.

'That is Poland. Everyone knows that about Poland. You see Warsaw, there and there . . .' Again his finger jabbed. 'Now it is what you say in English, very tedious.'

'Surely not,' I said.

But I did not know if this was true, if all the photographs and film footage could revive the horror at what had actually happened. We can only bring back to life what we personally know. For me it was only to turn the pages of a book that stretched back across all history, more and more of the same dreadfulness. My eye fell on a group of small children and I wondered what had become of them. Their faces were blurred and they were all half-smiling, distracted in that instant from what had already happened and what was to happen next, though it was the very worst that could happen. He was waiting for me to speak and all I could think was that it was only for show. There could be no exaggeration of such things, yet he needed to exaggerate. It angered me that such a man should want to make an impression on someone like me.

'I'm sorry,' I said. 'It's so awful. Were you . . . ?'

Then, from the room I had passed in the corridor, there was a loud thump and a sharp cry followed by a shuffling sound. I glanced at him, the bottle still unopened dangling from his hand.

'My wife . . .' he began, then shook his head and opened the bottle. 'All day she sits there, making her tapestries, stitching her white eagles and beautiful, unreal flowers. It is flowers she loves. If she stands on a chair, she can see the real ones wild in Mr Foster's garden.'

'She is Polish too?' I asked

He did not reply but took a book from the shelves and handed it to me. It was called *The Warsaw Ghetto* and consisted mainly of photographs. I leafed through it as he spoke.

'My wife never looks at it. She is half-Jewish only. But she was there, in another ghetto.' He reached up and took another book from the shelves. This one was called *The Lódz Ghetto*. 'You may take those,' he said. 'That was not her ghetto either but they were all the same. She never looks at these books. She never comes into this room because of the photographs. Sometimes I look at the books as if I might find her face there. Since I first met her in Scotland, a maid, quite alone, she never told me what happened until one night when we first loved each other and then she told me as day began breaking across our bed. Since then never. So why do I keep these books and photographs? Because I could not throw them away. Unthinkable you call it, absolutely unthinkable.'

I continued to leaf through the books. Page after page of the utmost cruelty and despair of a kind which everyone has seen somewhere, at some time. And suddenly I felt resentful that he should want me to take these books, that he should expect me to speak when I could not possibly have anything to say, as if there was some deficiency of feeling in me to which he wanted to draw my attention. I got up to go but again he filled my glass.

'Oh no, thank you, really,' I said, tapping my chest where a major attack of heartburn had begun to build up. 'Must be off. Expecting a phone call. Daughter's just had a baby.'

He lit a cigarette and at first I thought he was offended but then he gave me a smile which was full of kindness, with no trace of condescension. He stood up and put an arm round me and led me back down the corridor to the front room where the two young men were still staring at the television. In the flickering gloom I saw under the window a heap of what looked like sleeping bags and knapsacks.

'Goodness gracious me,' he said, imitating the upper classes in his Polish accent. 'You came to mend my blasted fuse and I was coming on all Polish at you.'

'Please. It was very interesting. I wish I knew more about it, that's all.'

'Why should you? If you did wish it you would know enough already. Look there at our new generation, watching their *Neighbours* and going to discos and wanting more money. That is why we wanted to win battles and be free, so that our young people can dance to loud music and watch silly television and have money. I think that is good. I think that is very good, don't you, Mr Ripple?'

We had reached the door. He moved his hand up my arm and squeezed it as if testing the muscle.

'Certainly,' I said. 'Do whatever turns you on.'

'Which is the same thing as turning the television on,' he laughed, pleased with his joke. 'Sorry I am boring. I ask you nothing about yourself and now you are a grandfather.' He opened the door for me. 'The future. Hope. I trust the child will be very happy. Boy or girl?'

'Girl.'

'Excellent. Absolutely excellent. Instead of children my wife and I have many other people's children coming and going to watch our television and sleep on the floor. Three cheers for the free market economy. Free for them and not very economical for us, I say to my wife.'

He gave another sharp laugh. Quite right too. I looked back at him as I went back up the steps. A trick of the shadows cast a deep black gash down his cheek. And then I believed that all he had said to me was simply out of friendliness and courtesy. I had left the books behind.

The war has started. A few people believe that it should not be occurring at all. Most people want a great deal of destruction and slaughter and want it quick. I run through the people I've known and wonder what they might be thinking about it. I am glad the subject didn't come up in my conversation with my daughter or with my wife. Jenners would have a lot to say, Hipkin nothing at all, nor Webb probably. Plaskett – hurry on to the next. Sidney? Hurry along again. The Colonel, he would simply have said it would be a hateful, ghastly massacre. Geoffrey and Gwen and Ruth, something too smug by half. The ballerinas . . . here we go again. More thumping down below. I look down at the moonlit street. No Volvo. Thoughtless, inconsiderate, stupid little bitches etc. I have a sore throat and feel rotten. I watched the houses opposite with my binoculars as the lights went off one by one. The frost lies along the crooked fences and bare branches like dust. Just have to sit here until the Volvo returns. Thank God for Gaviscon . . .

A few moments ago I heard a car drive up and the banging of two doors. I went to the window and saw Foster lurching towards the house with a woman on his arm. She seemed to be holding him

370

upright. As they reached the bottom of the steps she looked up at me, then back down the street as if to see whether they were being followed. Her blonde or grey hair spread out high around her head so that she seemed at first to be wearing a large fur hat. In the lamplight, her face was white and her lips were black. She was not a young woman. As they climbed the steps, he pulled her towards him and kissed her violently. She tried to push him away and her mouth opened wide, the blackness filling her face, her head tossed back as though she were yelling silently to the heavens. I imagined a laugh as he thrust his head forward and kissed the air. Then he lunged behind her up the steps and I lost sight of them. He should not have been driving, I thought, and was mightily grateful to him for the thumping stopped and the world fell silent. I took my temperature. 102°. I swallowed three aspirins with a glass of whisky, honey and lemon and woke late after a fitful night. The world was still silent and from my bed the white sky was smudged grey like old paint. Perhaps there had been a snowfall. My temperature had gone down to 100°. I went down to get my Sunday newspaper. I paused outside the ballerinas' flat but heard no sound. I went down again and brought back their *Observer*, which I left outside their door. Then back to bed to read all about the war, warm and comfortable as my temperature came down and the sky thinned and whitened and it became a clear blue day.

Chapter Three

More time has passed. The war is nearly over and the suicide rate will soon be back to normal again. Not much has happened. I am now working two afternoons a week at the launderette. I also check the accounts of the restaurant next door, which belongs to the same people. They are Asians of course but I have not got to know them. They have an unhealthy respect for me though the way I do their books is without fault (my mother looking over my shoulder, the old fear of being found out). Putting figures to dirty clothing and quantities of grub is not what you might call Ripple in his prime, but there we are. Virginia's husband has got another job, in the office supplies business, and she tells me he is enjoying that, though the money is not so good. The baby flourishes. Adrian and Jane are all right too. The air above Kuwait is filled with black smoke. Saddam Hussein is where he was before.

I have not seen the Poles again, though I often see the young people coming and going, girls too, amazingly and differently pretty, since you enquire. I've greeted one or two of them and get such candid smiles in return. I have learnt to say '*Dzień dobry*', whatever that may mean, and their faces really do seem to light up when I say it. I have borrowed several books about Poland from the public library and I am sad and glad for them at the same time.

I bump into the ballerinas from time to time. No smiles there, rather a sort of wan watchfulness and no wonder since at any moment they will be whisked away above the roof-tops in a high wind. Foster invited me to his flat again. No sign of any female occupancy. Twice he has returned late at night with women, perhaps the same woman, with abundant hair and large dark lips. He told me more about his past in Africa. I do not understand why since I know he has no wish to impress me. His voice droned on and his dead eyes gazed high out of the window. I wished he would tell me which, if any, of the delicate little bowls and dishes was an ashtray.

'Oh yes,' he began as if carrying on where he had left off. 'Never a dull moment. Camping out with huge log fires outside my tent, the carriers gossiping away all night. That was the life. One night fetched out by the chief, said there was a lion prowling among his cattle. There it was, eyes glinting. It was one of his bloody cows. Damn near shot it. Had a snake under my mosquito net one night. Felt the weight of it sliding up over my balls. The wife couldn't stand snakes. Wouldn't come on tour with me. Often wondered, since you ask, if Dickenson was having it off with her in my absence. Well, fair's fair I suppose, what with one thing and another. Not that it crossed her mind or if it did, bloody quickly. Never asked her. She never asked me though she'd have drawn the line at native bints. So did I, up to a point. They weren't called blacks then, you know. Penicillin made a difference, I mean knowing it would. They were riddled with it, the Afs. She was sick a lot, but nothing to put your finger on, so Dickenson said, blushed when he said that, they both did. If you must know, I wondered about the house-boy, became a chief in the end. Dickenson did himself in, poor sod. October, when else? Shot himself. Won't go into details but he lived for a day, much of that rattling about in the back of my Land Rover on the way to the hospital. Nobody had the faintest idea why. Handsome bugger. Good at his job, no doubt about that. Really bloody cared, tearing round his dispensaries. If it was daylight he was on the job. Worshipped him the Afs did. Perhaps that was it. Because they died a lot, you see. Fifty per cent infant mortality, kids in their first two years. Perhaps that was it, never being able to do enough. Of course had to wonder why he was there in the first place, why any of us were come to that. Flunked his medical degree, they said. Could have been a broken heart. Could have been any damn thing. He was keen on my wife, you didn't have to be a raving genius to know that, the way he looked at her. Mind you, you could hardly blame him . . .'

And so he rambled on, then suddenly stood up, before not after looking at his watch. He stared at me for a while as if trying to remember who I was. Talking to me had been no different from talking to himself. Yesterday he came back to return the package of cheroots I had put on a table beside me, waiting for the signal. He refused my offer of a drink and stood at the window, gazing down the street. It was a bleak and drizzly day and the gaudiness of his attire made him look like an out-of-work entertainer. Again, his flat voice ground on as if compelling him to hear the sound of his own thoughts and confirm their worthlessness.

'. . . Christ,' he went on, 'miss the great wide African spaces sometimes, I can tell you, the clean blue air, the thorn trees, the colours, poinsettia, hibiscus, bougainvillaea, those things, the dust and blackies in rags going about their business. Had to watch what you called them: munts, coons, kaffirs, wogs, it was a quick way of telling who the shits were actually, words like that. Afs, blacks, chocolates if you gave a sod. Still can't get used to them in suits and ties. Politics has a lot to answer for in my humble opinion. Some funny names they had. There was this bloke in Chief Singani's area asked the DO for tax exemption, ten bob a year it was, because he had twins. Bossy little twerp he was, the DO, I mean. Said their names were Ophelia and Winterbottom. Should have given him exemption for life, I said. Dickenson told me he'd given a woman a bottle of medicine to rub on her chest and she had a baby shortly afterwards she called For External Use Only. I miss the skies on a day like this . . .'

'Wouldn't have suited everyone.' I said chattily. 'The heat and snakes. Your wife . . .'

At that he pressed his hands down on the window-sill, then turned and took a pace towards me, the hand at his waist clenched into a fist. Then he sighed and fingered his yellow silk cravat as though in anger that he had been about to betray himself.

'Must be off,' he said. 'Business to attend to.' At the door he stopped and said, 'Wouldn't have suited you at all, my friend, and I think it would be preferable all round if you left my wife out of it, if it's all the same to you.'

'I'm sorry,' I muttered. 'I only . . .'

'So long as we understand each other, that's all. That's what you're thinking, it's him who should have left his wife out of it. You may be right. None of us should have been there, stayed all comfy with our little odds and ends and pretty herbaceous borders in Sidcup, pushing pieces of paper about, couple of weeks each year on the Isle of Wight, sand-castles for the kiddies, paddling and clowning about on donkeys. And now that we've left, the place is completely buggered up, whose fault is that? Nobody gives a toss really. What we call civilization. You were well out of it.'

374

But he did not sound bitter now, looking past me at the blackening clouds, groping for the door handle behind him. Then he gave a loud grunt and bared his teeth. 'If I were you, old chum, I wouldn't give it another thought. Stick to your patch. Look what happened to Dickenson. Go turn on your telly and have a wank or something. Nothing personal. Dancers been good little girls, have they?'

But he didn't wait for an answer and closed the door very quietly behind him.

This is three days later. I met him in the street outside the house and he nodded in the direction of the basement flat.

'Poor sods. Not much going for them is there? Poland. Phew!'

I walked with him to the corner and he pointed at two black people in conversation outside the launderette. 'They've come on a bit, haven't they? I like to see that, Africans in suits doing business as if the place belonged to them. Can't see anything wrong in that, myself. Where you happen to be and make the best of it. Better here than there. Willy wet-legs are what I can't stand.'

At that he glanced at me as if deciding which side of me he drew the line or was too sure about that to bother having to think about it. I stopped outside the launderette. He knew I worked there.

'All right is it, in there? Not much you can tell your Patels about the numbers game. On the fiddle are they?'

'Of course they're bloody not,' I said. 'Why should you think that? And their name isn't Patel.' That was no willy wet-leg talking.

'Didn't think they were. Why should they? Do all right without it.' And he left me with a shrug.

About a week ago I met the Pole again. It was to be for the last time. He came up to see me on the pretext that he needed to check the water tank in the loft outside my flat. It was about six in the evening and I had just returned from the launderette with a bag of washing which I was sorting through to decide how little of it needed ironing. I had heard him coming up the stairs very slowly, pausing every few steps. I invited him in and offered him a drink. He lowered himself into the sofa, raised his head and closed his eyes as if he wanted me to take a good look at him. He was again wearing a dark grey suit and white shirt and his tie was blue with small wings scattered about it. His shoes were highly polished and his engraved gold cufflinks glinted. I wondered if he was dressed like that only for me. He had shaved too and, held up to the light, his face was stretched smooth like a film of rubber, the last of the colour in it as if drained into the hollows of his eyes like a fading bruise. It was the face not of an old man but of someone in the prime of youth, tired out and very sick. I had only been aware before of his assurance and dignity and for some reason this made me ashamed. When I gave him his vodka he sat up abruptly as if he had been asleep.

'That's better,' he said, tossing it back and wiping his mouth with the back of his hand. 'I shouldn't, the doctor tells me, but it seems to make an improvement.'

His face loosened and there was a sudden tinge of pink in his cheeks. His eyes shone moistly and he gave a short, loud laugh, raising his fist above his head as if some victory had been won. 'Ha,' he said. 'You see, we shall never surrender. You know our proverb: so let us be fools and hope.'

Then equally as suddenly, he slumped back into the sofa. It was as if he was acting in a play, or rehearsing some grand dramatic effect but it was only a show, an imitation of how life might have been. He sighed and shook his head. The moment had passed. And then he smiled at me, ashamed perhaps that he should pretend to be anything more than a foolish old man who did not want to see pity in my eyes. I wished I could think of something to say without any sympathy in it. I raised the bottle but he shook his head.

'No, Mr Ripple. Vodka too is the mother of fools. Let me tell you, how do you say it in English, my days are numbered.'

'As I understand it, that's true of everyone in any language.'

He looked at me as he had when we first met, sizing me up and finding nothing at all to go on. 'I do not have a good heart any longer and soon . . . That is all right at my age but . . . you have a wife?'

'Not any longer. I mean she is now somebody else's.'

He did not seem to hear that and spoke down at his hands, which he pressed and stroked as if trying to smooth out the wrinkles in them. 'My wife does not know, I think, that I shall not be living for ever. She does not know I see the doctor and when I went to the hospital she thought I was in Scotland on business. What business would I have in Scotland, for Pete's sake? My pills are hidden behind my books. She thinks I am the same as when I flew aeroplanes and went dancing all night. She trusts me fearfully, always to be there. I am all her family and all her friends.'

'A lot to ask, I see that, but simplifies life at Christmas,' I said. This was very silly but my only thought then was that I wished he would keep his private life to himself.

'No children. Once I took her to the Polish Club but it was always the country, the nation they talked about and freedom and the Reds and they were right and they sometimes sang and listened to Chopin. And my wife sat in a corner and there was a woman there who whispered to her it was all the Jews again. She never wanted to go again. Sometimes I go, for some of them are good, brave people and are a long way from their homeland, which they love. And now I tell her the long dark night is over and the Communists are finished and I shall take her back there. And the young people say she can buy anything in the shops but they tell her too it is not so wonderful and I know it will be like a long grey dawn in the middle of winter and not so different from the night. She does not know what to believe. She only knows what I tell her and she does not seem to care at all. It only matters that I am there to tell her something, anything at all. She can only remember and want to forget.'

He paused and let me refill his glass. 'As one gets old,' I said, 'shouldn't one try to let the past go, or remember the best in it?' Why did he always make me speak such nonsense?

He shook his head vigorously. 'Remembering is not choosing. When it is all people have? Never mind those things. And now, you see, one day I will leave her. There is money but if I am not there, how will she know . . . I have to tell you, honestly, Mr Ripple, I am worried, my wife living alone there with her sewing and tapestry. She will be frightened, Mr Ripple. And I am frightened.'

He glanced at me apologetically as if he had gone much too far. 'But why am I telling you this? It is none of your business. You have given us a home, you people. What more should we ask? I apologize, another boring old Pole who rambles on about his country. What must you be thinking . . . ?'

'Nothing really. I . . .'

He shrugged. 'No, it is nothing of course, the past, the curse of the past. I only say that one day, maybe once in a blue moon, you can show her about the poll tax and pension rights and such things and save her from too many young people coming and going. I have told her you are a good man, Mr Ripple, not so much I think.'

To this I replied rather hastily, clasping my hands together. 'Come, Mr Bradecki, we mustn't be too gloomy, must we? I mean, aren't there . . . ? And the young people, I could hardly . . .'

At this, he drained his glass and went to the door. 'I am very sorry,' he said. 'Certainly not, but then you will have to solve your own electrical troubles. Goodbye for now, Mr Ripple, and I thank you from my heart . . .' He really seemed to mean it.

He closed the door behind him but I knew he would come back. For a minute or so I listened for the sound of his footsteps on the stairs and imagined him waiting there. Then, as I was about to turn on the television I heard the door open behind me. I turned to see him standing there, very upright, his head held high, his face gleaming and grey as stone, his eyes blinking as if getting used to a bright light.

'Look after her, Mr Ripple. You must look after her.'

He reached out a hand towards me and I saw there were tears in his eyes. I told myself that this was just another little moment of drama and he'd gone outside to rehearse it. I did not move and he withdrew his hand, looking down at it as if his presumption shocked him. Then he stared at me for a long time and slowly shook his head.

'It is all my Polish nonsense, Mr Ripple. But I am telling you. One day you must take her back. Take her back. It is what I think you should definitely do.'

And then he left. He did not close the door and I heard his footsteps going slowly down the stairs, pausing from time to time as if I should continue listening and would less easily forget his disappearance from my life, the footfall on the stair down into the silence of his final winter. Though I write this some months later. At the time, I only jotted down the things he had said, embarrassed that I should have been so confided in, as he might have entrusted me with an unfinished manuscript in a language I did not understand.

I largely forgot about him for a couple of weeks after that. Or tried to, for I could not rid myself of the discomfort he had caused me, the urgent courtesy in his voice. I heard my mother say, 'Keep yourself to yourself, then you won't be disappointed.' And he made me think too of my father, who had no strength and looked on silently, without judgement, always fearing the worst.

The ballerinas helped me to put him out of my mind. The following Sunday, I again delivered their newspaper, knocking on their door this time. Not so brazen of me as you might think, for the night before the door had opened and shut into the early hours, the din thumping on like an amplification system badly out of control augmented by a wide choice of cheerful, high voices belonging to quite the most loathsome people in the world by a long chalk. How I longed for the return of Foster in his silver chariot. What I had decided to say was: after that bloody awful racket last night I'm telling you straight if it happens again you're out on the streets and sod the weather.

The door opened and I said to the girl standing there, 'Newspaper?'

She took it and then, though not at once by any means, she said, 'Would you like to come in for coffee? The place is a bit of a mess, I'm afraid.'

So indeed it was. The room was littered with cushions and cups and glasses and plates and bottles and quite a few garments. There were even some pillows and blankets lying about. It was a bright day and the dust danced over the debris in the rays of the sun. She cleared a one-armed chair for me and went into the kitchen where a good deal of muttering went on, to do no doubt with how welcome I should or shouldn't be made to feel, considering. After a while they came back bearing coffee in mugs. They were both wearing black slacks and T-shirts, the one white with the words 'Come dancing' printed on it, the other orange with two pairs of lips where the breasts should have been. Their faces looked as if they had recently been fiercely but only partly scrubbed and their hair was drawn back into ponytails so that in the dusty blur I could not tell at first which was which, the one who had come to the door this time not presumably being the one who a few moments earlier had enquired what the fuck the other one had invited me in for, Christ honestly. They perched on the arms of a sofa under the window so that with the sun in my eyes the process of differentiation began sluggishly, or here and there. I was making a sound far back in my throat, which I ended by taking a sip at my lukewarm coffee: no hanging round in there waiting for the kettle to boil.

'I'm Annelise, she's Michelle,' the one who had asked me in said, undoing whatever tied her hair back and shaking her head so that it fell to her shoulders. Previously darkish blonde, it now looked mud-brown in the sun dust and unwashed for a very long time.

'That's better,' she sighed. 'Rather overdid it last night.'

379

With some apology looming, I took my chance. 'It was a party, I hope? Couldn't help worrying whether there was some fearful scrap going on. Glad to see you came through it all right, I really am.'

Michelle stared at me. Absolutely clear now who had come to the door the first time and who had been saying what in the kitchen. The black hair, of course. She raised a leg and pointed her foot at me. She was wearing red socks and no shoes. If I had reached out I could have pinched her toes.

'An opening night,' Annelise said. 'And I made such a bish. Oh God!'

Michelle looked crossly at her and said, 'Don't go on about it, Annie. I'm sure nobody minded. It wasn't your fault.'

'Of course it was my fault.' She stretched her mouth as far as it would go and gave a hiss of pain. 'Michelle is brilliant. She's got a solo and the Dutch want her. I'm just a no-no.'

Michelle said nothing, being intent on estimating how long it would take me to finish my coffee. I was absolutely determined to get back at once to the subject of the party; very well, some other time.

'I think it's incredible what you do,' I said. 'Was it a dreadful bish or just forgetting to come on stage or falling over or doing a leap instead of a twiddly bit?'

Annelise tossed back her head, her hair staying close to it, heavy with dirt or whatever it was she sprayed it with to keep it in place while dancing. 'Only came on late, that's all, got out of line. It was nothing except that it was *everything*.'

She looked at Michelle who said 'Ts' and examined her foot. 'All right, Annie, it happens.'

'Oh no, it doesn't,' Annelise said. 'You wouldn't do anything like that. It's always all right in class, in rehearsal. I never bish then.'

There was a long pause while coffee was sipped. Annelise's voice remained in the air, plaintive and unanswered, certainly by Michelle, whose frown continued regardless. If I had not been there, they would have started quarrelling. No doubt who would have got the better of that.

'For what it's worth,' I said, 'I used to find that too. I was in finance, that sort of thing. You think the figures are spot on, then you find you've missed a nought, or somebody has and you blame yourself or not if you can possibly help it and then you become doubly efficient for fear of being found out and you forget how unimportant it is, or was or ought to be and you wonder if you can trust yourself . . . I know the feeling.'

This sounded even more daft than it reads but succeeded in bringing them together again, for they exchanged glances and almost managed not to smile at all, their feet now wagging up and down in unison.

' . . . Not the same thing at all, of course,' I went on. 'I can see the arts are really a different thing, league altogether, of difficulty, exposure, er . . .'

Michelle got up and strode past me to the kitchen, very close and absolutely not saying anything as she glanced down at me glancing at where her slacks were tight, extremely so. I gave a throttled sort of cough. When she had gone, Annelise said to me quietly, 'She's a star, she really is. It's all right for her.'

There was no answer to that either. We had been left together. I wanted to ask all about the life she led but Michelle would soon come back and not expect to find me there. Commiseration, or whatever Annelise wanted of me, would take time with the curiosity that went with it. But what could I possibly have to contribute, whatever she told me? I looked at her and away again. She had read my disapproval as aimed at her.

'Don't tell me. I'm lucky to have got as far as I have. There are hundreds who don't.'

'You mean because bits or most of them turn out to be the wrong size or shape?'

She attempted a smile. Her face seemed to have shrunk around her eyes, which gazed blindly at me as if behind a magnifying glass. It wasn't mere sadness but a longing for life as though she was a convalescent with a wasting illness. She needed a long holiday in the sun, lots of rest and masses of food. She needed to recover from too much exercise. She needed to become damn all use for ballet. A loud continuous clattering noise began in the kitchen which had nothing to do with washing-up.

'That or not enough dedication or talent,' she had said and now added, 'The trouble is that the second, in my case, never quite matches up to the first. Size and shape are all right.'

'Yes, I can see . . .' Then (forgive me just this once more) I said, 'They keep you on your toes, I bet?'

That must be the commonest silly joke in ballet circles with fathers of twins running it a close second, so mercifully Michelle then returned, looked sternly at Annelise and said, 'You've come to tell us not to make so much noise, haven't you?'

She looked down at my empty coffee cup and decisively did not ask if I would like another. This was my last chance. If it hadn't been for knee scratching and throat clearing, you could have heard a pin drop.

'Oh no, not at all. One can absolutely see that after all that thing one needs to let one's hair down. I'd be the last person . . . I mean it's not as if I had to be up at the crack of dawn or needed my beauty sleep . . .' I rubbed my chin and flicked an eyebrow and could see them relax and grin slightly, if not wholly out of relief. 'There's little harm possible there. No, you mustn't give it another thought, truly. You enjoy yourself while you can . . .'

I stood up slowly, simulating excruciating backache which I could see from their concern or impatience they thought real, had every reason to. Annelise made way for me and almost took my elbow as I hobbled to the door.

'That makes a change from that dreadful man Foster. He threatened to chuck us out,' Michelle said.

'He threatened worse than that,' Annelise said. 'He's our landlord so he's got a key and we *know* he snoops about when we're not here, rummaging in our drawers, we're sure of it.'

I reached the door in three sprightly strides. 'But a jolly sight worse if you were in them,' I leered or whatever the word is.

He would never go as far as that, or anywhere near it and I should have stood up for him. That word I do know: ingratiation, but thanks all the same. Anyway, they got the joke because they ignored it, or rather Michelle winced with her nose and Annelise widened her eyes, both of which I did too, mumbling 'sorry'.

Going back up the stairs, I said 'Oh well' at frequent intervals, and thought of Foster fondling their undies, followed by me doing something like that too or whatever. There was page after page of analysis in the newspaper about the war: the bombardments and body counts and bragging, but I did not want to have to think about that instead. Wild beasts were on the rampage and snow had begun to fall. I wanted to sleep for a very long time and wake up to a world smothered in snow and at peace with itself, a fire burning in the hearth and nothing happening at all, the black trees streaked with white, a long cold stillness before the buds began to burst and spread and the full-blown leaves swayed and rustled in the wind and the first blossom fell again. Such words these are to summon calm and beauty but they are only to keep terror at a distance and assuage desire. It is now midnight as the snow flutters thickly through the light from my window and there is no sound anywhere except this machine clacking away in fits and starts. Poor little Annelise, who only wants to dance always to perfection and live up to her art. I imagine them lying there below me, naked in sleep.

I was away visiting Virginia when the Pole died. It was Foster who told me outside the front door. He pointed with his thumb down at the basement flat and said, 'Curtains, poor old sod, heard I presume?'

I looked down there, expecting the window to look different in some way. 'Sorry?'

'Anyone could see he had it coming. Decent old cove, but a bit haughty for my taste. Superior. Perhaps he was, who knows?'

'You mean . . . ?'

'Yup.' He drew a finger across his throat. 'Comes to us all one time or another.'

I thought how much harder it would be to get to like him after this, that the death of a neighbour should mean so little to him. 'I'm sorry,' I said. 'He seemed a good man. Is his wife . . . ?'

'Couldn't say, to be frank. Must have a word in her ear some time about the rent. Give her a day or two of course. They've been getting it dirt cheap since you ask. Well, he was useful, you see, electrics, painting, carpentry, plumbing, the lot. Sure to be relatives. Polaks all over the bloody shop. Ealing, South Kensington. She'll want to move, shouldn't wonder. Apart from anything else, the place isn't much more than a squat for illegals. No objection personally, don't get me wrong, but the law is the law, there for a reason, usually at any rate. Unemployment, in that general area. Well, I suppose they fill in for the loafers and scroungers and serve them fucking well right if you'll pardon my French. I could get double for that flat or near it.'

'Perhaps she doesn't have anyone,' I said.

'Everyone has someone, for Christ's sake. And what's wrong with Poland these days now they've booted out the Commies, that's what

I'd like to know? Saw this film the other day. There she'd be a bloody millionaire.'

'What's she like? Is she . . . ?' He was the last person to ask this and I wished I hadn't.

'Bit of a misery, since you ask. Doesn't look at you. Hardly heard her speak more than half a dozen words, if that, and those were in her own lingo. Cheery good morning and you might as well be chatting up the sparrows. Bit of a non-person, if you ask me. But don't you worry, I'll break it to her gently, give her a couple of weeks. I'll miss him, superior bugger. Once he sent up a couple of lads to do the place out, your flat mainly. Marvellous job. Dead cheap. Didn't feel so bloody law-abiding then I can tell you. Students they were. Not bad English either. Must be going, if that's all?'

'Yes, that's all thanks.'

'Pop in for a chinwag some time.' He put a hand on my shoulder as if at last he had decided to approve of me. But his face was as lifeless as ever and again it puzzled me that he should talk so much.

I met Michelle on the stairs later that afternoon.

'Hallo!' she said cheerfully – things going well for her, I assumed, which reminded me they probably weren't for Annelise. 'You heard about the Polish gentleman?' I nodded. 'You knew him quite well, didn't you? He was so like dignified.'

'Not well, no.'

'He was so kind to us, fixing things and wouldn't take money. He looked so lonely, hurt somehow.'

'I know.'

'It's their country, isn't it? One of our dancers is Polish.'

I shook my head and left a pause. 'Both of you keeping well, are you?'

'You mustn't take any notice of Annelise. She has her ups and downs.'

'The problem is keeping them in time with what the others are doing.'

That did make her smile, I'm glad to say, not much but enough. I'd never seen her smile before, indeed never expected to. It drew attention to her mouth, small in width but the smile pressed her lips together and plumped the lower one out. There was moisture all over it and that plus the creasing at the corner of her eyes were what some

384

other lucky sod need not take as a signal to get stuffed, indeed soon enough if not immediately he could . . . oh, scrub it. She was human after all. It had taken a death in the house . . . 'Don't worry about her, really,' she was saying, the smile suddenly replaced by that altogether needless frown.

'I'll try not to.'

I made exaggerated way for her and watched her trip on down the stairs, or an inch or two above them. She was a star all right. She was absolutely stunning too, while I was on the subject.

I spent three days with Virginia. Her husband, as I have mentioned, had lost his job in agricultural machinery and was now in stationery supplies, which meant he had a company car and was on the road a lot. It was a bit of a comedown but he almost persuaded me the job had prospects.

'Upwardly mobile in the stationery business,' I said. 'Doesn't sound quite right somehow.'

'That wasn't particularly funny,' Virginia said, to protect her man, putting me down. Well all right, so I added, 'Why not try the transport business, then you'd really go places.'

He made a protracted gagging sound which was what he thought a laugh was supposed to sound like and Virginia looked angrily at me. She hadn't understood that I simply didn't want him to be solemn, when he had everything, a wife like that, a child like it, a job with a car. But it wasn't my teasing him that she minded, for all his self-doubt. It was that she thought I was trying to show up what little sense of humour he had.

He went on about its being a new company and was on the up and up (great restraint shown by me here). It was mainly for Virginia's benefit of course. Not that she gave a damn with her new baby guzzling from her on demand, eyes blissfully closed, an example I would have liked to have followed when unable to think of a reason for leaving the room such as half-way through the soup course. Her man did not know where to look either, the filthy hypocritical lecher, though less uniquely vile now with all that blatant lesbian incest going on under our very noses. Why couldn't people leave my daughter alone? She was very affectionate towards me too and we had some good laughs together. With her baggy postnatal attire and limp and no perceptible attempt to make herself attractive aside from partly combing her hair, she exuded contentment and love, as if she had found life to spare, more than enough for the baby alone. All her husband and I had to do, as it were, was to put in for it. I prepared the meals, short of actually cooking them, drove her here and there, did some of the housework and shopped etc. I called her madam and she called me Thomas. I called her husband 'squire' when he was there but it was a strain for him to enter into the fun, if such it was. He was taking his new responsibilities very seriously and more than once seemed to want to catch me on my own for a heart to heart, beginning on the first occasion by telling me how handy the money had come in. I wanted none of this but on my last evening, Virginia left us alone in the living room and as I was about to follow her, he frowned deeply, brought his fingertips together under his chin and said, 'We are sincerely most appreciative. I've had to take a significant reduction in earnings, you see, so I decided the most prudent course to follow was to extend the mortgage. The way I see it is I've worked it out as follows . . .'

This seemed a build-up to showing me a full set of household accounts so I hurried out to the kitchen with a murmur about potatoes and returned not too soon with a glass of wine for each of us. There wasn't, as I had feared, a large ledger open on his lap though he was leafing through the stubs in his cheque-book.

'Drink up,' I said. 'I must say it's good to see Virginia so happy.'

He smirked rather too readily, then assumed an intensely solemn air as if what he aimed to get on to next was how much he intended to set aside for her funeral.

'Yes,' he said. 'I think she's keen on more . . . on, well, quite a large family, more . . .'

'Children,' I suggested.

'Yes, that's it,' he said as if the idea hadn't occurred to him in quite those terms.

'Yes. And the job may not expand as fast as all that, though there's a chance of a raise in . . . it's a competitive business, stationery. We mainly deal in the basic products: exercise books, Scotch tape, paper clips, ballpoint pens, writing paper, that sort of thing, but there are some new products coming out. For example, you know jiffy bags, well . . .'

I crossed my knees tightly and stroked my knee very thoughtfully – which is what he was also doing, I realised too late. 'So she'll do the expanding, even if the business doesn't,' I said. 'How many might she have in mind? Just the half dozen or upwards of that?' I tried not to sound disapproving but at that moment I was not overcoming my revulsion at how much shagging there still was to come.

'Sort of three or four I think.'

'Sort of more or altogether?'

'We'll have to address that question as we go along I think.'

'Very wise. One whatsit at a time.' I kept the sarcasm out of my voice since it was clear he was taking me very seriously. In the long run, however, losing count of one's grandchildren would go along with other things not adding up. So that aspect of the topic too was not one I cared to keep on stream.

'We intend to plan our strategy very carefully,' he was saying.

More visions then of what exactly would have to be talked about and how and at what stage in the proceedings etc. Then there was the military imagery, softening up, thrusts, flanking movements, body counts, studying the calendar and the like. I saw them sitting at a table poring over charts covered in sums of money and rows of little stick people, some with triangular skirts. I went across and put a hand on his shoulder. He really did need cheering up.

'Whatever you decide will be all right by me,' I said.

'Thank you very much, Dad. I truly appreciate it.' No doubt at all he thought that was tremendously big of me.

At that point Virginia returned. 'As good as gold,' she said inappropriately.

'We've just been discussing . . .' he began.

I wasn't having any more of this nonsense.

' . . . the future,' I said. 'What else is there to look forward to . . . ?' And off I sped into the kitchen again. There was earnest muttering from the front room and I thought they might be forming a committee of which I would be asked to be treasurer. But of course they had nothing at all to worry about in any known scale of things.

So it went on. Those were happy days. I could see why Virginia wanted more children if that was the effect it had on her. Her approach to motherhood was quite different from her mother's. She was not sure or knowledgeable and never looked anything up in a book. She wanted to find out about it for herself. She had not had the baby at home or in a bathtub and her husband had not been present. 'He dreaded my asking him,' she told me. 'I couldn't have coped

387

with that too, his trying not to be squeamish and not knowing what to say to mother.'

About whom I then asked, had she been on balance slightly too helpful?

'Oh no, Dad,' she said. 'She's changed. She didn't interfere at all. She was marvellous actually, in the background doing things, but there . . . She's very worried about Brad who's very ill and not taking it well. He's bitter and unreasonable and she doesn't know how to deal with it. They were always deeply in love and she's simply very sad. She talked about you quite a lot.'

'Oh dear, how thoughtless when otherwise . . .'

She came and kissed me on the side of my forehead. 'She knows that with all her left-wing ideas and having all the answers and things, she was sometimes overbearing and humourless and dogmatic and then leaving you like that.'

'She did go on a bit about the television, grant you, but looking back I can see how right she was, wanting the world to be a better, kinder place and understanding why it wasn't. Perhaps it was just that the words weren't quite right, the tone of the voice, not hers, I mean, it was the vocabulary and then of course she must actually have done a lot to help and set an example and so forth. While I . . . But there were good times, weren't there?'

'Oh yes. Hundreds. She wanted Adrian and me to be happy, that's all, not just thoughtful and successful and *good*. Which can be boring for children and there were you bumbling about . . .'

'Thanks.'

'Well, you did rather dither and we never knew what you were really thinking . . .'

'Nor did I. Still don't, come to that.'

'We hated it when you split up and you took us out and it was so awkward and we didn't know what to talk about and Mum and Brad were so decent about it and then the accident. Adrian and I never talked about it though, the whole thing, there was just a sadness in the air and we had other things, adolescent things, to worry about and then there was his . . .'

'So you always knew about that?' She nodded. 'All of it?'

'Oh yes. Webb and all that and there were never any girlfriends. He was ashamed of it and miserable as soon as he realized, fairly early on. I can remember wondering why he never laughed at anything.'

'Was Mum any help, or Brad or whatever his name is, the demon driver?'

'Yes and no. They sent him for counselling and Brad kept on giving examples of famous homosexuals, the Greeks and writers and actors and so on, but that only seemed to make it worse since he didn't want to be famous or like any of those people.'

'Counselling. How perfectly frightful.'

'They call it "coming out" now, but Adrian only wanted to be left alone. You know what he's like. He didn't want to sign up for anything.'

'I should jolly well hope not.'

'Anyway it's all right with him now, isn't it?'

'Jane, you mean. That and the fact that he's going to be tremendously successful. He still doesn't give anything away. Perhaps sometimes he'd rather be shacked up with a bloke but sex, or whatever it's called these days, isn't everything.'

'Of course not.'

'Hold on though. Just running a quick check and so far nothing much else . . .'

Then the baby intervened and she bared her breast and manoeuvred the nipple into its mouth. My wife used to go away into another room to do that for which I was grateful to her, as for much else if only after the event. But I do not want to go any further into that since those days have been sufficiently recorded and I must not be tempted to write it all over again more generously to us all, less honestly as I have already said more than once so far as I can remember. But the question persists: what was the real truth of it? Our understanding of people and events we can alter with hindsight, or should we learn to settle for what was true to us at the time? On such matters I pondered as the baby finished feeding and I went upstairs to pack and waited with Virginia for the taxi to arrive. There was now only conversation to be made.

'Planning on a large family, are you?' I asked.

She blushed faintly. 'Yes, Dad, I think I am. Any views on the subject?'

'Sure you can cope, that's all. And what about your deaf people? There's a shortage of speech therapists I've been reading somewhere.'

She squeezed my hand. 'I can do both. I really believe I can.'

'There's my taxi. What view could I possibly have? From a great distance, the bumble-bee's of the marathon runner. Enough of that. Oh yes, and thanks and love to the proud father. He's a good bloke. You're a lucky woman.'

I could see she was glad I added that, though I'm not sure how far I meant it or she believed I did. And thus we parted. I gave a final wave as the taxi drove off and in that moment was overcome with a great fear for her. Not only that hers was such a happiness that could not last because it was too much, but because nothing lasted and in store for her, as for us all, was age and then the only end of age, as the poem says, and no meaning behind it all which we, the unbelievers, could ever decipher however much we thought about it or tried to write it up as I have been trying to do in all its ordinariness. She was smiling broadly and holding the baby up and it wore a stunned, bewildered look as if it already knew what life would be like much of the time.

And so I returned to Highbury to learn of the death of the Pole as I have already recounted. Virginia phoned as soon as I returned home simply to say how glad they had both been to see me and looking so well too. Her man had been told that day he had been given a rise and more responsibility, which meant that he would have to spend more time away from home. But that was the price that had to be paid. Yes, she was very happy and life went on. I think she was also telling me that they expected nothing more from me, money I mean. But one can never be sure of such things. It has to be in the back of one's mind. And these days I don't look the picture of health exactly, whatever my daughter says. They had not mentioned how much money he was still having to give to his mother. That was the most comforting aspect of it all somehow.

Chapter Four

I left it for four days before calling on the Pole's widow. I did not want to intrude too soon on her grief, or interfere – or to be bothered, was that it? I went down at about midday on my way to the launderette and rang the bell. After a long wait I was about to go away with a feeling of relief when the door opened slowly and I saw her for the first time. It is still my most vivid memory of her.

In the shadow of the doorway, she seemed simply curious at first, but as the door opened wider she raised her hand to her mouth as if to stifle a cry. Her black hair was parted in the middle and encircled her face like a cowl. Her dress too was black with a white lace collar high under her chin and it hung loosely as if handed down and still too big for her. In that first instant, she seemed to stare at me with hatred, then she slowly lowered her hand and I saw that her lips were quivering. They were thick with lipstick and her face was coated with powder and it was a terrified child that looked up at me, entreating my forgiveness. The words I had prepared sounded like gibberish, as she might hear them.

'My name is Tom Ripple. I live in the top flat. I knew your husband slightly. I just wanted to say how deeply sorry I am and please do not hesitate at any time if there is anything, anything at all, I can do to help.'

I had written my telephone number on a scrap of paper and offered it to her. She pressed her lips together and nodded but did not take it. For a moment she searched my face as if trying to recognize me. Then the fear seemed to sink within her, leaving a painted mask, blind and desolate. I was about to go but she opened the door wider and stepped to one side.

'Please,' she said.

There was no sign of occupancy in the front room as if it had been hastily tidied up and left empty for a long time. It was as if the dust had soaked into it and it was beyond the reach of light or air. There was a vase of what might once have been red roses on the television set and an empty decanter and row of glasses displayed on the sideboard like an unwanted wedding gift. The only picture on the walls was of distant sunlit mountains covered in snow but this too seemed blurred with dust, a sullied vision of grandeur. She had gone ahead of me and now turned at the entrance leading to the corridor.

'You like coffee?' she said, her voice hushed and stilted as if she was reading to herself from a phrasebook.

'No, thank you,' I said. 'Really, I just called to say . . .'

'Tea you like?'

I shook my head, unsure of what she expected of me. She stood there completely still, her hands clasped at her waist, the black dress hanging loose and lopsided, the lace collar curled up on one side, her face a child's again, wary, trying to remember its manners. I wished she would not stare at me so that I could leave her alone, my duty done.

'Please,' she said again and I followed her into the corridor and then into the room to the right. 'My husband room,' she said quietly, pointing at the closed door at the end of the corridor, as if he were in there working and was not to be disturbed.

The room she led me into was vivid with colours and as we entered the sun came out and bathed them with gold. The divan against the far wall was covered with a patchwork counterpane and half a dozen small cushions each with a different pattern of flowers and leaves. The two small armchairs on either side of it were scattered with branches coming into blossom and the sun shone through the half-drawn curtains striped in shades of silver and brown like trees in a forest. On the floor was a dark red and orange Persian carpet which gleamed as though under water. The room blazed like a garden run wild. There were real flowers too, a white azalea on the table and a red cyclamen on the ledge above the divan, both in full bloom. On the divan lay an unfinished tapestry of a white eagle on a red background, the wings and gold crown complete, the head and body and tail and claws a threadbare outline like a phantom coming to life. On a long shelf opposite the window various household items – balls of wool, an open sewing box, coloured bottles and jars – were neatly arrayed and I thought how capable she was of organizing her life, of surrounding herself with familiar comforts, of keeping herself busy.

392

And I thought too I had no business there and wherever she was she would create this little home for herself full of brightness and life. She had gone ahead of me to a kitchen beyond and now returned.

'I make coffee for you?' she said. 'Please you sit.'

I thought she was trying to smile but it was only a trembling of her lips, as if the room concealed something of which she was ashamed. She seemed to have no wish for me to stay but went out again, returned with a cup of coffee for me and sat opposite me on the divan, watching my hands as I raised the cup to my lips. I forget now exactly what I said, that it was a lovely room and what a fine day it was and how nice it had been to have a real winter again. She nodded slightly but said nothing, as if I was talking to someone else and if she were patient I would soon tell her why I was there. She lowered her eyes and gazed round the carpet as though looking for something that had fallen there. Then suddenly the powder seemed to crack, the wrinkles creasing across her forehead and from the corners of her eyes, the sunlight streaking her hair with grey. And as the mask crumbled, she became again a timid child who believed she could never again be loved or made happy.

'Shall you stay here?' I asked. She shook her head but it wasn't an answer or a denial. 'Perhaps there are friends you could go to?' But she continued to stare at the carpet and I thought I could not go on quizzing her like this, like some nosy welfare official. Perhaps that is what she thought I was, or that I had come to tell her she could no longer live here.

'Your husband said that you might like advice about your affairs, taxes, bills and things. I could easily . . . it would be no trouble.'

She stared at me as if reading my lips and I realized she barely understood me.

'Please?' she said, faintly.

I replied very slowly and deliberately. 'If you would like my help with your bills, papers, poll tax, electricity, gas, that sort of thing.'

'Sorry,' she said, 'I no understand.' I gave her the piece of paper with my telephone number on it and made a circular motion with my forefinger.

She nodded again and said, 'Thank you,' and followed me out into the corridor. I had almost reached the front room when she seized me sharply by the elbow and pointed to the door of her husband's room.

'There,' she said.

She opened the door and stood back. The lamp was still burning dimly on the desk where he had sat that day and poured vodka for me and waved his hand across the photographs on the walls. I turned round and she was right behind me. She now looked angry as she pointed to his desk and said, 'You see.'

The papers were strewn about as if he had been working on them when he died. She pointed abruptly at them as if what they contained was evil and dangerous, as if she blamed him for not taking them with him. I moved a pace forward and heard her close the door behind me.

I glanced at the papers – statements, invoices, bills, letters in Polish, pages of accounts – but I could not touch them as though his death had tainted them and they should be bundled away and burnt. I switched off the lamp and left. She was nowhere to be seen, so I called out 'Goodbye' from the front door and was half-way up the steps when I looked back and saw her watching me from the window. Her mouth was open and her hand was raised as if she was calling out to me. She seemed in that instant small and vague and far away like the people in the books her husband had shown me, exhausted by despair and the terror of abandonment.

On the way to the launderette, I tried to imagine her sitting in her bright little room and taking up her tapestry and stitching away at the eagle, waiting for the young people to return and those of her kind who would come and comfort her and take charge of her life. She wouldn't want to be troubled by strangers. The young people would be company. She would get over it. People did. But as I pushed open the door of the launderette and breathed in the clammy air of soap suds and stale clothes, I knew that none of this was true and that she had been crying out to me soundlessly, unaware that I was watching her.

As I made my way through to the office, the people glanced at me as though it was my fault they had to sit there observing their dirty clothes go round and round like that, their private lives made public. I have never seen people smile in a launderette or look at each other or talk. Like a doctor's waiting room, guessing or not wanting to guess the worst. 'Afternoon, all,' I said cheerily, then 'Lovely day.' No response of course. And it wasn't a lovely day of course, not the weather, which was neither one thing nor the other. It was the day the ground offensive was about to begin. On the floor the newspaper headline declaimed 'HIGH NOON!' Oh what an absolutely ripping time the media were having.

The owner was in the office with a man I had not seen before. They stopped talking but did not greet me as I got out the books and began working on them. I felt them staring at me behind my back and said cheerfully, 'A good month. Look at that. The best since October.'

The owner came and looked over my shoulder. 'The children are liking the snow very much but that is making more clothes to get dirty. But not eating in restaurant so much, staying home and watching telly.'

'Yes, you have a problem there. If you're not careful you'll have to start cooking the books.'

This was a joke he'd once made to me and it bore repeating. But not today. For weeks we had carefully avoided talking about anything but the business. I reminded myself of how much he still owed the bank and of the size of his family and then of the taunts his children might now be having to endure in school. I did not know what he thought but looking over my shoulder I saw the other man scowl at me. Only the figures in front of me put us on the same side, that and repeating a few weak jokes from happier times. He wished he had remembered to laugh, perhaps.

'More bad weather, wearing more clothes, more mucky, more money,' he said. 'It's a dirty business, this launderette. You help me to clean up, Mr Ripple, I hope.' He put a hand on my shoulder and I thought I heard a snort of disgust from the man behind him.

I laughed too loudly. 'Nobody's clothes are quite the same,' I said. 'But I'm sure they'll be able to iron out their differences.' I'd prepared this and I think he might have enjoyed it but the man behind him said sharply, 'This is not a time for jokes and foolishness.'

He pulled his hand away from my shoulder and they left me to it. One day perhaps we could enjoy the banter again but not soon, not for a long time.

I mentioned this episode to Adrian and Jane at supper that evening but they did not want to talk about the war. All Jane said was, 'It's the dreadful glee of it all. As if it was the latest war movie, but even better because real.'

Adrian watched her with the contented but incredulous expression of a man in love. Then he told me what was uppermost on his mind, that he had moved to another accountancy firm and it meant much more responsibility.

'Gone up in the world have you?' I said, taking out a handkerchief and mopping my eyes. 'Remember me, guv? Give us a fiver for old times' sake.'

Adrian made a face and Jane winked at him but they didn't want to say any more about that either. So to fill the silence, I told them about Mrs Bradecki and asked what they thought I should do.

Adrian looked at Jane, who sighed and said, 'I had a Polish friend at school and used to go round to their house sometimes. They were very kind to me but they never talked about the past as if their daughter should be shielded from it in my presence. She wouldn't tell me anything but I read about it and there were the films and so on. I've just thought sometimes that here we are, bickering and whinging away in our playpen with all our little envies and hatreds and pomposities, paddling in the shallows while out there in the ocean of history the ideas became monsters . . . I don't know. Perhaps they felt guilty that they'd escaped. My friend didn't talk about it simply, I think, because the subject bored her and she was ashamed of some of the Poles who came over and did nothing but complain and make demands: you have so much, we have so little. Besides she was exceedingly pretty and could have a marvellous time without . . . no, that sounds catty. I wasn't jealous. I liked tagging along. You could see how much her parents wanted her to enjoy herself, but at the same time it hurt them she turned her back on her origins. She even wanted to change her name because it was always pronounced wrong . . .'

'What happened to her?' Adrian asked.

'Drama school. I've seen her once or twice in small parts on television. Not the same name. Perhaps she's married. Children. Anything.'

'You didn't like her very much, did you?'

Jane thought for a moment. I had never heard her speak ill of anyone and now she chose her words with care. 'I think I began to disapprove. She was, in a general sense I mean, far too promiscuous for her own good, too available. She did not hold herself back. She was always in debt. I loved her, you see. It was as if she'd been set free from some long imprisonment and hadn't long to live. She had a tremendous sense of fun but she had to work at it all the time. I did rather get left behind.'

396

'Slept around, did she?' Adrian asked, as though trying out a new vocabulary. I remembered my golf club days, the banter at the bar. There was a slight drawl in his voice I hadn't heard before. Was he developing the first signs of self-importance?

Jane did not answer. There was something to be fetched from the kitchen and when she came back, she changed the subject to the recession. Mrs Bradecki was not mentioned again. They had listened attentively and Jane had said I should do what I thought best. Adrian had nodded.

More time has passed. The war was soon over. Negligible loss of life, it has been said – well, only the 100,000 or so Iraqis. There will probably be a victory parade since we've always done these things so well. I feel sorry for two or three of the television commentators (who shall remain nameless: I do not want to spoil my chances of being invited to take part in one of their programmes). However, I am sure they will soon find some other reason to display their self-infatuation, condescension, loftiness and smugness to the nation at large. Next time perhaps they'll make sure there isn't so much bloody ignorance in it too. I also feel sorry for the press. You could see what a satisfying time they were having too. They deserve their victory parade.

I am writing this some little time after the event. The day after my evening with Jane and Adrian, I caught bronchitis, which led to pneumonia and an anti-smoking campaign. (I am not sufficiently enjoying my first armistice cheroot right now.) It has been no time for scribbling, or come to that for anything that might be described as thought. There must be times in everyone's life when one just sort of mentally waddles on regardless, living by rather than for the moment, if that can be called living, though there is peace in it when you get to my age and living is increasingly something you once did or thought at the time you were doing, or would have got round to doing if you'd thought about it. I worried about others even less than I usually do, but illness is like that, the discomfort and fatigue and premonition there is in it. It should extend the common ground but it didn't, not in my case. I was not ennobled by it. I never expected to find my name in the Honours List of life. Now I must try to continue scribbling. It helps to convince me that I have any thoughts or ideas (though that would be pushing it a bit) at all. Or life for that matter, if that means some sense of continuity. Otherwise there'd just be the moment: sensations, memories, feelings, the task in hand plus desires of course. Now you see them, now you don't. More flux than fucks (I may or not leave that in if I go over this bit again. It really belongs somewhere else where I am addressing more basic matters). So I ramble on because it seems to hold the muddle together, or that small part of it that can momentarily be held, and becomes all the evidence there is. Of what, I hear you ask. 'Why don't you piss off?' is the approximate answer to that.

But my illness had one happy aspect. The ballerinas have been very quiet because they know I have been sick. I had asked Annelise to get me some pills from the chemist. She was very kind and came up every day after that to ask if I wanted anything. I thought what a good nurse she'd make if there was one bish too many one day and she was banished from the Garden, as she calls it. I had borrowed a videotape of Rudolf Nureyev and Margot Fonteyn dancing excerpts with the Royal Ballet and could see how the smallest bish in the chorus would spoil the whole show, which might explain that look of cautious rapture they all wore. I thought too how some other occupation might give her back some of her colour and flesh (not to put too fine a point on it). I was feverish at the time, you understand, and it was she who kept me company in both body and spirit.

She used to come in for a few moments and look around her at the dreadful shambles the place was in. Perhaps I made her feel better, wheezing and flabby and unkempt in the yellow towelling dressing gown I had bought for Maureen's benefit, now stained and creased and mangy looking – a fitting extension of myself, in short, suffering too as I was then from a bad case of the adjectives which always seem to come in threes. Once she ordered me to bed and fetched me a hot drink. It was then I showed her the videotape. Margot Fonteyn had just died. I began saying how absolutely lovely she was but this brought on a fit of coughing while she gazed at the cover of the tape and I thought through the tears my coughing had brought on that there were tears in her eyes too.

When I had spluttered and gasped to an end, she patted the blanket where my knee was and said, 'My parents wanted me to be like her, someone very special. My father even invented a name for me and sometimes called me his little Margot when I started lessons and everyone said I was so full of promise. You remind me of him in some ways. He is dead now.'

I mopped my eyes and said, 'Thanks for that. My father was a grocer and wanted me to be prime minister but the competition further south had the same idea.'

She let out a brief, shrill laugh and caused me to spill a large spoonful of Lemsip on to my dressing gown, at least the right colour. All this brought on a fresh bout of coughing with a great deal of phlegm in it so I waved her away. She looked back at me from the door and twiddled her fingers at me. The combination of pity and amusement on her pale, forlorn little face helped me to sleep in the usual manner and is with me still.

I had more or less forgotten Mrs Bradecki when some weeks later I was returning from a convalescent shuffle round the block and met Foster at the front door.

'You do look like death bloody warmed up,' he said. 'Been ill or something?'

'Pneumonia,' I said.

'Know what they call that? The old people's friend.'

'I had the other kind.'

He was looking particularly fit and dapper and, my walk having left me tired and breathless, I felt like giving his grey silk cravat a sharp, tightening tug.

'You should give up those crappy little cigars of yours.'

'I have.'

'Changed my life, giving up smoking did. Got up the wife's nose. Clean living that's the thing. You could go to pot in Africa easy as that.' He snapped his fingers close to my nose. 'The outdoor life, the whole of bloody Africa out there for the taking. Live hard, play hard.'

I went through the motion of gently serving a tennis ball. 'Fishing,' he almost shouted. 'Don't call that exercise. Talking of which, how are our cute little chorus girls these days? Giving you any trouble?'

'None at all.'

'I should bloody well hope not. Said you were a good mate of mine and any complaints they were out on their dainty little bottoms. I could get twenty quid more for that flat, or sell it off, couldn't I? You know what you paid for yours. Well then. So just say the word, old fruit.'

'Thanks, now if . . .'

He held me by the elbow. 'Madam Polack now. No rent from that quarter since the old boy snuffed it. Well grief is grief, say I, but it doesn't make the world go round. Had a word with her the other day, soul of tact I was. Trouble is that after all these years she hardly speaks a word of bloody English or pretends she can't. Eyes jumping all over me as if I was covered in insects. Sad really when you come to think of it, but can't hang about for ever waiting for the tears to dry up.'

At that point a boy and a girl came up the steps from the flat whispering fast in Polish. They looked up at us with alarm and I said '*Dzień dobry,*' which they repeated with broad smiles, the girl adding, 'Good morning. It is a very nice day, isn't it?'

Which in that instant it then became. As they hurried off down the street, chatting loud and fast, Foster looked after them with an even more contemptuous expression than usual.

'That's the other thing, isn't it? Half a mind to ask to see their work permits. But then, good luck to them and all that. What do you think?'

I recalled their eager, grateful smiles. 'I don't see the harm in it. Just a few . . .'

His face darkened. 'A few, is it? You could have fooled me. The girls. You know what they're after, don't you? Bloody husbands. Citizenship. That's a thought, eh, Ripple, my lad? A pretty little Polish lass to tuck you up at night and cook your breakfast and lots of lovely cock-a-doodle-do in between.'

I watched them turn the corner, hand in hand, and moving very fast. Foster was glaring at me, accurately reading my thoughts, which I tried to offset with a wince of disapproval and a 'ts'.

'Don't tell me,' he said, gripping my elbow. 'Hardly bears thinking about. Anyway, now's your chance. The place won't be a doss-house for cheap Slav labour much longer, if I have owt to do with it.' He pushed his face closer as if it was I who was under threat. 'Get the message? If I were you . . .'

He released my elbow and opened the door. I gave him what I hoped was a neutral smile which probably came over as wholly servile. One of his willy wet-legs in a word.

And so I felt obliged to pay Mrs Bradecki a second visit, or rather failed after three tough days of inner debate to argue myself out of it.

It was as if she had been expecting me for she led me through immediately to her husband's room where the papers lay as I had left
them. The lamp had been turned on again. On the floor inside the
door were several unopened envelopes, which she picked up and
gave me. So far we had not said a word and I had hardly caught a
glimpse of her face, which she seemed to want to keep hidden from
me. Now, as she began closing the door behind me, she stared past
me at the desk as if she had just woken up in a strange place and
remembered she would never see her husband again. But there was
no grief on her face now, simply a paralysed bewilderment and I
would no more have spoken to her then than I would to a corpse.

The door closed and I looked around me. At the edge of the desk
was a half-empty bottle of vodka and a glass lying on its side. There
was another glass on the floor. On the small table beside the chair
where I had sat was the full glass where I had left it and the book he
had given me about the Warsaw ghetto, the page still open at a photograph of three young women and two boys who were about to be shot.
There had been that look on her face too, on the dumb far side of terror.

The papers told their story soon enough. There was a bank statement showing a balance of £957 and two building society accounts,
one in his name and one in hers, with about £10,000 in each. There
were unpaid electricity, water, TV rental and gas bills. Their television licence and community charge had been paid. In a neatly kept
rent book he had recorded his monthly household expenses: the rent
was £600 overdue. There was a file for a Polish club he belonged to
with half the correspondence in Polish and half in English. He
seemed to have been on its board of management. Nothing there to
detain me. There were also two box files containing letters going back
several years about visa applications, most with a tick in the top
right-hand corner and a few with a cross, the former having attached
to them a copy of either a letter of invitation from several different
names and addresses to the British Consulate in Warsaw, or of a letter
of recommendation to some other address in Britain. There was an
index of names and dates on the inside cover of one of the files and
there must have been several hundred names in all. He was apparently at the centre of some network; of interest to Foster no doubt, but
of no concern to me.

In another set of files, bound together in white ribbon, was a record
of his earnings and his income tax returns, all meticulously kept to

the smallest detail. On the inside front cover he had stapled a copy of his advertisement in the local paper: his name, address and telephone number followed by 'All electrical and plumbing services plus household repairs, decorating and carpentry. Twenty-four hour service. Lowest prices.' He had evidently been the only man in England to report all his cash earnings, indeed any of them, to the Inland Revenue. The same may be true of Scotland and Wales, though I cannot swear to this. There was no sign of any life insurance policy.

There was also a file containing his RAF papers and his medals. They included a letter of commendation from Air Chief Marshal Dowding and another from the king. The signatures might even have been original. One of the medals I recognized as the Distinguished Flying Cross and the bar half-way up the ribbon presumably showed he had won it twice. I glanced up at one of the photographs above the desk – all those indistinct, grinning, daredevil faces. They seemed to be having the most tremendous fun, but somehow it all had a swindled look. In the background was an aeroplane riddled with bullet holes. I wondered what had happened to them all. I looked for his face among them and could not find it.

He had been ready for death and had tidied his life away. I imagined him laying it all out for me so that I could quickly see what had to be done. My task would soon be complete: letters to the Social Security, local authority, Inland Revenue, bank and building societies, the bills to be settled. But at the back of my mind I knew that £20,000 would not allow her to stay where she was indefinitely, even if she kept up the stream of lodgers and they contributed to her rent. That was no business of mine. Surely the Polish Club would be keeping an eye on her or what was it for? I remembered his last words to me. 'Take her back! Take her back!' At the time it had seemed simply part of the act. Now it was laughable, except that there was nothing funny about it at all.

I knocked on her door. She opened it cautiously and at first did not seem to want me to come in. 'I've been through the papers,' I said. 'Everything is in order but there are one or two . . .' I held out the bills and realized that I had spoken much too loudly and slowly as if she were a simpleton, or I was, simpletons together. But that was how she looked, her mouth hanging open and her eyes narrowed as if she had forgotten who I was or had been expecting someone else, hearing noises from her husband's room. Then she looked up at me and whispered, 'Come in, please.'

The curtains were drawn and all the colours had faded as if summer had given way to a sodden grey autumn. She was still wearing her loose black dress and lopsided collar and stood sideways to me gazing at the curtains as though they were open and she was searching for something in a dim landscape a long way off. Her shoulders were outlined through her dress, rising and falling and I could hear the shivering sound of her breathing.

'Would you like me to come back some other time?' I asked.

She shook her head, then turned and said very calmly, 'Please you sit.'

Her eyes seemed disdainful now as if she had decided to treat me as some insignificant minor official who was only doing his job, which suited me fine. I perched on the edge of the chair and fingered the papers, then slowly began telling her what needed to be done. I offered to write all the necessary letters and then asked if she'd like me to prepare the cheques now. She nodded so I wrote them out and handed her the cheque-book. She added her signature very slowly, pressing the pen into the paper as though she was signing against her will. She gave me back the cheque-book with a shrug as if it was too late now to change her mind.

I stood up and said, 'I'll send all these off and let you have copies of the letters. There is really nothing at all to worry about. I've arranged the files on the desk, so you know which is . . .'

But she wasn't listening and went past me to show me out. At the front door she raised her hand and withdrew it as my fingers touched hers. Her eyes were half-closed and she did not look at me. I had not asked her how she would live or whether she had anyone else to turn to because she wouldn't have understood what that had to do with me. I had done my duty and expected no gratitude. She wanted me to know perhaps that she understood the limits of duty. Or worse than that, my indifference. Well, that was her problem. Such were my thoughts, and the shame that went with them, when I reached the top of the steps and met the girl I had greeted a couple of weeks before. She smiled at me with intense longing, or politely it might have been.

'Ah,' I said, 'I've just been to see . . . I hope . . . Are you, do you think . . . ? Is there . . . ? I was wondering if there's . . . Are you staying here long . . . ?'

While this lucid questionnaire was going on, she continued to smile at me, which became the confusion itself of course, her limpid (?) blue eyes alight with expectation, the glimpse of teeth between her lips, each delicate crease or wrinkle . . . 'Want to become a British citizen, do you?' I succeeded in not adding.

'I am here for three months for short stay and English student. I am very interesting in your country.'

'Frankly, I think you'd be jolly interesting in any country.'

'Please?'

Excuse now for a wink or whatever. I put a finger to my lips. 'You're not working of course, are you?' Then the wink. She looked away.

'Absolutely I cannot work, only sightseeing and tourist and learning English.'

I tried again. 'Mrs Bradecki. Is she your relative? I wonder if you happen to know who is now responsible for her?'

'Responsible? My relative, Mr Bradecki invited me as his guest, and my friend too. He is a very kind man. He wrote he is responsible.'

'Not any longer he isn't. Who is going to look after Mrs Bradecki now, I think that's what I'm asking.'

'Soon I go back to Poland. I am Maria. Maria Wysinska.'

Somewhere along the line the smile had narrowed into mistrust. Why don't we continue this conversation up in my . . . 'Make a lot of money, did you?' I asked.

She blushed. 'No much money,' she said.

'That's Mrs Bradecki's problem too, you see, so I wondered . . .'

She frowned, delaying our betrothal even further. 'Mr Bradecki say he did not want money. Poland needs money. My boyfriend is starting a business. I am going to have language school.'

'I wish you luck,' I said, doing a chummy thing with my eyebrows.

This cheered her up and she said, 'You can come to my country too. My boyfriend says we need foreign capital and stock exchange for making a market economy and learning management know-how for small business and command economy with state enterprise is useless.'

'Lots there to get one's teeth into by the sound of it. But it was kind of you to ask. Do you . . . ?'

But she left me then and I watched her trip down the steps and let herself in. No hope for Mrs B from that quarter, I thought, but for the future of Poland it might be another matter.

Her affairs were soon settled. Everyone was very prompt and helpful. I visited her again and set up a simple filing system for her. I pointed out how much money she had but drew no conclusions from it. Once or twice she said, 'Yes, I understand,' watching me as if reading my lips and frowning slightly, stroking the papers on her lap but hardly glancing at them. Still she did not thank me. I did not mind this for I did not exist for her except as some agent of fate in the absence of somebody else. I began to wish, oh yes, that she did not exist for me either. We were like actors rehearsing for two utterly different plays. Once I saw her in the local supermarket, choosing very little very carefully. In her dark brown overcoat with perhaps the same black dress showing beneath it, she seemed so conspicuous and diminished as she intently examined the shelves, constantly putting out a hand and changing her mind, then peering again to examine the label. She was wearing a black scarf so I only caught a glimpse of her face. Her black, darting eyes seemed angry that she should be reduced to such trivial choices and for herself alone. But it was something beyond anger or despair and was quite beyond my understanding. She was like a refugee who had wandered from those terrible black photographs into this sumptuous paradise which was the measure of the best life we knew, I and the other customers there, and there could be nothing more foreign to us than she was, or unsettling, or ignorable. When she began coming towards me I went quickly up the next aisle to avoid her. To save her the embarrassment of surprise, of not knowing what to say? Of course not. It was to spare myself . . .

It has taken me several evenings, in between some quite good television, to try to put all this into words in the hope that once having done so I would be left in peace, not only to watch television but also to do some reading and to listen to some 'good music'. This usually reminds me of Maureen of course. Piano music is my favourite. Schubert and Chopin though there are a violin and a cello sonata or two I like as well, in fact a very great deal, though more, I suppose, for the memories they seem to arouse than for what they are in themselves. Not only of Maureen but in a more general way, of some world of longing and love which I have completely missed out on but which I must once have got some inkling of. I have about thirty records and tapes now. If I met Maureen again I think we would get on better this time or for longer. I do not know why I don't phone her for old times' sake, invite her to a concert out of the blue. In case you hadn't suspected, it's what might happen afterwards or later, or mightn't or certainly wouldn't that I think about too. Or a bloke might answer the phone or she'd give me the brush-off. Not worth the risk. I can't trouble Jane with it, not again. She has full confidence in me. Not so Foster.

Foster glanced at the cheque for the rent as if it might be a forgery, then folded it twice and put it in his top pocket.

'Wouldn't get too involved if I were you,' he said. 'Do people a favour and they become dependent. Came across it in Africa. Rescued a man from drowning once, decent old cove really with four wives and children you gave up counting. Never left me alone after that, old clothes, money, school fees for the kids, tin of fruit, any damn thing. All right up to a point but in the end I had to tell him to bugger off. Walked in all the way from his village. At least twenty miles. Went on coming to see the wife when I was on tour. Brought one or two of the kids with him. The ones with something wrong with them. Bloody great big ulcers. That sort of thing. The wife had a soft spot for things like that. Saw the old chap skulking about one evening. Didn't say anything of course. We didn't go into things like that. You see, she had sod all going for her, did she, and dishing out aspirins and ointment, the odd bob or two, salts, cough mixture, added something extra. But she made a home for us, no doddle that, I can tell you, in the middle of bloody nowhere. Especially the garden. Lovely that was. She wouldn't have servants, not at first. Then later, about the time Dickenson died . . . so I turned a blind eye to all the charity palaver. She needed her own life. Had a heart of gold really. So what I'm telling you is watch the dependence unless you've got a bob or two to spare. Mind you, retired accountants usually do. Suffering can get you down if you don't watch it. Like poor old Dickenson, told you what happened to him, didn't I? So she can't stay on there for ever, can she now?'

'I'm sure it can all be sorted out. Don't worry about me, I'm as hard-hearted as they come.'

'Done your duty, have you? Glad to hear it. Not so bloody common these days, sense of duty. All right, I'll give her a couple of months. So give her the message, will you? Asked her myself what her plans were, very tactful I was, don't fret yourself, but might as well have been talking to a brick wall. Had a lot of time for that husband of hers. Lot to be said for Polaks.'

I nodded as if agreeing with every word. 'It's hit her pretty hard . . .'

'Stands to reason, doesn't it? Must be off now. Keep up the good work.'

That evening I listened to some Beethoven played by a pianist called Brendel. This should have helped me to think big but had the opposite effect. It had not been a good day at the launderette either. The same man was there again and while I tried to get on with my work he started waving his arms about and ranting on about the filthy Zionist Americans and Saddam Hussein was a great man and the Muslims in Britain were treated like dirt and then, lowering his voice, with a hiss followed by a gurgle, he mentioned the name of Salman Rushdie. The owner kept on trying to silence him, glancing at me and saying, 'I agree, I agree.' I was surprised he went on like that with me in the room, not being noticeably of Arab stock. But true anger is like that; it doesn't matter who is listening in. He began swearing revenge and I wished I could believe he might be drunk. I then decided to stop working and turned to listen to him. Suddenly he seemed to become aware of my presence for the first time and shrugged and fell silent.

Then there was a long pause and tears came into his eyes and he said to me, 'I am sorry. I am only very sad. All the glory and thanksgiving of the soldiers coming home, having bashed the towelheads. How would you be feeling, sir? My son in school is called Saddam and my daughter is asked where she has parked her camel. They are called Muzzies. They cry and they are frightened.'

'Not all the other children surely?' I asked quietly.

'It is enough to be murdered by one or two people, isn't it?'

The owner looked at me with shame. 'He is not meaning what he say about Saddam Hussein, Mr Ripple.'

The visitor shook his head and a tear spilled down his cheek. He mopped his eyes, shook my hand and left. My uppermost thought was that this was somewhere I should not be. I wanted to be home again, listening to music, hoping it was not so loud as to disturb the dancers but loud enough that they would know me to be a cultured chap.

I wonder whether I should go in for CDs. I cannot see myself acquiring many more records since I'm getting to like the ones I have a little bit more on every playing. In fact, each time I listen to them, the more I hear in them. This could go on and there is only so much time one has. And some of it, as now (*The Holberg Suite* by Grieg), draws me back, as I've tried to explain, to time lost and vanished happiness, but somehow it is for all loss, what never was or might have been or came and went very swiftly. I wish there was a way of connecting what I'm listening to now and what I feel about it to the angry Muslim. If my former wife were here, perhaps I could put this question to her. She might not think it altogether silly now, while undermining her respect for the interest I was beginning to take in the arts.

Chapter Five

I have called by to see the widow again on three occasions. The young people seem to have vanished and the front room smells damp and stale as if it hasn't been occupied for years. On each occasion she showed me to her husband's room where some fresh bills or correspondence were laid out for my attention. Much of it was junk mail which I threw into the waste-paper basket. As I came and left, I tried to make conversation: the weather, the poll tax, some news item on the television about her part of the world – but she did not respond. Or I tried slipping in some questions: did she have friends to visit, what had happened to the lodgers, was she thinking of returning to Poland some time? But I do not think she heard them as questions. She had closed herself off, her body draped in that worn black dress with the high warped collar, her hands locked together like a knot of bones gripping the last of her strength, her face hidden from me like nakedness. Still she has not thanked me nor again offered me coffee. I am sure now she thinks I am an official of some kind with a job to do. There is little now to be read into her eyes: a fleeting obstinacy perhaps or perplexed innocence. She has only spoken to me twice. On the first occasion I said that her poll tax bill might come down but the government hadn't made up its mind, that it didn't used to be like that under the former regime. I was in the doorway of her room where she sat with a new eagle tapestry on her lap, this time beginning with the golden beak.

'Always we pay taxes,' she said with hardly more than a whisper, watching her hand pull tight the golden thread. 'Some people too much money.'

This was my opening but I did not take it. One day soon Foster would increase her rent, or worse but oh my God, I said to myself again and again, I don't want it to have anything to do with me. This time she followed me to the door and touched me on the arm.

'Passport no good?' she said.

I had once mentioned this to her as a way of finding out if she was thinking of returning to Poland, as her husband had wished. So the question seemed promising but then I realized she was simply afraid it was illegal to possess an out of date passport.

'Miles out of date, I'm afraid. Tell you what. I'll get you a form and we'll fill it in together. But you'll have to get a new photograph taken.'

So today this is what we have done. I took her to a photographer with a bald head and eyebrows in a constant state of the highest surprise above small granny spectacles. He showed me the photographs and her face stared out at me, the mouth twisted, as if the lace collar was strangling her.

'Would you like me to do these again?' he said. 'In passports one isn't supposed to be expressive or whatever you call it. I'm something of an art photographer too, if you can credit the fact and I catch faces like that, showing emotion. Unguarded's the word. Kids of course, they make funny faces like that, trying it on before they've felt it or in that general area.'

'Perhaps you should,' I said. We looked at her standing at the window staring out into the street as if waiting for someone.

'I only said a touch of a smile because she was glaring at the camera like God knows what as though I was going to shoot her or something. Quite a face. Relative is she?' I did not respond. 'Well, let me tell you, I've made quite a study of faces. Had an exhibition once in one of the local galleries. So I know whereof I speak. Breath of sea air, a good square meal, have herself a bit of fun and sun. None of my business but like I say I know my human countenance.'

'On second thoughts, don't bother,' I said. 'She probably isn't going anywhere.'

'Not English, is she?' he said, putting the photographs in a small brown envelope.

'Why do you say that?'

'Like I say, I know my physiognomy. Jewish. Armenian. One of those. The old fashioned dress, heavy shoes for a start.'

'She's a cousin of mine actually. From Derbyshire. Farming stock.'

He scrutinised me carefully. 'Could have fooled me. You don't seem the exotic type exactly. No harm in that. On the contrary.'

I put the photographs in my pocket and turned to leave.

'Thinking of paying were you?' he said. 'Or not, as the case may be.'

He had said it jocularly but I coloured nonetheless. 'Oh,' I replied casually. 'So they have to be paid for these days, do they? Snapshots. You might have warned me. You're not the only photographer in these 'ere parts as they say in Derbyshire.'

'Yeah, I know that,' he replied, putting on an accent somewhere between Dorset and the Deep South. 'But I guess you'll find we're all the same these days, working for money.'

'Good God! You can't be serious. It's the overheads, is it?'

'Not really, it doesn't make much difference whether they wear hats or not.'

I acknowledged that one with a tap of his arm and we left. We went straight back to fill in the form. She sat opposite me on the sofa in her familiar posture, hunched, leaning forward, hands clenched, answering my questions with a whisper. She would not look at me. None of it seemed to matter to her now. As soon as the passport arrived she would bind it with her husband's in an elastic band and put it away at the back of his desk.

When we had finished, I prepared the envelope and took a last look at the photograph, the inane half-grin a grimace of submission.

'Now is all right,' she said.

I smiled at her, hoping for a smile in return but she reached for her tapestry and began to work on it as if she were quite alone. She did not see me to the door and I hurried back to my flat, wanting above all to shake off the memory of her. Spring was in the air. I was overcome with longing to walk in Kew Gardens or on the Heath, to bring back my own memories, to restore me to myself. I put on a record. Mozart. I had bought an interesting new novel. There was some promising telly coming up so I did not go for a walk. I listened to the Mozart twice.

I am writing this two weeks later. I haven't been feeling all that well and tell myself it's the remains of the pneumonia. Yesterday the doctor told me to take a good long holiday as if I was slaving away somewhere and am not on perpetual holiday already. I seem not to have the energy I once had though admittedly there used to be such huge quantities of it that a little less should hardly notice. I feel like a good night's sleep just after I've woken up from a good night's sleep.

The pains in my chest are usually relieved by a swig of Wyeth Mucaine 500 ml suspension which contains Oxethazine, Aluminum Hydroxide Mixture BP and Magnesium Hydroxide BP which you'd think should cure just about everything though I suspect there may be too much Hydroxide BP in it. There is a pain like heartburn, milder, which comes and goes and is helped by a swig of whisky rather than the above so on the whole I prefer it. Like my dreadful cheroots I often get puffed but I'm cutting down on them, lighting a stub when I feel like another, or another instead so that as soon as possible it becomes a stub. I am cutting down on the drink too, more soda and ice added when the glass is half full until what I am drinking is iced water. However this whole procedure starts earlier and ends later so the bottle itself does not seem to last that much longer. The more exercise my bladder demands, the less the rest of me gets. If I saw the doctor again he would tell me what I can pretty well guess already: that I'm not getting any younger and I ought to look after myself. Also, if you hadn't noticed, this writing is not getting any easier which has to do with reading more and finding out how the professionals do it. They seem to have such a big vocabulary though sometimes the words in all their craft and abundance get in the way so that that is what you notice as if behind them they were trying to hide some lack or shortage: like wondering why someone should take quite so much trouble over their dress. Who are they trying to impress? But in the main, it takes up too much time and the writing not getting any easier has to do with other things, namely not getting any younger and not feeling like it and having other things to do etc. Or not to do, rather. Actually though, what it has to do with is not being able to find oneself more and more fascinating as the years pass, indeed just the opposite. And all this is a way of not getting round to relating what occurred late yesterday afternoon.

I was returning from the launderette when the Polish girl called up to me from the window of the Bradeckis' flat. There was absolutely no doubting how thrilled she was to see me again after our long and cruel separation. A few moments later she joined me in the street looking flushed with desire, our betrothal imminent. Right beside us was the Volvo which meant that Foster might have us in his sights. I took a very deep breath and did not say any of a wide range of complimentary things about her new frizzy, or uncombed, hairstyle which zig-zagged downwards on one side towards where the top two buttons of her blouse were undone, the spring weather permitting that, then glanced back up again to the blatant lust in her eyes and parted lips and variations of the flush, then down again to whatever might have been made more accessible to the spring breeze . . .

'Yup,' was how I summed all that up, her having said something. Then, 'I thought you had left.'

As if reading my thoughts, she made her lips disappear and screwed up her eyes which gave her an old and ugly look, to set up a contrast or something.

'Please sir. I am sorry to troubling you but here is a letter for Mrs Bradecka from my mother in Poland saying she can visit a friend, old lady who is there. My mother is writing to me to show the letter to Mrs Bradecka. It is in English of course.'

'Excellent,' I said.

'She is not wanting to go.'

'That's rather up to her, isn't it?'

She drew close and through the breeze, I got a whiff of her breath or of what she had added to herself, or of herself. 'She is afraid if somebody is not going with her.'

'What could be better?' I said, not wanting to clear the huskiness in my voice with a crude cough. 'You're about to return yourself. She'll have her passport in a day or two. I'll help with the ticket and visa. Order a mini-cab. Bob's your uncle.'

'My uncle is very sick in Ealing. My mother is there who can meet her. She is a very good English teacher and translator for you.'

'So you will be able to take her?'

She shook her head. 'Soon I must go. Visa problem.'

'Ho ho, caught up with you, have they? Just give me a date and I'll see if I can't fix it all up in no time.' The wistful tone in my voice came out as weary bank-managerial. I was appalled to see I was rubbing my hands.

'Maybe I go to Germany,' she said. 'With my boy-friend.'

'Ooh, I wouldn't do that if I were you.'

'Please, Mr Ripple, you go with her,' she said. 'She never go otherwise.' She drew closer. That whiff again. I confirmed: definitely no bra. She knew I had.

'Oh no, I could never do that. You see . . .'

413

There was a pause while we both looked at the window of Foster's flat. He was quite clearly there, silhouetted beyond his lace curtains. A couple on the other side of the street were staring at us too, nosy twerps. I tried to draw back from her but she laid a hand on my wrist where it was stark naked, and let it rest there, lightly, tenderly. Then she took it away and said, 'I give you my mother's telephone number. She is meeting you and taking you to best hotel. Four star. Warsaw is a very nice city now with shopping everywhere, supermarkets and old town and churches and restaurants and castle and casinos and park where Chopin's statue is and very big opera . . .' These run rapidly past me as she scanned my face to discern where in all that my interests might lie.

'Hold on a sec . . .' I began, but she pointed to the pen in my pocket and, under Foster's close scrutiny, I gave it to her and she reached inside a fold of her skirt and brought out a page of a letter on which she wrote an address and telephone number hastily in mid-air while I don't think I said, as the pen dried up and she shook it, 'Come along up to my room and we'll fix a date for the wedding. Do they have sex before marriage in Poland?'

She finished writing, gave me the letter and said, 'Thank you very much Mr Ripple. Mrs Bradecka is saying you are very helpful man.'

Then she left me and went back down the steps. She did not look back. My hand was raised in vain. The smell lingered, whatever it was. As did I, to stay with it: dried petals, cold cream, orange juice, a hint of toffee or sour mouth-smell and the thing was I could imagine it in perpetuity . . . Come along, I have a book to get written. It is late now. Down to the last ice-cube. The page of the letter is beside me now, the address and telephone number scrawled in the margin. All the lights are out opposite, bar two and their curtains are closed.

When I finally untransfixed myself and went back up to my flat, Foster was standing in his doorway.

'How's tricks?' he asked.

'Fine,' I said.

'Not as young as we were,' he said, giving me that scornful stare of his.

'How do you figure that out?' I asked, my onward progress barely faltering.

'It's how others see us, really.'

'Ah, I hadn't thought of that.'

414

I went up the stairs briskly two at a time, greatly regretting this as soon as I turned the corner. It was only a slight pain but persistent and I didn't feel like any supper or rather any supper that was available to me. It's all right now, the last cheroot extinguished, the last ice-cube crunched, the binoculars back in their case. I wish that smell would go away.

Ten days have passed. In the end I decided to have another word with Jane about Mrs Bradecki. I read her the page of the letter. There was a touch of irritation in her voice when she said, 'Oh Dad, what on earth are you waiting for?' Then she added, 'What fun! I mean Poland. Do you the world of good.' From anyone else I might have taken exception to that as if I was lacking some key factor in my life, had been found wanting. Bloody ridiculous. The next day I spoke to Adrian, hoping for a view from him too but he only said he was keeping busy and mentioned a Kuwaiti and a Japanese bank in the same sentence, sounding much alike. There was an edge in his voice. Had he and Jane fallen out? The thought was dreadful. Adrian hurt is so easy to imagine and remember.

Now to the letter: '*Please tell Mrs Bradecka that I am very sorry that her husband has died and he will now never see Poland again. He was always very kind to help you and other people to come to England. Everything is different now but some say it is not better. There are too many problems with the economy and political disagreements. Perhaps Mr Wałęsa will do something. I hope education is not everything and some of the other leaders are too intelligent in a way so they are always disagreeing. Money is a problem for us and many people but some people in Warsaw have got it. You can see the new shops everywhere and thousands all over the streets. There is a lady who came to see me the other day who knew Mrs Bradecka a long time ago in the war. She is alone now and has no children. Her husband was nomenklatura but he is dead now. Her name is Anna Konopka. She thinks that Mrs Bradecka can come and see her now that her husband is dead. She wrote once before but there was no reply and Mr Bradecki would not have liked . . . *'

It was only then I realized that the letter could only have been in English for my benefit and at Maria's instigation. And so finally I went down to see Mrs Bradecki again this evening. We sat in her artificial little garden as the sunlight left it and the colours dimmed into each other. It was a warm room but I felt chilly as if we had stayed outside too long through the twilight. I was as direct as I knew how, giving her the letter and asking her if she would like me to arrange her ticket and visa. She responded with the faintest of nods, avoiding my eye. I told her I would order a cab, that I would phone the number in Warsaw with her date and time of arrival. In the dying light her face and hands stood out whitely against the fading flowers and she began to breathe heavily. At first I thought she was trying to control her shivering but then I realized she was weeping, the streaks of light down her cheeks, her eyes wide open staring down at her knotted hands. She was utterly still now and made no sound, just letting the tears fall. She was on her own, deep into her past. A tear dropped onto her hands. Still she did not move. It was as if she was hardening herself, letting her whole life shed itself out of her. Perhaps I should have put my arm round her but she seemed so distant and alien I just sat there watching the tears fall onto her knuckles. It was not for more than perhaps half a minute but I remember it now as the whole length of the passing from light to darkness. Finally, I stood up and said, 'Please don't worry. Leave it to me.'

When I reached the front door I looked back. She was standing where I had seen her husband that evening, outlined against the dim lamp in the corridor leading to his room, the red shade dangling above her like a funny hat.

'You come with me,' she said very clearly and firmly. There was no emotion in her voice. It was matter-of-fact, a simple command.

'Of course.' I said. 'If you would like me to.'

And now, at one in the morning, no lights on in the houses opposite. I sit at this typewriter, unable to sleep, and think only that I wish I hadn't said that, that I will get out of it somehow. And then I hear Jane's voice saying it will do me the world of good and see Maria gazing up at me with that expectant innocence and the rise of bare flesh beneath her blouse. And I know I have absolutely no choice in the matter. There is so much I am missing. It is the insufficiency of what I know as unhappiness, or its short-lastingness perhaps.

This is the eve of our departure. I bumped into Annelise this morning. It seemed a long time since I had last seen her. I told her I was off to Warsaw in what I hoped was a worldly manner.

'Keep an eye on the flat,' I said. 'And if you wouldn't mind taking the dog for a walk.'

'Warsaw. Gosh, how interesting. I'd love to see those countries. When you come back you must tell me all about it.'

'And you look after yourself. When I come back I must see you dance.'

She smiled slightly with unparted lips, perhaps at my politeness since I had more important things on my mind. I do not know why I didn't tell her I was taking Mrs Bradecki home. 'I hope you have a really lovely time.' she said and meaning it.

Then she went on down the stairs cautiously and with a limp. It was only then that I realized how unwell she had looked and unhappy and tired. Perhaps she was grateful I hadn't asked her how she was though the absence of common courtesy would have offset that.

I have made two other calls: to Virginia who told me a great deal about the early vices and virtues of Ann and said she hoped soon to be starting a new part-time speech therapy job where they had a crèche. The goat-fingered groper, her husband, had already been made a Deputy Regional Sales Representative. He was on the road a lot and they'd given him a brand new estate car. There was a pause. 'He told me to tell you', she said, 'he'd leave it to you in his will.' Another pause. 'A pity it's not a saloon then,' I said. Anyway, more than a fair share of happiness on that front, my trip to Poland making no great impression. I phoned Jane too. She sounded cheerful. I asked her to give my love to Adrian who, though it was past eight, was not back from the City.

'He's not overdoing it, is he?' I said.

'It's his life,' she replied with not the slightest trace of a sigh. 'You mustn't worry about him.'

'If you don't then I won't,' I said.

'Ah,' was all she said to that before, somewhat casually I thought, wishing me a good trip.

Was something wrong there? Why had she told me not to worry?

A nice thing happened the day before yesterday. I received a note from Sidney, enclosing a Christmas card from the Colonel's wife. He said: *'The new owners of your nifty little bijou country retreat gave me this the other day. Found it under the doormat or somewhere and the vicar gave me your address. You should see the wonders they're doing to the place. Retired folk can always find the time, can't they? Especially the garden. Vegetables too. Should add a bob or two to the price of the place.*

Lousy property market these days. I'm thinking of packing it in, not for the first time. Tried it once, calculating motor insurance premiums in Norwich. Godawful. Perhaps when I've got that bloody shambles of a so-called Crafts Centre off my hands. But what else am I fit for? Yours in potential penury, Sidney.'

The card had a portrait of Hogarth on it, paintbrush and palette poised in front of a blank canvas. She writes: *'How is life in windy old Suffolk? I miss you guys when the sun is tall and the leaves are silent. Also you kill each other less than we do. Sarah is expecting. The poor old sod would have got a terrific kick out of that. I miss him like it was yesterday. Keep the flag flying but not too big and not too high on the mast. With love, Agnes.'*

I do not remember the vicar asking for my address but in his line of business this may not be necessary. I have no idea what Sidney can have meant about the garden. Mind you, with all that spadework I'd done the rest should be what Foster calls a doddle. But vegetables? At first I resented what this would mean to the general colourfulness of the place. And then I thought of the Hambles and their home and what all that had meant to them. I liked the idea of people like the Hambles sitting out among the health-giving improvements they had made to my garden.

Foster came up to my room to say goodbye. He would not accept a drink. The way he looked at me now was somehow less contemptuous, more resigned. There seemed a weariness in him as he stood slightly stooped staring down at the street where his Volvo was parked. But if anything he was more smartly dressed than ever, his brogue shoes highly polished, his twill trousers sharply creased, his plum waistcoat and hounds-tooth tweed jacket looking brand new. But his voice was at its most harsh and brusque.

'No need to hurry back. In my experience not to be sneezed at, you only miss the old country up to a point. Don't think for a moment that travelling broadens the mind. Like hell it does. We colonials used to drink through the night talking the most frightful piffle listening to Ivor sodding Novello and that ilk. Smoke gets in your eyes and I'll see you again and we'll gather lilacs, no wonder we couldn't think straight and all those Afs out there in the darkness banging away on their drums and getting up to God knows what mumbo-jumbo.' He began to chant. 'I'm in heaven, I'm in heaven and my heart . . . Jesus

418

wept. Music's got a lot to answer for in my humble opinion. Sometimes made me want to go off and shoot a bloody elephant. Not all of it, grant you, the stuff my wife . . . Schubert, Chopin, Schumann, whatever they're called, those. Off you go then and keep out of trouble.'

As he left he put out his hand and I took it. He had only done this when we first met and he held on for several seconds. His grip was curiously gentle now and his flesh seemed soft. But his pale eyes had hardened again into that look of disdain when there is nothing left to hate.

Passport, travellers' cheques, shirts, socks, underwear. Christ, take a look at those! Must have had those since before my marriage. Only took them to the launderette a week ago. What had I put in with them to mottle the old off-yellow with a new tinge of mauve? In my Maureen days I had carried out an underpants and socks replacement programme. No need to keep that. And look where the off-yellow darkens into threadbare khaki, the unbleachable stain of a life-time. I dropped it into the waste-paper basket. Then put it back in my suitcase. Who else was going to see it at this juncture? Except Annelise to whom I had given the key of my flat. I could imagine her holding it aloft with her finger-tips as if it is conceivable she could think less of me on that account.

Chapter Six

It seems a long time ago, my trip to Poland, and is hard to relate. My notebooks aren't much help for in them I seem mainly to have recorded trivia, like someone who witnesses an epic battle and sees only the surrounding scenery, the puffs of smoke and the colours of the uniforms.

We were due to leave at nine in the morning and I went down at about eight to make sure she was ready. The door was open and I found her sitting in the front room, her suitcase on the floor beside her, already wearing her dark brown overcoat. She looked up at me as if I was still a stranger. Her eyes were bruised with fatigue and in the gloom her face startled me with its whiteness like a clown's.

'Everything all right?' I asked, rubbing my hands.

She nodded and I think tried to smile like a child I had failed to humour.

'See you in an hour,' I said, pointing at my watch and holding up a forefinger. She turned away from me and put her hand on her suitcase, then grasped the handle tightly as if I had come to take it away from her. It was bound together by a strap and the handle had been wound with string that was black with age. I don't suppose she had slept any more than I had. We were like patients in the waiting room of a dingy hospital, met by chance, discharged too soon. The world outside was not yet ready for us.

In the taxi and at the airport I cannot remember whether she spoke at all until we reached the departure lounge. I was brisk and efficient, presenting our tickets and passports, fetching her coffee, pointing out our flight on the departure board. She seemed to have shrivelled, submitting herself to me, waiting for me to tell her where to go, always following a little behind me as if I would not want to be seen with her. The officials were all very friendly but they seemed to frighten her as if she thought they were trying to catch her out. She watched me as they ran the detection thing up and down me and I saw her flinch when it reached my keys and bleeped. She had tried to take trouble over her appearance. One of her cheeks was over-rouged, her top lip was smudged and there was a streak of powder across her forehead. One eyebrow was darker than the other. It was as if she had done it without a mirror or had given up half-way. In the departure lounge I tried to cheer her up, reading from a Polish phrasebook in an exaggerated English accent but she only repeated the phrases to herself as if trying to learn them by heart. Perhaps she thought I was making fun of her language so in the end I gave up, bought *The Times* and tried to make a start on the crossword. She sat very still, her eyes closed, her hands clasped on her lap, the knuckles sharp as if the bone was about to wear through.

As soon as we were on the plane and I had shown her how to fasten her seat belt she closed her eyes again. Then as we took off she turned her face to the window and I could see her eyes reflected there, staring out at the dwindling earth and the rush of clouds and then above them into the deep blue air as if she had seen it all a thousand times before or was not seeing it at all. She refused all refreshment and when, settling down to my first whisky, I asked her if she had flown before she murmured, 'First time. You many times?'

'Oh Lord yes. It's as easy as flying.' Why was it that in her company everything I said sounded especially silly?

'Please?' she said.

At that point a stewardess came by and smiled down at us in a practised manner, offering us trays of food. I took mine but Mrs Bradecki turned back to the window.

'Are you sure you won't have a drink or something?' I said. She shook her head as if in irritation. 'If I can call you Dorota, you can call me Tom.'

'Please?' she said again.

And that was that. Towards the end of the flight, I put my hand briefly on hers and said, 'Please don't worry. I'm sure it will be all right.'

For an instant her hands relaxed and she looked down at my hand. Then she turned back to the window and glancing at the reflection of her face I thought she had started weeping but it was only streaks on the glass. My fingers where I had touched her felt as cold as ice.

Maria's mother recognized us at once. She was a tall, austere-looking woman and seemed very nervous, steering us through the crowd speaking half in English, half in Polish. A young man helped us with our suitcases to the taxi but then vanished. Behind me in the taxi, Maria's mother spoke very rapidly as if to bring Mrs Bradecki up to date with a great deal of history in a very short time. There was no embarrassment in her voice and she chattered on as if they were old friends. Once or twice I glanced back and saw Mrs Bradecki gazing out at the city, the buildings like barracks in various shades of grime and the trees coming into leaf along the pavements as if indifferently planted there to hide them. Each time I turned round Maria's mother smiled sheepishly at me as though Maria had warned me about her. And then the Palace of Culture rose up hugely before us opposite the new glass Marriott Hotel like giant monuments facing up to each other across a battlefield. The woman pointed here and there and gabbled on. The city was now plastered with hoardings as if an advertising convention was taking place and had run out of control. There was even a tram painted pink advertising Barbie Dolls. All along the streets and around the Palace were stalls selling cheap goods and the people swarmed among them as though ordered out on a shopping spree that was badly letting them down. We drove on past buildings which seemed as though work had stopped on them a long time ago, their crumbling drabness brightened here and there by shop signs which looked second-hand or painted over in too much haste. And everywhere the people hurried along the streets, as though their surroundings did not belong to them and they had come here by accident from their real lives elsewhere. It was the Palace which dominated it all, the pillars at its base reminiscent of classical times, then knobbly ledges mounting up to an onion-shaped dome and a spike and up there too was an advertisement: for Digital, as it might be to give it the ultimate finger. And I imagined our modest little church in Suffolk with an advertisement for Heineken on its tower saying this was the resting place which other biers could not reach.

Suddenly the woman said to me, 'Like a giant, dirty old wedding cake, isn't it? The Russians up there once like gods. Now they are down at the bottom selling rubbish. Capitalism is traffic jams and sex shops and advertising and the mafia and everybody wanting what they cannot have. It is better than socialism, isn't it, Mr Ripple?'

'I wish I knew,' I said. 'It is not very beautiful.'

422

'Now you see the old town,' she said. 'This we could make beautiful.'

We drove down a handsome street to where there was the rust-coloured castle I had read about and then got out of the taxi and walked through a narrow street to the old town square. Mrs Bradecki did not come with us. The woman told me that all of it, in fact almost everything that I had so far seen, had been rebuilt after the war. I told her, as all tourists must, that it was hard to believe. It was a calm early spring evening and the people were wandering about as though nothing of great moment had ever happened there and it had been like that for hundreds of years. Later I visited the museum in the square and saw the city as it was at the end of the war, destroyed utterly, and it seemed afterwards as though the people there had just woken from a terrible dream and found themselves in some picturesque film set and did not know if they were still dreaming. The tall, differently coloured and decorated buildings caught the sunlight and I turned to the woman and said, 'Would Mrs Bradecki not want to see this?'

'I do not know what she wants to see,' she replied.

She had now lost all her nervousness and I saw how like her daughter she was, the frank, wide-set eyes and measured smile. And yet her well-dressed grey and white elegance seemed a concealment of what I might judge in her and find wanting. On the way back to the taxi, she asked if I had been to Poland before and how was Mrs Thatcher. She told me her daughter was now in Germany and how kind I had been to her. She asked whether I was a businessman who had come to make an investment in Poland or was interested in a joint venture. I wished my replies were not so brief and non-committal since she was trying so hard to say all the right things. The questions continued in the car as if she had forgotten about Mrs Bradecki altogether. But I had nothing to say. There were too many impressions and somehow I could think only of my mother and how it would have been if I had brought her here instead of Mrs Bradecki. She would probably have been most struck by all the cars parked on the pavements. She was against cars and we never had one. 'Your father's got enough problems on his hands without having to worry about engines,' she said once and on another occasion, 'If there were fewer cars, there'd be more room for buses.' Though she never actually said so, I am sure she voted Labour if she voted at all. My father would never be drawn into political comment. I suspect he sided with the Conservatives because they seemed vaguely safer. It would have annoyed her that the pavements made for ordinary people should have been taken over by motorists. My father would have thought that you could have seen it coming but would not have said so. My mother's main doubt would have been what on earth I thought I was up to coming to Poland at my age, there was more than enough that needed seeing to at home.

We finally arrived at our hotel. Maria's mother helped us to register and said she would come for us the following morning. Mrs Bradecki was clearly exhausted and began saying, 'Thank you,' over and over again as if in a hurry to be left alone. She seemed to have little idea where she was. At the reception desk she held out her hand for the return of her passport and when the clerk spoke abruptly to her, she reached further forward, spreading her hand and curling it into a claw like a beggar. Maria's mother took her gently by the elbow and led her away towards the lift. I followed with her suitcase, which she snatched away from me as the door of the lift opened. As the door closed, Maria's mother smiled at me and shook her head as if I had delivered Mrs Bradecki into her care in some institution for the insane and I would never see her again. And in that moment as the door shuddered shut, I caught a glimpse of her hunched in the corner of the lift and wondered if indeed she was mad. There was hatred in her eyes as if I had tricked her here against her will and was now turning my back on her.

Later that evening I phoned her room to ask if she would like to have dinner but there was no reply. I had a drink in the bar which was like any other hotel bar – too many men hanging about waiting for something to turn up and Elton John or someone like that whining away to fill the void between wanting and thinking. After a meal of mushrooms, wild boar and too much Bulgarian wine, I wandered the streets for a while, where a few lighted signs tried to flash out a bit of capitalist good cheer to keep spirits up in the long night ahead, like jolly messages in a graveyard. On my return I put my head round the door of the casino. The lobby was full of men lounging about as if waiting for an audition for a cast of crooks. There were some women too from the same scenario but looking a good deal more alert about it. One of them brushed past me and said, 'Hundred dollars, good time.' A man beyond her was glaring at me. I took a second look at the woman and at two or three of the others round and about. There wouldn't be any bloody nonsense about it if you knew what was good for you and if they seemed utterly shagged out and pretty cross with it, you could still have a preview (or broad hint) of the shape of things to come. My hesitation was bringing the man to his feet so I hurried away to the lift.

I was dropping off to sleep when the phone rang. A voice said huskily, 'You like make love?'

'You bet,' I said. 'But not just at the moment. I'm in bed.'

'I come in your room?'

'No,' I said. 'I'll do that.' And put the receiver down.

Which was what I did, wishing for a short while I had said yes, just naked curiosity of course, until the face loomed back etc. I slept fitfully, waking up each time to the memory of Mrs Bradecki and the hatred in her eyes and her outstretched hand wanting her passport back.

(I realize I should be calling her Mrs Bradecka throughout but will leave her name as it is to avoid confusion. It's a nice Polish tradition to make a wife that little bit independent of her husband. If only in that respect, 'Good morning, Mrs Rippla' doesn't seem appropriate somehow. Foster always called them Bradekky which lowered my opinion of him at the time.)

She was not in the dining room at breakfast and again I phoned her. Still no reply. We had arranged to meet in the lobby at ten and on my way from breakfast at about nine-fifteen she was already there waiting. I was standing above her before she saw me and I startled her.

'Had breakfast?' I asked. 'Sleep all right?'

She stared up at me like a suspicious child, afraid to trust me. Her hair was neatly parted and combed and she wore no make-up. She was dressed in a dark green skirt and pale green blouse with frills down the front and at the wrist. They were faded and badly creased as if they had been folded away in a drawer for a very long time. She patted her hair and stroked her skirt as though I had come to inspect her, then began to stand up.

'Not yet,' I said, raising my hands and sitting down beside her. 'Plenty of time. It's a lovely day. Did you sleep all right?' I repeated.

'Very nice,' she said meekly.

'That's good,' I said. 'So did I, on and off. It must feel funny to be back after all these years.'

She looked round the hotel lobby, her face suddenly eager and for the first time I could imagine her when she was happy long ago in her childhood. Her eyes rested on the casino sign.

'What is that?' she asked. It was the first time she had asked me a question.

'It's where people gamble. Bet.'

'Bet? Sorry.'

'Oh, you pay money and if you're lucky you get more money back.'

'Sometimes not lucky?' She frowned at me as if reproving me.

'Definitely. In fact, the odds are more often than not, unlucky.'

'Are you gamble, Mr Ripple? My husband do pools. Maybe you better on horses?'

'Oh yes, absolutely terrific. You should see . . .' And I jogged imaginary reins up and down, accompanied by a series of clicking noises. She looked at me as if I was off my rocker. I stopped that and said, 'No, I never take risks. It's been the problem.'

'Ah, risiki,' she said, staring at the Casino sign, then murmuring, 'Casino important for Poland.'

I think that was what she said. She continued to stare at the sign and I mumbled an excuse and left her. There had been something new in her expression, wishful perhaps or even resolute. Or that was what I wanted to believe.

Maria's mother drove us to the park and we began walking through a rose garden towards the statue of Chopin that Maria had told me about. Nothing had been said and when we were about fifty yards away, Maria's mother suddenly gripped my arm and we stopped to allow Mrs Bradecki to go ahead on her own. She did not look back. At first her stride faltered and then she hurried forwards, almost tripping over. Maria's mother tightened her grip and led me towards a bench. Then she pointed at the statue and said, 'Now we leave them alone.'

Standing alone under the statue was a tall, large, grim-faced woman who was looking nervously about her. Her arms folded under her breasts, she gave the impression of a severity long practised now caught off guard and at a loss, become mere stubbornness. She did not notice Mrs Bradecki until she was a few paces away and then they were facing each other like mistress and servant. I do not think anything was said for a long time and then the woman pointed beyond the statue towards the trees and they moved off together side by side along the path down into the park. My companion got to her feet, nodded at me and we followed after them at a distance.

Suddenly the city seemed a long way away. There was only the abundance of trees coming into leaf, the fresh undergrowth and the long sloping walkways and the people strolling and children and dogs, then some old-looking buildings which my companion pointed out to me: a palace, an orangery with statues inside it, a small temple and then another garden where the roses had begun to sprout. It was a warm, blue day with an occasional sharp breeze, reminding of winter. We walked in and out of the patches of sunlight, occasionally stopping to watch a red squirrel or a bird. For a long time we hardly spoke, or rather I listened as between long silences she told me about the park and the gunfire that had once ripped through it, wounding the trees.

'Soon,' she said, 'they will be in full leaf and then we can forget again. We begin not to know how much we have forgotten.'

On a stretch of water opposite the palace there were ducks and a few swans coming to be fed and a flock of gulls screeching and generally getting in the way. Here the people had gathered, families mainly, not talking much, before moving on into the trees, slowly in and out of the sunlight. It was as I remembered from my dreams all those years ago, grave and shadowless as if time had stopped as the first leaves had begun to dapple the branches and the sun came through them and lay on the earth and the grass as if the light was within them. There were birds flitting about and flowers here and there, daffodils and buttercups and golden shower, some violets too and daisies, like remnants of vanished gardens. The damp brown leaves of the old year clung within the undergrowth and along the edges of the paths, becoming the stone and the earth, dissolving the light. Though all was changed year after year and nothing was the same, no flower, no leaf, it was all as it had always been, the old people, thoughtful in memory, taking the air, parents and children in the perpetual onset of spring. The Webbs and the Hambles and my family were there with me and the children that might have been mine moved away from me as they had in my dream. And for all that timelessness, every one of us was there that day by the utmost chance and we might have been other people, utterly different, and it was all those other unseen people in their multitudes who were there too.

We kept them in sight a long way off. They never looked back to see if we were following them. And Maria's mother began telling me about them. The woman's name was Mrs Konopka and she and Mrs Bradecki had known each other as children. Their parents had perished in Treblinka. She said that a book had been published shortly after the war with accounts by Jewish children of what had happened to them. Mrs Konopka's story had not been used and many years later she had asked her to translate it. She promised to show it to me. The children became separated and it was only long afterwards that Mrs Konopka discovered her friend was still alive. But by then she was married to a man who became a prominent party member and contact could not be made with the Polish community in Britain. I asked if they were both Jewish.

'They were friends', she told me, 'because their fathers were Jewish and their mothers were not and wanted to stay with their husbands. It was only by accident that she learnt that Maria was going to stay with the Bradeckis and so she asked me to write. You see, her husband is dead and everything is changed. She was true to him all those years and now she is becoming old and can be reminded. I was born at the end of the war but I do not wish to be reminded either. There are no Jews now.'

I asked if she had known Mrs Konopka well. At first she did not answer and began talking about her work as an English teacher. Then she said suddenly, 'She was a *nomenklatura* woman and had a good life. We hated those people sometimes.'

'Only sometimes?' I asked, without knowing what she meant.

'Because even in school we had to be on the right side. My husband too was a good party member. So we hated them more but we thought it would go on for ever until Mr Wałęsa came and the Pope and we had hope but fear too. Now I make money teaching English and our daughter is happy and will marry a clever man who is a new businessman and consultant. I am not such a good woman, Mr Ripple.'

'What is goodness? For us, it is easy. We do not have to do much or go far. But for you . . .'

'Once her husband helped us. A long time ago. He found my husband a good job and obtained a car for us. He was not a bad man, her husband. He believed. My husband did not believe. He was only humble and frightened. She did not ask me to write because she knew Mr Bradecki hated them.'

428

'Then why did you?'

'For my daughter, I think. That she should think better of me and of her father. She is ashamed of him being in the party and now he is frightened he will be chased from his job in government. He too is not a bad man. He is my husband. He only loves his family. Now we only want to be happy and my daughter to be happy. I wrote because my daughter wanted me to write when she told me Mr Bradecki was dead. I do not think I can be so happy now. Once we felt safe. We were not responsible for ourselves. Seeing them together now does not make me so happy. We only want to go far back into the past and not remember things that were so terrible in between. We wanted our true history not lies and now that we have our true history we have been waiting for we do not want it. I want my daughter to think I am a good woman . . .'

I recorded all this in my notebook in snatches for that is how she spoke to me, with long pauses in between as if she had to think carefully what to say next, to make sure her English was correct or wondering whether she could trust me or because in speaking her thoughts she might be endangered or untruthful. It was all beyond my comprehension and I thought of all the choices I had never had to make. And I was saddened that this honest, self-possessed woman with her prim, correct English who had done no wrong could be so troubled by herself, who had a husband who was about to lose his job and a daughter who was ashamed of them.

We had made our way back to the lake, where the people had gathered round a peacock with all its feathers out, quivering and making advances at a peahen. There were two other peacocks and another peahen, which took no notice, and finally the peacock was left alone and its feathers shrank and folded and drooped behind it. The people smiled and pointed at it and I noticed how smartly dressed the women were, the men less so but far from shabby and I thought of a similar gathering of ordinary folk in Britain, tatty and scruffy as if to flaunt their poverty. The wrong people seemed to be in the wrong place. It was there that I asked again about Maria and said what a charming girl she was. And for a moment I saw her hope and eagerness in the face of her mother before something silenced it, something she could never explain to me. 'She will have no memory,' she said. 'As if she were born at the beginning of time.'

Eventually we joined up with Mrs Bradecki and her companion, who had come to rest on a bench by the rose garden where we had begun, sitting under the statue of Chopin with the wind-torn willow tree above his head, overarching it like a massive angry bird. They glanced towards us as if they didn't want us to come any closer, but they seemed to have run out of things to say to each other. Side by side they seemed to have nothing in common, Mrs Konopka straight-backed, her grey suit stiffening her like a uniform, her face set as though she had done her duty and that was that, with Mrs Bradecki huddled beside her, head bent in an attitude of submission. But as we approached them, they leant into each other and their arms touched, then they abruptly drew apart as if surprised in some intimacy they must now disown. They seemed not to have spoken for a long time and to be waiting for us to turn away so that they could be alone together again. We turned and they followed us back to the car and nothing further was said.

At the hotel Mrs Bradecki went straight to her room and Maria's mother told me they had arranged to meet again later that evening. I was not invited. They had moved back into their own lives and my duty was done. Maria's mother asked me to supper the following evening to meet her husband. Her last words to me were, 'She has a house in the woods outside Warsaw. Now they can be together. When they are like that those people are strangers to us. A thousand years more strange than I am to you.'

I wandered the streets again that afternoon through the acres of stalls around the Palace of Culture and in and out of one or two shops. I then went to the Marriott Hotel for a drink and it might have been any such hotel anywhere, the mirrors and false foliage and marble and gleaming steel. The waitresses even had name-tags and split skirts. I wondered what on earth I was doing there, alone and bored and out of place in some grand, impersonal waiting room of life. My guidebook had told me I should visit Kraków and because it was the only idea I had I went to the registration desk and booked a car for the following morning.

Back at the hotel I found Mrs Bradecki in the lobby, her suitcase packed. She pointed at the cashier's desk and gave me money to change for her. I asked if she was checking out.

'I stay my friend,' she said firmly, as if forcing herself to it, avoiding my eye. 'Hotel too much money.'

Then Mrs Konopka arrived and took her suitcase without looking at me and they left. Not then nor at any other time had she addressed a single word to me. I hoped Mrs Bradecki would look back but she did not. I wished I had asked for a telephone number but there was no need for that now. My duty was done but I felt no relief. I wondered if I would ever see her again and could only recall her gaping eyes when Mrs Konopka came and took her suitcase, as if something had woken her in the dead of night.

The next day I did some sightseeing, taking a taxi to the old town and going round the castle. I bought some glassware for my children and some Russian dolls for Ann. I bought a wooden box with a pattern on it for Annelise and went back into the shop and bought another for Michelle. Then I walked to the Palace of Culture to wander among the street traders. There were even more of them than I thought there were and scattered all over the city too, as though the advertising convention was being run in conjunction with the Quinquennial Convention of the International Bazaar Federation. I never saw anyone buy anything. Perhaps having the choice was enough.

Over the way there was a building calling itself the British Institute, so I felt I had a duty to see what it did. On the ground floor was a reference library and information centre. It was bright and modern and there were some attractive posters on the walls, the one facing the entrance of the back of a naked woman, so not quite as eye-catching as it might have been from the other side. I sat there for a while reading *Private Eye*, checking the 'Eye Love' column mainly, and glancing through *The Economist*, which I had only looked at once before, in a dentist's waiting room, when in view of what was to come (root canal treatment since you ask) I may not have been sufficiently in tune with its godlike flippancy. There seemed to be a lot of younger people coming and going who wanted to know about Britain and I saw them through Foster's eyes, disapproving but hoping they'd make it.

At one point I became aware of a man standing a few paces away and staring down at me, either as if I had no business there or as if he knew me but couldn't quite put a name to it. I had never seen him before in my life, knowingly. He was quite tall with a balding, woven-celery suit with a hole in the elbow (I observed later), half-eye glasses, greying hair and a lost but intent air about him. I waited for him to say 'Buzz off' or 'Haven't we met somewhere before?' though from his expression it would have been when one of us was not quite coming up to scratch. Then with a last look at me, a very close look at quite a lot of me and what I was reading, he went to the woman at the enquiries desk and asked if the latest issue of *Country Life* had arrived. She smiled patiently at him but did not reply. Then he left glancing this way and that, as if looking for some excuse to meddle. I asked the woman who he was. She was a pale and slender girl with glasses, which gave her prettiness a judicious air. No nonsense there of any sort.

'That was the Director,' she said with a weary smile.

'Oh, it's just that he seemed to know me, or as if I shouldn't be here. Perhaps he thought I had swiped his copy of *Country Life*.'

That patient smile again. 'I always tell him we do not take *Country Life*, but he is retiring soon and likes looking at pictures of houses. So I give him *The Times* so he can do the crossword and forget about where he will live.'

'Oh I see. A nice place you've got here, I must say.'

'Once it was a café. Can I help you please?'

I shook my head and thanked her, then went up to the library on the first floor and chose a P. D. James. There was a long queue at the issue counter and when I got to the end of it I was told I had to become a member before I could borrow anything. It wasn't much so I paid up. Then I toured the rest of the building. There were potted plants on the window-sills and framed posters on the walls. In the reception room was a map with coloured pins all over it indicating a network of libraries, teachers' colleges, lecturers, management centres and studia, whatever those might be. On the second and top floors there were smart black and white signs indicating various offices: Scholarships and Visits, Film Library, English Language Unit, English for Management Advisory Service, Hall and Cinema, Administration and something called 'Know-How Fund'. There were several eager-looking young men in that office being nicely dealt with by three women so I decided not to disturb them, though whatever the fund did I'm sure I needed it more than they did at my age. I continued my tour of the offices. There were a lot of people coming and going and more than once someone asked me if they could be of help. I said I was just looking around and nobody seemed to mind that or not all that much. I do not naturally have the air of someone who is up to mischief. Everywhere I encountered more attractive young women, all of them smartly dressed as if they were about to go to a cocktail party which perhaps they were, to judge from the glasses laid out in the hall which was surrounded by posters advertising cultural events. It was the range of charm and ways of smiling, or of not doing so just for the moment that I liked – what my mother called 'well brought-up, not like some I could mention'.

I went back down to the reference library and began reading my P. D. James or the first two pages of it, as much of it as I needed to before realizing I had read it before. So I left it there, wishing the room was still a café because I felt like a drink. The Director came and went for no particular reason that I could detect but this time he ignored me. I hoped he would find somewhere nice to live in his retirement. He looked ready for it all right. I hoped he wouldn't miss it all too much. He had certainly presided over a satisfactory staff recruitment policy. I hoped he would soon get rid of that suit. I remember him now and wonder if he was only a figment of my imagination.

Dinner that evening with the Wysinskis was something of a strain. I noted down immediately afterwards as much of it as I could remember. Mr Wysinski did not speak any English at first and I am sure his wife did not translate half of what he said. He spoke incessantly, mainly about all the mistakes the old regime had made. He seemed at first to be apologizing to me, or through me to the Western world at large, or to his wife for what he had known all along was inefficient and foolish, a blame without guilt. His wife translated neutrally, keeping her distance but wanting me to think well of them both. The food and drink were plentiful and they watched me to see how much I appreciated it. They thought I was more important than I was, a successful English businessman, though surely their daughter must have told them I lived in a small flat in an unfashionable part of London and worked part-time in a launderette. It was as if my very presence carried some magic authority. The more Mr Wysinski drank and spoke, the more watchful his wife became and then, towards the end of the evening he began breaking into English and she ceased translating altogether. His vocabulary was mainly abuse: rubbish, nonsense, foolish and, most frequently, stupid and the names came tumbling out of what I gathered were leading politicians. His plump face began to redden and sweat profusely and he waved his hands in the air as if conducting a rebellious choir. 'No hope,' he said again and again, 'Church, Russia, elections, Wałęsa, Gorbachev, democracy, freedom, stupid, all is stupid and people knowing nothing, nothing, Mr Ripple . . .'

His wife tried to calm him down but she did not seem to be embarrassed any longer, as if in the act of clearing the table and bringing coffee such matters counted for nothing beside the daily routines of life. Sometimes she nodded at what he had said, that he should be reassured of her love or that I should know she had once been proud of him and should not think him ridiculous or contemptible. Drinking heavily now, one vodka after another, and beginning to crouch over the table and stare in front of him, he seemed to have run out of things to say, so to change the subject I asked about Maria.

They brought out photographs of her at various ages and gradually they were restored to each other. Pointing and laughing, they were suddenly very happy, telling me she was so clever and lively she must become a successful businesswoman, which seemed a bit of a waste but that is the sort of thing people like me think. I remembered her looking eagerly up at me in a London street, then turning the corner, hand in hand with some appalling lecher. As the pages turned, the smile of the child seemed to become more flirtatious and wilful and my mind turned to Annelise, her limp, her cry of apology when I spilt Lemsip onto my dressing gown, her sorrow and sense of failure, her loving father.

They began asking me about my family and in replying I thought how complacent I must sound, how simply and easily fulfilment had been come by, or satisfaction, how comfy it all was. It was a future they wanted for their daughter, the past contained in the pages of a family photograph album. And suddenly the evening quietened. Mrs Wysinski was standing behind her husband, who was hunched over the album in a cheap, underpadded brown armchair, gripping it as if it was his last worldly possession. He reached back to take her hand where it rested on his shoulder. I had so far asked no questions but that gesture seemed to free me to do so.

'Those years,' I said. 'They must have been difficult. For everyone.'

There was a long pause while they stared down at the album. It was open at a photograph which Mrs Wysinski took out and handed to me. It was of Maria alone in front of a tall church, her head slightly on one side, not smiling this time. It was a windy summer's day and she was wearing an autumn-coloured dress pulled in at the waist, which showed off the shape of her. One hand was held to her head to prevent the wind from blowing her hair across her face and she was frowning into the sun. There were pigeons around the edge of her shadow.

'On that day,' she said, 'Maria was angry with us. Because she knew we were against Solidarity and wanted martial law.'

'Stupid,' Mr Wysinski said again but now in hardly more than a whisper. He looked at me, the sweat drying on his cheeks like tears. His eyes were large and moist and he reminded me in that instant of Foster, the spent scorn behind them, but then he laughed and held his hands up in a gesture of surrender.

'But now, she is not angry now.' He reached back and patted his wife's hand. 'It was not my wife she have anger for then. Only me.' Then he said loudly 'Vodka?' and pointed at my empty glass.

Mrs Wysinski tapped him on the shoulder. 'Mr Ripple is not a Polish drunkard like you. He does not have a party card to tear up.'

I offered my glass and Mrs Wysinski fetched the bottle and handed it to her husband. 'Maria,' she said and paused. 'Maria is going to be manager in the horticultural business. My husband has a friend. He still has many friends. She was so angry on that day because some of her friends had parents who were Solidarity. Now this is not so good for her.'

Mr Wysinski smiled proudly. 'My daughter not so stupid, Mr Ripple.'

And so the evening came to an end. I had wanted to talk about Mrs Bradecki and now, as we waited for the taxi, I said I hoped she would be all right. Mrs Wysinski left the room and came back with a brown envelope. 'This is for you,' she said. 'I translated it a long time ago. But I think the English is not so bad.'

Her husband glanced at it as if it was none of his business. When he said goodbye, he put a hand on my back and said something in Polish. She translated for me. 'My husband says you are very sympathetic to listen to him who knows nothing about democracy and the free market economy.'

'Perhaps there are more important things to know about,' I said.

They waited for me to continue and I felt like a conjuror whose trick was about to fail, as if I should reach forward and produce a gold coin from behind his ear. I bumbled on. 'Money. Buying and selling. Getting and spending. Everyone for himself. We have our

435

own poverty.' Then a phrase of Jane's came to me. 'We who know the price of everything and the value of nothing.'

Mrs Wysinski (or Wysinska as she should properly be called) did not translate and they shook their heads in unison. 'You can say things like that if you have money and hope,' she said. 'You can say many fine things like that.'

And so I left them. My last impression of Mr Wysinski was that he was close to tears though he was smiling broadly. His wife stood sternly beside him like a hostess glad to see the last of a guest who had behaved badly. I do not remember if I thanked them. I had not brought flowers as Poles do, or a gift of any kind, as though my very presence, my Western omniscience, were generosity enough.

That night I read the account she gave me. A note was attached to it which read as follows.

Dear Mr Ripple,

I am sorry about the translation, which is not perfect. Soon after the war, Mrs Konopka told someone about what happened to her and Mrs Bradecka. As I told you in the park, it was for a book about Jewish children and their experiences but in the end they did not use it. She gave it to me one day when my husband and her husband first joined the party together and we were friends. I think now she has forgotten she gave it to me. It is a long time ago and she made a new life, being married to the nomenklatura as we call it. You must not tell her that I have given it to you. It is only that you should know about your friend, Dorota Bradecka.

Sincerely yours, Elzbieta Wysinska.

Before the war I was very happy and my best friend was Dorota. When the Germans came we lived in the old town and then we had to go to the ghetto. Our fathers were Jewish but our mothers were Aryan and we had to stay together. That is why we were best friends though Dorota was younger. One day when there was an Aktion, I went to my aunt who was married to an Aryan and lived as an Aryan. She gave me bread to sell sometimes and sent me to work on a farm. The work was hard from sunrise to sunset but my aunt gave them money and they did not know I was Jewish. Sometimes I went to the ghetto but my parents sent me away quickly. I lived like this for two years. I was only eleven years old.

Dorota's parents lived in the next house to ours and they also had a son who was older. He used to wander here and there selling cigarettes and newspapers. I liked him because he was always so brave and cheerful and he used to pull my pigtails but only gently. He told us the Gestapo came sometimes and searched him but he kept everything in a suitcase and they never found it. He said the other boys sometimes called him Jew-boy but they did not hate him. They only ordered him to give them things. When he was arrested by the Bahnschutz he was beaten and he gave the address of a friend of his mother's and they sent him there. His parents told him not to come back but to find work on the farms because his life was dangerous and they did not see him again. Dorota would not leave them when they tried to send her away too. Once when I went back she was crying all the time because her brother and father were angry with her. Her mother could have taken her away because she was Aryan. I heard them discussing this many times. She could have come with me to the farm where the farmer would protect us because we did not look so Jewish and they needed someone more to help them. But I did not live in the house but in the barn where it was very cold sometimes but they gave me plenty of blankets when I asked them. One day I came back to the ghetto, I was nearly there when an Aktion started. I saw two men in the secret police who knew me and I hid in a doorway where other people were watching too. I saw my parents and Dorota's being pushed into a truck and when it started driving away I saw Dorota running after it but they would not take her because there was no more room, though they had taken some children. She was screaming very loudly and ran a long time and I heard her mother shouting to her very angrily. I found her later outside her house and took her with me to another house where there was a friend of my mother's but they would not let us stay because they were afraid of the Ukrainians. We went to a priest who had some documents made for us and he said we could work for him. Then we went to another aunt but she was very sick and spat blood and her mother came on the second night and asked why she was harbouring Jews. Her husband was a Jew and one evening when he came back from the ghetto, two Ukrainian policemen and a Gestapo officer came and they found him hiding in the bathroom and they took him away. He was shaking and sobbing and she tried to go with him but they could see she was very sick and left her but next day the militiamen came and took her away too. We watched from the doorway. She was coughing very much. When she saw us she waved but she had stopped crying now. She used to

437

make cakes and sell them in the square and we stayed there for a few weeks and did the same. Every day the militiamen came and took away more people but they left us alone. Once a man pointed at us where we were sweeping and said, 'Those are Jew-girls,' but they were in too much hurry. So we could not stay there. We were near the ghetto and every night we heard screams coming from there and we even saw they were killing small children by breaking their heads against the walls. The lady next door tried to be kind to us but she was very frightened. She tried to send us to a home but we didn't have any papers so we were sent to another home on Dwoecki Street where there were other children. The other children did not all like us but the Mother Superior knew we were Jewish and let us stay there. Every night Dorota cried. Then after a few weeks, my mother found us. I was very happy but she would not tell us anything, only that she had been told to go home because she was Aryan from a good family. She told me that my father and Dorota's parents had been sent somewhere on a train. Dorota's mother had been told to go home too because she was not Jewish but she refused. But she did not tell Dorota this. For a time we lived like this, making and selling cakes but it was not so safe and some people were saying we were Jewish children. Then one evening my mother went to the ghetto to fetch some things to make us more comfortable in my aunt's flat and we never saw her again. Somebody told me she was hiding a boy there and she was shot but I do not know this. Then we went to another friend of my mother's who had a large house near Lwów and we gave her twenty thousand zlotys my mother had given us and she looked after us as if we were her own children. Nearby there was a German soldier whose girlfriend told him we were Jewish but Mrs Stoklowska gave him money and other things to keep quiet about it. He kept his word and when we met him he always winked at us. One evening a man came to see Mrs Stoklowska and he said how well I acted the part of an Aryan girl. He was a friend of hers but he searched my room and found a photograph of me kneeling to take communion which my parents had had taken by a photographer they knew. The man then pointed at Dorota and said, 'So you are the little Jewish girl. When did you last go to church?' Mrs Stoklowska said she had come from Kraków to stay with her because her parents had too many children to look after and she was soon going back there and Dorota was her niece. Dorota then cried in front of the man but she was not frightened at all and the man put his hand on her head and said he was sorry he had called such a nice little girl a Jew. But Dorota could not *stay there after that and Mrs Stoklowska tried to find her another home but other people knew her story and were frightened. Then one morning she was not there any longer. Mrs Stoklowska told me she had been sent to another farm where she was hidden with the cows but the mother of the farmer's neighbour saw her one day and she was taken to Oświęcim. The farmer said he did not know where she came from but he needed someone to look after the cows but they did not believe him and he went with her and some other people. The war was nearly over now and the farmer's wife came and told Mrs Stoklowska that she had been happy at the farm and was glad to go where she might find her parents and brother. So I thought she was dead. Then someone told Mrs Stoklowska that she had survived. But we heard many things in those days and nobody knew what to believe. Then Mrs Stoklowska sent me away too because the same man as before was not so friendly now. I do not know what happened to Dorota. I have told everything I know at the present time.*

I phoned Mrs Wysinski and told her I would be driving to Kraków for a couple of days and asked her to tell Mrs Bradecki, should she ask after me, though I made it clear that there was absolutely no need for her to do so. I thanked her for the evening before and she said, 'My husband is very sorry he talked so much nonsense.'

'Oh no! Not at all. It was extremely interesting.'

'Interesting, Mr Ripple – maybe we are tired of being interesting. The British people have seen on the BBC that Polish politics are only quarrelling and our president is a dictator.'

I had seen this programme and had thought how much it had to do with life – angry and troubled and trying to be honest and starting from nothing. Whereas our own political life . . . I am still trying to work this out. I should do more reading perhaps. I could say none of this, of course, but managed, 'Well, our politics by comparison seems bickering and deceit and playing with numbers. I mean . . .' How smug I sounded.

'You must not try to be nice to us, Mr Ripple.' She said this very gently.

'We've got to try to be something,' I said. 'But really, I do thank you.'

'It was our pleasure,' she said and I think she meant it.

I drove to Kraków by way of Częstochowa where there is a monastery with a long history and the famous black madonna which the guidebook told me has a deep meaning for Poles, having kept their faith alive, and their faith in themselves which seems to be much the same thing. And it has worked many miracles which some say come from within. I arrived there when there was a service in progress so it was some time before I could get close enough to see the madonna properly. The people were of all ages quietly milling about, a casual sort of reverence it seemed, a natural part of ordinary daily life, not like going to church at all. The walls were covered with little badges and shields and necklaces and all manner of tokens, with crutches here and there to bear witness. Millions had been made happier by coming to this place, gazing at the madonna from a distance, the glitter of silver and gold round a small, sad face with two scars on the right cheek which might have been tears. Or not just sad but with a patient and weary anger which gave back to them their endless wretchedness. I cannot tell from the guidebook what expression Jesus is wearing since his face is almost pitch black. The people shuffled back and forth and came and went with a plain, everyday seriousness, sometimes chanting quietly along with the priest, as if they had nothing better to do, were just getting themselves back into focus from time to time. Whatever it was, they were inside it and it was inside them. And I was there as a tourist, a voyeur, and now I don't want to go on trying to write about it any longer. I wished the vicar was with me. Whatever he missed, I think he would have found it there.

Kraków you can read about. The Pope's city. Very old and beautiful and worn and dignified. There was lots to see: the Wawel castle, the old town square and market and St Mary's church with its huge lavish altarpiece, starlit roof and dusty splendour lighting the gloom here and there like a misty autumnal nightfall. There were people kneeling in prayer and taking confession among the sightseers and I was one of them, curious, there for the experience. What business did I have in their house, in God's house? Then I drove out to Nowa Huta where there was another city of hideous huge tenement blocks and steelworks filling the air with filth which seemed to have come back down with the rain and soaked into everything. It was a damp and muggy day and the stench of it was everywhere. They say this other city was built there near the old city out of some monstrous spite and envy, to cast a cloud over the past and its humbled confusion of glories. I do not know. But I remembered the hymn from my schooldays and now understood the meaning of 'dark Satanic mills'. No wonder they wanted to build churches here too and the authorities tried to prevent them. I tried to tell myself that the human spirit cannot be stifled for ever but how does one live through the lives of others? I wanted to describe what I felt but am left now, weeks later, with thin fragments of memory which come and go across the fringes of imagination but do not enter it, images merely which do not change what I think and what I am so that in truth I am unaffected by them and go on much as I was in this book of my meagre and inconsequential life. I have not been deepened or enriched. I have knowledge which I did not have before but I can do nothing with it except write it down. It is not even understanding.

I then went to Auschwitz, the worst place in the world, someone has called it. I do not begin to know what I could say about that. Or if I should even try. What could I add? Perhaps that must be left to those to whom it happened, the witnesses, the rest of us only continuing to watch and listen.

On my return to Warsaw, there was a message waiting for me from Mrs Wysinski that I should phone her. She told me that Mrs Bradecki and Mrs Konopka were going to Treblinka the next day and, too quickly, I offered to drive them there. But then she told me Maria was back and would come with us, so it was not too quickly at all. With nothing else to do that afternoon I drove to a southern suburb and wandered the streets and into courtyards. The pavements were full of pot-holes and the derelict buildings seemed temporarily occupied or long since deserted. Some were still spattered with bullet holes. It was like wandering through a forsaken graveyard. Here and there were giant refuse bins mottled with rust and grime like huge satchels on wheels, their contents spilling out as though they had outlived their purpose and had been forgotten except by a few rummaging old women. The graffiti were mainly in English: PERSONAL JESUS, SLAYER, HOOLIGAN, DEATH, PUNK NOT DEAD, SADDAM GLEMP, GAME OVER, VANILLA, FUCK EVERYONE, WELCOME TO HELL, SEX PISTOLS, EXPLOITED and, most ominous of all, CFC. It was like a built-over wasteland that belonged to no one, dumped upon, crumbling, dirt soaked, abandoned. Yet here and there too people were sweeping the pavements or raking the patches of grass between the trees or putting out window-boxes. And there were one or two shops with fresh lettering and bright awnings as though a few brave settlers had begun to move in and were staking their claims. Oh yes, and there were pedigree dogs everywhere being led along: Afghan hounds and Alsatians and boxers and collies and dachshunds and Doberman Pinschers, even a Rottweiler. Perhaps, I wrote in my notebook, it is only in England that most of the dogs are mongrels. We love them so much we are quite happy to let them loose to go bonking about all over the place, which is not the only thing they do all over the place. On the main street an unusual number of shops and stalls were selling flowers or displaying them rather and I noticed again how smartly dressed the women were but there was a despair in them too as if they knew the colonisation would make little difference in their lifetime. The trees coming into leaf were playing their part too. I remembered reading somewhere that the first shop to open in Warsaw after the war was a hat shop. That no longer surprised me, the bravado and swank of it.

In the afternoon I went round the Royal Castle, rebuilt and restored in all its golden glory in twelve short years and I thought that people who could do this could do anything. Yet between the hope and despair, I read somewhere, there was a gulf as deep and wide as time and between them the will might fail and the squalor would then expand like a fog, leaving behind only the monuments.

That evening I went to a song and dance show at the Palace of Culture with laser lights shooting all over the place and phosphorescent figures looping about and a large cast of excessively lively young people who reminded me I had been young once if not quite like that. It felt as though the laser beams were going through me like the latest medical experiment which might work better on others. There was a black American at the centre of the cast, imported to give the show an authentic flavour perhaps. You could see they liked having him there and he liked it too, because he had done that sort of thing many times before and they were having a go at it for the first time. And so to bed. The musical took place in an underground station in New York and a plump and shabby man with a suitcase had shuffled across the stage from time to time, on his way picking up an orange. In my dream that was my part, unnoticed by the lads and lasses, most notably the lasses, with my depreciating luggage laden, as the poem puts it. I carried the suitcase everywhere, stooping with the weight of it, ignored, stumbling into pot-holes, trying to find an empty rubbish bin to put it into. But it was a deep and restful sleep. The phone had not rung again. Perhaps they'd now seen the face etc. which went with the number. When I awoke to a bright late April day, it was Annelise I left behind, or so my notes tell me, twirling and leaping about, her limp quite cured, criss-crossed in her standard frilly white get-up by coloured laser beams, much too engrossed to notice me either. I felt well that morning as if the warning signals in my chest towards the end of the show had been intended for someone else. An extra couple of Gaviscon tablets had done the trick. Too much cheap Bulgarian wine, that was all.

My notebook from now on is not much help though there is little more to tell. The day began excellently: after a phantom Annelise, Maria in the flesh. Mrs Bradecki and her friend were late so we had a long time (about four and a half minutes) alone together in the lobby. My oh my. She was in lively mood with a wide variety of smiles and her hair definitely a lighter colour and tangled widely about as if she'd hurtled to meet me after hastily drying it following a shower. Some lipstick too now and eye shadow. No record of any smell, then. Believe me, she really did greet me with the most unqualified delight.

I offered her my hand, which unlingeringly she took. 'Aren't you supposed to be in Germany making money?' I asked, blushing alas.

'Now I come back here and start public relations with Japanese, learning the ropes, you say.' Here she clapped her hands together without making a sound, already well into Part One of her training perhaps.

We sat down in a deep, leather-looking sofa. I touched her arm just above where the sleeve ended. 'The more public you keep them the better would be my advice.'

She looked around her, pretending not to have heard, or because she hadn't understood me, or had perfectly well. Her smile had gone. Start again, somewhere in the avuncular range. I looked at my watch and she looked at hers with a slight shrug and compression of her lips. I looked at hers too or at the arm above it, the drift of golden hair bringing to mind what might be guessed about the colour etc. of it elsewhere and on from that ad infinitum. All right, not that avuncular.

'I should think the Japanese are pretty fussy about punctuality,' I attempted. 'Make watches that keep the time to a thousandth of a second.' I showed her mine, the one Adrian had given me. 'This one's an antique, at least a year old. Only keeps time to a hundredth of a second. Don't know why I keep it frankly, turning up for appointments three hundredths of a second late. You should see the way they look at you, even worse than the Swiss. The Japanese frown and say, "You velly rate, Mister Lipple. Lecommend commit hali-kali before hard bargaining begin."' I made a two-handed fist and with a gasp then long gurgle plunged an imaginary samurai sword deep into my stomach. She put a hand to her mouth, thinking I had come to harm, then looked around where the cast of crooks and others were staring at me too.

I quickly withdrew the sword and lowered my voice to brotherly with just a hint of a drawl. 'No, what I mean is I think it is a job you will be absolutely marvellous at, public relations, or any other job come to think of it whether or not you're actually doing it. The Japanese are jolly lucky in my view.'

At this point she made me aware that Mrs Bradecki and Mrs Konopka were among those near the casino sign who had been watching us and we went over to them. They were standing apart as if they had decided to have nothing more to do with each other. Mrs Bradecki was wearing a faded flowered frock and a dark green cardigan and had her brown overcoat over her arm. The black scarf round her head bared her face and made her look cowed and lost, a peasant up from the country ashamed of her poverty. Mrs Konopka was dressed in a dark blue suit with a matching blue silk scarf at her neck with a large amber brooch on her lapel and her blonde-dyed hair glossy and sleek as if she had just come from the hairdresser. She stood grim-lipped at her full height, as a woman who had toughened herself over the years to suspicion and hatred. It was impossible to see how she might have been as a child or wounded in any way, or laughing. As I approached her, she nodded at me as if I were a supplicant. It was to Mrs Bradecki that I spoke.

'All set to go then?' Again that creepy rubbing of my hands.

'We are ready,' she replied, looking up at her companion as if waiting for an order. Then she smiled at me very fleetingly or it may not have been that, simply a remembered politeness and then a shadow seemed to cross her eyes as Mrs Konopka spoke to her rapidly in Polish. As Maria and I walked behind them towards my car, I asked her what Mrs Konopka had said.

She shrugged. 'I do not know. It was a Jewish thing. Something about a long journey. It doesn't matter.'

There was a question I had to ask her. 'Have you been there before?'

'At school to Majdanek only. We had to go. My mother said I must come today with you. She said that before it was Communist propaganda, to show what they saved us from.'

'But the same for both of you, surely?'

'She think it is better and maybe you are tired of her after the other night at our house.'

'Goodness gracious no. I mean . . . Anyway, I'm delighted . . .' But was less so, wondering whether it might have been the other way round. I wrote her a thank-you letter but did not see her again.

'I am not so glad, Mr Ripple.'

And so we drove off, the two women in the back and Maria beside me. After an hour's stretch of road through the city's outskirts, we reached open farmland and an hour or so later turned right through a pine forest. The countryside seemed bare and orderly, cultivation going on here and there in tidy fields with horse-drawn ploughs and elderly folk bent over, jabbing with hoes. There were horse-drawn carts too and if it hadn't been for the occasional tractor, it might have been a landscape from the last century. The villages looked prosperous enough with their square, three-storey houses made of concrete blocks, most of them looking unfinished for rather a long time. The few people about seemed at least as well clothed and fed as they do in Suffolk, especially the children. Around the houses was the usual functional disarray of agricultural paraphernalia, ducks, preoccupied chickens and plots of vegetables and flowers. It all seemed very contented, country folk going about their everyday business in that unhurried way people have who are tuned to the seasons and the customs of the past. Timeless etc. But it wasn't like that at all, so I've read. Tranquillity in the eye of the tourist.

It was a warm, hazy spring day, the high, vague clouds moving slowly and thinly across the sun. For a long time Maria and I spoke little. She seemed nervous, as if waiting for the two women to say something she could interpret for me or perhaps wanting to overhear

445

them. But they were silent. From time to time I glimpsed Mrs Bradecki in the driving mirror staring out of the window into the far distance or with her eyes half closed and flickering as if she was trying to stay awake. Once she seemed to be asleep but in that glimpse her eyes suddenly squeezed tight as if in the fierce concentration of prayer. Mrs Konopka was out of my vision but once I turned round and she too was staring out of the window, her expression rigid and unaltered. I glanced down at the seat between them, where their hands rested, not quite touching. Maria and I had become strangers, met by coincidence, both wishing we were somewhere else. And what could we have said except to wonder how these farms and pinewoods would have seemed all those years ago to the people squinting through chinks in the railway cars, dreaming of the day when they would be out there again with their loved ones, joking, arguing, watching the clouds drift across the sun?

In the end I could not bear the silence and asked if she had been there before, remembering too late I had asked her that already. She looked away. 'Perhaps,' I said quietly, 'it is only necessary to be reminded once?'

'We are reminded all the time,' she replied impatiently.

'People like me, I meant.'

She paused for a long time. 'How do I know? You can always be so certain. I cannot think of anything different we can be saying or feeling about it. The past is always the same.'

I glanced in the driving mirror to see if we had been overheard. Mrs Bradecki was staring at me and looked away as if she was ashamed of me. I lowered my voice and stumbled on, 'Perhaps for you and me, not for them. For us, for me, I mean . . . Don't we owe you anything? . . . So you're going into business. Looking forward to that?' No reply to that. 'Wonderful opportunities for the young, now. The world at our feet. Creating the new Poland. Your parents are proud of you. They expect much of you. Good time to be setting out in life, making plans . . . Exciting.' The usual twaddle of old farts chatting up the young.

She stared in front of her and did not even nod, so I asked about her time in Britain and she began telling me about the jobs she had done, mainly as a waitress, the mistakes she had made, getting the sack for coming late one day because she had misunderstood the time, how the English had sometimes been kind to her but they knew she could not complain. I ran out of questions and wished she would ask me about

446

anything at all. But what was there to know? And so I asked her to teach me a few words of Polish and that was how the rest of the journey was spent. She pointed out things to me and told me their names in Polish, which I repeated, forgetting them almost at once. But not all. I have beside me the phrasebook with the words she underlined in it: sky, car, green, poor, good, bad, sad, wonderful, girl, love, hope, foolish. And we had these little conversations about plane travel, car repair, asking the way to the station and the museum, buying vegetables and stamps; and these I read over to myself now, remembering how it suddenly became all right, rehearsing those silly, unlikely phrases while she laughed at my pronunciation, for I have absolutely no gift for languages. I remembered mouthing out my French homework in a growling accent and my mother being no help at all. 'Knowing you,' she said, 'I doubt you'll have occasion to visit the Continent much.' And my father added with his little cough, 'You never know, it might come in handy like in a restaurant or if he becomes a scientist or such like.' To which my mother replied, glaring at us over her spectacles, 'I've never heard of the French going in for the sciences much. They have other fish to fry.'

I exaggerated my difficulties and made her smile but not much and not often. Once, towards the end of our journey, I had to slow down to cross a narrow bridge where the road ran over a railway line. I tried to say in Polish, 'How fast are we going?' which is followed in the phrasebook by 'Two pints of milk please.' This made her smile the whole length of the bridge, pointing to a man not too far away who was leading a cow as if taking it for a walk. And I laughed too in my somewhat staccato, choking manner so that she felt the need to touch my hand on the steering wheel, to keep it steady, if you will. And then I heard both phrases spoken very distinctly and turned to see Mrs Bradecki leaning towards me.

'English often very bad too,' she whispered.

'Bad?' I said. 'Some of the time we're perfectly bloody appalling.'

This made Maria laugh and I swerved dangerously so that she touched my hand again, letting it rest there, I thought, a fraction longer. Mrs Bradecki would have seen that. But by now we were turning right into the pine trees where the extermination camp had been.

At the side of the car park was a low building with a few photographs and maps on display. Little trouble had been taken over its upkeep.

There was also a kiosk selling guidebooks and postcards, cigarettes and sweets. For a few moments we stood there by the car, not sure which direction to go in. Then Maria pointed to a sign beyond the building and we moved towards it.

'Wait a minute,' she said suddenly. 'I leave something in the car.'

I followed her back to the car to open it for her and was about to put the key in the lock when she nodded towards them where they were turning the corner and said, 'No, they must go alone.'

And so we followed them at a distance beside the concrete sleepers which showed the way the trains had come carrying 800,000 people to their slaughter from all over Europe in little more than a year. The place had no other purpose at all. Here and there on the sleepers were small bunches of spring flowers and one or two miniature Israeli flags. We reached the point where a railway station had been built to look like any other railway station. Here they undressed and were led to the gas chambers, after which their bodies were dumped in a mass grave, doused with petrol and burnt. Now there was only a pathway of cobblestones leading to a simple monument of two columns of granite blocks across the top of which further blocks had been laid and carved with contorted figures. And stretching beyond it were hundreds of jagged chunks of rock of different shapes and sizes, some of them inscribed with the names of towns, embedded in expanses of concrete or in the soft fresh turf as if planted at random like a stunted, petrified forest. Here too a few more small bunches of flowers had been laid against the rocks and there were people wandering about, reading the inscriptions. Maria and I drifted apart and I watched the two women walk slowly side by side among the stones and then beyond them to the edge of the pine trees. It was a cool afternoon with the clouds high in a vivid blue sky. Fresh grass and weeds and wild flowers were spreading across the brown turf and in the distance birds were singing. It was a scene of ordinary calm and beauty on a fine spring day. I looked again towards the women. They were standing close to each other and I wondered how long they would stay there. Maria came up behind me and said, 'If my parents had died here . . .' But she did not finish.

I could not imagine whether I would have come to such a place if people I had loved had died here. It would not be the same as visiting a graveside to pay one's respects. I shook my head. Maria took my arm and pointed at the women. Mrs Bradecki seemed to be enfolded in the other woman's arms, then she broke away and covered her eyes with her hands and raised her head and her hands slid down to her mouth as she stumbled forwards into the trees. Mrs Konopka began walking back towards the monument and seemed to be looking around for us.

'I think we have finished,' Maria said.

We walked towards the monument and as soon as Mrs Konopka saw us, she turned back to where Mrs Bradecki was standing at the edge of the trees, her hands now hanging at her side. As her companion approached she briefly held them out and they walked towards each other and locked arms and went slowly back to the railway track and stood at the centre of it and looked into the distance where the sleepers stretched away into the pine trees. Then they turned and separated and walked quickly away towards the entrance and did not look back to see if we were following. When they were past the monument, Mrs Bradecki stopped and stared back at it for the last time. Did she then see her parents as she had throughout her life, but more vividly, stripped and terrified, hearing the voices, the screams, two in a multitude? I cannot know, but as we approached her, her eyes lifted above us and she gazed slowly across the whole sky and down to the level fringes of the trees. It was an expression I cannot describe and was as if the mask of grief had been swept from her face by the cool spring air in the stillness of this place and she became in that instant the young woman she had never been, baring herself to the eternity of blank blue skies overarching the world, resolute, undeluded, infinitely lonely. And she was further from me then than ever, as though history had drawn her back and she stood there as a witness of all that might have been and could never be restored. I can only say that she was changed and now seemed at the mercy of nothing.

We came up beside her and she showed no surprise. 'Now we are going home,' she said. She had spoken briskly like a command and walked on ahead of us, saying something in Polish. I asked Maria what she had said.

'She said that every day of her life she has been here and it is happening all the time.'

'Are you sorry you came?' I asked, for since we arrived she had seemed bored and indifferent.

449

'For you it is the same. It is other people, other times. History has many terrible things like this. We must listen to them weep, my mother says.'

'We don't often think about it though, do we? We don't know how to and if we did, we wouldn't want to much, would we? How could we then get on with our lives? Our silly, busy little lives.'

'You say we are not mattering so much.' She sighed. 'For me it is only to start loving my parents again.'

'I don't know. Until something terrible happens to us too.' Now I was just chatting to her.

Again she looked bored and hurried slightly ahead of me to the car park. I stopped at the kiosk and bought a guidebook. The women were waiting at the car and I did not look at their faces when I opened the door for them. Before driving off I looked into the driving mirror and saw that Mrs Konopka had begun to weep. Her stern, official face, accustomed to lies and authority, had given up the struggle. Her eyes were screwed up and her mouth hung open in a grimace of pain, then with a groan that seemed to come from deep within her, she leant forward to hide her face from me and began fumbling for a handkerchief in her gold-trimmed black leather handbag. Then she pressed it to her face and into her mouth to stifle her sobs, her body heaving beyond her control.

'Is it . . . Would you like . . . ?' I began.

Maria reached across and turned on the ignition and nodded sharply at me to drive on. When we had reached the road through the forest, I glanced back again and saw Mrs Bradecki leaning towards her companion and whispering to her and their hands joined and clasped tight between their breasts. I looked at Maria and we smiled at each other as strangers might and we knew we had to start a conversation about anything at all, so I asked her about her boyfriend and she told me he had trained as an architect and was still in Germany, that they were going to start a business together and soon they would have their own flat. He wanted to design furniture and they had a friend with a workshop. She produced a photograph of him from her handbag and he looked very dashing with blond hair falling across his forehead and a sly expression, sure of its uses and the success that would come his way in abundance. She wanted me to know how much in love with him she was, that it was all she cared about. When I asked her a vague question about Poland's political

450

future she shrugged as if that meant nothing to her. And then I told her about myself, my children and new granddaughter and the ballet dancers in the flat below me, and my father who had been a grocer and never thought he was quite up to it and was surprised that anything had come of me at all. I told her about my wife, that we had split up but now got on quite well together. I told her about my work and my time in Suffolk and the people I had known there and the church I used to visit and my faithlessness. I told her everything about myself. And as we talked, I became aware that the women behind us had fallen silent. I did not look in the mirror again. We were pretending we were alone. How well I came to know the drift of pale golden hair along her arm.

When we reached the hotel, Maria got out and went with the women to find a taxi. They did not say goodbye to me. I expected Maria to come back but she got into the taxi too with the briefest of waves. She too had not said goodbye, as if there was no need for it, the gulf too great dividing my past from her unbounded future. I had not enquired whether Mrs Bradecki would be staying on. We were booked to fly back on the following day but now, once more, she had ceased to be my business. I had done all that might have been expected of me. I did not know when I would see her again. I did not know what I would tell Foster. I knew where she hid a key to her flat and could go down there from time to time to make sure it was all in order. I could open the windows and let in some fresh air and clean the place up a bit. I could deal with any bills. If she returned it would be ready for her.

That evening I went to a concert at the National Philharmonic Hall given by the cellist Yo-Yo Ma. He played with great passion, sweating and making rapturous faces and not seeming to mind at all that the hairs of his bow were beginning to break off and float loose. I wondered how many there were and whether they still came from horses. Presumably he had a spare in his dressing room. The female pianist was exceptionally adept at keeping up with him but of course they must have practised a fair amount together. There was nothing wrong at all with any of it so far as I could tell. The passion was right and real but wouldn't have been much use without the dexterity; the other way round too, I suppose. I promised myself I would buy a record of his on my return and this I have now done. It is Elgar's

Cello Concerto and I quite often play it, imagining all those loose hairs wafting across the sound. It becomes more beautiful each time I listen to it, so I am careful not to do it too often, in case it wears off, the immense sadness or yearning or whatever it is of it.

And while I listened to the music that evening I found myself wondering if Maria had read Mrs Konopka's account of her childhood. Of course she must have. She must have known too that her mother had given it to me. And so what we had witnessed that day we were seeing through the same eyes, were briefly at one. The music then, as it sometimes does now, piercing through sadness, seems to be pleading for some impossible redress against the terrible enormity of things. And then I may remember Maria beside me. So personal. I can't help it. I wish I could.

452

Chapter Seven

But now I have drifted into the present again. Many months have passed and I must decide what to make of all these papers which surround me. Bits typed and the scribblings in my notebook. There are so many loose ends everywhere. I wish it did not seem so long ago and that I could bring it to life again, as it was then. But time slides by and I should not try to refashion it, weave in a pattern of threads, or make something of it all that stands apart or above it, like meaning you can take out of it or point at, or as if thereby I might 'slip time's halter' as it was put in a book I was reading the other day. The best I can do is try to remind myself. So I must resist the temptation to go back over what I wrote all those years ago when the children were young and make myself out to have been less unfunny or silly or whatever than the way I unwittingly portrayed myself, indeed believing that I was showing myself to be quite a guy, as the Americans say; as in, say, ten years' time I'll look back on this and think, 'Oh, my God, you can scrub that lot out for a start.' Though in ten years of course I may not be here at all, or all there to coin a phrase. So I try even harder now to get it right, imagining for example that Ann will come across it one day and I begin to think I am writing it for her rather than just for myself when I would have no reason not to be honest or take more trouble. It is best to believe, perhaps, that truthfulness and consideration for others are what really matter rather than wanting to be thought well of, those and a certain untargeted cheerfulness. And if when I'm not here this finds its way, as it almost certainly will, via the dustcart to the incinerator, to be recycled into something useful, that will be perfectly all right by me, just as everything was perfectly all right by me before I was born.

That was by way of not getting on with the story. From time to time, as perhaps I have not sufficiently remarked, I had suffered from breathlessness and twice I had what are called palpitations, which I mistook for some kind of deviant digestion. Then, three days before my departure for Poland I had a bout of what I have since learnt to be angina pectoris – one of a number of complaints in the cardiac range whose names I have since become all too familiar with. It was, I have to say, painful and put me into a state of shock. It nearly gave me a heart attack. But it passed and I put that down to an evening's chewing of Gaviscon tablets. Indeed I persuaded myself I felt as right as rain, though looking out now at black clouds and a relentless downpour swamping this piece of the world I must have known I was deceiving myself.

Or so the doctor told me when two weeks after my return from Poland I fetched up in hospital after my second myocardial infarct. Though I sent a telegram to Jenners to ask him to get up a petition, this led to a triple bypass operation and a strict regime combined with what my doctor had the gall to describe as a perfectly normal life: avoid obesity, nervous tension, mental strain, fear, anger, joy, grief and anxiety to say nothing of moderation in all things. Tobacco and alcohol have also been mentioned more than once if my memory serves me. Fearfully and anxiously avoiding all these things instead of doing relaxing things like drinking and smoking seems to have a built-in fallacy somewhere, though I cannot quite put my finger on it – as one of the nurses said to me one memorable evening when she was searching for my pulse and I thought, feeling ghastly at the time, indeed scared out of my wits as I waited for the trolley to come and wheel me off, that there might not be a pulse to feel and it wouldn't be more than a second or two before the rest of me caught up. 'Don't pull the sheet up any higher just yet,' I said. 'Ah there it is,' she said. Which made me feel immensely better and I had the terrific pluck to say to her, 'These triple bypass jobs, work out all right normally, do they? High success rate does the bloke have?' '100 per cent', she replied. 'You'd say that if it was more in the region of ten per cent, wouldn't you?' She touched my nose very saucily, 'Dead right I would. See you tomorrow and we'll continue the discussion then.' Such a pretty girl she was and I decided the last thing I might have done in my life was to fall in love. And so, by now drugged out of my senses, I put another question to her, 'Tell me, nurse, if you were sure I was going to snuff it and I asked you to put up a screen and let me see you without any or most of your clothes on, what would your response be, having in mind your duty to the welfare of your patients?' Though I said it in far fewer words than this, I expect, and in the wrong order. 'Ooooh, Mr Ripple, with you I'd go a lot further than that, I would. What a pity you're not going to snuff it then, isn't it?' 'I'll have to think about that . . .' I said. By now I was very sleepy and slightly less frightened and my last thought before I woke up and it was all over was how nice it was, however ill one might be, to be entirely in the hands of others who know exactly what they are doing and what's best for you and if you want anything, just ring the bell. Not like life.

I don't think I need to write any more about my heart trouble. Those who have been through it won't need reminding and those who haven't will want to skip it as if thereby they might skip it in life, a knack I have yet to acquire.

So on with the story. On the second day after my return from Poland, Foster called. He seemed exactly the same, the empty staring eyes on the edge of anger and the garish, mismatching turn-out, now a black and yellow check waistcoat, gold corduroy jacket and bright red cravat like a gush of blood. He sat down in my armchair, stretched back and held out a cupped hand, waiting for a drink to be put into it.

'So, Ripple, got rid of Madam Polack have you in the land of her forefathers?' I said I didn't know. 'Well, she'd better make up that gloomy Slavic mind of hers PDQ. I'm going to advertise.'

'Leave it a week or two,' I said, bringing him his drink.

'Oh all right. But eighty quid the absolute minimum. There isn't the quid pro quo now you see, pardon the pun.'

'I see that.'

He stared hard at me as if he expected more from me. 'You're not looking up to much if you don't mind my saying so? Not been overdoing it, have you, caught some awful Polish bug?' I shook my head, poured myself a drink, lit a cheroot. There was a pause while he closed his eyes and drummed his forehead with his fingers. When he looked at me again, there was a moment of bewilderment in his eyes as if he had forgotten something. Then the old suppressed ferocity returned and he said, 'You know in the so-called good old days when we were shoving our noses in on the Dark Continent it might be yonks before you could get to a doctor. The wife, now, got malaria.

Temperature up in the 105s. Just had to sweat it out, swallow the tablets. She was a wreck for weeks. Her own fault for not taking her Novaquin. Poor old thing. Then I broke an arm, falling out of a tree since you ask. Twelve hours jogging about in a Land Rover over dirt roads at the start of the rains. Don't know how lucky you are. I could tell you some stories. The Afs, Christ, they must have bloody suffered, miles from anywhere, most of them had something and sometimes slicing each other about a bit if you know what I mean. Bloody lucky. Toothache. Bingo! And now they don't have to cut you open, do it with lasers. Hardly worth the bother of being sick at all. Didn't do to be sick in Africa, I can tell you. Dickenson was all right up to a point but we all know what happened to him, poor sod. Nursed the wife a treat, I'll say that for him. No names, no pack drill. Well, I was sodding grateful to him, wasn't I, getting her on her feet again, up to a point? And if that meant . . . oh hell. And then Dickenson doing himself in and she losing the baby. Whose, I hear you ask. Am I boring you? Do say, for Christ's sake.'

I shook my head, though now feeling distinctly unwell, what there was in store for me sending out signals. He leant forward and thrust out his hand as if, had I been closer, he would have taken me by the scruff of the neck.

'All that aside, we had a high old time, the open spaces, the stars, the sun, a bit too much of that, and actually getting things done, better crops, healthy cattle, saving life. Dickenson was a bloody hero really, a bit of education too though we know where that leads to, don't we, politics but can't object to that, can we, seeing us off the premises for a start. Not that anyone who wanted to stay on couldn't. We did for a while, or I did, bit of teaching, game control, tsetse fly stuff but you had to make a new start some time. Then back to this place. Wife had a bob or two plus the golden handshake, lumpers they called it. So there we are. You miss it on a day like this, drizzly, damp, mean little, cold little, dreary little, stuffy old England. Still, they say it's a bloody shambles there now. You can't win, can you? And now AIDS as if the poor buggers didn't have enough . . . Sod it, that's what I say . . .'

He rambled on like this, his voice becoming quieter and almost inaudible. Twice I filled his glass but he hardly seemed to notice, gazing out of the window and tapping his forehead from time to time. He left as abruptly as he came. On the way out he laid a hand on my shoulder and said with sudden gentleness, 'Look after yourself, Ripple, I would if I were you. You look as if you try to enjoy life.'

And that was the last I saw of him. He did it on the night I had my operation. Out on a moor in Yorkshire in the middle of the night, a hose from his exhaust. Annelise told me when she came to visit me in hospital. The police had come round with a solicitor or someone. There had been no suicide note, not then. The solicitor, she said, had told her his wife had been in a mental hospital for many years, what was wrong with her not improved by rapidly advancing Alzheimer's disease. The suicide note was in fact a letter to me and I did not get it until my return. I think Annelise had recognised the handwriting but did not want to risk upsetting me further. It did not say too much.

Dear Tom, if I may,

This is really a bloody selfish thing to do, don't tell me. But the wife won't know the difference. Keep the flat tidy. She loved it at first, her little bits and pieces and pottering in the garden until she didn't know it was hers and started wandering off and pottering in other people's gardens too. I couldn't let anyone else near it. Can't help remembering the old days in the beginning, seeing her making such a beautiful garden out of nothing, crouched by a swimming pool, running her finger through the water. God, we were happy for a year or two, I can tell you. All good things come to an end, sod the lot of them. Year after year driving a minicab, well you can see your tomorrows, can't you? My squalid so-called love life compared with those lovely dancing girls coming and going, when they can't stand the sight of me. The estate was a bit of a mess, house in the wife's name, but I've managed to fix that now. Seemed like a good idea at the time. Didn't feel like taking it away from her when she was losing everything else. So now she's got nothing. There are a few cousins but haven't kept up – stuffy lot – but they don't want to know so what I've done is leave enough to the wife's hospital to see her through and the rest I've left to a charity. Details with the bank. There's a solicitor bloke, stupid fart but professional with it. The house is in pretty good nick, thanks to our Polack chum. So there we are. I'm doing this, if you must know, because all the time, non-stop in fact, I feel fucking miserable. Bought a new cravat and gold waistcoat yesterday. They'll jolly well find me looking my best. Can't get the wife out of my

mind, what she was once, the day I first saw her, bloody lovely she was,
tending her garden, me too for that matter, with such love and that's
the word, believe me, and what she is now, a completely gaga, ugly,
bad-tempered stranger. So curtains, old fruit, and look after yourself.
Didn't like the look of you at all when I drank all your gin that day.
Knew you weren't fooled for a moment by all that tycoon rubbish. Could
see you were a quizzical sort of bugger. Don't know if there's a hereafter
when we might meet up again but frankly the way I feel now I don't give
a toss one way or the other. It's my fleedom at last as the Afs used to call
it. Wish I'd made a better job of the self-government.

Regards,
John Foster.

Looking back over what I wrote about him at the time I see him now
quite differently of course. It wasn't anger or contempt at the edge of
his emptiness but sheer misery but I'll leave it as it was. Thus we
often get things wrong. Or should I say, defeat not scorn, that and a
spent capacity for any sort of happiness?

Mrs Bradecki came back from Poland a week after I returned from
hospital. I'd been down to the flat and tidied it up a bit, in fact quite
a lot, hoovering and dusting and wiping and letting in the air and
doing the washing-up. She hadn't bothered with much of that after
her husband died. She phoned me and I went down to see her. She
seemed little changed but in the dim front room with the curtains
half-drawn it was difficult to tell. She was still wearing her black
dress but her face was darker and she looked at me steadily, almost
eagerly, as though I puzzled her or there was something she wanted
to tell me. She brought me coffee and as we sat there in silence for a
while she suddenly smiled and patted her hair and I saw that she had
had it cut and the ends had been curled. I noticed too that she had
painted her fingernails and was wearing small orange earrings,
amber perhaps. Briefly the sun came out and I saw that she had
coloured her cheeks and shadowed her eyes and her mouth shone
with lipstick. She had done herself up for me. The sunlight faded
away and still we just sat there, looking at each other with small,
polite smiles. I must have said something but it was nowhere near
the question I wanted to ask her or telling her I had a bloody great
scar down the middle of my chest or that Foster was dead. It was

something like, 'Welcome back home again and what lovely weather we've been having.' I opened my arms and looked around me.

'You make very nice for me,' she said quietly.

'That's nothing. A touch of the duster here and there, beating the carpets . . .'

'No, please . . .'

I began telling her about her electricity bill, which appeared to be a mistake unless she did really owe the electricity board £4,786,296. I fetched it for her and said sternly with a wag of my finger, 'You really must try to remember to switch off the stove or perhaps I left the hoover on?'

She stared at it for a long time. 'What I do?' she asked.

'Borrow money from the bank.'

I was standing behind her and she reached back and touched my arm. 'You like my husband sometimes, trying make jokes.'

Then I went towards the door and she got up and just stood there, her hands to her side, her head up. 'Thank you, Mr Ripple,' she said. 'You kind to me. I no think you better on horses. I think you have very good legs.'

I made an extended series of clicking sounds and then a long drawn out whinnying noise. She looked amazed and put a hand to her mouth and I left. And so it was. Nothing of any moment had been said, nor has it since. Soon we were to become conspirators.

About a week later, she showed me a letter which said, 'I am a friend of Maria who is saying you can give me inviting letter in English that I am your guest for two months and pay all my support and accommodation. If you agree Maria say Mr Ripple will write proper letter for my visa and friend too. Mr Ripple she say is absolutely helpful and friend of Poland.'

I have written several such letters now, confirming this and verifying that. Some have her signature, one or two have mine and yesterday I even forged Foster's. Jane has signed one. The young people are beginning to turn up, never more than three at a time. They seem to get work quickly enough. One or two have only stayed for a few days before disappearing altogether. I have told Mrs B she must insist on rent. I go down to meet them. They all shake my hand vigorously or the boys do. The girls allow their hands to be held briefly and they always seem cold and frail. Which is not at all how the rest of them seem or might be and oh my Lord I can't begin to tell you how glad they seem to be meeting me, the brightness in their eyes, the gratitude, the longing, sod the lot of them as Foster would have said, there's no bypass for that and stop thinking piss.

Anyway, one day soon an official from the Home Office will turn up accompanied by members of the police force and invite me to account for myself. I shall say that it is utterly disgraceful to let such riffraff in to sully this fair land of ours when all they want to do is work and some of them even get married and what could be more depraved than that. 'Shit,' I'd say as they marched me off to the police station, 'just think of it, all those busy young Polaks all over the place, scroungers and fiddlers and layabouts the lot of them, lowering the whole tone of the place. Social pollution, that's what it is, as though there weren't enough bloody foreigners fouling up the place already. Laying on royalty and fancy horses and men in funny costumes for their president is one thing but giving them the idea they might be welcome is quite another. Czechs and Hungarians and Lithuanians are one thing but Poles, Christ, I ask you. And don't give me any of that history crap . . .'

More time has passed. It is taking time to sort out Foster's estate so I took advantage of that to pay one of the Polish lads to build some steps up from Mrs Bradecki's flat to the garden. She works incessantly there and is doing wonders to it. The dark-brown soil is freshly turned and weeded and flowers and shrubs have been planted at organized intervals. There is mauve and white and yellow and a wide variety of greens. Yesterday something red came into bloom. I bought her a new lawnmower and some of the blue-powder fertilizer and the lawn is becoming the lushest for miles, only in patches admittedly but spreading fast. One of the Polish lads has repainted the garden bench and table with Dulux white gloss and repaired the bird bath so that it holds water and breadcrumbs can be put around its rim. He did not charge for that. You can see what I mean, the way they'll turn their hands to anything and what's more look so damn cheerful about it, as I said earlier lowering the whole tone of the place.

I have just pushed my typewriter to one side and leant out of the window, causing a tearing sensation along the gash down my middle, but not serious, more a lengthy itch.

'Very nice, Mrs B,' I called down. 'No slacking, mind you.'

Her uplifted face was contorted because the sun was behind me. 'Slacking please?' she called back. I put my palms together and rested my cheek on them. 'You go sleep now?'

I pointed at my eye, then at her. 'Oh no,' I said, 'can't let you out of my sight.'

I waved and returned to this blank page, wanting to fill it up somehow. I think of taking her a cup of tea and some biscuits and sitting down there with her on the bench. But the truth is we seem to have nothing to talk about now, except the garden. Yesterday I saw Annelise down there chatting away, watching her at work. Michelle joined them for a minute or two. I cannot imagine what they have to talk about, cultural matters perhaps. The truth is too that I am suddenly feeling very tired and think I should sleep. Just looking at her working away in the garden seems to have taken a lot out of me.

Resumed later after sunset. It seems increasingly nowadays that I cannot help rambling back and forth out of the chronology of my life, but internally of course there is no such thing. Memories and thoughts, which are increasingly the same thing, come and go in no particular order, looming and fading, in their own time, disordered and unbidden. They are quite random. Time has become only the light and the dark, the hands on one's watch in different places, a calendar on the wall, numbers, the world outside more or less green and blue, brown and grey. That is what is out there but what takes place in the mind has no regard for that, it has its own schedule, one is not quite sure if it is trying to tell one something. As the poet says of life: 'Whether or not we use it, it goes and leaves what something hidden from us chose.' I have no idea what this means, though I know it is beautiful and suspect that must be because it is also true.

As you would expect, I had several such meditations in the hospital. You can skip them. They're not thought out, which is the point I'm trying to make. The aforementioned nurse was there when I came round from the anaesthetic. She was holding my hand. 'All my clothes on, you see,' she said, pulling her shoulders back a little, hinting at what I was missing. I hope I managed a wan smile. She ministered to me in various ways, with an astonishing mixture of briskness and calm. I did manage, however, to say, 'I feel half dead, so you could take half of them off.' 'You're a dirty old man,' she

461

said. 'Yes,' I said, 'but aren't we all?' 'How would I know?' she said. Doesn't that make me sound a plucky, jovial sort of chap? In fact I was still shit scared, uncomfortable too, though glad to be alive. She was going along with me as I tried to cheer myself up. I wonder if all the nursing profession is like that. Of course if they hadn't wanted to live their lives beside death and suffering, they wouldn't have become nurses in the first place. A special class of person by definition.

The doctor came later and gave me the thumbs-up sign. 'I'd be glad to put my signature on that one,' he said. 'Ten out of ten.' The nurse winked at me. I must say he did look far too young, still learning by his mistakes. Adrian and Jane came to see me on Day Two. They brought flowers and two Agatha Christies. I was too drowsy to say much. Adrian looked sternly at me as if I had been making a fool of myself and was paying the price. Jane said that I should take a long holiday in the sun. The flowers they had brought were yellow and white roses, barely beyond the budding stage and they bore all the sunlight I thought I should ever need. I told Adrian he looked tired but it was Jane who replied, 'Your son works too hard. He is too conscientious but that's why he is going to be the best.' He shook his head. 'There are lots better than I am.' She touched his hand. 'See what I mean.' Then they got on to some episode in the City in which they were both involved and I am ashamed to say I fell asleep. When I woke up, the nurse had put the flowers in a vase beside me and there was sunlight on them and I missed Adrian very much.

They came to see me twice more, the first time bringing fruit and the second time a crossword puzzle book, the *Daily Telegraph* unfortunately. They did not stay long. Once or twice Adrian looked at his watch. I hope he is not too preoccupied in relation to Jane too. I told them a bit more about my trip to Poland to add to what I'd told them over the phone. They said I should try to write it down if I didn't have anything better to do. I wouldn't have dreamt of telling them that I'd already written a fair amount about my life, which included them. I can just see the expression on Adrian's face.

Virginia came to see me about a week after the operation. The nurse told me she had phoned regularly and sent her love. She apologised and said she was sorry Richard had not come too but he was very busy now, making his mark.

'So into the forgery business now, is he?' I said, taking her hand. 'Counterfitting. Or shop design. Somewhere to put the cash register. There should be money in that.'

She did smile a bit then, in fact the beginning of a giggle, then took her hand away. 'He thinks you make fun of him,' she said. 'He's not very sure of himself, having been laid off twice now. He's really too nice to compete and impress. He needs every bit of confidence he can get. This stationery job, I'm afraid I don't see it lasting. They're a new local company and the big boys have European partners. He's very worried and doesn't sleep and another on the way.'

'I'm sorry,' I said. 'But if he wants a safe job why doesn't he try Chubb or Durex for that matter . . . what was that you said?'

'I'm pregnant.'

'Are you indeed? Then he does worry too much.'

There was a pause. 'You don't sound very pleased.'

'I read the other day, the *Evening Standard* I think it was, they're looking for cold shower salesmen. Why . . . ?'

She sighed. 'Come off it, Dad, at your time of life.'

'Of course I'm pleased. Haven't asked you about Ann.'

'Ann is all right.'

'That was my impression too.'

When she left there were tears in her eyes. I think they were from happiness.

This morning I stared at my binoculars on the window-sill and couldn't for a minute or so remember what they are called. Two days ago, I typed out my telephone number on a letter I was writing to the local authority, I forget now about what. It was the number of our house near the North Circular Road. In the last three days I have completed a total of eleven clues in *The Times* crossword, only two so far today and it is approaching midnight.

Up the road I have begun to notice a slight lad in a space suit and safety helmet coming and going on a scooter at all hours. Yesterday I took my longest walk so far since my operation and went past the house on the corner where the scooter was parked. The lad had just got off it and removed his helmet. Not a lad at all but a black-haired, black-eyed, wide-mouthed beauty. I raised my hand by way of greeting and said good afternoon. No response at all. Pity about that.

Wonder what she does for a living. Sometimes I hear the sound of a piano coming from that house. Spanish-sounding music of late. I walk past the house almost every day but I have not seen her again. I'm not sure I really want to.

Annelise came to see me in the hospital too. She said Michelle sent her love. They loved the little boxes I had brought them. By then I was able to get up and shuffle about in my dressing gown. So yet again she was not seeing me at my best. What a crying bloody shame. She could not stay long, she said, because she was on the way to rehearsal. After she had told me about Foster, I said I thought she was looking better and indeed she now had some colour in her cheeks and the black shadows had gone from under her eyes, and these shone, nervous and alert as when there is something good to look forward to. She was fidgety, crossing and uncrossing her trousered legs and moving the top half of her body about as if already limbering up. Her upper garment was a loose deep red and gold floral smock-like thing but not so loose that I was able in all conscience to say she seemed to be putting on weight too.

'Really,' I said. 'You're looking good.'

She lowered her eyes. 'I hope you get well soon,' she said. 'Being ill doesn't suit you.'

'Oh no? Well in that case, this is the last time . . . But you?'

She hesitated. 'I'm not sure. I'm truly not sure. Michelle tries not to patronize me but you know how it is . . . For myself, all those years of slog and not having a sort of normal physical life but it would have broken my father's heart. He went around telling everyone I was with the Royal Ballet and he brought his friends to see me and I could almost see him pointing and saying, "There she is, seventh on the left." And my mother saying "Shush, Harry . . . " He adored me and if I packed it in he'd have . . . well it would be awful. So I have to go on, but it will be the same old thing year in, year out, more and more bishes and I'm not sure I enjoy it any longer . . . I'm dancing now as well as I ever have but it won't last and so many others coming along. Oh God . . .' She closed her eyes and took a deep breath. 'It really would have bust him up. He lived for me . . . You see, in his background there weren't any arts at all, my Mum too, and it's sort of a whole world of the imagination which lets you see things differently and better and gives you, like, alternatives . . . But I'm so selfish, only talking about myself and poor Mr Foster and you cut open.'

'You talking about yourself, believe me, is . . . oh, never mind. But why the gloom? You seemed when you came in so exceptionally, well, happy.'

She blushed and raised her tiny hands off her lap and crossed her fingers. 'Oh, that's something else.'

'A bloke?' I asked. 'Touch and go?' She nodded vigorously. 'The more there is of the one, the tougher the other would get.' I squeezed her hand. 'Good luck. I only hope he's good enough for you. Also in the dancing business, is he?'

But that she did not answer, looking hurriedly at her watch and getting up to go.

'Get well soon,' she said, but her mind was on other things.

My former wife also came to see me. She was on her way to another hospital where Brad was. She is very grey now and lined and all her old assurance has gone. She had with her the typescript of a book wrapped in brown paper which she laid at the foot of my bed. She told me it was about delinquency and she and Brad were writing it together but it was nowhere near finished. She began to tell me about a theory that the effect of some misery or psychological damage skipped a generation, the spreading or deepening of harm over the years and its coming out in another disorder. Part of the book was a series of case studies to validate this.

'I do not think I can finish it without Brad,' she said. 'He likes me to discuss it with him, the tiniest detail.'

'Then he must believe it will be finished.'

'No, that's the point. All the details he finds fault with. He wants to go back over every single argument. It frustrates him terribly. And he's very weak. He keeps on saying, "We've got it wrong. We've got it wrong." '

Her voice trailed away, all the certainty collapsed out of it, the sentences dispersed about a void. We talked a bit about the children then and I hoped she might find some satisfaction there, what credit there was being largely hers. We recalled a few episodes from their childhood, the walks in the park, a snowman, a school play and further back to the days after they were born. But no mention of Webb or Hamble. It was as though we were embarking on a long search,

465

stumbling at first and finding little. We remembered the days at the seaside without the bad temper and rain and they became suffused with gaiety and beneficence as the sea glittered under the sun. In our minds we were restoring time and making it anew and in that short time, my wife at my bedside, we were not deceived. And all the time we were thinking, oh once we were young and in one another's arms . . .

When she got up to go, she said suddenly, 'That day in the park, I guessed then about Adrian. Three in one car, five in the other.'

'Ah . . .'

'I'm sure you've forgotten now. I was so tactless and you told me off. The jokes. They only get one so far, don't they?'

'Yes,' I said and looked away.

She put her hand on mine and let it rest there for a moment. 'Concern or love, they leave so little room for anything else. Or death for that matter. I'm sorry, Tom.'

I shook my head. Sorry for what? But she gave me no chance to reply. When I looked back at her she had already turned away from me.

So there we are. Time passes. I must bring this to an end. Things are happening on the property front. Foster left his money to the Save the Children Fund. The rest of the house is on the market. I wish I could afford it but I spoke to Jane the other day and she seemed interested. An investment. I did not need to tell her that would solve the problem of Mrs Bradecki, who hasn't been paying rent for some time now. I nearly forgot: the vicar sent me a kind note wishing me a speedy recovery. I do not know how he found out that I had been ill but in his line of work the good news travels.

He added:

Why not drive out for a service one Sunday and give thanks? Bring your sister and that lovely voice of hers. We could do with a bit of class and vigour, God alone knows. However, mustn't complain. Your friend Jenners has worked miracles, if you'll pardon the expression, raising money for the restoration fund. Hope we can now track down a few more worshippers to offset the tourists. I'm not one for charging but the eye of the needle and all that. Churches are excellent places to shed the loose change weighing down their pockets after purchases of iced lollies, gasoline, picturesque postcards, junk food and the like. Roll on the ten-pound coin, even if it's called something else, the same in twelve languages. They've begun chipping away again at the St Christopher, which is turning out to be even more remarkable than we thought. Your friend Sidney asked me if it had been painted in blood. He would. There's even talk of a new organ. Some pressure from on high for drums and guitars and happy hours (bring your own sacraments). I even have a colleague who shall remain nameless who's organizing a weekly Jog for Jesus. One bishop has drawn the line, I hear, at Jesus Jeans. I've been asked to organize a series of singalong teach-ins at a church in Ipswich, each centring on one of the apostles. Any ideas? Rock for St Peter. Rap for Judas. Revivalist music for Lazarus, though he's not an apostle. I'm in doubt about St Thomas. The highlight of the series might be for virgins only, devoted to the Mother of God. The aim would be to bring in the early teenagers by when, so I'm told, it's likely to be too late. (The lovers are all in school, remember?) Must go now. Got to clear the altar for a buffet, set up the speakers on the font. Oh yes, had you heard about the crafts centre folk? Upped and left. Fiddled the books. Talk of orgies. Naked bodies observed prancing in the woods by moonlight. Recitations and amorousness of a fairly indiscriminate (catholic) sort. Just the sort of thing we're supposed to be going in for these days though at a different time of day and with more clothes on. My own view is that it's been greatly exaggerated. One of the trainees with a history of mental disturbance got pneumonia and her parents laid a complaint. It was the misuse of public funds they minded, of course. One must be prepared for everything these days. Who knows where it will all end? One of the things on the list of the restoration fund is central heating though the weather is getting warmer and winter in general seems to be on the way out. We could always break off for a spot of PT and a few press-ups. Would Cantuar draw the line, I wonder, at volleyball in the nave and showers installed in the vestry? Tried your joke about losing one's marvels on an evangelical colleague (bearded, green corduroys with turn-ups) the other day. Just looked at me. Oh well.

God be with you and get well soon, with or without His intervention.

Yours (still) faithfully.

PS. Is this a prayer you've ever come across? 'Let us confess to God the sins and shortcomings of this world, its pride, its selfishness, its greed; its evil divisions and hatreds. Let us confess our share in what is wrong

and our failure to seek and establish that peace which God wills for
his children.' A pretty tall order but right of course. Underneath that
nothing else much matters, does it? The thing is, you couldn't get away
with saying things like that except in a church of one sort or another.

A few more bits and pieces. Earlier this evening I phoned Maureen. A
man answered. I nearly put the receiver down there and then but
plucked up unimaginable courage to ask whether she was in. 'She's
at choir practice,' he said. 'Who shall I say called?' His voice was,
how shall I put it, protective and not inviting further enquiry. Gruff
in a word. 'It was about *The Messiah*,' I said no less gruffly. 'Come
again?' he replied. 'We'll just have to wait and see about that,' I said.
'I'll phone again.'

Which of course I won't. I hope he is treating her well. I didn't like
the way he said 'choir practice' as if that was another expression for
having it off with somebody else for all he knew. Surely she should be
teaming up with one of her tenors or basses, someone she could be in
tune with? I remember her with affection and gratitude and no little
shame. I hope she's had a chuckle or two at my expense too. I think
of her often at night, close up, unclothed etc., her body merging and
changing into others and back again, unheld by the imagination, just
fancifulness, all there but the soft feel of flesh or in other words nothing there at all. I listen to her singing. I count her teeth. We could not
love each other for long. How sad it all is.

Oh yes! In the *Sunday Times* last week there was a photograph of
Plaskett (remember him?) above a story about Handsworth
Holdings, a Stoke on Trent manufacturer of lingerie, lacewear and
children's clothes, taking over a sock manufacturer in Cardiff. I cut it
out for some reason. He has an austere and pensive look which is
intended to inspire trust and confidence. He is trying very hard
indeed not to look like an absolute shit. He is succeeding so well, I am
prepared to believe he no longer is. But then I remember Hipkin. I bet
there are some redundancies in Cardiff in the sock industry and
Hipkin is one of them. The story uses the word 'rationalization'. That
is what he is trying to personify. He makes me feel irrational. If they'll
take me back at the launderette I shall wonder which of those garments mingling and churning about have been rationalized by
Plaskett or are now likely to be. I can imagine him dipping his hand
in and plucking them out, limp and damp and ragged, leaving

behind only the unbedraggled, cost-effective underwear of life. In that context, I wonder how his wife is and what underwear over the years she's been able to compare with his. That line of thought. I look again at his authoritative face. The story says he's going to double exports, mainly in the Common Market. Perhaps he'll develop a line in frilly French knickers. Do French women wear different knickers from other women? I have no idea. How little I know about the world. And I'll know less and less the more they clean up the advertisements. Perhaps that will take longer in Greece and Italy. Knowing Plaskett as I did, I'm sure he'll do his market research or get someone to do it for him. But I won't be buying his shares for some reason.

Now, towards midsummer, the light is dying. All day long there has been the sound of lawnmowers from the gardens between our row of houses and the houses opposite. Plenty to see, too, between the trees, people lounging about, gardening, eating and drinking, playing with their dogs and children, a constant murmur between the lawnmowers. Mrs Bradecki has mowed her lawn too. I waved down to her but she was too busy to notice. All day long everything has seemed perfectly all right in this part of the world. I am really beginning to feel very well again. The doctor is pleased with me. The dancers are on tour somewhere. I have a top-price ticket to see them in a month or so. Annelise gave it to me. She said it was a complimentary but I suspect she paid for it. And in this dying light, last of all, before I pour another of the almost pointlessly weak whiskies the doctor allows me and light up my daily cheroot (which are three times the size at least of the ones I smoked before) I think of Hamble and wonder if he is still out there somewhere, tending his immaculate vegetables in his world of memories and stopped clocks, as if in that tending and care the world may be kept going as it always was so that she is still there beside him or bringing him tea or laughing at his little jokes which are no longer to cheer her up because in death she is restored to him, a living dream. And somewhere out there too, Mrs Webb is living alone and has nothing restored to her, except what never was or might have been before it was cancelled out and time was cut short in the sound of an echoless gong, a frying pan brought down on a bowed, retreating head. Two childless couples. Ah! How much I have had to live for. And now it is four in the morning and I cannot sleep. I pour myself a large forbidden whisky and sit at this desk, in front of this typewriter, and must try to come to an end. How silent the world is. I have never known such silence.

In times like this I ask myself what is the point of it all, and that must be true of most people, though Jenners's OBE might be sufficient point for him and for Sidney it might just be to go on buying and sell- ing houses and hoping to get laid tomorrow and so on. But for most there must be, or conceivably might be, something out there that makes life less utterly pointless than it gives every indication of being: God or an after-life or a previous life etc. Well those are lives too and the thing about them is that they don't seem to need anything to give them point, while giving point to us. We need meaning, they don't. They carry it about with them, God or our future or previous selves. Why can't we have it now? Unless every God has another God beyond Him, or there's an after-after-life going on for ever. Why shouldn't the same question be asked about eternal life as about this life? Religion is always doing that, pushing the answer back a stage, the ever-receding conclusion. If supernatural lives give purpose to ours, that's hardly to say more than that natural lives should do so too. But we know that only too well already, God knows. Multiplying lives doesn't help, however supernatural they may be. I seem to get nowhere in that direction at all. Out of my depth again. Thanks.

Perhaps it's much easier, if false, to come to the conclusion that the only point in life is what is already to be found in it somewhere. Not only fulfilment (OBEs and things) because only very few can have that and it leaves out the vast majority of people who only want more to eat for themselves and their children and somewhere nicer to live and to feel well and contented and less frightened much more of the time. There must be some measure in there somewhere more general than achievement: satisfactions you might call them, the basic expe- riences, what life is, the ordinary moments of affection and beauty and common kindness that are infinitely precious and the worse the life is, the more in danger, the more precious they become. I do not think I have paid enough attention to these things in my account. Perhaps none of us do, those in that small minority who are always wanting more of what we can't or shouldn't have because we have more than enough already if only we knew it, achievement all along the line. So are the precious things the point and the purpose? I saw a cartoon once of two bored-looking angels conversing and one says to the other, 'So what's the point of it all, do you reckon?'

'What's it all about then?' But then I do not remember that taxi driver but the day my son and I had egg and chips in a rotten café and went out into the park where the leaves were falling. If you'd asked me then I wouldn't have referred you to Bertrand Russell. The question would not have occurred to me while another, which would not have been a question at all, more of a vague, inexpressible query about happiness or love, was being answered.

But in the small hours of the morning none of this will do at all. What I suppose should worry us much more is not the search for some guarantee we will go on for ever, however pointless that may be, but how the appalling injustice of things can ever be put right. If there were a God, there'd only be one question worth putting to Him constantly: how are You going to make it up to people for the terrible things that have been done to them? I cannot think at the moment of any other question that matters in the slightest. And make it up to them so that they and their loved ones know that You will or have. Justice is the only thing that matters when you come to think of it, some equalization other than death itself. The rest is just words and stories and music and wanting to live for ever – and in that at least one thing is certain, come to think of it: no one is going to be disappointed, which is more than you can say about anything in life. And if there is no God, no purpose, nothing of that sort at all, the most that can be done, here and now, is to minimize unhappiness, seek ways of doing so, so that we find ourselves perpetually falling short; while knowing too that for that great fearful, suffering multitude, wretched beyond description, no difference can ever be made at all . . .

Yesterday evening just before sunset I put on some Chopin, one of the piano concertos. The window was open, letting in the first chill breath on the warm summer air. I looked out and saw Mrs Bradecki sitting in the garden, having mowed the lawn. She looked like a child surrounded by a golden carpet on which, the ragged shadows seeping towards her, she was afraid to tread. She looked up and we waved at each other. Then a minute or so later, there was a knock on my door. I opened it and she was standing there, looking meekly but firmly at me as if I was blocking her way. I stepped aside and she walked past me and sat down, gazing in front of her with an expression of indescribable longing, somewhere midway between joy and grief or rather both at the same time. Her hands were clasped on her lap, but not tightly, as if resting in each other. I was about to ask if she wanted coffee or whatever, then realized she had only come to hear the music. So I said nothing and went into the kitchen and pottered about, a difficult thing to do without making a sound, especially in kitchens. Eventually, as the music was coming to an end, I went back. All I can really say is that she was utterly still, utterly silent and tears were streaming down her face. I was right in front of her but she did not see me. I have never seen such weeping and in that moment had never heard such music. I went back into the kitchen and for some reason concentrated for a long time on the dirt under my fingernails. When the music had finished I returned bearing, I hoped appropriately, a full bottle of vodka, but she had gone.

Another long evening. I hope nothing happened in the houses opposite while I was away. Out with the thingummies, binoculars. About ten-thirty. People's bedtime. Still quite a lot of lit, uncurtained windows. As usual nothing going on at all. Hey, hold on a sec . . .

PART FOUR

PART FOUR

Chapter One

The years have passed and now a new millennium will soon be upon us. Since leaving my top-floor flat about five years ago I've added to this account from time to time, increasingly unsure what the point of it is. As soon as I start to think it may have given substance and continuity to my life the opposite becomes true, if anything.

It was an encounter at the corner shop this morning which sparked off thoughts about the millennium. The only focus I'd given it up to then was an upturned dish pinned down with spikes and a huge body underneath you'll be able to crawl about in – that surrounded by a series of zones covering aspects of human experience. There is a desperate look about it – remembering that once upon a time people used to build things like cathedrals. Then there is what it is costing. Perhaps that's it: to bring into focus the fatuous extravagance mankind is capable of. Oh well, no doubt I'll find myself not alone somewhere raising a glass as the hour strikes. There'll be the same old illusion in the air, much multiplied, of heightened resolve and lasting transformation – these offset by the usual range of fears and regrets, failure and disappointment etc., all of it whooped up into something that feels significant, different, hopeful, for a second or two. A time of reckoning. But not long into 2000 the only reckonable transformation will be in the numbers at the top of the page. We'll all still be crawling about in the same old body, our zones of experience all too human, all too familiar . . .

That was last week. Beside me now is the folder containing everything I've written since I left my flat. I came across it when looking for brochures about cookers, mine having started to turn on and off as if it had a life of its own. Looking through those – all offering a range of options I can manage without – my thoughts turn again to the millennium . . . Just another day on the calendar perhaps, but up and down the land beacons will be lit on hilltops, buildings finished, parks embellished, village halls renovated and goodness knows what else by way of celebration and renewal. So what better time to be reminded of what can never be renewed and merits no celebration? The raising of glasses to those who have passed on . . . What was that bloke's name? Nondescript sort of chap . . . On the glummish side, suddenly chuckling about nothing at all . . . Scribblings to be chucked out with the garbage by whoever lives here next: thoughts, memories, events higgledy-piggledy, shapeless, dispensible, very lifelike. The stroke of midnight, raise your glasses. That's two thousand years of Christendom behind us. Where's it got us? What next? Kissing, laughter, booze, funny hats and in the shadows round the edge, the unmodified sadness, the private little millennia explored for what isn't there, before the next day dawns, the floor is swept and the bottles roll out from under the sofa . . . My resolve thence heightened to have another look at what's in the folder . . .

Another day. Where was I? It was Mrs Felix at the corner shop who set me thinking about the millennium.

'And what plans are *you* making for the millennium, might I ask, Mr Ripple? Having a little celebration, are we? Taking stock? Pros and cons? Hope you're going to help with the beacon? Mr F and I, we're both of the view that we're lucky to be alive to see it. So jolly well should you be. You are, aren't you? Going to visit that Dome, are you? What's your opinion about that, I wonder? The hugest waste or the hugest good fun? And what about that wheel thingummy?'

That is the way she talks. She is a retired schoolmistress and asks a string of questions without pausing between them, each requiring a quite different answer.

I assumed a gruff or lofty expression. 'Ah yes, that millennium one hears about. Can't seem to relate to it somehow.'

She plucked my sleeve and her pink but withering face came closer, its nerve ends sending messages from one part of it to another.

'You can't do *that*,' she said gleefully. 'It's only a date. You can't have relations with a *date*.'

I sighed and mumbled, 'Ah me! As I recall only too well, too bloody often too bloody true . . .'

476

She did not hear this, being busy buying a Snickers chocolate bar which she gave to me. 'See if you can't relate to that, then, Mr Ripple.'

I pocketed it saying, 'Gosh, thanks,' while she fumbled in her handbag.

Then she looked up, plucked my sleeve again and gave me a surprised smile, expressing that if our conversation continued I'd be talking even more nonsense than I had already. I could tell she would have enjoyed teaching, watching the puzzlement of all those unanswered questions flitting across her children's faces, preparing them for life that way.

Continuity then, if not substance. Here it is, the last thing I wrote in my flat concerning what I saw in one of the houses opposite:

She was pulling a dark green dress over her head, revealing substantial breasts in a white bra and white knickers. Youngish looking. Long hair. Black. She began fiddling with the clasp of the bra, then, as if hearing my instructions, slid her hand down the side of her knickers. She was right up against the window and seemed to be standing in front of a mirror, enacting what had already occurred or what was to come. It was round about eleven. I groped so swiftly for my binoculars that I knocked them off the window-sill, then having got a fix on what she had done in the meantime – nothing, hand still under the elastic, breasts thrust forward – attempted to find her through the binoculars. Windows, brickwork and rooftops, a tree or two whizzed about until a couple of hours or so later, I did. She was standing facing me. She was smiling. She was young all right. I thought for an instant she was raising a hand to me, but it was to draw the curtains. It was all so fleeting, the instant before she drew the curtains, that I couldn't be sure if she was naked. Oh dearie, dearie me, what had I missed in those hours spent roaming the brickwork etc.? I slammed down the binoculars, deciding to make enquiries the next day about a tripod, more powerful binoculars while I was about it. I did nothing of the kind. All those years looking up after dark at lit, uncurtained windows and never before having seen a thing. That was as good as it got. I've never seen her again. I'd never seen her before. She was only spending the night there, perhaps. She'd seemed happy with what she'd got or was getting. Love is blind or sees only what is close up in the mind's eye. It doesn't care one jot about Peeping Toms out there in the world who take the long view and aren't getting anything.

I lost the binoculars in the move and didn't replace them. I've had no further use for them. Let the world keep its distance. It was unfinished business . . . A clean slate, I wrote at the end, having had a close look at a lot of those – gleaming in the light of a full moon, the sky having cleared after a heavy rainfall. It was that, the lovely scarred purity of the moon, the few frail clouds skimming along either side of it, that I was looking at when she appeared before me that night. It is only now that I remember the rain on the roofs glistening in the full moon, can persuade myself that I was in the habit of contemplating higher things, my sights only temporarily lowered, my vision emasculated; that can't be right, surely?

Some updating. Jane and Adrian bought the rest of the house from Foster's estate, the proceeds of that going, as he specified in his will, to the Save the Children Fund. His solicitor said it was the shortest will he had ever seen. I suspect the reason Jane and Adrian bought it was so that Mrs Bradecki and I could go on living there. (Jane's idea, though what she said was that it was as good an investment as any.) They went to live in New York for a while. Virginia had more children and Richard had more jobs. I went back to do the accounts for the launderette and the neighbouring restaurant. After six months or so the dancing girls moved out, first Michelle who became a 'principal' dancer in Holland . . . ('To keep the others up to the mark, I assume?' I suggested, no longer caring whether they smiled simply out of kindness – anything to lighten those pallid, careworn faces). I missed them.

Especially Annelise who got married and went to live in Kent. I vividly recall that at first there was only her overwhelming happiness when she floated in to say goodbye. She sat down and took a mug of coffee in both hands while I told her, not having to choose my words with care, that she and Michelle had been one of the very nicest things in my life so far. She hunched up, bent her head as if finding fault with her coffee, then suddenly stopped telling me about how kind and clever etc. her man was – a solicitor – and about the flat they had found in Canterbury near the cathedral, and the dancing school she could get a job at. For a moment I thought she had stopped breathing. Then I saw tears dropping on to her hands and heard two big sniffs.

'Good grief,' I said, 'I've heard about tears of happiness but . . .'

She was shaking her head and more tears fell. I considered sitting beside her and putting an arm round her shoulders but offered her my handkerchief instead. She took it but only let it dangle down around the coffee mug.

There was a further series of sniffs, then she looked up at me. 'Sorry. I'm being silly. I just suddenly missed Michelle, that's all. That whole wonderful life. Stuck away in a bloody flat in bloody Canterbury. Kiddies, if I can have them, housework, washing-up . . .'

Her tearful face was utterly different – the black smudges round the bleary eyes, the lips, smudged too, quivering. That sweet prettiness had been replaced by something forlorn that a companion, a child, might learn to dread. I did not want to see any more of that, so sat down beside her, not putting an arm round her shoulders.

'Hold on a sec,' I began. 'Aren't you supposed to be in love or something?'

I felt a slight shrug of her bony shoulder.

'Sorry,' she said again. 'I don't know what came over me. Must go now.' She turned and gave me a sudden, fierce hug. 'Love isn't everything, is it?'

Fortunately she didn't wait for an answer, jumping to her feet, then bending down to give me a quick, hard kiss on the cheek. 'Hope you keep up your recovery. It's been nice knowing you too.'

It was all no less formal than it sounds. I was being dismissed from her life.

'He's a bloody lucky chap if you want my opinion,' I tried much too loudly. 'The kiddies will be too. Send me a Christmas card. I'll let you know about love not being everything . . .'

She was opening the door and not listening, I suspected. Love was everything to her then again. She blew me a kiss.

'Of course I'll send you a Christmas card. Every year for ever. Promise.'

I didn't believe for a moment she would. But she has: from the same Canterbury address. She always signs it off 'with lots of love' and a cross or two, followed by a brief, noncommittal note: 'Life goes on'; 'So the years pass'; 'As you can see, still in Canterbury'; 'If you're ever this

479

way . . .' Nothing about a husband, kiddies, a job. Last year the note was longer. She wrote that Michelle had gone to the States and was 'a real star nowadays. Brilliant old Michelle! I wish she'd write.'

I have been tempted more than once to write and ask for her *news*. But I never knew her well enough and I don't want to be told there isn't any. That is the form my love for her takes, being kept in ignorance of her boredom and unhappiness. I'd like to tell her that no, of course love isn't everything; the trouble begins when you try to work out what else there is. Her Christmas cards, though, make me very happy. Thus to be remembered at all, that heftily outweighing the evident misery in them – that's love for you.

Mrs Bradecki still lives there, virtually rent-free I should imagine. I went to see her a couple of years ago. I made a few notes about it. It was early summer. She led me past the sleeping bags to the garden to show me how well she was looking after it. The lawn had been freshly mown, the flower-beds recently dug and replenished with good dark soil of the sort that Agnes once urged on me in my garden in Suffolk. We sat on the bench and talked about it. She had made herself something of an expert, showing me several books and pointing out a number of shrubs – I had no way of knowing how badly she was mispronouncing them.

Michelle and Annelise were succeeded by a couple who spent much of their time quarrelling, or at any rate shouting at each other – this sometimes drowned out by music of the thumping variety, lack of it rather. When we passed on the stairs or in the street, they couldn't manage even the most elementary greeting, one look at me having convinced them I was disgustingly old or repellently fascist or crassly intolerant or all of these. I didn't complain about the din, suspecting that if I did they'd turn it up louder. When they shouted, I enjoyed their loathing since it took some of the burden of it off me. When Adrian and Jane came round one evening I was about to suggest they might like to have a word about them with their letting agents when Adrian told me they weren't paying their rent and were about to be chucked out.

'Oh poor things,' I said, hoping I'd see them one day huddled in a doorway, their hands outstretched, in appalling weather – well perhaps not quite.

'You don't sound too sorry,' Jane said.

Then the music started up below. I looked back at her, removing all expression from my face.

'Far be it from me . . .' I began.

She gave me one of her sweetest smiles and nodded. 'Absolutely,' she said.

How clearly, blindingly, I see her now at that moment. There is more to be said about Jane. It's in there somewhere. Some time.

I'm not quite sure why I decided to move. The years were passing and on the spur of the moment one spring morning I took a train to the seaside town where long years ago we had spent those happy family holidays. As I wandered along the beach the memories began to return: Virginia sliding off a donkey, Adrian showing me a shell he'd collected for his mother's sewing box, her saying what a thoughtful child he was becoming, French cricket, Virginia's scream when a blob of ice-cream fell on to her naked thigh, our laughter then . . . and so the past continued to dart across my mind as I made my way back to the station and on the journey back, until dusk fell and the train clattered into the half-lit dinginess of London. The train shuddered to a halt and as I stepped on to the platform, through all that sooty dankness the smell of the sea returned – the cry of gulls, the brightening haze of the sky as the sun came through, the waves heaving and breaking, something glinting far off at the water's edge . . . And in that moment I believed that if I'd listened long and hard enough the voices would have sounded clear in the wind, that if I'd suddenly turned there we'd be on our knees round a sand-castle, hurrying to finish it before the tide came in. Back in my flat I began missing it more and more often. And in the small hours of the morning I even sometimes came to believe that if I went back, the years would fall away and I would hear the voices as if I lived again in the past itself.

So it was I found a little house within walking distance of that stretch of sea. We had been happy then. It was where people were happy, the seaside, on the rim of the world. So I told myself. But the vivid expectancy of that day never returned. There has been no adding to it. I have heard no voices. The memories have become rarer and more indistinct. Time is not so easily cheated.

481

(This added later. It is Remembrance Day. Of course there's a great deal more to memory than that – a hankering after the past etc. No doubt books have been written on the subject. We seek former happiness but the more we find it the more we are reminded of what we have lost and that's best forgotten. The smile fades from our faces. It is also the burden of what cannot be altered, cannot be undone. These loom across whatever happiness there was, blotting it out. In memory we do not find happiness for long, if at all. The burden is never lifted. Nor should it be, today of all days when we may forget ourselves in not being forgetful of others. What we are reminded of then is that we are not alone. There may be a kind of happiness in that, in losing ourselves for an hour or two, in a moment of selflessness. An old soldier said, 'We did what was our duty and now can only pay homage.' You could see on his face how much there was he could never forget. He had long since given up thinking about himself but may have found happiness in being able to speak for others, both dead and living. That is as it may be. I couldn't just leave it that I came down here for memory's sake. I couldn't be happy with that.)

Could I have thought like that earlier, I wonder. Have I become wiser? If I have changed, is it only because there is more of the past to be reflected upon, without feeling any the wiser for it?

If I'm going to carry on with this, a few facts. My house is in the middle of a row half-way up a hill. There are several similar streets above and below us. It is about half a mile to the top of the hill where there is a view of the bay. That's where I assume Mrs Felix's beacon will be lit. At the bottom of the hill it is a short walk to the seafront past a few shops, including the aforementioned corner shop where I buy my provisions. This I do regularly, so I don't get too puffed lugging the stuff back up the hill. (I told my doctor this, having previously confessed that I still allowed myself the occasional cheroot. 'Feeling like a cheroot?' he asked. I didn't immediately get this, replying, 'Not just at the moment, thanks.' He gave a chuckle, clutching my arm. 'Getting puffed, I meant.' I nodded in acknowledgement. I find him altogether too breezy in regard to my health, making it clear there's sod all more he can do about it beyond the tablets, the sensible living etc. He's right of course. If he wasn't breezy, he'd be putting the wind up me. Once he asked if I might consider joining a health club and I made a face. 'Don't be like that,' he said. 'It won't kill you. But if it does, think how healthy you'll feel.')

The other people on the street and round and about are a mixed lot. For instance, five houses away the front garden, or yard, contains two partial motor bikes, assorted surplus building materials, discarded toys, two or more black dogs and one or more of, I think, three children whose mother is constantly telling them very loudly to keep quiet, the dogs too. One day I stopped at their gate to return a football which had found its way into my front garden. She came towards me, adjusting her formerly golden housecoat and stroking back her hair, as if to show me how badly her face needed what little October sunlight there was. It seemed I had interrupted her in the middle of putting on her blood-coloured lipstick or she had run out of it, for it only covered most of her lower lip, this further accentuating the fact that she hadn't had a moment all summer to hold her face up to the sun. I tossed the ball towards her.

Her voice was thin with fatigue. 'You're thinking we're one of those neighbours from hell.' She looked around her at the gathering children and dogs and smiled, suddenly becoming a girl again, getting ready for a party. 'Can't pretend it's a sodding paradise, grant you that.'

I'd learnt from my neighbour that she is a single mother and it is her brother who uses her yard to fix motor bikes in. He is an odd-job man who at that moment appeared behind her. I'd seen him about, walking lopsidedly, his head bent down and sideways, a marked disfigurement of the shoulder which makes it difficult to offer him a greeting since he might have difficulty in returning it. His open mouth suggests speech might be difficult for him too.

I shook my head vigorously at the three children who barged past her to seize the football. 'What do you say to the gentleman?' she shouted.

But they were too busy quietly and carefully setting out the pros and cons of who the ball belonged to. The dogs started barking. The woman began looking ashamed, from sixteen or so, hardly more than a child, becoming a weary, worn-out forty. She glanced up at me.

I shrugged. 'Granted. You've got the devil's own job . . . Sorry, I don't even know your name.'

She gave a little laugh, losing in that instant almost all her years again. 'It's Rosie. Not like my prospects, you're thinking.'

Her brother's expression did not change. I suspected that it could not. I left them to it, the woman shouting at the dogs or children, the last words I heard as I turned the corner being, 'Oh Christ Almighty, what will people think?' All those years ago, my wife would have taken such a person professionally under her wing. She would have been a 'case' to be kept an eye on . . . I want to take that thought back, for goodness alone knows how much comfort she gave or misery averted.

The point is that she'd moved in at least six months before and that was the first time I'd spoken to her. The other point is that the neighbouring front yard has been transformed into a beautifully tended little garden with geometric flower-beds, a patch of weedless lawn, two bird baths, several stone animals and fishing gnomes and even a basin-sized pond. The couple who own it often sit out on the little bench under the window, apparently oblivious to the state of affairs next door. They too are small. At first I thought they might not like people stopping and admiring their miniature estate, their dream of a lifetime come true. But when I did, not having observed them at first sitting so quietly on their bench, I said, 'How very nice,' and they replied happily in unison, 'Yes it is, isn't it?'

They spend most of their time just looking at it, cherishing it. Perhaps they believe they have made it nice like that for the sake of the neighbourhood, to set an example. I suspect that footballs and goodness knows what else from next door end up there frequently, that the dogs get in and ruin the flower-beds. I suspect, too, that they do not mind in the slightest. They are quite inviolate with their little patch of orderliness and beauty. They remind me a little of the Hambles without the sorrow in their lives. Day in, day out, they live in exactly the surroundings they have chosen. There is no envy in them. They have chosen their own lives. Grown-up children perhaps, some modest employment, no matter: this was what all along life had been for. They are the Tomkins.

I have mentioned the Felixes who provide another contrast. They bought the large detached house at the end of the street about two years ago. They have made a large number of improvements to it, including a mahogany door covered with ironwork, hanging baskets of flowers on either side of it, a paved path, a wrought-iron fence and front gate. Their house has a name as well as a number. It is 'The

Beeches'. Why, I don't know, there being no trees of that substantial woodland variety in the vicinity. Perhaps the people who first lived there couldn't spell.

Otherwise, the houses look much the same: some intermittent fresh paintwork, net curtains as a rule, some minimal gardening, variously overflowing dustbins, things dumped usually in black bags the dustmen don't like the look of. People come and go, keep to themselves. Various walks of life – briefcases and tool-boxes, suits and dungarees, Volvos and bangers. A racial mix too with two Asian families and a black couple who wave at everyone. Did rather, because they only stayed six months. I hope it wasn't because not enough people waved back. More single people than couples, at a guess. As I say, it's a cross-section. The streets above and below us seem to be much the same. The main thing I've noticed is that people expect to remain unnoticeable. This suits me admirably. I do not seek to impose myself, am not imposing, or not so as you'd notice.

Shortly after I moved here, Adrian and Jane came to see me. Adrian tried to hide his surprise, I thought, saying that so long as I was happy . . . Jane said little, once taking my arm as we walked along the front, as if to reassure me that it was as good a place to live as any. When she said goodbye there was a look in her eye I might have called 'faraway' – but not as though she wished she was somewhere else. Quite the contrary. It was as if she was concentrating hard on how the moment might be recaptured years hence. Very much here and now . . .

I paused for a moment to see if I could find a note of what, if anything, I wrote at the time, then gave up. I won't be able to say more about Jane for some time yet, if ever.

There is a handwritten note about Virginia who came down with her husband and their three children for their summer holiday.

Found a boarding house for them. It was not a happy occasion. They were to have stayed a week but left after four days since indefinite rain had been definitely forecast. But the gloom spread far deeper than that. Richard had lost yet another job and couldn't find another. He should never have been a salesman, though I don't know what else he should have been. All that self-effacing anxiety and humourlessness. Virginia told me firmly over the phone that there

485

were to be no jokes about the stationery and transport businesses etc. I was ashamed that she needed to tell me this. The misery was written all over him. They came round on two afternoons and I was grateful that the insatiable demands of the children made it impossible for any conversation to take place at all. If it had just been the three of us what could I possibly have said remotely tactful or encouraging or anything at all? Virginia glanced at him from time to time as if she expected him at any moment to burst into tears. His eyes darted about as though seeking a flicker of hope in the encompassing despair, but knowing there was as much chance of that as of the clouds suddenly lifting and the sun breaking through. Once he glanced across at me as if to say, 'Don't tell me: your daughter has married a complete dud. I'm sorry, I've let everyone down.' I wished I could tell him that he hadn't let me down, that he mustn't feel sorry for himself, that he must take life by the scruff of the neck and look it in the eye, that, as I'd read somewhere, the best way out is always through, that he must seize the day and never lose heart . . . All that high-sounding piffle which even I knew cannot touch that depth of despair. He reminded me of Hipkin all those years ago, beyond reach. Besides, I was sure that Virginia was giving him every ounce of the support a man could ever need. It was of course his pride he needed back. It wasn't life he should be looking in the eye but other people. How could I possibly convey to him that I held him in esteem whatever anyone else might think, that employability isn't everything? I didn't say anything, though, apart from 'Good luck with the job hunting' as they said goodbye.

'Thanks,' he replied.

'Don't worry about us, Dad,' Virginia added.

'So long as you don't worry about me,' I thought – but gripping Richard's elbow instead, I said, 'Everything will be all right, I just know it.'

As they got into their car, I cursed myself for not having offered them money. That was the least I could have done. The pride meant they couldn't ask. For that reason they couldn't have accepted it either? Pride is the worst of the sins we are told. It is sometimes to be swallowed. I looked at their faces as he lowered his car window and they gave their last waves, the children momentarily sweet and lovable. The sun did then come through for an instant and I remembered that day in Suffolk when I first met him – the brand-new, over-polished car, the excitement of their love, the prospects, when time was only what would allow them all to come true. What a smile he had given me then through the open car window. So vulnerable, so hurt his expression was now. What I just knew in fact was that it almost certainly wouldn't be all right at all.

As they drove off, I began swallowing then – enough pride for the lot of us, leaving nothing behind but an empty glass and a bare plate. Or it wasn't pride at all, mainly preventing whatever might have turned into tears . . .

How sensitive that makes me sound. I must try to be truthful. I've got my pride. The note ends: 'Mainly felt pissed off with him. Don't be such a drip. Stop feeling so bloody sorry for yourself. Get on your bike. Where's your pride, for God's sake?'

I recall now that a tear or two were shed later. Nothing to do with Richard. More simple than that. It was remembering Virginia, her continual hurt, the way she looked at him, sharing his humiliation, seeing then in her face the vulnerable child on the day she told me Mrs Hamble was dying, or in hospital after the car accident, or the day her mother left us, or getting the giggles at Harrods until neither of us knew whether she was laughing or crying – countless such occasions, one image superseding another, slightly altered, the unending layers of sorrow . . . Well, Annelise, one can't help loving one's children, as by now you may well know. Year by year they change, are lost and found again but in whatever is their distress there is no alteration or solace at all.

That's some bringing up to date, encouraging me to oil my typewriter, buy a new ribbon and some paper, put my notes in some sort of chronological order. I watch the world go by from my window – all still going on across the rag-bag of memories – these, then, to be interspersed with events of the moment.

Yesterday morning, for instance, I saw Mrs Felix marching towards me, keeping to the centre of the pavement in a manner that made it clear there'd be no time for idle chit-chat on this occasion, thank you. When we were a few yards apart and I stepped aside, she faltered, her open mouth not saying, 'Well?' Soon the questions would be unleashed. Her husband was catching up with her, having been into a shop.

I said hurriedly, 'Never thanked you for the Snickers. The Dome. All those zones. Pretty knackering, should have thought. Let alone the body. Probably not, on the whole. Wouldn't mind going up on the Eye though . . .'

Very evidently she didn't for some reason have the foggiest idea what I was talking about. Then the thought sped into my mind that she hadn't given me the Snickers bar, had simply been asking me to hold it while she returned change or whatever to her handbag. Her mouth had slowly closed and she was expecting me to step aside, her husband having reached her. He looks like an eager-eyed, very grizzled schoolboy with his round specs, loose, low-hanging trousers and fringe of hair, even a couple of spots on his forehead. It was as if she was taking one of her more scholarly senior pupils on an outing. For reasons to be explained later, he believed me to be a graduate of Oxford and a distinguished academic. This now had the effect of making him open his eyes at me as wide as he could as though I had said something of wondrous subtlety. I stepped into the road with a two-fingered salute and nodded them past.

When they were a few paces beyond me, I heard Mr Felix say, 'What in heaven's name was all that about?'

'Sh! Haven't the foggiest,' she shouted.

'What an extraordinary chap,' he then said, looking back at me, astonished to see I was still standing there. He twiddled his fingers.

As he walked away baggily like an elephant, I twiddled mine in response, thinking: Some small error there, and no mistake. I wish. Or do I? Had I been less ordinary, how much more might I have made of things, what more might I have understood, more might I have done? But then there would have been less to write about, less need for it rather, my usefulness to the world speaking eloquently enough for itself. It might have been beneath me too, going on about myself. Doing good in the world, I wouldn't have had the time for it either. At any rate such is my understanding. Perhaps I am getting above myself. There is certainly nothing out of the ordinary about that.

'Snickers are your favourite,' she said as if deeply offended.

'First I've heard of it,' he replied.

Chapter Two

Next in the folder are four undated accounts which were written during a period of three months or so: my first meeting with John Brown at the Connaught Hotel; the visit of my former wife; a meeting with an estate agent; and a note about my neighbours.

About a hundred yards along the front is a small hotel with a bar I sometimes go to. There is a sitting area with a view of the sea. It has leather chairs and tasselled red lamps on the tables which make it dim enough for others sitting there to be only vaguely visible. In the summer months one might not get a chair but most of the time it is deserted. The bar too is dark and often there are no customers there either. It is a good place to sit alone for a while, particularly as the sun sets over the sea. That and the shapes and colours of clouds are never the same and are peaceful or uplifting to watch. I cannot remember exactly where we stayed all those years ago but it was hereabouts.

I'd stay there longer if the cheroots and drink weren't rationed. Am much tempted to, in the belief that gazing at clouds and sea etc. is of an altogether higher order, a sense of the infinite – spiritual may be the word – making one feel both diminished and elevated at the same time, in fact a great deal so, so that one wonders whether one shouldn't have it further elevated by more nicotine and alcohol, notwithstanding the diminishing effect of those at some later date. It has an ultimate feel about it – there's nothing beyond it, other than certain music – so that how often one experiences it, how long one's life lasts in other words, ceases to matter, if it always feels the same. A sense of timelessness is conveyed. The ordinary senses are taken over or transformed into something else. The music too is enhanced by nicotine and alcohol. As with the clouds etc. the effect is of what can never be better, finer, more wonderful, than it is now. Rationing in matters spiritual seems inappropriate. (They don't tell you in churches, so far as I know, that the Holy Ghost can't hang around for long or there's not enough of it to go round or too much of it will damage your health.) You can forget yourself then. Forget the morning after also – not to mention the afternoon – when the very last thing you can forget is yourself. Time then hangs heavily.

This is the sort of thought I allow myself in the dingy, dark-red sitting area of the Connaught Hotel, my chair so placed that I can move my eyes from the clouds etc. to the bar with the barest turn of my head – the other reason for wanting to drink more and smoke more being further sight of the girl serving there. There have been several over the months from various parts of the world – all charming and nice to look at, the usual. It is a subsidiary reason, need I add, indeed wholly insignificant in the scale of things touched on above, though radically altering the reflection that at times like that – the sunset, the Schubert – it doesn't seem to matter at all, or nearly as much, when one snuffs it. A turn of the head and, oops, mortality matters then all right. Nothing timeless there, indeed reminding of nothing but time. How it passes. Time was. It will not come again. The insignificance swells into a haze of longing, a taking leave of one's senses. Nothing subsidiary about her, those before and those after, ad infinitum. From one infinity to another with a slight turn of the head. Hardly spiritual. Just senseless.

Back to the sunset or the moon on the water then. Our bit of beach cannot have been far from here, half a mile perhaps. That was another kind of experience beyond which there is nothing. Time past. 'Can I get you something else, sir?' she may come over and ask in the middle of such a meditation. 'All in good time,' I may reply; or pay, having had my ration, saying, 'Perhaps another time.' The tip is huge, telling her something about the iceberg. She really does have the loveliest smile. They do. I turn my back on the sunset, memories. I do not wait for the voice that says, 'Time, gentleman, please.' My patience with the spiritual is not infinite. 'Thanks,' I say. 'Until the next time.' There are the other thoughts too, of course, dealt with previously – the context, the comparison with other lives, other deaths. Well, one's insignificance then is truly huge, commandingly subordinate.

So much for that, a distillation of the sort of thoughts one has in a deserted hotel by the sea. I've not dealt with this before so far as I can recall. No point in jotting down what recurs regularly. The milkman left a bottle of milk this morning. Pretty sunset. Cumberland pie underdone. Charming barmaid. Running out of Fairy Liquid. Nice Mozart piano concerto on the radio. Opened new tube of toothpaste.

Anyway, I was wool-gathering in this manner, hoping the barmaid had not found me too insubordinate, when a voice from the other end of the sitting area said, 'That one's from New Zealand, in case you're wondering.'

I raised my glass of wine to the light. 'Oh? Seems all right, though.'

He jerked his head towards the bar. 'I meant her with the spindly legs.'

'Oh.'

I had noticed him, or rather the barmaid bringing him two or three glasses of what looked like neat whisky.

He leant forwards into the glow of the lamp. 'Saw you having a bloody good dekko, that's all.' He raised his glass. 'Join me?'

I went over and sat opposite him with my back to the sea. His face in the red lamplight was very dark, as if badly sunburnt – this highlighted by thick, nearly white eyebrows and a small moustache to match. His close-cropped hair was darker but also whitish. His voice had sounded out of practice, the throat uncleared. There was a lilt in it. Welsh perhaps. He was wearing tinted glasses so at first I could get no idea of his eyes.

'Normally wouldn't have bothered you,' he said. 'But realize, did you, you were talking to yourself? I don't mean out loud. Lips moving.'

'Good God, I'll have to watch that. Find a mirror to sit opposite.'

'Our lovely lassie noticed it too. Gave me a look as if to ask whether I thought you were two fingers short of a noggin.'

He drank most of his whisky. 'We all do it,' he went on. 'You can't not. Think, I mean. It would be nice, wouldn't it, to stop thinking?'

'Except that then we wouldn't know how nice it is,' I suggested.

'Death, you mean?'

'Something like that.' I was ready for another drink, beyond my ration. 'What'll you have?' I raised my arm to catch the barmaid's attention but she was already looking at us, staring in fact. I pointed down at our glasses and she nodded.

'She knows already,' he said. There was a pause. A conversation beginning with death might not have a lot of life left in it. 'Seen you here before. Usually sit over there.' He pointed towards a recess on the far side of the bar.

'I don't come here often. It's quiet . . .'

'Talk to yourself without being overheard.'

The barmaid came with our drinks and a bowl of peanuts and I paid, telling her to keep the change. He looked up at her and whatever face he made caused her to smile. She didn't smile at me. If anything, I guessed, he was quite a bit younger than I was, but older looking. I've not really aged all that much, though not enough hair or lines on my face to judge that by, admittedly.

There was another pause. He raised his glass and put it down again. 'Come here to lay your bones?'

'I suppose now you come to mention it . . . What about you?'

His eyes, I now saw dimly, were very pale and staring hard at me. His reply was barely a grunt, a scoffing noise. I then noticed his hands, the long fingers and neat nails. I found myself wondering about him: a convicted murderer, paedophile, crook or con man of some sort. The eyes continued to stare, sizing me up. Perhaps he was having the same kind of thought about me – though I'd never have made out as a con man, not enough confidence for it. It is a comfort to have no secrets when everyone else has something to hide, but their thinking you must have too makes you feel uncomfortable. I was deciding not to like him, and needed a reason. At any moment he'd ask to borrow twenty quid. Would build up to that. He had the gaze of someone practised in inspiring trust. Suddenly I realized who he reminded me of: the unwavering stare, the jokey, carefully impudent voice. It was Webb pretending to show an interest in one thing while thinking about another. I noticed my hands were fiddling with each other and I was having difficulty returning his gaze – was looking decidedly shifty in fact – the last person you'd trust, or perhaps the first if untrustworthiness can be trusted never to look like its opposite.

He was expecting me to continue. I had no choice.

'Not a bad place to retire. I was made redundant, in the financial field, roughly. Not done much since. Children grown up. Married. Them, I mean.'

He was listening hard. His hands were still. 'Got a family yourself?' I asked finally.

'Oh yes, well, we've all got one of those.'

That was dismissively said, of me not of them. Who had invited whom over? Who had made a personal bloody comment about whom having a good look at a barmaid from New Zealand?

'What line of business were you in then?' I asked.

'Oh, this and that.' He was getting up to go and put a hand on my shoulder. 'Yup, lay my bones here. Wouldn't have taken you for a financial man, frankly.'

'What would you have taken me for?' A ride, I was thinking.

'Good question. Shouldn't jump to conclusions. I drop in here from time to time. May bump into you again.' His hand gave my shoulder a squeeze. 'Just one other thing, old chap.'

'What's that?'

'Oh never mind, it'll keep. My shout next time.'

He got up and moved into the light. His hair was not white but pale ginger. On his way out he leant across the bar and said something to the barmaid which made her laugh. There was a swagger in his walk which made me even surer he was not to be trusted, that I didn't like him. That he'd made the girl laugh, the unreflecting joy in it, may have had something to do with that. Making them laugh is better than nothing – what it does to the face, the noise it makes, what those suggest – soon including the absolutely nothing it is therefore no longer better then.

When she came over to ask if I'd like another, I thought at least I'd try. 'One of your regulars? Or only doing his National Service?'

She looked at me in a flummoxed fashion, the dutiful smile rapidly on the wane. 'Sorry, sir?'

'Never mind. I won't have another, thanks.'

'If that'll be all then.'

She took my glass, avoiding my eye.

'It's a long way from New Zealand,' I tried next.

'I wouldn't know about that, sir.'

'But . . . I thought . . .'

Then she did smile, just. 'That's what he's got into his head. It's Zimbabwe.'

'Ah yes, of course. I'm sorry.'

She was turning now, my empty glass in her hand. 'It's not your fault.'

Suddenly I remembered Foster, what he'd said about somewhere like that, his defeated wife languishing in the African heat, then he himself finally defeated. Perhaps this slender creature, endeavouring to be polite, out of her element, had survived something of that kind. Certainly she would be wishing she was somewhere else. I looked around me in the reddened, wintry gloom. Nobody would want to be here, having to be polite to an elderly stranger like me with only one thing on his mind which had nothing whatever to do with Zimbabwe – who couldn't give a toss about whatever it was she, and Foster, had left behind them. I really didn't want her to go just yet.

'What isn't my fault?'

She stopped and turned her head. 'Your not knowing, sir. You don't have to apologize.' She smiled again then, very sweetly. 'You probably don't even know where Zimbabwe is.'

'Actually, I do. Know a bit of the history too.'

'A bit is better than knowing nothing, like just about everyone else. Nobody really cares if it's a long way away.'

'Miss it, I expect?'

She gave a deep sigh and wouldn't answer that, returning to the bar. She wasn't there when I left a few minutes later, not having been able to switch back on my senseless thoughts of infinity, timelessness and all the rest of it. Foster kept on coming back to me, then Annelise. It was as if I had bumped into them in a foreign country I had once passed through. They meant nothing more to me than the barmaid, for a while anyway. As I climbed the hill to return home, the sea exploding against the promenade wall behind me and the rain building up, the faces came and went, Mrs Bradecki, the Webbs and Hambles, Plaskett and Hipkin and all the Suffolk folk and now the stranger in the bar was added to them – that pale, semi-visible searching gaze catching me having a 'dekko' at a barmaid's retreating form, her manner of moving. He might just as well have said: all those years and what have you got to show for them? What have you learnt? How have you changed? Infinity and timelessness can be had by anyone at any time. Lend me fifty quid, would you?

Home again, I put on a CD. Schumann. Some heartfelt songs about love. Which brought to mind that stretch of beach and the happy times there, and thence my former wife. She phoned me the other day to tell me that her man had died. They had not quite finished their book. His last words were that they had got it all wrong. 'Professional to the end,' she said. 'Of course I promised him I'd get it right, I knew what his doubts were, mine too.' She sighed. 'Was it all worth it, I wonder?'

I should have arranged to meet her. Perhaps I shall. I remembered the days when she had no doubts, as she did too. Once she knew everything worth knowing, the worth of everything. Now she was wondering whether it had all been worthwhile. I didn't want to hear her say that again. If that is what useful, caring people end up thinking, of how much less worth are those who couldn't care less and aren't useful to anyone. No one really cares if it's a long way away as the girl said.

My wife's call prompted me to phone her back a couple of months later to say that if she was ever in this part of the world I'd love to see her. She came down for lunch, at the Connaught, as it happens. I may vaguely have hoped the Zimbabwean barmaid would be there, but I can't remember now. Anyway, she wasn't. It was quite a cheerful occasion on the whole. She had picked herself up. The book was being seriously considered by a publisher. The idea of specific wickedness or virtue skipping a generation was being talked about, could be tied in with a fresh awareness of the role of grandparents – the disinterestedness of affection displaced from dysfunctional parenthood into a sense of renewal offsetting the inevitabilities of old age. I jotted that down as soon as I could: that much hadn't changed. But now she spoke the jargon hesitantly, glancing up at me as if expecting to see a smile on my lips. How old, how very old she had become. And lonely too. She asked me questions about my house, wanting to be invited back there. I do not know why I did not want her to see how little or how much I had changed. There were the books now and the small collection of classical music CDs. I still feared her judgement or, worse, her approbation: how nicely I was coming along in my old age – one of her delinquents who'd turned over a new leaf, falling though they were about him, brown and shrivelled.

We talked about Adrian and Virginia of course. Once, the thought of Adrian becoming a capitalist (which he now was on a very impressive scale, doing the sums for massive take-overs, and hugely benefiting from them) would have horrified her. He had done particularly well out of privatisation. I'd expected her to express, or hint at, misgivings about all this, but she only dwelt on his happiness, his sense of achievement, his marriage. The pleasure in her voice was untainted by principle.

'Don't you wish, though, he'd made the same mark in some field less er . . . ?' I asked.

She gave me a shy, almost flirtatious, look. 'You don't, do you?'

'Most certainly not. But then you know me, no scruples at all.'

'I must say I'd much rather Adrian was doing that sort of thing than a lot of the other people who do.'

'Jane too of course.'

She paused and looked away. That was the first inkling I had that something might be wrong. She wasn't going to leave him, not that, pray to God. The skin across my back turned cold. Jane . . . The moment passed and she had begun talking about Virginia.

' . . . still no job, but she's got part-time work at a clinic. There was some temporary thing in the offing.'

'He's not taken it at all well, I'm afraid.'

'No. A recent report has clearly demonstrated that the tendency must be resisted to underestimate the effects of unemployment on the underlying cohesion of family . . .' There must have been something about the way I had my fork poised with a chip on it in front of my mouth. 'Sorry, Tom. Hark at me. Here I go again. I did inflict an awful lot of jargon on you, didn't I? No, he hasn't. But Virginia has been wonderful. One's heart goes out to her . . .' I nodded and put the chip in my mouth. 'Adrian has lent them rather a lot of money; she insisted it was on loan of course.'

'Easily repayable when they read out my will. No problem there.'

She smiled, then frowned. 'Adrian, you see, has far, far more than he needs. No sign of children and now . . . He'd love her just to have it, but Richard's pride etc. etc.'

And now? What did she mean by that? 'That's the trouble,' I said. 'There's something of the loser about him. Not much for the pride to feed on so turns into something else. Outwards . . . Not sure. Your line of country this.'

There was another long pause. She looked very tired. Tired too of all the analysis and jargon. In fact we were thinking almost exactly the same thing. I know that because it was she who said it.

'We had pretty good children together, didn't we?'

I only had to nod. 'Do you remember when . . . ? Not far from here?'

'It was having to pack up and go home. That's what I remember. Their faces. They so *loved* it . . .'

By then the meal had come to an end. I wasn't inviting her back. We could have had a wallow together about the good old days, improving on them, no doubt. One can choose to remember only the best. Cheating maybe, except that that is what we may choose to live up to. I paid, helped her on with her coat, that once having been something she could perfectly well manage on her own, thank you very much. I held her arms for a brief moment.

'Thank you so much for coming. We must keep in touch . . .'

'Whenever you're in London . . .'

We went out and stood on the hotel steps. She looked up at me in the full sunlight and I saw in her face how she had been in the beginning, how too I had foreseen then how she would look now. And from that followed all the other thoughts I'd had about her and written down. It was simple. It wasn't just that I hadn't made her happy. It was that I hadn't done that because I'd been wondering how happy she was making me. And now . . . oh how haggard she looked, beyond her years! The wind blew her hair apart, exposing a bald patch, pink edged, grey as bone. She continued to gaze up at me. Her eyes too, once so dark, seemed to be turning grey. This sure, knowledgeable woman so vulnerable. I was ashamed. I was about to say how sorry I was when she touched my arm.

Her voice sounded young and hesitant, as it had been in the beginning. 'I'm so sorry, Tom. I shouldn't . . .'

I couldn't say I was sorry too, not now. As always she had the last word. I could only shake my head. At least I put my arm round her and gave her a squeeze.

It was that sort of an ending. I watched her walk along the front towards the station, a small, frail figure having difficulty against a blustery wind. Down there to her right on a cold, deserted beach a family was enjoying a summer holiday, running in and out of the water, splashing, fooling about, building a sand-castle before the tide came in. She turned and waved. There was such clarity in that movement. It was almost defiant. Her mouth was open as if she was shouting. It was too far away for me to tell whether it was only the broadest of smiles. The clarity was timeless, though it all had to do with the passing of time. I'm out of my depth here again, paddling in the shallows. But it was probably love I felt for her then too, of a kind – a mutual forgiveness and understanding, and the glimpse of how we had once been together. I could tell Annelise in my next Christmas card that love, for sure, may not be everything but it comes in many shapes and sizes and it's something when for most purposes there is sod all else.

Yesterday morning I was boiling a late egg when there was a knock on the door. A woman was standing there whom I hadn't seen before. She was wearing a navy-blue suit with thin white stripes, a silk-looking floral scarf and very large, oval-shaped blue earrings, one of which she was fiddling with, the immaculate, vivid red fingernails turning it almost grey even though the sun was out. She had taken a lot of trouble too with her face so that what it might look like in its natural state was impossible to guess. The fingernails didn't quite match the lips but perhaps weren't supposed to. Her hair was matt blonde and recently done so that it seemed to puff out from her head like something fresh from the oven. Little of this, of course, registered at the time or only skimpily. My immediate thought was that she was too smart for our street and had probably got the wrong address. She certainly wasn't a district nurse or chiropodist. Something to do with cosmetics or public relations, perhaps, or both. Mainly, I registered the eyes as one does. I do not remember their colour now, only that the painstaking beautification around them suddenly reminded me of Maureen: take me as you find me, this is the best I can make of myself, like it or lump it – whilst anxious to suggest it might be well worth finding out what lurked behind all that. The voice, though, was that of a practised salesperson, aiming at or disguising posh, unsure as yet of its clientele, not of itself. No self-doubt there, unlike Maureen who always seemed to be practising how to speak, listening to herself. Singing was another matter. There was no doubtfulness then, as if that was what the voice was for; talking was only what had to be done with it in between. That was another difference: however similarly done up, you couldn't begin to imagine this woman singing for all she was worth in a choir. What she said was, 'So sorry to trouble you. I've tried the houses next door but no one seems to be in.'

I looked up and down the street as though what she had said needed confirmation.

'To get to the point,' she went on, 'my sister is thinking of buying number 27 and wanted my advice on the neighbourhood, services . . .'

I should have invited her in, but I never do this. Perhaps I'm an inhospitable old misery but I do not like the idea of people reaching conclusions about me other than behind my back. I do not live chaotically or dirtily; I just don't want anyone looking about and saying, or thinking, 'Like to do the odd spot of reading, I see, use the library do you? Ah yes, the great explorers. Old photographs, fascinating . . . A bit of the old classical music, relaxing don't you find it . . . ?' Or arriving at a judgement about my choice of corn-flakes, muesli rather.

'Delighted . . .' I began with a smile which must have been welcoming enough because she returned it, revealing teeth over which no less trouble had been taken than over the rest of her – smiles believed, wrongly in my experience, to be the key to whatever lies beyond the façade. In this case, though, it only made me wonder whether she lived alone, then what other bodily things it had to contend with, first thing in the morning for example.

The smile remained, thus cancelling itself out. 'Why have a sister who's an estate agent,' she continued, 'if you can't ask her advice about property?'

Her voice had sunk into posh, acquiring that hushed tone when figures are being bandied about, offers considered. The similarity with Maureen vanished altogether.

'Ah,' I said, looking mournful, 'I'm afraid I can't ask my sister's advice about anything.'

That killed off the smile. 'I'm so sorry,' she said with a frown. Practised too. Or perhaps not. She need not know that I'd never had a sister.

Again I looked up and down the street. 'There's not a lot to be said about it really. Bus stop at the bottom of the hill. Rubbish collection on Thursdays. Street sweeper every other February or thereabouts. Milk delivery. Medical centre about eight minutes' walk. Good local minicab service. Local convenience store at the bottom of the hill. Sells most things. Post Office not far from the medical centre. Main shops in the town at the end of the bus route. Schools, supermarket on the route . . . Some churches here and there. Some old-looking. Some newish. Clearly labelled I seem to remember . . .'

She was becoming impatient. No teeth now. 'Neighbours . . . ?'

'Yes, there are a number of those too.'

'I mean, are they noisy . . . ? Parties? You see, my sister . . .'

I remembered Mrs Felix twice charging up the street and banging on doors to silence loud music in the early evening but had heard nothing since then – except once or twice in summer when the windows had to be kept open. We could all rely on Mrs Felix.

I wanted her to go now. In the background there was some lovely piano playing on Radio 3.

'No worries on that score. The conductor deciding against a rehearsal. Now if you'll forgive me, I'm expecting . . .'

499

'The conductor what? But of course. I'm so sorry to have disturbed you. You've really been most helpful.'

'If your sister does move in, I look forward to meeting her.'

She took a long, hard look at me as if at a property whose basic specifications would be hard to embellish.

'If she does buy it, it *would* be nice if you could call and . . . She . . . Make her feel welcome. She . . .'

Her expression had now quite changed. The smile had returned with even more teeth showing, but the façade seemed to have slipped out of focus, as if more work had to be done on it and soon. The eyes had panic in them.

'Of course,' I said. 'I'd be glad to.'

'I seem to have struck lucky.'

'Yes, well, I like it here. Or can't think of anything much *against* it.'

'I didn't mean that.'

She was already turning so I didn't see her face again. She had not wanted me to. She had said something nice about me. Naturally I enjoyed that except for the fleeting relief that came with it: nothing the slightest bit daunting about him, pleasant enough considering . . . I've noted before, I think, that the impression I seem to give is one of neutrality. I feel pretty neutral about that. Taking sides does not come naturally to me, unlike preferring to be thought nice than not – just to be on the safe side. Cruising along nicely in neutral, going slowly downhill. No need to get into gear, to dress myself up in any way . . . I thought roughly that, while mainly regretting I'd judged her too soon, almost certainly unfairly – Maureen too, even more so perhaps, in making that connection. (Perhaps most of us get people wrong on first acquaintance, quite badly wrong – nice people anyway or rather those who turn out to be that. It seems to be different with shits: Plaskett, for instance, who came over as that from the outset. Can they believe you'll like them when you get to know them? Or don't they give a shit, to coin a phrase? Nice people like to be liked and to like others. Mrs Plaskett was very nice, as I recall. She certainly liked her husband. She couldn't have thought him a shit. Nor could their children. Nor could his parents for that matter. Perhaps we are more likely to find something nice about shitty people than something shitty about nice people. One would get everyone more or less right on first acquaintance if the difference were only in how much they seemed to care whether they were liked or not. Of course most people one doesn't get to know better at all. How nice or shitty they are is for others to discover and they too of course could be nice or shitty ad nauseam . . .)

If she'd met either of my neighbours instead there would have been nothing to disturb her about them either. My house is number 13. At number 15 lives Phil Badgecock. He retired long since from the Post Office. It is surprising how little I have spoken to him. The first time we met he said that, to be honest, there wasn't a hell of a lot to tell me about himself, in fact sod all. He'd spent most of his career in the sorting office. He was never a delivery man. And there's not a lot you can say about sorting mail, even with the new technology and that. It was the door-to-door people who had the stories to tell. His hobby, he told me, was collecting matchbox covers and old cigarette cards and there wasn't much mileage in those either, conversationally speaking. On most mornings he goes for a walk along the beach whatever the weather and the rest of the time he seems to watch television. Or rather when I pass his house it's always on. His wife, he told me, had left him for a parcel van driver when they'd only been married for a year and he'd not much fancied marriage since.

'Couldn't get that sorted then?' I said.

'If I had a quid for every time . . .' he replied but without rancour.

At the end he said, 'Can see you're one of those likes keeping to himself. Seen those books through the window, hope you don't mind. And that classical music. Well, so am I. Man after my own heart. I don't mean the music so much. Like I said, I was never a door-to-door sort of bloke.'

His greeting is always friendly with a comment about the weather. He does not dawdle. He had shown no interest in what I had done with my life. He is an ideal neighbour, in short, completely without any trace of neighbourliness.

My neighbour on the other side is quite the opposite but an ideal neighbour too. Her name is Emily Hirst. On most mornings she cleans other people's houses. She always wants to have a chat. About her cats mainly, of which there are four. I know that because almost every time I see her she tells me, one by one, about their ailments and funny ways etc. They often come and see me so I feel no need to acquire a cat of my own. She apologizes for them, though each time I say I enjoy having them, which I do. She is an immensely cheerful

501

woman, even when she tells me about her 'late husband'. That is what she calls him. She never gives him a name. 'I called him that when he was alive. He was even late for our wedding. Have you ever heard of the bridegroom coming up the aisle after everyone else? Lost at least four jobs because of it. At the last count. Couldn't get up in the morning. Best time of day, he used to call it. No point wasting it getting tired again.'

She has a married son in Australia whom she went to visit once. 'I was in the way, you could tell. Didn't know where to put myself. I thought she was a bit bossy, to tell you the truth. He was henpecked. I told him one day: who wears the trousers in this household, I'd like to know. She heard me. Well that was that. So much for Australia. Can't say I cared for Australians come to that. She was Australian, mind you . . .'

She tells me these things in passing, as it were, stopping me in the street or when we happen to be in our front gardens at the same time. 'Oh there you are, Mr Ripple,' is how she greets me, as if seeing me had come as a lovely surprise. I try to avoid her – when I see her going out or coming in I stay put until she's vanished. But I do like her. I like her very much. Her cats too. She has a soothing effect on me. All that bubbling over. She has no designs on the world. As she puts it herself, she takes life as it comes. And when it starts going, she'll take that too. I've never seen her walking far down the street because there's always someone to stop and talk to. I even saw her deep in conversation once with Mrs Felix or rather she was talking and Mrs Felix was listening for a change.

Once she said to me, 'Our Mr Badgecock is very interesting, all those cigarette cards he's got.'

I wonder what she tells people is very interesting about me. She never invites me into her house and I never invite her into mine. When one of the cats has gone to sleep on my bed or wherever, I bring it tenderly out. Be that as it may, my estate agent would have been even more reassured, for quite different reasons, by either of my neighbours. 'I'm always there if you need me,' Mrs Hirst says. Mr Badgecock would never dream of saying anything like that. But it's nice to know he's there too if you need him. I hope they think approximately the same about me.

502

Chapter Three

The millennium is increasingly in the news. I expect there'll be some local occasion to attend e.g. at Mrs Felix's beacon. There's something to be said, I suppose, for hearing the clock strike on one's own – to prepare oneself for the lonely day when the clock stops altogether and there's nothing more to be said at all. Raising a glass of champagne at the mirror – wishing oneself well and being wished well in return – seems silly and self-regarding. Or not, remembering that much of our time we spend regarding ourselves, worrying about how others regard us, not wanting to appear silly or to have too high an opinion of ourselves. We do it constantly – so when better than the night a new millennium begins, looking silly only to ourselves while having a high opinion of ourselves for recognizing that? Then telling oneself to press on regardless and failing to raise a smile. Trust you not to get the joke. I did but it wasn't funny. In self-regard one cancels oneself out, feels all the better for that. Oh vain thought!

I read somewhere that the tone of desperation in the lonely hearts columns has noticeably grown as the millennium approaches. 'The clock ticks more loudly and becomes the mournful sound of a tolling bell.' That was how someone put it. Possibly. Which makes me think of Maureen and wonder whether she ever thinks of me. Perhaps she is still advertising. Occasionally I glance at those columns looking for someone in search of late companionship in a choral setting. I hope she has found happiness. I look for her face in the congregations in *Songs of Praise*. The elderly folk especially do seem much uplifted, enduringly heartened by their love of God, or at any rate by gathering with others to express that. Perhaps Maureen has been amongst them and I have not recognized her. I hope her memories of me bring a smile to her lips. Perhaps she too glances at those columns from time to time, knowing she'd spot at once that clever dick trying to grab the attention with double entendres and self-deprecation. I don't do that any longer. I don't want to come across the advertisement of some desperate bugger who's having a lonely millennium and realize it's me. 'Fat, cheroot-smoking, turning over new leaf after triple by-pass etc . . .' Ah well, God bless you, Maureen. Sing your heart out in the love of Jesus. When things went wrong in the shop my father would sigh and say, 'O Lord, have mercy!' And my mother would reply, 'It's not His mercy you're needing, it's His help with the turnover.' I wish I could be like those elderly folk in *Songs of Praise*. But as the days pass, I would feel increasingly uncomfortable among them. It would not be the tunelessness of my singing, but my deepening unbelief, my growing awareness of our infinite capacity for self-deception. I try to believe too that in this general area I may be deceiving myself.

I have often wondered what my parents would say if they came to see me. I imagine my mother saying, 'Haven't made much of yourself, have you?' It wouldn't be in the least hurtful, since making much of oneself, she implied, could only be too much by half. She wouldn't have wanted me to go too far up in the world, the world being what it was. Those high-ups, she once said, the depths they sink to. My father? He'd have looked around and thought I'd made myself comfortable enough, still wishing though that I'd taken over the shop, while recognizing that would have made me less comfortable likely as not, and neither of us would have drawn much comfort from that. He wouldn't have said anything much at all, continually looking at his watch and repeating more than once the time of the train they had to catch.

Back to the millennium. I've considered laying in a few delicacies to offer my neighbours who might pass by with greetings of goodwill on the morning after. The corner store is very well stocked for the needs of someone like me, with frozen lamb cutlets and pork chops etc. To relieve the monotony every six months or so of ready-made Cumberland Pie, Fisherman's Pie or Cauliflower Cheese etc. As the festive season approaches, Mr Patel, the owner, tries very hard to meet his customers' needs with Christmas puddings, Mr Kipling's mince pies, crackers and the like. He does not like to be found wanting. Nor his customers.

I learnt this shortly after I arrived, when coming across him in the street with his wife and two children, and saying to him that

504

his wonderful store stocked everything I should ever need – a pity though about the *foie gras* in white of quails' eggs I'd become used to when dining out at Bogdilliano's especially after the opera. I really didn't think he'd heard me. We then talked about other things such as how happy they were to live in our street, how friendly everyone was, how well the children were doing in school – though he didn't have to tell me that, one look at them being quite enough. Shortly after we parted I heard Mrs Patel berating him at great speed which, from the way she had nodded at everything he'd said earlier, seemed out of character.

When I went into the shop two weeks later, he beckoned me eagerly into a store-room at the back and showed me with immense pride a carton of . . . you've guessed. 'I keep these only for you, Mr Ripple.' I simulated great delight, of course, and for the next twenty-four weeks bought a tin of the stuff. It was not on display. As soon as he saw me coming he would wrap a tin in a brown paper bag and slip it into my carrier bag with a wink when no one else was watching. The problem grew, of course. How was I to tell him I didn't want him to reorder when the carton was finished? It was not only expensive – the produce of Alsace and Lorraine – but pretty revolting. Mrs Hirst's cats liked it though. So I had to tell him my doctor had warned me against pâté; it was altogether too rich. He was very disappointed, asking what little delicacy he could get me instead. His wife was there too at the time, rapidly nodding. How does one thank such people? Only doing their job, some would say. I wouldn't.

My doctor, incidentally, does not warn me against rich food although my cholesterol count stays stubbornly higher than it should. 'Quality of life, Mr Ripple,' he said to me once. 'Don't forget that. Enjoyable things often not good for one. The longer it is, the less fun, if that's how one gets one's satisfaction.' He glanced up at my raised eyebrow. 'Oh dear. Sorry. Life, I mean, what must you be thinking?' He snickered at this point while scribbling out a renewal of my prescription. 'Butter, cheroots and so forth, jolly sight nicer than marge, mineral water and chewing gum. Anything within reason, that's my advice; though there too, what do people say about faith going beyond that?' He left that in the air, flourishing the prescription at me.

'I have complete faith in you, doctor,' I said feebly.

'Don't tell that to your vicar,' he replied with a high snort.

I thought of the only vicar I'd known and wondered what had become of him in his war against the modernizers. I could have told him anything, he had so little faith in himself – which so far as I know may make him a better Christian.

I am digressing, the consequence not of mineral water and chewing gum. It is one o'clock in the morning. I remember Mrs Patel's face now, the expression of alarm when I said the pâté was doing me harm – as if I had told her it had slowly been poisoning me and I did not have long to live. The thing is this: she wasn't worried in the slightest about their reputation, their licence, the health inspectors or whatever – she was worried about me. I don't know how you can tell when people have no thought for themselves, but you can, like anything truly rare, I suppose.

My eye wandered to the top of the dresser where I had put the bowl the Ranasinghes gave me all those years ago. It had broken into three pieces in the move but I'd glued it together fairly successfully. The cracks show and there are several chips around the rim. But still it shines in all its kaleidoscope of colours, transforming whatever light there is into a shimmering brilliance. The brighter the light, the more the cracks show of course. Which is why I no longer keep it on the window-sill, to catch as much light as possible. It is still my favourite possession. It reminds me too of my mother. Even she liked the Ranasinghes. I shall always regret that she never told them so. Every time I look at the bowl I wonder how they are getting on running my father's shop. They think of us often too, speak about us from time to time, recalling too the bowl. I am quite sure about that. The bowl itself seems somehow to convey that vivid certainty.

The night deepens. It has begun to rain. I shall wake up with regrets and a headache. So to end this digression. Ever since that day, when I go to the shop, I assume a particularly brisk and healthy manner so they can see how much good their food is doing me. I make comments to that effect. I only wish I could do something about my paunch which I pat when buying a delicacy, sometimes too even licking my lips and saying daft things like 'Live dangerously, eh?'

Once I met Mrs Patel and her children, a boy and an older girl, halfway up the hill on my way back from the shop. I was puffing and sweating and generally giving the impression of someone not long for this world. Fortunately, I saw them coming from some distance and so could put down my carrier bags to do up my shoelaces. I had partly recovered my breath by the time they reached me. They did not seem to be stopping, but suddenly did.

'Good morning. And a lovely one it is too,' I said, not taking a breath.

'Say good morning to Mr Ripple,' she said, slapping the children lightly on the back.

Which they did. I wished I wasn't sweating and breathing so heavily.

The worried expression returned to Mrs Patel's face. 'We can deliver everything for you,' she said. 'It would be no trouble at all.'

'Good heavens no,' I replied. 'My doctor strongly encourages my walks up and down the hill. Does me the world of good, he says. Honestly.' Three intakes of breath were needed to say this.

She was now pushing the children forward and about to walk on, her expression even more worried if anything . . .

'But thank you very much all the same,' I continued.

They walked on and I heard the girl say, 'He's an old man, isn't he, Mama?'

'*Very* old,' the boy added loudly.

So now when I see the children on their own, I assume an exaggeratedly antique demeanour with a laborious shuffle and a bent back. They are not quite certain whether to look compassionate or to laugh. I put them in a terrible quandary, challenging their impeccable politeness. Serve the little blighters right.

To bed now. Turn out the light. As on every night I shall turn from the stairs and see the bowl still mysteriously glowing through the surrounding darkness.

Some weeks have passed. The notes and typed material are now in some sort of order. The following was written soon after the estate agent's visit.

Two months or so later there was a removal van outside number 27. I was as good as my word, giving her a day or two before knocking on her door.

At first sight she could hardly have been more different from her sister, a good deal older for a start, though, on reflection, her lack of make-up may have accounted for that. There was a similarity in the eyes, the momentary panic in them, and in the mouth, the way the teeth showed.

'I told your sister I'd call. Tom Ripple from number 13. Welcome to the street. Do please let me know . . .'

At first it seemed as though I might as well have been speaking in a foreign language; she just stared at me, so much so that I had to repeat what I'd said, doing so very slowly.

'Oh I'm sorry, sorry, sorry,' she replied. 'Of course. How kind. Thank you . . .'

There was a noise behind her and she half turned, moving sideways, it seemed, to block my view. I had caught a glimpse of a small white face and a fringe of black hair.

I stepped back. 'Do please call. Truly. At any time.'

She became even more flustered. 'Thank you so much. I'm sorry. I wasn't expecting . . .'

Then rather abruptly she closed the door. I thought I heard a raised voice speaking three or four words. It might not have been hers, which was like her sister's, though less confident, careful to be neither one thing nor the other, copying some ideal in that inimitable English manner. She might have been addressing a pet, of course . . .

A week earlier I bumped into the man with the tinted glasses I'd met at the Connaught that winter evening. It was at the corner store. We were both reaching for a carton of milk. He was still wearing the glasses, which seemed to have thickened in the garish light so that his eyes were now quite invisible. The darkness of his face had faded into a whitening pink.

'Given up, have you?' he said loudly, making me jump since I had not seen him standing there beside me, concentrating as I was on cheeses, remembering in that instant Virginia lying in hospital, laying her hand on mine, her eyes filling with tears. That voice: 'Don't, Dad! Please!'

I stared at him for a short while. 'No, not really. I think I'll hang on for a little time yet. See in the millennium, at any rate.'

He raised an elbow. 'The drinking, I meant. Haven't seen you at the Connaught lately.'

There was no need for any comment on that. I reached out for a package of ten Kraft slices to add to my milk.

'Bloody millennium,' he said. 'Sod all difference it'll make to me.'

'Rather agree with you,' I replied, turning away, then taking another packet of Kraft slices from the shelf.

'Who makes a *difference*? It still goes on.'

I shrugged. 'It's all the same to me.'

He was following me down the aisle. We both put a jar of Nescafé into our baskets. 'Ripple you said your name was,' he said, his throat still uncleared. 'Didn't make many waves in *your* life then?'

I made sure he could see I wasn't smiling, or not much. After my school days when my name had its uses for those who did not envisage me embarking on any rough waters in life, only Plaskett had tried to raise a laugh with it. It was at the bar of the golf club when he introduced me to one of the MDs we (he) needed to impress. He was a tall man with a sad air, as if something hurtful had just been said to him. Slapping me on the back Plaskett said with a single guffaw, 'My assistant sales director, Tom Ripple. But makes a splash when he wants to all right.' The MD shook my hand without the trace of a smile, whilst giving Plaskett a glance of contempt which made him blush and shut him up for at least ten seconds. The conversation turned to the bunkers on the seventh or some such.

When he left, Plaskett whispered to me, still flushed, 'Not a man I care to do business with, frankly.'

After lunch I found myself having a pee next to the MD in the men's cloakroom. He barely glanced at me but on his way out, stopped at the door, took a card out of his wallet, made an amendment to it with the pen in his top pocket, then handed it to me with the barest twitch of an eyebrow and a slight compression of the lips as when preventing a smile. I never saw him again. His name was Christopher Prebble and he'd crossed out the 'r'. It has remained a lovely coincidence and ever since I have often thought of him – sometimes imagining us in partnership, introducing ourselves and absolutely keeping the smiles off our faces.

About six months later Plaskett told me he'd been convicted of insider trading on quite a grand scale and had been sentenced to two years in gaol. 'Told you, Tom, didn't I?' He was smiling that smile of his, with slightly more smugness than venom in it on this occasion for a change. I considered sending him a note saying that he'd been an absolute brick, humiliating Plaskett that day, but didn't of course. I'd liked him. It is difficult to like crooks, thieves and so

509

forth. But Plaskett's pleasure at his downfall caused me to like him even more.

I still do and often wonder what became of him. I had hoped he liked me, or would have done had he known me. When I remember Plaskett it is usually Hipkin I remember at the same time, alongside Mrs Plaskett. But sometimes it is Christopher Prebble. I picture his tall, bowed figure walking along the front, a ruined man, his life a wreckage, his marriage over, if he had one. Sometimes he pauses at a bench where another figure sits, head in hands, who looks up at the sea from time to time as though there was something there he might be missing. It is Hipkin. He sits down beside him and says, 'You won't believe this, old chap, but I once met a man called Ripple.' Then hands over his card with the 'r' crossed out. Even Hipkin smiles at this, having long since forgotten me. Then I remember Plaskett again, who is perhaps on a boat where the waves sparkle under a blazing sun.

These thoughts were straying through my head when we reached the counter. He made way for me, saying, 'See you at the Connaught then? Look, bloody silly joke, I know, sorry, but when your name is bloody boring like Brown, without even an "e", John Brown, I ask you, you get envious.'

'Even worse if it's Green then?'

'Oh very droll, I'm sure.' He looked out into the street which shone damply in the wet sea air. Beyond it the sea itself looked much the same though crinkled and flecked with white as though strewn with litter. 'Bloody miserable, isn't it? Bloody, bloody miserable. That's life for you. Oceans of the stuff.'

I could think of no reply to this as we went out into the street together and began walking in silence in the same direction towards the hill.

'I'd not take any notice of me if I were you,' he said after fifty yards or so. He stopped, had clearly come all that way with me to say something since he was now turning to go back the way we had come. It was not much to have said and impossible to reply to.

'Why on earth not? I mean . . .' was the best I could do.

'I can't see the funny side, unlike you by the sound of it. You have that, what, facetious, look about you.'

'I'm sorry.'

510

'Oh, don't be sorry, matey. Don't you be sorry.'

He was staring at me fairly close up, his eyes shining but very pale, colourless. Then abruptly he left. Facetious? That was what my mother used to call me, my father adding that I should listen to my mother and that I'd have to start to take things seriously if I wanted to get on in life. I knew what my mother was thinking then: that seriousness hadn't got *him* very far, had it – running a shop he'd inherited from his father? Perhaps she was thinking that there might be something to be said for facetiousness after all. I've never really been sure. No one takes much notice of me. In my experience people take the least possible notice of those who are constantly being serious; they avoid them like the plague, they're too unsettling, all that pondering they do on how serious life is when you think about it, even more so when you don't. So much so that it becomes increasingly hard to take them seriously. Or am I just being facetious?

It seems to have been round about then I recorded in a handwritten note that one day I caught up with Mr Tomkins as he turned the corner of our street and went towards the bus stop. I'd never seen him, I wrote, without his wife. Often one saw them, arm in arm, their briskly striding little figures side by side, keeping in step. I raised a hand and said, as everyone else must say to them unfailingly, as I do, 'Garden's looking very nice.'

The effort to sound as though I really meant it had the opposite effect, as happens. Sincerity should be effortless. 'Sincerely, you have to trust/believe me,' makes the hand clench round the small change in one's pocket.

And he replied eagerly, as if no one had ever remarked on his garden before, not quite looking me in the eye, 'Thank you. It is, isn't it?'

Since their inseparability was the main thing about them, I added, 'The wife keeping well, I trust?'

His reply was almost a squeak. 'Oh no! She's not my wife. She's not Mrs Tomkins or anything like that. Just fancy!'

This huge and daring confession rather took me aback. 'I thought . . .' I began.

'She's not well at all, not at all well.'

I said how sorry I was and waited for the confession to continue.

'She'll recover. She always does. I never get a thing. Never catch anything off her. All right, the sniffles perhaps. She's the one who takes the vitamins.'

I made as if to go, frowning at my watch and muttering something about a speedy recovery.

'Mrs Tomkins, she was just the same, not a day's illness in her life, except for the last one of course. You can't have everything in life.'

'So your wife . . . ? I'm sorry.'

'I was referring actually to our dear departed mother, God rest her soul.'

'Oh I see. How proud she would have been of your nice little garden.'

At that moment the bus appeared, stopping at the brow of the hill. At the same time Emily Hirst was striding towards us. Normally she would stop for a chat but she walked past, saying, 'Garden's looking very nice, Mr T.'

'Thank you. It is, isn't it?' he replied.

The bus arrived and as he got on to it he turned and said, 'She's my twin sister, you know. She looks after me. I look after her. We both look after the garden.'

He smiled broadly as if a hugely funny thought had entered his head, being married to his twin sister perhaps. I raised my hand as he moved up the bus and sat by the window to give me a final wave. He was still smiling, as if what was hugely funny now had something to do with me. I wished I could be sure what. I brought to mind their wonderfully neat and tidy little garden, was glad that I'd admired it. But was it, perhaps, a substitute for some other happiness there might have been then – their dead mother and goodness knows what other sorrow in their lives? He seemed to have been happy simply recalling it, looking forward to planting new seeds, to all the other things he and his sister would be doing for it when they could spare the time from caring for each other – that was all . . .

Like much of the rest of the material in the folder, that note is undated. I'm not sure why. A kind of laziness perhaps. Nothing fancy to do with disrupting the relentless passage of time. The material has simply accumulated but sorting it out now to give it some continuity, the unchronological jumble does seem to have a certain verisimilitude about it, if that is the word. But it's a nuisance too, being unsure of the order of things. The higgledy-piggledy is all very well if left well alone. Muddling along is natural, it's what we do best. Articulateness makes life difficult, has hardly anything to be said for it at all.

For instance, I've just come across another handwritten note about a window cleaner who lived in the house opposite when I first came here. His van was parked outside with a ladder on top of it. He saw me watching him as he got into it, at once got out again and came to greet me, arm outstretched, grinning broadly. He had carefully trimmed, neatly parted, thickly greased, black, perhaps dyed, hair quite at odds with his disarray in other respects – a large, loose mouth with detached, skew-whiff, rusty teeth, big dissimilar ears and one half-closed eye. It was as if the head's surface was having to keep up appearances for the rest. In his doorway stood his wife with her arms round two small children, their arms raised to wave him goodbye. I had some music playing on my recently installed CD player.

'Like the classical, I see,' he said. I nodded. 'In my walk of life you hear every sort of music ever invented. I like all of it as it happens, except in the home. You're very welcome and if there's anything, don't hesitate . . . Clean your windows too if you ask me ever so nicely.'

That was with a wink which involved a major distortion of his ample mouth. Beyond him his children's arms were still raised, their hands flapping.

In my adolescence I had fanciful thoughts about being a window cleaner, the things one would see, the propositions one might receive etc. Not any longer of course, oh no – having to climb ladders, I mean. But I still idiotically said, 'Seen a thing or two in your walk of life, shouldn't wonder.'

He glanced back across the street. 'That's a lovely family you're looking at. I have her believe I've never seen a bloody thing, if you must know. All she worries about all day long is that I'm careful up those ladders. She doesn't think of me peeping through windows, only my getting up there and down again without breaking my bloody back. I only do the domestics. Less far to fall.'

His smile had gone and I felt ashamed. 'Sorry,' I said, then stammered on, 'Was never much of a social climber myself. No head for heights. Half-way up the career ladder, missed my footing . . .'

He was gazing at me, my growing discomfiture, with no trace of a smile, then suddenly slapped my arm. 'Bit of a jokester, I see. I like that. At least having a try at it. Cheer oneself up a bit anyway.'

And so I was put in my place, deserved to be. The point of writing this down is not only that. The window cleaner moved soon afterwards and later I saw him in town high up a very tall building on a platform that hung from the roof. It was sickeningly precarious. I thought of his wife and children waiting for him, not wondering what he was up to, or not for long, such trivial guesswork hugely overshadowed by wondering whether they would ever see him again.

I'm not sure why I bothered to record all that; perhaps it was just to remind myself that there are those who make their livings dangerously. (A phrase comes back to me, God knows where from: Those that go down to the sea in ships and occupy their business in great waters.) I see that little family assembled to wave goodbye, imagine their silent, continuous prayers. And I am glad to be reminded of that, of the insufficiency of humour too, though long since discovered for other reasons, when at any moment anything dreadful could happen, and does. I think of that friendliness, that glistening head of hair, the need to keep up appearances against all the odds. I've no idea of his name but I think of him every time I look at his doorway. He stands for something. I remember him driving away, that large lop-sided smile back on his face, waving both ways, at me and his family.

'Can see you've got your feet firmly planted on the ground,' he shouted before revving up and driving off.

I turned off the CD player: some song about rising up above the tribulations of this sad world. Inappropriate in the circumstances.

There is something else in this, I think. That any man or woman or family might be chosen. It is not just that everyone has their story to tell, true though that is. It is that everyone, however differently, can be seen on the edge of some catastrophe. It is thus that sometimes before I sleep I see the window cleaner, whose name I never knew, falling with his platform from the top of a high building and I wait for the cry that never comes.

To return to John Brown. Shortly after the meeting in the corner shop I saw him one afternoon pushing a wheelchair down the front. He was walking away from me, but once turned and raised his head, opening his mouth wide, taking a deep breath of sea air perhaps, but it looked like a silent yell. An arm shot out in front of him, pointing, but there was nothing out there to point at. He leant forwards, then they vanished up a side street.

The next time we met at the Connaught, he told me a little about himself, that he'd been some sort of transport manager in the north. We paid for our own drinks, he having consumed a good deal more than I was allowed to. No sign that he was going to touch me for a bob or two. We eyed the Zimbabwean girl, shrugged, grinned. Much of what he said about more or less anything was that it was a load of bollocks, it could be taken or left, a toss need not be given etc.

All of which made me want to cheer him up. So coming back from the gents I began singing, 'Oh I do like to pee beside the seaside, oh I do like to pee beside the sea.'

Wretchedly unfunny, don't tell me, but he burst out laughing and couldn't stop, was quite convulsed, so that I had to call the barmaid over and ask for a glass of water. Eventually he calmed down into a series of gasps.

'Not very funny when you come to think of it,' he managed finally.

I nodded. 'Not in the slightest.'

He took off his tinted glasses and wiped away the tears.

'If only you knew how much one needed a laugh,' he said. 'God, if only you bloody knew.'

He left soon after that, waving from the door and blowing the barmaid a kiss. She raised her hand and gazed after him for a long time with a wistful look. Perhaps she was dreaming of the Zimbabwean bush. Then she realized I was staring at her and gave me the loveliest of smiles, thinking no doubt of a rogue elephant or some other elderly wild beast at a watering hole . . .

Chapter Four

The anniversary of Jane's death. It is late and pouring with rain. Having dozed off this afternoon after a walk along the front I cannot sleep. A Schubert Impromptu is playing on my CD player. I have taken out the folder with her name on it. There are a dozen or so unnumbered pages of typescript in it. I spent little time on them, recognizing perhaps that however hard I tried I could no more bring her to life in language than I could in fact.

In the notes of the CD Schubert is quoted as saying that everything he wrote came from his knowledge of music and his sorrow. Everyone is drawn into the heart of that sorrow but without the knowledge, which the note says 'could not be exceeded', that wouldn't happen – the point being that without its equivalent in words in my case, there is so much feeling I cannot hope to express, wanting to being the most powerful feeling of all. And if it is not expressed how can we be sure of it, how can it endure?

From what I've gathered too, he knew that much of the music he wrote, particularly towards the end of his life, wasn't likely to be heard except among his small circle of friends, so that in effect he was writing for us. It was Jane's family who introduced me to Schubert. It was when I went up to spend Christmas with them. During tea it was a family tradition to listen to music for half an hour or so. I forget what was played but I remember saying that I didn't really know much, indeed anything, about classical music, was an ignoramus in that particular regard, putting it pompously like that. To which Jane replied that I could do worse than start with Schubert 'who'll never let you down'. To which her father added, 'The late works especially, Tom, will take you straight to the heart of the matter. He was dying. And so young. Pretty desolate, really, not where everyone wants to go.' 'But it's just so lovely most of the time, that's all,' his wife added. 'So personal to each one of us somehow.'

I could hardly tell them that my sole recollection of Schubert was the evening Maureen came to stay, my thoughtful preparations for that, meticulously laying the table to the accompaniment of a Schubert Impromptu while she had a bath upstairs. I was keen to impress her in both respects. Whether I did or not I cannot now recall.

Be all that as it may. This is what I wrote at the time. The account is in two parts.

I met her when I went up to London to see Mrs Bradecki, who seemed as contented as she could ever be with her little flat and garden – so far removed from all she had once lived through, surrounded by memories of her beloved husband. Indeed, when I left, saying I'd see myself out, I heard her speaking in Polish, not as if to herself, but in quite lengthy explanation. I am sure it was him she was talking to, having forgotten my presence though I was still within sight – telling him perhaps where she intended to put this shrub or plant those flowers or, to judge from her tone of voice, asking for his opinion.

On the way out I heard some music playing faintly and noticed a new CD and cassette player on the sideboard with a rack of CDs and tapes on the wall above it. I remembered then Jane telling me a year or so before that the player was something she had given her 'so she could listen to Chopin to her heart's content'. (Adrian and Jane are still letting her live there rent free of course.) I assumed the music to be Chopin and stopped to listen. Mrs Bradecki had followed me in and I said how nice it was. When we said goodbye I told her how nice her garden was looking. Very nice. To which she replied, 'Everything is very nice, thank you, Mr Ripple.'

Jane. We met in Waterlow Park in Highgate. I had never been there before. She'd had lodgings nearby as a student. It was one of her favourite places, she said. When her parents first came down to see her, it was there she had taken them. She and Adrian had gone there on their first date. She told me he was away on an assignment. I should add that it was she who phoned me, saying she'd like to see me. Visiting Mrs Bradecki at the same time was her idea too.

We met at the entrance to the park and she embraced me as she always did, her arms round me, holding me tight for an instant.

There were no tentative pecks on the cheek or mwah-mwah noises. It was a late spring day with a few clouds moving fast across a deep-blue sky. Most of the trees were in full leaf, the rest due to catch up in the next week or so. The gusts of wind were making them rustle, altering them with even more shades of green. From time to time shimmers of silver slid across them and there were patches of pale gold too here and there. The shrubs in the recently raked flower-beds were thickening nicely and some were in flower – azaleas I remembered from my Suffolk days, Agnes pointing out to me that they looked mighty pretty but not for long, rhododendrons too, but what youthful prettiness, she added with a wink, did?

We had the place largely to ourselves and for a long time just walked. We didn't even ask the usual polite questions. Or rather I did not ask her how she was because she was clearly not well – the taut pallor of her skin, the eyes shadowed beyond exhaustion. It seemed more than just a female thing. There was something too about her deep brown eyes. The whites gleamed and they seemed to have grown larger. When she held my arms before our embrace, it was as if she was staring at something beyond me, or rather seeing me from afar as one among many, almost as a stranger. We reached a bench which she pointed at and there we sat. She took my hand, turned it over and examined it.

'If you're thinking of telling my fortune,' I said, 'start with my life-line. Save time on the rest.'

She closed my hand into a fist and held it tight. Then we gazed into each other's eyes for a moment . . . I do wish the phrase wasn't such a cliché, that it had never been said before. But no, that is not what we were doing. It is too vague. There was puzzlement there and longing and an awful uncertainty. The moment quickly passed. As we had walked along the path in that lovely reawakened park I'd wondered if there was something she wanted to tell me about Adrian, that they were going to separate, had found other people, or one of them had, the usual miserable tangle. But now I suddenly knew what it was she had to tell me. I looked down at our hands, fear and love leaping up in terrible conjunction to seize me by the throat.

'I think you've guessed,' she said very quietly.

'Not really. I . . .' But I had, I had.

'Six months if I'm lucky. It's pretty well all over my insides. That's enough to be going along with. Or not going along with. You won't want the details.'

She patted my hand and smiled. I don't think I've tried to describe her smile before. It went with a raising of the eyebrows as if she'd done something slightly shocking and had been caught out. It was a smile of the utmost candour. It almost closed her eyes so that when it stopped she was looking at you as if it was such a lovely surprise that you were still there, especially if you were smiling too.

'No,' I said. 'But what . . . I mean. Well, Adrian. Does he . . . ?'

She shook her head and stopped folding and unfolding my hand for a moment. 'He's got this consultancy helping to set up a Europe-compatible accountancy system in Hungary. Absolutely loves it. Comes back on Sunday. I shall tell him then. He knows I've not been well, been having tests.'

There were so many questions I'd never dared to consider about their marriage, children mainly of course and what led up to that, how they really were together. What had always struck me about them was their casualness with each other, no shows of affection but absolutely no kind of tension, unease at all. When they looked at each other it was with the plainest trust and respect. And dependence. Perhaps because I was seeing her too through my own eyes, Adrian's expression had seemed that much more in her thrall – or almost that, simply believing that there was no one remotely like her in all the world. He was dead right about that. I had thought him the luckier one by a long chalk. Well, not that long.

I was thinking this when she said, 'I just want you to know this, Dad. Adrian is the most remarkable man I know. You see, and there can't be any more beating about the bush now, or not much . . . How to put this? There not having been the usual intimacies, or not often and not always very conclusive, something else took their place which steadily grew and flourished like a tree, something not shaped by the ups and downs, the dissatisfactions of desire . . . Sorry, language problem . . .'

I took her other hand and examined it as she had mine. 'Not the breaking of waves, the repeated fresh collapse . . .'

She laughed. 'You'd better do more work on that. Doesn't it ring a bell, the collapse bit?'

I couldn't place it at the time but found it later in the little book the vicar gave me: that vision of the sea, the white steamer stuck in the afternoon, the children grasping at enormous air, the rigid old feeling a final summer. Only the last line about helping the old too, as they ought, came dimly back. It's all the wrong way round, I thought. But these reflections were swift and frail. I simply hadn't registered what she'd told me, her voice had sounded so matter of fact. I glanced up at her. She was very thoughtful, very far away. In that moment it suddenly became true.

'Adrian, how on earth will he . . . ? What's the scenario, thing . . . ?'

'That's the worst. My parents, my brother too.' She looked up at me, that smile there again, as if we were having some sort of fun, not a trace of complaint or self-pity. 'And you, Tom.'

I shrugged. 'Me? Couldn't give much of a toss either way, to be frank, whether you're here or not.'

A sob burst from me and I began to weep uncontrollably so that I had to leave her there on the bench and walk some distance away into the shadow of a tree. What a truly tremendous amount of use to her I was being, I told myself, what a terrific tower of strength I'd be for my son. But grief does not heed persuasion and it was some time before it ran its course. Meanwhile she left me alone until I blew my nose and wiped my eyes for the last time and I felt her arm round my shoulder to lead me back to the bench. We sat there for a while, saying nothing. I was glad she did not take my hand, thus setting off the whole bang shooting match again.

When she spoke her voice was exactly as it had been. I imagined this was how she was at work, calm, authoritative, uncontradictable.

'I want to spend my last days with my parents. There's a very good cancer department in the local hospital. I'll need constant attention if I'm to die at home . . .'

'Oh for God's sake, Jane,' I blurted out. 'You could hire a nurse . . .'

'He could come up as often as he wanted. Every night if necessary. It's only an hour and a half by train . . .'

'Of course, of course, I'm sorry. And your parents will want . . . I didn't think.' My voice went hoarse here as if I'd tried to make it like hers. 'You'll let me know, won't you, the sort of thing I should say to him?'

'No, no, Dad. You'll know that.'

The wind had turned cold or we had sat there too long. Briefly a cloud hid the sun and she shivered. The pallor of her face was tinged with grey which seemed to have seeped down from the darkness under her eyes. I suggested we find a café for a cup of tea.

'In a moment. This place is so beautiful. Quite lovely. Spring. Early summer. I will never come here again. Couldn't with Adrian. It was here we settled very quietly into our love. It was here he told me . . . Oh just look at it all! Look at that restless tree, that bursting shrub. That sky, the deepest blue as if dusk had already reached it . . . And do you know, at this instant, it is so huge that I believe I couldn't be happier, simply that one is blessed to experience such things. But always the darkness soon comes. It's the same for everyone.'

Again she shivered. I was cold too and without a word we got up and walked back to the gate and up the hill to the village where we found a café. She said she'd like hot chocolate and a sticky bun, so I ordered the same. What she had last told me reminded me of that dreadful café, so different from this one, where all those years ago Adrian had told me he was homosexual and the waitress thought we were lovers. How I wished I had been a better father for him then and always, for a far better father now was what he needed. I wished I could say any of this but here in this cosy, genteel place where the waitress wore a short black dress and a frilly white apron, there was nowhere to flee to, no open space to summon my strength, what little there was, had ever been, of it.

Jane held her cup in both hands, warming herself. From time to time she looked up at me with a slight wistful smile, her dark eyes consoling me. I smiled back. For a while we said nothing, then suddenly she said, 'I forgot to ask. How's Mrs Bradecki?'

'Fine, I think.'

'There's no reaching those people. Even now . . . What they've known and seen and had to live with. That account of her childhood you showed us. We can't identify with what we haven't experienced, can we? Some people seem to think they can. The empathizers. The second-hand witnesses. I do rather wish they wouldn't . . . As for the rest of us, don't we feel we are unable to care as much or as often as we know we should?'

I didn't know what to make of this but nodded all the same.

'At least now she's as happy as it is possible for her to be,' I said. 'Thanks to you and Adrian.'

'Hardly. I looked in a month or so ago. You could hear the Chopin in the street. One of the concertos. Wonderful. She does love that garden of hers. Was quite talkative for a change. Spoke very warmly of you. Mr Ripple is very nice man.'

Naturally, that pleased me and I mumbled that that was nice, thinking: there seems to be a lot I'm finding nice today. I might have said more about Mrs Bradecki but Jane had been reminded of something and raised her hand a few inches off the table.

'You remember when you returned from Poland, those terrible places you went to, you didn't say anything about them. And then you were taken ill and had your operation . . .'

I remembered clearly that when I mentioned the camps, simply that I had been there, Adrian had said, 'I couldn't bear to go to places like that.' And I'd replied with a shrug that I didn't know, I just had. We'd waited for Jane to add something but of course she was right and there was nothing more to say at all. The horror was always there. It was absolute, final. As final as a bright early summer day with the trees in full leaf and people strolling beneath them. How glad I was then that she would never read what I'd written about my visit. How glad, for that matter, that she will never read this.

I frowned a little at the lazy thoughts I was having.

'It doesn't *help*,' she said, 'but this ordinary, common sorrow of ours . . . Compared with the magnitude of that, it gives us just an inkling, we can begin to imagine, just begin, multiply it out, take away the terror . . . No, I'm sorry, that's quite wrong. That connection. I mean, when all one comes out of it with is a sense of having been, of being, most extraordinarily fortunate.'

I shook my head. This didn't seem right.

'Do you want me to go on?' she asked. I nodded.

'I can tell myself that sort of thing anyway. I want you all to know that I am really very prepared . . .'

'Do you believe in an after-life, that sort of thing?'

She shook her head. 'Unfortunately not. That's the point. Somewhere in between the unspeakable dreadfulness of the world and the beauty of things there is peace to be found. By some anyway. Here and now.'

I did not know, still do not know, whether I went along with any of this. It is too abstract for me. I should find out. But there she was, thinking only of how best to spare others. There was a long pause. I could not say what I was thinking. In all she said, all she was, there was no trace of self-consciousness. How far that removed her from me, rabbiting on interminably about myself.

'You don't want this sticky bun, do you?' she said, looking down at it as though it had been abandoned there a long time ago.

I hadn't started my own either. 'Typical,' I said. 'Take my daughter-in-law out for a slap-up tea, spoil her something rotten, then she tells you she's not hungry. Honestly . . .'

She laid her hand on mine, squeezing it. I had to snatch my hand away and make for the lavatory. Door locked. Someone else in there of course. I could not look back at her so began weeping again at the door, muttering that it badly needed a coat of paint. At least no one else is going to read any of this.

When I returned she was standing up, buttoning up her coat, wrapping her scarf around her neck.

'Please, Jane, a little longer.'

She sat down. 'I was feeling cold, that's all.'

At first I couldn't think of anything more to say to her. Then I remembered another café and Adrian's misery that day, a day in autumn where we chased falling leaves, a taxi driver asking Bertrand Russell: 'What's it all about then?' But mainly I remembered the silences.

Wanting to break one now, I blundered into saying more than I wanted to. 'About Adrian, I don't know what to think except that I'll be there for him. No, that sounds awful – too American by half. Sorry, old chap, father's not here, gone on a world cruise, back in six months. You see, I feel I've never really known him, always had this sense that I was trying too hard or not nearly enough. As a boy he seemed remote . . . So now . . .'

She looked hard at me, almost sternly. 'He often talks of you and his mother. He loves you. You are his parents. It's as simple as that. Worries about you both. Virginia too, how to give her money. There isn't any sort of judgement.'

'For or against.'

'Precisely.'

My left hand lay on the table, exposing my wrist. For some reason that day I'd replaced my Timex with the very expensive watch Adrian had given me which told the time to the nearest hundredth of a second.

'Adrian gave me that. Hardly ever wear it. Only for special occasions. He's, you've always given me nice presents. The CDs, the books. Last Christmas, though, those ghastly *red* socks. What would people think, always putting his foot in it.'

She laughed. 'Every time someone cracks a bad pun, Adrian says, "Dad would like that one." He grins a lot when he says that.'

I made an exaggerated wincing face, raised the back of my hand to my forehead and groaned. Then I noticed that the smile had gone from her face. For a moment it had been quite lit up, full of joy as it had been earlier when she looked up at the trees, at the sky, following for a while the swift passage of clouds.

'I really think I must go now, Dad. My car isn't far.'

I stood up beside her. 'Let me walk you there.'

She touched my arm. 'This last bit I'll do on my own.' She paused and looked at me with an uncharacteristic frown. 'You do realize, don't you, that I have had the most blessed of lives?'

We went outside and again she gave me that close embrace, holding me for a long time, or rather it was now me who was holding her. The tears were welling up again, so that when eventually she stood back I could not see the expression on her face, not even if she was smiling or shared my sorrow.

'Goodbye, Dad. And thank you.'

She turned and walked away. I just stood there, blinking, so that at one moment she was vividly clear and the next had vanished in a blur in the surrounding crowd and traffic and houses. It was when she was clear that she turned and blew me a kiss. She was smiling her broadest smile, for all the world like a young lover, looking forward to the next time, confident that that would be very soon. Then she was fuzzy again. Then she wasn't there at all.

I stood there for a very long time. The waitress was standing beside me, handing me a bill.

'Didn't you like the buns then?' she asked. I shook my head and took a twenty-pound note out of my wallet. 'You still have to pay for them, you know.'

'Keep the change,' I said.

She looked at me at first as if I was off my rocker. She could see I'd been weeping, I suppose, so instead of thanking me she said she was sorry. People often do, without knowing what for. They are seeing others drinking at the pool of unhappiness which everyone shares.

'There was nothing wrong with the buns so far as I know,' I said.

'That's all right then,' she replied, returning to the café.

As she opened the door her dress was blown high up her thighs and she tried too late to hold it down. Oh yes, even then, even then . . .

I never saw Jane again.

Adrian called me a few days after his return from Hungary. He simply said how glad he was that Jane and I had met. He'd like to see me. Could I come up one day? We fixed a date. I asked if Virginia and his mother knew. He said they did. Both phoned me the following day. Virginia hardly knew Jane. It was a terrible thing, she said. Such a waste. How did I think Adrian was bearing up? I said I didn't yet know. This was about nine months after their bleak holiday visit. Richard had a part-time job. It was a bit infra dig, she said, clerking for a transport concern but there might be a managerial opening later if he played his cards right. There was a pause here. She was expecting a joke perhaps. I asked after the children instead. She worked half time too at the local hospital, so looking after them was shared between them. They were coping all right. After their visit I'd sent them a 'loan' of a thousand pounds, so 'thanks to me' they'd cleared up most of their mortgage arrears. I'd played my cards right, you might say, coming up trumps.

I wanted to ask how Adrian had seemed to her. She would have told me if there had been anything more to their conversation than the passing on of news, if he had sounded distraught etc. Or would she? I did not know how close they were, indeed had ever been. Suddenly the memory returned of that visit to the park with the Webbs and Hambles – the awkward handing round of food, the French cricket, Virginia constantly glancing at Mrs Hamble and vice versa, the love in the dying woman's eyes for the child she never had. I very nearly asked Virginia if she remembered all that. But she had never spoken of the Hambles again that I can recall. Her thoughts had filled up with other things. Once when I mentioned that I'd passed our old house and seen Mr Hamble at work in his garden she made no comment at all. It was as if all that had never happened. Then so vivid, so all-consuming. Sad. Our conversation petered out. There was the noise of squabbling children in the background so her thoughts had doubtless begun to drift away too.

My former wife phoned. This was her territory. In the old days she used to do some 'bereavement counselling', attended a course on it if I remember correctly. She said that Adrian might be in need of a support group. She said that care of the dying, the drugs, had improved enormously in recent years. She said that when Brad died she thought she'd never get over it. I said nothing because I could think of absolutely nothing to contribute at all. It was the voice of expertise talking. Finally she said, 'I do know, Tom, that the words are no use at all. But we couldn't just say how awful it is, then hang up, could we?'

'No. I just don't feel like a member of any support group, that's all. There's Adrian. There's Jane. There's her people. I don't seem to be able to think beyond that.'

'Sorry, Tom. I was being the most frightful theorizer again. We had a laugh about that at the end, Brad and I. We sent for a bibliography on grieving. Decided that, as respectable scholars, we shouldn't read any of it if there wasn't time to read all of it, to get a fully balanced view. He didn't want me to spend the rest of my life reading about how I felt about his not being there to discuss it with. He was a good man, you know.'

I said I was sure he was, the children had liked him. Which they had, or not disliked him in any specific way. On that note we said goodbye. I do not know why I did not try to share memories with her, the cardboard bowler hat, the seaside holidays and all the rest of it. Perhaps it was simply that I didn't want my memories corrected, amplified in any way. True or false, however partial and selective, they had become a whole, a complete world which I did not wish to be further elaborated on, like the final draft of a chapter of a book. I now feel the same about Jane. If I were to meet someone who knew her and wished to talk about her I would make an excuse and take my leave. I have tried to work out why this should be so. I should be hungry for facts about her. But the picture is finished. It is not unlike pieces of the loveliest music. They shouldn't be tampered with in any way.

I met Adrian in his flat for lunch. Jane had left the week before to stay with her parents. He would spend the weekends with her and most evenings during the week. We embraced, clumsily, for it was the first time we had done so. He was very calm, his movements slow, visibly under the strictest control. He poured two glasses of wine and we sat opposite each other at the dining-room table. The flat was impeccable, nothing out of place, the furniture gleaming, the kitchen spotless, the carpets freshly hoovered. The air smelt of artificial lavender. There were three vases in prominent places without any flowers in them. Was this how Jane had wanted to leave it for him, or had Adrian made it impersonal like this, to neutralize the spirit of her presence?

'Jane said she so enjoyed her afternoon with you. She's very fond of you, you know.'

'And I of her.' Was this the best I could do? Should I tell him what he knew already a thousandfold? Well, he wasn't saying anything, so I did. 'She's the most wonderful woman I've ever met, that's all.'

He nodded slowly. It was very strange – as if he was considering carefully what I'd said, deciding whether or not he agreed with it. I told him I'd spoken to Virginia and his mother. He did not respond to that either at first, getting up to pour himself another glass of wine. It crossed my mind for a moment that he'd rather I wasn't there, that I had interrupted a train of thought and he was afraid of losing the thread.

'We're worried about Virginia,' he said. 'You see, we've a lot more money than we'll ever need. I'm coining it, frankly. So is Jane, even more so actually. Was. We'd like Virginia to have a chunk of it, quite a large chunk, but wouldn't it be humiliating for Richard, them both?'

'Yes, it would.'

'What we thought was this. Could we give it to you and you could say that it was what you were leaving her in your will and now was when they needed it. A sort of advance. Live for seven years and it's tax-free. Something of that sort.'

'Couple of snags there, Adrian. If I've got a large chunk of money with seven years to live, Virginia knows perfectly well I'd be off like a shot to the Costa Brava or the Canaries and live it up. Or a round-the-world cruise. The birds would come flocking. You know me. The main chance. Bloody silly idea, frankly.'

He smiled that shy, knowing smile of his. One could see how some would find him irresistible, of either sex I suppose I should add.

'Jane said you'd say something like that.'

'Oh she did, did she? She hardly knows me.'

'She knows you all right.'

We discussed the idea for a while and I agreed in principle. Wasn't it wrong, though, to deceive her. To lie to her? That was what Jane had thought too. So that is what we settled on mostly – truthfulness versus kindness and all that moral caboodle. We ate some cheese and biscuits, drank more wine and then he had to go.

There were no summary parting words. I simply gripped his elbow very hard and muttered, 'Let me know . . .'

And that was that. He remained very calm, almost offhand, as if to show me how he would have to be for her, that in their last days together their companionship, if that was the word for it, would deepen further; the tree would spread its leaves, blotting out for a while the mounting black clouds and the coming dusk.

It is that sort of an evening now . . . I have just returned from the seafront in something of a hurry, having seen the clouds massing above the cliff like a herd of huge wild beasts on the rampage. I just made it in time. Or not quite. I sit here with a few spots of rain on my cheeks, wondering whether now is the time to finish what I have to recount about Jane. As I have said, I did not see her again but three times when Adrian was there she spoke to me on the phone from her deathbed. She told me my son was spoiling her something rotten, waiting on her hand and foot. She'd finally confessed to him how much I'd hated those red socks. She said we shouldn't lie to Virginia, but there was nothing to stop her leaving her something in her will. She said I had been incredibly stingy only to have offered her a sticky bun that day when she'd been absolutely *longing* for scones and a chocolate éclair, what sort of a father-in-law was I? No sense of humour for a start . . .

She did all the talking, knowing that I wouldn't know what to say to her. She was trying to make her voice sound normal but there was a husky, breathless edge to it as if she had to break up her sentences to put strength back into it. The effect was to make her sound flirtatious.

It was she who drew attention to this. 'Adrian says my voice sounds very sexy these days.'

'Now you come to mention it.'

'Ironical. I'm dying to make a pass at you.'

'Did you think that one up?'

'No, Adrian did. He said it was just about appalling enough for you . . .'

'I really haven't the foggiest idea what you're talking about,' I said.

But Adrian had come on the line and they both missed that. He said rather abruptly he had to ring off because the doctor had arrived . . .

That is where the first account ends. The remaining pages were written some months after the funeral, though I scribbled some notes whenever the silence of echoes and images became unendurable. As I remember, I wanted to get it over with, increasingly aware of my failings of expression, aware too of my fading grief – that acceptance she most wanted for us.

The end came sooner than expected. Adrian called at dawn to say she had died peacefully during the night and to tell me when the cremation was. Peacefully. They always say that, not knowing what nightmares there might have been at the end, what parting accusations there were of things said and done, or not said and not done.

I went straight to the crematorium from the station. In the waiting room Jane's parents welcomed me as though I was the person they were by far the most glad to see. I have mentioned them before, too briefly, but there's not a lot you can say about people like that. Just the sort of people you'd expect Jane to have as parents. And vice versa. Quiet, professional, thoroughly decent folk with a sense of duty to the world. They were stricken. Adrian introduced me to Jane's younger brother, a plump man with glasses and the face of an eager boy. You could guess that normally he did a lot of laughing. He hadn't been at home that Christmas because he was in Africa, Zambia I think it was, as a VSO volunteer. There would once have been great gaiety in that household, no longer now. I couldn't help wondering whether Adrian would have had a somewhat subduing effect on them. He'd seemed on edge that Christmas – my presence having something to do with that no doubt. I remembered Adrian telling me that Jane and her brother used to spend a great deal of time talking on the telephone and Jane often used to shake her head or burst out laughing. There were thirty or forty other people there. I asked Adrian if Virginia was coming but she said she hadn't been able to get away. Because of the children.

When we went into the chapel a tape was playing some simple piano music. Something quite often heard. By Bach, I believe . . . I expected a vicar of some sort to conduct affairs, but instead Jane's brother stood up, took a folded envelope out of his pocket which he only referred to once. He spoke very tentatively, looking down at the floor or up at the ceiling. Whatever he had prepared didn't seem any use to him now. I cannot remember it all.

He said that Jane hadn't believed in God but there were those there who did and were convinced she was on her way to a better place. For them, her beloved friends and relatives, she hoped that instead of a Christian funeral service they would accept some readings from the scriptures in the old and lovely language bequeathed to us by Tyndale – this was where he referred to the envelope – since this was something they all shared. The music they would hear as she finally left them was written when the composer was only nineteen, inspired perhaps by thoughts of his mother who had died four years earlier. He said finally that he'd thought of writing a proper address about the sort of person Jane was or of asking someone else to do it. But nothing he or anyone else could say could do justice to that extraordinary person they all held individually in their hearts. I saw several heads nodding at this point. In the front row Jane's parents were absolutely still, their shoulders pressed together, their backs straight. You could tell they were holding hands very tightly.

He then read, falteringly, the psalm which begins, 'Lord, who shall dwell in thy tabernacle or who shall rest upon Thy holy hill.' After which he returned to sit beside Adrian on the other side of the front row.

This was followed by I Corinthians xiii read by a woman of about Jane's age who couldn't continue when she reached the line beginning 'When I was a child . . .' She just stood there, her lips pressed together, the Bible shaking against her breast. After a while Adrian got up, put a hand on her back and looked down at her with a tender, questioning smile I had never seen before. She smiled back, took a deep breath and was able to continue to the end, the tears falling down her cheeks every time she blinked. Her voice remained clear and steady even though some of the tears trickled into the corners of her mouth. An old childhood friend perhaps.

Then an elderly man stood up and said that Jane had asked to see him a week before she died. She wanted him to say something about Adrian, how wonderful her marriage had been, that there could never possibly have been anyone else. She'd then asked him to read at her funeral something they had studied at school. So he'd chosen a poem he'd read to her sixth-form class called 'Whitsun Weddings'. She'd led an argument about what the last line meant, saying how sad it was. For once, he said, he thought she'd been wrong. He was disappointed she'd decided not to read English at university for she

530

had an exceptional love of language. She thought she wouldn't have made a good teacher and the law would make her useful in other ways. Perhaps he shouldn't say it, but he hoped she wasn't wasted on the City. It didn't surprise him she wanted Tyndale to be mentioned. They'd spent a wonderful afternoon comparing his New Testament with the Authorized Version. When she came back to see him one day she told him she'd been reminded of the poem on the train journey up and how much she loved it.

Like the poem about the sea it was in the book the vicar sent me, though I'd forgotten it and it was as though I'd never heard it before.

He read it very plainly, not putting on a special voice, and hesitated quite a long time before the final line. It seemed sad to me too and Jane was usually right. Finally, her brother returned and read the Beatitudes.

Then a song was played, sung by a beautiful female voice, and we waited for the coffin to start gliding away but it stayed there as if held back by the music, to be enveloped by it in complete stillness. When it finished, it was played again as the coffin slid away until the music was playing across a huge empty space. Meanwhile some knelt and others remained standing, among them Jane's parents, he very upright, gazing up at the roof, she with her head bowed. After the last echo faded no one moved for a very long time as if they wanted the music to continue and for as long as it did Jane would still be there among them.

Outside, Jane's parents shook hands with everyone or embraced them. Several were weeping. Only those who loved her most could not afford to weep. As I approached I heard her father apologize that there would be no reception but they did want to see everyone if they wouldn't mind leaving it for a week or two. There were flowers to be looked at, the labels to be read. Slowly they all drifted apart into the car park, stopping for a word here and there, then dispersing to their cars. They seemed to be making as little noise as they could. It was as if something was holding them back, some reversal of time they should hold themselves in readiness for – or as though they were reluctant to enter the noise and bustle of the world again where they would begin to forget.

Adrian took me by the elbow to his car and drove me to the house. I said the service had been beautiful which wasn't as totally inadequate a word as any other would have been. He said he wished now he'd done one of the readings. But he couldn't have trusted himself. Anyway he didn't have the voice and delivery for that sort of thing. All right for financial statements at board meetings. 'And bored is what they usually are,' he added, glancing at me.

I nodded. Not the twitch of a smile.

'Not bad for a beginner?' he asked.

I pursed my lips. 'Four out of ten and that's generous.'

We were drawing up at the house and he gave me a fleeting grin. There were three or four people there beside the immediate family. Jane's father gave us sherry and her brother handed round nuts. I found myself talking to a maternal aunt about azaleas of all things. There must have been a pot of them somewhere. The aunt left and Jane's mother came over. It was clear she was starting to grieve now beyond endurance. Too much had been held back. Her voice was too loud and beginning to crack. Her eyes were staring and filling with tears.

'She couldn't have children, did you know that?'

'No, I didn't know that.'

'Oh if only . . . to have seen her in someone else. She would have been a wonderful mother.' She began to gabble, her voice now broken, out of control. 'The last line. Somewhere becoming rain. That's fertility. It shouldn't have been sad at all. She tried all the doctors, everything. It made her so unhappy. She wanted to give Adrian a child, us grandchildren. You too. Some poor little so-and-so for him to tell his dreadful jokes to, she said . . .'

Now the tears began to spill out. She was shaking and muttering over and over again how sorry she was. Her husband came and led her away. Adrian said he'd give me a ride to the station. I wasn't sure how much of that he'd heard so said nothing. Jane's father came with us to the car, his arm round Adrian. He said he was so glad I'd been there, as if I'd had an alternative. I couldn't think of anything to say to him. When we shook hands he gave a slight shake of his head as if to prevent me from trying. What memories he must have had of his little girl, each year losing one child and gaining another, slightly different, equally adored. And finally all those lovely, living faces overlaid by the one enduring face of death.

I asked Adrian in the car who had written the music at the end and he said he wasn't sure. She listened to a lot of classical music. Most of it wasn't really his cup of tea. It was often in the background while they worked in the evenings and it was vaguely familiar.

When we parted, he said, 'Her mother was right, Dad. We could never have had children. So in that too we had to acquire a great self-sufficiency of love on its own. Jane put it like that once. She did mind terribly. But now? At least there are no little ones to put through this as well. That was one of the last things she said.'

That is what I wrote at the time. I did not discover until a year later the name of the music she had chosen to accompany her departure. I was in the kitchen busy preparing my supper. All right, putting a ready-made Cumberland pie in the oven. It was playing on the radio: 'Litanei auf das Fest Aller Seelen.' Schubert, who else? Which is where this chapter began. I bought the CD and played the song often for a week or two. But it never affected me again quite as much as it did when I was putting Cumberland pie in the oven, suddenly coming from nowhere and filling my little house like that. It brought me solace and a sudden peculiar joy. It was as if Jane and I were listening to it together, lifted into some other world. Which I suppose we were. The CD note talks about 'grief consoled but still weeping'. That's quite good as far as it goes. The sorrow was not surmounted but somehow dispelled into all sorrow. That's not much better. I have not played it for a long time now. I don't know why. I quite often play some of his other things. Perhaps I am saving it up for the time when I shall shortly be joining her in the hereafter or oblivion.

Blessed are the pure in heart.

Chapter Five

The next pages of material are mainly about Bridget and Mrs Felix.

Recent arrivals have included three female students at the far end of the street on the way to the bus stop. Whenever I happen to be passing (crossing the street to do so) they can be seen in their front room lounging about on the floor or on a sofa, usually eating with their fingers and watching television. To judge from what one can see of the room, their studies are not in the fields of hygiene or interior decoration. They never draw the curtains; indeed there are none to draw. I said there are three of them. Those are the ones I see most often, there being several others to be observed through the window or coming and going, and not only in the evening for some kind of social get-together. I wonder if one day I shall see heads down over books etc. Sometimes I glance up after dark at the upstairs windows. They are never lit. Bulbs broken and never replaced in all probability. When they first moved in they frequently played popular music. It was out of my earshot unless I stepped out into the street. Mrs Felix soon put a stop to that, standing in my path one morning and saying in a warlike manner, wagging a finger at me, 'We can't have that, you know. Quite disgraceful. Spoken to the landlord.'

I wondered what offence I had committed, casting an eye back to see if my sack of rubbish was out of sight, even glancing down at my fly zip. I had not shaved and did look pretty shabby – indeed had resolved that very morning to buy a new jacket and pair of trousers. I had believed hitherto that my appearance might be that of an endearing old codger enjoying his retirement but the day before had caught sight of myself in a shop window and heard myself mutter they shouldn't let filthy old tramps into respectable places like that. Anyway, Mrs Felix had that effect on me, convincing me that I was letting the side down. She rummaged in her handbag

534

and I quite expected her to give me the address of a dry cleaner or men's outfitters.

'Sorry?' I mumbled.

'Those so-called students. That dreadful music. I put the fear of God up them. Said I wasn't the only one who'd had enough of it. Was speaking for the residents.'

I'd heard no other comment about the music, which had seemed not all that loud by contemporary standards and never late at night. Mrs Hirst had said to me, 'Those students, they seem to have a good time, I'll give them that. I wish I'd been one. Didn't have the brains for it or never found out if I had. The music was different in those days. More tune, less thump. At that age you've got to have a good time, else when can you?'

'Lowering the tone, are they?' I asked Mrs Felix. Not the twitch of a smile. 'In both senses,' I added helpfully.

'They certainly are. Turning it off altogether. Mark my words, Mr Ripple.' Here she paused, looking me up and down as if the fear of God was what she was minded to put up me too. 'So *slovenly*! When I was an undergraduate we had a bit of pride, to say nothing of self-respect.'

Whilst working out what the difference between those might be in her case, it occurred to me that she was expecting thanks.

'What would the neighbourhood do without you?' I asked, taking a long pace to one side, clearly making way for her.

'The fear of God,' she repeated. 'One has a duty to speak up. This is a respectable neighbourhood. As you so rightly observe, Mr Ripple, can't allow a lowering of the tone, now can we?'

'No need to bring the Almighty into it, surely?'

She didn't know what to make of this, the flattery of it, but leaving in doubt too as it did whether I might be a fervent believer offended by blasphemy. I tried to imagine her as a student with a bit of pride but failed; what she had had was an enormous quantity of it. She was moving on now, then turned back.

'Were you at university, might I ask, Mr Ripple?'

I sighed. 'Ah, those were the days!'

She was about to ask which one, what I'd studied; or if not then at some other time. This had to be forestalled. And anything to take that superior look off her face. The reply I gave was nevertheless ill advised. 'Christchurch College, Oxford. History as a matter of fact.'

I wasn't sure there was such a college at Oxford, though it sounded familiar enough. She thought so too.

'Ah, the House!' she exclaimed. I looked around, wondering which one she was referring to. 'My husband was an historian too. He was sartorial. You and he should get together. Now that was a *real* education. The so-called subjects they study nowadays: environmental this, media that, feminist the other thing.'

Again she looked me up and down, but approvingly now, as if recognizing a uniform; I had become a scholar and an eccentric. We belonged to the educated classes. How I had wished sometimes that I'd been to university, got a few A levels come to that. Not only would I know more, I'd have learnt how to express things better, or more easily, though these may not be the same thing. She seemed to be waiting for some response, perhaps about her husband.

'I was a pretty natty dresser myself. Once upon a time. Like Mr F, the picture of elegance. But now. Appearances. What do they matter?' I indicated my own clothing with a dismissive gesture. 'Neither of us been near our tailor for yonks.'

She was gaping at me, beyond wonderment. It was then I realized she'd told me what college her husband had attended. I gave a sharp laugh and repeated, 'Those were the days.'

She had no idea what I'd been talking about. Oh well, I thought. Too late now. But her anxiety was suddenly broken by a broad smile and she gave my forearm a squeeze.

'Such wags, you lot. Oh dear oh dear oh dear. Lowering the tone. Must tell Cedric that one.'

With a guffaw and a final squeeze of my arm she sped on her way. So I had become an educated man and a wit to boot. A diversion here. One thing about my former wife was that she never made me feel less educated than she was, less moral perhaps, certainly if unintentionally that all right, but not stupid. A key aspect of superior morality seems to be that one shouldn't think of oneself as morally superior, compare one's morality favourably with that of others. A key aspect of being morally inferior on the other hand, provided one recognizes oneself to be that, is in comparing one's thoughts and behaviour unfavourably with those of the morally superior. As a general rule, though, the morally inferior recognize nothing of the kind. They have expressions for the morally superior like 'holier than thou' or 'self-righteous' or 'hoity-toity' etc. Perhaps that's why the morally superior keep quiet about it, even perhaps in converse with themselves. The same is true of superior knowledge which allows that everyone is knowledgeable or ignorant in their own way etc. The ignorant tend not to mind being that, apart from having a tendency to call other people bloody ignorant and having expressions for those with superior knowledge such as 'smarty boots', 'clever dick', 'egghead' and the like. I haven't a clue whether I am right or wrong about any of this . . .

Anyway, Mrs Felix left me standing there, a graduate of Oxford University. There and then how I wished I was! Though if I had been I wouldn't have been there then or at any other time. Well, there might be some fobbing off of Mr Felix to be done. Perhaps Oxford graduates have learnt how to do that. I don't think I've met any. Jenners perhaps. Like him, I could acquire some half-eye glasses quizzically to peer over. Practise a change of voice. He could of course look me up, blow my cover. I could hear Mrs Felix say to all and sundry, 'Complete fraud, Ripple. Says he went to Oxford. Never been near the place.' Who in the street would give a toss? Mr Badgecock? Mrs Hirst? The window cleaner whose name I never knew? The Patels? The students who were lowering the tone? I would feel obliged at some stage in every encounter to say, 'When I was at Cambridge.'

Soon afterwards I found myself sitting next to one of the students in the bus: a bleary-eyed girl with cropped hair and perfectly formed lips who'd made no effort to amend her looks. Nor was she wearing scent of any kind – all those male students to be warded off perhaps having something to do with that. Indeed her general air was one of defensiveness. I was bringing some books from the library and she had a number of books on her lap also. Mine were three thrillers with an Anthony Powell at the top fortunately. She knew me by sight well enough to say, 'Hallo there.'

I glanced down at her books and said, 'Of making many books there is no end; and much study is a weariness of the flesh.'

The words were inscribed in large letters at the back of the issue counter in the library – just the sort of thing a graduate of Oxford University might say, I hoped.

She giggled and clutched her books tighter. She wasn't, thank goodness, going to ask me who'd said that. Might even assume that I had.

'What are you studying, if I might be so inquisitive?'

She wriggled again. 'Media studies.'

As a graduate in history from the University of Oxford several centuries ago I couldn't plug into that. 'Ah!' I said therefore. 'In my time . . .'

She looked away from me out of the window, shifting her thigh further away from mine.

'I gather Mrs Felix was rather hard on you about your music.'

She glanced back at me briefly. 'Ignorant, superior cow!'

'Yes, well . . . Media studies. No deficiency of channels career-wise in that sphere of endeavour I dare say.'

She gave me a long frown as if trying to remember when she'd last heard people speak like that, if ever. 'It's all right.'

After a pause I tried again. 'Otherwise, it's not such a bad little street. Convenient.'

She leant back and closed her eyes. 'Said she was speaking for all the residents. We should show some consideration. Did we know how fortunate we were. In her day something or other. A lot of that sort of crap. Talk about the generation gap.'

'She's right about fortunate. Wish I'd gone to university. That's another gap. Those who know and those who don't.' I put my hand across. 'Sorry. Introduce myself. Tom Ripple.'

She took my hand limply, no name offered in return – lest perhaps I use it in calling a familiar greeting across the street.

Instead, she looked away and muttered, 'Bridge it.'

'Oh absolutely!' I replied enthusiastically. 'Spot on! That's just what we must all try to do all the time. There are too many divisions in society. We simply mustn't allow them to, well, divide us. We have our common humanity, our sense of community to . . .'

She gazed at me, lost in wonder, but not it seemed at what I had been saying.

'It'll be all right,' she said gently at last, parting those lips. The teeth were no less perfect. 'Sorry, I expect Mrs Felix is a friend of yours.'

I gave a high, dismissive laugh. 'Good heavens, no! Mrs *Felix*! Fuss about nothing, frankly, if you ask me.'

We were close to our stop and she got up, saying, 'Sorry. Must rush.' There was to be no danger of my walking back alongside her.

'That's all right,' I said, wishing I knew her name, then realizing I did.

538

'It's been nice talking to you,' she said, seeming with a smile of sorts to half-mean it. 'See you around.'

My mouth was hanging open. It was too late to shut it now. She had been showing me kindness, I might have thought, had it not been naked pity. She strode away, her loose dress doing wonders for her walk. She hadn't even glanced at my books.

A week later I met Bridget with her friends. She returned my greeting with more of a grunt than a 'good morning'. I could imagine her telling all and sundry I'd tried to chat her up on the bus, one of those boring old farts who can't stop leering and spoiling the fun for others etc. And the most fearful gasbag to boot. Little chance of getting to know them then. And that's all right, to coin a phrase. We Oxford graduates are bound to find it difficult to communicate with students of new-fangled subjects when all's said and done. It's our superior knowledge.

That afternoon I found myself standing next to Mr Felix at the counter of the corner shop.

'Gather you were at the House?' he said.

'Whose . . . ?' I began, then remembered. 'That's it. You were at Oriel. Never mind.'

He smiled his ungrown-up smile. 'You always were an arrogant lot. Who did you . . . ?'

I made my escape, glad to see that he had a lot to tally up and pay for.

As I puffed my way up the hill, I remembered the student in the bus, thought of her being berated by Mrs Felix, on my behalf too. I wasn't sure whose side I was on, though. I'd have known if I'd lived next door to them all right. I wouldn't have been so superior about live and let live then, the less so as a graduate of Oxford University with erudite books to ponder on and music of, say, the operatic variety to listen to. Evidently superior knowledge and superior morality don't always go together. It could even be that a higher than average proportion of academic folk are shits.

When I next see Mrs Felix I shall tell her I've met one of the students and, to tell the truth, had rather liked the music they used to play. If Mr Felix is with her I shall add, 'My tutor at the House played in a jazz band.' Take sides the other way. I won't of course. I remember imagining long ago stepping out into the world with

Webb and Hamble, thinking of myself as half-way between them, with a bit of both of them in me. And now I find myself midway between Mrs Felix and a student of media studies. All things to all men. Above suspicion. Neither fish nor fowl. For some reason this makes me feel inferior all along the line – not having been to Oxford, having said I had now being an aspect of that. As I'd thought: knowing more, or less, and being better, or worse, than other people goes round in circles, one can't be sure of anything. Best to be sure of nothing then. Which may be characteristic of some of the morally superior and those with superior knowledge, come to think of it.

When I saw Mrs Felix yesterday she showed me a great deal more respect, asking how were we this glad, confident morning. After I'd muttered that she was very well considering, how was I?, she asked me to drop by for a glass of sherry the following evening. I had become an educated man, one of them. My heart sank. A friendship loomed, making me feel decidedly unfriendly. I accepted of course.

Their house was furnished much as I'd expected, though I'd never been into one owned by an Oxford graduate before, again except possibly for Jenners.

Mr Felix welcomed me in with a sweep of his arm like half an embrace, saying, 'Welcome to our humble abode.'

I am not making this up. People do say that, even graduates of Oriel College, Oxford. Mrs Felix was standing in front of the fireplace, as if inviting me to have a jolly good look at what civilized living was all about. Which I did. Books floor to ceiling on three walls. Overwoven, threadbare rugs from some middle or far eastern tribal mountain region. More records than CDs but a quantity of both. Pictures, or reproductions of them, portraying: a full frontal but indistinct female nude, a pot of flowers with faces peering out from among them, and a collection of precariously stacked, highly coloured boxes. No Mona Lisa here for me to make a daft comment about. No wife to tick me off about it either. I smiled at the picture with the boxes, glanced around the bookshelves. There were a number of ornaments, figurines, vases etc. about, each with a story to tell, no doubt, some of them to do with their value now compared with when they had been acquired. The sofa and chairs, once golden perhaps, now unwashed yellow, were littered with mud-spattered

cushions to match the carpets, though not exactly – from a neighbouring mountain region perhaps. I accepted a glass of sherry from
Mr Felix, saying I preferred sweet anyway, nearly adding that that
was what my tutor used to offer me at the House.

The questioning, ruthlessly, began. There were the television programmes and films and Oxford-based thrillers which had given a fair
idea of the sort of life led there. I invented a tutor called 'dear old
Spencer-Mallett' who'd done most of his work on the Crusades. I'd
played cricket for the college second team. I'd only got a good second
class degree, what with the carousing one used to do and larking
around with the drama society and the pubbing of course. Punting
on the river too. I was then asked what school I'd gone to, about
which I told the truth, not wanting to have to invent details of my
time at Eton or Harrow on top of all the rest. In any case, my accent
could not be made to sound of that sort. The only time I've tried it
was at a meeting with a merchant banker who said it was frightfully
good of me to have taken the trouble to turn up when I'd just been to
the dentist.

'One of your scholarship boys,' I added, looking hard at Mr Felix
as if to spot the smallest trace of snobbery there. There was none,
since he was glancing at Mrs Felix who said, unbelievably, 'And jolly
good for you too!'

'And you, Mr Felix?' I asked.

'Ardingly. Not that that means anything nowadays, mind you. The
rest, much the same story. Nothing to shout about.'

Mrs Felix was not minded to agree with this. 'Why should one be
ashamed of what is nowadays called a privileged education? Why
did people from humble backgrounds such as yourself, Mr Ripple, so
want to go there? Because it was the best, that's why.'

I thought of my mother telling my father that just because he came
from a humble background that was nothing to be humble about.
There was nothing to be proud about either – there was far too much
pride and humility about in the world when you didn't have any
choice in the matter. From something she'd read or seen, she told me I
didn't want to go to those Oxford and Cambridge where the students
were always climbing over the walls in the early morning and no one
did a stroke of work and there wasn't proper plumbing so they all
had chamber pots under their beds – never mind I wasn't nearly
clever enough, I certainly wouldn't be any cleverer when they'd

finished with me. My father didn't respond to any of this. Oxford and Cambridge were so far removed from him she might as well have been talking about Marco Polo's journeys to the Orient.

Mrs Felix had started to talk about the students.

'. . . I pointed out to them in no uncertain terms that the privilege of education should mean consideration for others and the setting of standards. You could see from the way they gaped at me they'd no idea what I was talking about. Had that dopey look. Probably on drugs. It wasn't as if the music wasn't so *mindless*. And those ridiculous studs all over their faces. Better than coloured hair, I suppose . . .'

Mr Felix was watching her fiddle with an earring and assumed an extreme version of his small boy expression, blinking behind his round spectacles and scratching his hair. Mrs Felix was looking hard at me, expecting my agreement. Then she said, 'You must surely agree with me, Mr Ripple. Coming from your background. Getting a leg up in the world.'

I drained my sherry, looked at my watch.

'Goodness gracious me,' I said. 'I do declare . . .'

Then I had a stroke of luck. My eye fell on a biography of William Tyndale on the rough-hewn coffee table which went with the carpets.

'Ah!' I said, pointing at it. 'Before whom we should all daily bend the knee, giving us a language, removing the Latin participle . . . The AV owes *everything* . . . Ah well, a call expected from Professor Brigstock. Some trivial detail about a little monograph I'm working on . . .'

Overdoing it, you might say. The Tyndale bit sounded very impressive, I thought, remembered from the day I'd spent reading about him in the library following Jane's funeral to take my mind off it, thus missing her all the more. They thought so too. I could tell from Mr Felix's stammered beginning about the Bible and the way Mrs Felix widened her eyes at me. She was about to press me further so I said, 'However, not my field, the language aspect. The Reformation on the other hand . . .'

With this I downed my sherry, thanked them and took my leave, saying, 'Do like the carpets. *Not* the Himalayan tribes. One can tell the difference, but not at a glance. That's half the fun of them . . .'

They stood together at the door, smiling inanely and I gave the friendliest of waves, my hand high above my head in the dotty manner of Oxford graduates or not as the case may be. The effect was spoiled when I turned and saw Bridget watching us. No doubt at all that Mrs

Felix and I were the closest of chums; indeed it was doubtless I who had put her up to complaining about the noise. I had to pass her on the way back to my house.

'Hi there!' I called. She looked blankly at me. 'Keeping in with the neighbours.'

Perhaps her mind was elsewhere, devising a documentary on bossy crones and old farts.

I did not see the Felixes for a while after that. When I did so they waved very cordially at me from the other side of the street . . . I had seen them coming and had time to assume a scholarly air, deep in thought, so that the sight of them came as a great and welcome surprise, lifting the burden of knowledge from my stooped shoulders. Evidently there had been no checking up. If pressed, I had unearthed an obscure research topic in the library on which Professor Brigstock and I needed to consult each other from time to time.

I found myself one morning at the bus stop with Bridget and two of her friends.

'Aha!' I said, turning, wondering which of the books was at the top of the pile I was returning to the library, one of the Ruth Rendells or the four essays on liberty by Isaiah Berlin.

(I borrow books like this from time to time. I don't read them word for word, indeed page by page, by any means. I just like to get the notion of what ideas and their expression at their deepest and best argued can be like. They make me feel inferior of course, except in wanting people to know that that's the sort of thing I read. Some people. Students for example. Both my neighbours would simply think I was keeping myself busy with books. I remember now that I tried to write about liberty once. Having had a taste of Berlin I couldn't bear to look at it now, the shallowness of my mind so starkly revealed. Gosh, how we can be put to shame by the paltriness of our thinking, others having thought and felt far more profoundly and intricately than we ever could. But they do it on our behalf, that's the thing, surely? Someone's got to do it. Someone's got to do a lot of things on our behalf and pretty paltry most of those things are too.)

They all had books as well. 'Great minds think alike,' I said, deserving the utterly expressionless, collective quarter-giggle I received in return.

Bridget looked prayerfully down the hill for the bus. The other girls stepped slightly back from me as though taking a sensible precaution. Both wore long dresses, one dark brown, one light brown of the hand-me-down variety. Their hair was similar too but with the browns the other way round. They seemed to have about the same number of studs in their ears. One of them had two studs in her nose. The other's two studs were under her lower lip. There was sticking plaster where Bridget's stud had been. Both the other girls were trying not to smile or to frown, to prevent their faces from revealing anything at all. No make-up of any sort on them either to disguise the spots or for any other purpose. They were all pretty in a forlorn, austere sort of way, as if where they were going was not a place of learning but a reformatory where the food was bad and their spare time was spent in prayer. I was staring at them.

'Bloody bus,' Bridget said.

There was nothing to lose. 'Not been having any parties recently?' I asked jovially.

'Give us a break,' she said.

'Oh no, no, no, no, no,' I replied. 'Not that. If you had, you'd have invited me. Music livens the old street up a bit. You've got to unwind. All work and no play . . . In my day . . .'

The other students also began to search yearningly for the bus.

'Doing media studies too, are you?' I asked next, trying to remove the anxiety from their faces; how differently would those look, I wondered, if the yearning was for a lover, not a bus?

'Social work,' said the first crossly, as though I really ought to have known.

'Environmental health?' said the second, not expecting me to have the faintest idea what that might be.

I nodded in what I hoped looked like approval. Which is what it was. Relevant things. I thought of all the good my former wife had tried to do. Brad as well of course. Things perhaps not on offer at Christchurch College, Oxford?

'To make the world a better place.' This to end my nodding as much as anything.

They exchanged glances, not mockingly but as if they hadn't thought of it quite like that before. Bridget was including herself, though media studies did not belong in the same category, so far as I was aware.

544

'Hopefully,' one of the other students said, smiling nicely, almost gratefully it might have been, plus more than minimal eye contact.

'I wish I'd had the benefit of a higher education. Mind you, if I had had, whether it would have been a better place with it, or made me better placed it wouldn't have . . . though God knows it might have improved my grammar . . . Well, obviously, the problem about the university of life is that there's no degree to show for it, though it's not just a matter of degree or rather is I mean you don't know whether you have done with more or less of it what . . .'

They watched me patiently trying to finish what I was saying. That is what they would have to be good at. Patiently hearing people out, not making them feel bloody foolish. I was saved by the bus which appeared round the corner at the bottom of the hill.

'Well, anyway, good luck,' was all I managed next, which seemed tame in that broad context, so I followed it with 'Fight the good fight!' and a raising of my fist.

It was at this moment that the Felixes drove past. It might well have seemed that the fist was raised at them and the students were grinning, at the arrival of the bus I hoped they thought. Bridget waved at them and I waved too. The other two got into the spirit of it and waved in an exaggerated fashion as if welcoming home a troopship from foreign battlegrounds. So the moment passed and we got into the bus. I would have wished to sit near them but that was not to be and I had to watch them from the back seat chattering and giggling at the front of the bus. However when I got off, I'll say this for them, though of course I'm really saying it for me: they all waved and one of them raised a fist.

I began by observing that there were several new arrivals at that time. Amongst them was a darkly-suited couple who got hurriedly into a Volvo every morning at eight on the dot with briefcases. One of them was usually taking a bite out of what was left of a piece of toast while the other spoke into a mobile telephone. Opposite me a few doors down was a man with a surreptitious, incognito look about him who came and went hurriedly at odd hours. He had a slight limp and always seemed to be looking the other way so that I still haven't seen his face . . . His trousers have turn-ups and are a good three inches too short. That is the sort of thing you notice when you can't see some-one's face.

545

Next to the estate agent's sister is an electrician with wife, baby and small, brand-new looking white van. When he saw me staring at him he hurried over and gave me his card. It was freshly printed. How young he looked, barely out of his teens, just starting out on life. A few houses down there was another couple who stood at their front window having the most fearful row when they were moving in, as though one of them was about to move out again and they were having to decide who's was what. Perhaps it was just about where to put what ... Anyway I observed them the following day cleaning the windows and tidying up outside. They were singing and quite often touched and kissed each other. I did not observe them for all that long. It was the sight of such a complete reconciliation that held my attention, that and wondering how long it would last. They had been very angry; the window was open and they were sharing it with the whole neighbourhood. I heard myself say, 'God help them.'

It is at moments like those that I wish God wasn't just a word: not that that would make any difference, there being as many unhappy folk who believe in Him as those who don't. What evidence do I have for this? God alone knows.

Just to round off then. The Felixes had come to deem me a person of superior knowledge while to the students my knowledge was inferior. Mrs Felix felt morally superior to the students and vice versa. Having lied to both, I could not feel morally superior to either. If I had not lied to the students, had had nothing to do with them, kept my distance, I should have felt morally inferior to them in my lack of achievement and relative indifference to the well-being of mankind. That is to assume I had bothered to think about those things at all – an inferior thing to say, come to think of it. I do not know whether the Felixes or the students feel morally superior to me. I do not know if I care whether they do or not. It does seem in this general area that we are all swirling around trying to place ourselves in relation to other people so as to give us a sense of ourselves without loss of self-esteem. That's what we care about – being thought well of, not inferior or superior in this respect or that. Once we recognize that, we feel all the better for it. We need to know where we stand in the eyes of others. We need to feel good about ourselves. Goodness and knowledge do not come into it. And so we often have to pretend to be what we are not. There can't be anything good about that. If Mrs Felix

546

accused me of being an impostor, I'd tell her she was right but it was only a recognition of her superiority to which those of us who are inferior cannot help but aspire. Whereas in fact I'd been thinking: don't you see I've been taking the mickey, you superior ignorant cow?

(Which brings to mind that what I seem to have left out is the combination of being intellectually superior but morally inferior and the other way round. I cannot think of anything more likely to be harmful than the former: those who are cleverer than other people are likely, very likely, to think themselves more moral too, having spent so much more time thinking about the rights and wrongs of everything – this meaning they can do or say pretty well what they like to and about other people. What they care about is that they know better than others. They don't care about how much better they are, whether they know that or not. The other way round is comparatively harmless. The morally superior with inferior knowledge have no desire to push their ideas down other people's throats, not having much in the way of ideas at all, least of all about how morally superior they are. To be considered further at another time. Not apropos myself; that seam is now exhausted. Did I not say somewhere that there was more unravelling to be undergone? No longer. I cannot pick up the thread and weave it back in. It is not only my stamina that is frayed. It is my belief in certainties. That is the temptation: to say you don't know a lot and you're no better than the next man and who gives a toss about that? Which makes it a blessing, the clear truth of it, the peace of mind it brings. I'm not tempted to take this any further. I don't care to. And that's the truth of it.)

Oh yes, I do know, thanks, that it should be Christ Church College. The Felixes could have caught me out on that. When I drafted these notes I wrote it as one word because I didn't know any better, making quite a few of you feel jolly superior I shouldn't wonder.

Chapter Six

Last week my doctor told me, with a glance at my paunch, that I'm in pretty good shape – considering. I thought to ask him: considering what? But I knew the answer: age etc. He needn't have added that. He should have shown me more consideration. As I was leaving he turned to his screen and mumbled, 'So you were previously a hairdresser?'

I hesitated, giving me time to wonder where he'd got that idea from. While having my blood pressure taken had I frowned at his sideburns, winced at the dandruff on his shoulders? I now looked around his head and nearly said I'd drop round with my clippers at closing time, give him a shampoo while I was about it.

'However did you guess? More of a short-back-and-sides man than one of your stylists. Had my own salon . . .'

He was looking at me in a puzzled manner and only then did I realize that what he wanted confirming was that I had been a professor. Nothing to be gained from correcting that if I wanted more consideration. Important he should believe I was still active, that there were more books, lectures etc. in the pipeline. I could be doing research into the general practitioner for all he knew. In academic circles and newspaper articles he'd want to be a GP I swore by – not to be referred to as 'my bloody doctor'.

So as I opened the door, I made the connection as best I could, petering out with, 'Still try to keep the old mind alert, no fancy language, snip-snipping away, keeping to the point, a circle of like-minded colleagues . . .'

He was still open mouthed as I closed the door with the gentlest of clicks. On my way home it did not take me long to make the connection.

I see Emily Hirst frequently. I can barely remember the following day what she talked about, so cannot be sure how much she repeats herself, other than about her cats, one of which between our meetings

548

seems to have extended the limits of established animal behaviour – the envy of humans who vary little from one day to the next.

One of the people she cleans for is Mrs Felix. The day before I went to the doctor she said as I handed back her ginger tom, 'Mrs F says you're a highly educated man. You aren't, are you? I told her there were no airs and graces on you. I said I'd seen you with books. She said you were high up at Oxford University. She asked if I cleaned for you. When I said I didn't she looked really disappointed.'

At that point Phil Badgecock came past, on this occasion stopping. I had gained the impression that his pace quickens when he sees Mrs Hirst. He doesn't stop to have a chat with me either, there being nothing new in his life or thoughts, he believes, worth drawing my attention to. If he had intended to say something, the moment he stopped he had forgotten what it was. Mrs Hirst wasted no time.

'You ought to show him some respect, Mr Badgecock. He was a professor at Oxford University. Hiding his candle under a bushel.'

Mr Badgecock was very alarmed by this, so that by blinking and smirking I assumed the mien of someone deserving little respect from anyone. The distinction between being up at Oxford and high up there was a finer one for Mrs Hirst than it might be for others. Mr Badgecock is the kind of person who is incapable of disrespect towards anyone. It would be impossible for him to show me more respect than he already did. A professorship at Oxford or anywhere else would hold no water for him.

He stared at me. 'Fancy that,' he said, turning to Mrs Hirst. 'I always took him for a thinking man, meaning no disrespect.'

With that he hurried on and I made to follow him.

Mrs Hirst restrained me. 'You wouldn't like me to come in one morning a week to clean for you, professor? I've got a vacancy.'

'How kind. But no thank you. It keeps my mind fresh, cleaning and tidying up.'

'Should have thought your brains had better things to do than dusting and wiping. That's my honest opinion.'

'I'm afraid Mrs Felix may have got the wrong end of the stick.'

She dismissed this with a flick of her finger. 'She waves it about whatever end she's got. I said she didn't surprise me one bit. You with your books coming and going. You can't get through reading and hoovering at the same time.' She watched Phil Badgecock's retreating shuffle. 'You couldn't want for a better neighbour,' she said. 'Respect or no respect.' At this moment she observed one of her cats climbing through my window. 'Naughty little Mogsy . . . You've not left anything out, I hope.'

'Apart from the whole fresh salmon on the kitchen table, nothing that leaps to mind.'

'You'd better hurry then, Professor. He likes his little bit of fish. You mustn't let them disturb your studies. After all, they're only cats.'

She began calling me 'the professor' after that. Then Phil Badgecock took it up. And before long I found in my daily greetings that that was how others addressed me. It was of course she who told my doctor. She'd told everyone she saw ('my neighbour the professor') and she saw everyone, adding no doubt something to the effect that they'd better watch their p's and q's in future and not mess about with me mentally speaking. Naturally, I did not like to disappoint them ('we've got this famous professor living in our street') so tried to live up to it, assuming a preoccupied air and a shuffling walk, spared from having to buy any new clothes. I stopped short of walking about in my dressing gown and slippers. The Patels called me 'professor' in every sentence. Their children stood exaggeratedly out of my path when they saw me coming and gave me a sort of salute. I still put on a bit of a limp and additional stoop for them on the understanding, probably false, that in Asian circles professors become more revered the older they get, unless that is only gurus. I quite like the way they lower their voices then fall silent when they see me coming. The only person unaffected by my distinction was Rosie, who shouts out 'Morning, professor' above the noise of her barking dogs and bawling children. The students, I thought, eyed me, if at all, with suspicion.

One morning I met Bridget with a pile of books under my arm. 'On my way to the library,' I said, unnecessarily perhaps.

'Keeping your hand in?'

'Goodness me, yes. So easy to get out of date, lose track of the latest . . .'

'What was your subject, if you don't mind me asking?'

'Oh, very marginal, or so it has become. History. The Reformation. Aspects thereof. Doing a little piece now on what happened to the East Anglian churches.'

'That's interesting. I thought you said you didn't go to university.'

'I did. But you see, I find it puts people off. They start not being themselves. Like being a vicar, wearing a dog collar. That gap we discussed.'

'Oh, I hadn't thought of that.'

She looked at me as if to say: if he was lying then he could be lying now. No matter. Our lives would not impinge on each other's. In her line of study she was being taught, I hoped, not to take anything at face value. She could easily turn me off given I couldn't turn her on, being a switched-on sort of woman already I mean. At first I wasn't sure whether I liked being a bogus professor. It was only necessary not to be found out by the Felixes. Once a week Mrs Hirst would remind them she lived next to that professor. If they found me out, Mrs Hirst would be the first to know and soon afterwards everyone would.

I felt rather as I did when I filled my briefcase with bricks to persuade Plaskett that I was a great deal busier than I was. I enjoyed fooling him. Fooling the world was rather a different matter. But then I became accustomed to it. We try to fool other people most of the time, that we are less foolish than we are; ourselves that we are less foolish than they are. We therefore suffer fools gladly, hoping to be found less insufferable in our turn. One of the ways of distracting attention from our foolishness is to play the fool, to indicate that our foolishness is something we are well aware of. We do not need to fool them any longer. 'Don't fool yourself' is therefore an expression I try to avoid, except when addressing myself.

Sometimes I think that that was where it all began, scribbling away about the neighbours and my family life etc.: wanting to discover if an average fool by reflecting on this and that can become averagely wise through truthfulness rather than exhaustion. Perhaps I got this from my mother who used to say, 'It would be foolish to lie to me, Tom,' and, 'If you're wise you won't trust a soul until you know better.' My father was constantly diddled by customers and suppliers. When this happened, my mother would shake her head and look at me as if to remind me not what a fool my father was but how easily the world could make a fool of him. She was never disloyal to him. She almost made his foolishness seem like a virtue. I suppose that I was somehow trapped between his foolishness and her wisdom. And now, writing that, I only know or care that I miss them. I wish I could have been and done more for them, shown them greater affection.

551

One relives what cannot be relived. Regrets what cannot be changed. That is foolish. But does not feel so. One cannot say: what happened happened, we are what we are, and there's an end to it – snap one's fingers at what life has taught one. Very unwise indeed I should have thought, or have foolishly been trying to find out . . .

Next there is a note about the woman at number 27.

After our first encounter I did not meet her again for a while. I often saw her get in and out of a car, always in a hurry. She did not look about her. On several occasions she had someone with her, a black-haired young woman who kept very close to her. Sometimes she was not there when the car returned. Quite often too I saw her in the front garden. She always had her back to the street as she weeded or trimmed or planted in what seemed a hectic manner, as if trying to meet a deadline. Once when she was away I saw Mr Tomkins and his sister standing at the gate, enthusiastically chattering and pointing, doubtless delighted that someone else in the street had standards. They never stop to look at my front garden, knowing that it still consists of a wonky-surfaced paved path held together by grass and weeds – mainly dandelions, these occupying much of the lawn too, and a 'flower-bed' round the edge with six shrubs in it. It is not a complete mess like Rosie's. I do cut the lawn with a strimmer, dig up the bed and trim the shrubs. I have even painted the front gate. Phil Badgecock and Mrs Hirst like everyone else on the street are minimally tidy with their front gardens. The poor Tomkinses. Setting an example which no one follows – such is the stuff of sainthood.

One day I did stop at her front gate when she was in the garden, saying to her stooping back, 'Settling in all right are we?'

She stood up and brushed a strand of hair from her face, then gave me a quick smile as if at once thinking better of it. There was a vague, alarmed air about her as if she had just woken up and had forgotten where she was.

'You gave me quite a fright . . . Yes, thank you.' She began rubbing her hands together. I should have said something final then, continued on my way, said anything at all, but was distracted by those hands. She looked around her and went on breathlessly, 'Not making much headway, I'm afraid. But I'd like it to look nice . . . Maybe even a bird bath one day . . .'

Still I did not move on, this time because behind her the lace curtain was parted and a face appeared. It was the face of a young woman who seemed to have been crying, though that may have been stains on the window. The mouth slowly opened and shut, enunciating words perhaps. The woman caught my glance and turned, then hurried inside as if for a second she had forgotten I was there. At the door she looked back. This time she gave me a real smile.

'Thank you so much for calling by.' Then she repeated, 'I do want it to look nice.'

As I walked on, I realized it had not been a real smile at all. It was how people smile when they are embarrassed or humiliated.

At the end of the street I stopped for a chat with the electrician. He was polishing his van and seemed in high spirits. His garden, like Rosie's, had a motor bike in it, though less dismantled. I asked him how business was. He is one of those who very much want to be asked that.

'Oh fine, professor, really good. More work than I can handle.'

'Family all right?'

'Brilliant.'

'You'd be able to see to that, in your line of work.'

This he ignored, glancing at number 27. 'Saw you talking to her. None of my business, mind you, but I did a bit of wiring for her and there was this humming coming from a bedroom. Moaning more like it.'

'There's all sorts of religions these days. Yoga, meditation, Hare Krishna. You see them advertised.'

'It was likely that then. I've got my work cut out for things like that. Sitting about, praying and things.'

'Not plugged into them myself either.'

He glanced at me, confirmed I wasn't taking the mickey. 'My wife's religious. Catholic. I'll get wired up into all that, I tell her, when the spirit moves me.'

Then he resumed polishing his van. His wife was watching him from the window, a baby in her arms. She was smiling broadly. It could have been at anything, or nothing in particular, other than being lucky. Brilliant all right. Plugged into the mains. I walked on, passing the house where the couple had had a blazing row while moving in, then made it up. I heard raised voices and my pace quickened in case they looked out and saw me lingering there. The only word I heard, first in her voice, then in his, was 'fucking'. Far removed, I surmised, from what they were doing.

From time to time, as I've said, I caught a glimpse of the other woman who lived at number 27, hurrying to or from the car, keeping close to her mother, assuming that was what she was. She was very thin but not tall and usually wore a long skirt with flowers on it in an autumnal setting, this in contrast to a shabby, brown, leather-looking jacket. Her hair was black and cut short. She always had her head down so I never got a good look at her face but it seemed small and round and white. But it was her mother who held the attention – that harassed, worn-out sadness. I imagined the moaning in the bedroom. There was only one conclusion: a woman with an ailing daughter. It had nothing to do with religion. Or everything to do with it.

There have been several television documentaries about people with various ailments and those who try to look after them, the strain on their love etc. I felt that I shouldn't pry, that the woman didn't want me or anyone else to stop by for a chat. So from then on, to choose my words with care, I passed by on the other side. This kept me in closer touch with the couple who got on better at some times than at others. It also meant that I had a closer look at the man with the short trousers who twice as I passed was putting out his rubbish. He was wearing a dressing gown or old brown overcoat, below which showed even shorter pyjamas. His spiky, grey-brown hair was uncombed, so perhaps he had recently got out of bed, though on both occasions it was the early afternoon. His response to my greeting was non-committal or in a foreign language. His face, under a narrow forehead, seemed unusually grey and small, deepening its lines and bunching them together. My impression of someone on the run was confirmed. I wondered why Mrs Hirst hadn't told me about him so I asked her one evening.

'Well might you ask, professor. Let's just say you wouldn't have a lot in common. That's my guess. I did take the trouble to ask if there was anything but he said there wasn't.'

I hadn't asked her about the woman and her daughter at number 27, expecting her to tell me in her own good time. One morning while I was handing back a cat, they came out and got into the car in that hasty, surreptitious way they have. We stopped chatting for a second or two and watched them drive off. Even then Mrs Hirst said nothing, indeed avoided my eye for a moment. Then she continued talking about a scandalous event involving the vicar at her church and a trip to the Holy Land from which we had been distracted. She had made it quite clear to me that some things lay beyond the reach of gossip; indeed as I had, more feebly, by not bringing the topic up myself. Her face had gone still, there had been a glimmer of compassion in her eyes, the vicar not qualifying for this as she returned to his travails in respect of church funds and the organist's wife. Her attempts to sound shocked were counteracted by her excitement: if I wanted to know the truth, she'd never cared for him thank you very much with his sloppy clothes like anyone else's and guitars strummed right there in front of the altar, even one of them once sitting on it wearing a baseball cap, and sermons about footballers and pop stars.

As she chattered on, stroking the cat with broad, long sweeps of her hand, I found myself wondering what had happened to the vicar in Suffolk with whom I had lost touch. His belief had been on the edge. Perhaps he had heard the call and become a stockbroker. I wished I hadn't lost touch with him. There has never been anyone else I could have talked to about matters of faith. All the books I'd looked at started off for or against and stayed that way. You either did or you didn't . . . Believe, that is.

Mrs Hirst was saying, '. . . You've got to ask yourself, haven't you? Whatever'll happen next? Perhaps we'll have a woman.'

'Follow the vicar's example . . .' I said with an unnecessary smirk.

I made as if to go, giving the cat a quick stroke which stopped it purring. On the opposite side of the street the man with the short trousers was walking past. They seemed even shorter than before. He was in a hurry. Mrs Hirst gave me one of her knowing glances.

'Can't swear to it but I reckon he's done time, if you want my opinion.'

'How do you figure that?'

'There's this man been visiting. Wouldn't be surprised he's his probation officer. It's the look of him too. Shifty.'

'Shouldn't we give him the benefit, I mean . . . ?'

'I'm not giving him any benefit. That's the government's job.' She laughed suddenly and even more suddenly stopped. 'If he was, I'd like to know what for. Wouldn't you?'

'I suppose I would.'

'There you are then. If he was a murderer you'd want to know. Or one of those sex maniacs.'

'Perhaps after all I wouldn't. If he was harmless.'

'*I* would. You don't know if someone's harmless until they aren't.'

'Best leave him alone. If he's paid his debt give him the credit. Live and let live.'

I remembered Webb, the noise of the frying pan clanging against his head, the way he crouched down and covered his face. For the first time there had been fire in Mrs Webb's eyes and loathing, her voice full of a vanquishing authority. I hadn't thought then that Webb should be allowed to pay his debt in peace.

'Will he leave *us* alone, that's the point, professor? Think of the kiddies.'

We were already some distance apart by now so I had to raise my voice to say, 'You keep me posted, Mrs Hirst. I hope things are soon sorted out with your vicar.'

She laughed again and the cat leapt out of her arms. 'You can't really imagine it, that's the thing. Him and the organist's wife. Talk about Laurel and Hardy.'

Her laugh turned into a scoffing noise . . . She had forgotten her sex maniac, imagining a grotesque coupling. I remembered telling her the first time we met that I had two children. 'Two? *Really*?' she had asked happily as if an outrageous miracle had occurred twice. It is as well that our imaginations are less active (fertile?) than they might be. Otherwise they would be thus engaged most of the time and we'd then find ourselves imagining other people's lives in more and more detail. As it is we hardly bother to imagine them at all. We couldn't give a stuff. We have been spared the relentless imagery of other people coupling. Or crapping for that matter. We have been spared caring about them as much as we might if the imagination were less sparing. 'Stuff you!' we think, not stopping to imagine who has or would want to. Or 'I don't give a shit', if you prefer it.

This was what I wrote at the time, thoughts about the woman at number 27 slipping from my mind. About the jailbird too. It was, as I've said, a time when nothing much happened. I waved dottily at the Felixes and they waved respectfully back. According to custom I 'owed' them. Assuming I'd liked them enough. Let them remain uncertain on that score. They'd have known for some time now that I'd become a professor. Mrs Hirst would be giving them constant intelligence about me. If they didn't believe it they could make enquiries and then tell Mrs Hirst that I was not what I purported to be. The process of unravelling would then soon begin. I would have to introduce into my conversation with Mrs Hirst a tale or two about my time in Canada, having looked up the name of some small university in, say, Nova Scotia where I had spent the bulk of my professional career. Some obscure research into the history of the Blackfoot tribe might then have to be invented, not at first sight compatible with Norfolk churches at the time of the Reformation – though, transmitted through Mrs Hirst, that would give the Felixes something to think about all right.

Bridget and her friends were sometimes to be seen in the street and they always greeted me in friendly enough fashion. Music could be heard in the evenings, albeit faintly. I'd not want to be questioned too closely about Nova Scotia and the Blackfoot by them, indeed about Canada generally. A book might have to be borrowed from the library. (The last time I was there, the assistant at the issuing counter said, 'And where are we venturing today, Mr Ripple?' She either thought I had commendably wide-ranging interests or couldn't decide what they were – aside from the lives of the explorers. It is true I do tend to pull books off the shelves at random. Like life itself my knowledge of it was to be left to chance.) There were still no curtains in the windows, no light upstairs.

Rosie was the gladdest to see me, waving cheerily, a break from the constant beleaguerment of life. And, as summer was then approaching, the Tomkinses were more often to be seen sitting in their garden, just looking at it, sometimes pointing, deciding how to reposition the gnomes and animals perhaps. The quarrelling couple continued to quarrel, swear-words echoing down the peaceful street like reminders of reality. Whenever one saw them, however, they were hand in hand, about to kiss or having just done so. It seemed like a display – virtue flaunting itself as if to make the reality unreal.

After Jane died I spoke to Adrian quite often to start with, though neither of us could think of much to say. He was keeping himself busy. He went off to continue his assignment in Hungary and told me there were other foreign assignments he was considering. 'My life is so bloody empty otherwise,' he once said. I asked on another occasion if he was seeing his mother who had lately moved to Somerset. He said they spoke quite often on the phone, but not for long. Evidently she did not know what to say either. I asked if she was finding ways of doing good down there. I did not mean it sarcastically, intended no comparison with myself who was doing no good to anyone at all. I did really hope that she was not wasted on Somerset.

'She did do a lot of good in her life, Dad. I don't think we should knock that. Yes, she does seem to be keeping herself busy.'

I thought how far removed from my son I was, that he could not detect sincere concern in my voice. How little he had to go on.

'Please, Adrian. I simply like to think she's keeping busy in all the ways she's so good at. I only hope they know how lucky they are to have her.'

'OK, Dad.'

It was too late. I hadn't convinced him. Didn't deserve to. I thought: I wonder if she knows how much he still misses Jane, whether all those words she'd used to help others would now do for her own son. I wished I was not thinking that. I wished I could tell Adrian that I missed Jane dreadfully too. That, in a word, I had been in love with her with no desire whatever to sleep with her or see her unclothed. On the contrary. I did not want to speculate further on this even in my own mind. There was a pause. Then he said, 'Mum really understands, Dad, though they didn't have a lot in common. It tended to be a bit one way.'

I knew which way that was: the way it used to be in the old days. How very much I wanted him to say that Jane had a lot in common with me. I wanted him to believe that I assumed it.

'Now, though . . . ?'

'Oh now, she just listens really. I want to see more of her. While there is still time and all that. More of you too of course.'

That afterthought. 'Any time. I hope you know that.'

'A large part of me wants to be alone. I talk to Jane. I mean, all that.'

'I talk to her too. Sometimes. Wonder what she would think about something or other.'

'When we talked about you we always seemed to end up laughing.'

'Thanks a lot, old son.'

'Oh Dad, for Christ's sake, you know.'

I'll leave it there for the time being. Soon I shall have to revise what I wrote about my next encounter with John Brown. He had not been at the Connaught the three or four times I went there after our last encounter at the corner shop. I asked the barmaid and she said he had recently been in twice. Beyond that she didn't seem desperate to continue the conversation. Though she did smile at me, I'll give her that. On the second occasion, when she brought my drink, I asked her how Zimbabwe was and she said it was all right in a way that told me she did not think it was all right at all. Or else that it was a particularly stupid question. I'd never get anywhere near the truth or otherwise of that. Were her parents farmers constantly threatened by former freedom fighters? Or were they safe and comfortable and happy etc? So I asked her when she was going back. That seemed a neutral enough question but other customers were requiring her attention.

'Will that be all, sir?'

'I'm afraid it'll bloody well have to be,' I didn't reply, watching her move off, bend forwards to clear a table. 'None of your business' had been in her voice. The words came back . . . Their parts and particulars, their ways of moving. Sod all that intervening cloth, I muttered.

She turned. 'Sorry, sir?'

My gaze had not sufficiently shifted back to the sea, blurred and specked now by squalls of rain.

I cleared my throat. 'Chance of any peanuts?'

These she brought. 'I hadn't forgotten, sir.'

I thanked her, looked back at the sea as if now she had become the last thing on my mind. Which was how she remained, first and last, until the rain lifted and I could return home.

The next time I went there, she smiled beautifully at me in a way that I knew had nothing whatever to do with me: good news from home, a smashing new boyfriend.

'Your friend's over there,' she said.

I looked towards the recess where he was signalling me to join him.

Chapter Seven

He waved me into the seat opposite. 'So where've you been, stranger? Long time . . . Drink?'

'Already ordered thanks. You know, this and that. The family.'

'Not in any trouble I hope?'

I had no wish to tell him about Jane. 'No, nothing like that.'

'You're a lucky chap, do you know that? How do you spend your day then? Killing time they call it. Spot on, dead right, that is.'

He was in high spirits, almost aggressive. His glasses seemed darker and the fall of the light prevented me from seeing his eyes at all.

'Bit of reading. Pottering. Telly. Bus to the town. Chatting to the neighbours. A walk. You know.'

'I don't as a matter of fact.'

He signalled to the waitress, pointing at his glass. He seemed on the point of saying something about her so I waited. Instead he only puffed out his lips. It was my turn to speak.

'Forgotten where you said you lived.'

He stared at me. 'No you haven't. Never told you.' He pointed down the front. 'Other side of bandstand. Few streets back among the bungalows.'

There was another pause. When I'd told him where I lived he'd said he couldn't be doing with hills and I'd replied that, according to my doctor, the puffing was good for me. The barmaid came with his whisky and a bottle of soda. It was at least a double. He looked up at her, touched her wrist.

'Thank you, my darling.'

As soon as her back was turned he puffed out his lips again and muttered, 'Jesus!'

Only then did I remember seeing him pushing the wheelchair down the front. Perhaps it hadn't been him at all. He saved me from wondering whether I'd ever ask him.

'Saw me pushing the wife along a short while back?' I nodded. 'How very tactful of you. Thought it was you, scuttling off in the other direction.'

'I didn't like . . .'

'That's all right. That barmaid now. Once it was my wife I said that to. Jesus must have been tuned in then. She was beautiful, every bit as beautiful as her.' He nodded towards the barmaid. 'Couldn't believe my luck. Let me tell you something. You only get one bite of that particular cherry.'

'What happened?'

'Thought you'd never ask. Stroke for starters, or not actually . . .'

He finished his drink and beckoned for another. I wished he wasn't so evidently the worse for wear, beginning a confession he'd regret later.

'I'm sorry.'

'Not half as sorry as I am. You see, fact is you look at a girl like that and you think two things: that's how it was once, with a girl like that, hands reaching across a candlelit table, eternal love, violins, all that stuff. You can't imagine anything different. Wanting a good look at her, all of it, then getting it plus bloody plus . . .'

I lit a cheroot and signalled for another drink. 'What was the other thing? Wishing one was younger, could ask . . . there's a fair chance she'll . . .'

'Oh Christ, not that, you old shagger. No. The other thing is that's how she'll end up one day, something like it. Washed up. Wrecked. One way or another. The dirty tricks department up there making notes already . . .'

We waited in silence for my drink. When the barmaid came, I thought I saw in her eyes a foreboding of what he meant: a flicker of dread, a futile summoning of hope. Her arm brushed my shoulder as she leant down to put my drink on the low table, her breasts dangling under her slackened blouse.

When she had gone I said, 'Pretty bleak stuff . . .'

'Like to come round some time? See for yourself . . .'

I realized now how drunk he was. His words were slurred and he might have been talking to himself.

There was no other reply I could give. 'Thanks. I'd like that.'

He'd soon forget about it. He was now gazing out at the sea. The sun had not quite set behind a bank of black clouds. There was no wind and the water gleamed like wrinkled ice. A man and a woman were running along the beach, close to the incoming tide. A boy was throwing a stick for a black dog. There were half a dozen couples striding along the front to get home before nightfall. My companion had fallen silent so I counted them, then counted them again as a seventh appeared, in far less of a hurry, older perhaps.

'I'll be off then,' I said.

'Be in touch,' he replied. 'Got another half an hour. Bloody paradise.'

With that I left him there, grinning at the barmaid on the way out. She was as far as it is possible to be from an afflicted old hag. She gave me her best smile – lips parted, teeth showing, tip of the tongue between them. All right, one's seen it time without number but it's always unique for a second, only for you . . .

That, I assumed, would be that. Hardly the most rousing of conversations with a comparative stranger in a seaside hotel. The walk up the hill puffed me out and I was worrying about Virginia, who'd phoned earlier to tell me that far from the management opening if he played his cards right, Richard had lost his job. She could go on to full time at the hospital but it wasn't much of a life, the children were a handful, Richard was feeling pretty low and was sometimes impatient with them . . . more in this vein. So it wasn't until I turned off the light that I remembered John Brown again and caught myself hoping that I'd never set eyes on him again. There was another hotel further along the front if I wanted to do any more gazing out at the sea of a lonely evening . . .

About three weeks later he phoned me.

'Brown here.'

For a moment or two I did not recognize his voice, nearly said he'd got the wrong number and hung up. 'Sorry?'

'Come off it, Ripple. Your drinking companion from the Connaught. Don't tell me you're on the water wagon.'

He was certainly not on that himself, 'companion' and 'Connaught' having become words of one syllable.

'Oh no, I . . .'

'Thought you had a thing for that kiwi barmaid. Lovely bum on her.'

'Not really. Well . . .'

'Look here. Why not drop round for a drink one evening?'

'That's kind. I . . .'

'Tomorrow then, about six . . . Got pen and paper handy?'

He did not wait for my reply and gave me his address.

So it was that I found myself outside his house the following evening. It had been a half-hour walk and I wished I'd taken a taxi. I also wished that my name wasn't in the telephone directory. In the sober light of day he probably regretted he'd invited me.

The bungalow was almost wholly similar to the others round it, the net curtains too and paved path and small fir-type trees and shaped flower-beds with mainly roses in them. When he opened the door, he looked startled. He didn't regret having invited me. He'd completely forgotten. It was the first time I'd seen him without his glasses. His eyes were the palest grey with a searching timidity in them which frightened me. All the aggression had been stripped from him as if he'd just been kicked out of his job or I was someone he'd been expecting for a long time who'd come to collect. The game was up. With his club tie, new-looking tweed jacket, gleaming brown brogue shoes and sharply creased twill trousers he was dressed up to be taken away . . .

'It was tonight . . . ?' I began.

He quickly recovered and reached forward to take my arm. 'Ah, Tom, glad you could make it. Come along in.'

Then a female voice called out, 'Who is it, darling?'

He led me into the front room where I expected to find a crippled woman in a wheelchair.

'Meet the wife,' he said. 'This is Tom Ripple, dear. Whom I told you about.'

She was leaning against the mantelpiece and put out her hand in a languid manner as if imitating a duchess. In the other hand she held a long cigarette holder with an unlit cigarette in it. There could be no doubt now that I was expected. She was heavily made up and very thin, this accentuated by a shiny, dark-green evening dress which clung to her body and exposed her shoulders. Her neatly waved blonde hair had a coarse, sprayed, skew-whiff look as if she'd just come from the hairdresser. It ought to have occurred to me at once that it was a wig but all I saw at first was that with her wide lips and large dark eyes she must once have been beautiful. It was when the eyes narrowed that I noticed the wig.

'Ah, one of his binging chums. How nice to meet you, Mr Thomas Ripple Esquire. What a very comical name, I must say. Did you find the house all right?'

The affected voice went with the languid offer of her hand – those words some way towards becoming 'nace' and 'hice'. I took her hand and she lurched sideways so that I had to tighten my grip to steady her. She grasped the mantelpiece and slowly let go of my hand. There was no sign of any wheelchair.

'We met a couple of times at the Connaught, sweetheart,' Brown said, pointing at a chair. 'Drink?'

'Whisky and soda, if you have it,' I said.

'We've jolly well got plenty of that all right, haven't we, Johnny darling?'

Her eyes drooped, her head fell forwards and she jerked it back, her hand sliding along the mantelpiece. I glanced at Brown. She was about to fall over. Why didn't he help her?

He went through to the adjoining dining room and returned with a drink for both of us. Then he went to his wife and put an arm round her, pulling her upright. Her eyes were now shut.

'My lovely Johnny,' she murmured.

'Come on, my darling, a little rest.'

'I want to talk to little Tommy Splash,' she said. 'Why can't I meet your friends any longer? *What* a funny name! He doesn't *look* very funny, does he, Johnny?'

But she went willingly, resting an arm along his shoulder as he eased her away from the mantelpiece and towards the door. Her left leg dragged slightly and her shoe was half off its bent foot. As they reached the passage she looked back over her shoulder at me.

'Tom, Tom, the piper's son, stole a pig and away did run. Mr Splash the soda siphon man.'

He was away for four or five minutes though it seemed much longer. While all this had been going on, I hadn't been able to look him in the eye, not wanting to see that timidity again. Now, as I looked around that room, I realized that what it had been was shame and defeat. This is how he wanted the room to be for a visitor, how he always kept it perhaps. Completely spotless. The porcelain shepherd and shepherdess at one end of the mantelpiece,

564

the gold clock with its works showing at the other. The pink carpet with white curlicues. The antimacassars on the pale gold settee and chair, the reproductions on the walls: a galleon in full sail; a country scene with cottages, smoking chimneys, a ploughman, black birds circling tall trees; people sauntering under the Eiffel Tower. The gleaming table and chairs in the dining room, the red, imitation velvet curtains held back by gold tassels. It was as if every day he looked round this room and said to himself: one day it will all be in order again, she will be sitting there, having done all this to welcome me home. There were no photographs, no flowers. I caught myself wondering why he had invited me there, at once wishing he hadn't . . .

His voice was loud behind me, in the tone of a command. 'Sorry to keep you waiting, old fruit. Gave you a drink, didn't I?'

He came and stood in front of me, rubbing his hands. He had put his dark glasses on. I raised my drink at him, glad that I could not see his eyes, that in the gathering gloom he had not turned on the ceiling light. He turned on a standing lamp in the corner. Its thick tasselled shade matched the curtains and shed little light beyond the corner of the carpet. He took his drink and sat down, throwing his head back with a deep sigh.

'There you have it then. Didn't know how pissed she'd be. Sometimes she makes an effort for visitors, or rather did when we had them. Come across it before, have you?'

'Don't think I have.'

'Bloody alky, that's what she is. One hundred per cent.'

I crossed my legs, which might have made it look as if I was settling in for a long chat so I uncrossed them again.

'I'm sorry.'

He went on staring at the ceiling. 'You're sorry. What the fuck do you think I am?'

'Can't imagine. Has she . . . has it been for long?'

'No, as it happens, you can't. It feels like bloody ever. Don't ask. Yes, she tried AA. Detox at one of those funny farms. Psycho-what-d'you-call-it. All worked for a bit. You'd think a couple of strokes would do the trick, wouldn't you?'

'I really don't know anything about it.'

He finished his drink and went to the dining room to pour himself another. He had his back to me when he said, 'You want to know the truth, Tom? I hope the next one kills her. Well, not all the time. You can see what a lovely woman she was. I remember the candlelight, the country strolls, the walks along the shore, all that stuff that happens at the beginning. Then the baby, couple of miscarriages first mind you. Wonderful little chap he was. Dream time. Terrific sense of humour she had. That's what a lot of it was . . . Tommy the Splash. Sorry about that.'

He came back and sat down, leaning forwards now, gazing into his drink. I guessed he hadn't spoken to anyone else for a very long time.

He seemed to need prompting. 'Yes, I could see that,' I said. 'I mean, what fun she might have been.'

'I still wish she was dead. Often. Then I remember . . . Hope too . . .'

His words were beginning to slur, his head to loll. I thought that perhaps he might nod off and I could slip away. Then he suddenly sat upright and stretched out his hand.

'Let me get you another.' I shook my head. 'Mind if I do?' He went back to the dining room, raising his voice again. 'I can tell you this for nothing. Sometimes she's not fun at all. Hunt the bottle. Once found half a litre of Gordon's in the toilet cistern. Never mind that. There's no darling Johnny then, I can tell you. Sleeps a lot, thanks be to God. Stuffs herself with pills too. I look at her and think, "Do us a favour, old love, don't wake up in the morning." Then she turns over and looks so peaceful lying there. It all comes back. The morning in that hotel after the first time. The strip of sunlight lying across the bed. The birds. Having a bloody good laugh. You said you had children?'

I waited for him to sit down again. 'Yes, two. A boy and a girl.'

'Ours was a boy. He seemed all right. Nothing special. Fat. Spotty. Bit dull, to be honest. Did well enough at school. All that. Got six GCSEs, or seven was it? Then on his seventeenth birthday he just scarpered. Her getting pissed all the time, me getting pissed off, who can blame the poor little sod? So she got even more pissed after that. Happy days!'

He looked up at me. Even though I could not see his eyes I could imagine the beseeching in them. He was waiting for me to say something, to show that he wasn't boring me to death.

'How's he getting along? Your son, I mean.'

'Haven't a bloody clue to be frank. Came back twice. First time stayed the night. She seemed better. One of her AA spells. Then the

566

next morning she just swore at him, totally blotto. What did he mean by leaving her in the hands of his bloody useless father . . . Didn't even finish his fried eggs and bacon. Cooked them myself, wanted to make a bit of a fuss of him. "I'm off," he said.'

'The second time?'

'When he came in she took one look at him and said, "Who the fuck do you think you are?" So he just turned round and went out again. The front door hadn't even been shut. The next day she had her stroke. Not much fun that wasn't. Paralysed down one side. Do you know something? I hadn't been so happy in a long time. Her in hospital. Bloody bliss that was. God, how I longed for her to have another one . . .'

'That's pretty terrible. I mean, your son and all that.'

He went to pour himself another drink.

'I know what you meant, thanks. Terrible. That's one of the words for it. Look, don't get the wrong idea. All her fault etc. I was pretty bloody awful to him too. He never liked me. Didn't hit him. Nothing like that. I hated him bloody loafing about, that's all. All the time with those earphones on. Suppose he thought it was my fault, what went wrong with her. Thing is, he might have been right. Partly anyway. The shrinkos said it went deeper than that. Bloody childhood, that sort of thing. But you know. You blame yourself, don't you?'

There was a loud thud from the other side of the front passage followed by a curse. I leant forwards, gripping the arms of my chair. He raised a hand to restrain me.

'Don't you worry yourself about that. Looking for another bottle. Fell over. She can get up. Mind you, I've been known to let her lie there for a bit.'

There was another pause while he gazed at the ceiling. I looked around the room. It was utterly impersonal. As if he had wanted to remove from it all sign of recent habitation. This, I thought, was what Adrian had done to his flat after Jane left. Sometimes we try harder to forget than to remember. Such choices are made for us. Our reckoning of our own lives is arbitrary, cannot be truthful. I looked back at him. He was holding his drink on his lap and staring at me.

'Can see what you're thinking. Every time I come in here, I want to find it like this. Spotless. Lifeless, that's what she calls it. Life being so fucking frightful, who can blame me?'

Again, he was waiting for my response. 'Your son, has he . . . settled down somewhere? Is he all right, I mean . . . ?'

'He was into this and that once. Moved to Sheffield or somewhere. Government pen-pusher. He wouldn't be married, I shouldn't think. Trouble is, awful thing is, she, we, always found him – what's the word – unprepossessing. Sullen, bolshie. She didn't love him much. I couldn't either. Not enough. Did try. We thought he was letting us both down, like he had a duty to make up for us both. It was the other bloody way round. We were awful. Every Christmas we agree to make it up to him. I mean we made him, for Christ's sake. But just look at her . . .'

'I'm sorry,' I muttered, thinking of my own children, my great good fortune.

'In short, Tom, if you want the honest truth, my life's been a fucking mess. In the end, had to stop working to look after her. Done sod all since. Not like you. Could tell straight away: there's a lucky sod. No problems in that quarter. You with your studies and books. Let me fetch you another.'

Without waiting for my reply, he took my glass and poured us both another whisky and soda.

'I'd best be off soon,' I said.

'Very good, professor. Better things to do than listen to the ramblings of a sorry old fart like me.'

'On the contrary, I . . . Where did you get the idea I was a professor?'

'Mr Patel in the corner shop.' Here he did a passable imitation of an Indian accent. '"Saw you talking to the professor, Mr Brown. He is our very good customer."'

'It's a misunderstanding. Honestly I'm not . . .'

There was a noise along the passage and I stood up.

'You run along then. Professor or no professor, you've got that knowing look about you, knowing better.' He stood up and took my untouched glass. 'Sorry, no offence.'

'Please, John, I'm not a professor. And I don't know better. I really don't.'

'You know better than to make a fucking mess of your life.'

We were in the passage and he was going ahead of me to open the door.

'I'm just bloody grateful to you, that's all,' he said.

The door at the end of the passage opened and his wife stood there, leaning against the frame. A bottle dangled from her hand.

In the dim light, she appeared as a young woman, except that the blond wig had gone and her hair was black turning grey, neatly parted, a lock of it arranged in a curl across her forehead. She was wearing a smart black suit and a white blouse. A large silver brooch in the shape of a bird was pinned to her lapel. I looked again at her face. The make-up had been removed and she seemed peculiarly still and self-possessed, the eyes gazing at me with kindness. It was the face of someone who has said, is about to say, 'Can I help you?' or, 'You are very welcome,' or, 'Please make yourself at home.' This imagined later, perhaps. Brown had me by the elbow, urging me towards the door.

'Be with you in a minute, darling. Mr Ripple's just leaving.'

Her voice was quiet and calm. The affectation had gone but there was something stilted about it as though she was remembering lines. Brown's hand tightened on my elbow.

'I expect he's told you that I've ruined his life. He's right. I have. Our dear little Simon's too. Oh well . . .'

'All right, darling . . .' Brown began.

Her voice now became sleepy. 'But it's still nice sometimes. When he wheeled me along the front. We're both happy then. Remembering. The beach. The sea. You see how I was. Just an ordinary shopgirl . . .'

'You became a senior assistant, sweetheart.'

'Underwear. I knew a lot about underwear, didn't I, Johnny? You thought so. You wanted me to show you the latest lines . . . My little nightly fashion shows.' She giggled.

'Be with you in a moment, darling. Just say goodbye to Mr Ripple.'

'Slowly, he used to say, take your time. That's why it's called lingery.'

She smiled at him and raised the bottle. 'Lovely man.' Then she waggled the bottle at me. 'Are you married?'

She gave me no chance to reply. 'You look as though you might be. Along the front, we have our moments, don't we Johnny? Not as good as frilly knickers. Different. But most of the time he wishes I was dead. Tell you that, did he?'

'No, of course not. He spoke of you very affectionately.'

'Bollocks, Mr Splash. Absolute total bollocks.'

I might have remonstrated with her, lied a little more but Brown was leading me towards the door, opening it and standing in my way.

569

'Thanks for coming,' he said. He was the drunkard now. Beyond the tinted glasses I guessed there were tears in his eyes. 'It meant a lot to me.' He lowered his voice. 'It won't surprise you why I'm a trifle fucking lonely.'

His wife raised her voice. It was suddenly harsh and shrill. 'Telling you what I looked like in fancy underwear, is he?'

He said over his shoulder, 'No, darling, I wasn't telling him that. I was telling him to come and see us again.'

Beyond him she waved the bottle high above her head. Then she let out a long wail, and pulled the door shut behind her, reappearing almost at once without the bottle, a cigarette dangling from her lips. She struck a match with a flourish but her hand was shaking too much to light the cigarette.

Brown went over to her. 'Hold on a sec, old girl,' he said, deftly lighting her cigarette with a lighter. She cupped her hands round his. I could see how once they had been together.

Brown returned to me. 'I meant that,' he said with a grin. 'Do come again, professor. Not that there's the faintest chance you will if you've got any sense.'

'I'd like to,' I said. 'See you at the Connaught some time.'

'Or at the shop.'

'Or at the shop.'

'Thanks,' he said as I turned and began walking down the path.

I heard the door bang behind me and waited at the gate. Silence. Perhaps he had gone in to her. Perhaps they were having a go at each other. I could not know. Then I was as certain as I could be that he had simply gone into the living room, poured himself another drink, taken our glasses into the kitchen, washed and polished them and put them away in a cupboard, leaving the house as if I had never been there. I even thought I could hear the sound of hoovering.

I met him again at the Connaught about a month later. It was like the evening we had met there for the first time, polite, distant. I could not of course ask him how his wife was, how his son was doing in Sheffield. He asked me about my children, and I told him about them, then a little more about my life. I avoided mentioning Jane, saying vaguely that my marriage hadn't worked out but no hard feelings. I came across as a contented man to whom a great deal had not happened. He expressed a few views about the bloody government, world events. But they were very far away from him. The world he spoke of was not his own. We got on to television.

'Takes your mind off,' he said. 'Something we can do together. For quite long stretches of time. Be together. Watch, experience together. Don't have to think or talk about it. Just watch and switch off. Doesn't really matter if it's cobblers or not . . .'

I nodded in agreement, thinking there was a research topic there to put Bridget on to. We left together. There was a new barmaid. He asked what had happened to the previous one.

'Gone back to Africa,' she said, bitterly it seemed, as though they deserved no better of each other.

'You from Australia?' Brown asked.

'New Zealand,' she replied abruptly.

Out in the street, Brown said, 'A bit rude, wasn't she? Clearly did-n't fancy you one bit.'

'Oh no, you're wrong there,' I replied. 'Was in there yesterday evening. She really came on to me. We're having dinner next Thursday. She said she hoped I wasn't a friend of that frightful man with the dark glasses, not her type at all.'

He laughed and squeezed my shoulder. 'Thanks, professor. Thanks. Really. Thanks a lot.'

'Just for the record,' I said finally, 'I'm not a professor. Nowhere near it.'

'You don't have to tell me that,' he replied, putting a hand on the small of my back. 'An ignorant sod like you.'

A couple of days later I received a letter on smart headed notepaper which said:

Dear Professor Thomas, if I may,

You probably thought I was a bit of a shit, what I said the other evening. As you saw, I was pissed. I'm sorry. She is too. Don't know how differ-ently I'd have put it, though, if I'd been sober. The main thing is I'm very glad you came, very glad indeed. Thanks. Classy letterhead, what? You can usually tell how people would like their lives to be. Standards. Respectability etc.

Sincerely yours,
John Brown

Chapter Eight

There is a gap in my account for several months after that, until I got round to buying a new typewriter ribbon, the effect of which was to give my thoughts a somewhat raucous, over-confident sound.

I replied to John Brown's letter on a card, simply saying, 'Thank you very much for your letter and for your hospitality. Meet you again soon at the Connaught if the place isn't overrun by trippers.' On the blank reverse side there were the things I did not say in praise of his drink or what a pleasure it had been to meet his good lady wife.

Why did I not phone him, arrange to meet him, invite him to my place? Often, I was on the point of it. Well, not that often. He might want my company, but did I want his? Was it that I did not want to be drawn into a friendship from which it would become increasingly difficult to extricate myself? I pictured drunken evenings of intense embarrassment, drives to beauty spots with Mrs Brown in the back, raving or fast asleep. I imagined more of their confessions, the total exposure of their lives. I wasn't even sure whether I liked him enough, or at all. Whether I liked her or rather could come to like her if she ever became the person she was capable of being, if there was such another person, it didn't seem worth the risk to find out. All of us, I suppose, should be capable of choosing to be other people. Better, I mean. But on the whole we don't. 'Spoil yourself a little,' we sometimes think. There are those like Mrs Brown who have been so spoilt by life that they have few, if any, choices left. Thinking thus, while Brown was waiting daily to hear from me, I was saving myself further embarrassment, choosing to do nothing. I wondered what advice Jane would have given me. I did call by at the Connaught from time to time on the off-chance of seeing him again there – on neutral territory. So it is, I've read somewhere, that animals in the

572

African bush feel less endangered by others while sharing the same watering hole.

Another visit to my doctor. With the weather improving I'm trying to take seriously his advice to walk at least twenty minutes every day: keep the old heart pumping etc. He shook his head and screwed up his eyes when I told him I did at least that around the house. 'What's preventing you?' he had the bloody cheek to ask, implying I had nothing better to do with my life, not going logically on from that to enquire what my old heart had to be kept pumping for. 'Do you good,' he insisted. He does seem to want to keep me alive as long as possible. That's his job. Perhaps it's enough: to keep life going for its own sake. Not the same as maintaining a car in good working order so that it will continue to carry you somewhere or other – more like taking it for a twenty-minute spin so you can hear the sound of its engine or the occasional hoot of its horn, for the sheer enjoyment of it.

After the check-up he sighed and switched to philosophical mode, giving me the following deathless advice, 'I'd just try to be as happy as you can. None of us lives for ever.'

He looked rather pleased with that as if he'd just stumbled upon the meaning of life. But it's made me wonder: how can one ever be truly happy with death in the offing? Or is it death which makes life so precious? Without it, happiness would lose its edge, we'd hardly know what it was. What about the other angle, though? Shouldn't having led a happy life make death more acceptable: I've achieved in life what I wanted, I've been a lucky chap and so forth? By the same token, not having led a happy life should make death less acceptable: I've missed out on life so I reckon I'm due a lot more of it in case something better turns up. Against that, the happier the life the harder it is to let go of it surely – the whole of it soon to go up in a puff of smoke? And the unhappier the life, the happier one should be to get shot of the whole sorry business. It seems from this there are two sorts of happiness. On the one hand, those passing moments, more common in memory perhaps, when one knows one is or was happy. The other sort is being able to feel one's life has been pretty happy by and large. The passing sort is what ought to make death acceptable: the accumulated happiness of having lived each moment as if it was one's last. Nor should one mind dying so much after leading a happy, meaningful life – for what more could there have been? One should mind it a lot that there are to be no more of those passing moments when one has been happy? Happiness and death: there seem to be pros and cons, ifs and buts, which cancel each other out. Then there are other people. One can be happy for them as one can be sad for them. What we can share, what can bind us together, is that we will all die one day. But we can't share another's death especially as we are all differently happy or unhappy. Then there's the question of how it is possible to be all that happy or happy at all when surrounded by so much unhappiness. We can't know moment by moment, happy or unhappy, when we'll die nor can we know whether at the end we will think we have led a happy life. We'll just jolly well have to accept it. Round and round it goes. In my own case I've no idea how acceptable death is. Where do I fit into the above? I've had my happy moments, more than my fair share no doubt, but have achieved nothing. Like death itself I'll just have to accept that. Best not to think about happiness and death at all perhaps, not in the same breath anyway unless it's one's last. Of course those who believe in some sort of after-life needn't be bothered by any of this: death is only a gateway etc. How happy that must make them, not having to be bothered about happiness, there being so much of an even better kind still to come and going on for ever. But how acceptable would that be, I can't help asking. One can hear the angelic voices beginning to grumble, 'Can't stand much more of this happiness – there's no end to it.'

To return to my philosophical doctor. I have no reason not to want to live as long as possible, but for no specific reason. Unlike John Brown who surely wants to – as long as possible after his wife. I wished I could get him out of my mind. I wish I could decide whether I disliked him enough not to offer him the hand of friendship. We don't, do we? Go out of our way. Unless under instruction from our doctor to walk twenty minutes a day in order to live longer to no particular purpose. When walking to keep fit or spending a long time with someone we have little time for, we would rather be somewhere else, usually at home, doing nothing, just thinking or reading or pottering about, being purposeless in short. It is this we live for. Pointlessness seems to be the point of it – for people like me who aren't professors or trained in serious or creative thinking so don't know how to spend their time fruitfully, not just thinking about ourselves, that is.

There are hobbies of course like golf and sailing and painting water-colours and train spotting and making model galleons. There are, or were, cigarette cards. Mr Badgecock and I could do some swapping. It would add a dimension to our neighbourliness. I do not know why I do not take up a hobby. I could if I put my mind to it. All those years ago I really wasn't bad at golf – I was appalling. I had the highest permissible handicap other than being perfectly frightful at it. If I did take up a hobby, I'd be likely to wonder if there wasn't a better way of using my time to make my life more purposeful. I should imagine it is one of John Brown's pleasures to think of all the things he'd like to be able to do with his freedom, or may be able one day to do with it, for their own sake, purposelessly, living only for himself. For him, to be free to have a hobby may have become the whole purpose of his life: anything would do as a celebration of his freedom. I have the freedom already with nothing to celebrate, and nothing would last for long.

Thus I came to the conclusion that I could leave a decent interval before getting in touch with him. 'Could' not 'should' you will notice. A decent interval would have been a matter of days. I let the weeks, the months, pass. He did not phone me, imagining no doubt that I had no wish to see him, or her, or them, again. He was becoming increasingly right about that. What a crying shame it was that we did not share a hobby like golf or chess or stamp collecting which would bring us together from time to time other than for each other's company by itself. Or what a jolly good thing it was we didn't share a hobby etc . . . You can see how much John Brown stuck in my mind. After returning one afternoon from a half-hour walk, feeling very tired but pretty satisfied with myself – much as ramblers must after a twenty-mile hike, the more so if they have encountered a toff or two to shout abuse or wave their fists at – I sat down with a cup of tea, lit a cheroot and recalled the detour I had taken to avoid walking past Brown's bungalow, thus making me feel both that much fitter and fit for nothing. Then I remembered death, followed by life vanishing in a puff of smoke and stubbed out my cheroot, not feeling at all happy about it . . .

That was roughly my thinking when one fine, fresh Sunday morning I decided on a walk in a direction I hadn't previously taken. About twenty minutes before I set off I had seen Mrs Hirst going that way in her Sunday best, this including a black hat with multicoloured feathers spread across it, giving the impression of an exotic bird having been shot and ending up there. I'd seen her wearing it on previous Sundays but until she mentioned the vicar's visit to the Holy Land with the organist's wife had assumed she was on her way for Sunday lunch with relatives or some similar ritual gathering.

When I went out into the street Phil Badgecock was in his front garden snipping at a shrub. I raised my blackthorn at him and called out a hearty 'good morning'.

'Off to church then, are you?' he called back, cheerfully for him, as if it was an activity he'd tried once but had comically failed at – like tightrope walking, say.

I stopped and turned to give him a good look at my dark green corduroy trousers, wrinkled grey shirt and brownish, anorak-type jacket, spreading out my hands in a priestly gesture. He stared back at me, humbly awaiting my reply.

A professorial turn of phrase seemed to be expected. 'As you may perhaps have remarked, I have foregone my ecclesiastical regalia this beauteous morning.'

'Saw it on the telly, professor. Your sort don't hold with any of that. Sorry I asked. No offence.'

This conversation needed to be kept going, already the longest we'd had since we'd first met. 'May one not worship God, I ask myself, if there is a God, in communion with His creation, if He created it?'

'A load too many "ifs" in there for my liking, professor,' he replied, giving a branch of his shrub a brisk clip. 'You go and enjoy yourself then and have a nice communion, God or no God.'

He turned his back on me and I proceeded on my way. Ahead of me Rosie was making spasmodic progress with her two dogs and three children, one in a push-chair.

As I stepped into the road to pass her, she shouted, 'Oh for Christ's sake I give up with you lot. Just bloody shut up!'

Then she saw me and put her hand to her mouth, withdrawing it to let out a giggle. For a while I walked beside her, hopping on and off the pavement, one of the children copying me in an exaggerated manner.

'Got your hands full, I see,' I said.

Her blush was fading already. 'Only taking them to their father, that's all.'

'That'll give you a bit of a break then. Not the dogs though?'

She let out a single loud laugh. 'You don't think the bastard . . . ? Sorry, professor. He just sees them, gives them a peck and a sweetie, me a tenner if I'm lucky. Look after them, that'll be the bloody day. He'd rather have the dogs to kick since you ask. Like I said, he's a complete won't repeat what he is.'

I finally overtook them, with a thumbs-up and a parting smile that I hope conveyed sympathy, the very most she got from anyone already if she was lucky. She smiled back, happily, even gratefully. I had distracted her from the grinding monotony of her life; oh, that it could take so little to do that, I thought, what a lovely, self-possessed free spirit she was being prevented from being. Pushed to the side of her own life, as the poem says. Pushed a long way, a very long way indeed.

I was thinking about Rosie, then Jane, then Adrian, then Maureen and others too, all coming and going like visitors bidding me farewell, when I realized I had reached a church. As I looked at the sign outside, an organ sounded and a hymn began. It was the hymn I had heard on my way to the station on the day I saw my father in hospital for the last time. I remembered him lying there, his hand moving under mine under the bedclothes, the feeling that it was the first time in my life he had spoken to me alone, uninhibited by the presence of my mother. In his dying he had displayed an eloquence I had no idea he was capable of – about the bits of him whizzing away in a million pieces, how the vicar hadn't mentioned Jesus once, how my mother never brought flowers which only reminded him of seeing them outside in the earth where they belonged, as yet another spring and summer came round. And so the singing began: 'The Church's one foundation is Jesus Christ our Lord . . .' I remembered my father saying at the end how much he liked a good sing – released from his life from time to time by that and by longing for the windswept sunlight across the sea.

I went in and stood at the back. It wasn't a large congregation, perhaps about seventy people, at any rate almost enough to give the hymn some conviction. This was largely due to one female voice soaring above the others who seemed, along with the mushy sound of the organ, to be dragged along behind it. It was a voice of great purity with none of the usual wobble or quiver in it. Even I could tell how true it was.

I saw my father among them bellowing out the words, my mother glancing across at him from time to time with a frown, perhaps because he was out of tune. She never sang herself. She just stood there, staring ahead, her mouth clamped shut as if to prevent herself from uttering any nonsense. I never heard her sing, or even hum for that matter, and believed that she simply didn't know how. We went to church seldom, nor did they ever discuss it afterwards. My father had seemed sheepish that he had let himself rip like that. And I had felt ashamed, recalling the heads that turned to see who was singing so loudly. It was for my benefit, my father once said, we went at all. 'It'll be good for the boy. The music and words. He needs to know about those.' 'So long as that's all there is,' my mother had replied. She went for his sake, not for mine. For she did not always look at him disapprovingly. I remembered how happy it made me when she half-smiled across at him, glad he was enjoying himself having a good sing. She also almost smiled when she surprised my father listening to his old Kathleen Ferrier record: 'my little bit of crackling' as he called it. 'I feel like a touch of the old church tomorrow,' he used to say. She never protested. 'I'd better be ironing your suit then,' was all she said in reply.

As I looked around the congregation, my eye was caught by a splash of colour near the front. After some cautious manoeuvring down the side of the church I realized it was the splattered bird on Mrs Hirst's head. She was singing with some vigour so that the bird seemed to be struggling to take flight. Then half-way down the aisle I saw the woman from number 27 and her daughter. The woman had her head down over her hymn-book and seemed not to be singing at all. Her daughter was hidden on the far side of her but suddenly she leant back, her head held high, and I realized it was her voice which rang out above the rest. It seemed strange that no one seemed to be glancing at her as they had at my father. Apart from the struggling bird and the young woman's mother, everyone was looking resolutely ahead, their hymn-books held well up, as if suddenly they would start marching. The hymn came to an end but the congregation at first seemed reluctant to sit down. It was now the vicar's turn.

I couldn't see him very well but he appeared nothing like young enough to have misbehaved with the wife of the organist or anyone else. The organist I could see clearly. Not only did he seem young enough, say about fourteen and a half, to be the vicar's great-grand-son, he was looking round at him with eager affection as someone may gaze at a great-grandfather, proud that he's still able to move about unaided. Clearly the offending vicar had left, which might be the reason why there'd been a tone of jubilant relief in the way the congregation had sung about the Church's one foundation, mystic union and the like. It was an elderly congregation, which surely wouldn't hang about for long if people started propping guitars against the altar, let alone sat on it. I hovered at the back, looking around the rest of the congregation to see if there was anyone else I recognized. The wounded bird seemed to have made its escape. All I could see now of the woman and her daughter were the tops of their heads.

The congregation then knelt and I found a chair to one side behind a pillar. Not being able to hear what the vicar was saying, or only intermittently through the rustling and coughing, I scanned through the hymn-book to look for one or two more of my father's favourites. My eye fell on 'Praise, my soul, the King of Heaven,' then on 'Come down O Love Divine.'

Suddenly I saw him with great vividness, his partly shaven chin, his gap-toothed mouth, usually so small as if it had shrunk over the years from not speaking up for itself, now large and round and bursting with self-assurance. I began thumbing through the prayer-book. My father had made me follow the service in it, running his finger under the line and once saying, 'That's language for you, Tom, that's real language.' And I became aware of the vicar's voice squeaking and pausing as if in imitation of a breathless old woman. The coughing had subsided as though everyone was making a spe-cial effort to hear what he was saying. The words were those I was looking at: '... as many as are here present to accompany me with a pure heart and a humble voice unto the throne of the heavenly grace, saying after me.'

Then the church was filled with a growling mumble to accompany what the vicar was intoning above them – far more loudly and surely than before as though he was having to speak also for some in the congregation who were reluctant to speak for themselves. I could just see the head of the organist bowed very low on his chest. '... We have followed too much the devices and desires of our own hearts ... We have left undone those things which we ought to have done. And we

579

have done those things which we ought not to have done. And there is no health in us . . .'

Again I saw and heard my father as he spoke these words, unable to understand what someone so gentle and cautious could possibly have done wrong or left undone – apart from last month's accounts and that surely wasn't enough to justify calling himself a miserable offender. My mother stayed silent, her head held high so that anyone who cared to open their eyes could see she wasn't having any of it. This seemed to me exactly as it should be, for what could she have possibly done wrong either, or left undone? Once when we were walking home in silence after a service, my mother said to me as we passed a shop which sold ice-cream: 'I know what the devices and desires of your heart are, young man.' Without being asked, my father went in and bought me an ice lolly. 'There,' he said, 'that should restore you, penitent or not.' I smiled a lot at that, not because I understood what he meant but because my mother was smiling, very broadly for her, and they glanced at each other and I was very happy.

These thoughts interrupted the vicar pardoning everyone that truly repented so that the rest of their life hereafter should be pure and holy – or at least until the following week. After that the Te Deum was sung, less lustily than before, quite right too in the circumstances, but also because the daughter of the woman at number 27 was not leading the way this time. In my search for them I discovered Mr Tomkins and his sister, huddled down well below their neighbours' shoulders, as if all that adulation was altogether too much for them. I thought at first they had remained seated. It seemed improbable that they too had unspeakable sins to confess, had vowed to turn from their wickedness and live.

After that came more prayers and a lesson read by a girl of fifteen or so with long black hair tied back by a red bow. It was about Jesus driving the money-changers from the temple. She enunciated each word very precisely which conflicted with her effort to convey maximum feeling, as if she was auditioning for a drama school or trying to persuade her parents and others in the audience that that was the direction in which she ought to be heading. It was wonderfully lucid nonetheless with the husky undertones of a child. This, I thought, was how Jane might once have been but without the self-consciousness. It was the topic that most reminded me of her, wondering what

580

she'd think of Jesus's intemperate behaviour, herself having been at the heart of all that, done well out of it. Then my parents powerfully returned, my father having dared to comment after a service at which the same lesson was read that Jesus knew what he was up to, giving the money-boys what for and what about the camel and the eye of a needle? The lesson ended and the girl stayed at the lectern for a moment or two, giving the impression she was waiting for applause and getting ready to bow.

Another hymn followed: 'He who would valiant be, 'gainst all disaster . . .' At the end of the second line, that voice rang out again above all the others and I found I was singing along too, quite loudly. Then at the beginning of the last verse the voice suddenly stopped. It was as though the rest of us had suddenly been left in the lurch, were grumbling along in the dark and the whole charade wasn't worth the bother.

Then came the sermon. Up in the pulpit the vicar seemed to believe he didn't have to try so hard to be heard, or had adopted his quietly persuasive tone. Or perhaps he'd been called upon at the very last minute and on the way out had grabbed a sermon he'd preached years before which he was now discovering was a load of rubbish he didn't know how to bring to an end. I strained to hear above the coughing and rustling what he was talking about. It did have to do with money, Jesus not being against making that, what with his father having to sell tables and chairs and having a good time at a wedding. Snatches too about the eye of the needle being an archway difficult to get through if your camel was overladen. At this point he raised his voice and spoke with some force about giving generously to the poor and those in reduced circumstances. This caused some whispering and head turning, a reference having perhaps been picked up to the stinginess of church pensions.

I was getting ready to leave as soon as the sermon ended when there was a loud sound of sniffling followed by an eruption half-way down the aisle as four or five people stood up to let out the woman and her daughter from number 27. They hurried up the aisle, the woman's arm round her daughter's shoulders. She was holding a handkerchief to her face and the sniffling had now turned into sobbing. As they reached the door the woman saw me. For an instant I thought she was pleading for my help and I half rose. But then they had gone. I followed her to the door and saw them, almost running now, disappear through the gate and down the street, the sobbing now having become a continuous wail. When I reached the gate, I saw them get into their car, the revving of the engine followed by the grinding of gears obscuring the start of the final hymn, 'Praise my soul the King of Heaven.' It was my father's favourite, which he sometimes hummed in the shop when a customer left, making the doorbell clang to echo the cash register. He seemed unusually happy then, perhaps at some exceptionally large sale or the settling of a debt, or because the customer was one of those he couldn't stand the sight of. But it caused me sadness too, knowing how much he longed to be bellowing it out in a church, having a good sing.

And so I made my way back, the sound of the hymn dying away – feebly sung now, with no praise in it, that high, pure voice no longer there to lead them on. As I reached our street, I saw the car outside number 27 but it was not the woman and her daughter I found myself thinking about, nor my parents, nor Jane, but the words of the confession. All the curtains were drawn in number 27 and it was utterly silent as if there had been a death there. It was John Brown who was on my mind and I vowed out loud to phone him that evening. I walked the length of the street, unable to enter my house. I had never felt like that before, unprepared for the deadening silence I would find there, as if my whole life had been broken up into that residual bric-à-brac and my body lay upstairs, covered in a sheet, awaiting the undertakers. Religion has a lot to answer for, I muttered, if that's what it does to you.

As I was about to turn back, Rosie appeared round the corner with her dogs and children who were now all crying. She was staring ahead of her and I guessed she had been crying too. Now in her exhaustion she couldn't even try to silence her children. As she reached me she said, 'Bloody charming . . .'

'One of those days, by the look of things,' I said.

'You could say that.' Then her patience snapped and she shouted at the top of her voice, 'O for Christ's sake shut up you lot.'

This caused one of the dogs to snap at my ankle. 'How was it?' I enquired, looking away from her face turned ugly by her anger and the redness around her eyes.

She began loudly, her voice gradually sinking to a whisper. 'Do you really want to know, professor? He was pissed out of his stupid

582

bloody tiny mind. His new bint was there, tarty cow. Pissed as he was. Five minutes they gave us. Kiddies began crying. And do you know?'

'No, I don't.'

'Well, you wouldn't, would you? He didn't give me a single bloody penny, not even enough for an ice lolly or a packet of dog biscuits. What's the Security for, he said. He couldn't in front of her, could he?'

'I'm sorry . . .'

'What am I telling you all this for? I'd better be getting along. It's been nice talking to you. I mean, thank you for listening.'

She really seemed to mean it. 'Let me know if there's anything . . .' I said.

She gave me a sideways look, gratitude quite cancelled out by the routine emptiness of it. No, it was the other way round. The only kind words she had heard all week.

And so I kept my promise to myself and phoned John Brown that evening. It was his wife who answered.

'Tom who did you say?'

'Ripple? I came round to your house a few months back.'

In the background Brown's voice shouted, 'Who the fuck's that?'

'Somebody says he knows us. Phoned us a few months back he says.' Her voice was no worse than slightly drowsy.

'What is it this time?' Brown shouted. 'Double glazing or new kitchen? Here, give it to me.'

'I'm perfectly capable . . .' she began.

'That's a new one, drunk and capable,' he muttered as he took the phone from her, causing her to give a little yelp. 'What is it this time?' he said. 'And the answer is no I don't sodding want it.'

'It's me, Tom Ripple. Sorry. Seem to have chosen a bad time. These telephone salespeople are a damn nuisance, don't I know?'

'Oh Christ, Tom! Jesus! Anyone who chooses a good time can sell me anything. How're tricks?'

'Fine. I just wondered . . . Missed you at the Connaught.'

'Frankly, old fruit, I thought you'd had a bellyful. Don't blame yourself in the least.'

'How is erm . . . ?'

He waited for me to finish but my question had got stuck, unsure what it might be, ought to be rather, other than never to have been started.

'Not all right, roughly speaking.'

'Just thought . . . Was thinking of going down to the Connaught tomorrow.'

'Not sure right now . . .'

His wife's voice pleaded in the background, 'Help me up, Johnny. Can't seem to . . .'

'Coming, sweetheart,' he said. 'First got to get rid of this ruddy salesman.'

'What's he selling?' she called out, evidently in some pain.

'You're not selling anything, are you?' he said to me.

'Not nowadays, no.'

'May see you tomorrow then. And thanks for calling. Never thought you would.'

'Why, I . . .'

'Just *coming*, darling, for fuck's bloody sake. Sorry about that. Cheery-bye.'

He didn't turn up at the Connaught the following evening. A good thing perhaps, because the recess was full of visitors from Belgium drinking beer. And that is what they seemed to talk about all the time I was there, the women too. There were ten of them on some neighbourhood or club outing perhaps. I knew they came from Belgium because three of them were wearing baseball caps with 'I Love Brussels' on them. It was the warmth and flatness of the beer that intrigued them. Or so I guessed from the way they gulped large mouthfuls of it, then spoke, the beer not always having been fully swallowed. They saw me staring at them and lowered their voices, one of the men pointing at his beer and saying, 'Inklish beer ferry goot.' I nodded and raised a thumb and elbow which made at least half of them laugh very raucously, albeit briefly. I left soon after that, waving at them which brought three of them to their feet with their glasses raised. One of them said, 'Cheerio!' And another said, 'Bottoms up!' Then they all laughed loudly and were still laughing when I went out, thinking two things: what a jolly business altogether the European Union promised to be; and that I was off the hook so far as John Brown was concerned.

On my way back up the hill I became unusually puffed. Indeed had to sit on the front wall of someone's garden for a while to get my breath back. The sun was setting in a clear sky and the sea was ablaze along the horizon. A few stars were beginning to appear between the wisps of cloud. The thought I had then, and I write this on the same evening, is that in some such circumstance I would breathe my last: glad that I hadn't shown a friend an elementary kindness; thinking what ghastly oafs a group of harmless Belgian tourists were; going on from that to the farce of European Union; wondering what I'd have for supper; what a lovely sunset it was and how insignificant we all are when for a second or two we contemplate the infinite vastness of the universe; must hoover the stair carpet some time; there must be a God; where did I put the Polyfilla; there can't be a God; and so on and so forth. We might like our dying thoughts to be less fatuous or more momentous than those we have previously had, except that then it would dawn on us at the last how fatuous and unmomentous our thinking had been. Which we wouldn't like one bit. The next time I saw my doctor and he raised the subject of my fitness I'd tell him I hadn't been able to get to the top of the hill without a rest, giving him the opportunity to tell me that at least I wasn't yet over it. Keep fit for what? I hadn't quite recovered from that moment of dread of walking into my house and going upstairs and finding my own body lying there under a sheet . . .

And so my mind wandered away from all that had gone before and I returned to myself, my health, my well-being, this scribbling away. It was all I was fit for. And so it was too that the next day I went by bus to the bank and then down to see Rosie with an envelope with £500 in it. There's not a lot I want to say about that. What a splendid chap that makes me? No, none of that. What I have omitted to mention, have tried to prevent myself thinking about, is that in her will Jane left me £10,000. It was, Adrian told me, so that I could buy some new red socks, a new Frightful Joke Book or two, a few CDs (more Schubert?), spoil myself a little. But mainly it was so I could give to charities I thought she might approve of. I was as sure as I could be of anything that Rosie was one of those. I couldn't explain any of this to Rosie of course.

She was much taken aback at first. I told her that I'd won a bit on the Lottery, not a jackpot though. It was to be a secret between us. She said she couldn't possibly etc. and tried to hand it back. So I took the envelope and said that there must be a misunderstanding, it wasn't for her, and gave it to the eldest child, suggesting he ask his mother's advice before spending it. I hurried away after that, not giving her time to say anything else but she caught up with me at the door and kissed me wetly on the lips. Her brother was watching, expressionless as usual, his head twisted to one side as if the whole business was thoroughly distasteful and I was up to no good.

For a while therefore I no longer felt any guilt about John Brown and his wife. I thought I could go back to church at any time, needing little, if any, repentance. Religion had turned out to be not such a bad thing after all, not so demanding by a long chalk. As my mother had said, so long as it was only the nice-sounding words and the music.

This didn't last. I could have afforded to give Rosie more, for even without Jane's gift I had more than enough. Should I have given it to her anonymously, causing her to worry incessantly where it had come from? For now, though it wasn't calculated, I'm sure, on her part no more than on mine, we never met, except to wave at a distance. It was as if we were avoiding each other. I did not want her to think there were strings or how jolly good I felt about it. She did not want to have to thank me again, explain what it had meant to her. Anyone can work all this out. Gratitude is a funny, complicated business. It creates obligations we would rather be without, though not the giving and receiving themselves. We wouldn't be without those. It's the owing we mind. I missed Rosie, even to the extent sometimes of wishing I hadn't given her any money at all. I missed the occasional chat, the ordinary daily neighbourliness of it. Once it had seemed the least we owed each other, it was as simple as that.

The things we have done and left undone and there is no health in us . . .

Chapter Nine

On the following Thursday morning I saw Mrs Hirst coming out of number 27. As I embarked on my daily walk late that afternoon she asked me over the fence if I'd seen two of her cats. They were asleep on my bed and I said it seemed a pity to wake them, I'd bring them round later if she wouldn't miss them too much in the meantime. She thought about that before replying, 'Oh all right then.' She seemed, as usual, to be in talkative mood, giving me the opportunity to ask her about the people in number 27. I couldn't tell her I'd been at the church service the previous Sunday – not wanting to express any opinion that might lead to – so I tried another opening.

'Liked your hat last Sunday. Very dashing I must say. Don't see hats so much these days. Sunday best for church?'

This seemed to fluster her. 'Oh thank you, professor. Thanks for the compliment. Much appreciated though I say so myself.'

There was a pause while we both wondered if the time of day had been sufficiently passed. I moved a couple of paces further on.

'Saw you talking to that poor Rosie girl,' she said. 'Honestly don't know how she manages. A really nice kid she was.'

'Still is.'

'I mean before it all got spoiled and everything. He was a right bastard, that one.'

'No change there by the sound of it.'

'There's nothing you don't know, is there, professor?' she said with genuine appreciation.

The conversation had been diverted so I had another go.

'Solved your little vicar problem, have you?'

'Him. He's not little. He's over six foot. We had the old vicar last Sunday. Bit past it, to be honest, but I don't see the harm in that.'

'Organist's wife in no immediate danger there then?'

She gave a little snort. 'Ooh no. Not him. It'd be the organist in danger from that quarter, if anyone.'

'I see. So what happened to the other one and the organist's wife?'

'Well might you ask. She came back. They say he's still in the Holy Land. Fat lot of good that will do him.'

'It's not the church on Albemarle Street by any chance?'

She glanced at me eagerly, as if after all I might be a believer, was doing a survey of the neighbourhood to decide where salvation might be most readily come by.

'St Peter's. That's the one. Have you been there? It's a lovely church. Used to be old-fashioned with the proper Bible and prayerbook and things. We had them out again last Sunday. You'd be very welcome, professor. You should try it one day. No percentage in just putting your head round. There's a really big organ.'

'And a happy organist again to go with it. Some pretty good singing seemed to be going on, I must say.'

She became even more animated. 'You ought to have dropped in, professor. Where's the harm in that? You don't have to buy tickets, you know.'

This was the opening. 'Does anyone else from the street go there?'

'The Tomkinses. They do.' Her voice tailed off and she paused. I waited, giving her a chance to continue. 'They're quiet with their little stone animals. Gentle. Too many for my liking. Two new tortoises, a mole and a ferret or something. Otter. But they do sing. He takes the collection. I'll give them that.'

'Do you think they mind that the rest of us don't try to follow their example: a street of perfect little gardens?'

'They want theirs to be special. Different. It wouldn't do if all the others were just as good, would it?'

'I'll have to think about that.'

'You be off on your little walk then. You won't be wanting to hang about talking about church and gardens. Sorry about the cats. Real animals, they are. So long as they're not taking advantage or anything.'

'Who knows? Perhaps I will. One day. I do like those hymns, the other bits. Used to go as a child.'

As I moved off she said, 'There you are then. And professor, Rosie's a good girl. You be nice to her.'

I raised my walking-stick and strode off for my 'little' walk. Sooner or later she'd have to tell me about the people at number 27. When she did,

I'd like to be able to tell her I'd already heard whatever there was to be known. But I didn't. I did not want them to be the subject of gossip. No more, apparently, than Mrs Hirst did. I remembered the way the woman had looked at me as they left the church. The shame of it, the desperation. But now the whole neighbourhood, or the churchgoing part of it, would be gossiping about them – the voice, the breakdown. I was asking myself what more I could have done. Could now do. The answer was nothing. Keep well out of it. It wasn't my virtue that needed satisfying but my curiosity, and that could wait. Not like virtue.

The last summer of the millennium arrived. Our suburb is a mile or so north of the main beach and promenade where all the big hotels are. The town centre had never seemed so crowded as though everyone was in a hurry to get rid of their money before it was too late. Under the promenade is a row of shops and stalls which sell the usual cheap seaside consumables. They are what people want. I take the bus down there sometimes on a fine day and wander about, the sea sparkling away as if those who cavort about there have been invited to plunder its infinite treasures and cannot believe their luck. In the middle distance there may be a few speedboats showing off; and on the horizon a cargo boat or tanker or two making no visible progress – bearing something of what is necessary to keep life going in the serious time between. At a distance all that larking about on the sea's edge seems as close to joy as it is possible to get.

I do not go down there, preferring to stroll along the row of stalls under the promenade, looking out for an empty bench. The jumble of goods – the hats and postcards and flags and beach toys and souvenirs and ice-cream and hot dogs, all that garish, higgledy-piggledy tat – seem to show how far, how trivially, we must go to endure the serious days and nights to come. Away from the glittering water the joy has been left behind. By the adults anyway. No one is smiling or seems about to. Or talking much. The words start and stop as if a new vocabulary is being invented for trying to have fun. The children are learning how not to get too excited, recently having been ticked off or expecting to be shortly. Holidays are also for finding out how little can be afforded. If it wasn't for the sun-tans you couldn't tell those who have just arrived from those who are about to leave. All good things come to an end as soon as they have begun. But down there on the beach it is utterly different: the ball games and sand-castles, the high-legged running in and out of the water, the shrieks and splashing, and when you listen for it, the laughter. Here and there are those who just sit in deck-chairs, watching or dozing. In abandonment or reflection, the emptying of the mind.

No, it can't be as simple as that. I sit there too, remembering, my mind going round in circles. It isn't the same for everyone. You can see faces raised to the sun smiling at what happened a long time ago. They are being reminded. For everyone there is a different loss along the way. Happiness shades into sorrow or is cancelled out. The mind is not emptied. When all the daily doings and worries begin to be forgotten, vacant spaces appear which have to be filled up. 'Where has it all gone?' we ask. There is more and more to remember. Memory spills over. The sorrow of loss, of waste, of forgetfulness. The happiness is washed away in it. That we all differently share sooner or later. What began as happiness – the smile on the face – has been stolen from us. The sorrow hardens and turns into theft . . .

I try like that to make my own thoughts less personal, less repetitive, when I remember our own seaside holidays further up the coast, to fill in the details, or let them come. Times past. Happiness turning to sorrow etc. as above: Adrian's knobbly knees, the swelling of Virginia's breasts, my wife's sustained uncensoriousness, the two stinking large dogs that lay around the boarding house dining room, the sand in the sandwiches – memories without end, returning again and again to the faces of Adrian and Virginia, without a care in the world. Before the end of innocence . . .

Such were my thoughts that late August afternoon as I waited on the promenade for my bus, trying to remember if I'd helped Adrian to build a sand-castle, how had we taught them to swim, what had we bought, refused to buy, in the shops and stalls . . . ? Suddenly I was overcome with tiredness and had to walk some way from the bus stop to find a bench. In my breathlessness I forgot the past and all I could think of was the time not long before when I'd had to sit on a stranger's wall half-way up the hill about to breathe my last. Then, as now, I was frightened. The mixture of thoughts had ended then quite differently under the starlight: there had to be a God. Now, not so. Not so at all . . . The whole thing was a complete farce and everything else was self-delusion. However different the mixture of thoughts, the fear was the same.

Just as I had decided that my end might not be nigh after all and my final verdict about existence could be further postponed, my bus appeared at the far end of the front. I was about to get up and walk back to the bus stop when I saw a black-haired female figure striding along the edge of the water. She was wearing a long green dress down to her ankles and was swinging her arms, a black shoe dangling from each hand. Among that swarming crowd, my thoughts now elsewhere, I would not have noticed her. But as she marched along with long strides, her head held high, all activity around her stopped for an instant as if she had cast a spell. Some stared at her with annoyance for she walked straight through the throwing of balls or rubber rings, a game of football or cricket. Twice she narrowly missed kicking down a sand-castle. She seemed to create around her an invisible cloud of silence. As soon as she had passed the activity resumed as if it had never been interrupted.

On and on she strode and I found myself following her along the front, my bus now forgotten. I had to walk fast but no longer felt in the least tired. Towards the end of the beach a man shook his fist and shouted at her when she kicked over a sand-castle but she ignored it completely. She saw and heard nothing. It was only then that I realized from the way she held her head, chin thrust forward, face up to the wind, that it was the young woman who had sung so beautifully in the church, the daughter from number 27.

When she reached the end of the beach she veered sharply up towards the promenade, then suddenly stopped and turned to face the sea, completely still as if waiting, listening for something. Then she looked back along the beach and I thought she was about to walk back the way she had come, that that was all she had been doing – taking a brisk walk on a late summer afternoon – and that she would now go back and join her mother. I was standing directly above her at the top of the steps, perhaps some fifty yards away, when she swung round and stared up in my direction, or above me and for the first time I saw her full in the face. For a moment her hair covered her eyes and was then blown back as she tossed up her head, closing her eyes and opening her mouth as if to exult in a sudden cloudburst.

She stood like that for perhaps half a minute. Around her were clusters of people in deck-chairs and children playing in the sand. No one seemed to see her there among them, vivid in her long green dress. Then she lowered her head, opened her eyes and came towards me, kicking up the sand, swinging the shoes high above her waist. Her eyes were fixed on me and there seemed to be fury in them. Her mouth was still open as if she was about to call out to me. As she came up the steps I moved a few paces to one side to let her pass. It was clear in that instant that she hadn't seen me and that she shouldn't be there. And that she was patently mad.

She stood for a while at the top of the steps, looking to either side of her, as if trying to remember which direction she had come in, or as if she'd been dumped at the side of the road in a place she had known as a child that had now changed beyond recognition. But for someone so evidently lost she did not seem in the least anxious. I cannot have been more than five yards away and might then have introduced myself, asked if I could help. Instead I had the fatuous notion that once she had put on her shoes she'd remember where she was and everything would be all right. I thought too that there was no reason for her to recognize me and I would only frighten her. And yes too, I was curious. No, I was primarily curious and the rest rambled on around that.

Suddenly she raised her hand and waved a shoe at a bus that had stopped at the other side of the road. As the bus moved on she ran across the road, making two cars screech to a stop with fierce blasts of their horns. When she reached the bus stop she stood there, feet wide apart, to wait for the next bus. There seemed to be no pockets in her dress to keep money in and on that side of the road the bus would take her in the opposite direction from our suburb – out towards the cliffs and on to the London road. I told myself firmly that she was probably quite all right and I should mind my own business, replying almost at once that even someone capable of believing that couldn't believe that. As I waited for a gap in the traffic another bus came and hid her from view. I quite expected that when it went she would have gone with it. But she was still there, looking down forlornly at her feet as if trying to remember why they were covered in sand and what had happened to her shoes. Perhaps the driver had refused to let her on because she didn't have the fare – as simple as that. If she'd had any money she'd have been well on her way up towards the cliffs. I crossed the road and stood beside her, resolved to say something before the next bus came. Don't worry, I almost said, your shoes are in your hand.

'Forgive me,' I began. 'My name is Tom Ripple. We live on the same street, I believe. You're at number 27 with your mother. I live at number 13.'

Intent on staring at her bare feet, she seemed not to hear me. We were out of the sun and a sudden gust of cold wind blew a few scraps of litter round our ankles. She clasped her hands together under her chin, the shoes still dangling from them. There were goose pimples along her arm and she had begun to shiver. Her dress clung tightly around her as if the wind had shrunk it and I saw that underneath it she was naked. The cold had hardened her nipples which were too large and stood out too far for her miniature breasts. A catch in the throat etc. Definitely not too anything at all, the breasts becoming definitive too. Her fearless look had gone and she looked pitiful as if she stood naked before a hooting crowd. She was still gazing at her feet and started wiggling her toes. An ice-cream wrapper clung to her ankle and beside one foot was a splodge of mud, to give it the benefit of the doubt. I tried again.

'Tom Ripple?' I held out a hand and repeated the name of the street. 'On your way somewhere?'

Such daft questions we do in reality ask and it may have been this that made her smile. But it was to herself, reminded of something. She looked up to where another bus was coming, then suddenly bent down, swiftly put on her shoes and unfolded a ten-pound note which had been screwed up in her fist. She began waving at the bus as if saying goodbye to someone on it. When it stopped, I did what I thought I should. Or had not got nearly as far as thinking that – simply that she must be prevented from getting on that bus. I did not want to lose sight of her. So I took her elbow and said, 'I'm catching the bus too. Frankly you look frozen. Why don't we have a hot cup of something?' I gazed up the street and mercifully there was a café about thirty yards away. 'Was just going myself . . . Bun . . . Come along . . . Don't even know your name . . .'

She was gazing at me like a child momentarily distracted from something much more interesting.

'Come along . . .' My grip tightened slightly. 'I'm far more harmless than I look.'

Now she looked at me as if trying to recognize me, remember whether I was someone she had liked or not. The bus driver was staring at us and I shook my head. The door clattered to but not soon enough to prevent me from hearing the words 'stupid berk'. I became aware of people staring at us as they walked past. I wondered how I must appear to them. Restraining my granddaughter from what teenage folly? That at very best. I begged her with my eyes, repeating, 'Come along. Warm you up.'

Mercifully, she then relaxed and, still holding her elbow, I led her to the café.

We found a table by the window and I asked her what she would like. She stared out of the window and did not reply. So when the waitress came I ordered cocoa for two and some biscuits. The waitress looked between us three times quite slowly, her pencil still poised above her pad.

'Did you want anything else?' she asked, slowly too, with a pout now. Someone had told her she had sexy lips.

'And when might that have been?' I asked.

I don't respond like that normally – shop assistants and the like only doing their jobs and not getting paid enough and customers knowing they're always right and don't you forget it. But I had this notion that my little pedantry might catch the girl's attention, even make her smile. For what I haven't mentioned is that, despite everything else, she also had the shrewd, enquiring look of someone of unusual intelligence. And then too, of course, I had heard that rapturous voice.

'When would what have been . . . ?' the waitress was saying.

I waved her away. 'Sorry, just the cocoa and biscuits.'

We sat there for a while. Her hair had fallen across her face so I could see little of it, until she lifted a strand of it with her forefinger and tucked it behind her ear. She did this slowly as if letting me inspect the finger, its nail bitten to the quick. Then she cupped her chin in her hands and stared unblinking out at the sea. At least she wasn't on a bus on her way to London. That was what I thought at first, until deciding that after we'd finished the cocoa I'd get the waitress to call us a taxi to take us home. I was also thinking it was a pity her arm was preventing me from having another look at those nipples. I stared out at the sea too. There was nowhere else I could politely look unless I spoke to her. When the waitress brought the cocoa and biscuits, lingering for another good long stare, it seemed right to try again.

'Let's get through this, warm us up, then we'll take a cab home. All right by you?'

She turned her face to me, still cupped in her hands.

Her voice was matter of fact, polite, simply curious. We might have been meeting at some social gathering. 'You're not my father, are you? You're not anything.'

'Well, there might be some, one or two, who wouldn't go quite as far as that.'

She nodded. 'I see you almost every day walking past. You always look up at my window but you can't see me, can you? I can see you.'

She smiled as if to console me but the moment I smiled back at her she sniffed and wiped her thumb across her mouth. I looked down at her hands which now lay on the table, spread out as if for inspection.

'You're just thinking I should stop biting my nails. All fathers think like that.'

Her voice was harsh and spiteful. It was not the voice that had sung so beautifully that day. I shook my head, though her exposed fingertips were raw and there were little scabs here and there where she had drawn blood, and that was exactly what I was thinking. I wanted her voice to change. Stupid though it may seem I just wanted her to stop letting herself down. Simply to become a bright, happy young woman who sang beautifully in church every Sunday. I took a sip of my cocoa, bit into a biscuit and said, 'I heard you in church the other Sunday. You've got a lovely voice.'

She frowned as if trying to work out what on earth I was on about, then turned back to the sea. I waited for her reply.

'It's rude to stare,' she said.

'I'm sorry. I . . .'

She shrugged. 'You can have my cocoa if you want to. Ghastly muck. That's all they ever give you.'

'Thanks. I was just curious. I mean, I thought whoever sang like that was going to be a professional singer.'

'I'm not allowed to do it in there. It disturbs the others.' She gritted her teeth, turning towards me, widening her eyes. 'So what do you want, Mr Nosy Parker? Walking past every day. Mr Policeman. Tranquillizers. That's what they call them. The stuff they put in my cocoa. To stop me singing. Shall I sing now?'

I became aware of the waitress hovering behind me and asked for the bill. There was a phone by the counter so I enquired if she could give me the number of a minicab company.

'I'll do it,' she said. 'No trouble. It's ten minutes usually.' She glanced at the girl and gave me a knowing look, all but touching the side of her head.

When I turned back, the girl was staring at me. The simple sweetness had returned to her face. It was as if it could never be recognized, was useless, without hope or help.

When she spoke her voice was gentle, almost a whisper. 'I would like to sing for you. We could go down to the sea. The wind carries it away. It just joins the universe. I only give it back. You wouldn't be able to understand that.'

I stared into her eyes as forthrightly as I could. I felt that if I willed it hard enough I could keep her like that, just like that, for ever. But her eyes were closing and she began mumbling to herself, or humming rather, as if singing herself to sleep. Her face was at rest. On the table her raw, scabbed fingers drummed some rhythm. The waitress returned with my change and to tell me the taxi would be there shortly.

'Is everything all right?' she asked.

I nodded. 'Thanks. That'll be all. Thank you very much.'

'Just so long as everything's all right.'

And so we sat there. Her eyelids were not quite closed and there was flickering behind them. She murmured on. Finally her fingers came to rest and closed into fists. She turned them upwards and I saw for the first time the scars across her wrists like miniature scourge marks. I counted them. Five on each side, equidistant and almost symmetrical.

I looked up and she was staring at me. 'There you are, Mr Policeman Busybody. You should put more stuff in my cocoa. Do you think I'm pretty?'

'Yes, I do. Very.'

Her voice became pert and proper. 'Quite pretty, I suppose. I've got rather a skinny body, I regret to say.'

She closed her eyes again and not long afterwards the taxi arrived. I raised her to her feet and she came with me without protest, half asleep. We were being stared at by the other customers as if they were witnessing an abduction. Not doing a thing about it, though. People don't. You read about it. Terrible things going on and people just watching. Interesting but too much trouble. The waitress stood at the counter, arms akimbo. I waved and called out, 'Thanks.' She did not wave back. For an instant I wanted her to become middle-aged, then old, as soon as possible. She would hate that.

As I eased the girl into the back of the taxi she put an arm round my shoulder and murmured, 'You're quite a boring old man. But that's not your fault. Walking past looking up at windows. I saw you looking at my breasts. I'm glad you're not my father. You couldn't do that then.'

I got in the other side and the cab driver gave me a look which he couldn't decide ought to be saucy or disgusted. The girl folded her arms, huddled into the corner with a deep sigh, closed her eyes and began humming again. I doubted if I would see her again, would certainly never again be alone with her.

'You seemed to be enjoying yourself down there on the beach.'

She stopped humming for a moment, then huddled down further and turned her face to the window. She seemed to be trying to prevent herself from shivering. Her face was now very pale and strangely shadowless. The goose pimples had returned to her bare forearms and now I could only imagine them stretched out as she drew the razor across them, first one, then the other. I had the utterly absurd, ignorant thought that I should say to her, 'Please don't try to kill yourself again.'

And then I heard myself say it, but so quietly that I did not think she could hear me. The humming had stopped and she breathed deeply, her chest heaving under her arms. I looked out of the window for a last glimpse of the sea as we drove away from the front. The sky had clouded over and people were beginning to pack their things away. Deck-chairs were being stacked and two men were putting litter into black plastic sacks. Some people had already reached the promenade, heavily laden with seaside clobber, their children lagging behind them as if, their freedom over, they expected to be carried too. Hands reached back to drag them on. Several stallkeepers were beginning to fold up their awnings and put up their shutters. The sparkle had gone from the sea which was pale green now, wrinkling and turning grey further out among patches of spray. There were no boats. For a moment the sun came out as if to summon everyone back, then vanished, leaving behind sharper edges of darkness.

When I looked back at the girl she was staring at me.

'Why ever not?' she asked. This was said in the simple spirit of enquiry, as if we were talking about someone else. She smiled at my puzzlement. I did not know what to reply. 'Come along, old man. You're supposed to know all the answers.'

I looked over my shoulder for a last glimpse of the sea, then back at her. She was smiling even more broadly, but it was the imitation of a smile now, a baring of the teeth, a semblance of menace.

'Because it would be a waste. A terrible waste.'

'The waste of a good voice you mean.'

And she began singing a high scale at the top of her voice. The driver's shoulders hunched and he looked round, muttering 'Jesus!' – whether in anger or admiration he probably did not know himself.

When she had finished, I clapped my hands a couple of times and said, 'Bravo!'

She sighed and closed her eyes again. 'There are lots and lots of voices. Lots of them. Some of them are in my head and I just want them to shut up. Actually I want you to shut up.'

'I'm sorry.'

'That's what everyone says. Everyone is always saying that. My mother is always saying, "Sorry, darling. Sorry, darling. Sorry, darling ... " '

Her voice trailed away and she seemed to fall asleep. As I watched her crouched in the corner of the cab she began to babble quietly, making no sense that I could decipher, her voice whiny like that of a little girl.

When we arrived her mother was waiting for us. She ran down the path, snatched open the car door and pulled her daughter out, saying over and over again, 'Where have you been, darling? Where have you been?'

I followed them up the path and stood at the foot of the steps. From the doorway she turned over her daughter's head and looked at me angrily as though I'd abducted her and had my way with her. She even seemed surprised that I was still there.

'I saw her at the far end of the front. I thought ... She was about to catch a bus ... I thought ... Do let me know ...'

She closed the door with the barest nod and I returned to pay the cab driver.

'You've got a right one there,' he offered. 'Pissed at her age.'

Giving him a tenner, I told him to keep the change. He offered me his card.

'Any time,' he said. 'Charge the same with or without the fancy

598

music.' This he thought very funny, chuckling away while he put the note in his wallet. 'Takes all sorts.'

He drove off and I went home and made myself a cup of tea. I took it upstairs, lay down and almost at once fell asleep. I did not notice the cat and when I awoke it was lying between my legs, purring loudly. It was the ginger tom. I had been woken by a knock on the door and I went downstairs. It was Mrs Hirst. The cat had followed me and she picked it up.

'I see you brought her back, professor.'

'That's it.'

'She's not right, is she?'

'Seems not.'

'Poor kid.' I nodded. 'Nothing to be done about it, is there?'

'I don't know, Mrs Hirst. I really don't know.'

'Nor do I,' she said, lifting up the cat. 'Do you mind me saying something?'

'What's that?'

'I don't think we ought to talk about it. They've got enough problems.'

'I wasn't going to.'

'I never have. Doesn't seem right. Gossiping about that. You a professor. You'll understand, I told myself.'

'I agree.'

She put a hand on my arm and left me. She'd never done that before. I almost called her back to say that she shouldn't hesitate to let me know if there was anything at all I could do . . . I glanced across at number 27. The upstairs curtains were drawn and I imagined the girl lying there asleep on her back, the scars exposed, her teeth bared in that manic smile. I heard her voice soaring up in the church, leading the others on. I saw her striding along the beach, oblivious to anyone else, even to the sea itself. I had slept through the onset of dusk. The beach would be empty now and the sea barely visible, glinting here and there to reflect the lights coming on in the hotels and boarding houses. Then I wrote some of this down, put a Fishermen's Delight ready-made pie in the oven and spent the rest of the evening watching television. P. D. James. Very gripping though I guessed the culprit too soon.

The following morning the woman from number 27 came to see me. I invited her in but she said she had to get back.

'I'm sorry about yesterday,' she said. 'I'd been worried sick. I was so overjoyed to see her I didn't think . . .'

'Please . . .'

'Where did you find her?'

'At the far end of the front. She'd walked the whole length of the beach. As I said, she seemed to be about to catch a bus in the wrong direction. I thought . . .'

'How can I thank you . . . ?'

'You needn't . . . I enjoyed her company.'

She put a hand to her mouth and I thought it was to stifle a sob but then she coughed.

'She said she had a lovely time. All by herself walking along the beach. I'm afraid she'll want to do it again and you won't be there to bring her home.'

'Is she . . . ?'

'Going to get better? No, she's not going to get better. This morning she thought I was her doctor in the hospital. When I went to wake her she just bared her arm for an injection. That is worst, sometimes not knowing me.'

'Yes, I can understand . . .'

Then she smiled. 'She thought you were one of the gardeners at the hospital. She said that you'd been very kind, buying her cocoa, then taking her to see where you'd planted out the dahlias. She said you were going to teach her how to grow vegetables everywhere to make herself useful for a change, something to live for.'

I could only nod. I did say that she mustn't hesitate and all the rest of it. She thanked me again and I could tell that she'd never ask for my help for there was none that I could give. She'd be the sort of person who'd say, 'You don't want to listen to my troubles.' She'd not want to talk about herself, the misery of her life and her deeply sick daughter. She'd not like to complain. Unlike those who have little or nothing to complain about.

As she stepped back to leave I said, 'I'm sorry, I don't even know her name.'

'Julia.'

'It's a lovely name.'

'Oh yes. We gazed down at her as a baby and thought: she's going to be so beautiful. Life would shower her with every blessing under the sun. We would see to that. Oh she was such a lovely, clever child . . .'

She saved me from having to reply to that by turning and walking away. My hand was raised to the empty blue sky.

The next morning an official-looking car came and took them away. The woman returned alone in the evening. I thought of her sitting alone, missing her child dreadfully and not missing her too and the shame of that. Go round. Knock on the door. Say, 'Thought you might like a bit of company?' No, my guess was that misery like that is not to be shared. The humiliation. The way she had glanced at me as she hurried out of the church that Sunday had not been a plea for help but a plea to look the other way. That was the image that came to mind: hands reaching out towards a retreating crowd and no one turning round . . .

Chapter Ten

A couple of weeks ago Mrs Felix knocked on my door, choosing to do
a lot of that rather than ring the bell. Looking up at me over her
glasses, she said she assumed of course I knew all about the beacon –
as if I was the sort of person who thought they knew everything but,
thanks to her, had another think coming. One or two 'good folk' were
coming for home-made mince pies and rum punch before they made
their way up there for the dawn of the millennium.

I had seen her coming and had prepared myself.

'What a convivial gesture, I do declare,' I said in what, albeit before
her time, might have had a professorial ring to it. Then I gave a
thumbs-up sign and switched to what might be taken for a Canadian
accent. 'You gutta date, ma'am.'

'Succinctly put. Very droll, I'm sure . . .' There was a pause as when
someone begins to change their mind and realizes it's too late. 'Early
days, I appreciate, but if you'd care to join us . . .'

'Too kind,' I replied. 'Too, too, too kind. Family willing.'

'But of course, my dear fellow. Only if you're free, naturally. Couple
of Cedric's old chums'll be there. One at the House, I fancy.'

I replied indistinctly, as professors might when speculating half out
loud on some truth that had yet to have several lifetimes more thought
devoted to it, 'The other being required to stay outside in the garden.
Poor old chap. A trifle on the chilly side. In the drear dead of winter.'

'I beg your pardon?'

I returned half-way or half the time to my Canadian accent. 'I was
but reminded of those long hard winters in Nova Scotia. Ah me! New
Year's Eve in a snowstorm. Hot puddings. Cold trifle. Arcadia.
Wolfville. Meanwhile out there the Micmac in their wintry wastes
wrapped in their sealskin . . .'

I gazed wistfully up at the sky and closed my eyes. When I looked
back at her she was staring at me as though I was completely off my

rocker. On my last visit to the library I'd done just enough reading on which to base a scholarly career in Canada – where almost everyone who teaches at a university seems to be a professor of some sort. I nodded vigorously as though she was about to say something with which I would profoundly agree.

'Perhaps another time when you're . . .' was as much as she could manage at first. Then she recovered her composure. 'Anyway, as I was saying, the point is you'd be very welcome . . . I do think, don't you, we should be there to witness the girdling of our beloved country with beacons of fire to herald the new millennium? From hilltop to hilltop.'

'Another time, another place, Mrs Felix.' I mumbled on. 'Ah yes. Now cold trifle and rum punch. Then the campfire and caribou steak among the Micmac in their tepees. The sizzling griddle. So elemental, the signals of smoke . . . The ancestral spirits . . .'

Her mouth opened and shut. I'd spoken in dreamlike fashion as one not quite of this world, giving her nothing to latch on to.

'McDonald's,' she said finally. 'Quite revolting. I do so agree. Take your word about the beverages. You wouldn't see me dead . . .' She was moving off with a wave. 'Do come if you can.'

I put my hands together in an attitude of prayer and bowed. American Indians didn't do this so far as I knew but she mightn't know that either.

'Sure do, ma'am,' I called after her with a wink and a leer to let her know what cruder replies there might have been to that, none of them academic.

Immediately after this I spoke to Virginia. I couldn't ask directly how keen she wasn't for me to see the new millennium in with them. Richard had found and lost another job. She told me this with a long sigh as if to say what else had she learnt to expect. Her job was keeping them going. The children were a handful etc. It was so hard on Richard, the humiliation of it. It was getting him further and further down. She can't have wanted me to witness this misery, could only say though that they'd love to see me. Of course. What about Christmas? Finally she said, 'Mum wants to come up. But, Dad, I love her dearly, I really do. But I can't be doing with any more silent judgement, any more advice. Certainly not about the children who can be pretty appalling.'

'Yes, but surely she could take them off your hands? Give you both a break.'

'You mean a candlelit dinner. Oh Dad, it just pours out of Richard then. After a glass or two. And when we get back Mum would tell us . . . oh you know. I'm being horribly disloyal.'

'You are rather. She simply isn't like that any longer. As I understand it, the key is Richard getting work.'

'You've got it, Dad. You usually do . . . Pray for us.' There was a noise of bawling children in the background. 'Must go.'

I did say a sort of prayer for her that evening before phoning Adrian. Without a God to talk to, I had to address it to Fate. 'Let her be happy. Let them be all right.' That was about all there was of it. The snag about talking to Fate is hearing in the background the sound of chuckling. Which is better somehow than the kind of eternal, resolute silence God seems to go in for.

Adrian was spending Christmas with Jane's parents but wanted to see the New Year in on his own.

'Not come down here?' I asked. 'They're lighting a beacon.'

'I suppose I should let go a little, but I haven't even begun to. On anniversary days I want to be alone with her. I talk as if she was listening. I can hear what she would say. Probably sounds a bit deranged. Sick.'

'Whatever the opposite of those things are, that's how it sounds.'

'Yep.' There was a pause. 'What about Virginia?'

'Not good, I'm afraid. Richard out of work again. She wants to battle through on her own. No witnesses.'

'Not Mum?'

'No, not Mum.'

'I spoke to her a couple of weeks ago. She certainly keeps herself busy. All sorts of voluntary work. They've got single mothers and the homeless and drug addicts even in Somerset. Committee this. Panel that.'

'What did she say about Virginia?'

'Same as you, Dad. Worried. Sad. Said she'd been so kind-hearted as a girl. Do you remember the Hambles?'

'Indeed I do.'

'It really upset her, Mrs Hamble dying. They sort of adopted her, didn't they?'

'Yes. She felt it deeply all right. Do you remember that jaunt to the park? The Webbs too.'

'Oh my, yes. I behaved rather badly. Something to do with French cricket and Virginia was being so bloody *good*.'

'Nothing to do with Webb then?'

'He was a horrible little creep of course. But he'd been pretty good to me. I remember feeling mainly sorry for him.'

'Not for her? Surely . . . ?'

'I must have thought that something or other was her fault. He was so pathetic. They both were. Real losers as they say nowadays. I wanted to hate him more than I could. And since then, well, enough said. The chat we had in that awful café and that nice waitress. It was all said then. As much as could be.'

'Needed to be. What's it all about then?'

He laughed but did not reply. I then went on to tell him about my memories of our seaside holidays, how the memories multiply, the happiness changing to sorrow and back again – some of the thoughts I'd written down after my encounter with poor Julia. It was the longest conversation we'd ever had. He filled in more details. His memories were much like mine – of fun and laughter and peacefulness between us.

He told me that Jane had often spoken of her childhood, the memories that suddenly took her unawares, especially towards the end. Sometimes they overwhelmed her. She quoted a poem by A. E. Housman which begins, 'Into my heart an air that kills from yon far country blows.' He said I should look it up. It was about remembering the happiness of childhood. But the point, as Jane explained it, was that the air was not sad or poignant or joyful or anything like that. It killed. That distressed her, Adrian said, when memories were all she had left.

So we returned again to Jane. The conversation ended shortly after that. We had forgotten Virginia. Perhaps there was nothing more about her that might have been said. If there was anything Adrian could do for her, he would already have done it. What Virginia had not said was that Adrian was such a success he only reminded Richard of what a failure he was. She probably avoided mentioning him. Sending money, even for the children, was out of the question. I could hear that plaintive voice saying, 'Of course your rich brother is so successful. It's all right for some . . .' Or words of that sort.

When I put the phone down my prayer was that Adrian and Virginia could be together again, getting along famously. As they hadn't as children, except on holiday. Then the memory of innocence would seem fulfilled, or rather an element of it would have remained. But enough of all that. I haven't yet looked up the poem.

A week or so ago I saw the window cleaner mentioned earlier. He was high up the side of a glass building on a slightly tilted platform. I'm pretty sure it was him. The point is that that was how I had once imagined him, no longer doing private houses – no longer working for himself but for some vast contractor who cleaned all the office windows in southern England. A number in an employment register now. If he ever did come to harm I would never know about it. Perhaps that's where our indifference comes from. Not just from not being able to do anything about it. But also from not knowing what difference it would make in the long term if we could. That couple going out into the world before settling down – provided the difference could be made up between what they had and what they needed. They had their differences all right, often needing more from each other than they had to give. I was able to tell myself very soon afterwards that I couldn't give a stuff about them. Guessing until the cows come home and never knowing. What difference could they possibly make to me?

'It's the same difference,' my mother used to say, usually with reference to people who had more than they needed. It wasn't a matter of degree. The differences that counted were among those who had less than they needed. She never minded my father giving credit to those who were hard up; and sometimes she told him a debt should be written off and the debtor, usually a single woman with several children, should be given a chance to start all over again. It would make all the difference to her life, she said, all the difference in the world. My father always seemed grateful for her approval in this respect since it was rare in others. Whatever generosity there is in me I suppose I learnt from them.

As I turned the key in my door, I remembered my father again. He lay in his hospital bed with about two weeks left to live. I do not think I have tried to record this before. We hardly spoke. Most of the time his eyes were closed and when he opened them they seemed to be searching mine for answers. Thinking he had fallen asleep I got up to go but, his eyes still closed, he gripped my hand and mumbled that he hoped I'd make something of my life, not that he'd set much of an example in that direction. I shook my head and told him I couldn't have wished for better parents. He opened his eyes. It was her idea calling you Thomas, he whispered, said she didn't want you taken in by any nonsense and there were precious few things in the world that weren't. 'I don't doubt that for a moment,' I said, understanding for the first time why she alone never called me Tom. He closed his eyes and began breathing deeply. I thought I detected a slight nod and a smile. This comes back to me so vividly now after all these years. I do not know why until that moment – turning the key in my own front door – I had forgotten it. Few things should be more memorable than how one came by one's name. Since then have I unconsciously tried to live up to it or live it down? Either way, I very much doubt it. No, I think I have wanted to forget that my father believed he had set me a poor example, that he did not believe I could not have wished for better parents – it was just something I felt I had to say. Had I failed at the last to bring him any solace or reassurance, which by any reckoning he deserved no less than anyone? I do not think like this about my mother. She needed no reassurance or comfort. Life had to end some time. She'd been luckier than many. No point in looking back. No need to make a fuss. That was one thing I should be in no doubt about at all . . .

It was some three weeks ago that I saw Phil Badgecock again. I was repairing my garden gate one afternoon when he came past. Though he wasn't slowing down, some kind of greeting was inescapable. Surprisingly he stopped.

'Didn't reckon you were the handyman type, professor. My gate's a bit rocky. Fix that too any time you like.'

He was evidently still in good spirits and wasn't in any hurry to move on. He had something to tell me.

'You seem in jolly mood these days, Mr Badgecock. Completed your collection of Famous Cricketers?'

'Oh no, did that long ago. You're on totally the wrong track there, professor.'

'The Lottery? The pools?'

'A long shot better than that . . .' He leant towards me across the wall. 'You'd like to know?'

'I would.'

'Told you she went off with that van driver, didn't I?'

I nodded, though for a moment I had no idea who he was talking about.

'Well, just you listen to this. Had a letter from her the other day, saying she couldn't stand it a moment longer. He was a complete and utter shit, always had been, and now the children had grown up she'd left him. "I think I made a big mistake, Phil." That's what she wrote. Bloody marvellous news that was.'

'Wasn't it all rather a long time ago?'

'Oh no, it's only nearly thirty-three and a half years. I warned her. I bloody warned her. I might be boring, I told her, but he's one of your Flash Harrys. But she wouldn't listen. She wishes she'd listened now, oh yes.'

'How did she find your address? After all this time?'

'That's the beauty of it. She'd only found out what town I'd retired to. It only took them two days to do the rest.'

'Have you answered it?'

He shook his head vigorously. 'No, professor, I certainly haven't if you must know. I had to stew for close on thirty-five years. It's her turn now.'

'People change though, don't they? They make mistakes, regret them, want a second chance, all that sort of thing.'

'I take your point of view, professor. Very wise and intellectual. But there's what you might call a bit of a snag.'

'What's that?'

'In nearly thirty-five years I've come to hate her guts. So I'm boring, am I? That's what I've lived with. Asking myself that question every bloody morning in the mirror. Every single bloody morning. And that was only for starters.'

'She might not find you boring now?'

'I'm more boring now than I was then. Stands to reason. Not working. She's not going to find that out, I can tell you that.'

'I see.'

'I thought you would in the end,' he replied, then walked briskly away.

He began whistling 'If you were the only girl in the world . . .' Their song once perhaps. He was a contented man. Perhaps I could add 'at last'. All those years eaten up by a wrong, imagining a jaunty man in a red van dashing about delivering parcels, returning to a loving wife and a life together which wasn't boring in the least. Day in day out. Now he could stop picturing that. He was getting his own back. He was in charge now. His imagination had been set free for that. Who was the master now? He was going to enjoy every minute of it, for the rest of his life. Imagining her misery. Something a lot worse than boredom. Thus may a man's inner life, his life itself, be utterly changed by a little accident of fate, a letter out of the blue. I pictured him reading it, then waving the envelope in the air and shouting to his unknown colleague. 'Well sorted, old chap!'

The first of November. I bumped into Bridget again at the bus stop, so we had a little compulsory time together. She'd already told me that she'd spent the summer with her parents in Scarborough and that her friends had abandoned her. We'd been standing outside her house when the man in short trousers came out of the house opposite. I hadn't seen him for a long time and had assumed he'd moved on or been locked up again. He was carrying a leather bag and was looking unusually smart. His dark grey trousers were the right length, his black shoes glinted in the sunlight, his tie was of the club variety and his green check jacket looked new. The oddest thing was that Bridget waved at him and he waved back with an everyday sort of smile.

'Morning, Mr Fogarty,' she'd called out.

'Morning, Bridget,' he replied with a surprisingly deep voice, raising the bag at her. His accent had been Irish.

I asked her now if she'd found anyone to share her lodgings yet. She shook her head. Her sun-tan had faded, leaving her even paler than before. She looked very weary, even of life itself. I was feeling pretty wan myself, my doctor having told me the day before with an expression of foreboding that I really ought to have another checkup. Since I'd have to wait 'upwards of four months' for that he prescribed some new pills to tide me over. My mind was more on all that than on Bridget. We need only the smallest excuse to think first and last about ourselves. And all points in between. Not even room for thoughts about God or any of that palaver. So it was with hardly any part of my active mind that I asked her, 'Another trip to Scarborough called for? Bask in the sun up there for a week or two.'

She looked away down the hill where no bus was arriving.

I tried again. 'Be going back there for Christmas, I expect, the new millennium?'

She nodded and her lips tightened.

'That'll be nice.'

'No, it won't actually.'

'Oh.'

'I took a place down here to get as far away from them as possible. I could have gone to Leeds. They don't know that.'

'Oh, I'm sorry.'

'You needn't be.'

It was only now she looked at me. Her skin had a stretched look. You could see where in later years all the lines would be, how pinched up her thin lips would become. I let her continue.

'They think I'm going to become someone important on the telly. When the credits roll they want to be able to say, "That's our daughter".'

'Not a lot wrong with that, is there?'

'They go on at me. Non-stop. All my bloody childhood. Have I done this? Have I done that? What's the use of this? What's the point of that? Am I trying hard enough? If I want to make something of myself . . . They wish they'd had the chances I'd had. Nothing happened, absolutely nothing, without an inquisition. And now it's have I got my name down for the BBC and ITV and Channel 4? I've got to get a good degree to get an interview. They're looking to me, they say. To make a real success of my life. They hope I'm not getting mixed up in all that student rubbish they read about. They haven't scrimped and saved to have me drinking and drugging it all away and going on demos.'

I saw her at the other side of a table being interviewed. The job would go to someone else. Yet again. She was going to let her parents down. I couldn't tell her that what they felt was love of a kind. They wanted her to be happy and successful. They wanted her to be successful so they could be happy. How far do we, can we, love people for their sakes and not for our own? One can get stuck for ever in that misery-go-round. She looked away from me and this time a bus was turning the corner. There was nothing sensible or helpful I could say. She stood up.

'Sorry,' she said.

'Well, if you carry on doing well on your course I'm sure that one day you'll make them very proud of you.'

'Actually, I'm not doing well at all. I can't seem to get on with the others. They're so full of themselves. I'm thinking of dropping out, doing something else, something useful.'

'Well, whatever you decide, I'm sure . . .'

The bus arrived and we got on to it. It was already fairly full so we could only get seats next to each other across the aisle. I was glad I hadn't finished my sentence for I was sure of nothing about her.

'Hope you soon find people to share the house with. Those other friends of yours seemed pretty nice to me.'

'Until I stopped them playing loud music in the evenings. I said we should be considerate to our neighbours.'

'What did they say to that?'

'"Crappy neighbours. That's their problem." And so forth. I also liked keeping the place a bit tidy, not dump garbage outside until the rubbish men came. Wash the dishes. Clean the bath. Hoover the carpet. You name it. They called me Goody Two-Shoes.'

'Crappy eh? Ouch! Well, that puts us in our place.'

'They thought you were behind it actually. Seen us talking. Called you "that stupid old gasbag".'

'Do you think you should have told me that?'

'Why ever not? I don't think you are. Who gives a toss what they think?'

'Bridget, you ought to know, I'm not a professor.'

At last she smiled. 'Of course you're not. I knew that.'

'Did they?'

'You were just a laugh to them. You're being a professor made it even funnier.'

I rocked back and forth, my mouth wide open. 'Ho ho ho ho ho.'

She got the giggles, or began to until people stared at us. We fell silent and did not speak again until I got off at the public library.

'Good luck,' I said. 'My advice is: whatever you do, stick to it.'

She gave me an exaggerated salute. 'Yes, professor.'

Then I began worrying again about my heart, my life itself.

The only other event worth recording in the last weeks before the millennium is that Mrs Hirst is going to spend it with her son in Australia. She was very pleased indeed about this. His wife had forgiven her or rather there were twins to be taken off her hands 'not to give her the benefit of the doubt'.

Her eyes widened as far as they could. Then she bared as many of

611

her teeth as possible. Together these had the effect of darkening a complexion already quite heavily rouged.

'I think I could get to like her in time.'

'How much time, that's the question?'

'The first five or ten minutes, let's say, I don't think.'

'Well, not years anyway.'

'I'll just have to count up to a hundred, won't I? I mean, when she gets to me.'

She was sizing me up as if she'd heard something disreputable about me. Extraordinary that I didn't cotton on sooner. As I waited for the question and thought up the first two or three of my excuses, Mr Fogarty came out of the house opposite and Mrs Hirst waved at him. I waited for the gossip.

'That nice Mr Fogarty,' she said. 'He's going to look after my precious pussies for me. He loves cats, he says.'

'But, Mrs Hirst, I would have been glad . . .'

The eyes widened but not so far this time. She gave my arm a squeeze.

'Get along with you. That's very kind, I'm sure. But that face you make when you bring the little darlings back. They're not exactly your favourite things, are they? Cats.'

'Oh, I wouldn't say that exactly. I . . .'

'Anyway, with his experience running a cattery near Leamington Spa he said.'

'But they do know me.'

'They do that all right. But I've never heard of someone asking a professor to look after their cats.'

'Come to think of it, nor have I.'

She was already on her way. The cats would be in and out just the same, I told myself. And I'd be just as nice to them as I'd always been. I do wish, though, she'd asked me first. I'd have said I was very sorry, I'd have loved to, but I'd be away a lot – hinting, perhaps, at a research trip to Nova Scotia to update my work on the Micmac. Knowing what I did now I'd have said of course I'd be delighted to. Being kind is like that, being jolly glad we only seldom have to be. It would be a kindness if . . . Sure it would be. If.

I see I haven't followed up that poem Adrian told me about, which had saddened Jane. The air that kills comes from a far country of blue remembered hills and spires and farms. It is a land of lost content, of happy highways where the poet went and ne'er will come again. My own childhood was spent in the inner suburb of a large industrial town in the Midlands. No happy highways there. Not unhappy either. Just boring, unmemorable.

Occasionally, though, we went out into the country and looked at views like that – the smoke drifting up from the farmsteads, the churches and hills in the distance. I could see that remembering all that, the vanished happiness of it, could easily take over from everything else. And could become deadly. Anyway, it's a very lovely poem. The opposite of deadly.

What I suddenly remember now is my father sitting at the side of the road, his chin resting on his knees as he gazed out over the landscape. Once he said, 'You've got to admit it's beautiful. Lifts the spirits.'

My mother, who had been gazing at it too, though standing up, replied, 'Only because you're here, not there.'

'That's neither here nor there. It's still beautiful,' my father said.

He looked up at her with a smile, a broad one for him, and she nodded down at him in acknowledgement, almost with pride I might then have thought. It was so rare. I do not know how old I was. Six? Seven? But I remember it so clearly now. It was the only time I heard him play with words. After that they stared at the landscape for what seemed a long time. I did too. Not because at that age one cares about scenery. I was simply happy. It was something we were doing together. The same thing. As if our lives had been lived towards that moment. It was the point of them. Something like that.

Chapter Eleven

I saw John Brown again about three weeks before Christmas. He was coming out of the Connaught as I was going in.

'Can't stop,' he said.

I put a hand on his arm: 'Oh come along. A quick one. You can't leave me alone with the barmaid. You know that. Couldn't keep her hands off me on my own.'

On our way to the recess I ordered a whisky for myself and he said he'd just have a Coke with plenty of ice. There was no sign that he'd already had one too many so I couldn't help raising my eyebrows. He wasn't wearing his dark glasses and there was something in his pale eyes I hadn't seen before: a shyness or guardedness, diffidence even. Then he sank back into the red gloom and I couldn't be sure.

'Since you didn't ask,' he said, 'I think, I *think*, we may be on to something. There's this clinic in London, a new drug. Fucking expensive. But half way there, slightly over half. Takes less to get her pissed though. Longer gaps in between. Two hours less sleep. I don't know. We've been to the flicks, out for dinner, drives up the coast, things like that . . .'

He was beginning to talk too fast in his excitement when the barmaid came - another new one. Young, blonde, shapely, lovely smile - lips, teeth, green eyes uniquely unimprovable upon. The usual, in short. Standard, but setting it too. When she leant forwards to put our drinks on the table, her breasts, or one of them, brushed my shoulder. Brown saw that very clearly, the expression on my face too.

'I see,' he said. 'Good thing I was here. How right you were. She was just telling me she couldn't wait for that dashing bounder Tom Ripple to come in again.'

I made a shocked face as if blowing up a balloon with great difficulty.

'All right. All right. All right,' he went on, then stopped abruptly, hunching his shoulders, closing his eyes and lifting his head as if summoning the last of his strength. I was sorry he'd been interrupted and waited for him to continue. Equally suddenly he relaxed again and smiled. There might have been a mist of tears in his eyes but they were so pale it was difficult to tell. There was a pause while we drank together.

'That's it really. The lad's coming down for Christmas. You're not a church-going kind of chap are you by any chance?'

'No, not really. Apart from going into churches from time to time. That sort. I like that a lot. The words and music.'

'Nor me. Never mind. Just say a prayer anyway. It'd be a paradise on earth. I'd settle for that. You can stuff your eternity. The here and now. A few remaining years of that. Jesus! Couldn't begin to tell you how lovely she was. Suddenly some days now it's like she comes into the room and smiles as if to say she's sorry she stayed away so long, she'd been held up . . .'

He leant forwards into the light, staring hard at me, as if something was seriously my fault. It was almost a look of fury but the mist was still there in his eyes.

'Yes of course I will. I know what you mean. I think it's, well, wonderful . . .'

He put a hand on my knee and squeezed it hard. 'You do that, old mate, you pray for us.'

Then he suddenly got up and left, having a word with the barmaid on the way out. She brought me a dish of peanuts, wearing a solemn expression.

'Sorry,' she said. 'Your friend said I should say sorry I'd overlooked your nuts.'

I giggled but as briefly as it is possible to do that, her face remaining, entirely dutiful and/or apologetic. The giggle might have been taken for throat difficulty common in people of my age. This time her breasts when she leant forwards were a very long way away from my shoulder indeed.

'Those were his very words,' she said as she left. And then did smile with a swift wrinkle of her nose.

I let out a yell which no one else heard.

I had a nice surprise three days before Christmas - a letter from Agnes.

My dear old chum, or whatever you limeys call each other these days. Just had to write to you. Was over your side of the pond a month ago to see Susie (do you remember her?) and my lovely grandchildren and we took a day off to visit our darling little village and see the house again. It was a mistake, I guess, bringing the Colonel to mind as it did, seeing him there digging away in his beloved garden and the rest of it. The church seemed all right with some new roof beams and roof-tiles. The Jenners' house is now a small family hotel. Your cottage unchanged but the garden has been extensively developed - I'd say improved but it would hurt your feelings terribly. I had a good look for signs of some of the cuttings I so generously gave you but couldn't see any. Complete waste if you ask me. Up the road they've built a little colony of new houses. Ghastly. It was Susie who said I should write to you. She remembers meeting you after the old boy died and you chatted so normally. You talked a bit about your family and that helped for some reason. The Colonel said you were a bit of a joker and after you phoned towards the end he said we ought to have got to know you better. I've remained single. Lonely. Very, sometimes. But haven't met anyone who comes within a thousand miles of him. Whatever's happened to all the laughers in the world? He said I should find someone to look after me pretty damn quick. I just miss him all the time. It's as simple as that. He'd have been so proud of Susie and her children. I can't stop myself picturing him playing with them in the garden when they were little. Must stop all that. This was supposed to be a cheerful letter. They were good days. Funny too. Do you remember the Jenners' carpet? Anyway, you're part of those memories whether you like it or not.

Fondest best wishes,
Agnes.

I replied almost at once at about the same length. I told her where I was living, what had become of my children and about Adrian's bereavement. I said that I certainly remembered Susie and what a lovely person I'd thought her - not spelling out just how lovely. I said she'd been damned rude about my garden and it was typical of how tactless and unperceptive Americans were. I said I missed her and the Colonel, that it was perfectly apparent how much in love they were and not all that hard to guess why, that it had been a good time in my life too. Finally I said that getting her letter was the most wonderful surprise, and that being reminded of times past was the kind of mistake for which it was sometimes worth paying the price.

The following day Annelise's card arrived. In it she wrote: '*Much as before, millennium or no millennium. The child still doesn't come. If it's a girl I'll make sure she doesn't become a ballerina if she wants to have children. Joke. Still teaching. Still at same flat in same street. Michelle has married a millionaire and lives in New York. Wow! Lots of love from Annelise.*'

I spent Christmas on my own. Adrian said that Jane's parents wanted me very much to join them. It was the third time I'd refused their invitation. He said it might cheer them all up a bit. But for us all, surely, the more cheering up went on the more one would be reminded of what it was aimed to be the opposite of? Also, I would be an outsider at an occasion of the most intense privacy - altering the things they might or might not have said in my absence. That sounds considerate but I see now that it was not. I can hear the disappointment in Adrian's voice. They wanted me there. They wanted normality, light-heartedness, the little Christmas rituals, the constancy of tradition, the funny hats and solemn music. They wanted to be kind and hospitable and provide good food and drink to outsiders. They wanted what Jane would have wanted. To give pleasure to each other and to all there present. When we say we should consider the feelings of others, it is our own we are usually considering - feeling good about our considerateness being uppermost amongst them. Being saved effort and embarrassment and going to trouble and putting oneself out are in there too. I should have gone. I would have enjoyed it. It would have done me good. I hope they invite me again next year. For my sake.

Both Virginia and Adrian phoned me. Virginia sounded quite cheerful for a change. I really did seem to have chosen the right gifts for the children; they hadn't yet been broken or cast aside and it was already six o'clock. She was less ebullient about the books I sent them, not the books themselves but whether they'd ever get round to reading them. The miniature imitation Ming vase and silver nutmeg-grater were much appreciated. More to the point though was that after Christmas Richard would be starting a new job doing the accounts at a large gardening centre, ordering plants and the rest of it. I said I'd heard of talking to them but wasn't telling them what to do overdoing it a bit? Surely even Prince Charles didn't go as far as that? She laughed and repeated the comment to Richard in the background. I heard him say something to her which took a long time. 'Richard said, do you remember? First a tractor then fertilizer? He'd been a bit slow on the uptake on that one, he said, but had used it quite often among his customers and colleagues. Ordering plants would come in handy with his new workmates. He says, thanks a lot Dad.'

There was a sigh in her voice. Undeterred, I said: 'Tell him to pay up promptly, not to sit on the cacti.'

'Oh Dad! Do you remember when you took us out after you and Mum split up? Your trying to cheer us up with jokes. And then in the hospital. It was so awful.'

'The jokes weren't that bad, were they?'

'Not the jokes so much. I mean . . .'

'I know what you mean.'

As soon as we'd hung up, I wondered if there were other reasons why Richard has lost all those jobs - other, that is, than telling the same joke over and over again and the humourless laughter that went with it. There ought to be a number of puns to be obtained from the gardening centre business. Perhaps I should think up a new one each week and phone it through to him. Richard joined John Brown that evening in my prayers.

Three days before Christmas I saw Mrs Hirst carrying her suitcases out to a taxi and went to help.

'I'm not sure I want to do this, professor. That woman . . . But I love my son, that's the problem.'

'You'll have a lovely time,' I said. 'Think of those beaches.'

'Think of them there while I look after the children more like it.'

'If you don't like it you can always come back.'

'Don't know about always. Won't be going again.'

As I opened the taxi door for her, I asked: 'Forgot to ask, Mrs H. Whatever happened to that trendy vicar of yours? Still wandering around the Holy Land in sackcloth and ashes?'

'Oh, I wish I had the time. He's settled in Hastings and she's gone to live with him. Unholy mess he's landed in more like it. Don't know about sackcloth. He's certainly made a right old hash of it, that's all I know. He's going to be defrocked, that's what they say.'

The taxi-driver looked at his watch and began hitting his steering-wheel. 'Seems only right after the things he's been doing to her.'

She smiled, then became suddenly thoughtful. 'I'd love to have gone to the midnight service again. Christmas won't be the same. All that sunlight and naked bodies if you know what I mean.'

I closed the door and she wound down the window. She laughed, 'If we get a woman, she'd have to be de-trousered, wouldn't she?'

I pondered this. 'I'll have to look into that,' I said. 'Let you know.'

'It was only a joke,' she replied.

I raised my hand. 'But it wouldn't be, would it? Anyway, God bless, have a lovely time. Send us a postcard. I'll keep an eye on your monsters.'

She fluttered her fingers at me. 'They're not as bad as all that,' she said as she wound up her window.

I waved until she was out of sight. It was quite sad.

So I spent Christmas on my own. Or not quite. At midday, there was a knock on the door and Rosie was there with her children. Their arms were outstretched to hand me gifts in red wrapping paper. Rosie was holding an iced cake with 'Happy Christmas!' inscribed on it. I stood back to let them in. 'We won't stop,' she said.

I took the gifts. I hadn't even sent her a card. 'Oh Rosie, you're very kind.'

'Seeing as how you were all on your own,' she said.

She had a lot of make-up on. I wondered if she wanted to hide from me all the sorrow and exhaustion which lay behind it. I wished her a happy Christmas all the same.

'The kids would like their Dad to be there. They wouldn't if they knew how pissed he was. My brother's been very good. They've had a few presents and stuff.'

'Sure you won't come in for a moment.'

'Must be off. We've got a nice leg of lamb. Doesn't seem any point in turkey and all that palaver with just us.'

'I've settled for a sprig of holly on my Cumberland pie.'

She was beginning to turn and did not smile. Her mind was else-where. Imagining Christmas as it might have been, or one a long time ago in her own childhood. Anywhere but here and now.

'Thank you so much, Rosie. You really shouldn't have.'

'Oh yes I should,' she replied.

The children had given me a packet of Hamlet cigars, a bar of Belgian chocolate and three handkerchiefs with the letter 'T' embroidered on them. The cake was dense with fruit and it was weeks before I could bring myself to cut it open. I had given them nothing. They had surely expected something in return. The children I mean. Another of the day's disappointments. Simply a pound coin each would have gone a very long way indeed. A fiver would have raised them up to the gates of paradise. God rest ye merry, gentlemen. Let nothing you dismay.

That evening I walked up the street. There was an elaborate array of coloured lights in the electrician's window and a single loop across the window of the Tomkinses. On their window-sill was a very small Christmas tree with a star on top of it. They were standing either side of it, looking out at their garden, discussing no doubt what they would be doing to it when spring came. Winter for them, with Christmas at the heart of it, was perhaps simply a time to take a rest along with nature and all its various flowering and foliage. He would give her a few packets of seeds and a bulb or two. She would give him a new trowel or stone animal. I waved at them but they could not see me. There was a huge wreath thing hanging on the Felixes' front door. The Patels had hung a smaller one on theirs. Out of respect for the customs of the people they had come to live among, perhaps. Their curtains were drawn so I did not know if they had put up any coloured lights. There were lights too in other people's houses round and about. Nothing too elaborate or showy. There was nothing in Mr Fogarty's window. I had not yet seen him come in to feed Mrs Hirst's cats.

I returned to my Cumberland pie and Christmas music on the radio. Afterwards I lit one of the Hamlet cigars and poured a glass of brandy. Before I opened my novel, the third in the Anthony Powell series, I began to have a sad thought or two about Christmases past when I was a boy, when my children were young, about those who had peopled my life and how they would be spending their Christmas. I even had a kind thought for Plaskett in that procession. But it did not last long. For I found myself unable to dwell on all that Christmas wistfulness. Instead I ended up wondering about the defrocked vicar and the organist's wife in a bed-sit in Hastings - people I had never met and never would. I was trying to imagine them. They might be having a lovely time in bed. Or he might be missing his vocation - presiding over a Christmas service, while she hankered after the sound of an organ. They might be laughing a lot, their love for each other being quite sufficient. Or sitting there asking themselves what on earth they had done and asking God's forgiveness. And so on ad libitum. Perhaps the imagination is there to release us from memory, from ourselves. The imagination takes flight, as the saying goes, and we grab hold of it. I really can't think what it is for otherwise, the pursuit of alternative worlds. How should I know? I went gratefully back to Mr Powell's but each time I put the book down that couple in Hastings returned until I heard myself say: 'They had it coming and serve them bloody well right.' It wasn't my voice speaking but that of a senior member of the congregation. I'd formed a judgement about them, though I didn't agree with it for more than a second or two. Another voice said; 'It is the triumph of passion and jolly good luck to them.' Then a number of other notions took over, one after the other, proliferating out to all men and women everywhere involved to some degree or another in the infidelity business, that is to say all men and women everywhere. The imagination does seem to release one from a sense of right and wrong. There is too much curiosity, too little discrimination, in it. It cannot be curbed because the question then leaps up: ah, curbed from imagining what, I can't help wondering? I slept well that night, thinking up scenes of dalliance featuring a vicar and an organist's wife pulling out all the stops, while the organist was doing that too some way away. That was how my Christmas ended.

And so to the arrival of the millennium. I arrived at the Felixes at about a quarter past ten. Mrs Felix welcomed me with open arms. Her mouth was widely open too as if stopped in the middle of bellowing out some rowdy carol. 'Ah, the great man himself! Ring out the old, ring in the new, what?' Cedric Felix appeared, swaying either side of her. His smile was distinctly one-sided and one of his eyes was half-shut, as if he had been in the process of bringing his face under control, or losing control of it. Their being evidently quite drunk could go either way. Mrs Felix ushered me in with an exaggerated sweep of her arm and introduced me, the arm still raised, to a Sheila and Shimon Something, and a Roddy and Roddy Wawawereminnihaha.

'Tim Ripple at the House too, Roddy,' Mr Felix said, handing me a glass of something pale pink with froth and fruit lying about on the top of it. 'You two should have a lot to talk about.'

The woman beside put out her hand; 'Rhoda Warmington. Roddy loves talking *endlessly* about his Oxford days, don't you, Roddy?'

She was completely sober, making it clear that there was nothing she had loved less for the past half-century or more. Her smile, though, made it equally clear she had jolly well better have got used to it. In her accent there was more than a trace of my part of the world. Roddy seemed sober too to judge from his frown and the thorough scrutiny he was giving me. The other couple were listening in until Felix said loudly: 'Never met a soul who was up with me at Oriel. Come and look at this . . .'

Mrs Felix's mouth was as wide open as it had been when she greeted me. Then Roddy suffered a paroxysm, striking my arm and slapping my shoulder with an expression on his face of someone who had been goosed - shock followed by delight.

'My God! I remember you! Changed a bit though. Haven't we all? Rowing man if I remember rightly or was it squash? Bit of a cricketer myself. Wasn't it you who parked that motor-bike on high table one night? Making a point about the meadow, wasn't it? We got some drinking done, by Jingo. And then, you swine, you went and bloody grabbed a first.'

Mrs Felix was looking at me with pride, while Mrs Warmington might just as well have been saying very loudly; 'Here we bloody go again.'

'So what did you get up to in life, Tim old thing? Shipley. Well, fancy bumping into you again.'

I said I'd gone to Canada, drifted into anthropology, speaking in an accent like Mrs Warmington's, believing this might help to make it clear I wasn't much for reminiscence either. Roddy took me by the elbow to the corner of the room. 'Mustn't bore the others, must we?' he muttered.

Mr Felix joined us for long enough to fill our glasses. 'You House lot. No stopping you.'

Then he began, slapping my shoulder again. 'Good old Shipley. Quite an athlete. Rugger too, as I recall. Do you remember . . . ?'

And so it went on. I only had to nod. Invent the odd episode such as the day Jenkinson fell in the river when he was out in a punt with Crayshaw's sister, that odd fellow with ginger hair who was thought actually to be reading books, that day in the quad old

Smithers stopped a complete stranger and asked where he, Smithers, was supposed to be going. He nodded but wasn't really listening, remembering names one after the other and saying; 'Wonder what happened to . . . ?' Mrs Felix came and went to listen in while Mrs Warmington joined the others to look at what seemed to be a book about carpets. There seemed to be more of them than I remembered from my previous visit, several of them on the walls. The couple nodded, pointing from time to time at a design perhaps. It was difficult to tell how bored they were. Just as I was thinking that, Mrs Warmington tugged her husband's elbow and said, 'Can't you see, Roddy, Mr Shipley's bored out of his mind.'

'He isn't, are you, Tim? Nothing wrong with talking about old times, is there?'

I shook my head. 'Not at all.'

'Except that it's old people doing the talking,' she muttered.

Though she was smiling, a bicker seemed to be in the offing so I went over to where the carpet discussion was going on. There was nowhere else I could go. Cedric Felix was holding a very large coffee-table book about carpets and rugs, turning the pages to make comparisons with the patterns and colours of the carpets illustrated there and those on his floor and walls. Mr and Mrs Something were nodding and saying 'how very interesting', their tone of voice sounding as it would if they'd been saying 'how extremely uninteresting'.

'Here comes the expert,' said Mrs Felix with a sort of abridged whoop.

'I wouldn't quite say that,' I muttered going behind Mr Felix so that I could look over his shoulder and remain fairly unobtrusive.

He pointed at a zig-zag and some concentric squiggles on the page and indicated their similarity with a pattern on a carpet on the wall.

'You see how it has flattened,' he said. 'And then that splendid curlicue motif. And here . . .' He turned the page eagerly to find another similarity. 'Of course the Afghan hill tribes didn't always . . .' he began. 'Or not all of them.'

Mr and Mrs Something were making no comment at all, nor asking any questions. At the other side of the room the Warmingtons were deep in conversation, probably about enjoying and not enjoying the company of old university chums.

'You were saying about the different Himalayan tribes, Tom if I may . . .' Mrs Felix was saying.

There was a silence while the Somethings and Mr Felix looked at me very enquiringly indeed.

'Not my field exactly,' I said, sipping my punch or rather getting a nostril full of mint. 'The Cree, Blackfoot, Stony Squaw, Micmac of course, they're another matter. But interesting parallels. Do we have . . . ?'

Mr Felix was obligingly turning the pages through the Afghan to the Himalayan section.

'There we are, you see,' I said pointing at random. 'That disguised protuberance. Evidently phallic but tentative, I'd say, and the further north . . . Among the Blackfoot you wouldn't get the squiggles so close, the semblance of water and that dark cavity.'

I looked around the walls and pointed at one carpet or rug at random. 'I thought so. You see the way the lines break there and there. It is not uncertainty of design, but deliberate omission. There is a comparative study . . .'

I was saved from having to keep this up by the arrival of the Warmingtons. 'Saw you two chewing the rag,' Mrs Felix said. 'You House people. Reckon you're the salt of the earth.'

'Oh I wouldn't say that,' Mr Warmington muttered.

'Or at any rate not again this evening,' his wife added, but with some jocularity, so that her husband sniggered.

'Seemed to have a lot of friends in common, 'Mrs Felix said.

'Oh my yes, old Tim Shipley and I . . . Wouldn't have recognized him. Could have sworn he was dead. Rowing man, you know. Was a bit of a cricketer myself . . .'

Mr Felix was mercifully putting the book down, saying with what sounded like irritation that his discourse on carpets had been interrupted.

'All right, Cedric,' Mrs Felix said. 'Another time. Enough old times and carpets. What about drinkies?'

I was able now to move aside with the Somethings. They seemed glad about that too. In fact they seemed to have no idea why they were there at all. I longed to tell them that I'd been making it all up. We began discussing the Dome which was, is, a very good thing indeed – I mean, its being a topic about which there could be almost no disagreement, like English tennis or cricket. At the other side of the room, the carpet book had been brought out again. They seemed sober and I needed to cadge

624

a lift from them up to the beacon. I wished I knew a little more about them – the negative impression they gave was positively unnerving. Mrs Something had been saying it was a stupendous waste of money but without much conviction – this perhaps because she was chewing an olive. Simultaneously they put hands to their mouths, he to yawn, she to remove the stone. Then, simultaneously too, they looked at their watches. They were both very bored, not looking at me or at each other or anywhere in particular. The lines on their faces had a set look, caused by years of facial movement that had now altogether ceased. I wondered what they talked about when alone. I have often seen this: couples sitting together at restaurant tables and not saying a word other than to choose what they wanted to eat or drink. Not a single word. I have also seen old couples holding hands, but less often, much less often. But they all started the same: I love you, I cannot live without you, I will never tire of you until my dying day. A silence had fallen, which was better, I thought with a smile that quite passed them by, than having to endure close questioning about Asian carpets or Christ Church College, Oxford. Oops, here we go . . .

Mr Something's eyes drifted slowly down from the ceiling to stare into mine: 'You at Christ Church too, I gather?'

I smiled again - pursing my lips with a single nod. This time it was at her. Neither smiled back. She too was looking hard at me.

'Go to reunions, do you? Go back at all?'

This seemed like an opening, a way into a reflection on the cruelty and sadness etc. of life. 'No, not any longer, not for a long time. It's those that aren't there, isn't it? The ghosts . . . You know . . .'

There being no response, I added: 'My children rather teased me . . .'

They looked at each other as if for the first time in ages - as if they had seen enough there already, too often, continuously once. After a long pause it was he who replied:

'We know. We know all right . . .'

And she whispered, 'Ah! Reunions. If only . . .'

It was as if an invisible hand had brushed across their faces. The lines seemed to loosen and the bored emptiness in their eyes clouded over as if before tears. He abruptly shook his head and touched her wrist and the moment had passed. The subject had been changed but now there was not boredom in their eyes. It was an absence of life.

I asked if they would give me a lift up to the beacon. 'Sorry,' he said. 'Of course. Of course. Let's go now.'

'Of course,' she repeated.

As we made our way out, saying to the others we would see them up there, they were again not looking at each other. Mrs Felix waved to us from the doorway, calling out, 'I'll bring a bottle of bubbly. Two bottles of bubbly.'

They got in the front and I into the back. 'Silly woman,' Mr Something muttered.

We drove in silence for a long while. Finally she said, 'Interesting, your knowledge of carpets. Your field anthropology, I gather.' The question had simply been polite. They couldn't have cared less about what I'd done, who I was.

'Well yes in a manner of speaking. Carpets a bit of a hobby. Your-selves?'

They did not reply at first. Then he said, 'Hobbies. There's walking the dog. There's the garden. There's television.'

We drew up behind several cars at the foot of the path up the hill. Candles and torches intermittently lit up the big black mound of the beacon. Laughter and the sound of talking reached us. As I got out I heard them whispering and she said, 'On second thoughts we don't think we will.'

'Oh, I'm sorry,' I said foolishly.

'Auld Lang Syne and all that. It was nice to meet you. Good luck with the carpets.'

I leant down and they both looked round at me. It was as if they had forgotten who I was. I had an image of two dead people walking side by side through a meadow, a dog running ahead of them. They had nothing to say to each other. Everything had been said.

The man raised his hand. 'Couldn't face it. Sorry.'

They drove off. I hadn't even thanked them for the lift. Perhaps I shall never know anything more about them. Specifically, what their grief was, why their lives had long since ended. I shall not ask the Felixes. I do not want to know. A lost child is one of the likelihoods.

And so the millennium was to end – waving after a car with a Mr and Mrs Something-or-other in it, something or other having smothered the life out of them. They are everywhere. What can we know of others? What can we know of how they would have been if everything had turned out all right for them? There are walks through the woods. There is often a garden.

Chapter Twelve

About fifty people had assembled at the top of the hill. I wandered among them in the erratic torchlight, glimpsing people of all descriptions, some silent and wearing a reverential or bored expression, others talking in low voices, more loudly if to their children. A man wearing an anorak and gumboots was doing something round the base of the beacon. I'd expected a large iron receptacle full of logs but it was only a pile of old building timber and chunks of furniture. Chair and table legs stuck out of it and on top was what looked like a whole wardrobe.

'Why can't there be fireworks?' a small girl complained. 'Because they're dangerous,' her father said. 'I only want fireworks,' she replied. '*Why* can't we, Mummy?' About ten yards further on a man with a glass in his hand said, 'On the telly we could be seeing the millennium coming in all over the world.' The woman with him replied, 'Fireworks, fireworks and more fireworks. They're a complete waste of money if you want my frank opinion. I mean they're all the same, aren't they? One big burst, then nothing.' The man groaned. 'So you've often said. In the meantime where the sod's that bottle got to?'

There were other mutterings in the darkness, the words 'historic' and 'remember' being used more than once. Mainly people were silent, their uppermost thought perhaps that the occasion ought to be shared solemnly with their fellow beings. 'It's not every day, is it?' an old woman's voice murmured behind me. Further on was a tall woman wearing a very long white scarf with tassels and a black trilby hat. She stood apart so that when she spoke, each word clearly enunciated, it was to everyone or no one in particular. 'All that flashy Dome palaver and celebrities. That's not it, is it? It should be for ordinary folk like us. Local communities.' In front of her, a man with a bald head and a beard pressed a woman's head to his chest. 'Don't worry, my lovely,' he said. 'They'll show the high-lights tomorrow. They usually do.' A beam of torchlight flashed across her face. She was gazing up at him, enraptured. She seemed not much more than fourteen. When I reached my point of departure I found myself next to a man who seemed, like the woman with the trilby hat, to be there on his own. He nudged me and pointed at the bonfire. 'Bloody waste, I call it. Could have got a bob or two for that lot.' There had been no one I recognized. Soon the Felixes and Warmingtons would fetch up with their champagne. I dreaded that, their noisy conspicuousness of which I would become part.

Then I saw them. Mr Felix was holding a torch at the level of his chest, turning his face into a skull as if to scare away strangers. I went over, not meaning to stay long.

'Ah there you are, Tom,' said Mrs Felix. 'Where are Simon and Sheila?' She sounded sober now and unusually subdued.

'They . . . They thought better of it.'

'Really! What could be better than this, I'd like to know?'

Mr Felix whispered something which caused her to nod.

Mrs Warmington said, 'What a shame. They seemed so nice.'

Mr Warmington added, 'Used to know Simon quite well in the old days until . . . Decent sort of chap I always thought.'

'Come along, Cedric, better open the bubbly, the time you take. Both bottles.' Mrs Felix said this so loudly it might have been to let everyone know that there were at least some people present who knew how to celebrate.

I said I wanted to have a word with someone and left them. The man in the gumboots was herding people away from the bonfire with open arms, saying, 'Stand back! Stand back!'

Everyone fell silent as he returned to the beacon and walked round it, here and there striking a match and setting light to it. The flames flickered and spread, then began shooting up with sharp cracking and whooshing sounds until the whole beacon was burning steadily. A man cheered, only two women following his example. Then some-one shouted, 'Oh look!'

On the horizon a glow had appeared where the next beacon up the coast had been lit. There were more cheers then, people heart-ened, or wanting to be, by the thought of beacons flaring up around the land, a surge of fellowship girdling the nation, as Mrs Felix had put it. Wanting not to feel alone. A man pointed at the horizon in the other direction. 'No bloody beacon there, I see. It was in the local newspaper. Lack of interest, idle buggers.' 'Ssh, darling, the children!' his wife said.

I moved on to the other side of the bonfire, as far away from the Felixes as possible. Beside me a woman's voice said, 'Isn't it lovely? I'm so glad we came, aren't you, Arthur?'

'Wouldn't have missed it for the world.'

It was Mr Tomkins and his sister.

'Hallo there,' I said, bending forwards so that they could see who I was. 'Quite an occasion.'

'Oh *yes*,' Miss Tomkins said. 'It's so nice to see you again. We observe you passing, don't we, Arthur?' Her voice was slightly affected, the 'nice' almost 'naice'. But about the rest of her there was no affectation at all. Her smile was quite unfeigned, as if I was a long-lost friend, though I had never spoken to her before. That was a thought.

He leant forwards and raised a hand. 'We do that.' His smile was similar, delighted to see me.

She began talking quite fast, as if she'd been waiting for me. I had to lean down quite far to hear her.

'They used to have one every year at the Hall. A huge bonfire with sausage rolls and cake and punch and lemonade for the children. All the people from the village came. That and the fireworks. Then there was the accident and Her Ladyship said they should have a fête every year instead. Didn't they, Arthur?'

'People missed the bonfire. Some did.'

'What accident was that?'

'Little Molly Farthing it was. She got a burn all across her chest and round her chin. Her hands too. The Farthings, he was one of the milkmen, were very nice about it, weren't they, Arthur?'

'Said it could happen to anyone. His Lordship gave her a lovely new bicycle.'

'All her expenses too of course,' she added.

The beacon was now blazing away, the flames leaping up and throwing out sparks and the red heat at the centre turning white. The cracking sounds were less frequent and there was hardly any smoke. We had to step back a couple of paces because of the heat.

'You were one of the villagers, were you?'

'Oh *no!*' she said with a chuckle. 'Not us.' She chuckled again, this time on the brink of outright laughter.

629

Arthur Tomkins rubbed his hands. 'We worked at the Hall for thirty-five years, didn't we, Alice?'

'Summer and winter for almost thirty-six years it was.'

'The Hall?' I enquired.

'Wendlebury Hall. I expect you've heard of Wendlebury Hall?'

I vaguely had without having any idea why or where it was. 'Sort of. I . . .'

'The gardens are open to the public,' Mr Tomkins told me as if that was that.

His sister became animated. 'You ought to have heard of it if you haven't already. The gardens. Well, for me and Arthur they were open all the time. Summer and winter. Her Ladyship said we must go and enjoy them.' Here she spoke with great emphasis. 'Just whenever we felt like it. We mustn't hesitate. That's what she told us. More than once. Me only being the housekeeper and him what His Lordship called a general factotum. Whenever anything needed doing it was please Arthur, would you mind, wasn't it, Arthur?'

'Those gardens. Almost every evening, wandering about. Well, you couldn't have fairer than that.'

'So long as we kept out of eyeshot of the Hall,' she reminded him. 'Not interrupting the view, especially if they had guests.'

'Just wander about, even pick a peach if the fancy took us.'

'A sort of butler, were you?' I asked.

Alice Tomkins gave an even longer chuckle than before. 'Him a butler! They didn't hold with butlers or things like that. Gardeners of course and a cook and a maid and the ladies who came in. Like I said, they had to have a dogsbody.'

'General factotum is the correct expression for it,' he said earnestly. Then he began chuckling too. 'Imagine me at my size in one of those fancy jackets with tails.'

They fell silent then, watching the blaze and remembering bonfires at the Hall, little Molly Farthing too perhaps. You could tell from the way they had spoken how happy they had been. And now after all that they had made a perfect little garden of their own. There won't have been any little stone animals or garden gnomes at Wendlebury Hall, only large classical statues and fountains and herbaceous borders and avenues of shaped yew trees. I needed to know.

'Well, you've certainly made a pretty little garden of your own now,' I said.

They did not reply so I looked down at them. They were staring into the fire, as if spellbound by it. For all those years they had enjoyed one of the finest gardens in England as if it were their own. That was what they must be remembering – strolling about among shrubs and flowers and plucking peaches. Contented then, contented now. People with no envy in them. How rare is that?

She murmured something so I had to say 'Sorry, I didn't quite . . .'

'Something's better than nothing,' she said, as if suddenly cheered up. 'Paradise can come in all shapes and sizes. Can't it, Arthur?'

'So can hell, if you think about it,' he replied. 'But we wouldn't be knowing about that, would we, the lucky ones?'

Nothing was said after that and they were no longer smiling. So I took my leave of them.

'Happy New Year,' she said but did not wait for my reply. 'Come on now, Arthur, or you'll catch your death.'

They walked away into the darkness with a final wave. One of them lit a torch and the light darted about in front of them as if in search of something. A group at the other side of the beacon had begun to sing 'Auld Lang Syne'. Echoless in the winter air it sounded mocking and self-conscious. After the first verse it petered out and a man's voice shouted, 'Happy New Millennium everyone!' A mumbling followed as people began to drift away with a last look at the beacon, as if wondering if that was that. Behind me a familiar girl's voice said, 'When are the fireworks, Daddy?'

I went back to find the Felixes and the Warmingtons huddled together with champagne glasses in their hands as if in an act of self-commiseration.

'There you are, Tom,' Mr Felix said. 'Just in time.'

He handed me a glass and poured champagne into it. I raised the glass.

'A happy New Year!' I said.

They murmured it back at me. Mrs Felix had her eyes closed and was swaying slightly. I had dried up whatever they had been talking about. Me? We often wonder that. It is a rule that people think about us, let alone talk about us, a great deal less than we think they do. I would have left them then but needed a lift back. That was where the silence led. With no more to say about anything, the past or the future, the hopes, the regrets, or whatever else is summoned up by

631

new years, let alone new millennia, we made our way back to the cars. The singing had begun again behind us, with more gusto now but by the time we reached the car park the sound had ceased and it had begun to drizzle.

I drove back with the Warmingtons.

'A bit of a non-event that was,' he said after a while.

'What the hell did you expect?' she replied.

'Oh I don't know . . . one ought to take stock, I suppose.'

'You do, do you?'

We drove in silence, the fully fledged row having to await my absence. My mind drifted to Richard stocktaking, what disastrous pun he'd try to make out of that. I closed my eyes in prayer that he would not have an industrious colleague called Lizzy, another with ambition called Rose or, God help us all, that he wouldn't say his wife didn't like to ingratiate herself. So I was unprepared for what Mr Warmington said next.

'Sorry, Eric, wasn't it . . . ?'

'Tom.'

He shook his head as if after a swim. 'I was sure it was Eric Shipley. I was equally bloody sure he came to a sticky end in Morocco.'

'Sure you're right on both counts. Didn't know him myself.'

'But I thought . . .'

Mercifully, the impending row had been brewing up in Mrs Warmington's mind. 'Not more bloody reminiscences about bloody Oxford.' she said. 'Now there's a resolution for the new millennium.'

He did not seem to hear this, the tone of voice all too familiar in the last millennium. 'I could have sworn you said you . . .' He looked over his shoulder at me.

'For God's sake watch where you're going . . . darling,' she said, the dots indicating an afterthought – so long after that it might have been the start of something altogether different and more apt to a resolute new start in life.

There was a long pause while I assumed they, or rather he, awaited my reply. Then he said, 'Poor old Simon. Had everything going for him. Bloody clever, nice with it.'

'Poor Sheila too.'

'Of course, I only meant . . .'

She leant towards him and put a hand on his thigh. 'I know what you meant, darling. Isn't that the way to begin? What we've been spared.'

He put her hand on his as we drew up at the Felixes, who had arrived just before us.

'You're right, as always,' he said as we got out of the car. 'Eric Shipley. I could have sworn . . .'

'Almost always,' she replied.

'One for the road,' Mrs Felix called out from her front door. Mr Felix was bending down trying to fit his key into the lock. She slapped him hard on the back and said without lowering her voice, 'Oh do get a move on, you old fuddy-duddy.' Then, even louder, 'Another bottle of bubbly in the refrigerator' – this last word having to be guessed.

I expressed my thanks and left the four of them on the doorstep. When I turned round they were staring after me – except for Mr Felix, who still seemed to be trying to fit the door-key into the lock. Little doubt about what might be discussed over the bubbly. Ripple? What sort of a name is that? Rum bloke. Professor? Knew a bit about carpets. Canada too for that matter. All a bit fishy if you ask me . . . and so forth until Mrs Warmington might yawn and whisper to her husband, 'What the sod does it matter?'

Or none of this. I've remarked above that as a general rule people talk/think about us a great deal less than we imagine they do. If they did, and we worried even more than we do already about what they thought/said about us, wouldn't it make us that much, that is to say a great deal, nicer, wanting to be spoken/thought well of being the primary source of social virtue? So the more we wanted that, how very much more virtuous we would all then become. Except that there can't be much virtue in believing that other people are thinking/talking about you more than they are, leaving that much less time and inclination to devote to other things, such as how to become more virtuous – while at the same time trying not to become less that, the less we believed other people were thinking/talking about us. Thus, as often, one comes full circle. A vicious circle it's sometimes called. However, at least one is applying one's mind to it and there must be some virtue in that, I don't care what anyone says or thinks.

Adrian, Virginia and my former wife phoned the next day. I suspected that Adrian had not seen the New Year in and we did not ask each other about that, the word 'happy' having to be avoided. He told me that his company was sending him to New York to head up the office there for a while. It is a big company. I cannot guess how rich he must be. He'd spoken to Virginia and told me again how worried he was he couldn't give her money. He'd vaguely suggested it but she'd said pretty sharply that with Richard's new job they could manage perfectly well. 'I could pay off their mortgage whatever it is and wouldn't even notice it.' We agreed that when he came back we'd think of something – giving money to me and my giving it to Virginia 'in advance of her inheritance' – that again. I told Adrian I'd miss him. He said he'd phone regularly and I told him that if he showed any sign of acquiring an American accent I'd put the receiver down. Of course I've nothing whatever against an American or any other sort of accent, but that's the kind of jovial thing one says when one's miserable. It was just like Adrian to worry about Virginia. It would have been just like Jane too.

Virginia was cheerful for a change. She said she felt in her bones that Richard's new job was right up his street and he'd make a real go of it. 'He's still chuckling about Prince Charles and ordering plants,' she said. My heart sank. I mentioned Adrian and New York to which she did not respond. I wondered if her love for him was affected by his success, how far, rather – Richard probably going on about that a bit or a lot. This I would never know. Did I even know how fond of each other they had ever been? As children they had bickered incessantly, trod on each other's toes etc. No more than is in the unpleasant nature of things: jealousy and the like.

This question was in my mind when my former wife phoned. I would avoid the use of the word 'happy' with her too. Because of Brad. But she said almost at once, 'Brad and I used to make quite a thing about New Year's Eve. Seeing it in. Resolutions. Singing. It wasn't like him. Celebrations of that sort. Hated parties but New Year's Eve was different. So I just stayed on my own, missing him a bit. A lot actually.'

There was a tearfulness in her tough, no-nonsense voice I hadn't heard before so I told her hastily about the beacon and what a non-event it had been.

'Brad used to say there was an inevitable artificiality in the customarily dictated . . . Oh dear, you're yawning, Tom, aren't you . . . ?'

'I'm doing nothing of the kind.'

She laughed. 'Oh, Tom, I do remember the way you could yawn without doing anything with your mouth at all.'

I did not want to be reminded, of that certainly, but more generally of how I had been then. So I changed the subject, saying I'd been speaking to Virginia and Adrian. She interrupted to say she had too, though neither had mentioned it to me. I didn't want to compare notes with her, not now, but there was still that unanswered question.

'How fond of each other were they, are they, do you think?' I asked.

She hesitated for a long time so that I almost repeated the question.

'The characteristics, the vagaries, of familial affection', she began, 'are notoriously hard to delineate. There are so many, often conflicting or incompatible, factors . . .'

There was another, sufficient, pause. I tried again. 'What I meant was: how much do they love each other?'

'I know what you meant, Tom. For all they have shared, they love each other as much as is possible for a brother and sister.'

'A very great deal, you mean?'

'Of course.'

'What they have partly shared, I suppose, is us?'

'Well, yes.'

'Isn't that something, then?'

'You could say it's just about everything. Or all there is or can be or something.'

'Well, you can't have everything, can you? Sorry if I . . .'

'It's nothing,' she said.

'Anything's better than that,' I said.

We both laughed briefly before wishing each other well and hanging up.

And so I found myself in agreement with Miss Tomkins and with such intricate profundities the third millennium began.

A couple of months have passed. Mrs Hirst has not returned. I have caught a glimpse of Mr Fogarty coming and going to feed her cats. To judge from how much more frequently they come to see me, he is not feeding them enough. Or they have come to expect the cat food I give them so that Mr Fogarty may have formed a misleading impression of what enough is. It doesn't seem to matter now how much time or when one or more of them spends sleeping round my house. A week ago all four of them were on my bed when I woke up so that I thought for an instant I had became paralysed from the waist down. One day I must catch Mr Fogarty and ask him if he's heard when Mrs

Hirst is coming back. He has lost his surreptitious look and once I heard him whistling. In the middle of March she sent me a postcard showing a female surf-rider doing a somersault:

'Dear Professor. Taken of me last week. This is the life. Back at Easter. I've sent Mr F more money for the cats. Hope they're not being a nuisance or anything. Best regards, Emily Hirst. P. S. Hope you haven't forgotten me!!!'

Well into April. Perhaps she'll just turn up one day. Must now try to write about my visit last Sunday to see Julia. I hadn't seen her mother for a long time so I was rather taken aback when she appeared on my doorstep. At first glance I thought it might be her sister since she had taken some trouble over her appearance, though still a very long way from what her sister would have meant by that. There was less grey in her hair, which was shorter and neatly combed back. Her complexion was smoother with some red in it, more healthy-looking than artificial. Some pale lipstick. Quite a lot of blue pencilling round the eyes. These were as they had been previously, though she was smiling: the look of someone accustomed to hurt who is trying to talk herself out of it. I had not noticed their colour before – a dark sea-green. Julia's eyes. Looking at her like this and getting over my surprise, thinking for an instant that it might be her sister, I did not take in what she was saying. The smile was simple embarrassment.

' . . . If you'd like to come along. About tea-time. She often mentions the nice gardener on the beach. She gets bored, just me all the time.'

My expression must have been one of alarm so she added, speaking very quickly, 'Of course I'd quite understand if . . . Please do say . . .'

'I'm sorry . . . ?'

She began rubbing her hands as if drying them, especially between the fingers. 'I was just wondering, it's really the most awful imposition, cheek really, if you'd like to come and see Julia with me tomorrow.'

'But of course I would. I'm so sorry. Please come in.'

She shook her head as if I'd proposed something outrageous. 'Tomorrow. I'll pick you up. About three.'

And so it was. We drove there the following afternoon. She told me she was now living with her sister and had a part-time job in a chinaware shop. I hoped that before too long she'd start briefing me about what to expect, what to say, what not to say etc. Eventually

636

she only told me that Julia was 'stable' now and that at last they seemed to have found the right medication. The institution was a newly built Roman Catholic 'retreat' and most of her fellow inmates were mentally 'backward' in one way or another. I asked then if there was anything I should or shouldn't talk about.

'Oh no, just the weather, any sort of everyday chat. She may not be listening to us much anyway.'

I then asked if it was all right if I gave her something, producing from my jacket pocket a CD of Elly Ameling singing a selection of songs by Schubert. I'd bought two of them for some reason. No, I'd had the reason that it might be a handy gift one day.

She looked down at it and smiled. 'Oh dear, yes. That'd be lovely.'

We drove up a long drive with meadows either side of it. In one there was a herd of black and white cows. In the other a pair of horses stood close together, very still, head to tail. I was suddenly back in Suffolk, as if they were those same horses. Another spring. A church graveyard, the headstones patched with moss and fungus which told little to nobody now. The bones laid bare. Another herd of cows, huddled closely together. Flimsy clouds approaching the sun. The screaming of skulls, or their uproarious laughter. The chords struck by the vicar on the organ . . . no, there was only one horse that day, a single horse with its head over a fence, waiting . . . the smell of pigs on the wind. A tractor too.

We drew up outside a long, single-storey building, got out and rang the bell. A nun opened it. She was already smiling, welcoming no matter whom. She did not say anything, did not need to, as we followed her down a corridor with uncurtained windows on either side. It was a lovely view unspoilt by time – the meadows, a copse of trees against a hillside, a cluster of farm buildings, a trickle of smoke, a few birds in a hurry. The clouds sped across the sun, trailing shadows across the grass as if wiping the sunlight. The carpet was garish with red and gold flowers and had been freshly laid. In a recess there was a small electric organ with an open hymn-book on it. Opposite was a tall bookshelf containing nothing but a few hastily stacked board games: draughts, snakes and ladders, Scrabble. Beside it was a folded ping-pong table with a broken hinge.

We reached a circular lounge with a further corridor leading off it. There were green armchairs all around it, two of them on one side occupied by women with their hands on their laps who stared in front of them. They did not seem to notice our arrival. Their hair was cropped to the same length and they were wearing identical floral frocks. Beside the entrance another woman had her head down over a children's book which she was colouring with great concentration, holding the crayon with both hands. She did not look up. On the other side of the room three chairs had been arranged in a circle round a coffee table which the nun indicated with a gesture of the utmost graciousness, her smile unchanged. We were expected.

'I shall tell Julia you are here and bring you tea. Would you like that?'

The silence was such that we both only nodded. We sat there for what seemed a very long time, staring out of the same window at the passing of the shadows. One of the women came across and offered her hand with a little curtsy. Her mouth hung open and she tried to speak but her tongue could not follow whatever bidding she was trying to give it. You could see it lumbering about with a life of its own. From somewhere far back, deep within, she knew she should be welcoming strangers. In the vacancy of her eyes there suddenly shone what might have been an apology. For what she was. Had her lips been touched in a miracle, 'sorry' would have been the first word she spoke. Or 'thank you'. She tried to say more but her tongue became even more encumbered, liquidly filling her mouth so that a trickle of saliva fell down her chin. She gave us another curtsy and returned to her chair. The other woman stood up, curtsied and sat down again, clapping her hands and making a whimpering sound. One of us now had to say something.

'How absurd,' she said. 'You don't even know my name. Susan Wetherell.'

She put out her hand and I took it. 'Tom Ripple.'

Again we waited. How I wished she'd tell me more about Julia. Perhaps she thought she'd told me enough the day I brought her back from the beach and the rest I could now see for myself. Finally she arrived, followed by the nun with a tray of tea things.

Her mother kissed her and introduced me. There may have been a glimmer of recognition, as fleeting as the glance she gave me. Her black hair shone, freshly washed and brushed. It was a little shorter, the fringe higher on her forehead. She was delicately made up, just enough to hide her natural pallor. Perhaps the nun had helped with

638

that and this was why they had taken so long. Her dress was dark brown with long sleeves and a high, frilly white collar. As she sat down a vagueness came into her eyes, as though she had recently been roused from sleep. I was right, sea-green like her mother's but with no expression in them – an unpeopled sea. The nun had a hand on her back, the smile still unchanged. I could imagine her saying, 'Just take this little pill, dear.'

Julia held herself very upright, as if in readiness, then suddenly looked up from her hands and stared alertly out of the window. A smile began until her mother said, 'I expect you remember Mr Ripple, darling.'

She looked hard at me, then back at the window, expectant now and with a slight frown. Her mother asked me how I liked my tea and began pouring.

'I'll be leaving you to yourselves now,' the nun said, giving Julia's shoulder a parting squeeze.

'Here's your tea, darling,' she said, trying to hand it to her, then putting it on the table. She shrugged and turned to me. 'I live with my sister now . . . Oh dear, I've told you that. She has this beautiful little cottage. Julia loves it, don't you, darling?'

Julia looked slowly away from the window and stared at her mother. 'Aunt Charlotte,' she said, 'you look just like my mother.'

She leant forwards and touched her daughter's wrist. 'Don't tease, darling. You know perfectly well . . .'

Again she turned abruptly away and again her mother shrugged.

'I expect you've lived in a number of places,' she said. 'You look like a travelled man. A professor, I believe, Mrs Hirst told me.'

'London. Suffolk. That's about it, I'm afraid. Very dull.'

She lowered her voice. 'I thought it would be a change for her. Not just me and, sometimes, Charlotte. An ordinary conversation. Just a normal person from the outside world. You can see here . . .' She looked around the room. 'We could just talk about, I don't know, gossip or something just natural. I hate to say this but Charlotte, my sister, there is such tension when Julia is there. Talks to her loudly in words of one syllable as if she was a child . . .'

I saw before she did that Julia was listening intently to us and gave her a slight nudge. A normal conversation from the outside world . . .

'I've never seen the beaches so crowded,' I said much too loudly. 'Still, we have them to ourselves in winter. It becomes our own sea again. My daughter brings her children down, not as often as I'd like. Husband works at a garden centre. My son's living in New York at present. Accountant. Clever chap. It looks as if Mrs Hirst is in danger of staying in Australia for good. Lot to be said for that by all accounts. Couldn't go back to London. A lot to be said for that too, mind you . . .'

I was now talking more to Julia, since she was nodding as if I had begun to sound interesting. I looked out of the window with a wave of my hand.

' . . . Takes a lot to beat this, though, the open, unspoilt countryside. The air. Wonderful for walks . . . Do you . . . ?'

'You love that, don't you, Julia darling? Your little walks.'

Julia was leaning forwards, concentrating hard on what we were saying. I wondered why we could not do that now, simply get up and go out and breathe the fresh spring air. There would be plenty of normal, natural things to talk about then: the trees coming into leaf, the sound of birds, the cows, those horses. And in the farmyard there would be chickens, a dog, pigs, a cat or two. From that stifling, uncurtained, over-heated room which smelt of new carpet with a tinge of insect repellent the world could only be seen through smudgy glass.

'They take her after tea. There's an enclosed area. She has to wrap up warm and not run away, don't you, sweetheart?'

Julia looked directly at me. 'You're a gardener. You've come to fetch me to show me your garden. Actually Aunt Charlotte's garden is perfectly hopeless.'

How normal her voice sounded, I thought, but that of a much younger girl – trying to sound grown up, showing off.

'I'd love to do that some time,' I replied.

'Isn't that kind of Mr Ripple?' her mother said, sharply it seemed, teaching a child manners.

Julia looked out of the window again and around the landscape, her face quite at peace now as if she was outside in the spring air. She raised her head, closed her eyes and breathed in deeply. Then she began, very quietly, to sing, as close to a whisper as singing can be. The words seemed to be German. Her mother nodded at my jacket and I took out the CD.

'Just look what Mr Ripple has brought you,' she said. 'Now isn't that kind of him?'

At first she did not seem to have heard. Then her eyes opened and I held out the CD. Slowly, still singing, she took it, opened it, slid out the booklet and turned the pages. She fell silent for a while, until she reached the song 'Seligkeit' which she began to sing, nodding her head from side to side and beating time with her finger. It is a song about great happiness and that was the expression on her face. When she had finished, she looked up at me, her expression remaining one of joy, perhaps including gratitude to me. I wanted to believe that.

'Say thank you to Mr Ripple,' her mother said.

But she looked back at the book, turning two pages until she reached a song about spring. This too she began singing in that clear, whispery voice, again perfectly in tune so far as I could judge. I looked across the room. The woman who had come to greet us was staring at Julia with what I thought was impatience, even anger, behind the blankness. Then I noticed that the fingers of both hands were beating time on her thighs. The other woman began to conduct with both hands, her tongue dangling out as a broad smile spread across her face. They did not seem aware of each other though they were sitting very close together. The woman with the colouring book was concentrating even harder, her nose almost touching the page. The nun appeared and Julia's mother nodded to her.

'That's lovely, my dear,' the nun said. She put her hand under Julia's arm to raise her to her feet. She was not smiling now. 'Come along now. We must go for our little walk. Bring the pretty music with you.'

She led Julia away, still singing. Her mother hurried after her and pushed the nun aside to hold her in a tight embrace. One of the women began clapping and the other waved vigorously, making a gurgling sound like choked glee.

'Goodbye, my darling lovely girl,' she said. 'I'll come again soon.'

But Julia did not seem to hear her and was still singing when the door to the corridor swung back behind her.

On the drive back Mrs Wetherell seemed at first not to want to say anything, so I asked as neutrally as I could what the chances were of Julia getting better.

'None really, but the medication improves all the time so she'll be able to spend more time with me. I know you must think we should be able to find a better place for her than that, and of course I'll go on trying.'

'I didn't . . . Beautiful surroundings.'

'Yes, and she has a lovely, spacious room. And they are kind to her. Very kind.'

'Well, they would be.'

'I know, that wasn't quite right. You see, she seems perfectly happy being on her own. So far as one can tell.'

'About most people for that matter. How does she spend her time? Reading?'

'No she doesn't read. There's the radio and television of course which she turns on and off at random. As if she suddenly feels lonely and wants a bit of company. But she doesn't seem to hear or see them. They're just there. The psychiatrist says they stop, break up, whatever's going on in her mind for a while. The voices. Perhaps. Who's to know? But they're not the main thing.'

I asked what that was.

She gave a laugh that told me how she had once been when she was happy – when her daughter was little, for instance, and did charming things.

'You saw for yourself. She has a collection of CDs, including the Hyperion series of Schubert songs. It's complete now. There are thirty-seven of them. I got her each new one as soon as it came out. She listens or sings along with them and already knows many by heart. One day she'll probably know all six hundred and thirty of them or however many there are.'

'Cripes.'

'Yes. But you see, she truly is happy then, if faces are anything to go by. It is quite another world. Everything is there somewhere. Every shade of feeling . . . Everything. I'm not so sure about the words . . . Without the music some of them do seem a bit artificial, the poetry of that time. Not my cup of tea really. The words I mean. Sometimes, anyway. But without them there couldn't be the music, could there?'

I could think of nothing to say to all this. What insanity was it, I've often wondered since, that found contentment, fulfilment in such a manner? Apart from the Ameling, I have four of the Hyperion CDs and have read the commentaries in the accompanying booklets. From those, and the music too of course, it seems pretty evident that the intricate beauties of that other world are just about inexhaustible, could be lived in indefinitely – evident even to someone like me who knows nothing about music. Living in it all the time, though, might

642

turn one mad. This late at night three weeks later. At the time the best I could manage was, 'I could see she liked the CD. I seem to have hit on just the right thing.'

'You did.'

Then I asked, 'Has she had a chance to sing them with a pianist?'

She lifted both hands from the steering wheel with a loud sigh. 'Oh dear me, yes. Twice. She wouldn't go on after the first line or two. Just shook her head and left the room. They were really quite good but she's heard the best so . . .' She laughed. 'I've sometimes thought I'd write to Graham Johnson or Roger Vignoles or one of those to ask if they'd come and play for my daughter one day . . . I'm sure they're very nice people but you can imagine the reaction. They might show the letter round . . . There'd be laughter . . .'

We did not speak for a long time after that. My mind drifted away from Julia to the other women there. And I found myself asking whether it would have been better if they had never been born. It is possible for people to choose nowadays that they should not be. A choice made daily. The disfigured bodies and ineffectual minds. Lives worth less than yours or mine? Lives that could never cause hurt or harm to anyone. Is there a better measure of worth, of virtue, than that . . . ?

The open country was giving way to suburban bungalows and then to thick traffic, offices and warehouses. 'Seligkeit' ceased to echo. I became aware of my companion again, her hands clasped tight on the steering wheel. There was much more I wanted to ask. Foremost, about Julia's father.

'Forgive me, but are there brothers and sisters? A father?'

'None of those things. Her father left. Later killed in a car accident.'

'Is that . . . ?'

'No, it isn't. She still doesn't know he's dead. The psychiatrist says there'd be no point in it. Or too risky. She thinks he's still around somewhere, is about to walk through the door. It is what she looks forward to. She imagines she receives letters. She once told me he'd been unavoidably detained.'

'I see. Was it her . . . was that why he left?'

'Oh no! Well, not really. She was already pretty far gone. It was me he didn't want any longer. Can't really blame him. I could only live for her. I tried so hard not to but . . .'

'I see,' I said again.

But I didn't. We were drawing up at my house. I thanked her very much. I did not say I would like to be taken to see Julia again. I do not know if she wanted me to say that. I do not know whether I wanted to see her again. I still do not know. This is for my sake. I want to remember her how she was then, singing 'Seligkeit'. For her sake? For her mother's? There is plenty of time to think about that. She did not, will not, ask me so as to spare me the embarrassment – or because that is not what she wants? It is late at night now. I wish my thoughts would fall into place. I wish I could sleep.

When I said goodbye to her outside her house she touched my arm very lightly and said with the start of a smile, 'You'll probably think me completely bonkers but sometimes when I hear a knock on the door I think I'll open it to find Graham Johnson standing there and he'll say he's just dropped by to run through a few songs with Julia.'

Then she turned and walked away with a hand to her mouth so I did not know whether the noise she made was a giggle or a sob. I was glad not to have to respond to that.

Chapter Thirteen

At last Mrs Hirst has returned. She brought back a large number of photographs which she says she will show me in instalments. 'Just a few at a time. Other people's snapshots can make you feel queasy, too many of them all at once like chocolates.' It could take the rest of my life. Those she has shown me already were taken mainly in a garden or on the beach. She pointed out various aspects of her son and grandchildren. Most of the former's limbs were on show. They were dark and very muscular. He was keen for them to be seen. Perhaps in Australia there is a cloth shortage and all short-sleeved shirts and shorts have to be manufactured as high up as that. He was always smiling more than can have been necessary and it was a fair guess that he spent much of his spare time playing games and swimming too, of course. Australia clearly suited him. It was difficult to believe he was an accountant rather than, say, a life guard. The children – both boys – were very brown too.

Mrs Hirst said nothing about her daughter-in-law, who was blonde and might have been very pretty if she hadn't always looked in a bad mood, squinting and frowning. This is a bad combination. Pretty women have no right to be other than cheerful all the time, the luck they've had, the wider choice it gives them of jobs and men (if that is luck, given the higher odds on getting let down) – and hence of what life has to offer more generally. It isn't the same with bad-tempered, good-looking men. When they look cheerful one tends to think, 'And why do you think you're looking so bloody pleased with yourself?' If they look bad-tempered it may be because some pretty woman has told them what they can do with their good looks. This can be quite a satisfactory thought, the edge taken off it by wondering what equally good-looking man will soon be letting her down instead. Mrs Hirst's son did not look pleased with himself, just pleased. Anyway, I had to ask whether she'd got on any better with her daughter-in-law.

'She made the effort, I'll grant her that benefit. He gave her more than one talking-to to my knowledge. She was always having to ask me would I mind doing this or that. So you could say it was like a policy. She has a nice side to her, I'll say that for her.'

'Caring for your son, being loved by him, that'd be a start.'

She thought about this, staring at a photo of all of them together, sitting rather formally on a terrace in front of a french window. They are all smiling apart from Mrs Hirst herself.

'I never thought of it *quite* like that. But to be honest he does love her and she does try to look after him.'

'When are you going back? It really does seem a good life.'

She shook her head slowly. 'I'm thinking about it.'

The pause needed filling. 'They still seem to want the Queen,' I said.

'It's not the Queen they want. It's the alternative they don't.'

'Not so different from us then?'

She frowned. 'Not so different. Like us sort of magnified. Except they never let you forget how great it is to be them.'

'So not much like us in that respect?'

'Oh no, they don't much like or respect us. That's a big part of how great it is to be them.'

'I see. But they enjoy our liking and respect, don't they? That should add to how great it is to be them – rather than us say?'

She laughed. 'Oh no, professor, they wouldn't want to be us at all. They wouldn't enjoy that.'

'Except in our liking and respect for them, I suppose.'

She considered that. 'We'd like and respect them even more if they let us forget how great it is to be them. That's what I think.'

'But surely that would make them feel even more how great it is to be them. Unless of course it gave them more liking and respect for us.'

She was becoming impatient. 'I don't rightly know about that. But you can't argue they've got a great climate and whatever else they can always enjoy that.'

At this point two of her cats came through my window, one of them jumping on to my lap, the other rubbing itself against my leg. I glanced at Mrs Hirst to see how upset she might be.

'They *have* taken to you, haven't they?' she said, grinning as if proud of the way her children were being nice to a nervous stranger.

'Cupboard love,' I said.

She gave my arm a hard squeeze. 'I know, dear. You're very kind to them. They like you. I always tell them that.'

'Mr Fogarty seemed to do his stuff all right.'

I should mention at this point that the day before I had seen what at the time had seemed an extraordinary sight as I waited at the bus stop. It was Bridget in a driving school car being given a lesson by Mr Fogarty. They had drawn up on the other side of the street and he was leaning across her in what had seemed at first a brazen embrace, Bridget welcoming it with a smile and a nod. It was only then I noticed the driving school sign and realized he was pointing out something about the levers on the steering column or whatever.

'Oh yes,' Mrs Hirst said. 'He was so conscientious. He loves cats, he says. The accounts neatly set out and everything. He wasn't once a merchant banker for nothing. He even had a little joint and bread and milk and a few veg waiting in the fridge for me.'

She had sent me a card too to say when she was coming back. Those were things I might have thought of. It just didn't cross my mind. It is the sort of thing she would have done for me.

'He's a driving instructor, I gather.'

'Didn't you know?'

'When he first moved in, do you remember you were, well, suspicious?'

She gave me a look of startled innocence. 'I've never had anything against Mr Fogarty. Oh no! He's a really nice man once you get to know him. The time he's had.'

She was getting up with Australian photograph album Volume One, so I had no need to reply to that, saying instead, 'Those were lovely, Mrs Hirst. I'd really like to see more of them.'

'We did these trips in their camper. And there were the sports and boats in the harbour. You being a travelling man you won't be wanting to see too much of all that. I expect Canada is even more exciting with Red Indians and Mounties and what-have-you.'

'Oh no, I'd like to. Honestly.'

And it was true. I did want to see more of her other life. There is far too much about other lives about which we know nothing. I had sounded as if I had meant it and she gave me a very gratified smile indeed.

'It's still nice to be home whatever the Australians think,' she said as she left, calling her cats to follow her.

But they remained where they were, both of them now asleep on my lap.

A few days later I found myself standing next to Mr Fogarty at the bus stop.

The conversation was easily started. 'Mrs Hirst seemed very happy with the way you looked after her cats,' I said.

He took my elbow. 'It's you she should be thanking, I'm thinking. Spending all their time at your place. Feeding them too I shouldn't wonder.' I nodded. 'Then you should be giving her a bill. Ghastly creatures, cats are.'

I shrugged. Only now was he letting go of my arm. His Irish accent had become very pronounced, suggesting he might have much more talking to do, there being no sign of the bus. But he had fallen silent. His wizened face was turned away from me.

'You're a driving instructor,' I informed him.

He gave me a wink. 'Is that what I am?'

'Saw you the other day with Bridget.'

'Ah, the lovely Bridget. Now there's a fine girl for you.'

'I wish. Told you that, did she?'

'A man with a jest ever on his lips I see you are. Where is that infernal omnibus is what I'm asking myself. It is no small wonder that people are wanting to learn to drive automobiles.'

'How do you like the street, the neighbourhood?'

'Compared with my previous environment it is a positive paradise. That I can say without any fear of contradiction.'

'Nice to hear it. What was wrong with where you lived before?'

'Nothing at all, professor isn't it, except for the little matter of my house going up in flames.'

'Heavens, how awful!'

'Furniture, every stick of it. All the clothes I stood up in. Saw you staring at my short trousers the day I moved in. Must have looked a sight. That's the limitations of Oxfam for you.'

'Sorry. Didn't mean . . . How did it happen?'

'I wasn't in residence at the time. Nothing proven one way or the other. Suspected arson if you want the gory details.'

'Good God! Really?' I asked, there being something about things said in an Irish accent that makes one wonder, to begin with at any rate, how true they are.

'No, I made it up. No, I didn't. Mrs Hirst will tell you. In a nutshell, I was giving lessons to the wife of this Protestant gentleman lived on the same street. After she failed her test three times I told him she'd better be sticking to her tricycle for the foreseeable. She was fucking hopeless but I didn't go so far as that. Then she told him I'd made a pass at her and, to cut a long story short, he called me a fucking Papist Fenian pervert.'

'Good God!' I repeated. He was holding my arm again and again winked.

'That was just by way of introduction. There are two commentaries to be made on that. Would you be caring to know what those are?'

'I would indeed.'

'Well, professor, the first is that in ancient parlance I'm as queer as a coot.'

I raised my eyebrows with a slight smile, encouraging him to add, 'You're not being of that persuasion too, are you by any chance?'

'No, or not so far,' I said. 'And the other thing?'

'I'm no less of a bloody Prod myself. Protestant born and bred as ever was. When I last checked. He wasn't to know that, though, was he?'

The bus had turned the corner at the bottom of the hill. 'There she is, fair ripping along. Look at that exhaust on the poor old thing!'

We looked in silence at the bus struggling towards us. As it drew up I saw it was nearly full so we would not be able to sit together. I said hurriedly, 'So you think he burned your house down?'

'My house was burned down, professor. That's all I'm telling you. He had these Orange friends in that pub of his. Me being a teetotaller all my life never went near the place.'

As we got on the bus I said I was sorry.

He opened his eyes wide at me. 'I knew it was you all along. You've got arsonist written all over you. I said "arsonist". So don't be mistaking me, ducky.' This time he winked twice.

He made his way to the back of the bus and I sat down near the front. When I got off at the library I looked towards him but he was reading a racing newspaper. I think he had forgotten about me. I wondered why Mrs Hirst had not told me all this. I mean to confront her some time.

John Brown phoned yesterday evening. He told me he was back at work and could we meet at the Connaught some time soon. I shall see him again next Wednesday. His voice had changed. The bitter edge in it had gone and he spoke more slowly. Mrs Hirst has resumed her cleaning work and seems in more demand than ever. Phil Badgecock I hardly see. He has a smile on his face now of a rather grim variety. I sometimes see the Tomkinses in their tiny garden. It is astounding how much they find to do in it, how much they have fitted into it, as if it is to be photographed for a pocket edition of the *Gardeners' Encyclopaedia*. They wave and smile at me but do not seem to want to engage in conversation. Perhaps they have told me all I need to know about them. Perhaps, at the time I pass by, their estate is keeping them far too busy. I wonder if the fruit-looking tree they have planted by their door is a peach.

The suited couple with the Volvo still come out early in the morning with bulging briefcases, munching. On every single occasion one or other of them is speaking into a mobile telephone, looking equally anxious and decisive. Perhaps the people they are speaking to think they have toothache. I have only once spoken to them. This was to point out that one of the Volvo's tyres looked flat. It was hard to imagine their changing it themselves – too busy for that. They looked at each other rather than at me, breathing slowly in through their nostrils. Just as they were about to say something an AA van drew up. So much for neighbourliness, I thought. I hope they are becoming as rich as they want to be, all that time and energy they are giving to it. I hope that when they are, they have not lost the habit of relaxation, the enjoyment of things for their own sake. Otherwise they'll just have to go on getting richer and richer, more and more decisive, more and more anxious. I watched the AA man changing the tyre from about twenty yards away. They watched him too, looking at their watches whenever the man glanced in their direction. My impression was that they drove off without thanking him. Not seeming to mind that, he wiped his hands on a rag then, seeing me, he made a disgusted face and spat in the gutter.

Neighbourliness. I passed Rosie's house this morning. Her brother was working on a motor cycle in their yard. I greeted him and he turned his twisted face up at me. He could have been smiling. I could not imagine him caring for Rosie and her children as he evidently did. I was sure she hadn't told him about the money I gave her, not wanting it to become a topic. Then Rosie came down the path to meet me. Her lower lip was cut and swollen. A mauve bruise had spread up from her cheekbone to her eye where she had tried to disguise it with powder. Both her eyes were bloodshot. There was another, darker bruise along about half her hairline. But she was smiling or nearly succeeding in doing so.

'My God, Rosie, what the hell . . . ?'

'We've got him this time, professor. Five years if I'm lucky.'

Her brother almost shouted from behind her. 'Fucking shitface! When he gets out it'll be me doing the fucking time. You can rest a-fucking-ssured of that.'

I had not heard him speak before. Despite the language it was a deep, composed voice, accustomed to clear expression, almost accentless. She turned round. 'Who'd look after me then, Johnny?'

She looked back at me. 'My little brother, professor. He's lovely to me. You should really get to know him.'

Johnny stood up, wiping his hands down his overalls. His deformed shoulder seemed more hunched than before. A broad smile suddenly twisted one side of his mouth, baring half his teeth in what would otherwise be taken as a snarl.

'Rosie never could look after herself, could you, Rosie?'

He went inside with a high wave.

'Isn't he a lovely man, professor? The kids are really devoted to him.'

'I'm sorry, Rosie. I mean, look at you!'

'Oh, so I'm not getting my date then?'

'Fraid not, Rosie. What would people think? I've got my reputation to consider.'

'You mustn't be sorry. He did it even worse to her if you must know.'

I had nothing to say to that, touched her arm and left. I turned round when I reached the corner and she blew me a kiss. Her own reputation had probably never bothered her one bit.

I met John Brown at the Connaught as arranged. He was wearing a blue blazer with gold buttons, a club tie of some sort, well-creased twill trousers and highly polished brown brogue shoes. His shirt was white and the cufflinks were large and gold and flower-shaped. He was very groomed around the head and was not wearing dark glasses. His eyes seemed to have gained colour, a darker grey now.

'Blimey!' I said. 'Sure you want to be seen . . . ?'

He called over the barmaid and ordered me a double whisky and soda. On my own I only drink moderate quantities of red wine these days. I wish I felt better for it, plus the pills – not just better than I would have felt without them. How much better that is I can only guess. The same goes for feeling better than I usually do now. Except I guess that then I'd still be asking how much better I had been or might be. Living in the present is no good for the health. Anyway, I was too puffed to ask for wine instead and he watched me trying to get my breath back.

'You all right?' he asked.

'Fine, absolutely fine. But just look at you!'

'Self-hire vans. Transport manager. It's what I was good at. What's bloody marvellous is that I find I still am. Better if anything.'

While I sipped my whisky he went on to explain how he'd got the job. Stroke of luck. Answered an advertisement. Family business. Then details of how many vans. Expansion and so on. He proudly gave me his card. There was a pause while I studied it.

'This is, well, a bit of all right,' I said.

'A lot of bloody all right, Tom, actually.'

There was another pause. 'And how's . . . ?'

'I was getting to that. I'd like you to do me a favour. The lad's coming down shortly to stay for a day or two. We'd like you to come for dinner.'

'That's very . . . But wouldn't you rather, I mean . . . ?'

'No, we'd like, you see, a dinner party. Not exactly that. A guest. Just to show . . .'

I said I'd love to. We fixed a date and time and after he'd established I had nothing new to report at all other than Adrian going to New York he told me more about his new job, the ideas he had for it – something to do with computerisation in there somewhere. He had ordered me another double whisky which I was hesitating to drink while he sipped away at his first Campari and soda. The barmaid had come and gone without any comment at all. New again. Blonde again. Everything else again, even more bloody so if anything. Shorter skirt. Larger bottom. Looser blouse. As he got up to leave, he saw me glance at her.

'See you then,' he said with a wink. 'And thanks, Tom. You're a trooper and a gentleman.'

The barmaid came over and asked if I'd like another drink though my second was largely untouched. I shook my head and turned away to

652

look at the darkening sea. There were still some people on the beach. A black dog prancing along the water's edge. Litter catching the last of the light in the straggling strip of seaweed. The sun had just set when I arrived. No clouds then but now they had gathered quite high up the sky. It was a very calm evening. The sea unruffled, gracefully slipping into nightfall. That mighty life still reassuringly going on while we sleep. I was drifting away into thoughts of eternity and other such ultimate (penultimate?) things touched on before when I became aware that the waitress was still there, standing slightly behind me.

'Good God!' I said, sitting upright and twisting my head against the stiffness that comes and goes. 'So sorry. Thought I'd said . . .'

She made a pouting face which on such creatures is the opposite of a pout – the submissive end of flirtatious. 'You've forgotten me,' she said.

I stared hard at her. Hair much shorter and blonder. Lips redder. Eyes made brighter, shyer too, by thicker pencilling.

'Of course! Zimbabwe! Gosh, I *am* sorry!' I shifted round to look up at her face, breasts (what a pity) in the way. 'Do forgive me! Of course!'

And so I would have continued if she hadn't said, 'I expect you've been reading. I went back to see my people.'

'Heavens yes!' She can only have meant her family rather than the whole population, or the white part of it. 'Are they all right? Sounds pretty horrendous. People getting turfed off their farms or worse.'

She was beginning to frown and her lips were pressed together, evidently distressed, so I began to stumble, trying to remember an article I'd read the previous Sunday and a television documentary a fortnight or so before that. 'The economy in ruins . . . Unemployment . . . Corruption galore . . . Mugabe completely bats . . . Still at least there's an opposition now . . . Elections . . . So who knows . . . ?'

Here I ran out of steam. She had begun to nod but the frown had stayed.

'My parents knew one of the farmers. They were both born there. They're not farmers but they know a lot of them. There was one we used to go and stay on when I was little. It was so beautiful. I thought that was all I wanted one day. To marry a farmer.'

I tried to imagine her little, long before any farmer could get his hands on her. She would have been a very pretty child.

'Jolly painful for your parents to have to pack up and leave then,' I said.

She clasped her hands in front of her breasts. So much for having kept my gaze steadfastly on her face. Her frown vanished and the teeth came back.

'Oh no!' she said. 'They'll never leave. I'm going to go back when I've got my qualification. They're wonderful, gentle, decent people. Mostly.'

Surely she cannot have been referring to her parents, I thought. She must mean the white population as a whole.

'It must be jolly hard for them,' I gabbled on. 'The complete mess being made of things. The breakdown of services. Remembering the old days. Trying to get on with the new regime.'

This came from the article which described the whites living in the past, owning most of the best land, which those who had little or none of it wanted some of. The way the article was written, their gentleness and decency didn't invariably shine through all that brightly. The documentary left the same impression. Again I petered out as her hands fell abruptly to her side.

There was a long pause. 'I meant everyone,' she said. 'Well, not quite everyone, but you know what I mean.'

I stopped nodding. For the second time I was missing the point. How was I to know that what she'd meant by the word had changed? I'd simply wanted to say the right thing, the sympathetic thing I thought she wanted to hear, would like me for saying: a common cowardice, not right at all. I realized none of this at the time and just blundered on.

'The bungling and corruption. The breakdown of law and order. Hard on them, your people, having to give up and start all over again.'

Her face had become set. Mouth tight shut, the eyes widening, then narrowing, a little. She was looking at me as at someone it is very difficult indeed to be polite to.

'I suppose that's how it must seem. The stories there've been. By everyone I meant everyone. All Zimbabweans.'

'I'm sorry, I only. It's just that . . .'

I stopped stammering. The straightening of her back in profile as she smoothed down her tight skirt reduced the guesswork, then increased it. I swallowed and cleared my throat. These instead of a long, loud groan.

She had relaxed again and gave me a forgiving or extremely tolerant smile.

'Can't blame you,' she said. 'It's how you see us. The sensationalism and stereotypes. You've got to live there. There's good and there's bad. But ordinary people. There's a future for everyone. That's why I want my qualification and in the meantime have to do dreary odd jobs like this.' The smile suddenly vanished again as if she wasn't adding: and talk to dreary odd jobs like you.

'Unless of course you find your farmer.'

'What makes you think I haven't?'

I'd forgotten Zimbabwe for a second or two. She was in the way of it. I had been ticked off. I could only nod and mutter, 'Point taken. Sorry.'

Which she may not have heard. But she gave me a lovely flutter of her fingers when I left a few moments later.

I got pretty puffed going back up the hill that evening and twice had to stop to sit on a stranger's wall, thinking: one should never suck up to people. It's wrong to try to say the right thing, as opposed to the thing that is right . . . Pretty girl though. That body . . . Put me in my place . . . I'd have risked getting it wrong whatever I'd said. I'd only wanted to be nice to her . . . Serve me right . . . And so on, travelling further and further from Zimbabwe. Whatever the rights and wrongs of all that, much interwoven as they seem to be beyond unravelling, there was nothing at all I might have said other than nothing at all. So it was the being so puffed etc. that bore me away from Zimbabwe. If the rights and wrongs had been clearer I doubt whether I'd have given more of a toss about it. When one can be bothered, it's right to show one cares about the lives and circumstances of others however wrong one may be. That's what I write now, having got my breath back, trying to think more of the world at large, less of myself. Which brings back the barmaid, though she probably didn't think much of me, if at all, in the first place. I picture her on a farm, arm in arm with a farmer. In the background are a very large herd of cattle and fields of corn. It is not Zimbabwe I care about now. Not in the slightest. Though that was all she wanted of me. That I should take an interest, try to understand. There is a wider world . . .

I must soon try to write about my evening with the Browns. I was going to make a start on it yesterday morning when Mrs Hirst came round to look for one of her cats. She had what looked like a photograph album under her arm.

She glanced at my typewriter and the blank sheet of paper stuck in it.

'I won't be interrupting you, professor. Can see you're all ready to do some of your thinking.' She took two steps towards the stairs. 'Don't mind me, I'll just nip up . . .'

I didn't want Mrs Hirst going near my bedroom or past the open bathroom door. She'd called me 'a confirmed bachelor' more than once and what she would see there would reconfirm it. (The last time she'd called me that, I told her I hadn't been, so regrettably couldn't join her in communion. She didn't find that funny, considering it blasphemous no doubt; or perhaps she did not register it at all, assuming that as a professor I talked in riddles a lot of the time.) Anyway, I got to the stairs before she did, knocking the album out from under her arm.

'Whoops! Sorry! I'll do it,' I said, stooping to pick up the album and getting up the first stair in one movement. It was quite breathtaking.

When I returned, still getting back my breath, I caught her peering down at my desk where some drafted material was lying about. She took the cat and gave me a look of both puzzlement and disapproval. I recalled that the material concerned the young lady from Zimbabwe. What I'd said about Mrs Hirst's photographs was underneath that, thank God, though she could have read the top lines of the previous sheet which queried the manufacture of short-sleeved shirts and shorts in Australia.

'Research I'm doing for the Scandinavian Ecological Institute,' I said casually. 'A little piece on the effects of the environment on the brain. Heat and dottiness. Cold and reticence. The Walla Walla in the Amazon jungle cut off the noses of those who are judged too inquisitive. The Iroquois aren't afraid of heights. Why do you think that is? But must get on. These Norwegians, you know . . .'

She moved towards the door, her blush already fading. My tone of voice had unflustered her but she thought, perhaps, she needed to regain my good opinion. She needn't have bothered. I already had a high opinion of her. How hard we may strive to give people a higher opinion of us when as often as not they are unlikely to have any opinion of us at all.

'You're so clever, you lead such a rewarding life with all your studies, professor. Mr Fogarty was saying to me only yesterday what an interesting man you are.'

'He's the interesting one I should say,' I replied too eagerly.

'What did he tell you?'

'His house burnt down. Problem with the neighbours. He's a driving instructor. But I'm sure you know much more about him than I do, Mrs Hirst.'

'Sad about his wife, wasn't it?' she said, her eyes widening.

'Good heavens! She wasn't in the fire . . . ?'

'I don't know about any fire. She went off with one of his customers. He said he must have driven him to it.'

'That sounds very tolerant of him.'

'He's off the bottle now, he told me. His children can't get over it.'

'The not drinking or the separation?'

She ignored that. 'He's got six of them. Grown up now. That's your Catholics for you.'

'You seem to have got to know him quite well.'

'Well, you have to if someone's going to feed your cats. There's more to him than meets the eye. He said that about you, your being a so-called professor. He was at university too, in Dublin's fair city.'

'What did he study, did he tell you that?'

'One of those long words. It wasn't history or geography or anything familiar. Like he probably told you, he used to operate a ferry in Bangkok. That was before he bred crocodiles in Nigeria.'

She was now well over the threshold and her cat was becoming restless.

'I must try to get to know him better.'

'That's what he said about you. I told him what Mr Felix told me about your knowledge of carpets and the Red Indians and that . . .'

I raised my eyebrows which she took for impatience to get on with my work.

'The photographs had better wait till next time, you being so busy with your intellectual matters. I must tell Mr Fogarty that about climates and the Walla Walla.'

'You do that, Mrs Hirst.'

And so making a start on my dinner with the Browns was delayed. I went up to bed after that, taking it very slowly, and after a chapter of Powell slept for an hour or two. That evening I could only find the energy to watch television, eat the heated half of an Oceanic Pie I took too soon from the oven, then return to bed to read more about

Scott of the Antarctic. It must have been that which I had in mind when I told Mrs Hirst about the effects of climate. Zimbabwe and the South Pole. What a wide-ranging life of the mind I lead to be sure. I don't think I'd be any good at fiction but when I next bump into Mr Fogarty I must have a further story or two to tell him. We have come to owe it to each other, to keep each other amused with our inventions in this humdrum world of ours. The unadorned truth does not take us very far.

Before I slept, or rather to put myself to sleep, I thought again about the barmaid from Zimbabwe, not just her breasts and rump etc. but the look she gave me when she put me in my place. Her fault for using a word in different senses. My fault for trying to be nice. Getting it wrong about her. She surely got it far less wrong about me. In fact not wrong at all: an old man trying to be nice. Usually, though, what you see is seldom what you get. There's always much more than meets the eye. How far was that true of all the people I had known? It's true of girls too of course. Increasingly. What you see is very decidedly what you don't get. And if you don't see that you simply don't get it. Etcetera. And so to bed . . .

Chapter Fourteen

I arrived punctually at the Browns by taxi. Brown greeted me with a click of his heels, a bow and a sweep of his arm. There was something different about him. He was wearing the same smart get-up as when I had last seen him – blazer, club tie etc. and had recently had his hair cut. There was a good deal of oil on it which highlighted the ginger. His face was gleaming too. He'd also had his eyebrows clipped. Of course that was it. He'd shaved off his moustache.

'Tom! Splendid, old chap! Enter do, and meet the family.'

He led me through to the drawing-room and stood aside with his hand on my back. In that first second or two I thought I was meeting a female friend or relative, a sister perhaps, together with a young man who'd dropped by on some official business – an estate agent or insurance salesman or someone of that nature. He was plump-faced and held himself very upright with his head tilted back as if trying to offset his squatness and paunch. This also had the effect of making it seem as if he was trying to see the bottom half of you from under his gold-rimmed glasses. He was wearing a dark grey suit with a Paisley tie and the whitest shirt I have ever seen. With one hand he was holding a glass of lager. The other held his lapel. There was a large gold signet ring on its little finger.

'Meet the one and only son and heir,' Brown was saying, his grin not there any longer. 'Down from the frozen north to visit his poor old parents. Simon, Tom Ripple.'

I offered my hand which he seized vigorously and actually shook. Almost as soon as he looked at me he closed his eyes. His hand went back to his lapel, grasping it even more firmly.

'Delighted to meet you. A pleasure, I'm sure,' he said, the voice northern but with a slight lilt to it, out of politeness to his father perhaps.

While this was going on, I was having to come to terms with how much Mrs Brown had changed. She was standing a couple of paces back against the fireplace with a glass of orange juice in her hand, half held out as if she couldn't quite remember whether that was what she'd asked for. She gave me a smile and said very quietly, 'Hallo, Tom, it's lovely to see you. I'm so glad you could come.'

What had disconcerted me was how much older she looked. Her hair, about equally white and brown, hung straight down as far as her jaw and she was wearing little make-up: no longer the long blonde hair dark at the roots, the unevenly powdered, artificially tanned cheeks, the caked eyelashes, the blatant lips. That whine in her voice had quite gone too. I smiled back at her and we both nodded slightly. It was a nice moment of recognition. Very nice. No, it wasn't that she looked older. It was that she had stopped trying to appear the slightest bit other than she was. The voice though was having to be acquired afresh.

'Simon was just telling us about merging job centres with social welfare offices, weren't you, Simon?' she said to the back of his head.

Simon turned to me, closing his eyes again. He lowered his voice, becoming more northern, as mine sometimes did in the old days when wanting to convey I wasn't to be messed about with. Never with Plaskett, though, especially when he took me up in the world. Then I cultivated a southern smoothie twang with a touch of estuary. Lately my northern vowel sounds have returned – from being on my own and having a chat with my dead parents from time to time. When I forgot myself once and spoke to mother in a southern voice she cupped her ear and said my recent visit to Holland had given me a funny foreign accent. She gave me one of her rare smiles when she said that.

'Actually yes,' Simon was saying, looking at the floor midway between me and his father. 'I was asked to do a report on the staffing implications, regrading, cutting numbers of course, the likely savings, a new organisational structure . . .'

He turned half round to his mother, closing his eyes but soon opening them again.

'Poor Mum,' he said. 'I'm afraid all that's very boring.'

She shook her head. 'Oh no it isn't, Simon. It definitely isn't boring at all.'

'Hey!' Brown said in the ensuing silence. 'Tom hasn't got his tipple.' I opened my mouth while I made up my mind. He gave a single laugh like an exaggerated yawn. 'Thomas Ripple needs his tipple.'

His mouth stayed open and I gave the air a mild upper cut. 'Scotch and soda. Is that all right?'

While he went to get it Mrs Brown moved closer to her son, close enough to touch him.

'Do go on, Simon. I'm sure Mr Ripple is very interested . . . You can see, he's already making quite a name for himself in that line of business, aren't you, Simon?'

'Well I wouldn't go quite as far as that. However it happens to be true that subsequent to my report they did request me to join a task force to streamline procedures. It's promotion, you see.'

He turned to look at his father who was returning with my drink. Again his eyes closed.

'So there you have it, Tom, the lad's no slouch, is he? Well, it's no more than you'd expect with such brilliant parents. Here's to him then.'

We raised our glasses and Simon squared his shoulders, finished his lager, and put his glass loudly down on the mantelpiece. There was another silence. I couldn't make out what was going on. There were the wariness, the awkwardness, the self-consciousness of course, to which I was adding. They were trying to make out what their son had become, comparing that with how he'd been when he'd left home all those years ago. Proud? Disappointed? A bit of both? And he was deciding what had become of them, though there was much less doubt there. He simply wanted to impress them, beyond just saying, 'So you see . . .' There was the change in his mother requiring some adjustment, but apart from that . . . It all mattered far less to him than it did to them. He'd soon be able to put them out of his mind, unlike they him. Or so it seemed.

'Well, John,' I asked. 'How's the transport business going? You had ideas about expansion if I remember rightly.'

He nodded and it was his wife who replied, 'He's really in his element. They're jolly lucky to have him, that's what I say. He's got so many ideas there's no stopping him, haven't you, dear?' She turned eagerly to me. 'I expect he's told you in one of your little powwows together.'

Her voice had now become natural too. She was speaking from the heart and you could hear the child in it. He was still nodding, not in agreement but as if he'd forgotten to stop. The confused, affectionate way he was looking at her at that moment I shall not soon forget: as if he'd just started to recognize someone he'd known a very long time ago. No, it was more than that. He was trying to revive, see through to, the first time he'd set eyes on her; then the falling in love, the courting, the glorious expectancy that it would last for ever – partly recovered, partly beyond recovery. And from that, in his look were all the lost years, the lost parenthood, the lost contentment, the lost love. I'm only guessing of course, only imagining. These are only thoughts and feelings that could be deduced. I had not experienced them myself. Well, if I'm right to any extent, having no special imaginative or emotional equipment, it says something, I suppose, for our common humanity. One can never know for sure, or at all. Among that doubt lies much of our general sorrow perhaps.

Brown had stopped nodding. Their son had said he'd get himself another lager and was moving away. She was returning his gaze now as if she wholly knew what was going on in his mind. She turned to me and I realized I'd been nodding too. She handed Brown her glass which was still half full and said, 'Be an angel, Johnny, and fill her up would you? Right to the brim.'

She put a hand on his arm and they looked away from each other. Suddenly the moment had vanished. They both gave the briefest of laughs. It was clearly an old phrase of theirs, and indeed he said, 'That takes you back. Yes, madam, I surely will. It will give me the greatest pleasure. Anything you say.'

While he was away, I was muttering something to her about the new job sounding quite a challenge when he came back with his son. He gripped my elbow. 'What was that you were telling the trouble and strife? Not interrupting, are we?'

'Only that being in the transport business you seemed to be going places.'

He gave me a sharp tap on my arm with his fist. 'Told you he was a bit of a wag, didn't I, sweetheart?'

She giggled. There was as much nervousness as amusement in it. 'Oh I get it . . .'

(I remembered then it was one of the things I'd said to Richard who'd not laughed at all – that and upward mobility in the stationery business being a contradiction in terms. So unfunny now. Jokes, unlike sorrow, soon wear thin. Virginia had rarely sounded so happy when she phoned me that morning. The gardening centre job was proving a huge success. He loved it. The accounts had been in a shocking mess and with his customary attention to detail he was really sorting them out. They'd already raised his salary. And it was such a lovely environment, being surrounded by flowers. 'So he's looking out for the bloomers then?' I asked. There was a long pause while I remembered her ticking me off about teasing Richard all those years ago. 'Not again, Dad, please.' I left another pause before saying I was sorry. Then she did laugh. 'All right. I'll tell him that one if you absolutely insist.')

Simon looked at her, then at his father. His face was blank. Either he hadn't heard what I'd said or didn't think it appropriate. He had the air of someone who was constantly finding things inappropriate. One of life's inspectors. He was making it clear that he had been interrupted, now going on again about unemployment, the delivery of social welfare services and what should be done about them. I began deciding I didn't care for him at all, would have cared for him even less if I'd come across him elsewhere. He was not just trying to impress his parents, though he was clearly doing that. It was the way he always was. His mother was gazing proudly at him, listening to him rather than to what he was saying. Brown prompted him from time to time as if to keep him going. It was easy to see the adolescent in him, the boy Brown hadn't liked at all: fat, sulking, humourless, unprepossessing – though I could not then remember the exact words he had used. In a pause, Mrs Brown said, 'I'd love to hear more, darling, but if you'll excuse me I must see to the dinner.'

She touched Simon's arm and left us, with a glance at her husband. Somehow the plain brown dress she was wearing made her limp even more noticeable. Again that cautious smile had passed between them. Their son seemed to be picking up none of this, none of the unease or gratitude or happiness. I could easily imagine him telling his friends and colleagues, his girlfriend, with a worldly sigh that he'd had to go down and see his parents, that there was no love lost there, that it had been boring, an ordeal, but one had to do one's duty. What reason did he have to be grateful for what must have been a miserable childhood, that too having made him what he was? I listened to him and thought how lucky I'd been with my own children, though doubtless fucking them up too to some extent, as the poem puts it. He went on and on, once asking Brown about his new job but at once using that to talk more about his own in that slow, knowing drawl of his. It was a performance which had become his manner. That is what I was thinking when Mrs Brown told us dinner was ready.

She had gone to great lengths. There were four red candles in two candlesticks on the table and place settings for four courses. The glasses and silver gleamed and the table mats depicting old hunting scenes had been highly polished. The price tag on mine hadn't been quite scratched away. The white, lace-looking table-cloth was new too because the creases from the packaging hadn't been ironed out. At the centre was a glass vase of yellow roses surrounded by some fluffy stuff.

We sat down in silence, I opposite Simon. From the way Mrs Brown's head was bowed I thought that someone was about to say grace. Then Brown got up and took round bottles of red and white wine. He went first to his wife but she smiled up at him and shook her head. Still nothing was said until he sat down and raised his glass.

'A welcome to Tom, but sure he won't mind, first and foremost a welcome home to Simon.'

'Absolutely!' I said.

Mrs Brown having brought her orange juice in with her, we all raised our glasses, mumbling and glancing at each other. The silence resumed while we ate the miniature but elaborate concoction in front of us which consisted of bits of tomato and cheese, a pâté of some kind and cubes of avocado pear surrounded by interwoven shreds of lettuce. There were strips of red cabbage too. The silence was filled with the sound of our eating. A draught was making the candles flicker, animating our faces, so nothing could be told from those. I said, 'Utterly delicious!' 'Talk about cordon bloody bleu!' Brown added. Simon just ate.

Simon helped his mother to take out the plates and to bring in the next course: a dark soup with squares of toast in it and wisps of greenery which could have been plucked from the furry stuff among the roses.

'Good old Brown Windsor,' Brown said. 'Can't beat it.'

I waited for Simon to say something similar but he had eaten his first course in three or four mouthfuls and now slurped his soup as if in a hurry to be getting on with some efficiency survey or to go on talking about it. He could have been eating at any old office canteen. That was the kind of thought I was having about him. If he wasn't looking down at his food, his gaze roamed about over our heads.

'Fit for royalty!' I added, giving the thumbs-up sign.

'Quite the little cook, aren't you, my love?' Brown went on, smiling across at her.

She smiled shyly back but it was first at me then, for longer, at her son. She hadn't yet touched her soup, resting her spoon in it and half leaning forwards as if waiting to be told what to do next. As Brown turned to Simon to ask him about his new flat, what sort of a kitchen it had, she began to raise the spoon to her mouth. But her hand was shaking and she put it down. Simon was describing in some detail what he intended doing to his kitchen. She nodded enthusiastically, saying, 'That's nice' several times.

This time it was Brown who helped her to take away the plates so I had Simon to myself. He was going on about his kitchen, so that was all right: tiles, a microwave oven, fitted cupboards, some new material they had for floors etc. only requiring me to nod. I could hear murmuring from the kitchen. It sounded peaceful and once she laughed, saying, 'O John!' Simon showed no sign of having heard this. He had not asked me anything about myself, nor seemed about to. That was all right too.

Then the Browns came back carrying the main course: a large oval dish with slices of meat around it most elaborately adorned and sprinkled with a mixture of vegetables and other bits and pieces, so intermingled that nothing was immediately familiar. There were also two vegetable dishes, one with new potatoes, the other with peas, and a bowl of green salad, the green mainly hidden by much else besides. Altogether the impression given was of a meal over which she had gone to an immense amount of trouble. She served us, her hand quite steady now, perhaps because what she was doing was evidently giving her the greatest pleasure, her eyes wide in the candlelight. We helped ourselves to the vegetables, then to the salad and began to eat. Someone had to say something.

'This is quite delicious,' I said. 'Scrumptious!'

Mrs Brown looked at me with a coy or grateful smile. She might have been blushing. The candlelight added an expression of laughter. 'I got it from Delia Smith, actually,' she said.

'My girlfriend swears by Delia Smith,' Simon replied, examining what was at the end of his fork before putting it in his mouth and chewing it with a liquid noise, his mouth not quite shut.

(I knew who Delia Smith was, having seen her briefly on the television before switching off or over to something else. I keep on bumping into cookery programmes. One imagines that millions of people must be spending a great deal of their time in the kitchen or thinking about food – this making one wonder what thoughts they would be having instead, if any to speak of, or what thoughts they are preventing themselves from having, or are spared from having, would prefer to be without. Food is filling a gap. Pleasurable in itself, it might be said: the senses of taste and smell to be aroused and satisfied like any other, all part of a civilized way of life – indeed some of those cookery people seem to believe they are talking about civilization itself. Perhaps there aren't millions of people copying down their recipes. Perhaps there are hardly any at all. They are just glad to be watching it being done so well and not to be having to do it themselves. Like watching gardening programmes, though one doesn't have a garden, or only a small, unchangeable one – except that then one is looking at the infinite colours and shapes of nature beautifully come into being and flourish. They don't need the sound. Cookery programmes without the sound look like extended, comical enactments of greed. How many people out there are in a state of disgruntlement that they aren't eating like that, that their wives, say, or they themselves can't be bothered to cook like that, that their kitchens aren't big enough, that they've got better things to do with any spare time and energy they have than use them up on all that food palaver – that, in a nutshell, it's all right for some? You can hear the muttering: how many helpers have they got behind the scenes I'd like to know, who does the sodding washing-up? Thus thoughts may be caused by cookery programmes which people would like to be spared, would prefer to be without. This leaves out those who hardly think about food at all while quite liking the taste of some of it, as well as not wanting to feel hungry. It would be nice to know whether these people are free to make use of the thinking time that would otherwise be spent on food on ways of nourishing the mind instead, or on seeking other paths to civilization – reading philosophy, for instance, or going to concerts or helping their fellow beings. Not thinking about food should be an aid to freedom. I've no idea whether those who spend a lot of time thinking about food are more civilized than those who do not. As I've said, that is because one cannot know what they would be thinking about to fill the gap, or what else they would be doing – like serving people other than at their dining-room tables. Perhaps those who hardly think about food at all think that it is just one of those umpteen things other people are happily engaged in they are missing out on – too bad but they've got other things to do with their time, these not necessarily being more civilized, indeed perhaps not civilized at all. Whereas people who think a lot about food have the air of believing that they are not missing out on anything, that food is as important as anything else in life or more so, that it is something one could never get fed up with or lose one's appetite for. In short, there is a lot in the topic of food to be chewed over. Sometimes it's overdone. And much of it turns out to be crap. When you think about it.)

'Good old Delia,' I said.

The food really was exceptional enough to be eaten in silence, giving time to have some of the thoughts outlined above. The point is that on this occasion at any rate food was being as important and civilizing as anything could be, Mrs Brown being so proud of it, Brown too, more so if anything. Whole lives were being restored. A homecoming was being celebrated. Their smiles in between the munching and swallowing seemed to reflect each other. Simon too was enjoying it, twice saying 'Terrific, Mum!' in between drinking several glasses of wine and continuing to talk about his new flat, the first person plural now creeping in. He did most of the talking since he was the only person happy to do so with his mouth full. That was all right. It was his occasion.

'We placed an order for the carpets the other day. It's quite amazing really. There is considerable similarity between Sally's taste and mine.'

'Oh, so it's Sally is it?' Brown said jovially. 'You aren't going to tell your old parents about her by any remote chance?'

'All in good time, I expect,' his mother said quietly, glancing proudly at him as he held out his plate for a second helping.

He began talking about her, that she worked in a Jobcentre, that she came from Darlington, that her father was with a gas company, that her main hobby was ice-skating, that she'd dropped out of teacher training, that she had a younger brother who was only interested in football but had nevertheless obtained good A levels. He spoke about her possessively but without much excitement, or affection come to that. I could see how much his mother hoped that at any moment he would produce a photograph.

'We're not engaged or anything,' he pronounced finally.

'Gone out of fashion that sort of thing,' Brown said. 'Your mother and I were engaged for six months. Very respectable it was in those days. I can assure you of that. None of your cohabitation in those days, oh dear me no. Save it up, that was the message in those days. Used to meet her at the shop every lunch time and we'd go to the caff round the corner and . . .'

'I don't think Simon or Mr Ripple are very interested in our courtship, Johnny,' she said.

'Maybe. Maybe not. What about you, Ripple?'

'Much the same . . .' I began.

Though it hadn't been, my former wife, as previously recounted, holding to all the latest ideas about bourgeois convention etc. – which was all right by me since there were no ideas to speak of on my side of things.

'Times have changed,' I went on. 'But perhaps it doesn't matter much, if people love each other and so forth.'

'Who said it mattered?' Brown said abruptly 'You do just as you please, old son.'

'I'm sure Tom didn't mean . . .' Mrs Brown began.

In the ensuing silence, Brown gave me a wink, then blew his wife a kiss.

'Tell you something else, Simon. Your mother's going back to work, aren't you, old girl? Marks and Sparks as ever was. And what's more I'll be going round there just like the old days to take her to lunch at the caff round the corner. Office not far.'

Mrs Brown stared at him as though what he was saying was too good to be true. Then she looked at her son who was enjoying his second helping even more than his first. He can't wait to start talking about himself again, I thought. He said nothing about his mother's job, that he was glad about it, though the movement of his head to go with the audible munching might have been nodding. Perhaps he would say something when he'd finished his mouthful. He put down his knife and fork neatly together at the centre of the

668

plate and held his stomach with both hands. I found myself at that moment disliking him even more – self-centred oaf are the words I think I muttered. It wasn't hard to imagine him as a bolshie, sulking teenager. And now so self-important. He couldn't even tell his mother how glad he was she'd got a job, indicated all that went with that, shown her a bit of love. There was another silence.

She pushed back her chair, to start clearing the table, I thought. Suddenly she reached out and squeezed, then held his hand. 'If you half knew, Simon, how happy I am, we are, to have you home again.'

Then an extraordinary thing happened. He stood up, put his napkin decisively down on the table, lurched sideways and fell to his knees so that I thought he had passed out. With a hoarse groan from deep in his throat he stretched out his arms towards her, fell forwards and laid his head on her lap. I glimpsed his face before turning away. His eyes were tight shut and his cheeks were wet. She had begun stroking his hair. I could not see her face. At first there was no sound, then he began to sob – sudden, gulping sobs which tugged at the table-cloth and in between them the sound of her murmuring, almost like humming.

Brown gave me a nod. 'Bring your glass.'

I followed him out into the living room.

'Drink up,' he said. I raised my glass and finished my wine. 'There you have it,' he said. 'There you are then.'

I nodded. 'Perhaps I'd better be off.'

'Perhaps you had. Pity though. She's done this incredible meringue thing. Delia Smith again if you can believe it. Took her hours. First shot she had to chuck out. Start all over again. And then four varieties of cheeses. No five. She sent me back for the Camembert. You can't have a dinner party without Camembert, she said.'

He was talking with difficulty, that abrupt, cut-the-cackle voice catching in his throat which he had to clear between each sentence. Unlike him too, he wasn't looking at me. He touched an eye in a way that I knew there were tears there.

He cleared his throat loudly. 'Don't know rightly what else to say, to be honest. All those years up the spout. It's never too late, is it? Fucked if I know frankly. Miraculous, I suppose you could say that . . . He's a good lad you know . . . Wanted us to be proud of him, held nothing against us . . . If only you knew . . .' He pushed his fist hard against his mouth and turned his back on me. He had been unable to continue.

'I'll be off, then,' I said. 'Thank her, would you . . . ?'

He raised his hand above his head and left. I glanced in at the dining room and they were still as they had been but there was a murmur of conversation going on now. It was only when I reached the door that I remembered I would have to walk home and had not brought an overcoat with me.

As I opened it and felt the gust of cold air, he came up behind me and said, 'Sorry about that, old chum. No way to entertain one's guests. Bloody rude really. Boot them out before the pudding and cheese.'

He had quite recovered and I held his elbow for a moment. He winked at me as if he was about to say, 'Not a word to . . .'

'I'd like to say a lot,' I mumbled. 'Well, it was all right, wasn't it, except for me being there? I mean . . . I mean, everything coming out right in the end . . .'

'Don't you bother yourself, old man. Forget all about it. Know what I mean? Some things must be left to speak for themselves, if you want my honest opinion.'

'Anyway, thanks again. And really . . .'

'I said, don't bother.'

But he gave me a wide smile and a tap on the arm. 'Our thanks too, old chap.'

I was half-way down the path when he called out to me, 'Let me drop you off.'

'Thanks, but no. The walk will do me good.'

I waved and left. There could have been no question of that. He needed all the time he could have with his family. Simon would soon have to return to Sheffield, his girl, his job. They must spend as much time together as possible. They had much to talk about, or no longer had any need to, as the case may be.

The air was chilly and I was underdressed so I had to hurry. There was a full moon and a few clouds passing round it, like crumpled piles of bed linen. They made me think of that pure white tablecloth in the candlelight, now perhaps folded away or bundled up for the laundry. It was that picture – that and the young man's head on his mother's lap, the pride and sheepishness on Brown's face when he said goodbye, the lavish food of which there was more to come, there were all the things I had thought – these and other memories got in the way then of any sort of conclusion I might have reached.

And still do. I am writing this several nights later but have got no further than thinking vaguely how little, how very little, we can know about people, let alone understand them. How trite that is. I have elaborated a bit on the reflections I had at the time about cookery programmes, but not by much – so far removed are our thoughts from what is happening before our eyes. It may be that all lives, if sufficiently delved into, could become whole books. But however deep and far you went it would never be sufficiently true. It would always feel as if there is more to be known, more to be imagined. That is where the imagination in books has such an advantage. It can decide what should be known about the people it creates. There need be no enquiry beyond that. Whereas in real life, that is where the truth begins and endlessly unfolds. Right to the end there is whatever unknown grief or suffering or whatever is yet to come. Curiosity about living people cannot be confined within the covers of any book. Nothing can be invented. Wherever you look, there is that universe of lives that can never be known. Novels are such a relief really, not that I have read many of them. People say they are an escape. Just so. Nothing wrong with that. Reality is there to be escaped from, or so it feels much of the time. I haven't the faintest idea how one would go about writing a novel, inventing people and imposing limits on them. Not that it matters if it's just fiction. It's not like having to do justice to real people.

So I reflect now, escaping from reality. I wrote to Mrs Brown to say how very grateful I was to have been invited to dinner to meet their son. I said the food had been out of this world, the setting splendid. I wished her luck in her new job. I said I hoped Simon had got back safely and that good news would soon follow on the marital front. I said I had enjoyed meeting him and they must be very proud of him. I've been to the Connaught a couple of times but Brown hasn't been there. I don't like to phone him. He has no need to escape now. At the end of a hard day's work they are surely content with each other alone and a bit of telly perhaps. They'll be longing for the day when their son brings his girlfriend to meet them. That's the kind of conclusion one readily comes to. But of course I'm only imagining it. I think that's all I want to say about the Browns for the time being, can rather. We can only try to fill in the gaps, let the truth unfold, in our own way, and exercise care. I cannot continue thinking about this any more. There are so many people who do it better. I wonder if there is a cookery programme I could be watching instead. Food for thought.

Chapter Fifteen

I caught a chill walking back from the Browns that night. This became flu which developed into pneumonia. My doctor cured this eventually with antibiotics though the coughing persisted long thereafter. Phil Badgecock heard it through the wall and said one morning, 'Nasty cough you've got there. Myself I gave up smoking when I retired from the Post Office.' Mrs Hirst told me I looked like death warmed up and a man in my position ought to take better care of himself...

The first time I went out, well wrapped up, I met Mr Fogarty. 'Had a scarf like that myself once,' he said. 'When I was up there in the Arctic working on that weather station. That was a cold year I can tell you, after the Zambezi. The Calgary stampede in between. Those Eskimos could teach us a thing or two about keeping warm. Now I recall, you're an expert on the Eskimos and that ilk, so Mrs Hirst has been telling me ...' I began coughing and he slapped me on the back. 'You and I must have a powwow one day about our different experiences.' Again he gave me that exaggerated wink. He might just as well have said, 'So long as neither of us believes a word the other one says.'

The first day I was laid up I phoned Mr Patel to ask if there was any chance certain provisions could be delivered. Within an hour he had brought them himself and thereafter phoned each morning to ask what I wanted that day. Sometimes he brought the order himself. Sometimes the children came with it. The first time they looked around the house with dwindling eagerness as if there was something they were not finding there. I fear they had expected a great deal to wonder at: hundreds of books, perhaps, exotic pictures and bric-à-brac, tribal objects collected from all over the world in my travels. Instead, apart from my coloured bowl, there were only other people's old photographs, a shelf with a dozen or so books, the TV set, a couple of easy chairs with loose,

673

pale-brown covers and matching cushions, a typewriter on a table and the CD player. It was all very untantalizing. Perhaps they thought the mysteries of my life were kept upstairs and my front room was only somewhere visitors came. At any rate, as I shuffled bent-backed into the kitchen with them and then to see them out, they looked up at me with no less awe – as though, when the coughing stopped, they expected me to utter forth words of the profoundest wisdom. When Mr Patel himself came, he always said that if there was anything else he would go and get it at once, no trouble. And there was always some little delicacy I hadn't asked for which wasn't included in the bill. He did not seem disappointed by my house, saying what a very lovely comfortable home I had made for myself . . .

My wife phoned round about then. Very chatty and relaxed. Why didn't I come down to see her in Somerset? 'Now that the past has been folded up and put away,' she said. 'Talk about old times.' There seemed a contradiction in that. She said she had quite a lot of photographs of the children when they were little. I replied that I'd let her know. But I don't want to do that. 'Into my heart an air that kills . . .'

That was a while ago now. I had more or less recovered when Adrian called to say his estate agent had told him Mrs Bradecki had been in hospital and it seemed to be something serious. So I went to see her.

She led me through to the little room where I had once sat with her husband. It was exactly as I remembered it – the photographs and insignia on the walls, the books on the bookshelf, the black leather armchair, the stained desk with papers lying on it, perhaps untouched since the day we had gone through them together after his death. The only difference was that in the corner there was a small divan bed. She had much aged since my last visit and had clearly been ill. She had once held herself so upright but now her shoulders were hunched and she walked with a shuffle. The skin of her face seemed to cling to the bone, magnifying her eyes and giving her an eager, almost childlike expression. But I had never known her so cheerful. She guided me to the divan and for a long moment grasped my hands in hers.

'You see, this is where I live now always in this little room.'

I said that I'd heard she had been in hospital and asked if there was anything I could do.

'Thank you, sir. The children are caring for me very well. And see . . .'

There was laughter in her voice and she pointed with a broad smile at the little window which looked out over the garden. I stood up and there it was, as immaculate as it had ever been. The bench had recently been painted white and there was a new stone bird-bath. The flower-beds had been freshly dug, the shrubs trimmed, the lawn recently mowed, and new paving stones had been laid across it.

'Lovely . . .' I began.

'I tell the children they must keep it good or off they go, as you say in English, no bloody nonsense.'

She clapped her hands and in that shrivelling face for an instant there was such gaiety that I could not believe she was ill at all.

As if the clapping had been a signal, there was a knock on the door and a young woman came in with a tray of tea and biscuits. In the dim light I thought for a moment it was Maria. And as she put the tray on the desk she smiled at me with Maria's smile – that same innocent, brazen openness of spirit, a gladness to see me as if she'd been looking forward to it for ages . . .

'Here is Dorota to meet you,' Mrs Bradecki said, reaching out to grasp the girl's wrist. 'One of my children.'

Dorota put out her hand with a slight bob and briefly I took it. She was still smiling, even more so, but said nothing and left.

Mrs Bradecki poured the tea and handed me the plate of biscuits. I had many questions but, reminded of Maria, it was her I asked after.

Again there was that joy in her face. 'She is now in Warsaw with two children and a very good business. She came to see me in hospital and asked if Mr Ripple was still living and when I see you I can say you must come and visit her and meet her children . . .'

I thanked her. There was nothing to add to that. Still living . . . I thought of the old joke about that being a matter of opinion. To see Maria again. Golden hairs on a forearm catching the sunlight . . .

And so, without prompting, she told me very simply that she was receiving treatment at the hospital and there were always 'the children' staying to look after her, shopping and cooking and making the garden nice. More than once she said how lucky she was. More than once too she said that it was only thank you very much to me and the young Mr Ripple . . . No, there was nothing wrong, there was nothing I could do, she was happy with the children.

I finished my tea and we stood up together. Again she gripped my hands. But at once she sat down again and indicated that I should see myself out. Dorota was in the front room, about to carry a suitcase into the main bedroom. I thanked her for the tea and she smiled. No more than polite but no less of a smile. I had to ask.

'You seem to be looking after Mrs Bradecki very well. I hope there'll always . . .'

She lifted the suitcase and didn't let me finish.

'Always there must be someone. Someone cannot go of course until there is another one.'

She was frowning and there had been a scolding tone in her voice. Mrs Bradecki was their responsibility. Of course. They were her children.

I reached the door. I wanted that smile again to remember before I left.

'The garden looks absolutely wonderful. No bloody nonsense about not looking after that she told me.'

She put down the suitcase and pointed at herself. 'It was only me who painted the chair. You see!' She made some bold brushing gestures and looked very pleased with herself.

I stood back aghast and flicked my hair and coat as if she had splattered paint all over me. 'Oi! Steady on there!' I said crossly.

It wasn't a smile I got. It was a laugh, or a sort of stifled shriek. Eyes screwed up. Teeth. You can imagine the rest. Or rather that's what I've been trying not to be doing some of the time – that and her hand held briefly in mine . . .

About a week later. I haven't been well. This afternoon I knocked myself out and slept into the evening so that now, close to midnight, I cannot sleep. I have put a blank piece of paper in the typewriter. Force of habit – as often as not these days blank is what it remains . . . Some updating to pass the time.

Mr Fogarty again. He crept up behind me at the bus stop and whispered, 'Thought you ought to know.'

Recovering, I replied, 'Know what?'

'Fogarty isn't my real name.'

'What is your real name?'

'Wetherby-Featherstone actually, since you insist.'

676

'I see.'

'Thought you ought to know, that's all, professor, you with your tireless seeking after the truth.'

'I knew already as it happens. You look so like your twin brother. Used to be a good friend of mine.'

He nodded thoughtfully, a finger at his temple. 'How very peculiar. That's not what he told me.'

With that he left me with his usual wink, a nudge added on this occasion.

A call from Mrs Felix some weeks ago to say they'd bought a couple of old Nepalese rugs they'd like my opinion on. I had the excuse that I was ill, beginning to cough and talk through my nose. She said I sounded it. She seemed friendly enough, respectful even. I wanted her to think I was a recluse, deep into scholarly research, not quite of this world. I must cultivate a manner of speaking that goes with that . . . 'How nice!' I replied. 'Used to have a couple of Nepalese rugs when I was up at the House. In the late medieval zigzag tradition.' No of course I didn't.

Wonder why Annelise didn't send me a card last Christmas? Very good news – a baby at last – or very bad – a child lost. Either way, an overflowing heart that cannot write. Or just that some people slip off the edge of one's mind. Perhaps next Christmas . . . I did get a card from the vicar. It said, 'We should be careful of each other, we should be kind while there is still time. That from the Hull Librarian, who else? Only to do with a hedgehog but it's good enough for me for the time being.' I don't know who the Hull Librarian is, but it's good enough for me too. The reference to a hedgehog was lost on me too . . . Suddenly now Maureen stands beside me, looking down at a BMW, her teeth bared in contempt. The bonnet is scratched with an insult. What did she say? 'If they could express themselves properly they wouldn't think like that'? An overriding notion, but of no use to me at this late hour. If I'd been able to express myself better, as well as Isaiah Berlin say, how much more profound would my thoughts and observations have been? Thank you for that, Maureen . . .

The other night I dreamt that I was coming home. I was wearing my army uniform with my new lance corporal's stripe. I was walking down a street I did not know. At the end of it my mother was standing on a wrought-iron balcony though we'd never had a house with a balcony. As I came closer I could see my father standing half behind her. They were both watching me as if they were not quite sure who I was. I raised my arm but they did not respond. As I was almost beneath them, my mother looked down at me and said, 'We've been waiting so long, Tom. What kept you?' Then I saw my father's face. His mouth was open and he looked very frightened until he saw it was me and smiled. 'It feels we've been waiting a lifetime,' he said. Then they vanished and I had no idea where I was in a strange street beside a house that was not my own . . . When I had walked down the street it was in full sunlight. Now it was bitterly cold and night was falling . . .

Read yesterday that those who have had bypass operations are likely to show signs of mental impairment about five years later. Well, that is a surprise . . .

Adrian is still in New York. He phones quite often. I cannot tell if he is happy, or fulfilled rather. In his voice I can only hear someone who is telling me that what he is doing is the job he does; he might as well go on doing it since it seems to be what he is good at . . . We are both thinking about Jane and not mentioning her. We do not need to. A CD of Schubert songs is playing now. The next but one is the 'Litanei' . . . Oh my dear, dear Jane, why did you have to go and abandon us like that . . . ? Once I got the date wrong and, thinking he had returned, phoned him. A male voice answered. He said Adrian wouldn't be back for another week and could he take a message? I told him who I was. 'Ah, Adrian's Dad. He's spoken a lot about you.' The voice was very friendly; a touch too friendly if there is such a thing. I did not make the usual reply to that, or a reply of any kind. 'Just tell him I called,' I said and because that sounded abrupt added, 'And give him my love.' He said he certainly would and his name was Mark by the way. The only thought I had, indeed have had since, is that he isn't Jane. That's all really – apart of course from hoping he's helping to make Adrian happy or less unhappy than he would be otherwise. If that is possible since he must be thinking he isn't Jane too . . .

Oh yes, Jane's parents have written to say they'd love me to come and see them with Adrian when he returns from New York. '*Please* come,' they add in a PS. I have replied to say that I'd love to. But I don't think I will. I'm sure I won't. I wish I knew what percentage of people are decent and kind like that . . .

Mrs Hirst is going back to Australia. She only has three cats now, one having been run over. Again, it is Mr Fogarty she asks to look after them. 'No hard feelings,' she said. 'But I know how busy you are with your books and such like and Mr Fogarty having once worked with leopards in the Amazon jungle.' I shall miss her. She wonders if she'll ever come back. Even her daughter-in-law wants her to settle there. She thinks she'll get used to Australians talking about being Australian the whole time. 'You can't ignore the climate, can you?' she added.

Julia's mother has sold number 27, or rather the sign has been taken away. I haven't seen her since the day we went to see Julia. I wish she'd come to say goodbye. I'd like to have asked her how Julia was getting along, how far she's got with learning all Schubert's songs by heart. I often see her sitting there, humming. I often see her striding along the beach that day, kicking over sand-castles. I wonder who'll move into number 27 . . .

Either side of us a long time ago the houses were empty. Then the 'For Sale' signs were taken away and people moved into them. That was at the beginning. I did not know then why I decided to write about my life. I certainly do not know now. I'm glad I've made the effort. Or am I? If I hadn't, what difference would it have made? None of course. None at all. A written life, an unwritten life. They will all be the same in the years to come or could it be that . . . ? Oh how that bowl glows in the dead of night!

I'm not at all well now. Something's wrong. Half past midnight. It can't be! Sod it, my watch has stopped. I should start wearing the one Adrian gave me which tells the time to the nearest hundredth of a second. Must get to the emergency clinic first thing in the morning. It will be all right tomorrow.

Author's note

Mrs Konopka's account of her childhood draws on statements recorded in *The Children Accuse* edited by Maria Hochberg-Mariańska and Noe Grüss, translated by Bill Johnston.

About the author

About the book

Read on

Insights,
Interviews
& More . . .

Meet Charles Chadwick

Robin Farquhar-Thompson

AFTER SCHOOL and national army service I had a place at Cambridge, but became restless and decided to follow my brother to Canada. I studied English and French at the University of Toronto, where Northrop Frye and Marshall McLuhan were beginning to make their reputations. By selling gardening tools, doing menial jobs at the Banff Springs Hotel, clerking at a campground, teaching Cree Indian children on a settlement in northern Quebec (now under water), doing post office work at Christmas, and reorganizing the library of the Royal Ontario Museum I was able to pay my own way.

I returned home, read *A la Recherche du Temps Perdu,* then, more by accident than design, I joined the Overseas Civil Service in what was then Northern Rhodesia. After six years as a district officer at various "bush stations" (including the Zambezi Valley, with people resettled from the Kariba Dam), I stayed on after independence to teach administrative practice at the National Institute of Public Administration. I married a violinist and had one son, then joined the British Council and did the full range of aid and "cultural" council jobs in London, Kenya, Nigeria, Brazil, and Canada. Finally, by great good fortune, I served as council director in Poland during the fall of the Soviet Empire, where I helped set up the so-called Know-how Fund.

After leaving the council I was a governor of the Hampstead (comprehensive) School in Cricklewood for eight years. Having previously been a supervisor for the Zimbabwe independence elections, I was invited to monitor elections in Ghana, Pakistan, and Cameroon (for the Commonwealth), Bosnia (for the Organization for Security and Co-operation in Europe), and Uganda (for the Foreign and Commonwealth Office). I ran the European Union observer team in KwaZulu-Natal for South African elections in 1994. Having remarried, I've more recently been kept fairly busy by a seven-year-old son.

As may be apparent, I do not have a great deal in common with Tom Ripple. ❧

> ❝ Having remarried, I've more recently been kept fairly busy by a seven-year-old son. ❞

Making a Ripple

BEFORE *IT'S ALL RIGHT NOW* found a publisher I'd come to accept it never would, and wrote this: "Ripple belongs to the infinite host of real lives lived almost entirely unknown, their inner lives known only to themselves and all slipping into oblivion, their stories untold—George Eliot's unvisited tombs." In being like them Ripple seemed that much more truthful to life. The assertion on the printed page that he is real would be a constant reminder of the fact that he is merely artifice.

There's the usual question about how autobiographical he is. The short answer is not at all. We have nothing in common as far as background, education, work, family, etc. None of the characters are drawn from people I have known in real life. That is not to say I do not share many of his views and uncertainties (though I'd express them differently). Insofar as I do, I like to think that it is to the extent that other people share them too: a love of Schubert and Larkin is one marginal example. In any case, I'm not sure how much it matters to know how autobiographical novels are. How important is it to know about Proust's or Powell's originals? Interesting, perhaps, but unnecessary.

All I remember now is that I began the

book about thirty years ago after reading *Something Happened* by Joseph Heller. It was a book I greatly admired and which taught me there was a certain way of writing a novel I hadn't tried before. *Something Happened* is about an ordinary man writing about his ordinary life in the present tense and first person singular. Indeed, without that novel I doubt mine would have been written at all. Ripple soon acquired a personality of his own and a voice or style I will come to later.

Ripple is about forty when the book begins, a nonentity with a wife, two children, and an insignificant job. What distinguishes Ripple from others like him is his decision to write about his life, beyond that, to find out what he would think if he started putting his thoughts into words. Our minds are full of fleeting, unformulated, haphazard thoughts that soon dwindle and disappear so we can only dimly remember, if at all, what they were; though it may be going too far to say as Virginia Woolf did that nothing exists until it is described. Most of us live largely unexpressed lives. In finding out what he thinks Ripple discovers he is capable of having thoughts he would not have had otherwise— "thoughts" to include feelings, ideas, and beliefs or lack thereof. Articulacy acquires creative power, almost as if it were a separate faculty. There are two striking phrases of Saul Bellow's: "The ▶

> " Indeed, without [Joseph Heller's novel *Something Happened*] I doubt mine would have been written at all. "

restoration of the single unique self from oblivion" and "to bring under cultivation a barren emptiness within oneself." Thus Ripple invents himself and reveals what would otherwise not have been there. Having found he is able to do so, he cannot stop speculating about things.

His quest (his favorite reading is the lives of the great explorers) becomes not for self-knowledge, but for an understanding of the wider world, for truths that might be found if he took the trouble to look for them. His wife, a social worker, is certain of everything. Her dogmatic, left-wing views enable her to be morally domineering and take charge of the upbringing of their children. He is also dominated by his dictatorial boss at the other end of the ideological spectrum. At the mercy of these certainties he is made to feel more of a weakling than he might have otherwise. Writing becomes his best means of escape. By the end of Part One he is cast out by both "extremes" of certainty and is free to make his own way in the world. At the beginning he finds himself between two other extremes: the simple old-fashioned decency of his neighbors on one side, and the snide and sleazy knowingness of his neighbor on the other side. I've made this sound much too schematic; it wasn't consciously in my mind at the time.

> " At the beginning [of the novel Ripple] finds himself between two other extremes: the simple old-fashioned decency of his neighbors on one side, and the snide and sleazy knowingness of his neighbor on the other side. "

Sometimes he takes refuge in wordplay, which is where his thinking often ends. Although neither vain nor complacent, I don't think he readily earns our admiration or respect. There are things about him, his lewdness for example, which make him less than likable. Perhaps he becomes more likable, or ought to with all that thinking he's done. If he is to be an antihero his quest must not appear heroic. Quest or search are the wrong words. Stumbling journey is more like it. He says somewhere, "Nobody wants to hear about an ordinary man's life in one fell swoop, and my story is perhaps best read in very small doses over a period of about thirty years."

Ineffectual at home and at work, he unconsciously comes to realize that "the unexamined life is not worth living" and that "know thyself" is, as Coleridge said, the greatest demand of philosophy. This is not a conscious thing, for self-consciousness gets in the way and becomes the object of scrutiny. Like an explorer he does not know what he will find along the way and what he will discover at the end. His curiosity and bewilderment take him beyond himself. He acquires a widening sense of the absurdity and sorrow of the world, and also of right and wrong, or rather rights and wrongs, of "those little nameless, unremembered acts of kindness and of ▶

Making a Ripple *(continued)*

love . . . " He articulates none of this.
Nor for that matter did I in writing it.

After his wife leaves him and he loses
his job Ripple moves to a Suffolk village,
then back to London, and finally to the
suburb of a seaside town. He makes a brief
visit to Poland. He meets a wide variety
of people, all of whom play some part in
broadening his understanding of the
world and the limitations of any kind of
certainty. Indeed, all certainties become
more and more elusive. Ripple's self-
awareness and the clumsiness of his
relationships give him a growing sense of
how little can be known of other people.
It seems to be true that the less knowledge,
or moral certainty you possess, the deeper
the possibility of understanding.

His style is that of a novice, awkward
and literate rather than literary. I hope
that nothing comes between the
experience and the writing, that the style
does not invite comment or get in the way.
Too often in fiction the characters seem to
be peering out through what Henry James
called "the deliberate chosenness" of the
prose. His style is that of someone who
sees people, events, and ideas afresh
without any previous suppositions about
how they might or ought to be expressed.
He intermittently takes out his typewriter
and says what comes into his mind,
or what he says is written up from
manuscript notes. I hope this gives the

> [Ripple's] style is that of a novice, awkward and literate rather than literary.

story an immediacy, with no meditation as to the manner in which it should be told. His theoretical musings too are from scratch—simply an aspect of finding out what he thinks. It is increasingly not self-knowledge he is after. There was never a lot there to know. Again, none of this would cross his mind. Nor, until now, has it really crossed mine. Perhaps all this is too portentous by half; Ripple's reply would be: Which half did you have in mind? I think too that what comes to the surface instead of a series of truths or conclusions, whether moral or otherwise, will always remain beyond the reach of language. Expression does not always clarify; it entangles. Doubts are seldom resolved; they multiply. There are few abstract certainties and no conclusions. As for people: How far can they ever be sure of themselves or of others? What can we know of anyone? The variations of sorrow and absurdity are endless.

In all this one can only hope to be fairly readily identified as an "everyman" or "antihero," which is what most of us are. The best I could hope for was to capture real life and create for the reader a sense of our common humanity, or get as close to that as I possibly could. ❧

> ❝ As for people: How far can they ever be sure of themselves or of others? What can we know of anyone? The variations of sorrow and absurdity are endless. ❞

Debut at Seventy-two

On Being a White-crowned First Novelist

Read on

THE QUESTION I HAVE to get used to is: What does it feel like to publish a first novel at seventy-two? There are the obvious things. First there's the incredulity, which still hasn't worn off, of being taken on by a top agent and then by Faber in the UK (of all people). When I told my brother, a retired Canadian academic, he said he hoped I was prepared for a call from Faber to say they were sorry they'd made a mistake, the book they were interested in was called *She's a Bit of All Right* by Charles Chapman. Not long after there was the acceptance by an American publisher. That was even harder to believe, for what on earth could the appeal in the States be of the story of a very ordinary Englishman?

The book was written over thirty years in four installments, at intervals of about eight years. For most of that time I had a job to do for the British Council, so writing this novel and a few other things were not uppermost in my mind most of the time except for a few hours on weekends and on some evenings. I'd come to assume the chances of publication were remote, to say the least, especially since it had grown to almost 300,000 words. It was hardly even worth contemplating.

<blockquote>
❝ [My brother] said he hoped I was prepared for a call from Faber [& Faber] to say they were sorry they'd made a mistake, the book they were interested in was called *She's a Bit of All Right* by Charles Chapman. ❞
</blockquote>

The character isn't dead yet . . . is still writing. If I'd delayed any longer the grim reaper would have taken a pretty steamy view of my presumption, to say nothing of removing the chance of publication altogether. As it was, I had to consider the possibility of submitting Part One on its own or Part Four with a preface.

Then of course there's gratitude to the agent and publisher for rescuing the book from oblivion, and indeed for the sheer good fortune of having chanced upon the agent in the first place. The temptation was to think it was bound to happen eventually and about bloody time too. It wasn't. Bad luck and disappointment of one sort or another seem to be in the nature of things for the unpublished writer. Self-doubt too, of course—simply not knowing if it was much good, or good enough. There must be thousands of novels out there that haven't had the same luck—a sort of parallel universe of books as worthy of attention as many of the books that have been published. Finally there's the answer that it must be roughly the same for a first novelist of any age: nice to get the recognition and encouragement, jolly good for the ego, fingers crossed that people will like it; quite regardless of that, the wish that one had done it better. More about that later.

Then other thoughts begin to emerge as mattering a good deal more. As the years passed I learned to persuade myself that what outweighed everything else— ▶

> " There must be thousands of novels out there that haven't had the same luck— a sort of parallel universe of books as worthy of attention as many of the books that have been published. "

the disappointment and the like—was the importance of continuing to do it as well as one could for its own sake. Italo Svevo said during a long fallow period: "Write what one must. What one needn't do is publish."

There have been other novels, some rewritten, some gathering dust. If you've been taught literature and read quite a lot of fiction, you may begin to wonder whether you might have a go at it yourself. And then you think that when the end begins to loom you wouldn't want to have to give yourself a good ticking off for never having really tried.

Overlying that is all the experience that has accumulated. Not one's own, but the experience of life itself. There are so many things and places, so many people, real or imagined, that have been moving or striking or funny or seemed important in some way, and you don't want them to all slip away unnoticed, unexpressed. There may be degrees of autobiography in all fiction, but surely it's silly advice to say one should only "write about what one knows"—as if personal experience was a boundary of one's knowledge of the world. Not wanting to let life go has to do with the passing of time, wanting to make it less vague, give it clarity, a stronger illusion of permanence. And beyond that there is what has been written before and how it has been written, either learned

> There may be degrees of autobiography in all fiction, but surely it's silly advice to say one should only 'write about what one knows.'

from or unconsciously assimilated, which has fed the imagination and set standards. A literary heritage in other words. What Eliot has called "the consciousness of the past."

The creative imagination does seem to be a separate faculty with a life and a persistence of its own. Some people, Henry James and V. S. Pritchett for example, have even spoken of the writer as a quite separate being from the person who does the living. There are a vast number of people out there who paint watercolors, make pots, do tapestry, write poems, make furniture, take photographs, and so forth. They want to show them to two or three other people, relatives perhaps, but not much beyond that—perhaps a little show in the village hall. It gives them pleasure that they want to share. While doing it they feel that this is what life is for. If there is no one to share the pleasure with, they do it all the same. It is not a question of tenacity. There is no virtue in it. For what is the alternative?

Then there is the imperative. To take trouble, to be "professional." I once heard a father give his son this advice: "It doesn't matter what you do so long as you do it properly." Brain surgeons, road sweepers, and everyone in between take pride in their work and don't cut corners. If you see someone out with their easel painstakingly painting trees and houses ▶

you don't feel like saying, "Come on, why bother with all that detail? You'll only stick it away in your garage or give it to Aunt Ethel and Uncle Frank, who won't know the difference."

In the writing itself what took over was the need for truthfulness: to ensure as best one can that the characters are really alive, fully human. It seems then that you are not writing for any kind of reader, or for yourself. If the characters come to stand for people in real life one wants to do them justice, to live up to humanity itself, though you'll constantly fall short. Surely each day everyone is profoundly affected by something they have seen or read or heard, and you think that fiction ought to try to be true to that. As Doris Lessing said: "The writer represents, makes articulate, is continuously fed by, numbers of people who are inarticulate, to whom one belongs, to whom one is responsible." So the reader may only be fleetingly in mind. The obligation is to the characters. Just as in real life, the value of those we care about is in understanding them better, for what they are to themselves and to others, for their sakes, not for the impression they will make on strangers.

Henry James believed the "air of reality" mattered more than anything else, what he called "the odor of humanity." He was once profoundly

> " In the writing itself what took over was the need for truthfulness: to ensure as best one can that the characters are really alive, fully human. "

shocked by Trollope for conceding to readers that his characters were only "make-believe." "Such a betrayal of a sacred office seems to me a terrible crime."

I've wandered too far from the question. Of course, one wants to be published, to be told one is some good at it, that one has acquired a recognizable skill, that one can give pleasure, move people or make them laugh, and all the rest of it. As I said earlier: all jolly good for the ego. But more important than all that, or what ought to be more important, is a sense of proportion. Penelope Fitzgerald once spoke about the *littleness* of fiction: "when I'm writing it down what a small thing it must seem . . . in the face of the haunting faces that television now shows us from day to day of the displaced, the rejected, the bewildered and totally lost." Phillip Roth has said "that the actuality is constantly outdoing the talent. The daily newspapers fill us with wonder and awe (Is it possible? Is it happening?), also with sickness and despair." And so if novelists try to create real human life, they are always writing under its dark and overpowering shadow.

With all that floating about in the mind, when the question of age comes up it seems increasingly irrelevant. Seventy-two, twenty-seven. Same numbers, different order. I'm sorry if ▶

> **If novelists try to create real human life, they are always writing under its dark and overpowering shadow.**

Debut at Seventy-two *(continued)*

all this sounds a bit pious—or "pi" as we say—which according to my father was for the English a crime even worse than murder or cheating at cards.